BENEATH
the
KAURI
TREE

ALSO BY SARAH LARK

BENEATH *the* KAURI TREE

SARAH LARK

TRANSLATED BY D.W. LOVETT

amazon crossing

Text copyright © 2012 by Sarah Lark

Translation copyright © 2018 by D. W. Lovett

Previously published as *Im Schatten des Kauribaums* by Bastei Lübbe in Germany in 2012. Translated from German by D. W. Lovett. First published in English by AmazonCrossing in 2018.

Published by AmazonCrossing, Seattle

www.apub.com

Amazon, the Amazon logo, and AmazonCrossing are trademarks of Amazon.com, Inc., or its affiliates.

ISBN-13: 9781503900585
ISBN-10: 1503900584

Cover design by Shasti O'Leary Soudant

Printed in the United States of America

BENEATH
the
KAURI
TREE

Child of the Stars

Dunedin and Waikato, New Zealand
1875–1878
London, England
Cardiff and Treherbert, Wales
1878

Chapter 1

"And until now you have been privately educated?"

Miss Partridge, principal of the renowned Otago Girls' High School in Dunedin, cast a stern look at Matariki and her parents.

Matariki thought the darkly clad woman with a lorgnette a bit strange. Miss Partridge appeared to be about the same age as her grandmothers from the Maori village, but no one there needed help seeing. The principal, however, did not strike her as imposing, nor did the furniture, undoubtedly imported from England, nor the heavy drapes for the tall windows, and the many bookshelves. None of it daunted Matariki. It was her mother's behavior that was unsettling. She had been anxious to the point of hysteria the whole ride from Elizabeth Station to Dunedin, nagging Matariki about her clothes and comportment, and worrying over the entrance exam her daughter would take that day as if she herself needed to do well on it.

"Not precisely, M . . ."

It was all Lizzie Drury could do not to call Miss Partridge "ma'am," and during their introductions, she had nearly curtsied. For more than ten years, Lizzie had been mistress of Elizabeth Station, a farm near Lawrence. It had been a long time since she had worked as a maid, but highbrow settings and polite society still intimidated her.

"Miss Partridge," she said, trying to make her voice sound firm, "our daughter was in school in Lawrence. But the settlement is slowly dying as the miners move on. What remains of it, well, we'd rather not send our children there. That's why we've arranged for private instruction this past year. However, the capacities of our tutor have been exhausted when it comes to Matariki."

With nervous fingers, Lizzie checked the hold of her coiffure. She wore her frizzy dark-blonde hair primly put up under a pert little hat. Perhaps too pert a hat? In front of Miss Partridge, the delicate blue and pastel flower decorations seemed almost too bold. If it had been up to Lizzie, she would have pulled her hooded cloak from the far corner of her wardrobe and put it on to look more serious. Michael, however, would not allow it.

"We're going to a school, Lizzie, not a funeral," he had said, laughing. "They'll take Riki, don't worry. And why not? She's a bright child. And if they don't, it's not the only girls' school on the South Island."

Lizzie had let herself be convinced, but before the severe eyes of the principal, she felt as if the earth would swallow her. However exceptional Otago Girls' High School was or was not, Matariki would always stand out.

Miss Partridge's gaze now became markedly disapproving.

"That is quite interesting," she said, and then addressed Matariki for the first time. "Dear, you have just turned—what is it?—eleven. Yet you have already exhausted your tutor's capacities? You must truly be a gifted child."

Matariki—on whom the irony of Miss Partridge's tone was completely lost—smiled. It was a smile that usually won over every heart. "My grandmothers say I'm smart," she confirmed in her soft, melodic voice. "Aku says I can dance more *haka* than other girls my age. And Haeata says I could be a *tohunga*, a healer, once I learn more botany. And Ingoa—"

"How many grandmothers do you have, child?" Miss Partridge asked, looking confused.

Matariki's large, light-brown eyes briefly lost themselves in the distance while she counted to herself the older women of the tribe. For her age, she was also advanced in arithmetic, though that skill had less to do with tutors, teachers, or "grandmothers" and more to do with her thrifty mother.

"Sixteen," she said.

Miss Partridge turned her gaze back to Matariki's parents. Her expression made Lizzie's breath catch.

"She means the older women of the neighboring Maori tribe," Michael explained. "Among the Ngai Tahu, it is customary to call all of the older women 'grandmother'—not just grandmothers by relation. The same is true for grandfathers, aunts, and uncles, sometimes even mothers."

"So, she's not even your natural-born child?"

The thought seemed almost to relieve Miss Partridge. After all, Matariki did not particularly resemble her parents. Though Michael Drury was dark haired like his daughter, his eyes gleamed as blue as the sky over Ireland; his face was angular, not round like Matariki's, and his skin was lighter. The girl could have gotten her delicate figure and curly hair from her mother—though Lizzie's hair was rather frizzy whereas Matariki's was wavy. Lizzie's eyes were also blue. The girl had not inherited her amber eyes from either of them.

"No, no," Michael Drury said, shaking his head decisively. "Matariki is our daughter."

Lizzie gave him a brief, guilty look, but Michael did not return it, instead fending off the principal's apparent displeasure. Michael Drury had his failings, and sometimes his careless manner drove Lizzie mad. But he kept his promises, including the one Lizzie had asked of him before Matariki's birth: that he would never hold Lizzie's past against her daughter.

Michael had never asked the question of paternity, although soon after Matariki's birth, it was clear that he could not have sired the dark-skinned, brown-eyed child.

Now Lizzie braced herself, convinced that the principal would not believe that Matariki was their daughter.

"I am her mother," Lizzie said firmly. "And beyond that, she is a child of the stars."

Hainga, the Maori tribe's wisewoman, had called Matariki that. The girl had been conceived in the tumult of the Touhou Festival. The Maori celebrated New Year when the Matariki star cluster first appeared in the South Island's night sky.

Miss Partridge furrowed her brow. "So, not merely preternaturally gifted but also celestially conceived," she said.

Matariki glared at the principal. The woman's words did not mean much to her, but she felt how they hurt her mother. And she would not allow that.

"Haikina says I'm a chieftain's daughter," she said. "That's something like a princess. I think, anyway."

Lizzie almost cracked a smile. She, too, had once thought that. Kahu Heke, Matariki's biological father, had lured Lizzie into his arms with the hope she would be his queen. But things had turned out quite differently, and the tutor, Haikina, had done the right thing by not telling Matariki everything.

Miss Partridge's gaze became more hateful, and Michael squared himself. He needed to step in—he could no longer watch while Lizzie shrank in front of this impertinent lady.

"Miss Partridge, Matariki Drury is our daughter. That's what it says on her birth certificate in Dunedin, and we are asking you to accept her for admission to your school. Though I wouldn't call her gifts preternatural, our daughter is smart. Her tutor can read and write well, and she's taught our children English with loving rigor, but she doesn't know French or Latin, and she can't prepare Matariki for further studies or for a society marriage."

Michael emphasized "society" almost threateningly. Let Miss Partridge dare to contradict him here. In the last few years, he and Lizzie had grown their farm into a very successful business that specialized in the breeding of quality sheep. Rams and ewes from Elizabeth Station received the highest prices at auction, and the Drurys were widely esteemed.

Nevertheless, Lizzie suffered from feelings of inferiority when they were invited to the sheep breeders' association meetings or parties. Both Drurys came from humble circumstances, and Michael, in particular, did not strive for social standing. Lizzie did exert herself, but she was shy. When she was in front of people like the Wardens of Kiward Station or the Barringtons and Beasleys of Canterbury, her otherwise wonder-working smile failed her first, followed immediately by her voice. Lizzie had sworn to herself that it would not be like that for Matariki. Otago Girls' High School should provide her with the necessary skills.

Matariki, however, did not tend toward shyness. Nor was she nervous when Miss Partridge finally asked her a few science and math questions. With a clear voice and without any note of Irish brogue or the Cockney accent her mother had struggled with all her life, she solved the problems. Haikina had been an ideal teacher when it came to speech and elocution.

The principal looked at her benevolently. "From a knowledge standpoint, I have no objections to your acceptance," Miss Partridge finally observed, somewhat peevishly. "However, it must be clear to you that, hmm, Mat-uh-riki will be the only girl with such an exotic background."

Michael bristled, but Miss Partridge waved her hand soothingly.

"Please, Mr. Drury, I say that only with good intentions. The best families in Canterbury and Otago send us their daughters, and some of these children are, well, they are not accustomed—"

"You mean to say that the sight of our daughter would so frighten these children that they would run straight home?"

"I mean it from your daughter's perspective," said Miss Partridge. "Most of these children, in the best of cases, know Maori as servants. Your daughter will not have it easy."

Lizzie raised her head and held herself straight, looking taller and more self-assured. For the first time that day, she looked like the white woman of whom the Ngai Tahu spoke with more respect than for any other on the South Island. As far as they were concerned, this *pakeha wahine* possessed more *mana*—power and influence—than most warriors.

"Miss Partridge, life isn't easy," she said calmly. "And if Matariki learns that lesson in no worse circumstances than dealing with a few spoiled brats in a girls' school, she's to be envied."

For the first time, Miss Partridge looked at Lizzie with astonishment. She had appeared mousy a moment before, but now . . .

And Lizzie was not done. "Perhaps you'll be the first to accustom yourself to her name, should she attend this school. Her name is Matariki."

Miss Partridge's mouth twisted. "Yes, hmm, that is also something we should discuss. Could we not call her Martha?"

***

"We'll send her to Otago Girls' High School," Lizzie said.

The Drurys had taken their leave of Miss Partridge, without making explicit arrangements for Matariki's entrance into the school, and Michael had immediately begun to curse the "impertinent biddy" as they emerged onto the street. Lizzie let him rage for a while, figuring that he would calm down while he retrieved the horses from the rental stables. When, however, he brought up the subject of visiting the Catholic girls' school, she clarified her position.

"Otago is the best school in the area. All the sheep barons send their daughters there. And they want to take Matariki. It would be madness not to send her."

"Those little rich girls will make her life hell," Michael said.

"As I just pointed out to Miss Partridge," she replied, "hell doesn't consist of plush sofas, English furniture, and well-heated classrooms. A few troublemakers might prowl around places like that, but not as many as in the prisons or

Australia's penal camps or New Zealand's gold miners' camps. We survived all that, Michael—a girls' school couldn't possibly be as bad."

Michael gave her a sidelong glance as he moved the horses into position. "She is, after all, a princess." He smiled and turned to his daughter. "Would you like to go to this school, Matariki?"

Matariki shrugged. "I like the uniforms," she said, pointing to a few students passing by. Lizzie caught herself thinking that her daughter would look charming in the uniform; the white blouse would complement Matariki's golden shimmering skin, her raspberry-colored lips, and her black locks. "Haikina says girls have to learn a lot, more than boys. Whoever knows a lot has a lot of *mana*, and whoever has the most *mana* can become chieftain."

Lizzie laughed a bit forcedly. She knew from her own painful experience that too much *mana* did not always serve a woman well.

"But what about friends, Matariki?" She was determined, albeit reluctantly, to point out the possible difficulties her daughter might face at Otago Girls' High School. "You may not make any friends here."

"Haikina says a chieftain doesn't have any friends. Chieftains are un, un—"

"Untouchable," Lizzie said, completing the thought. That, too, awoke unhappy memories.

Matariki nodded. "Then that's how I'll be."

***

"Should we stop by the Burtons' residence?"

Lizzie asked the question reluctantly as their carriage rumbled through the roughly paved streets of Dunedin. Reverend Burton had always been her friend, but she still eyed his wife, Mary Kathleen, with mild suspicion. Kathleen had been the love of Michael's youth; they had been engaged, and he had carried a torch for her for years. His marriage to Lizzie had nearly fallen apart due to his revived passion for Kathleen. Lizzie would have liked to break off contact with the Burtons altogether, and she knew that Reverend Burton would have understood. He did not like to see Michael in Kathleen's presence any more than Lizzie did. But there was Sean, Kathleen and Michael's son. Sean had only gotten to know his father on the verge of adulthood, and even if the two had never quite warmed to each other, they ought not to lose touch completely.

"Aren't they in Christchurch?" Michael asked. "I thought Heather had an exhibition there."

Heather was Kathleen's daughter from her marriage to Ian Coltrane. Years ago, when Michael was deported for grain theft, he was forced to leave behind his fiancée, Kathleen, in Ireland. She had already been pregnant with Sean, but Kathleen had not been allowed to wait for Michael's return. Her father married her off to Ian Coltrane, a horse trader who promised to be a father to her child. Though the marriage had not been a happy one, they had nonetheless been blessed with two children together—Heather and Colin. Heather, the younger of the two, had made a name for herself as a portraitist. That week, a gallery in Christchurch was exhibiting her work. Kathleen and Peter had traveled there with Heather to celebrate the event.

Michael did not seem particularly eager to pay the Burtons a visit. Though everyone got along perfectly well, it must have been strange for him to see his old flame married to another, let alone a clergyman of the Church of England. Michael and Kathleen had grown up together in a village in Ireland where they were raised Catholic. Perhaps being around the well-read, highly educated Peter Burton still intimidated Michael a bit—or perhaps he felt daunted by the equally well-read and well-educated Sean.

Michael might be able to accept that a pastor was smarter than he, but he was sensitive about his son's attitude. The boy had let it be known early on that he wanted nothing to do with his biological father, though his demeanor had mellowed somewhat since Kathleen had married the reverend and Michael had married Lizzie.

"And Sean is in court," Michael said. Sean had studied law at the University of Otago and had just taken his first position as a lawyer in training. "If we want to see him, we'll have to stay in the city. Should we find a hotel?"

Dunedin was about forty miles from Elizabeth Station, and Lizzie's heart became heavy at the thought that she would soon live so far from her daughter. She was of two minds about spending the night in town. Though she loved the luxury of the finer hotels and would gladly have enjoyed a celebratory dinner and a glass of wine with Michael, Haikina would worry if they did not return that evening as planned. Haikina had fretted over Matariki's entrance exam just as much as Lizzie had. Besides, the younger children took advantage of Haikina. It would not be fair to leave her alone with them without having agreed to the arrangement in advance.

"No, let's go home," Lizzie finally said. "Sean might already have other plans. We shouldn't surprise him. It would be better to see him when we bring Matariki to school."

Michael shrugged and steered the horses toward the mountains. The road was wide and well paved, though not heavily trafficked. Things had changed a great deal in the years since Lizzie and Michael had arrived in Otago. Back during the gold rush, Lawrence had been called Tuapeka, and hundreds of people had poured into Gabriel's Gully. The area still looked like a wasteland. The gold diggers had dug it up so many times that the vegetation had been completely destroyed, leaving a muddy bog that would take years to recover.

Now the gold deposits around Lawrence were largely exhausted—in any case, those to which the miners had access. Lizzie thought with a smile about the reserves on Elizabeth Station. Only she and the local Maori tribe knew how much gold the river on her property carried, and everyone had an interest in keeping it quiet. That gold had financed the Drurys' farm, made the Maori tribe wealthy by the standards of the Ngai Tahu, and would now pay for Matariki's education.

The gold miners had moved on to Queenstown, and the once large and lively settlements they had founded shrank to sleepy villages populated by a few farmers and traders. Naturally, some scoundrels and adventurers remained— too old, too tired, or simply too lazy to try their luck once again elsewhere. They still panned in the forest's rivers around Lawrence—another reason Michael and Lizzie were loath to leave Haikina and the children alone on Elizabeth Station. If they planned on spending the night elsewhere, Lizzie would ask the tribe for protection, and the chieftain would send a few warriors to camp along the river.

This time, however, the Drurys need not have worried. When they emerged from the mountain forest and onto the path to Elizabeth Station, they could already see movement along the river. Hemi, Haikina's husband, was panning for gold above the waterfall, and Haikina was fishing. In the pond below, Kevin and Pat, Michael and Lizzie's sons, were splashing around.

Hemi waved to them and continued sifting his pan. Haikina dropped her fish trap on the bank and ran to the carriage. She was a tall, slender young woman with hip-length, straight hair. Probably to do justice to her position as a teacher, she wore a dress like those of white people, the *pakeha*, as the Maori called them, but she had tied up the skirt casually, drawing the eye to her long brown legs.

"How did it go, Matariki?" Haikina asked excitedly.

Matariki sat up straight. "The right education makes the heart as strong as oak," she said, proudly repeating the motto of Otago Girls' High School.

Lizzie looked at her daughter, astounded. Where did she learn that? She must have read it somewhere and remembered it.

"I just don't know how strong oak really is," Matariki remarked. "Maybe oak isn't even as hard as kauri or totara wood."

Michael had to laugh. "Good Lord, we really are at the edge of the world. The children are growing up without ever having seen an oak. It's very good wood, Riki, absolutely suited to a strong heart."

Haikina smiled. "So, they'll accept you?" she asked hopefully.

Matariki nodded. "Yes. But only as a chieftain's daughter. And they're going to call me Martha because the principal can't pronounce Matariki."

Haikina embraced the girl suddenly. "They called me Angela in the mission school," she said.

Kevin and Pat caught sight of their parents and ran to them without drying off. Pat, the youngest, boarded the carriage and hugged Michael. At age eight, Kevin felt he was already old enough to go to school in Dunedin and envied Matariki her privilege.

"If you get a new name at school, then I want a name like the greatest chieftain," Kevin shouted.

"The greatest chieftain is Te Maiharanui," Matariki shouted even more loudly. "And it's Hone Heke. You can't have a Maori chieftain's name at school. Just a *pakeha*'s. Maybe Captain Cook? Or Prince Albert?"

Lizzie laughed, but Michael wore a stern expression. "Kevin, you have a good, old Irish name. You're named for your grandfather, and he made the best whiskey in west Ireland, not to mention how he played the fiddle and—"

"You're named for Saint Kevin," Lizzie corrected her husband, glaring at him. "He was a great, holy man. He founded the monastery in Glendalough. And he probably didn't make any whiskey. Though I'm not sure. Don't worry, no one's going to rename you."

"Only girls get new names," Matariki announced, taunting Kevin as she stepped down from the carriage. "And I'm getting new clothes too."

Michael arched his brows. "It's going to cost a fortune," he said to Hemi, who walked up and handed him a bottle of whiskey. Michael took a drink and grimaced at the Maori. "You need money again, do you?" He pointed to the gold pan.

Hemi sighed. "There's news from the north," he replied, "and 'requests,' if you want to put it that way."

Principally, it was Lizzie—and later Matariki—who established the connections with the Maori. Lizzie spoke the language of the Ngai Tahu and had lived among them. Michael didn't have Lizzie's standing with the Maori. He suspected the warriors thought him a coward. However, Michael counted Hemi among his few true friends from the Maori village. Hemi had attended the mission school like Haikina, where he learned good English, and had then worked on a large sheep farm. He had only just returned to the tribe—and, especially, to Haikina.

"Requests?" asked Michael. "Don't tell me your *kingi* has the idea of collecting taxes."

Hemi laughed grimly. Until just a few decades before, there had been no central rule of the Maori in New Zealand. But then someone had the idea that the tribes would have a stronger negotiating position with the whites if they were represented by a single "king." Tawhiao, originally the chieftain of the Waikato tribes, was now the second of these kings.

"That would likely be the end of his kingship," Hemi observed. "But there are already levies and voluntary tributes, mostly from the chieftains rebelling against the *pakeha*. And we Ngai Tahu are happy to buy our way out of that. Let them fight on the North Island. We'd rather live in peace with the *pakeha*."

The tribes on the South Island did mostly resolve conflicts through negotiations.

"Rebellious chieftains—sounds like Kahu Heke," Michael remarked. "Is he still up to his nonsense with the Hauhau?"

Hauhau was a Maori name for a branch of the Pai Marire religious movement that championed Maori traditions and the winning back of the Maori lands on which the *pakeha* had settled. Kahu Heke had always promoted this view—although before the emergence of the Hauhau, he had hardly believed it possible. In place of a *pakeha*-free New Zealand, he had adopted the dream of a Maori nation under a strong, assertive *kingi*, and for a time he had envisioned himself as such a ruler. He had planned to offer a generous olive branch to the whites: Lizzie Owens, the *pakeha wahine*, was to have been his queen.

Ultimately, Lizzie had chosen Michael, and Kahu Heke had recognized the Hauhau as his springboard to power. Yet things went wrong from the start. Kahu Heke's troops had killed the Anglican clergyman Carl Völkner, and Kahu had subsequently gone into hiding.

"Unfortunately, Kahu Heke knows a bit too much about our gold," Hemi sighed. "We think he's behind these repeated requests to financially support the glorious fight for our land. But what are we supposed to do? They might send Hauhau missionaries and give our people a taste for human flesh." He grinned and clapped with the gold pan.

"As long as Kahu Heke stays where he is . . . ," Michael said. He took another gulp of whiskey just as he saw Matariki strip off her clothes and leap naked with her brothers into the pond. She would have to learn not to do that at Otago Girls' High School.

***

Matariki Drury was a happy child. She had never experienced unfriendliness or rejection. Without exception, everyone loved the adorable, lively girl. Of course, the question of her parentage had occasionally been the subject of talk in Lawrence, but no one let the girl hear it. In the former gold-mining town of Tuapeka, plenty of citizens had unsavory pasts.

Lizzie and Michael now were counted among the richest and most esteemed citizens of the region; they were among the rare gold seekers who made a fortune and kept it. Now, Matariki Drury had even been accepted into the renowned Otago Girls' High School, and when she went into Lawrence, she was held in admiration.

Lawrence, however, was nearly twenty miles from Elizabeth Station, so Matariki could more often be found in the houses of the Maori settlement. There she had friends and "relatives" who loved her too. Among the Maori, children were always welcome. Matariki weaved flax with the Maori girls and made dresses from hardened flax leaves. She played the *nguru* flute with her mouth and nose, and she listened to the stories about Maori gods and heroes. At home, Michael told tales of Irish saints and heroes, and Lizzie explained viniculture.

Lizzie had worked as a young woman on the North Island in the house of governor James Busby, who was one of the first to bring wine grapes to New Zealand. Though Busby had not been particularly successful, Lizzie had tremendous ambition as a vintner. Matariki helped her mother with the grape harvest and from her learned not to give up and to be optimistic.

***

On her first day at Otago Girls' High School, Matariki was in great spirits, whereas her mother was rather nervous as they stepped through the heavy doors of the dignified building. It was the first day after vacation, and the arriving girls bustled about. Most students did not live in Dunedin but on sheep farms, some far away. Matariki, too, would board in the dormitory.

Lizzie told Matariki to wait in the entrance hall while she followed another mother to the secretary's office. She had a stack of forms to fill out, but she was unsure about several things. Michael had not been able to accompany them because of an important livestock auction on the same day, and Lizzie longed for his easygoing self-assurance.

Matariki eyed the paintings on the walls, but they did not hold her attention long. It was considerably more interesting to watch the lively schoolgirls as they greeted one another. She noticed two Maori girls in light-blue dresses, bonnets, and lace aprons carrying the students' suitcases and bags. They did not seem happy, and none of the schoolgirls exchanged a word with them. Matariki was about to say something to them when a tall blonde girl called to her.

"Are you new? Why are you standing around? Take these to the housemother. They need to be ironed. They got rather wrinkled in my suitcase."

The blonde girl pressed a pile of blouses and skirts into Matariki's arms and then gestured as if shooing a chicken away. Matariki made her way obediently in the indicated direction, though she had no idea what a housemother was or how to find one.

Matariki asked a dark-haired girl who rolled her eyes theatrically. "Didn't they show you when you started here? You must come straight from the jungle."

While her friends laughed, she pointed the way. Matariki found a room in which a plump woman was distributing bedding and towels to the schoolgirls. Matariki waited politely in the line until the woman noticed her.

"Are you bringing me something instead of fetching something?" she asked amicably.

Matariki curtsied as Haikina had taught her.

"These need to be ironed."

The woman furrowed her brow. "Is that so? Tell me, are you the new maid? I thought she wasn't to come until next week. No one could learn the ropes in this confusion. And she'd have to be older." She eyed Matariki confusedly.

"I'm Mata—uh, Martha Drury," Matariki introduced herself. "And I don't know how to iron yet. But I'd love to learn. And history and geography and literature." She began to list the school subjects she could recall.

The housemother boomed with laughter, relieving Matariki straightaway of the bundle of clothing. "Welcome, my dear. I'm Miss Maynard, the house-mother. And you're the girl from near Lawrence whose name our esteemed principal can't pronounce. What was it again? Matariki, right? Well, I don't find it so hard. I'm from Australia, dearie, and the aborigines there have truly remarkable names. Can you imagine someone named Allambee? Or Loorea?"

Matariki smiled. Miss Maynard was nice. At once she no longer felt so out of place.

"Well, and now just show me who foisted her ironing on you. We'll give her something to think about, Matariki. The little sheep baronesses always tend to forget during the holidays that no one picks up after them here."

Except for the Maori maids. The thought shot through Matariki's head, but now she recognized the curious looks of the other girls following her and the housemother. The Maori maids watched, too, just as amazed as the *pak-eha*. They, however, lowered their chins sheepishly. Were they afraid of the housemother?

"They're so awfully meek," sighed Miss Maynard when she noticed Matariki's empathetic gaze. "We get them from the mission school, you know. It seems they curtsy and pray there more than they study."

Matariki now realized that none of the schoolgirls curtsied as Miss Maynard hurried past, though they greeted her enthusiastically—the housemother seemed beloved of everyone.

Finally, she gave the blonde girl, whom she addressed as Alison Beasley, an earful. Alison got her laundry back with the order to iron it herself—and while she was at it, to show the new students the ropes.

"The first-years will be expecting you tomorrow morning at ten o'clock in the laundry room, Alison—I'll be there too. And for the next few days, you'll be responsible for seeing that the little ones come to class looking proper."

Alison frowned, annoyed. She was already a third-year, came from a large sheep farm, and at home was surely not used to helping around the house or being responsible for anything.

"Oh yes, and to avoid further misunderstandings," Miss Maynard said, raising her voice so that all the girls in the hall and in the rooms with open doors heard her, "this is our new student, Matariki Drury. She has nothing against being called Martha, but she certainly will not be ironing your clothes."

Alison glared mockingly at Matariki. "So, where does she come from?" she asked. "Not likely from one of the big sheep farms."

Miss Maynard raised her voice again. "Alison, you won't believe it, but there are very smart and valuable people who do not come from sheep baronies."

Matariki returned the older girl's gaze with her own composure. "It's true," she said amiably, interrupting the housemother's sermon. "I'm an actual princess."

***

Lizzie was horribly concerned and relieved almost to tears when Miss Maynard brought Matariki back to her.

"Matariki got a little lost," Miss Maynard explained. "But it gave us a chance to get to know each other. Your daughter is quite an extraordinary girl."

Lizzie frowned, glancing suspiciously at both Matariki and Miss Maynard. Did the housemother mean that in friendship or mockery?

"The other girls thought I was a maid," Matariki said.

Miss Maynard bit her lip. "The incident is embarrassing for us, Mrs. Drury. We—"

Lizzie glared at her, enraged. "Those girls have already started trying to tear her down?" She seemed ready to deal with Matariki's future schoolmates directly. Lizzie might tend toward shyness around authority figures, but she would fight for her daughter like a lioness.

"I'm very sorry. It was just . . ." Miss Maynard searched for an excuse.

"It was funny," Matariki said cheerfully. "I have always wanted to be a housemaid. Like you were, Mommy. You did say you liked it." At that, she curtsied primly, giving her mother and Miss Maynard an irresistible smile.

Lizzie smiled back. Maybe these girls had meant to hurt her daughter, but Matariki was strong. She did not need anyone to fight for her.

Miss Maynard was smiling again now too—mostly with relief. "As I just said, a very extraordinary girl. We're very proud to have Princess Matariki Drury with us."

***

Matariki's school year turned out much like her first day. No matter what Alison or the other girls attempted in order to tease or annoy the half Maori, it proved all but impossible to hurt Matariki. The girl was not naive, and she understood her classmates' mockery and innuendo. However, she refused to take it seriously, and so she ignored the cruel remarks about "beggar princesses" and Alison's attempts to call her "Cinderella."

Miss Maynard tried to place Matariki in a room with the most tolerant and understanding girls. She quickly realized, however, that Matariki did not much care with whom she shared the room. She was friendly to everyone but did not try to get close to anyone. As soon as school was over on Friday at noon, she rode home as fast as she could go, reaching Elizabeth Station before dark. Her father had rented a stall in the stables near the school for a small but strong horse that created a sensation among the young sheep baronesses. Grainie came from the Wardens' stables on Kiward Station in Canterbury; she was a Welsh cob mare of the best pedigree. With Grainie there, Matariki was not dependent on her parents to pick her up—a circumstance that somewhat unsettled Miss Partridge.

"Nevertheless, it is forty miles, Mr. Drury," she offered to Michael for consideration. "If something were to happen to the child . . ."

Michael Drury, however, merely laughed at that, as did his daughter.

"Grainie runs like lightning, Miss Partridge," Matariki explained proudly. "No one can ambush me. I'd be gone too quickly."

The well-traveled roads around Dunedin now posed little danger of highwaymen. The Ngai Tahu were slowly reclaiming the land laid bare by the gold seekers, and they kept an eye on Matariki as soon as Grainie set so much as a hoof in the area around Lawrence and Elizabeth Station.

To remain fit for the long trips on the weekend, the horse needed to exercise during the week. This gave Matariki an easy excuse to get away from school as soon as she had completed her homework. She skipped evening activities like playing games and sewing, as well as choir and theater auditions, during which the other girls nurtured their friendships.

"Martha prefers talking to her nag," Alison Beasley scoffed once again— Miss Maynard remained the only one at the school who used the girl's proper name.

"A princess knows her own worth," Mary Jane Harrington, another victim of Alison's mockery, said on Matariki's behalf. Mary Jane was overweight. "As far as I know, the Kiward cobs have a considerably longer pedigree than the Beasleys on Koromiko Station."

Miss Maynard smiled at that to herself and moved Mary Jane into Matariki's room at the next opportunity. In the years that followed, though they didn't form a true friendship, Matariki and Mary Jane had a superb mutual understanding.

A few months later, a long-legged, light-brown dog joined Matariki on one of her rides. Afterward, half-starved and fearful, it hid itself in the straw next to Grainie's stall.

"The mutt can't stay here," said Donny Sullivan, the owner of the stable in Dunedin. "I'll be damned if I fatten up that critter."

"You don't need to do it for free, you know," Matariki responded.

The next Friday, the dog ran after Matariki all the way to Elizabeth Station and slept in front of the door to her room. Matariki rejected her parents' offer to keep the animal on the farm. Instead, she slipped at daybreak to the stream above the waterfall. The Drurys had tried to keep their gold source a secret from the children, but the Maori were less careful, and Matariki was not stupid. On Monday, she "gilded" Donny Sullivan's palm to let her dog stay in the horse's stall. He was to lock it in there every evening. Otherwise, Dingo—as Miss Maynard named him, after the dogs in her Australian homeland—would find a way into the dormitory, where he would stretch himself out in front of the door to Matariki's room.

"Well, he can't brag of any particularly exceptional pedigree," Alison noted maliciously. "Or are you claiming he's a prince?"

Matariki merely shrugged her shoulders meaningfully.

"He," said Mary Jane, "makes up for it with character, at least."

***

Matariki Drury did not have any problems and did not cause any—in contrast to her biological father, as Michael Drury and Hemi Kute affirmed in her third year of schooling in Dunedin. It was summer, and the men were drinking beer at a campfire near the stream in front of Elizabeth Station while Lizzie and Haikina experimented with skinning, butchering, and cooking a rabbit. Michael had shot it when Hemi was panning for gold. Some ship had brought the critters to New Zealand, and lacking natural predators, their population multiplied explosively. The Ngai Tahu, though, quickly learned to prize the animals as a new source of meat. Like the invasion of the *pakeha*, they accepted the rabbits as decreed by fate.

"Te Kooti sees the critters as new messengers of the god Whiro." Hemi grimaced. He was uneasy about the Ringatu and Hauhau movement. Kahu Heke had once again "requested" donations. "He cut out a rabbit's heart and sacrificed it to the gods."

"Weren't Whiro's messengers supposed to be the lizards?" Lizzie asked. The god Whiro was considered the representative of everything evil on earth, and the lizard was sacred to him. "Those I never really wanted to eat."

"They're more likely to eat you," Haikina laughed. "If the gods want you dead, they'll send one, and it'll eat you from the inside out. Rabbits just eat the grass out from under the sheep. In which they really hurt the *pakeha* more than the Hauhau. Te Kooti really ought to love them. But he's for anything that brings him attention."

"Including the ritual killing of a bunny? I don't know about that." Michael raised the whiskey bottle. "Don't you Maori have anything better to offer?"

Hemi responded with unexpected seriousness. "*Tikanga*, you mean? Old customs? Yes, we do. You know that." Lizzie and Michael and their children were invited to the tribe's festivals. Lizzie and Matariki would sing and dance along, but Michael always felt out of place. He sighed with relief whenever things switched to whiskey drinking and chatting. "All that stuff the Hauhau are digging up, though—"

"They're reaching back to rituals from the South Sea. Back to Hawaiki where we come from," Haikina added, seeming no less concerned. "With some of it, we don't even know if it was ever practiced on Aotearoa." She called New Zealand by its Maori name. "It's been a long time since we Maori ate our enemies," Haikina said. "But you hear things about the Hauhau. Te Kooti is supposed to have slaughtered people in the most gruesome fashion during his wars."

Te Kooti and his men had kept the North Island on edge between 1868 and 1872 through a series of surprise attacks. In one battle, almost thirty *pakeha* had died, many women and children among them.

"I can't imagine Kahu Heke participates in something like that," Lizzie said. Generally, she did not talk about Matariki's father, especially not in Michael's presence. Naturally, her husband had learned at some point who had sired

Matariki and under what circumstances, but within their marriage, Lizzie's relationship with Kahu Heke had never been a subject of discussion.

Now, however, Lizzie could not hold it inside. She simply had to express her concerns. Kahu Heke was, after all, no bumpkin warrior. He had attended the mission school until graduating high school. If he had been more patient and more moderate in his views, he could have been an attorney or doctor. But Kahu, a chieftain's son, was proud, cocky, and easily offended. The indignities to which he had been exposed at the mission school and by various employers on the North Island had enraged him and turned him into a burning nationalist.

At first, his actions had been childish. Like his ancestor Hone Heke, whose audacity had loosed the Flagstaff War in 1845, Kahu also got people to talk about him by knocking down flagpoles and damaging *pakeha* monuments. Only after his uncle Hongi Hika declared him his successor did he begin to take politics seriously. But to that day, he still had not succeeded Hongi Hika. The Ngati Pau had elected a chieftain with rather moderate views, and he kept completely out of the fights against the *pakeha*.

"Kahu isn't stupid," Lizzie objected. "And that stuff the Hauhau are preaching, there's no way he believes that some ritual will make warriors invulnerable or that you can poison someone with the water that runs off the roof of the chieftain's house."

Michael wanted to make some spiteful remark, but Hemi stopped him. "Him, no. I assume, anyway. I never had the pleasure of meeting him." When Kahu Heke was the guest of the Ngai Tahu, Hemi had still been in Dunedin. "But the average Hauhau is a warrior, not a student. They recruit from the big tribes on the North Island who were always happy to fight one another. Now a few of them are moving together against the *pakeha*—but if you ask me, they want to see blood more than anything. They want to believe in something, to be enthusiastic about something, and if easy loot happens along, all the better."

"Kahu couldn't support that," Lizzie said, but she was concerned.

Haikina nodded. "Right. But when it comes to these things, he never had any scruples. And that scares me. You never know what gets into such people's heads—which crazy custom or *tapu* they might think of next to set off a new war."

Chapter 2

"They're very different stars." Heather Coltrane leaned against the railing of the massive sailing ship, looking up into the sky, her back turned to the sea.

"Yes, and I would never have thought I'd see them again." Kathleen Burton, Heather's mother, had directed her gaze to the land, for the first lights of London could be discerned on the horizon. The stars had never much interested her. Kathleen's orientation was practical at heart. Even now, she thought less wistfully about her early life in Ireland than about the cities in Europe apparently being better illuminated than in New Zealand. When their ship had cast off on a summer evening almost three months before in Lyttelton, Kathleen had lost sight of the land after a few minutes. At least Dunedin, her home on the other end of the world, possessed gas lighting.

"A penny for your thoughts," laughed Peter Burton, lightly kissing the nape of his wife's neck.

Even after their years together, he could hardly be near Kathleen without the desire to touch her, to pull her close and protect her—perhaps because it had taken so long before all that was finally allowed him. The reverend had loved Kathleen for many years before she told him yes, and he was still proud he had not surrendered to the ghosts of her past. Kathleen had been fleeing her violent husband, Ian Coltrane; then, after his death, the love of her youth, Michael Drury, had reappeared. After all that, the final hurdle before their marriage—Kathleen's conversion from the Catholic to Anglican Church—ultimately had seemed an insignificant stumbling block.

Kathleen turned to her husband and smiled. She could not possibly admit to him that she had been thinking about streetlights.

"I was thinking about Colin," she claimed. "How strange it will be to see him again."

Colin Coltrane was the younger of Kathleen's sons and her middle child. After the violent death of his father, Ian Coltrane, the boy had been difficult, and Kathleen had consented to send him to a military academy in England. It had not been easy for her. As an Irishwoman, she carried a natural aversion to the British Crown. Yet the school had done Colin good. He had finished with good grades and since had been serving as a corporal in the British Army. Now he was stationed with the Royal Horse Guards in London—and was hopefully looking forward to seeing his mother and sister.

"We could have gone to Ireland too," Peter said, brushing his straight, light-brown hair from his face. The wind was blowing from the land; even in early summer, it was mostly cool and rainy in London. "Then you could have seen your whole family. We're going to be descending on nearly my whole tribe while you see only Colin. We won't be coming back to this place again in our lives. Maybe you can take this opportunity."

Kathleen looked into his friendly brown eyes. Peter's concern made her happy, but she shook her head decisively.

"No, Peter, I wouldn't like that at all. Look, there on the Vartry River, nothing's changed. The people are poor under the landlords' rule."

Three years before, Father O'Brien, the priest who had baptized Kathleen and Michael and taught them as children, had died at well past ninety. Through him, Kathleen had remained in loose contact with her family. Since his death, she had not heard any more from her brothers and sisters. Her parents had been dead for years.

"If we pop in there, we'll seem as rich to them as Croesus. I'd rather not stoke any envy."

Kathleen pulled tighter the extravagant tulle tie that fixed her small dark-green hat in place and held her hair back like a headscarf—a style from the latest collection of her tailoring workshop—wearable with any sort of travel dress. The Gold Mine Boutique in central Dunedin provided well for its proprietresses. Claire Dunloe and Kathleen earned considerably more than Peter Burton's parsonage in a suburb of Dunedin.

Peter grinned at his wife. "And most of all, you don't want to have to support your tribe from the goodness of your own heart from now on. Which someone would no doubt suggest—or which you'd think of yourself if the poverty is really as bitter in Ireland as they say."

"The poverty is surely bitter. So it is with the failed gold miners in Dunedin too." During the time of the gold rush, Peter Burton had always maintained a soup kitchen for penniless immigrants, and now his parish supported the families of the failed adventurers stranded in Dunedin. "Lord knows I don't owe my family anything." Kathleen grew more agitated. "To them, I was dead as soon as my belly showed I was carrying Michael's child. Not a spark of interest in my life after they sold me off to Ian and shoved me off to the ends of the earth. So, don't tell me about Ireland and my family. I belong in Dunedin. With you."

Kathleen placed her hand in his, and the thought shot through Peter's head that a more open wife would likely have embraced him at those words, but he could not expect public affection from her.

Heather, her twenty-nine-year-old daughter, smirked at her mother. "None of our relatives seem particularly lovable," she said. Heather was not exactly looking forward to a reunion with Colin. "I hope yours are nice at least, Reverend."

Peter laughed at the form of address. Through the childhoods of Kathleen's offspring, he had been Reverend Burton—and even though Kathleen's oldest son, Sean, had ultimately brought himself to simply call him Peter, Heather never would.

"My relatives are typical English country gentry," he answered her. "Prim, conceited, set in their ways, and guaranteed not to look particularly well upon us, although Uncle James was compelled to bequeath his estate to his lost nephew in the Pacific, of all people."

Heather giggled. "Although his justification really was rather mean spirited." With a serious expression, she recited from James Burton's will: "'I do bequeath my estate at Treherbert, Wales, to the only member of the Burton family who ever did anything sensible with his life.'"

Peter shrugged. "When you're right, you're right," he said. "But it's best not to expect the tribe to welcome us with open arms. Look there, London. A world-class metropolis with museums, libraries, theaters, palaces. We should spend a few days here, indulging in a little culture. I'm sure I can find a colleague who will put us up."

"And many, many soup kitchens." Kathleen furrowed her brow. "I know you, Peter, and the people you know work in the poorest quarters of the city, helping beggars and urchins. Within two days, we'd be at the point of you listening to their stories while I make stew. I won't hear of it, Peter Burton. We'll be staying in a proper hotel—nothing showy, but nothing shabby either. We'll meet Colin there, if possible tomorrow. And then we'll travel on to Wales."

Peter raised his hands. "Peace, Kate, I approve of the hotel. Anyway, I'm foregoing an audience with the queen—even if I do have a thing or two to say to her, precisely regarding the charitable sector. But until we've arranged our meeting with Colin, I may show you two around the city, may I not?"

***

The next morning, Kathleen contacted Colin at the Hyde Park Barracks. Following that, they visited the National Gallery at Heather's urging. Kathleen's daughter had inherited her mother's artistic talent, as was clear in her portraiture. The sheep barons of the South Island fell over themselves to be eternalized in oil by Heather Coltrane—and to have their wives, children, and horses painted as well. Heather once painted a prize-winning ram of Michael Drury's, and since then, the Sideblossoms, Beasleys, and Barringtons all wanted pictures of their animals. Heather made good money, although she now mentioned mournfully that she would not likely ever make it into the National Gallery with a picture of the Beasleys' stud horse.

"Here, perhaps not, but in New Zealand for sure," Peter joked, and Kathleen laughed along, happy that Heather was clearly enjoying herself and once more showing signs of life.

It had not been easy to convince Heather to travel with them. She was in mourning. Not because of any death—on the contrary, it was a joyful event that had robbed Kathleen's daughter of her joie de vivre. Her friend of many years, Chloe, the daughter of Kathleen's friend and business partner, Claire, had fallen in love and married. Yet the girls had always spoken of opening a business together like their mothers had with the Gold Mine Boutique. Chloe had imagined running a gallery in which she would sell paintings by Heather and other artists. But then, Terrence Boulder, a young banker who was to lead the branch of the Dunloe Private Bank on the North Island, appeared, and Chloe did not give Heather another thought.

There was nothing to hold against the young man. He was smart and friendly, educated, and open-minded; Chloe's mother and her stepfather, Jimmy Dunloe, could not have wished for a better son-in-law. After a grand wedding, the social event of the season in Dunedin, the young couple had moved to Wellington. Since then, Heather had been moping, despite her commissions and successes.

That afternoon, Peter visited a colleague—as Kathleen had expected, the man worked in the most dilapidated area of Whitechapel—while Kathleen and Heather went to Harrods.

***

At the hotel, there was a message from Colin, suggesting they meet around seven o'clock in the hotel's foyer.

"Seven! It's already six. We need to change, Heather, at least spruce ourselves up a bit. And hopefully Peter will come back on time. Do you think it's worth sending a message? It's possible he's lost track of the time talking to his friend and—"

Heather rolled her eyes and calmly pulled her mother toward the stairs. "Colin has seen both of us in evening gowns and in our nightgowns—and I don't think it matters to him either way. He doesn't think much of us to begin with. I hope the army's driven out all his back talk and his belief that the male Coltranes are so much above the female creatures of the world."

At first, Kathleen wanted to object, but Heather was right. Their relationship with Colin had never been good. The boy had worshipped Ian, which was no surprise, since Ian had shamelessly spoiled him, preferring him to the other children. Colin alone had remained with his father when Kathleen finally fled her marriage—and it had not been to the boy's benefit. When Kathleen had taken him back after Ian's death, her son could no longer fit himself into the family. Colin hadn't wanted to go to school or to remain in any apprenticeship Kathleen secured for him. And even worse, he lied and stole.

Kathleen hoped the army had at least driven the worst attitudes out of him. Still, she was in a hurry to get to her room and fix herself up for her son. When Peter arrived at six thirty, she was already wearing a proper, but figure-emphasizing, dark-green evening dress. She had put up her golden-blonde hair

25

and affixed a tiny, extravagant, green hat. A small veil danced along the side of her face without obscuring her large, luminous green eyes.

Kathleen Burton was a beauty—even now, at forty-seven years old. Her complexion was marble white, and her high cheekbones and full lips made her features seem noble. No one would come upon the idea that this British rose came from an unknown Irish village.

Peter whistled jokingly through his teeth like a boy from the streets, as he often did, when he saw his wife in front of the mirror.

"Your son can be proud of you in any case," Peter said as he exchanged his simple brown suit for a frock coat, under which his priest's collar looked strangely displaced. He was only doing it out of love for Kathleen. Peter hated formal clothing—perhaps because of his years in the gold-mining camps where he had tended his flock. He had rarely worn his vestments there, where the men had more need of hospital tents, soup kitchens, and medical care than preaching. "No one in his barracks has a more beautiful mother. Will he be inviting us into the officers' club, by the way? I've never seen one from the inside."

Kathleen shook her head, blushing slightly.

"No, as you know, that can't be. He—"

"Of course, he must still use the name Dunloe." Peter laughed. "I had almost forgotten. Think of poor Jimmy. But perhaps he's rather proud of the strapping lad in the red coat."

Kathleen did not find the matter so amusing. It had caused her bitter pangs of conscience to pretend her son was English and Jimmy Dunloe's progeny. Claire's husband had suggested the plan to her because it would hardly have been possible to admit the son of an Irish horse trader to the Royal Military Academy. Colin was now in the Royal Horse Guards and so protected the queen herself.

A knock on the door prevented Kathleen's need to reply. A page bowed and announced that Reverend Burton and his wife were expected in the lobby. She looked herself over once more in the mirror and let Peter help her into her coat.

Kathleen was surprised by what she saw when they reached the hotel lobby. Heather was conversing enthusiastically with a tall blond young man in the red uniform of the guards. They turned to Peter and Kathleen as they came down the stairs, and Kathleen noted to her relief that Heather was smiling. She, at least, had no intention of playing the sullen one that evening, and she looked lovely in her wine-red dress and matching hat.

"Mother, Reverend."

Colin approached with a friendly smile, kissed his mother's hand with perfect form, and bowed no less correctly to Peter Burton, who was startled at first. Colin's striking resemblance to his mother had not stood out to him so much in Tuapeka. He had resembled his father more. But then the boy had been a surly youth with lanky limbs and a devious expression. Now, in contrast, he was a young corporal with an open, amicable gaze—an exceptionally good-looking man with aristocratic facial features and soulful brown eyes. These, Kathleen had not given him, but Colin's eyes didn't have the black spark of his father, who, people whispered, had gypsy ancestry.

"It pleases me greatly to see you, Mother, the reverend, and, of course, my charming sister again. I hardly recognized you, Heather. You've grown up into a breathtaking beauty."

Heather blushed, and Peter revised his unqualifiedly good impression of Colin. The flattery was a bit too much, even somewhat inappropriate, toward his sister. Heather was shorter than her mother and had fine, curly ash-blonde hair. Her delicate features and her soft, dark eyes had something Madonna-like at second glance. But Heather was far from as eye-catching as her mother, who in her younger years had brought a whole room to silence when she entered.

"Where shall we go, Colin?" Peter asked in the somewhat awkward silence after Colin's little speech. "Or should I say Corporal Dunloe?"

He spoke amicably, but an expression of displeasure crept onto Colin's face. "It's not my fault that I'm not yet a sergeant. And I use the name Coltrane now," he blurted out.

Kathleen shrugged. "Whatever your rank, you look grand in your uniform," she said happily. "Will you recommend a restaurant? Peter was speculating about an officers' club, but that—"

"That would likely not be appropriate," Colin said brusquely, looking at Kathleen with some irritation. "I mean—," Colin began to explain, but Heather interrupted him.

"I, for one, am hungry as a wolf," she said gaily. "And I'm cold. To wit: 'It'll be summer in England when we arrive, Heather. You only need to pack your light clothing.' Perhaps they call this summer here, but to my mind, 'rainy season' fits better."

Heather's comment made all of them laugh and led to a graceful change of subject. As he led them to a steak house near the hotel, Colin described the monsoon rains in India, where he had spent the previous year.

"So, you didn't like it in India?" Kathleen asked.

"No," said Colin tersely. "Thoroughly backward rascals, delusional maharajas, and officers of the Crown settled into jobs for show." He seemed to want to keep going, but he then squared himself, breathed deeply, and twisted his face back into a smile. "The horses, however, Heather, those are interesting. Can you imagine? They have Marwari horses with upturned ears. I'm serious."

Heather, an equestrian, listened with interest while Kathleen and Peter exchanged concerned glances. India belonged among England's most important colonies—only the year before, the Prince of Wales had visited it—and there was constant unrest. Kathleen had been concerned when they had ordered Colin there, but for young soldiers, service in India was surely a springboard. Colin, however, had returned after one year. Had he let himself be replaced simply because he did not like the weather and the natives?

"But you do feel at home here, Colin?" Kathleen inquired with concern. "I mean, it's surely an honor to be in the Royal Horse Guards."

"Did you play polo in India?" Heather asked at the same time.

Colin did not quite seem to know which question he should answer first, and his expression wavered between smiling and reluctance.

"Naturally, little sis, I was always a good rider, wasn't I?"

"And that's why you're in the Royal Horse Guards now?" Peter asked. "Presumably one has to be a very good rider to—"

Colin pursed his lips. "Oh, nonsense," he blurted out. "Any beginner could ride the few formations we perform when it's the queen's birthday, or when we ride behind her carriage as an honor guard—it's laughable. I didn't go to the Royal Military Academy for that."

"So why do you do it, then?" Kathleen asked. She did not like interrogating her son, but she almost felt she had gone back in time to when every day at dinner she had tried to draw out of him the reason for his latest dismissal from an apprenticeship.

Colin seemed reminded of that as well. He made a face as if in a fit of rage, but then he brought himself quickly back under control. "Well, in the army, one does what one must," he mused moodily. "And I don't cut a bad figure on a horse, you know. Perhaps it simply pleases the queen to have handsome young corporals around her." He smiled winningly. "Or handsome young sergeants."

Kathleen could not return Colin's smile. Queen Victoria was generally held to be extraordinarily prudish. She surely did not spare a second thought to the men who guarded her.

"You're expecting a promotion soon, then?" Peter could not get Colin's comment when they met out of his head. "Are you vexed that it did not come when you were in India?"

Colin shrugged, seemingly apathetic. "It can take time. In the army, they don't give much thought to poor Irish beggars who want to make something of themselves."

Kathleen lowered her gaze immediately, but Peter furrowed his brow. No person in the army was supposed to know about Colin's Irish extraction. To his superiors, he was a Dunloe—perhaps born under somewhat opaque circumstances on the other end of the world but still an offspring of a banking family with contacts all the way to the royal palace.

"I'm considering . . ." Colin inhaled deeply. "What would you say, Mother, if I were to return to New Zealand?"

***

"Armed constable? What is that, anyway?" Kathleen asked.

She had not wanted to ask the previous evening. Colin had been so enthusiastic about his return home and his new prospects among the Armed Constabulary Field Force that she did not want to raise any objections. After all, he should feel welcome even if she did not have a good feeling about any of this. But now, on the train to Cardiff, Kathleen aired her concerns.

"The Armed Constabulary is a mix between an army regiment and the police, armed, as the name suggests," the pastor explained. "It was formed in 1867 and legitimized with a law from Parliament. Under the pressure of the Maori Wars, if you ask me. Back then, it looked like there was going to be a proper uprising. There were even soldiers from England on the North Island, but they were so far out of place and supposed to fight fellows like that Te Kooti in his own country. We've seen often enough where that leads. One doesn't understand the other, and in the end, it turns out bloodier than it needed to be. It did come to a few massacres—on both sides. And finally, they decided in Wellington to send the English home. The armed constables took over the fighting. Apparently with success: Te Kooti ultimately gave up and sought shelter from his *kingi*."

"But where did the men come from?" Kathleen asked. "Certainly not from British military academies?"

Peter shook his head. "No. Most of them seem to have been recruited from settlers and local police forces—and not without reason. They knew the area. Aside from that, they took on Maori, which was also well advised. Not all of them were in revolt, after all, and surely it contributed to calming the situation."

Heather, who had been drawing quick charcoal sketches of the English landscape viewed from the train window, broke out laughing. "That's one way of looking at it. At the university, anyway, they said instead that the tribes fought all the more fiercely with one another. In East Cape and Gisborne, there were supposedly civil wars."

Kathleen shrugged. "Either way, the battles are past. Why do we still need armed constables?"

She did not ask the question she wanted to pose: "Why do we need Colin?" Yet, it hung almost palpably between them in the elegant first-class compartment.

"To prevent further battles?" Peter said. "They still need to recruit people; otherwise Colin couldn't return."

"His sergeant apparently put in a good word for him," observed Kathleen, still somewhat tense.

Colin had presented the matter as if the Armed Constabulary were simply waiting for him, and his British superiors had approved his transfer.

Peter nodded—soothingly, he hoped—and was grateful to Heather for not saying more. Kathleen had to know that one could praise difficult subordinates out the door.

***

Peter's brother, Joseph, had sent a carriage to the train station to retrieve his relations from New Zealand. The Burtons owned an estate in Roath, a small town a few miles east of Cardiff. Although Roath was centrally situated, according to Peter, it was still stamped by village life.

Cardiff itself had originally been an idyllic little city itself, but since the boom in coal mining, its small harbor had grown into one of the most important industrial ports in the world. The city showed the signs of a settlement that had grown too quickly: ugly, hurriedly raised houses, shanty towns around the city center, and many migrants who sought their fortune or at least a livelihood by more-or-less legal means. However, beautiful buildings, arcades, and government buildings also sprang up. The city was clearly changing, and it reminded Kathleen in some respects of Dunedin during the gold rush.

"For those of us in Roath, the growth in Cardiff is a decided advantage," explained Joseph Burton, a plump, red-faced man who allowed one to imagine what Peter would have looked like if he were not kept so busy by his parish. Joseph, too, had straight brown hair and symmetrical features. Instead of having laugh lines and creases like those that characterized Peter's face, Joseph's cheeks seemed rather more bloated, and there were bags beneath his eyes.

"They're already building in our neighborhood. Naturally only the better sort, you understand: bankers, ship owners, businessmen who make their money in coal without getting the dust and filth in their eyes." Joseph laughed. "In Roath, they practically get to live in the country, but they are in their offices on the harbor in a jiffy. For that, they'll pay just about any price. We even sold a little land and made a humble profit."

Joseph Burton's appearance was anything but humble. His coach was exceedingly elegant, hitched to four beautiful horses and driven by a liveried servant. Peter praised the lovely horses but rolled his eyes when he faced Kathleen. It was completely unnecessary to send a four-horse team. After all, there were only three people and three bags to transport.

Naturally, Joseph was expensively dressed, his frock coat definitely bespoke.

"We have them made in London," he said when Kathleen asked him about it. She was heart and soul a tailor, after all. "On Savile Row. Here in the provinces, you can only get whatever's sold to the masses, but it must be worse for you lot at the end of the world."

Joseph passed an eye over Peter's already somewhat worn brown suit. Kathleen immediately began feeling embarrassed. There were plenty of good gentlemen's tailors in Dunedin, but Peter simply didn't place importance in his outward appearance. At least Kathleen was sure that Heather's riding clothes and her own, too, could withstand any scrutiny.

Heather was not so easily impressed. She did not like Peter's brother or his pretentious ways. She wondered to whom the "we" referred. What a shame that her stepuncle was now sitting across from her in the coach. That made it impossible for her to discuss her impressions with Peter.

The coach traveled through Cardiff's attractive center and the less appealing outskirts. The road to Roath led through lush green pastures and fields, and Roath itself was marked by a vast lake-dotted landscape. The stables, haystacks, and ivy-covered cottages seemed small and dollhouse-like to the New Zealanders. As they traveled through this landscape, it wasn't long before mother and daughter had a change of mood. Kathleen thought of Ireland, and Heather felt herself transported to the fairy tales of her childhood.

The Burton house lay amid a parklike landscape on one of the lakes. The building was a dream of red brick, its façade decorated with high windows, bays, and little towers. It was surrounded by ancient trees, its approach paved with bright gravel. Really, the Burtons owned a castle.

"Well, not a castle exactly," Peter said when Kathleen later accused him of understating his family's estate. "It's just a manor house. Like I said, country gentry. And the family did not have all that much money anymore, at least until my little brother made his 'humble profit' with land speculation. But all the better. Then they won't envy us the house in Treherbert."

A great deal of money had gone into furnishing the entrance hall, the apartments, and the guest rooms. Kathleen could estimate the value of the furniture and textiles, since the Gold Mine Boutique ordered its materials from England. Moreover, everything was arranged in the very latest fashion—which no longer astonished Kathleen once she met Joseph Burton's "we." Joseph's new wife and his son from his first marriage also occupied the house. Joseph had been a widower but had remarried a year before. Peter and Joseph's aged mother occupied rooms in the house's upper story. Their father had died.

"Didn't he say something about a son?" Heather whispered as a girl approached them in an elegant receiving room. She had dark hair, pale skin, and a fairylike beauty.

"Welcome to Paradise Manor," she said softly.

Joseph Burton laughed behind them. "She's renamed it," he explained. "Before, it was simply Burton Manor, but Alice has a knack for poetry. Allow me to introduce you. This is Alice Burton, my wife."

***

"Dear Lord, the girl's younger than Heather," Kathleen said when she was alone with Peter.

Both of them had worn frozen smiles as Joseph and Alice showed them the house and then offered them tea. Kathleen still found the English tea rituals somewhat uncomfortable, and the procedure in Paradise Manor reminded her so much of days long past in Ireland that it almost made her skin crawl. Then, she had been the somewhat awkward girl serving the tea—and longing for the sweet tea cakes served alongside it. The young Mary Kathleen had served in the landlord's manor house, and although occasionally she was allowed to take some bread home, she was constantly tempted to steal leftover tea cakes to share with her beloved Michael Drury.

Kathleen smiled encouragingly at the shy blonde housemaid who poured the tea with shaking hands. Alice had rebuked her sharply when a few drops spilled to the side. Surely the young housewife did not have it easy asserting her position, but Kathleen and well-raised Heather winced embarrassedly when Alice made a scene with the girl.

"Where did he scoop up this Alice of his?" Peter asked later. "She doesn't display the most proper behavior even though she is clearly trying to. And she's hardly older than his son, if I remember correctly."

"I, for one, will be happy to get out of here as soon as possible," Kathleen stated. "No matter how lovely the surroundings. And as much as I like your mother."

Peter's mother rarely left her rooms on the upper floor of the house any-more, ostensibly because she had difficulty climbing the stairs. However, during their short conversation, Kathleen had gleaned that Alice's décor did not particularly please her. Kathleen liked the old lady considerably more than her young daughter-in-law, but she did not want to judge Alice. Perhaps she had good reasons for marrying a much older and less attractive man.

"My mother knows that we want to be on to Rhondda soon. I think she likes you. She spoke very positively of you. However, there might be a problem with the house at Treherbert. The way things look, Randolph's moved in there, after Joseph and Alice married and before Uncle James died. Now he's claiming the house. Presumably, my uncle wanted to change his will in Randolph's favor."

Randolph was Joseph's son from his first marriage. Kathleen could not blame him for fleeing his father's house.

"Perhaps we can come to some agreement with him," she said. "There is a village that belongs to it with tenants living there—or was it a mine? When we have possession of the estate and make him steward . . ."

Peter shrugged. "Would you feel comfortable as an absentee landlady while someone else brings in your rent?"

Kathleen blushed. Things were only getting worse. Sitting through teatime had been difficult enough, but now she was supposed to be a landlady?

Chapter 3

It was beautiful March day in Dunedin, sunny and warm enough to seem summery to Matariki. The long Christmas break had ended only two weeks before, and the new school year, her fourth in Otago, had just begun. When her parents had first brought her to Dunedin, the harbor immediately fascinated her. Michael had steered his team onto the coastal road in the direction of Parakanui, and Matariki could not get enough of the view of the idyllic coves, beaches, and the Pacific, which gleamed deep blue and sea green.

During her time living in Dunedin, she left the study rooms whenever the weather permitted, taking her assigned reading with her on her daily rides. South of the city were plenty of beaches, and she would tether her horse and leave it to graze while she went to the beach and did her homework. Her favorite spot was a remote cove off the coastal road; here, Matariki imagined residing in her own hidden fortress, waiting for her fairy-tale prince—although her books for school rarely encouraged daydreaming as much as *Romeo and Juliet*, which she was now reading.

Her attention really left much to be desired. Instead of underlining passages that could help her with her assignment on the characterization of Romeo, she let her gaze wander over the deep-blue sea. Her birth father's people had overcome it in canoes, and Kahu Heke was himself a courageous sailor. Years before, he had helped Lizzie escape arrest on the North Island by bringing her from the Bay of Islands to Kaikoura in the war canoe of the Ngati Pau. They had sailed around half the North Island and navigated the channel between the South and North Island. Matariki found that considerably more romantic than sword fighting in Shakespeare's play. Distractedly she scratched Dingo, who had stretched out beside her. Suddenly, though, the dog leaped up and barked.

Two men thrust themselves out of the shadows on the other end of the cove, as if materializing from thin air, and raised their arms defensively as the dog rushed at them. Horrified, Matariki saw the guns in their hands.

"Dingo!"

The girl cried out as a shot was fired, but fortunately the bullet did not hit the dog. Dingo broke off his assault and rushed back to Matariki's side. The trembling animal pressed against her, Matariki looked at the men. Her book fell from her hand.

"Don't move." The man spoke Maori, but it sounded unusual. And he looked strange. Matariki had never before seen a young man whose face was so completely covered in *moko*, the traditional tattoos of the tribes. Among the Ngai Tahu, this custom had become increasingly rare. Haikina and Hemi had not been tattooed at all. Other members of the *iwi*, the tribe, had smaller tattoos on their noses and foreheads. The two men who now approached her in an odd mixture of threatening gestures and defensiveness, on the other hand, looked truly martial. The traditional polygons and spirals wound themselves across their cheeks to the chin, making the sight of their encircled eyes appear wild and their foreheads low. Both men wore their long hair tied into warrior knots, and the rest of their appearance was of the Maori warrior prepared for battle. Over loincloths they wore long skirts of hardened flax, a sort of colorful sash around their upper body, and small figurines of the gods, *hei-tiki*, of bone around their necks. However, they were not threatening Matariki with war clubs and spears but instead with modern firearms. One aimed a revolver at her, the other a hunting rifle.

Dingo barked again. One of the men raised his gun; the other shook his head and said something, but Matariki only understood the word *tapu*.

"You're Matariki Heke?" asked the man who pointed the weapon at her.

Matariki put her hand over Dingo's snout. "I'm Matariki Drury," she said, determined not to show any fear.

In fact, she was more shocked than afraid. While the men seemed warlike, it also looked like they were in costume—the Ngai Tahu only put on such outfits for festivals. So, to Matariki, they seemed less like soldiers and more like *kepas*, group dancers about to begin performing a *haka*.

"It's time for you to acknowledge your duties to your tribe," the other man said. "I had thought that she—"

"She's grown up among *pakeha*," the first observed. "She may not know her purpose."

"I'm going now," Matariki said.

She had no idea why the men were there, or why one of them was still pointing his weapon at her, but they seemed to want to discuss the matter with each other first. Perhaps they would just let her go. Perhaps she had just been in the way of whatever they were up to. Were they smugglers? Nothing that they could be delivering illegally readily occurred to Matariki, but that was not her problem. She slowly moved to stand up.

"You're not going anywhere." The man waved his revolver.

Matariki raised her hands placatingly. At least Dingo was behaving. "I, I won't tell anyone I saw you, agreed?" She forced herself to smile.

The man with the weapon seemed to have come to a decision. He reared up before her—although he did keep a distance—and looked even more like the lead dancer in a group.

"We've been charged with retrieving you. You belong to your people. May the sacred House of the Ngati Pau endure forever."

Matariki's heart suddenly began to beat hard and fast. The whole scene seemed like a poor performance by the theater club of Otago Girls' High School. Yet these men had weapons, and they were not props. After all, they had nearly shot Dingo. The "sacred House of the Ngati Pau" did, of course, clarify some things. Though the men were Maori, they were apparently not members of an *iwi* of the Ngai Tahu.

"Who, who exactly gave you that charge?" she asked cautiously.

"You are going to have to take on the responsibilities of a chieftain's daughter."

He pressed closer to Matariki, who forced herself not to back away. In battle and defense among the Maori, it always first came down to awing the opponent. If he was sufficiently impressed, he would often break off his attack.

Dingo started barking again, but this time no one paid attention to him. The men seemed to be more concerned that Matariki was not fleeing from them. Matariki found the expression in their eyes more than strange. Naturally her courage should irk them, but in reality, she had nothing to wield against them. The taller of the men was around six feet, and even the shorter one wouldn't have needed a weapon to overpower the barely fourteen-year-old Matariki. To kidnap her, he just needed to throw her over his shoulder. Nevertheless, he seemed to prefer negotiation.

"Your father sends us. *Ariki* Kahu Heke. We're going to take you to him."

Matariki frowned. She was confused and increasingly concerned. Might these men be crazy? "But Kahu Heke lives on the North Island. How are we supposed to get there? Fly?"

The men shook their heads. They gestured energetically with their weapons, directing Matariki to go ahead of them, toward the rocks from which they had emerged.

Matariki had to wade into the water and Dingo had to swim, but she knew the cove well and knew that it was completely safe to round the rocks while the sea was calm. Through the shallow water in which tiny fish swam and past the rocks, they reached the next cove, which was often flooded. Today the gravel beach was visible, and on it sat a gleaming outrigger canoe decorated with carvings. To Matariki, it seemed massive. Surely twenty men could occupy it. The two men could not have rowed it there alone. A folded sail lay in the boat. Matariki vacillated between disbelief, fear, and the desire for adventure. Doubtless the canoe was seaworthy, and the men seemed serious about spiriting her away to the North Island.

"But, but I don't know. What am I supposed to do? What are the duties of a chieftain's daughter?"

Matariki's head was spinning. She sought support from the rocks. The men who had followed her into the narrow inlet reacted with alarm, almost fear. One seemed to want to duck when her shadow almost touched him.

"There, over there!"

The man energetically indicated Matariki should either climb into the boat or stand behind it. He wanted Matariki to keep a distance between himself and his friend. He did not answer her questions, but Matariki's thoughts raced as she climbed over the canoe. What might Kahu Heke want from her? What were the duties of a Maori princess?

Marriage politics was the first thing that occurred to her. Did her father want to marry her off? To some Maori prince to win the support of his tribe for the Hauhau? No, that was laughable. Matariki brushed her panic aside. She had once read a report by missionaries who lived on the South Island in which they disparaged the custom of marriage between brother and sister in chieftains' families. Afterward, she had asked Haikina if that was common among the Maori.

"Among us, no, not for a long time. But it's supposed to continue on the North Island," she had said. "Don't look so horrified. It has advantages and disadvantages."

Matariki vaguely recalled a lecture on *tapu* and a strong royal line, but she did not need to worry about that now. As far as she knew, she was Kahu Heke's only child, and even if there were a son, too, he could hardly be of marriageable age.

The men had consulted briefly with each other; they seemed to feel safe now that Matariki stood on the other side of the canoe. There was no possibility of flight here. At most, she could swim. The taller one with the gun now began an explanation.

"You stay there, chieftain's daughter. Behind the canoe. Your dog too. And we'll stay here in front, understand?"

Apparently, the man wanted to divide the cove between them and Matariki and Dingo. Matariki did not know why.

"I think I'm supposed to sail with you. But I can't just go. I have to inform the school. And my parents will worry. And my horse—"

Grainie stood tethered on the beach, but Matariki did not really worry so much for her. Eventually, she would tear herself free and run to the stables.

"You won't be informing anyone," grumbled the taller man.

"Your family is the tribe of the Ngati Pau," said the shorter man. "You are only responsible to it. We will sail at high tide."

Matariki chewed her upper lip. That could be several hours. By then, they would have long since missed her at school. But nobody would know where to look for her. Perhaps she had mentioned the beach to Mary Jane, but she definitely had not described it, and it did not have a name. True, a search party could ride up and down the coastal road, and she did not doubt Michael would do so, but would Miss Partridge inform her parents soon enough?

***

No one worried much when Matariki did not appear at dinner. Sometimes she was late when she had been off riding. Miss Maynard did not become nervous until she saw Matariki wasn't in her room at bedtime. She asked Mary Jane if she knew anything, but she did not. And, no, they had not fought, and Mary Jane didn't know of any spats with the other girls.

Sarah Lark

"She just rode away. Like every day," Mary Jane said.

"But that's how it always is," said Miss Partridge when Miss Maynard pulled her aside. "The girls always cover for one another when one of them leaves. Have you checked the other rooms? Is there a party somewhere?"

Miss Maynard shook her head. "It's too early for a party. And besides, Matariki Drury wouldn't be invited to something like that. I asked in the stables as well. Her horse and dog are also still missing. I'm worried. Should we send someone to Elizabeth Station?"

Miss Partridge rubbed her forehead. It would make a bad impression if Matariki was annoyed by something and arrived sobbing at Elizabeth Station. Though that had never happened with the Drury girl, it certainly had with other charges. When the school had not reacted by informing the parents immediately of their daughter's disappearance, there had mostly been trouble.

"Could it be that she has, hmm, a beau?" inquired Miss Partridge disapprovingly. "I mean, these Maori girls ripen early. It could certainly be . . ."

Miss Maynard did not dignify this with a response. "I'll go back to Mr. Sullivan's," she said. "I'll have him send a stableboy to the Drurys'. I have a bad feeling about this. Matariki would not simply disappear without telling anyone."

***

The sun had gone down, and as the moon rose, Matariki shivered in her thin summer clothes. The Maori men lit a fire on their side of the cove and wrapped themselves in blankets. Over the fire, a stew of meat and *kumara*, or sweet potatoes, bubbled. Matariki was hungry. Fine, this was an abduction, and victims could not expect particularly friendly treatment, but she was a chieftain's daughter, and Kahu Heke could not have intended her to starve and freeze.

Matariki had snuggled into the canoe's leeward side, but now she stood up. "Can I perhaps get some of that?" she asked angrily. "Some of that food, some of those blankets? Or is it *tikanga* in the sacred House of the Ngati Pau to let a chieftain's daughter starve?"

The men winced anew as her shadow, created by the moonlight, fell in their vicinity. They whispered excitedly with each other as they had before. Apparently, they were of different opinions. She overheard the word *tapu* several times.

"We'll give you the black blanket," the shorter one decided, and he threw it over the canoe to her. "Here. That's yours now, understand?"

40

"Don't touch the others." The taller man spoke, sounding fearful.

Matariki looked at the pile of blankets the men had on hand. There was no shortage. They could easily have given her another and possibly another still for Dingo, who also was shivering. All the others were blue, however. Was there some *tapu* related to blanket color?

She took the black blanket without thanks and pointed to the food. "And that?"

Once more, there was quiet though frantic discussion. Matariki thought she heard something like, "We can't let her starve the whole journey."

"Do you know how to build a fire?" the shorter warrior asked.

Matariki arched her brows. "The sacred House of the Ngai Tahu," she remarked snottily, "is always properly heated."

"Good," said the man. "Then you can come over here and take this wood." He separated a pile. "And here is a pot. Here are *kumara* and dried fish. Take it and cook for yourself."

Matariki sprang up to get the items, but the men pointed their weapons at her nervously. She had to wait until both had withdrawn behind the rocks on the edge of the inlet. Threatened from there by their weapons, she slowly climbed back over the canoe and carried the supplies to her side of the cove. Until this point, she had found this situation strange, but now the men's behavior frightened her. It seemed she was in the clutches of madmen. And there was no possibility of escape.

***

Donny Sullivan's stableboy galloped the entire way to Elizabeth Station and woke Lizzie and Michael Drury around three in the morning. Lizzie ran to Matariki's room, and Michael ran to the stables, but Miss Partridge's hope that the girl might have simply up and ridden home did not bear out. While Michael harnessed a team, Lizzie lit a few torches—the sign for danger or trouble worked out with the Maori village. A short time later, ten Maori warriors were with them, prepared to fend off any assailants of the Drurys or their gold source by force of weapons. They confirmed that Matariki had not fled to the Ngai Tahu either.

Hemi and three other warriors who spoke at least some English joined the Drurys for the trip to Dunedin. Around morning, they all arrived at Otago Girls' High School, where the massive warriors, some of whom wore *moko*, frightened the principal half to death. The sight of them made Mary Jane burst into tears. Michael and Lizzie believed the girl didn't know anything, but she did recall that Matariki liked to ride to the beach. Michael divided up the search teams and headed out.

Lizzie took over the continued investigation in the school. She was deathly pale when she returned to Miss Partridge's office after a brief inspection of Matariki's room.

"Miss Partridge, we need to inform the police. Something serious must have happened. My daughter—"

"Now, let's not jump to conclusions." The principal strained to remain calm. "Girls will be girls. Martha may have run away. She could be with some, hmm, beau."

Miss Maynard inhaled audibly. Lizzie merely stared at the older woman coldly. "Miss Partridge, my daughter's no fool. She would never run away without taking some money at a very minimum. But her allowance and the money for the stables are still in her trunk. She didn't take a change of clothes either. According to Mary Jane, she's only wearing a riding skirt and a thin blouse. She would have frozen overnight. And she knows that. She's spent plenty of nights outdoors."

Miss Partridge rubbed her nose once again. "But if she's with a—"

Lizzie held up her hand to stop the woman. "As for any possible beau, she's never spoken of a boy, to me or to her roommate or her friends back home. Since the Maori, as I'm sure you were about to remark, are rather liberal on this point, my daughter would have seen no reason to remain completely silent about a relationship. So, please call the police, or shall I do it myself?"

***

The police officer was gathering information when Hemi returned with Weru, his search companion. They had found Grainie on the coastal road and then searched the surrounding inlets.

Miss Maynard moaned in desperation when Hemi pulled *Romeo and Juliet* from his bag, laying it on Miss Partridge's desk. He also had Matariki's riding boots.

"We found even more," he declared. "Perhaps you should take a look yourself, Officer. Michael already knows, Lizzie. We're all meeting at the cove."

***

Half an hour later, the Drurys were standing in a desolate inlet lit by the morning sun, which one could only reach by wading through water or being lowered down from the rocks. Hemi and Weru were both skilled trackers, and they found the trail of Matariki's little feet, Dingo's paws, and the bare feet of two men. They followed all of the tracks into the water.

"She was reading on the beach," Hemi said, reconstructing the events for the Drurys and the officer. "She had taken off her boots. And then these men must have appeared, and they followed her into the water. No, Officer, Matariki went first, and they did not drag her. We then waded around this rock and discovered this cove. There was a canoe here." He pointed to recognizable indents in the gravel. "And here was a fire and there another—no idea why they needed two, but they seem to have spent the night here until high tide. And now, look at that."

Hemi led the group to the back of the cove where the smaller fire had burned. At about hip height, a penciled note had been written on the pale rock.

Kidnapped, Kahu Heke, North Island, two men, weapons, M.

The letters were of uneven size and rather awkwardly written. Matariki must have written in several stages and surely in almost total darkness, maybe even behind her back. No doubt she had been under watch.

Lizzie rubbed her eyes. "I should have known. The Hauhau and their crazy ideas about *tikanga*."

The officer looked at her, horrified. "The Hauhau, you say? For heaven's sake. You don't believe, do you, that they want to eat the girl?"

Hemi shook his head. "A chieftain's daughter? Certainly not that. On the contrary, they won't touch the girl. But we still need to try to find Matariki. Isn't there some kind of coast guard, Officer?"

"There'll be patrol boats," Michael said. "I'll pay for them myself if I have to. Money's no object. I won't leave my daughter to these madmen!"

Lizzie only stared at her daughter's note. "He won't harm her," she whispered, "but we won't find her until he wants us to."

Chapter 4

Kathleen, Peter, and Heather took the train to Treherbert, a village in Rhondda in the south of Wales. There had been coal mining in the area for twenty years, but the area had been added to the train line to Cardiff only a few years earlier.

"It belongs to the South Wales Coalfield," Peter explained to his family. "Which is the largest in Great Britain, almost sixty miles long."

"Is the area pretty?" asked Heather unassumingly.

She had not liked the atmosphere in the Burton house in Roath any more than her mother or Reverend Burton did, but she would have loved to paint the landscape.

"It used to be. As a boy, when I visited my uncle, there were tiny villages, hardly populated, waterfalls, mountains, lakes, rivers clear as glass. But that was before they started mining coal in grand style. Back then, it was considered difficult—there were hardly any roads, no rail connections, and most of the coal lay relatively deep beneath the earth. Nowadays, the Rhondda Valley is completely open to mining. That hasn't contributed to the land's beauty."

This description proved understated as Heather and Kathleen saw when the train crossed the first mining settlement. The lovely green countryside gave way to a black wasteland, marked by coal heaps and hoist frames. The Burtons could taste coal dust on their tongues, and after Kathleen wiped her face with her handkerchief dipped in eau de cologne, black marks showed on the fabric.

Mining towns hugged the tracks. Even in Treherbert, the first thing a traveler saw was a housing row. In front of the newer houses were tiny lawns, which seemed gray and sickly. No wonder with all the dust.

"These houses are so ugly," Heather pronounced.

Peter shrugged. "At least they're houses," he replied. "The mine owners have them built and rent them to their workers for relatively little money. That counts as very progressive."

"And it is," Kathleen blurted out, "in comparison with the shacks we called home in Ireland. These people have work and a roof over their heads. You've been spoiled, Heather."

Heather laughed, but her discomfort was evident. "While they are working, the people here have a few hundred feet of earth over their heads, if I understand it right," she said. "And they die of the black lung."

"We died of hunger," said Kathleen.

"Now, let's not fight about who has it worse," Peter said, trying to appease them. "Surely it's going better for the people here than for the Irish during the famine—the flourishing pubs attest to that." The first of the pubs could be seen right from the train station, and it seemed busy although it was only late afternoon. "Though Heather is without a doubt spoiled." He laughed and tugged affectionately at the veil on his stepdaughter's elegant hat.

They left the train station and stepped onto the dusty street. No cabs were in sight.

"Perhaps we should ask in the pub if they have cabs for hire here," said Peter. "We can't go by foot. The house is outside of town."

Peter walked to the pub while Kathleen and Heather kept an eye on the luggage. In Wales, as in Ireland or New Zealand, women were not welcome in a pub.

Nevertheless, Peter met a woman wearing a worn blue housedress at the entrance, and she was moving as if to storm the taproom. However, she did not dare enter; instead, she threw open the door and desperately called inside.

"Jim Paisley, I know you're in here. And it's no good hiding. I'm not going anywhere. This time I'm not going to go. I—"

"Shall I look for your husband inside?" Peter saw tears in the eyes of the careworn woman. Without a doubt she had once been pretty. She had curly chestnut-colored hair and deep-blue eyes. "I'm a pastor—perhaps he'll speak with me."

The woman sighed and wiped her tears away. "You can try, though so far our own pastor hasn't had success showing him the error of his ways. Maybe he's still sober enough to listen. He needs to give me his pay. The children are starving. If I can't feed 'em, they don't get anything done below. The foreman's patient, but someday even he'll have enough of my Jim."

Peter nodded in understanding. "I'll send the man out to you," he promised. "What was his name? Jim Paisley?"

The woman nodded and brushed the hair from her face. The loose strands seemed to indicate she had put it up in a hurry.

"Heavens, how I must look, Reverend. You likely think I belong with all the drunks and good-for-nothings inside," she said. "But when Violet told me Jim and Fred went directly to the Golden Arms after work, I ran out at once. As long as he's only got three beers in him, you can still sometimes talk to him."

Peter, who knew this type of man, smiled encouragingly and entered the pub. The barkeeper overheard Peter's conversation with Mrs. Paisley. He looked distrustful at first but thawed on seeing Peter's clerical collar.

"My word, a pastor, and here I was thinking you were fooling with the women. You the reinforcements for our Reverend Clusky? This backwater has three pubs and only the one church. So, by that measure, there's need of you." He laughed. "Jim Paisley is the fellow there." The barkeeper pointed to a tall, reddish-blond man, just then cheering with his friends. "The one next to him is Fred, his son. He already drinks just like him. But try your luck, Reverend."

If Mrs. Paisley already had the barkeeper's sympathy, her husband had to be in a bad way. Peter moved closer to the miners' table and cleared his throat.

"Mr. Paisley, I am Reverend Peter Burton. Your wife is outside and would like a word with you."

"Oh, would she?" The man looked at Peter and laughed an ugly laugh from his coal-dusted face. "Then maybe she ought to be a little nicer to me instead of always cursing at me and nagging. It's embarrassing, you know, all that clamor in public." The men around him nodded in agreement. "Beer for you, Reverend?"

Peter shook his head. "I won't contribute to drinking away the money your wife needs for the household. Mr. Paisley, ahead of you lies a whole week in which you and your children must eat. How many children do you have, anyway?"

Paisley grinned. "Three," he informed him, "but Fred here, my big boy, he's already working hard with me."

He indicated the youth next to him, a strong redheaded boy, who appeared to be about fifteen years old. If Jim Paisley had looked the same in his youth, it was no wonder his wife had fallen in love with him. Fred Paisley was a handsome boy with flashing blue eyes and shining white teeth. His features were appealing, if a bit rough.

"Well—have you paid your mother your keep today?" Peter turned to Fred.

The youth grinned awkwardly. "I will, I will." He dodged.

"If anything's left." Peter shook his head. "Why don't you run and do it now, Fred? Your mother's waiting outside. Keep a couple pence for a beer after every shift and give her the rest. For your siblings." Peter looked the boy square in the eye.

"It's just two girls," Fred muttered. "They don't need much."

"Come out, Jim, Fred!"

Mrs. Paisley had decided not to rely on the pastor. Peter had seen women in the gold-mining settlement act this way. If she raved long enough in front of the pub, her husband would have to respond. Some men swallowed their pride and split their earnings with their wives. Usually they forgot the episode after the next few hours of drinking themselves silly. More often they beat their wives when they arrived home. Others had less compunction and beat their wives right there in the street. Then the women only received black eyes and no money at all. But that was the risk. More than one woman had assured Peter it was worth it.

Perhaps it was the intervention of the pastor that made Fred and Jim Paisley choose another option. The boy pulled out his wallet and counted the few shillings of the week's pay he had been given that afternoon. He pressed a third of it into the pastor's hand.

"Here. Give this to my mother." He turned back to his beer.

His father did likewise, grumbling.

Peter stood at the bar with a handful of money and did not know what to say.

"Now, piss off, Reverend," Jim Paisley yelled at him.

Peter fled outside.

"It's not much," he noted as he handed the woman the money. She, however, was so happy that he feared she would kiss his hand.

"It's enough to survive." She was joyous. "If I skimp and save and Violet earns a few pence somewhere. She's always looking for work. I am too. I do the reverend's laundry. So, if you need . . . but you already have a wife."

Mrs. Paisley must have realized that Kathleen and Heather were with Peter. They were waiting next to the bags, which reminded Peter about the carriage.

"We're here for only a short time," he explained to the woman, "and now we need a cab to the Burton house."

Mrs. Paisley's eyes widened at the mention of the manor house on the river. Did the miners know that an heir was expected here? Then she shook her head regretfully. "There are no cabdrivers here. The mine owners have their own carriages. And the rest of us go by foot."

Peter sighed. "It's a bit far for that. But the barkeeper mentioned a church. Where would that be? Surely the pastor could help arrange some transportation."

Mrs. Paisley nodded energetically. "Saint Mary's is only two streets over. And here's Violet." She indicated a scrawny girl, perhaps twelve or thirteen years old, who was running across the street toward them. "She can help carry your things."

The girl stopped somewhat breathlessly in front of them. Even through her concerned expression, it was clear that Violet would be a beauty. She had shining turquoise eyes and finely arched brows. Her chestnut-brown hair was tied into two thick braids, which reached halfway down her back. Her skin was pale, her cheeks rosy after the quick run. Her lips gleamed cherry red and were full and finely carved. She wore a dark-blue dress that had been mended many times and was tight at the chest.

"Mother, do you have, did he . . . ?"

Mrs. Paisley held the money out to her daughter with a smile. The girl's face relaxed; her eyes brightened.

Mrs. Paisley gestured gratefully to Peter. "With the help of Reverend—"

"Burton," Peter said. "And here are my wife and daughter." He pointed to Kathleen and Heather who were coming toward them with the luggage.

"The reverend and the ladies want to get to the church," Mrs. Paisley explained to her daughter. "Why don't you take them straight there and help carry their things? Where'd you leave Rosie?"

"Mrs. Brown is watching her," Violet told her. "She's in high spirits. Her husband dropped off the money before he went to the pub, and he worked loads of overtime. And she wants to make candy with Rosie."

"Rosemary is my younger daughter," Mrs. Paisley said. "My name's Ellen, by the way. Again, many, many thanks, Reverend."

Ellen Paisley stowed the money in her pocket and turned to go. Violet reached reflexively for the heaviest suitcase. Peter took it from her. "You can help my wife," he said with a meaningful glance. Kathleen could have carried her own luggage, but Peter was sure Violet would more readily accept money in thanks if she had done something for it.

The church was not far. Saint Mary's was a simple brick building. The parsonage next door mirrored the miners' houses but stood on its own on a small, not-well-tended piece of land.

"I told the reverend I'd clear a few beds to garden," Violet said, excusing its sorry state, "but he says nothing will grow here either way. He's right. The coal dust gets on everything."

She carried Kathleen's bag up the three steps to the door and knocked. A stocky, dark-haired man opened the door. He smiled at Violet amicably.

"Well, whom've you brought me?" he inquired. "Visitors?"

Violet curtsied. "This is Reverend Burton and Mrs. and Miss Burton—of London, I think."

"Burton, did you say?" The pastor looked at Peter probingly as if searching for a family resemblance. "Come in and welcome. Violet, thank you. You can also take the laundry with you to your mother."

Violet's beautiful eyes brightened anew. And even more so when Kathleen gave her a penny for her help carrying the luggage. For the Paisley women, this really seemed to be a lucky day: on top of the hard-won pay from the men, they had a laundry order from the pastor and a penny from visitors.

In a flurry of curtsies and thank-yous, Violet left with the laundry basket.

"A nice girl," Peter observed, "but the father . . ."

Reverend Clusky turned his eyes toward heaven. "And that boy Fred is just as much a good-for-nothing. Please, let me take your things, Mrs., Miss Burton. And tell me, is it a coincidence your name is Burton, or are you perhaps the rightful heir to the house on the Rhondda River?"

Peter nodded. "The latter. But we don't intend to settle here. In truth, I just wanted to sell the house and the land as quickly as possible. However, there seem to be difficulties."

Reverend Clusky sighed. "You can say that again. Randolph Burton acts as if the estate belonged to him. He's emptying the wine cellar at breathtaking speed, and he's scared away the servants. Those he hadn't already let go have left of their own accord. He's running the estate into the ground. Word has it he's

49

already sold half the furniture and smashed some of it when boozed. He's frenzied, Reverend Burton, against God and the world. Although I can't begrudge him that."

The cleric's gaze wandered to his fireplace mantel decorated by a few simply framed photographs. An old daguerreotype showed a serene-looking matron, likely Reverend Clusky's deceased wife. The more recent photos, however, made Kathleen gasp for air. The delicate creature at first depicted as a girl with long dark hair and then in a bridal gown beside a stocky man was clearly Alice Burton.

Reverend Clusky noticed his guests' gaze. "Ah, one of the reasons it will hardly avail me to try reforming the young man," he observed, "although I'm anything but happy with what Alice, my daughter, has wrought. If only she had taken the son. I think in truth she had an eye for young Randolph Burton, for she was constantly in the Burton house when James Burton received a visit from his nephew and grandnephew. Dear Lord, I still blame myself for not preventing it. Though I wouldn't have had anything against a union with Randolph. But alas."

Peter laughed tiredly. "Alas, my brother fell for her, body and soul," he said, completing his colleague's sentence. "Not that there's anything wrong with that either. Joseph was a widower, and your daughter surely was not dragged by her hair to the altar. So, there's no reason to fault the two for their happiness, as long as they find it."

Reverend Burton raised his hands as if in blessing. "As long as they find it," he repeated, and it sounded like a prayer to God. "Be that as it may, Randolph sees things differently. He feels they went behind his back, possibly robbing him of his inheritance. His father apparently has reduced his allowance. From what I hear in Cardiff, Alice requires a lot of money to be happy."

Clusky did not seem to think highly of his daughter. But for Kathleen, his story explained much: Alice's good breeding but lack of experience with servants, her pleasure in playing the lady of the house, and her affectation. A pastor's daughter who had escaped the *triste* life in a backwater like Treherbert, a girl who surely had already been halfway promised to a younger colleague in a neighboring parish, Alice had fled with the first man to come along, ready to pay the price for that. Kathleen could not condemn her.

"Despite what happened, that's no reason for Alice's, well, stepson to seize other people's houses," she said.

Reverend Clusky nodded. "Of course not, but young Mr. Burton raged when his father married her." He ran his fingers nervously through his hair and then went to a cabinet from which he took a bottle of whiskey. "Dear Lord, please do not force me to tell the whole ugly story. Would you care for a drink?" He took glasses from the cabinet when Peter nodded. "And a sherry for the ladies?"

His guests were silent as the pastor poured the drinks.

Reverend Clusky took a large gulp before continuing. "It seems to have been the younger Burton who first promised my Alice he would take her with him to Cardiff," he began. "Well, and the way things look, the elder gave him cuckold's horns to wear. And then tightened the purse strings when he got angry."

Perhaps even before that, Kathleen thought. For Alice Clusky, that her young beau no longer had the means to spoil her might have been a strong argument in Joseph's favor.

"As I said, please let me spare you the details. But that was when Randolph came back here, held his great-uncle responsible for all his misery—and provided increased revenues to all the pubs and billiard halls in the area. James Burton did not have much strength left to restrain him. He died shortly thereafter."

"Without changing his will, correct?" Peter asked.

"Without changing his will, of that I'm certain," Reverend Clusky declared. "I was witness at the drafting of his final will and testament, which was then given over to the notary. Your uncle was a very proper person, Reverend. He would not have slipped some handwritten note into a legacy hunter's hand. Not to mention that he was anything but happy with young Randolph. Nor any more so with my, well, son-in-law, Joseph."

Peter sighed. "So, we'll now have the unpleasant task of kicking the boy out," he said. "Wonderful. And here I'd hoped to be able to set sail again in a month at most. I hope you don't get seasick, my dears. Our return trip may not be until winter."

Chapter 5

Lizzie Drury was proven right. The canoe containing Matariki and Kahu Heke's men might as well have been swallowed by the earth. Nevertheless, the Dunedin police organized patrols, the settlements' fishers and former whaling stations were put on the alert, and what was more, the Maori tribes on the east coast of the South Island kept an eye out for the interlopers. At least, the *iwi* of the Ngai Tahu did, but the warlike Ngati Toa tribe, which occupied a few small enclaves on the northern tip of the South Island, protected the kidnappers.

The two men of the Ngati Pau had set sail right at high tide—after they had forced Matariki to take her place under an awning at the front of the boat. Dingo had leaped in with her, which precipitated a renewed discussion about the animal. Again Matariki heard the word *tapu*, but also "guardian"—although she did not understand whether this referred to Dingo's dubious aptitude as a guard dog or to some sort of magic.

When the men spoke quickly and quietly, she had difficulty following their Maori. Many words were different or at least pronounced differently than among the tribes on the South Island. The men seemed to have difficulty, too, when it came to her dialect, so it might not always have been rudeness when they did not answer her questions.

This confirmed Matariki's first impression: her father may have sent his strongest and most reliable warriors, but not his smartest. On land, she would surely have succeeded in tricking them and fleeing, but on the open sea, that was impossible. And even after the men hid her in the land of the Ngati Toa after a relatively short sea journey, there weren't any opportunities to escape. The warriors of the Ngati Toa worked hard to please the Hauhau, and they guarded Matariki around the clock. Yet she soon asked herself why they did not simply tie her up or lock her away somewhere. It would have made life easier for the guards. But no one touched her. It was almost as if a sort of invisible barrier that no man dared cross surrounded Matariki.

On the third day of her imprisonment, as her initial fear of the massive men who always formed a circle around her subsided, Matariki attempted to overcome the barrier herself. She nonchalantly went over to the warriors and stepped between them. And again their behavior astonished her: instead of driving her back determinedly, the men at first gave way in terror. One of them fired his gun only after the ring around Matariki had almost opened wide enough that she could have run into the fern forest. The bullet pelted the ground in front of Matariki's feet, and the men directed her to return to her area.

So, they would use their weapons—and she had better not let it come to the point of being injured.

What was more, over the next few days, it became apparent that among the Ngati Toa were a few men who were more cunning than Matariki's two abductors. It did not take them long to figure out that Matariki almost cared more for Dingo than for herself. Whenever she contradicted them or tried to exceed her boundaries in any way, they took aim at the dog, and Matariki could only behave.

Her worry for Dingo made her regret she had brought him, though he did keep her warm under the blanket at night. She had only the one blanket, and the men would not allow her at their fires. They placed wood and food at Matariki's disposal, but she had to light her fires and prepare her meals herself. Since her abduction, Matariki had not seen anyone other than the warriors. Probably the tribe did not even know that it had a prisoner. These were just a few young warriors currying favor with rebels they admired from the North Island.

Matariki did not understand any of it, and it hurt to be shut out in this way. Her own tribe in Otago was welcoming. After the appropriate greeting ceremonies, it bade welcome to any other Maori and most *pakeha* to its fires. Here, on the other hand . . . According to what her kidnappers said, Matariki was supposed to recognize the Ngati Pau as the tribe to which she belonged and had responsibilities to fulfill. But her "tribal brothers" sat laughing and chatting together with their friends from the Ngati Toa while she sat alone by her fire.

After they had set off again and Matariki was sitting in the canoe, watching the South Island slowly disappear behind them, the term "untouchable" occurred to her; she recalled her childish pride in knowing the word and Haikina's laconic information about the life of a chieftain on the North Island. Could it be that it was not disdain for her that kept the Hauhau at a distance but rather something like awe?

Matariki slowly began to long to see her father. She had a few words for him.

***

Matariki's abductors certainly did not distinguish themselves in *whaikorero*, the art of eloquence, but they were good seamen and conquered the Cook Strait without difficulty. Still, Matariki was a bit afraid when no land was visible, so she was relieved when the southern point of the North Island appeared on the horizon. However, her kidnappers did not stop near Wellington; instead, they sailed farther along the west coast to come ashore in the land of the Te Maniapoto.

Matariki wondered whether her parents had alerted the officials on the North Island, and she hoped they were not too worried about her. She was sure the Ngai Tahu trackers would have been trusted with scouring the coast and that they would have found her note.

Matariki estimated that their canoe had rounded half of the North Island when the craggy coast gave way to gently rolling hills. Here and there, coves, which would make excellent harbors, came into view. Finally, the men steered the canoe closer to the shore, and they were visibly cheered by the sight of a river mouth—so much so that one of them even informed Matariki of the river's name.

"The Waikato River," he said, pointing to the mouth. "We're almost there."

Matariki sighed with relief and allowed herself to eat her last piece of flatbread at noon. As she nibbled on it, she watched the coast. Green forested hills, the river's current—it all looked beautiful, but there were no human settlements in sight. Not that it was unusual. Even the *marae*, the gathering places of the

Ngai Tahu, often lay hidden. Finally, though, the men steered the canoe into a cove. The entrance was not easy to find, as it could not be seen from the sea. This hiding place was surely chosen carefully. At first, Matariki worried because the strong breakers tossed the canoe dangerously close to a crag, but the landing itself proved simple, and as soon as they rounded the cliffs, a sandy beach appeared. The sand was dark, and Matariki knew this was from volcanic activity many thousands of years ago. At some point, the mountains must have spat fire.

Matariki's captors indicated that she should remain in the canoe until they had pulled it ashore. Yet she would gladly have swum, and Dingo seemed to feel the need as well. He leaped happily into the shallow water.

At first glance, the cove appeared desolate, but then Matariki noticed movement in the bushes above the beach. Finally, a Maori warrior emerged—as impressively muscular and lightly clothed as Matariki's kidnappers. Those two waved enthusiastically up to him and made gestures likely equivalent to the *pakeha*'s victory signs. The man displayed his joy, but he made no move to help his tribal brothers unload the canoe. Her kidnappers exhausted themselves pulling the boat onto land while the Maori warrior did not lift a finger. Eventually, he raised his spear as if in greeting and left—likely to notify the rest of the tribe of the canoe's arrival.

Matariki's captors finally ordered her to climb out and wait. Matariki wondered whether a greeting ceremony was planned and whether they would request a recital of her *pepeha*. The telling of one's life story belonged to the *powhiri*, the formal greeting ritual, which, among other things, determined whether the visitor came with friendly or hostile intentions. A young girl was hardly a danger to a tribe, or so important that she would be honored with dances, prayers, and welcome ceremonies. But, she reminded herself, this tribe was awaiting a chieftain's daughter.

Matariki went back through the facts for her *pepeha* in case she needed to recite it: Her mother, Lizzie, grew up in a London orphanage. Her birth father's ancestors had come to New Zealand—Aotearoa—in canoes. Then Matariki had to describe the region from which she came, perhaps the path she had taken to arrive there. Matariki had no desire to do all that—at heart she shared Michael's view that the tribes overdid it with their greeting rituals. Besides, she was hungry.

Suddenly, there were noise and movement in the forest of trees that bordered the beach, and people came toward them. Matariki expected curious women and children, but this group consisted exclusively of men with a warlike appearance. They strode stiffly to the beach, marching like an army with spears and war axes. If this had been aimed at filling her with fear, it had succeeded. She felt queasy and recalled her parents' and fellow tribe members' comments about the Hauhau's attitude toward cannibalism. Might the cooking of a chieftain's daughter have a place in the cult?

Matariki was determined not to let her fear show. She stood up, squared herself, and stared defiantly at the procession. The men lined up facing her; then a tall, muscular Maori warrior emerged from the ranks, which respectfully parted for him. He was slender for a warrior, but his face was covered in tattoos like the others, and his gleaming black hair was tied in a warrior's knot. He seemed vaguely familiar to Matariki, and in looking closer, she recognized that his hairline was the same as hers. His eyes stood slightly aslant and were amber colored, similar if a bit darker than Matariki's. The man carried the insignias of a chieftain: the battle ax and the staff, as well as a valuable black-and-white striped shawl.

Matariki approached him with as much dignity as he did her.

"Kahu Heke?" she asked. "Father?"

The man almost twisted his mouth into a smile but then mastered himself. Smiling at the sight of his daughter was probably not compatible with the *mana* of a warrior chieftain. Nevertheless, he moved toward Matariki and bent down to exchange the traditional greeting of the Maori, the *hongi*. Matariki laid her forehead and nose on her father's hard, tattooed face.

"*Kia ora*, Matariki," said Kahu Heke. "*Haere mai.*"

Welcome. That probably wasn't how they would greet their lunch. Matariki could not help herself from struggling with a certain amusement. It was all so strange—the dignified chieftain, the silent warriors—where otherwise the tribes tended toward such lively greetings. Among the Ngai Tahu, Matariki's kidnappers would long have since exchanged jests and *hongi* with their old friends. Here, however, the two sailors stood just as isolated from their tribe as Matariki had from them the whole journey. Untouchable: Matariki vacillated between shuddering and giggling hysterically.

Kahu Heke turned to the kidnappers. "Hanu, Kahori, *haere mai*. You've completed your task. You can be certain of your tribe's thanks and the blessing of the gods. You can now go and clean yourselves."

Matariki furrowed her brow. Both men had just been swimming. They were surely cleaner than Matariki herself and the sweat-covered warriors. Hanu and Kahori bowed briefly before disappearing inland.

Kahu Heke, who noted Matariki's confusion, smiled. "That's part of it," he said, speaking curtly and, to the girl's amazement, in English unaffected by a Maori accent. "They had contact with a chieftain's daughter—for days, they were too close. Had they died after this offense against all these *tapu*, they probably would not have been permitted to enter Hawaiki." The souls of deceased Maori wandered across the sea to Hawaiki, the myth-shrouded land of their fathers. "There is, however, a cleansing ceremony, which they're undergoing now. Do not worry about them."

Matariki rolled her eyes. "I'm not worried," she answered angrily, also in English. "They kidnapped me. Their souls can wander somewhere else for all I care. What's this about, Father? If you wanted to see me, Otago Girls' High School is no prison, and my parents would surely have welcomed you to our farm, or in the *marae* of the Ngai Tahu."

"We'll speak of this later, child." He turned back to his warriors. "Greet Matariki, daughter of the stars, chosen of the gods."

The men raised their spears and let out a sort of war cry. Matariki once again fought back a hysterical fit of laughter. For a moment, she thought it looked as if the girls from her school were staging the Treaty of Waitangi. Finally, she smiled at the men and made a gesture that approximated a Roman salute. The warriors seemed content with that.

"Follow me, Matariki." Kahu Heke's request sounded quite formal. "Be sure my shadow doesn't fall on you, and yours doesn't on anyone else. We'll be alone soon. Then we can speak."

The troop of warriors formed a solemn procession and led Matariki to the Maori camp. Kahu Heke's peculiar tribe did not, however, have a fenced-in *marae* with a meeting lodge, kitchens, and storage huts. Instead, there was a camp with tents, which surrounded a giant flagpole. There were no women or children. *An army camp,* Matariki thought, feeling her amusement give way to an inner coldness. Naturally, Kahu Heke was a warrior chieftain, not a paternalistic tribal elder chosen by the *whole* tribe, including the women. But what was she supposed to do here? Matariki tried desperately to remember what Haikina had once told her about chieftains' daughters.

Back at the camp, the warriors turned their attention to the fires on which sweet potatoes and meat were roasting. Apparently, they had broken off their mealtime preparation to organize a suitable reception for Matariki. Matariki's mouth watered. Surely now someone would give her something to eat.

Kahu Heke remained on the edge of the camp, careful not to come so close to the fires or tents that his shadow could fall on them.

Then he began a speech. "Men! Today is a day of joy for all who believe in the Pai Marire—and even if they do not know it, for all of God's chosen people."

The men reacted with an enthusiastic cry. *"Rire, rire, hau!"*

They chanted the meaningless words again and again while Matariki reflected on where she had heard the expression "chosen people" before. Not in the Maori language to be sure, but often in Reverend Burton's church and during the devotion and Bible study in school. God's chosen people were the Israelites, enslaved by the Egyptians. But what did that have to do with the Maori?

"You all know," Kahu Heke immediately clarified, "that the archangel Gabriel once appeared to our great leader, Te Ua Haumene, to give him his message on his way: freedom for God's chosen people. To fulfill God's will, the Maori nation must throw off the shackles of the *pakeha*. Enough with the exploitation and land theft. Enough with robbing Papa of her *mana*."

Matariki's head spun. Her father was somehow mixing up everything she had ever heard about religion. He was jumbling the Old Testament, the Israelites, and the archangel Gabriel with the legends of the Maori about the creation of the world through the separation of Papa, the earth, and Rangi, the sky. She found all of it pretty nonsensical, but it seemed to excite the men. They forgot their fires and the preparation of their meals and began, as if in a trance, to run around the flagpole in the middle of the camp while continually chanting, *"Rire, rire, hau, hau."*

"We have a duty to rid ourselves of the *pakeha*'s priests and false teachings," Kahu Heke yelled. "Only *tikanga* is truly pleasing to God—the old customs of our homeland, our people, make us unconquerable. *Tikanga* makes us immortal. Let us think of the natural priesthood of the chieftain and his children. Atua—God—has sent us his priestess today. Blood from the blood of a long line of proud *ariki*."

Kahu Heke gestured for Matariki to step forward. The girl blushed in embarrassment—which did not happen often. She was being put in a position in which she did not belong. Every man and every woman in her own *iwi* would have declared her insane.

"This girl—Matariki, Daughter of the Stars—will lead you from peace to war, will transform you from warriors to holy warriors. Immortal, invulnerable—without mercy, unconquerable!"

The men cheered, and Matariki hoped she would disappear.

"Now, celebrate, men. Celebrate the liberation of Aotearoa while I do my part to prepare my daughter for her purpose. Pai Marire, *hau, hau!*"

Kahu Heke briefly fell into the men's chant. Then he turned to go. Matariki followed him again and sighed with relief when they left the camp. Only one of the men followed them—at a great distance—along a worn path through the forest. After a few strides, they reached a clearing. The chieftain's lodge, similarly provisionally built like the huts in the camp, stood under an overhanging kauri tree.

Kahu Heke invited his daughter to take a seat with him on a few rocks in front of the hut. The young warrior remained on the edge of the clearing where a fire already burned. He busied himself with the preparations for a meal, and Matariki hoped he was cooking for the chieftain. In any case, as "God's priestess," she seemed to be freed from kitchen duty.

"What was all that?" Matariki asked.

Kahu Heke now permitted himself another smile. "You did well," he praised her. "Would you like to speak English or our language?"

Matariki shrugged. "It doesn't matter to me," she said. "I just want some answers. What is all this about, Father? I'm no priestess. I'm not even a *tohunga*. I don't know anything about the old ways. At least not any more than any other Maori girl."

"You're very cute, particularly when you get excited. Just like your mother. But you have no *moko*," Kahu Heke mused. He acted as if he had not heard Matariki's outburst. "Well, that can still perhaps be remedied."

"I won't under any circumstances be tattooed." Matariki grew angry. "No one does that anymore. I—"

"Very soon we will all proudly wear the symbols of our tribes again," Kahu Heke insisted. "Even the Ngai Tahu—no matter how much they've already acclimated to their occupiers."

"But that's stupid." Matariki raised her voice. "There are no occupiers. We are all one people, *pakeha* and Maori. That's what Captain Hobson said in Waitangi: *He iwi tahi tatou*."

Kahu Heke snorted with rage. "We are not one people. And the Treaty of Waitangi was nothing but deception. The chieftains had no idea what they were signing."

The Treaty of Waitangi was a framework that Captain William Hobson and the governor, James Busby, worked out in 1840. Forty-nine tribal chieftains— entirely those of the North Island, since the Ngai Tahu had not been a party— had signed it, formally establishing the equality of the Maori and *pakeha* as citizens of New Zealand. Later, the British Crown would use that same treaty to assert claims of land ownership and justify land confiscation.

Matariki shrugged. "Then maybe they should have paid better attention," she replied. "But whatever the case may be, I can't change it. And I'd like to return to the South Island soon. Without tattoos. What does *rire, rire, hau, hau* mean, anyway?"

Kahu Heke sighed. "It doesn't mean anything, Matariki. Those are empty words. But they help the warriors find themselves, their people, and their strength."

"So says the archangel Gabriel?" teased Matariki.

Kahu Heke rubbed his forehead, touching his hair as he did, and hurried to put his hand on his nose and breathe in deeply.

"The god Rauru," he remarked, "lives on the chieftain's head. By touching my hair, I've disturbed him. Now I must breathe him in again. Please pay attention yourself so that you do not carelessly touch your hair, Matariki, when one of the warriors is watching." He pointed to the young man on the edge of the clearing. "It's a *tapu*."

Matariki laughed. "Now you've given yourself away, Father. You don't even believe all of that yourself. The archangel Gabriel didn't appear to anyone, and—"

Kahu Heke breathed in again as sharply as if inhaling the archangel personally. "See, Matariki. Our leader, Te Ua Haumene, saw the archangel. That cannot be verified, but he claims to have. Then, he founded the Pai Marire religion."

"Good and peaceful," Matariki translated the name into English, "but it sounded very different just now when you spoke."

Kahu Heke tousled his hair, this time forgetting the god Rauru. "Since then, many have been inspired by the archangel Michael," he admitted. "He is more warlike. But only one thing is important in all that: The gods and Christian angels turn to our Maori leaders. Te Ua Haumene names us the new chosen people. We'll no longer be told what to do or be preached to. We'll take back our land with God's help."

"And you need me for that?" Matariki asked.

Chapter 6

Ellen Paisley dragged herself back to the miner's house she shared with her family. She pulled Rosie, her four-year-old daughter, behind her, trying to ignore that the little girl was whining—as she had been for hours. Violet could not watch her. She had been working at the Burton house for a week. Reverend Burton's wife had hired her to help her and her daughter with the cleaning. Ellen had heard nothing more specific—she had worries enough of her own—but Reverend Burton seemed to have set his nephew's head back on straight. Violet reported that, though the young Mr. Burton still lived in the house, he was forced to behave himself in a half-civilized manner. Apparently, the apartments were a wreck when the pastor took over the estate. The women had now taken on the garden.

"Otherwise, they'll never be able to sell the house," Violet precociously repeated Kathleen Burton's words. The pastor from New Zealand, his beautiful wife, and stepdaughter had quickly become Violet's new role models. She raved about Heather, in particular. "She paints so well. I'd like to be able to do that. And she showed me pictures of her home. It's so beautiful there—the air is really clear, and the mountains always have snowy caps. Can you imagine, Mother, even in summer? The rivers are clear. No one dumps their rubbish in there. And there's no coal dust."

Violet looked wistfully into the distance. Surely, she was dreaming of accompanying the Burtons to their island at the end of the world.

Ellen could hardly blame her—she would love nothing more than to flee. The money Jim had handed over on payday was the last. He had said as much as soon as he got home. Apparently, he had had enough of working for the fore-man. According to Jim and Fred, father and son had quit in grand style after the foreman had called them lazy. Mrs. Brown's husband, however, said Jim Paisley had been fired. Fred was thrown out right behind him—after threatening the foreman with a pickax.

At first, Ellen had not taken the news too seriously. In the last few years, about twenty mines had opened around Treherbert, and the owners almost all hated one another. So far, it was easy to find new work. However, the mine owners' enmity did not necessarily affect their foremen. On the contrary, the foremen liked to grab a beer together and exchange stories of good and bad workers. Jim and Fred Paisley did not come off well there, particularly not after the story with the pickax.

Days passed before the two of them found work again. And then it was not in a real mine where the miners moved downward and dug out the coal underground; instead, it was in a level, for which they dug a horizontal passage into the mountain. From everything Ellen had heard, this was not a promis-ing approach in Treherbert because the coal lay relatively deep, but opening a level was considerably cheaper than building hoist frames and shafts. Ellen had briefly wondered how the owner, a country gentleman who lived nearby, decided to try his luck with coal mining. He could hardly have much of a sense of it, or much experience in judging workers. Otherwise he would not have hired Jim Paisley as a foreman.

Ellen chided herself for her unkind thoughts about her husband. Jim had a great deal of experience, and perhaps he really would prove himself. The new boss had paid the men only pocket money as an advance. The real pay would start when the coal mining started.

"What if there's no coal there?" Violet had asked when her father revealed these conditions. She had received a box on the ear right away for that.

"Where Jim Paisley digs, that's where the coal is," he had snorted.

Ellen found these assertions unsettling. If it indicated that the new mine owner was leaving the placement of the shafts to his foreman, there could be trouble ahead, since that wasn't something Jim knew about.

Nevertheless, the family could bear a week or two without pay. Violet's work for the Burtons was properly compensated, and she brought laundry with her, which Ellen did at home. If the Burtons stayed a few more weeks—and it looked like they would since the negotiations for the sale of land were dragging on—the Paisleys would be able to survive. By then, Jim would hopefully decide to crawl back to his previous foreman at the Bute mine or to one of the other mines.

That was what Ellen had thought until the housing management's letter arrived. The miner's house in which her family lived belonged to the Bute mine. They preferred renting to Bute workers, and would give them time to pay if they were a little short. However, if someone worked for a different mine, or not at all, the management evicted anyone who didn't pay. Ellen had stared, uncomprehending, at the paper where they were threatened with eviction on the Monday after next.

"I'm sorry, my good woman, but my hands are tied," the housing employee said when Ellen went to his office with Rosie to beg for an extension. "Your husband is two months behind on the rent—the foreman had already warned him. We generally do that so as not to upset the family. Most of them do pay, sooner or later. Worst case, we take directly from their pay. Since your husband no longer works for us, we need the houses for our own people. Not that we throw someone out just because he goes to the competition. But then he has to pay the rent, regularly and in full."

Ellen did—with the help of the whining Rosie, to be sure—negotiate another week's extension, although she had little hope that something would change in that time. She and Violet could not gather three months' rent themselves. And who knew how long it would be until Jim was paid at the new mine.

Ellen unlocked the door to her house and began peeling potatoes. There would not be more than a thin soup so she could save some money for the rent. Perhaps if she could make a partial payment, she could talk the manager into another extension. Ellen cried silently. Life with Jim had never been easy. His drinking, his beatings when he took out his frustrations on her, the sympathetic looks of the neighbor women for whom it was going at least a little better.

Yet it had once gone much better for Ellen herself. She tried to comfort herself with dreams of her happy childhood, thinking about her parents' house in Treorchy, which stood on the edge of the village, and its garden—back then the valley was not yet full of coal dust and soot. Ellen only recalled sunny days, the gold-gleaming grain fields, a glowing blue sky, picnics in the meadows. Her father had been a cobbler, and she had sat in his shop in the afternoons, play-ing with leather scraps and listening to his conversations with the farmers and craftsmen he measured for boots. But when the first mines had opened, miners poured out from every corner of England into the Rhondda Valley. Jim Paisley had been one of the first in Treorchy—then a handsome young man with a square jaw and flashing eyes, and lips that smiled wonderfully and kissed even more wonderfully.

Ellen had laughed when he came to her black as midnight from the mine. She had met him at the Rhondda River where he swam and scrubbed himself. It wasn't long before she had filched scented soap from her mother's well-guarded stores and happily scrubbed him with it. Eventually, he had pulled her into the river with him. They had fooled about, splashing each other like children, and following that, they took off their clothes. Then it had happened. Ellen had enjoyed every kiss, every touch, every time he thrust inside her.

They had soon been discovered, by neighbors on the river, which led to angry inquisitions and prohibitions. Under no circumstances should Ellen Seekers, the cobbler's daughter with the proper dowry, marry a newly arrived miner, let alone one such as Jim Paisley, who even then liked to take his money to the pub.

The whole situation escalated when Ellen's mother caught her daughter with her hand in the household's money box. "Just a few coins," Jim had said. "I'll pay it back too." There were tears, excuses, a second chance, which Ellen wasted as well because she forgot everything in Jim's embrace. Ultimately, her father threw her out. It was for her own good, he claimed. She would have enough of Paisley before she ever managed to drag him to the altar.

Ellen, however, possessed a bit of jewelry and a few dresses, which she took with her. That was dowry enough for Jim, and he was not opposed to a proper ceremony either. The money sufficed for a boozy wedding and for a used table and chairs for a hut a farmer rented them in Pentre.

Back then, one mine after the other was opening in the Rhondda Valley. It did not even occur to Ellen at first how often Jim changed jobs. Fred was born in Pentre, and shortly after their move to Treherbert, Violet was born. And, later, Rosie. Ellen worried through her pregnancies with her daughters. By then she knew what she had gotten into with Jim Paisley, but there was no turning back.

***

"What if you just go back to Treorchy and speak with Grandmother and Grandfather?" Violet asked.

She knew something was wrong as soon as she walked in and saw her mother crying at the kitchen table. Violet had been in high spirits on her way home. Heather Coltrane had given her a dress, and Kathleen had shown her how to alter it. Peter Burton had mentioned the tough negotiations with a mine owner who wavered on whether he wanted to buy the house. Maybe he would buy it with the land around it, or perhaps not. It seemed to Peter that selling the whole property to one buyer was unlikely. So, the Burtons would be in Treherbert a few more weeks.

When her mother pushed the letter from the house management over to Violet, the girl almost cried with her. In the Rhondda Valley, there was no alternative to the mining company houses. And even they were overcrowded. Whoever had snatched a larger apartment sublet to one or two young men. Naturally, there were still a few farms in the area, but the farmers did not like the miners there, and certainly none of them would share a house with the Paisleys. Violet had no illusions. They would have to leave Treherbert and move to another mining settlement, so this was the end of her employment with the Burtons and her mother's laundering. In a new town, they would have to start fresh, at first dependent on her father's and brother's pay. Unless . . .

"How long has it been since you saw them last? Fifteen years? No one can hold a grudge that long. At least not against their own daughter."

Violet had been trying to convince her mother for years to reestablish contact with her parents. The Seekers, she argued, could not do worse than throw her out of the house. And if she took Rosie with her? Who could resist her little sister's rosy cheeks and curly strawberry-blonde hair?

"I'm ashamed, Violet. It's embarrassing to show up like a beggar."

Ellen wiped her nose. Jim and Fred would be coming home soon—if they managed not to stop at the pub for too long. She did not want to look like she had been crying when they arrived. She needed to speak reasonably with both of them. Perhaps this new mine owner could be talked into forking out more money this once. Ellen wanted to find out what the man's name was at any rate.

"Then I'll go," Violet said determinedly. "If you won't do it, I will."

***

"I don't understand why you're in such a hurry, Reverend," Mr. Hobbs said.

Mr. Hobbs was interested in the land Peter had inherited. He was an incredibly wealthy mine owner, but he could not make up his mind about buying one of the parcels of land. He had just revealed to Peter that he would come once more with two of his most experienced foremen. Did Peter have anything against test drilling?

Peter found the back-and-forth frustrating. With as much restraint as he could manage, he explained that he wanted to sell the land quickly. If the drilling could be done right away, he had nothing against it. He certainly did not want to deceive anyone, but whether he sold the land for industry or agriculture did not matter. What was important to him was that the sale finally get going.

"Now you want to get into the mining business too. You won't be able to oversee the mining from afar, certainly not from New Zealand."

Peter frowned. "Now that I what?" he asked. "Mr. Hobbs, the last thing that would ever cross my mind or my wife's would be to open a mine. First, I know nothing about coal mining, and second, I love my position as a pastor. I have a parish in Dunedin waiting for me. And as for my wife, she already owns a 'gold mine' she would not trade for a few coal tunnels."

Malcolm Hobbs smiled incredulously. "Oh? But isn't that your land south of town where they're digging a new level? You see, I would have sworn you were going to offer that parcel to Arnold Webber because his mine is next to it. And now you're digging yourself. I must agree with you on one thing: you know nothing about coal mining. There's no coal on that land, Reverend. Perhaps a couple of hundred feet below ground, but you could bore ten tunnels into the mountain, and you wouldn't find anything there."

He laughed, bent over, and crumbled some soil between his fingers as if its consistency could tell him whether a coalbed might lie beneath it.

Peter was now quite confused. "Levels are the horizontal shafts, isn't that so?" he asked. "Into my mountain, you say? Are you sure you're not confusing it with another?"

Hobbs shook his head, grinning. "Certainly not. My people looked at the land too, Reverend. If we'd suspected there was coal there, we'd have bid against Webber. I know, you see, where it is. And as for Webber, he told me just yesterday he wanted to make you another offer. He needs land for worker housing. But, as mentioned, you're digging there yourself now. Gave him a good chuckle, Reverend."

"I'm afraid under these circumstances, you'll have to excuse me, Mr. Hobbs. I need to see what's going on. If someone is digging, I would like to know who and why."

***

"Sooner or later they have to find something." Randolph Burton turned, annoyed, and spoke to his foreman.

"We're not all that far," Jim Paisley assured him, "but soon we'll have to support the tunnels. I'm not concerned myself"—Paisley looked at the roof of the roughly thirty-foot-wide passage carved into the mountain—"but others say the thing could collapse."

Randolph Burton instinctively ducked and looked with concern at the four people with pickaxes and shovels straining to dig the tunnel deeper into the mountainside. Here he had just been happy to have escaped the rain, which seemed to fall more heavily from one moment to the next. But what if it was not safe here? Until then, he had never spared a thought to the possibility his tunnel could collapse.

"You'll need to order wood, Mr. Burton. I could do it for you if you gave me the money. And while we're on the subject of money, the pay, well, I'm not so greedy myself, but the others . . ."

Randolph Burton eyed the passage's walls grumpily. Perhaps this Paisley had missed some coal seam. Randolph was proud of his freshly acquired knowledge of mining. Even before his great-uncle's death, he had sought the company of foremen in pubs and even sounded the mine owners themselves for information. After all, they met at social functions—at least, they had always invited Randolph while his great-uncle was still alive. Randolph had tried to convince his uncle James to make a foray into coal mining. It must, after all, have been laughably easy. Supposedly the South Wales Coalfield was the largest in all Britannia.

"There's coal everywhere here," Randolph had pressured his great-uncle. "We only need to dig it out and get rich."

James, however, had only laughed at that. "It's not just lying in the road, boy, but often very deep beneath it. I'm not about to turn my land into a coal pile—if that's what you all do after my death, I can't change it. But just look at the river, the hills, the forest. It's all beautiful, Randolph. I treasure it. And I'd like to die with just this view out my window and with the birds' song in my ear. Not with a fat balance sheet in hand."

It cost a pile of money to dig a level like this into the mountain, but one could afford it easily with the Burton inheritance. Randolph only hoped to mine the first wagon of coal before his uncle Peter caught on. Then everything would look different. Surely the reverend would no longer want to sell and instead would leave management of the Burton mine to him, Randolph Burton. That sounded marvelous: the Burton mine! The thought alone raised Randolph's spirits. He would live here like the Webbers and the Hobbs—or acquire an estate near Cardiff like the Marquis of Bute. He could send the reverend some money every month. For the poor in New Zealand or wherever else. After all, his uncle was always droning on about how he would use the proceeds from his inheritance for charitable ends.

If only so much investment did not lie in front of these wonderful dreams. Tools, pay, now wood. Randolph was getting in over his head, particularly since Peter and his family took possession of the house before he had been able to sell the furniture and valuables to further his ambitious mining project.

"But you're sure there's coal in this mountain?" Randolph asked Paisley once again.

Perhaps his father could be convinced to provide an advance on his inheritance. After all, that man ought to have a guilty conscience. He had just informed him in a letter that Alice was expecting a baby.

Jim Paisley nodded. "There's coal everywhere here."

Outside, the rain was whooshing down with such intensity that the men could not hear the hoofbeats of Peter's horse. Only when the pastor entered in a soaking-wet coat, water dripping from his hat's brim, did Randolph and Jim look to the tunnel entrance. Peter had heard Paisley's last words.

"You're right, Mr. Paisley," he said. "It doesn't surprise me to see you here. Your daughter told me of your new foreman position. She mentioned besides that your employer couldn't be the brightest."

Paisley needed a few moments to grasp this remark. Then he grimaced. "I'll beat the hussy black and blue."

Peter shook his head. "That's not going to conjure the coal from below, Mr. Paisley. That's where it lies, or at least where it would if it existed. It's not up here in the mountainside, Randolph. Who gave you this ridiculous idea of a level? You're making yourself a laughingstock. And me along with you; it is my land, after all, in case that's still not clear to you. How are you paying for this digging? You've"—Peter counted quickly—"hired five men. Or wait, are those women, Randolph?"

Peter looked horrified at the rather delicate forms just then shoveling away the rubble that Fred Paisley's pickax had left behind.

Randolph shrugged. "Women are cheaper," he explained. "They're often employed in levels. While in the mines—"

"Women bring bad luck belowground," Jim Paisley affirmed.

Peter Burton rolled his eyes. "Girls, you can stop with the shoveling now. And you, too, Fred Paisley. What you're doing is dangerous on top of everything. This could collapse, especially now in this rain. Dear God, Randolph, this isn't rock and coal; these hills are nothing but earth." He turned to the workers. "Naturally, you'll get your pay."

"All of it?" asked one of the women. "Including from last week and the week before?"

Peter rubbed his forehead as Randolph glared at the woman. "Our agreement was quite clear that you would be paid when we found coal, Mrs. Carlson."

"We need the money," another said.

Peter breathed in deeply. "You'll receive your payment, madam. Don't worry. The same does not apply to you, however, Paisley. According to what your daughter Violet tells me, you've been working in Treherbert for more than ten years. You should know how deep underground the coal is buried here. So, if you get into nonsense like this, you need to face the consequences."

Paisley did not seem to have done much work, anyway. Peter noted that the foreman was the only one not covered in dirt but was instead clean and well dressed.

Paisley and Randolph both started to reply, but Peter bade them be silent with a gesture. "We'll speak later, Randolph, before your departure for Cardiff. You'll be on the next train. And you, Paisley, take Fred home—or better, to Mr. Webber. Tell him he'll receive a small discount on this land if he hires you and your son. And then try and keep that job for your wife and daughters' sake. My good women, please come by the Burton house tomorrow. I don't have any money on me now, you understand. Early tomorrow, I'll arrange everything with the bank. You can help my wife in the garden for the rest of the week, so you won't lose any of this week's pay."

The four women departed, grateful. Resigned, Peter looked out into the pouring rain. "Hopefully your father will pay me back the money," he said in Randolph's direction. "And now, everyone out before the entrance collapses."

Peter led his horse out into the rain now falling in a deluge. He longed for a cup of tea or a whiskey. And for Kathleen's face, her smile, and understanding. Had Randolph loved Alice Clusky just so? Did his crazy ideas perhaps only aim at winning the young woman for himself, after all? Peter sighed and watched the women go. No warm fire, no tea, no whiskey, and no comfort awaited them. Instead, there would be housework, children, and men unashamed to send their wives and daughters into the mines.

Chapter 7

At first, Kahu Heke wasn't definitive about what his daughter could do to save the Maori people. This was partly because their privacy was interrupted by a young warrior who had been cooking on the edge of the clearing. He approached them shyly, a strange device in his hand.

"*Ariki*, the food is prepared," he said reverently. "First for you. For daughter is cooking on fire."

Matariki was amazed by the difficulty the warrior had expressing himself. This wasn't a new dialect, but it sounded as if the young Maori had only recently learned the language of his people. However, she forgot all about linguistic issues the moment Kahu Heke sat down by the fire. The young warrior was careful not to cross his shadow when he stepped beside him and put the strange device to his lips. It looked like a sort of horn with an opening at each end. The warrior shoveled food into the opening at the top, and it ran through the smaller hole into Kahu Heke's mouth.

"I cannot touch the food; it's *tapu*," the chieftain explained. "If I were to use bowls and spoons like the others, that would require an elaborate cleansing ceremony that would be cumbersome and a mockery of the gods. Hence, the feeding horn. You get used to it, Matariki."

Matariki grabbed her forehead, but she was careful not to touch her hair so she didn't have to embarrass herself by breathing in Rauru afterward.

"He's not going to feed me," she said curtly with an eye on the young warrior.

He was quite handsome. He had only a small tattoo near his nose, which made him look more amusing than dangerous. Matariki thought it emphasized his dimples. The young man had an oval face, short dark hair that he seemed to be growing out so he could tie it into a warrior knot, friendly brown eyes, and a beautiful, full mouth. Matariki would have pictured him more as a poet than a warrior. To become a warrior, he would have to practice filling people with fear.

In fact, he seemed to be fearful himself. He looked shocked by her decisive words.

"I made mistake?"

Kahu Heke shook his head. "Everything is all right, Kupe," he soothed the boy—in English. The warrior relaxed.

"He doesn't need to feed you, Matariki." The chieftain switched back to Maori. "For the children of the *ariki*, the *tapu* are not as strict. Your food must be cooked separately, but you're spared the feeding horn. So, calm yourself. Are you hungry? Your food will be done soon."

Now it was clear why her abductors had avoided her the whole journey. Apparently, no one could come within three feet of a North Island *ariki*'s family without bumping into *tapu*.

As for the cleansing of Matariki's traveling companions, there seemed to be a problem, which was presented to the chieftain by an agitated messenger. "Hanu and Kahori have begun the cleansing ceremony. We lit a holy fire and cooked food. Then we rubbed it on the hands of the sullied like you said. But who's supposed to eat it now? I mean . . ."

Kahu Heke bit his lip.

"You said," the warrior recapitulated, "the highest-ranking woman in the tribe must eat that food. But there are no women here. Only . . ." He cast a shy look at Matariki.

"I am most definitely not eating anything those two had between their fingers," she said. "Besides, I would have to touch what the men have already touched, and I cannot."

"She's right. That cannot be," the chieftain said seriously. "Send them here. I will free them from the curse by spreading my cloak over them."

The warrior's eyes widened. "That is a most gracious, *ariki*," he said.

Kahu Heke shrugged. "Hanu and Kahori have performed for their people a great service," he said, and turned to go.

Matariki bit her lip as he disappeared into his lodge. She had thought he would keep her company while she ate and reveal a bit more of the mission for which she had been brought here. Yet it was probably *tapu* for a chieftain to watch his daughter eat. Once again Matariki did not know if she should laugh or be outraged.

The young man, Kupe, approached her shyly and spoke in Maori. "You eat now. I cooked bird. But you take yourself, otherwise *tapu*."

Matariki stood up with a sigh. She understood: she would not be served. Hopefully he was a good cook—although "cooked bird" did not sound promising, and the stew, which had sweet potatoes swimming in it, did not look very appetizing. Matariki made a face of disgust.

Kupe noticed her reluctance. "It's kiwi," he said. "Roasted tastes good. Cooking like this is better. Evil spirits don't like."

Matariki rolled her eyes. "You really think the spirits could gobble up this stuff if you made it a little tasty? You are wrong."

The young man blushed. "Can you maybe say again? I not have understood."

"It's nothing," Matariki murmured, a bit embarrassed. Her parents had raised her to respect the religion of the Ngai Tahu in the same way the tribe respected Lizzie's Christianity. "But why don't you understand Maori? Are you from a different tribe? The warriors here are of different tribes, right?"

Kupe shook his head, and it seemed he didn't understand much of what she said. Maybe Matariki's South Island dialect was hard for him. But then she had a flash of insight. Kupe differed in every respect from the others. Hardly any tattoos, his short hair . . .

"You speak English, right?" she asked.

He nodded, beaming. "Oh yeah, yes. But," he said, slipping back into Maori, "I should speak not that. Is language of enemy. I must our language learn."

Matariki sighed again. "Tell you what, you'll learn tomorrow. We'll make a trade, all right, Kupe? I won't tell anyone we spoke English, and in exchange, you'll keep me company while I eat."

"It's *tapu*," he said, but didn't look worried.

Hanu and Kahori had always shown fear when Matariki came too close to them. Kupe, however, only seemed to fear breaking protocol and falling out of the chief's good graces.

Matariki grinned at him. "Afterward I can spread my cloak over you," she offered. "Or my blanket. Unfortunately, I didn't have my jacket on me when your charming tribal brothers took me captive. But I'll make do."

Kupe now smiled too. In English he said, "I think when it comes to *tapu*, you sometimes have to improvise a bit."

Matariki sighed with relief. Finally, here was someone with whom she could talk. And not just because they spoke the same language.

"Where do you come from?" she asked as she ate the kiwi soup. The Ngai Tahu cooked better. "You are Maori, right?"

Neither Kupe's facial features nor his body type indicated a mix of *pakeha* and Maori.

The young Maori nodded. "I'm from Poverty Bay," he said. Matariki noticed he used the English name for the bay. Her father would surely have chided him for that. "From Gisborne; I was in an orphanage there."

Matariki looked up at him, confused. In the meantime, Kupe had taken a seat beside her but now scooted a bit to the side in order not to risk her shadow falling on him. He did not look at her either, but he no doubt noticed that she found his story strange. Maori children generally did not land in an orphanage. Even if their parents died, the children were lovingly cared for by their respective tribe.

"All the children of my tribe grew up in the orphanage. In 1865 there was a typhus outbreak in Opotiki, and many tribe members died there. Te Ua Haumene determined they needed to be avenged. He dispatched warriors who killed a missionary."

Matariki had heard this story. She wondered if her new friend knew that her father had to answer for the murder of Carl Völkner.

"After that, they wanted to drive out all the *pakeha* from Poverty Bay," Kupe said.

"Which they did not appreciate." Matariki knew that too.

Kupe looked at the ground. "The whites beat the Hauhau back. And then they came to our village. We had nothing at all to do with it. We didn't know anything about the Hauhau. But they did not want to hear it. They killed the chieftain and pushed out the tribe, confiscating its children." Kupe spoke dispassionately, as if he had recounted the tale often, but then his rage surfaced. "We were to be raised as respectable Christians." He spat out the words.

"They put the whole village's children in an orphanage?" Matariki asked, horrified.

Kupe nodded. "I can't remember our old village at all anymore. I was very little. But the older children told us about it. Before they separated us. We went to various homes, so that we no longer spoke Maori with one another. We little ones quickly forgot the language. That's why I have to learn it again."

Matariki would have liked to lay her hand on her new friend's arm to comfort him, but he would pull away from her: *tapu*. Matariki played nervously with the jade pendant she wore around her neck, a *hei-tiki*, a Maori god in miniature. Haikina had given it to her for her last birthday.

"It was terrible," Kupe said, continuing his story. "In the orphanage, they beat us all the time. We were always told the Maori weren't good for anything. If someone spoke even a word of Maori, they would lock him up for a day, even though we had long since started acting like *pakeha* children. I could not even remember my tribe, and I wasn't stupid or lazy. I always had good grades. I might have gone to university. There were scholarships for theology. But then I heard about the Hauhau in King Country." That was the *pakeha* name for Waikato and its surrounding districts. "To the missionaries, it sounded like the devil resided here, but for me it was a chance. Ultimately, I fled. And I did find it: my tribe." He sounded proud.

Matariki could understand Kupe's joy, but she also thought the whites surely were not the only ones to blame for Kupe's bad childhood. Without the Hauhau's provocations, the *pakeha* would never have thought to attack Kupe's village.

"I also have a new name," the young warrior announced enthusiastically. "Kupe—a hero's name. Kupe was the first settler on Aotearoa."

Matariki knew the legend; however, the story of Kupe and his family's settling of New Zealand could be seen multiple ways: no doubt it had been brave of him to leave Hawaiki and steer his canoe into the unknown. Yet there was not much left for him to do but flee. Kupe had murdered a tribe member and stolen his wife. Then later, he left Kura-maro-tini and their children to seek new adventures. Matariki's stepfather, Michael, might have called Kupe a hero, but her mother spoke with disdain of fortune hunters. Though, it was better not to tell her new friend all that. Kupe looked happy when he spoke of his life among the Hauhau.

"They called me Kurt in the orphanage."

Matariki laughed. "They called me Martha at school," she revealed. "Kupe is a nice name."

His eyes beamed at her comment. At times Kupe seemed almost childlike, though Matariki thought he was a good three years older than she was.

Matariki now had to ask some practical questions. "Where can I bathe here, Kupe? Preferably without violating any *tapu*. There must be a stream or a lake around here, right? I need to wash my hair, at least. As best I can without touching it."

***

An hour later, Matariki had washed herself in a clear stream. Kupe had been sure to look away when she took off her blouse. Another sign of his *pakeha* upbringing. Maori girls did not think twice about baring their upper body to their tribe members. Matariki found Kupe's behavior touching—especially when, blushing, he handed her a small bowl of soapy water.

"If you just pour it over your hair and then wash it out, you don't need your hands."

Matariki found these *tapu* bizarre, but she did as he instructed. She lay flat on her back and let her hair fall into the water. While the stream washed away the soap, she stared up at the lush green tops of the kauri tree, which rose majestically beside the stream. She wondered how long it had needed to grow to this height—supposedly kauri trees could live to be four thousand years old. If this one had held watch over the stream for only a quarter of that time, its seed would have sprouted before the first Maori had settled the land. It was possible no white person had ever laid eyes on it. Matariki did not know exactly where she was, but if there were *pakeha* settlements in the area, Kahu Heke would surely have sought another location for his camp. If her father got his way, the trees and ferns here would never give way to a *pakeha* ax.

The girl tried to imagine an Aotearoa without the whites, without the brick buildings, schools, and sheep herds. She could not quite do it, and it was nothing for which she longed. Still, she liked it in the here and now. Matariki's hip-length black hair floated in the water, the current stroked her scalp, and she thought she could feel the stream playing with her locks from roots to ends.

"Like that, you really look like a sorceress," Kupe said as he looked at Matariki's abundant black hair surrounding her like a mermaid's.

Matariki sat up when she heard Kupe's voice. "I'm not, though," she asserted. "I'm a completely normal girl. But, since we're talking about magic, do you have any idea what I'm supposed to do to make you and the other members of the tribe invulnerable?"

Kupe shrugged. "Your father will probably tell you. He wants to see you—before the ceremony this evening."

Matariki wondered how to dry her hair without touching it. She could have used her riding dress, but she had no desire to sit all night by the fire in a wet skirt—assuming there was a fire for her. The dress was dirty and ragged anyway. She desperately needed new clothes. And warmer ones. After all, winter was looming, and every night was already freezing.

Matariki ignored any thoughts of *tapu* and wrung the water from her heavy black locks with her bare hands. As she was returning to her father's lodge, a provisional shelter in the clearing caught her eye. Was she supposed to live there? They certainly would not let her into the chieftain's hut.

Kahu Heke stood in front of his lodge. "You've had time to collect yourself, Matariki," he said. "Do you feel spiritually prepared to take part in our ceremony this evening?"

Matariki shrugged. "Depends on what I'm supposed to do," she replied. "See, I still don't have any magic against bullets."

Kahu Heke seemed to be losing his patience. "I told you, girl, you need to view it metaphorically. We don't need to start with a grand ceremony."

"Father, once again, I'm not a *tohunga*," Matariki said, making her position clear, "and I'm not going to be one. When I was little, I went around with Hainga a little and know a few medicinal plants. And I can dance different *haka*."

"Well, that's something," Kahu Heke said happily. "You'll dance, of course; that's part of it. For summoning the war gods too. But as I said before, we won't start with that; we'll do that by, hmm, by the new moon?"

Matariki raised her hands in a gesture of helplessness. "Father, I don't know when one does this, or what exactly *this* is. I need help. Is there a *tohunga* who can stand at my side?"

Kahu Heke bit his lip. "Well, Hare says he once participated in such a ceremony when the tribes still fought against one another in his youth."

"Hare is a priest?" Matariki used the English word. In Maori, she would have said *tohunga*, but that meant someone who had specialized knowledge in a particular subject, not necessarily just the spiritual. One could, however, be a *tohunga* in spiritual matters but at the same time be a carpenter or midwife. "Priest," on the other hand, meant someone who had totally committed his life to the spiritual, so "priest" seemed the more appropriate term for what she was asking in regard to Hare.

Kahu Heke ran his hand nervously through his full hair, and Matariki noted again with amusement that he forgot to breathe in Rauru afterward. "He's, hmm, well, I'd call him *tohunga* in *whaikorero*. He leads the ceremonies when I'm not present. He gives very moving speeches."

Matariki shook her head. "Hare is a master of eloquent speech," she specified. "You could also say a storyteller. And he's supposed to reconstruct such an important ceremony? Based on what he saw once as a boy? Or maybe not?"

Kahu Heke now remembered Rauru, and he inhaled reverently. "Matariki, I told you. The precise procedure of the ceremony isn't important. What's important is stirring the men's hearts. Their own spirit makes them invulnerable. Not this or that god."

"And if the gods see things differently?" she asked impertinently. "Perhaps we're angering them by simply making something up. Anyway, Hainga would never do something like that. That would really be *tapu*."

Kahu Heke began to pace in front of his lodge. Matariki stood defiantly where she was, without dodging his shadow.

"Just leave what's *tapu* to me," the *ariki* finally said, aggravated. "You don't do anything but dance. Today, anyway, some *haka* you know."

"Like this?" Matariki asked, looking down at herself. "Father, I don't have a *piu piu* or *poi poi*. It's not going to work."

The young girls' dances did not make an impression through grace of movement alone. The traditional dancing skirts made from hardened flax leaves produced a rustling sound to accompany the girls. In addition, the girls swung flax balls on long strings. They, too, made noises and underscored the rhythm. Matariki knew how to make *piu-piu* skirts as well as *poi-poi* balls, but it would take weeks to harden the flax for them, not to mention sewing the tops in the tribal colors.

"I can't exactly dance in an old riding dress."

Kahu Heke could not dispute this. Although he was not sure whether the chieftain's daughter was to be naked during the decisive ceremony. Hare had hinted as much. However, by no means did he want to risk more stubbornness from Matariki.

"Very well," he finally said. "You will not dance tonight. I'll send a warrior to the next village. He will acquire your dancing clothes. You need to dress like one of us, anyway."

"Always?" Matariki asked, horrified.

Traditional Maori clothing was attractive but not especially warm. For that reason, the Ngai Tahu preferred *pakeha* clothing when there was no imminent festival or ceremony.

Kahu Heke did not answer. Instead, he again raised the matter of tattooing.

Matariki's eyes flashed angrily. "I already told you once, I don't want *moko*. For one, I don't like them. And they hurt. And the ink can inflame the skin."

Hainga had told the Ngai Tahu girls about various plants that had once been used to soothe inflammation after the tattooing procedure. Yet the remedies had not always worked, which was probably another reason that the practically minded Ngai Tahu now largely did without *moko*.

"You're a chieftain's daughter," Kahu Heke said sternly. "The pain—"

"That's just it." Matariki smiled triumphantly. "I'm a chieftain's daughter, and no one can touch me. So, no *moko*. Who's supposed to stick me?" She glared mockingly at her father. "And who stuck you? Did they not take it so seriously back then among the Ngati Pau, or are you not even truly a chieftain's child? Wasn't Hongi Hika just your uncle?"

"I have royal blood enough," Kahu Heke declared, leaving the question of his *moko* unanswered. "Now, come, Matariki. The men await. They will dance around the *niu*, and you should at least show yourself. Even if you don't join in the ceremonies tonight."

Chapter 8

It was growing dark, and Violet was slowly becoming scared by her own courage. The trip from Treherbert to Treorchy stretched on, and she was carrying Rosie because her little sister had long been tired. What was more, the light drizzle that afternoon was slowly turning into a downpour. Violet was soaked to the bone, and her old shoes were falling apart when she finally reached the village's first houses.

In contrast to Treherbert, Treorchy had not come into being solely with the founding of mines. There had been a town here before the first mines opened, so there were more freestanding cottages, and the streets did not all look the same. Treorchy had originally been tiny, and even now, after it had grown enormously through mining, Ellen's stories were enough to help Violet find the Seekers' house.

Violet's heart was pounding when she put Rosie down and opened the garden gate. There were a trellis fence and well-tended flower and vegetable beds. Violet made sure Rosie did not step in the beds as they walked up to the door. There, she stared at the door knocker shaped in the form of a lion's maw. A brass door knocker—that was a luxury. In the mining houses, no one could afford something like that, nor did anyone need one. Most of the time, miners' families left their doors open; otherwise, a simple rap was enough to announce a visitor.

Everything here was so different from back home in Treherbert. The mailbox was made of brass, too, with enamel designs. And in front of the door was a colorful mat with lettering: "W-E-L-C-O-M-E," Violet spelled out. That gave her courage.

"I want to go home," Rosie whined.

Violet took a deep breath and knocked. Then she took Rosie by the hand. "Can't you smile at least?" she muttered.

The door opened, and Violet squinted into the light of an oil lamp. The man who opened the door was lean and pale with a bearded face. His eyes, which were just as blue as Violet's, showed complete bewilderment.

"Ellen?" he asked.

***

A few moments later, Walter Seekers had overcome his confusion. Of course, it could not be Ellen standing in front of his door. But, in the dim light of the lamp, young Violet bore an uncanny resemblance to her mother. Now, the cobbler could not get his fill of looking at her—Violet Paisley, Ellen's daughter. Walter Seekers could hardly believe his visitor was flesh and blood.

Nevertheless, he soon recovered his thoughts enough to bring his granddaughter and the little one with her in out of the rain. Now Violet sat in front of the fire with Rosie in her arms. She was trying to dry her clothes and not to look too inquisitively while Walter made tea.

"And what's the little girl's name? She'd like a cup of hot chocolate, wouldn't she?" Walter asked uncertainly. "She's not your child, is she?"

Violet chastised her grandfather with her expression—something he knew all too well from his daughter. "Of course not. I'm thirteen years old. This is Rosemary, my sister."

Walter Seekers—*My grandpa,* thought Violet—had tears in his eyes.

"Rosemary," he whispered, "after my wife who's departed. Ellen named her after her mother."

Violet knew about the naming but not that Rosemary Seekers had passed.

"She died a year ago," Walter told her sadly. He placed a steaming cup of tea in front of Violet and a hot chocolate in front of Rosie, then opened a tin of tea cakes.

"I wish she could have seen this. We always thought Ellen would come back. Rosemary was so sure. That devil—sorry, dear, he's your father, but he was always a good-for-nothing. And Ellen had to see that someday."

"Mother's ashamed," Violet said.

Walter sighed. "She got that pride from my Rosie too. But tell me, Violet. Why are you here? What can I do for you?"

Violet reported Jim's unemployment and the eviction notice while Rosie stuffed herself with one cookie after another.

"But now Father has a foreman's job digging a level," Violet concluded, so as not to make her father look all that bad. "Only, he hasn't gotten his pay yet. When he does, he'll be able to pay the rent easily. Perhaps . . . perhaps you can help us with a few shillings?"

Walter Seekers sighed and then expressed the same considerations that had plagued Violet the last two weeks. "Oh, child, if your father doesn't have the money now, then he's never going to. What sort of mine is that supposed to be: broke two weeks after opening? Besides—a level in Treherbert?"

Walter Seekers was a cobbler, not a miner, but he had lived long enough in the region to learn the most important facts about coal mining.

Violet shrugged.

"I think, first thing, I'll drive you two home now. Your mother doesn't know you're here, does she?"

Violet shook her head, embarrassed. "She said I shouldn't come, but, Mr. Seekers, I—"

"Grandpa," Walter said, a broad grin on his face. "I've waited long enough to hear it. And it doesn't matter what your mother said. She'll surely be worried to death about you and little Rosie."

Rosie had meanwhile climbed into his lap. She was cautious toward men, but Walter Seekers's beard fascinated her, and his voice was calm and friendly, not loud and aggressive like their father's and his friends'. Walter gently stopped her from tugging on his beard.

"We can walk back," Violet said.

It was surely an imposition to have the old man hitch a horse in the pouring rain. Besides, by now her father would be home, and when he saw her grandpa bringing them home . . .

"Oh, nonsense." Walter was already reaching for his coat and then went into his bedroom, emerging with a rain-tight cloak. "Here, this was my Rosie's. You'll both fit nicely underneath it. It'll be like a tent. Rosemary, look, you can hide in there."

Rosie laughed and began at once to slip underneath the cloak, popping out again with a cheerful "coocoo" as Violet wrapped it around her.

"Thank you," Violet said. "Can I, can I help in some way? Maybe with the horse?"

Violet had never come within more than a few yards of a horse, but she offered anyway.

"Can we take the cookies with us?" asked Rosie.

Walter furrowed his brow when he saw Violet's expression at her sister's request.

"Tell me, Violet," he asked thoughtfully. "Are you going hungry?"

***

When the horse was finally hitched and Walter Seekers had thrown a few tarpaulins on the wagon to protect his young passengers at least somewhat from the rain, he also heaved in a basket of foodstuffs he had been able to assemble quickly: bread, cheese, some dried meat from which Violet could hardly look away, butter, and milk. The girl could scarcely recall the taste of butter. She pictured her mother's face when she unpacked these treasures.

Lucy, Walter Seekers's old but well-cared-for cob mare, trotted as soon as she was on the paved road to Treherbert. Likely she hoped to put the journey through the deluge behind her as quickly as possible. In the meantime, the evening had grown completely dark.

"Are there stables to rent in Treherbert?" Walter asked, pulling the tarpaulins over himself and his granddaughters. It did not help much. "I don't think I'll make it back tonight. But Lucy will need someplace dry to sleep, and so will I."

"You can sleep in my bed," Rosie generously offered her grandfather. Violet bit her lip.

"I don't know," Violet murmured.

Walter Seekers smiled at her. "I know well enough," he said. "Your father and I are not exactly friends. And by this time, he's probably long past sober."

Violet nodded, relieved that her grandfather had saved them the acknowledgment that a drunk Jim Paisley was not exactly pleasant.

"Don't worry, I'll find a place. I know the Davies' coachman quite well—been making his boots for years." David Davies was among the largest mine owners in Rhondda. His coachman traveled a lot. "If you tell me where the Davies' villa is, I can hole up there."

Violet had no idea where the incredibly wealthy Mr. Davies lived, but now the weak lights of Treherbert had come into view, and she first had to direct her grandfather to Bute Street, where they lived in the oldest section of town. In truth, she had expected to find the house unlit, or at most a candle burning in the window. Then again, her mother must be worried. Indeed, they could see from the street that something was happening at home. The lamps were burning in the living room and bedroom, and loud voices rang out.

"I'll kill you and that little slut."

"Let go of her, Dad," Fred shouted.

"You leave your wife alone, or we'll fetch the police."

The courageous Mrs. Brown from next door sounded considerably more determined than the audibly drunk Fred.

Mr. Brown would probably have been even more convincing, but he never involved himself in others' affairs.

"Daddy's hitting Mommy," whispered Rosie as she burrowed into the cloak.

Violet could not leap down fast enough from the wagon box. However, her grandfather was even more spry than she would have thought. He simply left the wagon on the street and ran to the entrance. The door was locked. Behind it, they heard Ellen's choked screams. Walter Seekers threw himself against the door, causing it to swing open. Violet wanted to run in, but Mrs. Brown stopped her and took Rosie, who had run after her sister and grandfather, in her other arm.

"I'll take the little one; she doesn't need to see this."

Violet muttered a thank-you and stormed into the apartment—where she glimpsed her grandfather laying out the twice as heavy but drunk and confused Jim Paisley with a powerful right-handed punch.

"Don't you dare touch my daughter again," roared Walter.

Fred, who had tried halfheartedly to pull his father off his mother, watched the scene, dumbfounded.

Ellen was curled up whimpering in a corner, holding her hands protectively in front of her face. She was bleeding from cuts over her eye and from her lip, and one of her eyes was swollen shut, but she did not seem seriously injured.

"Mommy." Violet helped her up.

Ellen stared disbelieving at the apparition who, full of self-confidence, was beating her husband.

"Dad," she whispered.

"You're not staying another night in this house."

Walter Seekers needed a little time to catch his breath, but then he looked in astonishment around the dilapidated miner's apartment out of which he had just beaten Jim Paisley. The cobbler was not easily riled, but when he was angry, he raged. Many years before, Ellen had experienced that herself. And now so had Jim. Fred had followed his father without another word; he was drunk enough that he might have taken Walter Seekers for some sort of avenging spirit out of hell.

The Paisley men were likely headed back to the pub. Violet attempted to put the apartment in order. That was rather hopeless. In his rage, Jim had destroyed half of the little furniture they had.

"He lost his job again," Ellen reported, still completely out of breath. "And for some reason he blamed you, Violet. I don't know why. I should have left him alone. Maybe he would have fallen asleep and forgotten it in the morning. But I had to tell him about the notice."

She pointed helplessly to the eviction notice, or what was left of it. Jim Paisley had torn up the paper and strewn the pieces across the floor.

"Leave him alone? Nonsense!" Walter Seekers worked himself up. "Don't act as if it had anything to do with you. How often did he beat you, Ellen? Once or twice a month? Every week? For heaven's sake, child, why didn't you come home?"

He took his daughter in his arms, very carefully, so as not to hurt her. "No matter, I'll take you all with me now. You won't stay here another minute. Those devils will be back as soon as the pub closes. Take what you want, Ellen, and you too, Violet. We'll be gone before he returns."

"But Fred, what about him?" Ellen was still too taken by surprise to think of fleeing. "He is my son, after all."

"Tonight, he was the accomplice to your abusive husband," Walter replied harshly. "When he's sober tomorrow, you can speak with him. He's welcome in my house, too, if he behaves. But tonight, he'll have to make do for himself."

Violet did not need more than a couple of minutes to pack her few pieces of clothing, a barrette Heather had given her, and a cheap notebook in which she occasionally wrote. Violet's greatest wish was to learn to read and write properly.

But she had never gone to school, and the bits her mother or the Sunday school pastor taught her did not take her very far.

"Done," she said, "and now I'll pack for Mom and Rosie. Grandpa, if you take them to the wagon, I'll be right there."

Violet threw Ellen's sparse wardrobe and a few clothes for Rosie in a basket. She took the doll Kathleen Burton had made for Rosie by sewing together rags and making a stuffing from sawdust. Rosie, who had never had a proper doll, was exceedingly proud of it.

Outside, Walter Seekers draped his daughter and youngest grandchild in the tarps. Ellen shivered and looked unsure. Her injuries hurt as well. However, her father and Violet would not hear any more objections. Walter was finally bringing his daughter home after all these years. And Violet saw her future more optimistically than ever before. In Treorchy, she would surely not need to work and could go to school. She would not be a poor, dirty coal miner's daughter but the granddaughter of the cobbler. She would live in a proper house with a garden all around, a house that belonged to her grandfather. Ellen would never need to worry again about whether her drunk of a husband paid the rent.

Violet would have liked to laugh and sing, but the weather was too depressing. The rain poured down from the sky. As Walter steered the wagon out of Treherbert, the effect of the torrential rain could be seen on the roads. He had to avoid mud holes everywhere and maneuver Lucy and the wagon carefully over the washed-out sections. In places, the road was completely flooded by the river, which had overflowed its banks, and they had to make a detour.

"Do we really want to try for Treorchy tonight?" Violet asked when Walter once again had his passengers climb out at an especially precarious juncture. Ellen was leaning on her daughter for support, and Rosie was crying again.

Walter looked at Violet wearily. "Where else can we go?" he asked. "The four of us won't be able to shelter at the Davies' stables."

"We could stay with the Burtons," Violet said. "If we go right here, it's only about a mile to their house. They'll take us in."

The thought of a house in which a warm fire was surely burning lifted Violet's spirits.

"That's the family you said you work for, correct?" Walter was somewhat mistrustful. "He's not a pastor who'll convince your mother to go back to that violent devil, er, husband because of her marriage vows, is he?"

Violet shook her head. "Certainly not. Reverend Burton isn't like that. Besides, we can't keep going this way."

That was true. The next thing would have been to cross the river, but the torrents of water had torn away the bridge. Walter Seekers considered briefly what other options might be open to him. However, the thought of several hours' driving in this weather helped him make a decision quickly.

"All right, so be it, girl. This way? Climb back in, Ellen. It'll be all right. And you, Rosie, stop that crying. Look, here, in this basket, there're still cookies. Didn't you want to eat these?"

Rosie contented herself with a few soggy cookies, and Walter Seekers steered the reluctant Lucy toward the Burton house. They moved forward slowly on the rutted field path, which had transformed into a muddy wasteland. The wagon inched up the mountain where Randolph Burton had made his level. Lucy pulled the wagon uphill, struggling valiantly against the rocky, slippery ground.

And then it happened: Walter Seekers saw too late the deep, rocky gully the water had cut when it washed away the road. Lucy overstepped the depression with a bound, but the wagon slammed into it, its axle splitting.

The cob mare remained where she was when the wheels jammed.

Walter Seekers cursed. "Looks like we'll have to continue on foot," he sighed, moving to unhitch Lucy. "Sorry, girls, all I can offer you now is the horse."

Neither Ellen, who was dead tired, nor the girls wanted onto the dripping wet horse. Violet thought with dread about walking through the mud. They still had a long way to the Burtons'. Walter took the oil lamp and used it to light their way. Violet took the basket of provisions. After all, one never knew.

"If we could at least find some woods or something where we could take shelter," Walter muttered.

After just a few steps, it became obvious that neither Ellen nor Rosie would make it all the way to the Burtons'. Their soaked dresses were heavy and freezing.

"I could go on ahead and maybe get a wagon or horses," Walter said.

"I can go," Violet offered, trying to determine by the landscape how much farther it was. The path and the mountain seemed strangely altered to her. There were countless footprints and wagon ruts, and rubbish lay to the side of the path. Then she saw the entrance to a shaft in one of the hillsides.

"Grandpa, look, we can take shelter there." Violet pointed excitedly to the dark maw gaping before them—not like a threat but rather as a refuge from the horrible weather. "There's a tunnel in the mountain."

"A tunnel?" Walter asked, amazed, and stopped right at the shaft's entrance. "Seems to belong to a mine. Be careful you don't fall if there's a shaft."

Violet had already run ahead.

"A level," she announced. "This must be the new one Father worked in."

Ellen nodded tiredly. "And that the reverend closed today. That's why Jim was so angry. He's—"

"He's a bastard," Walter remarked curtly. "Can you enter there, Violet? Is it safe?"

All Violet saw was shelter from the weather. The tunnel led at least one hundred feet into the mountain, and it was dry. Walter followed her with the oil lamp, which illuminated the smooth walls and the ceiling, which was slightly taller than an average man.

Walter sighed with relief. "We can stay here," he decided, "until the weather improves, even if that's not till morning."

Violet wanted to say something, but her grandfather bade her be quiet. "No, Violet, I'll not hear of you going out and trying to get to your employers. For one, something could happen to you, and for two, it would be an imposition on them to hitch a team in this weather—and who knows if the path is fit for driving. No, we'll remain here and set out on foot tomorrow."

He moved determinedly to lead Lucy into the tunnel, but while Ellen and the girls staggered with relief out of the wet, the horse refused to take even one step forward. Walter tried halfheartedly to force the mare inside, but Lucy would not be convinced.

"Then stay outside, you stupid nag," Walter cursed, and let go of the reins. "I'll tie her outside. In the meantime, you all settle in. Over there, Ellen, as far inside as possible—it's warmer there."

Ellen warmed her hands over the oil lamp, and Rosie comforted herself with the contents of the food basket. Never in her life had the little girl seen food like this, and she chewed with her cheeks full of cheese and dried meats. Violet made sure that her mother ate something. Ellen looked very pale, her wounds had started bleeding again, and her eye was still swollen shut. Reverend Burton surely would have called a doctor or treated Ellen himself. He was supposed to have led a field hospital in the goldfields. For now, there was nothing to be done, and Ellen would not die of her injuries.

"I just need rest, dear," she said as she noticed Violet's concerned expression. "We'll just lie down to sleep, and—"

Her words were swallowed in a thunderous roar, and it felt as if the earth were shaking beneath them. Another storm now? Violet gave up once and for all the thought of reaching the Burton house that night.

"I feel sick," Rosie announced. "I think I'm going to throw up, Mommy."

Violet sighed. "That's what happens when you stuff yourself," she said. "Just don't throw up here. It'll smell all night."

"I'll take her out," Ellen said, already half-asleep.

Violet shook her head. "Nonsense, I'll go. I'll also see to the horse, Grandpa. Maybe she wants to come out of the rain now."

She did not like the thought of Lucy dripping wet. She had already grown fond of the horse—and she wondered why the animal seemed so set against entering the tunnel. After all, the mare had hardly wanted to leave the stables.

"I need to throw up."

Rosie's whining grew more urgent, and there was another roar of thunder. Violet picked up her sister and carried her outside. Lucy whinnied at her. The horse sounded fearful—or insistent? Her grandfather had tied the mare to as protected a place as possible at the entrance to the tunnel. Lucy, however, seemed to want to get away. Violet was afraid of the stomping mare. She carried Rosie far from the entrance to the edge of the road, where she threw up at once. Violet held her hair and wished she were out of the rain—and then everything happened very quickly.

The thunder roared again. However, somehow it did not seem to come from the sky but from the mountain itself. Violet saw from the corner of her eye how Lucy, with a final desperate effort, tugged on her line and freed herself as a powerful mass of mud and rock collapsed in front of her. If the horse had not freed herself, she would have been buried. While Violet stared in shock at the tunnel entrance, it thundered some more, more masses of earth fell from the hillside into the entrance, and a boulder rolled toward Violet. She pulled Rosie away from the slope and heard Ellen screaming. Or were those her own screams? Or Rosie's? A torrent of water poured down the hillside, washing away earth and debris with it. The tunnel's entrance was no longer visible. The whole world seemed now to consist only of rain, collapsing earth, and thunder.

Suddenly the thundering stopped, and the collapsing earth came to a standstill. Violet ran to the mound of rock and earth behind which the tunnel's entrance lay. She began to dig with her bare hands.

"Mommy," she screamed and sobbed, but no one answered. Violet finally gave up. "We need to fetch help," she said flatly. "Come with me, Rosie. You have to come along."

Violet pulled herself together. Part of her wanted to remain to cry and scream and even to die. But another part of her remained coolheaded, looked at the disaster site as someone only casually involved, and knew above all that she needed to get Rosie out of the cold and rain. She cautiously approached Lucy, who had stayed nearby and was now picking at grass on the side of the road. The old mare looked at her amicably.

Violet lifted Rosie onto the horse. "You'll ride for now. No back talk. Hold on tight. You can do it. We need to get help for Mommy and Grandpa. And if I carry you, it'll take hours."

***

Lucy dutifully padded along next to Violet and even allowed her to hold on to her mane when the path became slippery. Nevertheless, it took an eternity for the Burton house to come into view. Everything was dark. Naked fear took hold of Violet. What if the Burtons were not home? Or if no one opened the door? Or . . . ?

She left the horse untethered in the garden, pulled the still-whimpering Rosie with her up the front stairs, and hammered desperately on the door. The knocking didn't seem to rouse anyone. Violet looked for rocks to throw at the windows.

Then she heard footsteps. The door opened, and she threw herself, sobbing, into Peter Burton's arms. "Reverend, Reverend, the tunnel, the level, my mother, my grandfather."

Chapter 9

The Hauhau's evening devotion was similar to what Matariki had seen at midday, though everything seemed more martial in torchlight, and this ceremony lacked her father's rousing speech. After his militant words, the warriors' monotone "*Rire, rire, hau, hau*" had sounded like a battle cry—but of the sort that reminded Matariki of school hockey games.

Now, however, the men's grim expressions and their cries frightened Matariki. The men, in sacred seriousness, surrounded the pole—called a *niu*—in the middle of the camp and chanted the syllables. Kahu Heke and Hare, the "master of eloquent speech" and self-proclaimed spiritual expert of this strange tribe, occasionally added names and comments. Some were taken up by the warriors, who shouted, "Pai Marire," "*Hau, hau,*" "Te Ua Haumene," or "In the name of Gabriel" or "Atua." A call for "freedom" was answered by the Hauhau with even louder cries. The noise in the clearing was deafening. Matariki could not believe that the civilian village of the Te Maniapoto could be that close.

The ceremony lasted hours, and Kupe looked completely exhausted as he stomped around the pole for perhaps the hundredth time. Most of the warriors seemed, however, to fall into a violent trance. Their cries spurred them on. A few swung their spears; others beat themselves on the breast. They seemed to desire nothing more than to finally have the foe before them.

To Matariki, it all appeared strange and terrifying—much more so than the martial *haka* her own tribe occasionally danced to stay in practice. That served as deterrence, but this was something else. This changed the warriors, and it was dangerous.

The men finally finished, and Kahu Heke withdrew to his lodge, followed by the cheerful Kupe who fed him before eating something himself. Matariki had lost her appetite; she only wanted to sleep, once she finally succeeded in getting the echo of the war cries out of her ears.

Matariki listened to Kupe's footsteps as he laid food in front of her hut. She expected him to move away again immediately, but he paused. Matariki sensed he was struggling with himself. His *pakeha* upbringing won, and he called out to the venerated chieftain's daughter.

"Good night, Matariki," he said in English.

For some reason, Matariki felt better as she answered him. "Good night, Kupe."

***

The next morning, the warriors' cries woke Matariki. Apparently, they conjured the spirit of Hauhau or whomever at least twice daily. She pulled her blanket over her head and tried to shut out the noise, but sleep was impossible. Around midday, she found *poi-poi* balls and a dress in front of her hut. It resembled the dancing clothes of the Ngai Tahu, but the sleeveless top was patterned differently—as would be the case since patterns varied according to tribe.

Matariki was happy to have a top to wear; she had feared that the ceremonies would require nudity. Though she was still boyishly slender, her figure was starting to become more womanly. Nevertheless, the dancing dress was too big on her. Matariki asked Kupe to find her some sewing implements, and as she altered the outfit, she wished she were in the village, where the women and girls would have helped her while making bawdy jokes about how Matariki's breasts were as tiny as the grapes from her mother's vineyard. Afterward they would all have admired her in her new outfit and laughed and danced. Matariki yearned for the normalcy of an average Maori village, and at the same time, she feared for these unknown neighbors. While the village did not lie within earshot, it could be reached within a few hours. Through the proximity of his camp, Kahu Heke was endangering this village much the way Kupe's tribe had been in the past.

Finally, it was evening, and Matariki uneasily followed her father into camp. The warriors had already begun to circle the pole.

"Join them," ordered Kahu Heke. "Let yourself be carried along. Do whatever comes to mind."

Silencing the men's yelling was foremost on Matariki's mind, but, fortunately, they became quieter when she joined them. Soon Matariki found herself in the circle of warriors around the *niu*, though they had to be careful to maintain their distance from her. When her father stepped toward her, the circle first parted to allow him in and then extended to avoid the shadows of the *ariki* and his daughter, which fell long in the twilight and torchlight.

Matariki was embarrassed. She had never danced alone in front of her tribe. She was too low ranked for a solo dance, and, mostly, the young girls performed group dances—only the very bold might sing a love song with a boy. The Maori warriors who watched her now seemed already to be in a trance and were surely determined to venerate her.

Bravely, Matariki began a *haka powhiri*—a greeting dance. She knew it well; she had often danced it with the other girls of the Ngai Tahu. And she liked it because there was nothing threatening about it. It introduced the dancers and the village and was performed after the warriors had carried out their show of strength in front of the new arrivals and the eldest woman had let out the *karanga*. Thus, it would already be established that there would be no conflict between the tribe and the visitors. Matariki swung her *poi-poi* balls and sang a song of snow-covered mountains, vast plains, streams rich with fish, and clear lakes. Her song described the region of Otago and the tribe of the Ngai Tahu. However, she wondered how many of the men understood any of it. In the meantime, she had heard many dialects—Kahu Heke had united men from all the tribes of the North Island under the flag of the Hauhau.

Matariki finished and enjoyed the warriors' applause. Her father, too, seemed content.

"Very good for a start, Matariki," he whispered to her, "and now, let out the *karanga*."

Matariki turned to her father, confused. "But I can't."

"Just do it." The *ariki* raised his arms, and the warriors fell silent. "The Daughter of the Stars will now call the spirits," he announced.

Matariki hesitated. Surely it was *tapu* for her to attempt the *karanga*. The privilege of establishing the spiritual bond between the members of a tribe and its visitors with this cry belonged to the oldest, highest-ranking woman of the tribe.

Considered that way, the privilege did fall to Matariki. After all, she was the only woman, so she summoned all her courage and screamed.

When Hainga on the South Island let out the *karanga*, the earth seemed shaken to its foundations, and the world of the spirits touched that of the people, drawing all listeners into a circle, which described the universe itself. The *karanga* was something sacred—Matariki's cry, on the other hand, hardly sounded different from that of her roommate, Mary Jane, at the sight of a mouse in their bedroom.

Nevertheless, her *karanga* made an impression on Dingo. The dog had not stood out much until then, but now his howl was infinitely more imposing than Matariki's cry. His howl turned into the frantic barking with which he usually announced intruders from whom he would then flee. He ran to the girl just before all hell broke loose on the edge of the camp.

"Hands up, drop your weapons! This is the Armed Constabulary. This is not a joke."

As if to prove it, they fired their first shots. Matariki saw the muzzle flashes in the twilight. Dingo cowered between her legs.

The surprised warriors ran around, confused and momentarily unsure from where the threat came.

"Rire, rire, hau, hau!" Kahu Heke shouted.

The warriors took up the call. A few charged the attackers armed merely with war axes and spears; others knew enough to fetch firearms from their huts. Bullets whistled over the village square. Cries of anger and pain mixed in with the wild calls of *"Rire, rire, hau, hau."* Matariki, paralyzed with horror and fear, watched as huts went up in flames and men fell. Dingo barked but was otherwise as frozen still as his mistress.

"Come with me!" Out of nowhere, Kupe grabbed Matariki by the hand.

"Quick, there are so many of them. They'll slaughter us here."

Matariki wondered if Kupe knew how many attackers there were. He was visibly panicked, and she thought he was using all his courage to look after her. Kahu Heke was nowhere to be seen.

Kupe pulled her in the direction of the clearing where her father resided. It was dark there, but the din of battle was nearly as loud. They did not stop, and it was only under the kauri tree at the river, where large ferns formed a thick jungle, that Kupe slowed down. Dingo had followed on their heels, and here they all calmed down for a moment.

"Up the tree," Kupe ordered, and pointed up a southern beech.

Kauri trees could not be climbed; their trunks rose without branches high into the sky. The beech, however, offered itself perfectly as a lookout point.

"But . . . Dingo."

"Up!"

Matariki climbed into the first crotch of branches and was touched when Kupe handed the trembling dog up to her. Matariki commanded Dingo to keep quiet while she hoisted the canine into the next crotch and then climbed after him. From here, she could overlook a portion of the camp. Kupe climbed even higher up the tree for a better vantage point.

In the clearing, the Hauhau's lodgings were ablaze. Several wounded or perhaps dead warriors were illuminated by the ghastly glare of the flames around the *niu*. Matariki didn't see any casualties among the armed constables, a few of whom crisscrossed the camp, likely looking for hidden warriors. Here and there, a few struggles were still under way, but the constables tried to take the warriors prisoner instead of killing them, and the majority did surrender. Others, however, still bellowed "*Rire, rire, hau, hau*" and charged the English, unafraid of death.

Matariki cried out when one of the militia did not know what to do about a powerful warrior other than to shoot him point-blank. She thought she recognized Hanu, one of her abductors. Yet she did not take any satisfaction in his death.

The English limited themselves to the razing of the main camp—apparently, they were not familiar with the custom of lodging the chieftain outside of it.

"Just *pakeha*," whispered Kupe, "no Maori."

"Maori?" asked Matariki, horrified.

Kupe shrugged. "They have Maori in their ranks, traitorous dogs."

Dingo whimpered.

"He doesn't mean you," Matariki said, stroking the dog. Then she turned back to Kupe. "So, this is something like a civil war among the tribes?"

Kupe nodded. "A few *iwi* of the Ngati Porou fight for the *pakeha*. In East Cape and Gisborne, there are many who—"

"It's all completely mad," Matariki interrupted him, but then her outrage caught in her throat, and she fell silent.

It was all crazy. But it was also deadly.

*****

Matariki, Kupe, and Dingo remained in the tree until first light. It was safer to wait to see whether the *pakeha* returned after questioning their prisoners. Under no circumstances did Kupe want to be taken prisoner. The constables might have taken Matariki back home, but they could also rape her or haul her to the nearest reformatory. After Kupe's stories about the misdeeds against his village, she did not trust the militia.

Toward morning, there was a surprise.

"The *ariki*," whispered Kupe.

From his position, he overlooked the clearing with the chieftain's lodge as well. Matariki roused herself from an exhausted half sleep.

"What?" she asked.

"The *ariki*, your father. He's below, in front of his lodge. And the surviving warriors are now gathering in the clearing. The *ariki* lives." Kupe cheered. "Kahu Heke! Kahu Heke! Pai Marire, *hau, hau*."

Matariki winced. She would have preferred to remain hidden longer, if only to think. She felt no need to see her father. However, the chieftain was looking up at them.

"Well, help us down, Kupe, if you're so eager to dance around a pole again." Matariki sighed and took the dog under her arm. "It'll be interesting to hear what the archangel Gabriel has to say about this now."

Kupe climbed down the tree first. Matariki slid down to the lowest branch crotch. Then she wanted to hand Dingo to Kupe, but the dog had experienced enough of the airy excursion. He wrested himself from Matariki's arms and leaped six feet to the ground, letting out a howl when he landed. Matariki was worried, but Dingo only hobbled a bit for a few minutes. Kupe caught hold of Matariki, who was carefully feeling her way down. They both landed in ferns under the tree.

"Now you've touched me." Matariki helped Kupe up. "And the world didn't end."

Kupe shrugged. "The bullets didn't rain on us yesterday either," he replied without looking at her. Matariki, however, forced eye contact.

"You didn't really believe that, did you?" she asked.

Kupe looked to the ground. "If I'd believed it, I wouldn't have run away, would I? Will you tell your father that I fled?"

Matariki raised her eyebrows. "Didn't he run himself?" she asked. "I didn't see him once the worst of the fighting started. Besides, you were looking after me. Then again, maybe a warrior chieftain becomes invisible when singing *rire, rire.*"

Kupe bit his lip. "You don't take any of this seriously," he said sadly. "But it's very serious. Deadly serious."

Not even Matariki could deny that, although even among the Hauhau, there had been fewer killed than she and Kupe had feared. Only three men, Hanu among them, had died in the hail of bullets. Four warriors lay wounded on the battlefield. The English must have thought they were dead, because they had taken the rest of the wounded away with the other prisoners. Kahu Heke's tribe had lost about twenty warriors, dead, wounded, or imprisoned.

The chieftain was organizing the transport of the wounded to the next Maori village. Proud and almost larger-than-life in his warrior gear and wide cloak, he turned to his thirty remaining warriors.

He thrust his spear into the sky and raised his ax. Then he cried just one word, "Vengeance!"

To Matariki's surprise, that was enough for the men. They answered at once with *"Rire, rire, hau, hau,"* and surely would have kept chanting if the chieftain had not bid them to stop.

"Men, the gods of our people have tested but not abandoned us. Look, there is Matariki, your chieftain's daughter. She has escaped the *pakeha.* The angel spirited her away and now leads her back to us."

The men shouted in excitement as Matariki set foot in the clearing. Once again, the girl lacked for words, but she could not help but admire the chieftain's finesse. Kahu Heke had just seen her in the tree. He had known that she and Kupe would soon come, and he orchestrated his approach accordingly. Matariki's appearance at the right moment would convince the men that divine powers were at play.

"The angel?" whispered Kupe, confused.

"Yes," said Matariki, "you've been promoted."

"The gods have given us a sign: it is not time to wait," said Kahu Heke. "It is time for vengeance, time to send the *pakeha* back to their own land. We'll ready ourselves. The ceremony that will make us warriors—unconquerable warriors—will take place tonight. Yesterday, we wavered. Do not deny it. I saw fear and confusion in your eyes. Tomorrow we'll march against them like a wall of steel. Pai Marire *hau, hau!*"

Kahu Heke stamped his spear on the ground in a manner Matariki recognized from *haka*. His portrayal of the warrior chieftain was perfect. It was hard to believe that it concealed a bold schemer.

Matariki rubbed her forehead. She knew it was precisely this genius strategist she needed to address if she wanted to stop anything. Her father could not truly believe that he would be able to defeat the entire Armed Constabulary with his thirty warriors, not to mention the civilian militia and, finally, the British Army. He would inevitably be defeated—and perhaps die in the process.

"When the first victories have been achieved, thousands will flock to us," explained Kahu Heke. "Every Maori wants freedom."

"And what about the Ngati Porou?" Matariki asked. "And the other Maori who fight on the *pakeha's* side? What about the Ngai Tahu, who don't fight at all but make accommodations?"

"We cannot allow ourselves to make such accommodations." The chieftain grew excited. Matariki had asked to speak with him while the warriors buried their dead. Hare led the burial solemnities, although that did not appear to be complicated. Once again, "*Rire, rire*" echoed deafeningly through the forest. "Matariki, wake up. While we make accommodations, they destroy our homeland. Do you know that the tribes here in Waikato are negotiating the construction of a train line? Through the middle of our territory? And they're fighting among themselves over who gets what. They—"

"So, they don't hate the *pakeha* all that much," Matariki concluded. "Not even here where you have a lot of influence. And what do you have against trains? They're fast and comfortable."

"You're blind," Kahu Heke said, "but that will not diminish your power. We'll carry out the ceremony tonight. For the men, you will represent the gates of victory."

"Gates?" asked Matariki.

"Yes." The chieftain looked at her, misty-eyed. "Traditionally, a man becomes a warrior—an invulnerable, deadly warrior—when he crawls between the feet of the chieftain's daughter."

Matariki could not help herself from blurting out, "Like Dingo?" She laughed. "Whenever there's thunder, he always runs between my feet. That doesn't make him invulnerable, though, as you can see."

Dingo came over when he heard his name. He was still limping a bit.

"Matariki, it's a sacred duty. And you can't compare elite Maori warriors with a stray mutt."

Matariki found this image amusing. "Father, how is this supposed to work?" She laughed. "The men are more than five feet tall and at least a foot wide. They won't fit between my feet no matter how I stand."

Her argument left Kahu Heke silent for a moment. Then he found a solution. "We'll have to place you on top of rocks," he said.

At the risk of annoying Rauru, Matariki brushed the hair from her face. "Father, we think up a crazy ceremony, we dance around with strange gestures, and then the men all run into the English bullets like Hanu last night? You should have seen him."

"He was a Hauhau," Kahu Heke said. "Now, go to your lodging, child. Someone will bring you food, and then you will speak with the spirits and prepare for the ceremony."

For the first time, Matariki felt true disdain. "Father, you don't speak with the spirits inside a hut," she said calmly. "Even I know that. And I know because I've lived among real Maori who don't make up their *tikanga*."

Kahu Heke waved her words away. "Whatever you do, just stay inside," he ordered. "Go inward. Search your conscience."

Matariki stood up and walked slowly in the direction of her hut. She knew a warrior would be standing guard as soon as she went inside. She had contradicted the *ariki*, so now she was a prisoner again. Just before Matariki reached her hut, she turned around once more.

"Maybe the archangel will appear to me," she mocked, raising her hand in salutation. "*Rire, rire, hau, hau.* And here I thought angels spoke in complete sentences."

***

Kupe appeared a short time later with flatbread and sweet potatoes. "No one has time to hunt," he said to excuse the meager meal. "Yet there's supposed to be a feast tonight. I think you'd better watch out for this one." He pointed to Dingo.

Matariki looked at him in horror. "They wouldn't eat the dog."

"Why not?" asked Kupe. "It was common among the Polynesians. Hare explained it to us. The first dogs probably came to Aotearoa as provisions. And these"—he pointed to the leather straps with which his *waihaka*, a short, hook-shaped club, was fastened to his wrist—"are supposed to be made from dog leather. And—"

Matariki shoved her flatbread aside. "That's enough," she yelled, pulling Dingo close. "We're leaving. You have to help me get away from here. However much you think of these people, you need to escape with me now. If my father and Hare carry out this ceremony, my dog won't be the only one to die—you'll all be dead in two days."

***

Matariki wanted to take her riding skirt and blouse—not just because she would freeze in her dancing clothes but also because she planned on reaching a *pakeha* settlement as soon as possible. She did not trust the idea of seeking sanctuary in a nearby Maori village. Almost all of the warriors there sympathized with the Hauhau. As Kupe had learned in the meantime, this had proved fateful for the group the day before. The *pakeha* had scouts in the nearest village. When Kahu Heke's men appeared there to retrieve dancing clothes, the English had followed them.

"This is more evidence that the spirits don't care whether I'm here or in Dunedin," Matariki said to Kupe.

He had been assigned guard duty in the afternoon and reported what news there was. However, he was not easily convinced to flee with her. At best, he would not betray her if she ran away.

"Look, I was the one who put the English on your heels," Matariki said. "If I hadn't been abducted, there would have been no need for the dress and no visit to the tribe. Then you all would have been able to go on happily screaming *hau, hau,* and no one would have discovered the camp."

"The gods wanted us to set out," Kupe mused, although only halfheartedly. "That's what the *ariki* says."

"To challenge the British Empire with a force of thirty men?"

"Someone has to start."

Matariki sighed. "Fine, I give up. But could you find my *pakeha* clothes somewhere? I'll try to reach the next town, but I'll stand out in this skirt."

Kupe hesitated. "It's *tapu*," he murmured, "your clothing."

Matariki wanted to shake him. "Are you really so afraid to touch my clothes?"

Kupe had to laugh. "I didn't mean it that way," he said. "But the *tohunga* sacrificed them to the sacred fire yesterday while you danced."

"The bastard burned my clothes?" Matariki yelled. "Fine, so be it. I'd run away from here naked. And I thought of something. When the warriors want to escort me to the camp, I'll tell them I need to speak with the spirits a moment. Back there on the rocks by the stream is a sacred place."

"It is?" asked Kupe.

Matariki rolled her eyes. "Maybe, maybe not, but Hainga sees spirits in every second rata bush and between rocks and the like. I'll say I need to converse with the gods there. The warriors will naturally have to stay away. The site is *tapu*—very, very *tapu*. I'll sing a bit at first to calm them. And then I'll make tracks."

"But your father—"

"My father will be suspicious. Of course. But with a little luck, he'll already be at the *niu*, speaking to the warriors." Matariki folded her blanket into a manageable bundle.

Kupe looked at her indecisively. "For sure?" he asked.

Matariki moaned. "No, not for sure. But most likely. Now, get to work, Kupe. You don't need to worry. You're not betraying your people by letting me go. I can't make all of you invulnerable. Strictly speaking, I'm not even a chieftain's daughter. Kahu Heke doesn't have a proper tribe. He isn't *ariki*, just a war chief, *rangatira*. And I'm certainly no priest. You're not breaking any *tapu*, Kupe. You have to believe me."

When Kupe looked at her, he appeared unsure but also hopeful. For the first time, Matariki noticed golden flecks in his soft brown eyes. In his friendly face, she saw admiration and reverence—but of a completely different sort than what one held for a priestess.

"If that's how it is," said Kupe shyly, "I mean, if you really aren't *tapu*, could I perhaps kiss you?"

***

Matariki could feel their kisses the whole long afternoon she spent waiting in her hut. Kupe's lips were soft, warm, and comforting, and it had been a good feeling when he held her to his firm, muscular chest. First, he had kissed her circumspectly on the cheek, but then, when she did not object, he kissed her on the mouth. Finally, his tongue had opened her lips and explored her mouth. A strange feeling but not an uncomfortable one. On the contrary, Matariki had felt warmth well up within her. She was light-headed—floating and happy.

When she parted from Kupe, she doubted her decision to go for a moment. But then she pulled herself together. She was not in love with him. At least she had not been a few minutes before. This love had no future here anyway—who knew what sort of punishment awaited a warrior who dared to touch a chieftain's daughter? If there was any hope, then Kupe had to flee with her. But he did not want to do that. Matariki was too proud to ask him again, let alone to seduce him so he would fulfill her wishes.

After their kisses, Kupe had looked at her longingly and then left without another word. Matariki had no doubt it was better to forget the episode and concentrate on escape. By herself. She was a little afraid of the wilderness on the North Island, but she reassured herself nothing could happen to her. She had spent half her childhood among the Ngai Tahu. She could make a fire, catch fish, and she knew every edible plant on the South Island. The flora might be a little different here, but she would manage.

As evening fell, Matariki heard murmuring in front of her hut. The men who guarded her made way for the *ariki*.

"Matariki, here, I brought you a cloak," the chieftain said. He did not open the fern curtain in front of the hut. Probably that was also forbidden for him. "You'll wear it now, when you come to the clearing."

"The clearing." Matariki could not help herself. She was going for broke. "You know the clearing is *tapu*, Father. Men died there. Hainga would say we may no longer set foot there. We must leave Papa to her mourning. Nature must take possession of it again."

Kahu Heke snorted. "This is the only clearing here, and we don't have another gathering place. But Hare says we can use the power of the dead. Their spirits will strengthen the living they accompany on their way to becoming invincible warriors."

Matariki fought back the thought of spirits also crawling between her feet. She needed to master herself. No matter what, she needed to get away.

***

The cloak turned out to be a true work of art, one of the traditional chieftain's cloaks with kiwi feathers weaved throughout. It was brown and plush, surely warmer than Matariki's blanket. Most of all, it was dark. It would help her evade possible pursuers when she escaped. Matariki was in high spirits. A horde of warriors afraid of touching her would not follow her into the jungle. Indeed, they might accidentally trip over her—it would be pitch-black, after all. With a little luck, she would have at least a half hour's head start. Matariki was short and delicate, the men big and heavy—another handicap for them in the fern forest. In any case, the warriors would not be able to pick up her trail until the following morning, and by then, she would have to have thought of something to cover her tracks.

It was totally dark when four warriors with torches appeared to bring her to the ritual. Matariki emerged calmly and majestically from her shelter. She frightened the men by letting out a sort of *karanga* as soon as she was in the open air.

"The spirits," Matariki declared theatrically. "They call us."

With a deep voice and relaxed dance movements, she recited from the last role Mary Jane had played in the theater club at Otago Girls' High School, one of Shakespeare's witches in *Macbeth*:

"Fair is foul and foul is fair:
Hover through the fog and filthy air."

The Maori warriors stepped back in awe.

"Follow me," Matariki called, and turned toward the stream's banks.

The men felt their way after her.

Then she made an imperious hand gesture. "Stay back."

And the men stopped in their tracks. Matariki's heart beat wildly, but she forced herself not to move more quickly. Calmly, as if the ceremony had already begun, she disappeared between the rocks. Dingo was the only one who followed her.

On a low boulder, Matariki found her blanket, a small packet with bread, and a note. She had no idea how Kupe had found her pencil nub—or whether he perhaps had brought his own writing implement to the camp. She held a page ripped from a notebook in her hand:

> *Martha, keep going upstream and you'll come to the Waikato River.*
> *Follow it upstream—in about two days' journey you'll reach Hamilton.*
> *I'm thinking of you. Without* tapu, *Kurt.*

Matariki stuffed the note into the blanket bundle. She permitted herself a moment of emotion before going into action. She ran the first mile along the stream, and then stepped into the water. She was not wearing shoes, but the cold water did not bother her, and it would erase her tracks. If she walked a mile or two in the stream, the warriors would never find her.

Chapter 10

The day was just dawning, and the rain had abated. Peter Burton stood in shock in front of the collapsed mineshaft his ambitious nephew had driven into the mountain without any consideration. The miners from the Bute, Webber, Hobbs, and Davies mines had not been scared off by the weather. They had been digging for hours—and risking their lives, as Malcolm Hobbs observed.

"More of it could certainly come down. Looks like the idiot tried surface mining first and stripped all the vegetation from the hillside. No wonder the earth was washed away and the tunnel with it. I don't believe anyone's alive in there, Reverend," Hobbs said.

That, however, did not stop the tall, burly mine owner from overseeing the excavation work or swinging a pickax himself. Peter also lent a hand, though the practiced miners naturally achieved more. The hope that only the entrance to the tunnel needed to be cleared was not realized. In the bright light of day, it became clear to even the last optimist that the level was gone. The mountain had buried the unsupported tunnel.

"It'll be pure luck if we find the bodies," one of the foremen said despondently. "We ought to simply place a cross on the mountain."

Peter Burton shook his head. "We can't do that to the girls. They wouldn't believe it either. Sure, the little one's sleeping, but Violet cried the whole night through. She would have preferred to come back with me, but my wife tucked her into bed with a few hot-water bottles. Dear Lord, really that ne'er-do-well nephew of mine should dig out the dead himself."

***

Kathleen did her best to keep Violet in the house, but it wasn't long before Violet ran from her. She arrived at the accident site at precisely the moment when the men were recovering her grandfather's corpse. Ellen was beneath him; he had tried to protect her with his body.

"Nothing could be done, girl. All that earth, if they were not crushed, they suffocated," a foreman explained.

"It surely happened quickly," Mr. Hobbs said, trying to comfort her.

Violet stared at the dead bodies with a pale, frozen face.

"They don't look dead," she murmured. "Maybe they're just unconscious?"

Peter shook his head and tried to lead the girl off to the side. "I'm sorry, Violet. They're dead." He crossed himself. "Do you want to say a prayer with me," he asked softly, "while the men place them in the wagon? We're taking them down to the church. Reverend Clusky—"

"It's my fault," whispered Violet, "all my fault. I found the tunnel. I wanted us to go in."

Peter pulled her close. "Violet, that's nonsense. Any reasonable person would have sought shelter in that weather. Normally a level would not have collapsed. You couldn't know."

"She knew," said Violet in a strangely monotonous voice. "Lucy, she said so. She told me again when I came outside."

"Who?" Peter asked, taken aback. "Who told you?" Violet looked over at his team of horses, and Peter understood. "Oh, the horse, she didn't want to go inside? Alas, animals sometimes have a sixth sense about these things. But you can't rely on those signs. The animal might have shied away from something else entirely. It's not your fault, Violet. Don't convince yourself it is."

"And I wasn't supposed to be the one to go outside," Violet continued. "Mommy wanted to go outside. She said—"

Peter did not know what else to do. "Violet, we should thank God that you went outside with Rosie. If she hadn't felt sick—"

"Mommy wanted to go outside," Violet repeated. "Mommy was supposed to go."

Peter held Violet even more tightly. "I'll take you home, Violet, to your father. He'll likely be sober now and able to understand what happened.

You'll have to find a way to live together. In any case, you now have a house in Treorchy."

Violet followed the reverend apathetically even as he stopped his carriage in front of the miner's house on Bute Street. She trotted behind him into the house, which she had left so overjoyed a few hours before. Mrs. Brown stuck her head out the kitchen window. She had taken over the housekeeping when she learned of the mudslide—the usual form of neighborly help after a mine accident.

"Reverend, Violet, I heard. Did they—? Oh God!" The miner's wife read the answer to her question in Peter's and Violet's faces. "I'm so sorry, Violet." She came outside and took the girl impulsively into her arms.

"It's my fault," said Violet. She did not oppose Mrs. Brown's hug, but she did not return it either.

"Oh, nonsense, child."

Peter Burton left Violet with Mrs. Brown and entered the living room where Jim and Fred Paisley sat silently.

"Mr. Paisley, Fred, I'm sorry that I have to be the one to tell you—"

Jim Paisley waved it away. "I already thought as much," he muttered. "The tunnel wasn't supported. Madness to go inside during the rain."

Peter felt anger rising within him. "You don't mean to tell me now that your wife and your father-in-law were at fault?"

From the door came a sob. Violet. Peter hoped she had not heard her father's words. He was struggling himself against the highly unchristian desire to strangle Jim Paisley.

Jim Paisley shrugged. "They didn't have any idea. I'm sorry about it too."

He did not exactly sound brokenhearted. Fred, who sat beside him, pale and obviously hungover, seemed in greater distress. His eyes were circled with red—he might have been crying. His gaze was glassy.

"But they didn't have to take off in the night," Jim Paisley added.

Peter balled his hands into fists. He hoped Violet would say something. Indeed, he knew the girl to be courageous and free—almost a miracle in these family circumstances. But Violet remained silent. Still, that was better than another, "It's my fault."

"Your wife seems to have had good reason," Peter said sternly. Then, however, he forced himself to be patient. Recriminations would get him nowhere with Jim Paisley. The pastor started again in a friendlier tone. "Mr. Paisley, with your wife's death, a few things will change for you. Your children now have only you. You need to assume responsibility for them."

Paisley stuck out his lower lip and furrowed his brow. "I've always worked, Reverend. Ain't my fault if the mine owners don't pay worth a damn."

Searching for sympathy, he looked from Peter to Mrs. Brown who had just stepped into the room, no doubt driven by curiosity. Peter rubbed his forehead. The woman surely had a good heart, but couldn't she have waited outside with Violet?

"Now, I got to find work too," Paisley continued. "How else are the brats going to live? And they want to throw us out of the house." His eyes flashed slyly. "Can't you do anything about that, Reverend? Now that we've had what you call a family tragedy. Maybe they'll give us an extension after all. Or my job back at Bute's."

Peter inhaled deeply. "Mr. Paisley, money isn't likely to be your greatest concern in the near future. You—or rather your children, although it comes to the same thing for now—have inherited a house in Treorchy. And my brother will pay an indemnity."

Paisley perked up. "An indemnity?" he asked. "How much?"

Peter inhaled sharply. "I don't know, Mr. Paisley, but I'll find out what is usual in such cases, and you will receive that. The fault clearly lay with my money-hungry nephew. His father will have to acknowledge that, or you and I will take him to court. After all, your family perished on my land."

"It isn't Mr. Burton's fault," Violet said in a monotone voice. "It's my fault."

Jim Paisley did not respond to his daughter. He didn't even seem to notice her. He apparently needed some time for Peter's words to sink into his whiskey-addled brain. Then, however, an almost unearthly glow spread over his face.

"I'm rich."

***

"You mean we should simply take them with us?" Kathleen Burton was packing her suitcase. Violet had helped wash, iron, and fold their clothing. Before the ship to Dunedin set sail, they would spend a few more days in London. "As long as their father permits," Kathleen added.

Peter Burton shrugged. "Why wouldn't he? He can't make use of Rosie, and as to Violet, sure, for now she does his housework, but he can find a wife for that quickly enough—now that the fellow's throwing money around."

"Can't anyone do anything to stop him?" asked Kathleen. "That money does mostly belong to the children. He shouldn't be drinking it down." She set a hatbox aside and looked at her husband. "Don't misunderstand me, Peter. I like the girls. I'd be happy to have them come with us. We'll find something for them in Dunedin. But it hardly seems right to me to uproot them like this— or to rob them of their inheritance. Half of the house and workshop and the indemnity belongs to the two of them. You don't really believe that their father will give it to them to take to New Zealand, do you?"

Peter sighed. "I don't believe that anyone can force him to. After all, it will be a long time before Violet is of age. Before she's twenty-one, he'll have squandered the fortune—whether she's here or in New Zealand. Here, though, she would have to watch him do it. Kathleen, the girls have no future here. And I feel responsible. If I had kept up with Randolph's machinations, her mother would still be alive."

Kathleen arched her brows. "Seems to me that just about everyone feels responsible for this woman's death except those who really are guilty: Joseph and Randolph and Paisley. God, I'm happy this house has finally sold. I can't wait to have eleven thousand miles between me and these cads again."

In the last few weeks, it had come to a few rather ugly confrontations between Peter Burton, his brother, and his nephew. As Peter expected, Joseph Burton had not wanted to pay for his son's mistakes, and Randolph showed no hint of remorse. He pushed the blame for the slipshod digging of the level onto Jim Paisley, who, Joseph said, "received his just deserts when his wife died there." Ultimately, however, the Burtons of Cardiff had come around. The Marquis of Bute was, after all, their neighbor in Roath, and other mine owners likewise had dealings with Burton's law office. Joseph did not want to lose face in front of them, let alone in front of his wife, Alice.

Alice was immediately pressured from two sides. Reverend Clusky asked her to work on her spouse, and at the same time, she was aware that the ladies of Roath, Lady Bute first of all, were whispering about the Burtons. Alice made quite a scene in front of her husband and inspired a space in Joseph Burton's heart for the Treherbert miners. He not only paid Jim Paisley a proper indemnity but also generously supported Reverend Clusky's collection for a school in the new mining settlement. Webber had presented the most modern plans for the land where Ellen had died, and Peter sold him the parcel at a favorable price and then promised financing for the school. He hoped it would comfort Violet if they named it after her mother, but nothing gave her solace. Violet had been living in her own closed-off world since her mother died. Though she emerged from it enough to do her work and take care of Rosie, she hardly spoke a word beyond her monotone, "It's my fault."

Immediately after his wife's burial, Jim Paisley had moved with his children to the house in Treorchy, but that had not been good for Violet either. In Treherbert, the neighbor women would naturally have taken care of the girls, but in Treorchy, they were strangers, and they lived not among miners but among respected craftsmen and small-business owners. There, too, the men sometimes went to the pub after closing shop, but they drank their beer rather moderately. So, they found the drinking tendencies of Jim and Fred Paisley contemptible. And Violet's confusion and silent mourning did not exactly forge bonds with the neighbors. The women talked about the girl, but not with her. Peter's attempts to pull her out of her isolation ran aground on her father.

"I'm sure Violet would like to go to school," the pastor observed when he brought the Paisleys the good news about the approved indemnity. "And now there's nothing more standing in her way. You can pay a woman to keep house for you."

Jim Paisley shrugged. "Violet's too old for school," he asserted. "They'd all just laugh at her there. Ain't that right, Violet?"

Violet just looked at her father. Peter was not quite sure she had even heard.

"You told me you'd like to learn to read and write properly," Peter addressed the girl. "Isn't that so, Violet?"

Violet nodded. "My mom could write well," she said without inflection.

Peter forced himself to remain calm. "Well, there you go," he encouraged the girl. "You—"

"It's my fault," said Violet.

Jim grimaced. "You heard it. She says that all the time. The other kids'll think she's crazy. I think Violet's quite happy cooking for us, right, girl? You do owe your mother that much, anyway."

Peter dug his fingernails into the cover of the sofa that Rosemary Seekers had surely treasured and cared for. Much as he wanted to, he would not attack Jim Paisley. As a pastor and a Christian, Peter had to leave Paisley untouched even if he could not love him. But he wanted to follow a commandment that God seemed to have forgotten: thou shalt prevent thy neighbor from ruining his children's lives.

***

"Paisley doesn't care for Rosie, and he's reinforcing Violet's guilt," Peter remarked to his wife. "Here, she'll never move on. In Dunedin, on the other hand: a new country, new impressions."

Kathleen raised her hands. "As I said, it's not up to me. I like the girl. As far as I'm concerned, she can even stay in our house in Dunedin. She could go to school, and the little one is adorable. There they'll easily find someone to foster or adopt them. But wait until you hear what the Paisleys have to say. I don't get the impression that it'll go as smoothly as you imagine."

***

Violet responded cheerfully to Peter and Kathleen's offer. Two months had passed since her mother's death, and she was slowly emerging from her cocoon of sorrow and guilt. She still felt responsible for the death of her mother and grandfather. However, she had Rosie, and their lives had to go on. Plus, other concerns were pushing to the fore.

The more Violet groped her way back to life, the more often she visited the village shops in Treorchy, went to market, and greeted neighbors, the more clearly she felt the rejection directed against her. The women would not talk with Violet, and Rosie found no playmates. When Rosie came home one day crying because other children had called their father a drunk, Violet knew their days were numbered. Jim and Fred were not spending their days looking for work as they claimed, but instead frequenting pubs and billiard halls. They had also discovered an enthusiasm for horse and dog races, and their wagers were growing bigger by the day.

Violet yearned to escape. Earlier she had risked confrontation—and had even almost won. She had enjoyed the triumph when her grandfather had fetched her mother from their house with the intention of opening the door to a better life for them. But that was now past, buried in the mountain tunnel. Violet had no illusions about her inheritance or her future.

"To Dunedin?" she asked when Peter and Kathleen laid out their suggestion of emigration. "With you?"

"Of course with us," Heather replied amiably. "On the ship, we'll have loads of time. You can model for me some more."

In the last few months, Heather had increasingly worried about Violet, and Kathleen had watched her daughter bloom as she cared for Violet. Heather taught Violet reading and writing, and had discovered her as a model. Violet's budding beauty, but also her sorrow and melancholy, had inspired Heather to evocative works. Two watercolors of Violet were already complete, and Heather intended to show them to a gallerist in London. Perhaps the pictures would represent her breakthrough as an artist. And the girls could fill a void for Heather. Kathleen had long sensed that, though her daughter remained unmarried by choice, it made her sad every time another friend became pregnant.

"And Rosie will come too?" Violet wanted to make certain.

Kathleen nodded. "As long as your father doesn't have anything against it. But he can't take care of her. We just want the best for you both."

She bit her lip. Did Jim Paisley also want the best for his children? Kathleen had her doubts. A man like Jim neither thought logically, nor did he want the best for anyone besides himself. He would not let his children go for free.

Violet smiled more radiantly than she had since before Ellen's death. "We'd love to come so much. I'll tell Father right away. He can keep all the money. From my inheritance, I mean. If he only pays the ship passage."

"We'll take care of the ship passage," Kathleen assured her.

Violet would offer her father her money to buy her freedom. Would it be enough?

***

It was like the time Violet had happily returned home, only to find Ellen sitting at the kitchen table, crying over a letter. But Jim Paisley was not crying or cutting vegetables. Instead, he had a glass of whiskey and half a bottle more in front of him. Ellen had admitted before the collapse that Jim had been on the verge of a fit of rage. Violet also felt a vague dread. Yet she simply had to tell him about the Burtons. Perhaps that would raise her father's spirits. The girl was too preoccupied with her own happiness to notice the letter Jim kept moving around between the bottle and glass, and it would be clear to her only significantly later how much the two scenes resembled each other.

Jim Paisley listened to Violet's excited report about the journey to New Zealand in silence. Outside, it was raining again. It was turning to fall in Wales; in Dunedin, it was spring now. Violet's heart pounded.

"They'll pay for the ship passage," Violet declared. "You don't need to pay for anything. We'll just be gone."

Jim Paisley laughed. An ugly laugh. "You want to take off? Like your mom? Don't you remember how that ended?"

He noted with satisfaction how the light went out in Violet's eyes. "But that'd suit you. You go off to make a nice life for yourselves and leave us here sitting in shit."

"Dad?" Violet looked at him helplessly. She would not have characterized the cozy house and the financial cushion that the indemnity and the sale of the cobbler's workshop had bestowed on her father as shit. "You can't. You have—"

"What do I have?" Jim Paisley stood up threateningly in front of her. "A house and money? That's what I thought. But this, the pastor just brought it." He threw the letter at Violet.

She labored to decipher the script. The letter was addressed to Jim Paisley. However, the sender had sent it to Reverend Morris, the pastor of Treorchy's church—doubtless to have a witness that it had arrived. And perhaps knowing that Jim could not read.

Violet struggled through the lines. She did not understand it all, but—

"I didn't know I had an uncle."

Her father rolled his eyes. "I don't believe it. Violet, the bastard's threatening your inheritance, and you're excited about a new relative."

"He's threatening . . . ?" Violet forced herself to read every word even though it took a long time.

> I would also like to register a claim on the inheritance of my parents as well as on a portion of the indemnity for the death of my father and sister paid by Mr. James Burton. I am likewise offering to assume the management of your children's assets until their majority. As you perhaps know, I am employed at a bank in London. Thus, I would deposit the money and doubtless increase it until my nieces and nephew are old enough to arrange for themselves.

To Violet, it did not sound all that threatening. Naturally, her uncle Stephen wanted part of the inheritance. That was his right. She now vaguely recalled how her mother had sometimes spoken of her brother. Stephen Seekers, however, had been much older than her mother. He had moved to London when Ellen was still a child. Violet would not have any problem entrusting her money to Stephen. It seemed just about anyone would keep it better than her father.

"But I'll spoil the bastard's fun," roared Jim Paisley. "'Portion of the indemnity,' as if! Did he put food on Ellen's table these last few years, or did I?"

Violet wanted to object, but her throat felt swollen shut.

"And he also wants to get his hands on the money for you brats. That'd suit him."

I would like to visit you on Saturday of the coming week to discuss the matter personally with you and your oldest children.

Violet hoped to already be on the ocean with the Burtons by Saturday of the coming week. This was Monday. The family wanted to leave Treherbert on Friday. On Wednesday, the ship would leave from London for Dunedin, New Zealand.

"You can have my money, Dad," Violet assured him. "And Rosie's. That'll be enough if we—"

"You don't really believe I'm going to let you leave, do you? What would I tell your dear uncle, Violet? That you made tracks? With the money? He'll never believe it. No, no, the bastard'll run straight to the judge and try to ruin me. You'll stay right where you are, Violet. And smile when Uncle Stephen turns up."

He grinned while Violet sank, defeated, into the chair across from him. Another dream demolished, another lost hope. Violet sought the way back into her cocoon of desperation and oblivion. She wanted to close herself off again, not to think, not to hope. But she could not find the way. She had already fought too far toward freedom. She was strong again; she was smart. Something had to come to her.

Violet thought feverishly, and then she did think of a way out. "Dad, what if we all disappear?" she asked firmly. "There's a lot of time between now and next Saturday. You can sell the house. The Suttons next door are looking for something for their daughter. Then you'll take the money. We'll go to London, and next Wednesday a ship leaves for New Zealand. Uncle Stephen will never find us there."

Child of the Shadows

Passage from England to New Zealand

1878–1879

Hamilton and Auckland, North Island

1878–1879

Dunedin and Greymouth, South Island

1879–1880

Chapter 1

Violet had not pictured the ship so massive or the sea so vast. After all the terrible experiences of the last few months, she could not have believed she would experience the sort of panic she did now as the coast of England disappeared behind them. Rosie fell completely silent and wide-eyed in her arms as she gazed at the seemingly endless and highly troubled sea. Violet's father already had thrown up in their shared cabin, so Violet began her sea travel with the unpleasant task of cleaning up after him. She had then fled to the deck, seeking the Burtons, but now she stood helpless before the sight of the sea and the feeling that her life up to that point was being erased before her eyes.

"That's just the English Channel, you know," Heather said, laughing. "It's not all that wide. True, you can't see the other shore yet, but there are people who swim across it."

Violet looked at her, confused, but somewhat comforted. If Heather was not at all afraid, she would be brave. She tried to ignore the wind tugging at the massive sails.

"And this isn't even a storm," Heather said. "Once we're on the Atlantic, it can get much, much worse. We should be happy about this wind. It's moving us forward quickly."

Heather faced contentedly into the fresh breeze. She had taken off her hat and tied on a scarf—perhaps so she wouldn't stand out too much among the steerage passengers. Now the silk ends of her scarf fluttered as if in competition with a few strands of her ash-blonde hair, which had loosed themselves. Heather seemed young and adventurous. Violet reached shyly for her hand.

She was endlessly happy the young woman had found her down in steerage. Entrance to the Burtons' cabins was denied to Violet. Even the viewing platform on the upper deck was reserved for the first-class passengers alone.

"And now, you two have looked back at England enough." Heather pulled Violet and Rosie away from the railing. "Enough moping. Instead, show me where they put you, since I'm already here."

Visits to steerage were not forbidden the first-class passengers, but the mixing of the classes wasn't looked on approvingly.

"But everybody's moping here," said Rosie, who had picked up a new word.

Indeed, the atmosphere in steerage wasn't particularly cheerful. Most of the passengers in the tight corridors and cabins were leaving their homeland forever and traveling to an unknown country. Many had been accompanied to the quay by their friends and relatives, and a few crying women continued staring toward the shore, as if they could still recognize someone there. The men, in contrast, were already drinking away their sorrows with the alcohol they had brought, mostly cheap gin. With that, Violet's father had explained to her, one avoided seasickness. Immediately afterward, he had gotten sick.

It was the same for a few others.

"It's really disgusting here," Heather said, growing agitated after passing the third puddle of vomit on the way into the hold. "And inside, heavens, it's as black as the pit."

Heather had been eager to see the lodgings of the poor emigrants. Her mother had told her sad stories of her own crossing more than thirty years before. Her worst descriptions paled in the face of this reality. Heather followed Violet down dark passages, finally taking a look at the tiny closets the travelers had to share, six to a room. Men and women traveling alone were naturally housed separately. Families, however, resided together, which, for Violet and Rosie, meant sharing the berth with her father and brother. Eric Fence, Fred's best friend and drinking companion, had also joined them. Eric had at first been inconsolable that the Paisleys were leaving Treherbert, but he received his first big win at the racetrack just before their departure.

Eric thought himself an expert when it came to horses. At the mine in Treherbert, the care for the work ponies had fallen to him, but Violet wasn't sure how he earned a heightened knowledge of racehorses. Still, the miners in the Golden Arms hung on his every word when he raved about an animal's chances of winning—only to bet with as little success as Jim and Fred. However, his weakness for outside shots had paid off. Eric Fence had raked in the monstrous sum of ten pounds in winnings and immediately invested eight of them in a passage to New Zealand.

"Brothers!" Fred and Eric had crowed. They hugged each other as they celebrated the win and the narrowly avoided separation. Eric paid for Jim's drinks that night, too, and by the end of the evening, Jim claimed the boy as his son and agreed to take him into his berth.

"When they came back home, he probably did not even know anymore how many sons he had," Violet commented bitterly as she told Heather the whole story. "And none of them thought about Rosie and me—except for maybe Eric himself. He can't take his eyes off me."

Heather shook her head, horrified. "You tell me if he dares to lay a hand on you," she said, though she didn't really know what she would do in such a case.

The best thing, Heather thought, would be to talk to the chief steward right away. Perhaps with his help, they could still find a berth for Violet and Rosie among the unmarried women. But Violet rejected this determinedly when Heather suggested the idea.

"I'd be free of Eric, but my father would beat me black and blue," Violet said. "And if he didn't, Fred would. I'll manage, Miss Coltrane, thank you. I keep my dress on when I sleep. The nights are ice-cold, anyway."

It remained that way for a while too. It was fall, and although they were sailing south, crossing the Atlantic was a cool, wet affair. Violet now truly became familiar with storms, though fortunately neither she nor Rosie suffered from seasickness. It was a bit different for the men in her family. Only Eric proved seaworthy. Jim and Fred puked their guts out.

At least, that was how Violet described it to Heather, Kathleen, and Peter, all three of whom came to visit below deck the next time. Kathleen had needed fresh air, to which Violet responded with a gloomy laugh.

"You certainly won't find that here."

She had just emptied another bucket over the railing, though it made her shudder to come so close to the tossing waves. The wind was again blowing strongly, and Violet feared being swept overboard. For that reason, she did not even allow Rosie to leave the cabin. The child cowered in a corner of her berth, staring with empty eyes into the half-light, which seemed heavy with the stench of urine and vomit. Violet did what she could to keep the cabin clean, but it was hopeless.

"And now there's water getting in," she told them. "Yesterday it was almost over my feet. I can't mop it out anymore. Might the ship fill up, Mr. Burton? Might it sink?"

Kathleen, who had more experience here than her husband, shook her head. "Not from the water in steerage. During my crossing, it was once up to our knees. It was dreadful. And I was constantly throwing up. I was pregnant with Sean, after all. Naturally, I dragged myself outside, but I was deathly afraid of bending over the railing."

Violet's father and brother spewed their latest meal wherever they happened to be walking, standing, or more often, lying.

"Mostly it's just gin," said Violet, resigned to fate. "They eat next to nothing, since they always feel sick. Just not from the gin."

"Well, you are supposed to take in lots of fluids," said Peter with mordant mockery. "Vomiting dries you out. I am truly sorry, Violet. And I feel a little guilty. If it weren't for us, your father would never have come upon the idea of emigrating. We've already inquired if there's still a cabin above we could book for you, but everything's taken."

The Burtons shared a cabin with Heather for the journey. However, the pastor was by nature discreet, and Kathleen had sewn a curtain before their departure, which created a tiny private space for Heather.

Violet nodded gratefully but did not reveal that she had made New Zealand so appealing. As for the offer of a cabin, she would have taken it, even if she could never have worked it off. She would have done just about anything to escape the moist, stinking nightmare in steerage.

"In a few weeks, it'll be better," the pastor comforted her. "Once we reach the Bay of Biscay, it'll get warmer, and the seas will be calmer."

Kathleen nodded. "But before that, a few of the toilets will overflow in steerage. Brace yourself, Violet. And try to keep Rosie halfway warm and dry. Besides that, you need to eat as much as you can. Heather will keep bringing something down for you, and the portions down here aren't too small, are they?"

Violet shook her head. Though the food, usually a hearty soup of potatoes and cabbage, was always cold when it got to the cabins—the passengers had to pick it up in the galley and carry it to their berths—it sufficed, particularly since Jim and Fred were sticking to liquid nourishment.

"There's hardly a passage without an outbreak of disease aboard," Kathleen warned. "And that's when the smallest and weakest die. So, keep an eye on Rosie."

"If cholera does break out, I'll smuggle her above," Heather said. "No one will look behind my curtain."

***

The weather improved after the first four weeks of the journey. As they sailed around Africa, occasionally land came into view, and the ocean sometimes lay smooth as a mirror in front of the ship. The captain was not as enthusiastic about the calm weather as his passengers. With less wind, the trip was slower, but the travelers saw dolphins and whales, which accompanied the boat.

Heather explained the peculiarities of the sea creatures to Violet, finding ever more joy in spending time with the bright girl. "They're not fish. They bring their young into the world alive and suckle them, and they have to emerge now and again to catch their breath. Sailors tell stories of castaways saved by dolphins."

"But the whale ate Jonas," Violet argued skeptically, using her Sunday school knowledge.

"That needs to be viewed metaphorically," the pastor responded, but then shied away from a more detailed explanation.

"Don't get any ideas about preaching that," Kathleen advised Peter, whose tendency to interpret the Bible metaphorically created difficulties with his bishop. At the request of the captain, Peter was now holding Sunday service on the upper deck. He had only offered when the passengers in steerage received permission to take part.

"God does not differentiate," Peter had declared firmly, and immediately recruited a few Irish musicians to accompany his flock's singing with fiddle and flute.

So, on Sunday, church service rang out with many voices from above deck—while every evening during the week, drinking songs echoed up from below. Past their first fits of homesickness, the people in steerage now celebrated their departure for a new land with music and dance in the narrow cabins. As if by a miracle, plenty of whiskey and gin always found its way there too.

Some of the crew traded in the booze secretly smuggled on board. Jim, Fred, and Eric were drunk every night, and Violet and Rosie's inheritance was being swallowed up.

"At least we have peace at night," mused Violet. "They come back late into the cabin. Rosie's already asleep, and I pretend I am."

Violet used the nights to browse through the books Heather had given her. She could hardly glean any coherent story from *David Copperfield* and *Oliver Twist*; when she had arduously made her way through one page, she had already forgotten what was on the previous one, but she tried. She desperately wished for a better life, and learning to read could only help.

***

Eight weeks of travel had passed, and the weather had become consistently good over the past month. Violet began to believe the Burtons' claim that in New Zealand winter was summer and vice versa. However, heat was not much easier to bear in steerage than the cold and wet. It was stuffy, and the stench of the unwashed bodies, the still-overflowing latrines, and the eternal cabbage soup combined into an unbearable strain. The thought of the ship's food nauseated Violet, though now she had to fight even to get her and Rosie's share. The men had recovered their appetites, but they weren't willing to get their own portions.

"That's woman's work," Fred declared when Violet asked him for help.

It was not that much to walk to the galley three times daily, but just as her father and brother were feeling better, so were the other troublemakers on board. Every day, Violet's path from the kitchen to their lodgings became more of a gauntlet. Young boys would wait in the passageways and demand a "toll," and the older boys pinched the butts of adolescent girls or groped their breasts when they tried to get through with the precious food containers. The first time, Violet dropped the pot in fright, but she soon discovered that her father's blows hurt more than the unwelcome fondling.

She had come to share her portion of food with a defender, a squarely built young brawler from London who was less interested in girls than food. He escorted Violet and other girls through the ship's hold unmolested, and Violet paid him for it with her food. If it were not for Heather and the Burtons' daily contributions, she would have starved.

Then, however, a fever broke out, and the passageways between the decks were blocked.

"So you don't bring your fleas up with you," one of the crew explained to Violet who had wanted to attend Sunday service with Rosie. "See, the doctor says that's what carries it."

The Burtons disobeyed the order not to visit steerage. Heather was horrified at the conditions, and Peter gave last rites to two women. Only Kathleen remained composed.

"I don't believe for a moment that there's a real outbreak," she declared. "During my first passage, it was chickenpox. Fortunately, I'd already had it, and the others in my cabin too. But I think we had twenty dead during the journey."

Peter, who had run a hospital during his time in the goldfields, agreed with her. "It's not cholera. Keep Rosie clean, Violet, and nothing should happen."

Indeed, the two women remained the only fatalities, and in Violet's cabin, only Fred got sick. Violet and Rosie followed Kathleen's advice to spend time on deck. Their London protector, whom Peter affectionately called Bulldog, which filled the lad with giantlike pride, pocketed a few coins from Heather and, in exchange, secured his best customers a sleeping place in a lifeboat. Heather sacrificed the curtain from her berth to serve as an awning for Violet and Rosie.

"Bulldog is good for other things too," reported Violet. "The men catch fish and grill them on deck, and he makes sure we get some."

"For free?" Heather marveled.

Violet nodded. "He's a fool for Rosie. She reminds him of his little sister in London."

Heather lifted her eyes and hands to the sky. "If only he'd start preaching peace and love."

"I hope not." Violet was horrified. "Yesterday he beat up three boys because they wanted to steal your curtain."

***

"And now, what ocean is this?" Violet asked Heather after they had not seen land in more than two weeks. Violet was continually taken aback that there were several oceans, and it was a mystery to her how the sailors oriented themselves.

"The Indian Ocean," Heather answered. "We're sailing straight across. The sailors say this is the most dangerous part of the journey. There's no land for hundreds of miles. But we seem to be in luck. The weather is good. A few more weeks, and we'll have made it."

***

Indeed, the rest of the journey passed peacefully. Life on board had settled down, especially given how weak even the strongest had become under the awful conditions. Violet examined Rosie every day for lice and fleas, and Bulldog collected rainwater for the girls to wash themselves. Unfortunately, the nights grew cooler again when the ship reached the Tasman Sea, and Violet and Rosie had to move back into the filthy cabin. In Violet's absence, no one had cleaned.

"I'm not sure if I wouldn't prefer to freeze," Violet unhappily mused to Bulldog.

"Go enjoy yourself on deck for a couple hours," he said to Violet, who was just then emptying another wash bucket into the sea. "I'll round up the lads."

To Violet's complete amazement, Fred and Eric appeared repeatedly on deck with full buckets. When Bulldog brought the girls back below deck, the cabin did not exactly gleam with cleanliness, but it was bearable.

"I couldn't get your dad up, though," Bulldog said. Jim Paisley snored in his berth. "Looks like he took his load again yesterday. Just where's he get the money?"

Violet knew if it continued like this, they would not even have a penny to make it through the first few weeks in New Zealand. Yet the money from the sale of the house in Treorchy should have supported the family for some time, until Jim and Fred found work.

"We're almost there," Heather comforted Violet. "Two weeks at most. Oh, I can't wait to hear from Chloe. No word from her in three months. She's probably pregnant already."

Despite their separation, Chloe and Heather had remained good friends. The postal service between the South and North Islands was good. They wrote each other regularly. In England, however, Heather had only received one letter in which Chloe had complained she wasn't yet pregnant. Yet surely that was just a question of time. One could read between the lines that Chloe and Terrence were trying, to their mutual bliss.

"Has your father told you yet what he's thinking of doing in New Zealand?" Kathleen asked Violet. "He knows there's no coal near Dunedin, right?"

"Well, I'm going looking for gold," Bulldog interjected. "They've got that, right?" He sounded only mildly concerned.

Kathleen laughed. "We had it. But the fields directly around Dunedin are mostly exhausted. Now, you'll have to head to Queenstown. But it's not all that far, unlike the coal-mining cities. Greymouth and Westport are on the other side of the island."

Bulldog shrugged. "I prefer looking for gold to coal. I'm gonna get rich. Right, Reverend? You were in the goldfields. You know."

Peter Burton turned his gaze toward heaven and folded his hands theatrically. "In this case, I can say the words, 'Everything lies in God's hands' in good conscience. Usually I like to add that you ought to help a bit, too, but in gold mining, it's really a matter of luck. Most of the miners are hardworking, Bulldog. Many shovel till they keel over. But few get rich. So, practice your praying."

Bulldog shrugged. "I can do that while I dig," he said.

***

The captain called all passengers onto the deck as the coast of the South Island appeared on the horizon after more than three months of travel. Kathleen again felt reminded of her first arrival—and was happy that this homecoming took a very different form. Back then, the weather had been foggy and overcast, the view of the tiny town of Lyttelton cheerless, her contractions painful. Today, it was sunny, and the coast showed off its dark beaches and bright cliffs, from behind which green forested hills greeted them. Here and there they saw small settlements, brightly painted houses, and boats from which fishers waved. Dunedin presented itself beautifully, and it was framed by shimmering blue bays, behind which Otago's mountains rose majestically. The hills were green, but Peter told the attentive Bulldog that once they had been white with tents when on a single day sixty ships of gold seekers had arrived.

"The city could hardly manage the onslaught. The people who sold digging supplies and tents became rich within a few days."

"And what happened to all the arrivals?" Violet asked.

The pastor shrugged. "Most of them are probably still here. Others are still moving from one goldfield to the next, but most prospectors eventually decided to seek other employment, perhaps doing what they were trained in back home.

Sometimes the gold does suffice for a modest existence: a shop, a farm, a workshop. New Zealand still has room for everyone, Violet. You don't need to worry. If your father and brother are willing to work . . ."

Violet sighed. That was precisely what worried her.

***

That afternoon, after spending hours gathering together her father's and brother's things—the two of them were so taken with the view of their new city that it did not even occur to them to clean out their cabin—Violet was once again in a more optimistic mood. She fell in love with Dunedin as soon as they left the ship.

The city was not a coal-mining town like Treherbert but not as big as London either. And Dunedin looked clean. All the buildings and streets shone as if freshly polished in the sunlight and unbelievably clear air. Violet felt she could almost grab the mountains behind the city with her hands; they seemed so near, and their contours appeared so sharp. On their peaks lay snow, which Violet admired.

"You'll get enough of it if you stay in this region," Heather laughed. "It snows all over Otago in the winter, but luckily it's summer now."

It was the beginning of February. Violet felt she was in a fairy tale for a few heartbeats. But then reality caught up to her. Her father and the two boys trampled across the gangplank, laughing at the feeling the ground was still swaying beneath them. Violet had the same feeling. It almost made her dizzy.

"That will pass in a few days." Kathleen smiled, especially sensitive to it herself. She leaned on her husband who offered her his arm.

"Dearest, today I'll carry you over whatever threshold you want," he joked.

Jim, Fred, and Eric looked with hazy eyes into the clear air. Wild confusion surrounded them. A few immigrants fell to their knees and thanked God for their safe arrival while others threw themselves into the arms of friends and relatives. Most of them hauled their luggage, trying to keep their excited children under control.

Violet clung to her bag; Rosie clung to Violet.

"What's going to become of you?" asked Heather.

She seemed a bit torn. Kathleen was already hugging her friend Claire who had come to the harbor in a delivery wagon that was painted black with gold lettering—"The Gold Mine Boutique"—to pick up the Burtons. Heather wanted to run to Claire and ask about Chloe, but she wasn't ready to leave Violet and Rosie to a fate named Jim Paisley, who was already directing himself, Fred, and Eric to the nearest pub.

Violet tugged on his jacket. "Dad, perhaps we should look for a place to stay first. We will need a bed for tonight."

Jim shook his head, laughing. "Nonsense. After a drink, we're headed straight to Greymouth. Why should I pay for a hotel tonight when we want to find work starting tomorrow?" Jim seemed to believe the coal-mining towns were around the corner. "You two stay here and watch the bags, and we'll be back in a jiffy." Violet's father set down his dirty duffel bag, sat Rosie down on top of it, and steered the boys in the direction of the pub.

"Is there really a night train?" Violet asked.

Heather shook her head. "I don't believe so. As far as I know, there's still no train to the west coast. You'll have to go to Christchurch first, through the plains. It's quite a long journey."

Violet blanched at the thought of a journey organized by her father. "Can't you take us with you?" she asked desperately.

Heather wavered. She would have been only too happy to do so, but her parents would not play along, despite the sympathetic look Kathleen was casting yet again at the girls. Violet and Rosie were minors. They couldn't be taken from their father. And Heather could see that Kathleen and Peter were withdrawing, even though they had guilty consciences. There wasn't much Heather could do, but she did not want to leave the girls to fend for themselves. She scribbled the address of her stepfather's parish on a piece of paper.

"Violet, if all else fails, come to us and sleep in the church. Peter often takes in new arrivals. Many come without any money or the slightest idea what awaits them. Here."

She pressed a pound into the girl's hand. "Take that, but don't give it to your father. Otherwise you'll spend all night here while he drinks it away. There are cabs, so, if all else fails . . ."

Heather kissed the girls good-bye. Then she turned and walked toward her friends and family. Kathleen and Reverend Burton waved to Violet and Rosie. The little wagon drove off.

Violet felt utterly alone.

Chapter 2

Matariki moved as quickly as she could; the cold kept her from resting too often or for too long. Her dancing dress offered almost no protection from the elements. The chieftain's cloak kept out the cold and rain considerably better. Matariki, however, did not want to get it dirty by sleeping with it on the ground. Even when she had to slog through thick undergrowth or muddy areas, she took it off. The feathered cloak was valuable, and she hoped to make enough money from its sale to telegraph her parents and keep herself fed until someone came to bring her home.

The area Matariki was struggling through was hilly at first, but then became flatter, which seemed strange to her. After all, the city of Hamilton lay near Mount Pirongia, a forested mountain of which the Hauhau had spoken reverentially. The mountain seemed rather small in comparison with the southern peaks on her home island, but at least Matariki could orient herself by Pirongia's peak. It had also been visible from Kahu Heke's camp. The Waikato River flowed through Hamilton, which was built on the rubble of several Maori villages and fortresses. Kahu Heke had depicted that to his followers as a sacrilege of the whites; however, Matariki had learned that those settlements had long been abandoned when the *pakeha* arrived.

Matariki reached the town two days after her flight from the Hauhau camp, yet she found the sight disappointing. She had been hoping for a city and always had something like Dunedin in mind, but in truth, Hamilton was no bigger than Lawrence in Otago. There were settlers on both the eastern and western banks of the river. Here, everyone was guaranteed to know everyone else, and surely it wouldn't take long before word made its way to Kahu Heke that Matariki was in town. This made it all the more important to organize her onward journey as soon as possible.

Matariki pulled the chieftain's cloak on over her dancing dress and made her way into town. After her days of lonely wandering and her time among the Hauhau, it was almost unreal to see *pakeha* and one of their typical settlements. Victoria Street, the main street of Hamilton, was occupied by two-story, brightly painted wooden houses with porches or storefronts on the ground floor. Matariki peeked into a grocery store. Somewhere there had to be a post office and a police station. Matariki had decided to seek the latter. She wanted to tell her story and ask that her parents be informed. She didn't care about revealing Kahu Heke and his people. Clearly, the authorities knew that there were Hauhau in Waikato anyway and had already cleared her father and his warriors from their camp.

It proved difficult to track down the local police, especially since people were not particularly helpful. The first woman she asked for help gave her a filthy look. The next woman spat at her, and others just gave her a wide berth. Three men standing in front of a pub seemed to be making derisive remarks. Nonetheless, Matariki went to speak to them.

"Pardon me, I'm looking for the police, or the Armed Constabulary."

On the South Island, this mixture of militia and police was not all that common. In Dunedin, there were just police stations. On the North Island, however, the armed constables seemed to be omnipresent, and although Matariki feared them a bit after the fight in the Hauhau camp, she was prepared to entrust herself to the officers.

"Look at this one; it can talk," one of the men shouted. "And not just that pagan gibberish."

Matariki glared at him. "I can speak English quite well, sir, and I'm not an 'it.' I'm a girl, more specifically, and I've been kidnapped."

The second man snatched at Matariki's cloak with lightning speed. The cloak did not have any fasteners, so Matariki had been holding it together in front of her chest. Now it opened, offering a view of her little *piu-piu* skirt and top. Dingo growled angrily but hid behind his mistress as he did.

"Well, I can guess who kidnapped you." The man yelled into the pub. "Hey, does Potter offer Maori girls?"

A bent little man—the proprietor presumably—stuck his head outside.

"Pardon me, sir, your guests appear to be drunk," Matariki said with dignity, turning to the pub owner. "But perhaps you could tell me where I could find a constable who—"

"She sure is a cute one," remarked the owner. He did not respond to Matariki; instead, he turned to the other men. "If she's one of old Potter's, watch out. They say the savages still ain't selling their girls. It's not like in India."

"Bet it depends on the price."

Matariki tried again. "Please, my good men, I don't know what you're talking about. But as far as I know, the slave trade is forbidden in New Zealand. I'm Matariki Drury of Elizabeth Station, Otago. And I'd like to speak with the local police."

"Oh, all the constables are Potter's customers too," the first man said. "They won't help you, sweetheart. But maybe if you do all of us here for free, we'd hide you."

Matariki turned on her heels. She had to find someone who would help. And she needed to get her hands on *pakeha* clothing as soon as possible. Perhaps she should try her luck among the shopkeepers.

Matariki crossed the busy road and entered a general store. A few women backed away from her as if she were a leper.

"We don't serve savages here," the shopkeeper said.

Matariki rolled her eyes. "I'm not a savage," she replied, "just dressed a little differently. I was hoping you might sell me some regular clothes."

The shopkeeper, a tall, scrawny fellow with bright, watery eyes, a crooked mouth, and bad teeth, shook his head. "You'd be the first rat that could pay," he said.

"I was hoping to trade," Matariki said. "Or sell something first and then buy." She removed the valuable cloak and laid it on the counter, revealing her dancing clothes, which drew shocked noises from the women. "This is a *korowai*, a chieftain's cloak. It's very valuable. The feathers come from rare birds, the pattern is sewn laboriously by hand, and the coloring is distinct. Only a few women in a tribe can make something like this. And in truth, a *korowai* is never given to *pakeha*. There's probably even a *tapu* about it. I'm willing to sell you the cloak. Can we do business?"

Matariki tried to make her voice sound firm, and to use the same words as her father when he praised the most valuable breeding ewes. The customers seemed to find that funny. Their laughter, however, was no friendlier than that of the men at the pub.

The shopkeeper eyed the cloak more intensely; his expression was devious. "It's used," he said.

Matariki nodded. "Chieftain's cloaks are part of the regalia," she explained, "like a queen's purple cloak."

The women laughed even louder. Matariki tried not to let herself be distracted. She let the mockery run off her like she did Alison Beasley's comments at Otago Girls' High School.

"They're handed down from generation to generation. Though, naturally, they're handled with care."

"And just where did you get the thing?" asked the shopkeeper. "Steal it?"

"I'm a chieftain's daughter."

Matariki had not finished saying the words when it became clear she had made a mistake. That had impressed the girls at school, not to mention the Hauhau, but at best, it aroused suspicion here.

"You look more like a bastard," laughed the shopkeeper. "But let's not be like that. Give it to me, and you can pick out one of the dresses. I can't just look on as an upstanding Christian man while a girl runs around so scantily clad."

Matariki shook her head. "The cloak is worth a lot more than a shabby dress."

The man shrugged. "Then go sell it somewhere else." He pointed to the door.

Matariki bit her lip. It was unlikely that there was a second store like that in town, but she had to look anyway. She left the shop without a word. Dingo leaped up to comfort her. In the meantime, he had discovered a butcher shop and peered over at it. From inside his shop, the butcher looked at Matariki. His offerings reminded the girl that she would eventually also need something to eat. Dingo whined.

"We need money," Matariki explained.

Meanwhile they had almost completely crossed the western half of Hamilton. At best, there would be a buyer for her cloak on the other side of the river. The bridge, however, was still being built, and people were crossing by means of two canoes tied together that were dragged from one bank to the other by a pulley system. The whole thing did not look very trustworthy, and the river had a strong current. And what if she needed a little money for the crossing? Matariki gave up the idea.

She looked across the street where a postal service carriage was stopped. No doubt it went straight on to Auckland. She was more likely to get an audience in the big city. Was there any possibility of smuggling herself inside?

What about stealing clothes? Dusk was approaching, and if she looked around, she would surely find a clothesline with *pakeha* garments drying on it. But if she couldn't find anything her size, she'd stand out in clothes that were too big almost as much as she would in her Maori clothes. Plus, someone might recognize stolen items.

Defeated, Matariki wandered back into the store she had just left.

"Thought it over?" The shopkeeper grinned.

Matariki nodded. "But I need more than just a dress. Also underwear, shoes and stockings, a shawl, and a few coins for a telegram to the South Island."

"Maybe a handbag and a pearl necklace too?" the man teased her.

Matariki sighed. "Please, I need help!"

"A dress, underwear, shoes—well, I suppose you can also have the old shawl there." The man pointed to an already rather ragged shawl. He also traded in used clothing. "But no money, sweetheart. Who knows what road that would take me down? Maybe I'm risking jail by helping you. Who'd you run from, anyway, heh? Your master probably. Or old Potter?" He laughed. "Probably took the cashbox with you?"

Matariki rolled her eyes. "In that case, wouldn't I have money instead of a chieftain's cloak?" she asked. "I didn't steal anything, sir, and I didn't run away from a"—she did not want to say the word—"from an establishment," she finally finished. "I was kidnapped. That's why I'm looking for the police, and that's why—"

"Fine, fine, save your breath. Even if it sounds like a good story, but you all do know your way around a lie. So, do we have a deal, sweetheart?" He grinned.

It took some time for Matariki to find a dress that came close to fitting her. The female citizens of Hamilton all seemed to be well fed. For petite girls like Matariki, the only items available were children's clothing, and then they were too short. Finally, she found a well-maintained green housedress. The shopkeeper, Mr. McConnell, as she gleaned from a sign in the display window, allowed her to change in the store's backroom and did not follow her. Matariki sighed with relief when she finally stood in front of the mirror in *pakeha* clothing. She still would not pass for a pure-blooded white, but she felt better when she halfheartedly thanked the man and prepared to go.

"What are you going to do now?" asked the proprietor.

Matariki shrugged. "Look for work," she answered. "I do need to earn money. We need something to eat."

"We?" asked the man alertly.

Matariki pointed to Dingo, who was waiting patiently in front of the shop. "And I need to send a telegram," said Matariki. "My parents, they—"

"Sure, sure," Mr. McConnell laughed. "Well, see if you find anything. But I'll tell you now that we don't suffer your ilk here gladly. What do you even have in mind?"

"Be a maid?" Matariki said. "My mother used to be a maid, and she liked it."

McConnell slapped his forehead. "But your type doesn't even know what tidy is."

Matariki refrained from enlightening him on how much emphasis Otago Girls' High School placed on the subject of homemaking alongside other studies.

"I can also take care of horses," she said instead, "and sheep."

She could still hear the man laughing when she stepped onto the street. She hated Hamilton more and more. She needed to get away soon—and not just because Kahu Heke could find her trail.

***

Over the next few hours, Matariki knocked on every door in the western half of Hamilton—and then thought about swimming over to the eastern half. It seemed hopeless she would find work in this tiny town—even a *pakeha* girl might not have had luck. People were quick to show Matariki the door and to speak unkindly. The people of Hamilton seemed to hate the Maori—she did not find any who lived there, and there wasn't any evidence of a nearby Maori village.

Night was falling, and Matariki was hungry and tired enough to fall over. She would have to go back into the woods in the morning to fish or find edible roots. Unfortunately, the flora on the North Island, as she had feared, was only generally comparable to that on the South Island. At least the warmer temperatures offered their advantages. In Otago at this time of year, it would already be too cold to spend the night outside, but on the North Island she could manage.

The girl dragged herself once more through the streets, Dingo following her. She could still ask for work in the stables—perhaps the owner would at least let her sleep in the straw.

***

"Are you the Maori girl?"

Matariki was walking past the McConnell store again when a voice startled her. The woman to whom it belonged was just as thin as Mr. McConnell, who was presumably her husband. She was occupied with locking up the shop under the light of a gas lamp.

Matariki turned to the woman. "My name's Mata, Martha Drury."

After she had been thrown out of the first few houses in Hamilton, she had resorted to using her *pakeha* name.

"It does sound like you're a Christian girl," said the woman snidely. "Are you baptized?"

Matariki nodded.

"Speak loud and clear. My husband says you talk normal. Step into the light."

Normally, the woman's commanding tone would have sparked rebellion in Matariki, but exhausted as she was, she obeyed.

"English is my mother tongue," she said.

The woman snickered. "You can braid your hair and put on a proper dress, so it seems you've got a little civilization. I told my Archibald straightaway that if she really can talk like a Christian, then she's from an orphanage. What did you do, girl? Did they throw you out, or did you run away?"

The woman was curious; perhaps she would at least listen to her story. And then offer her some bread? Matariki was prepared to beg.

"I really did run away, madam," she said politely, curtsying. "But not from an orphanage, from a Maori camp. I—"

"I might be able to use a girl like you."

Matariki's heart almost skipped a beat. Was that a job offer?

"I was telling Archibald before: my parents in Wellington, they also had a girl out of an orphanage. She didn't work so bad. Sure, got to keep an eye on you all—and the cashbox locked. But otherwise, come on in, girl."

Matariki followed the woman into the shop, sighing with relief—Dingo, who wanted to run inside after her, however, only earned a kick. He yelped. Matariki was sorry, but she was not worried. Dingo would wait for her somewhere.

She stood across from the haggard Mrs. McConnell, who eyed her closely. That gave the girl time to study her future employer herself. Mrs. McConnell was not yet very old; Matariki guessed she was younger than her parents. But wrinkles had already carved themselves into her face, pulling down the corners of her mouth. Her eyes, as watery blue as her husband's, sat close together. Her eyebrows were sparse, and even Mrs. McConnell's hair seemed thin and colorless. She wore it in a stern bun, not a strand in her face. Mrs. McConnell was pale but had surprisingly full red lips. Her mouth reminded Matariki of a frog's, but when the image shot through the girl's head, she was too tired to laugh.

"You're devilishly pretty," the woman finally observed. "You'll be a constant temptation for Archibald."

Matariki swallowed. Her mother had only hinted at the problems she had experienced with employers. However, it was enough to make her nervous now.

"I'm no . . . ," Matariki ventured, looking the woman in the eye. "If I wanted to lead someone into temptation, I'd be over at old Potter's."

Mrs. McConnell snickered. "Very well, and I'll keep an eye out. You'll help around the house, clean, wash, cook. I'll show you how if they didn't already in the orphanage. You'll stay out of the shop, understood? I'll show you your room."

Matariki followed her through the shop and, to her horror, downstairs to a cellar. Here, a portion of the goods were stored. A closet was separated from the main room, similar to a potato cellar. Mrs. McConnell opened the wooden door.

"You can sleep here."

"That, that looks like a prison," Matariki blurted out in horror after peering into the tiny chamber, which contained a pallet bed and a chair. More would hardly have fit. A tiny window looking out at the yard at ground level was barred.

Mrs. McConnell snickered again. "Well, we used it for one too, when our sons were little. If one of them misbehaved, a few hours in here, and they regretted it."

Matariki stepped back in shock. Her instincts told her to quickly put distance between her and a couple who would lock up their own children. But it was warm and dry, and, exhausted as she was, the pallet was like a four-poster bed. Surely Mrs. McConnell would give her something to eat. They could negotiate everything else in the morning.

"I'm hungry," said Matariki.

Mrs. McConnell made a face. "First you work, then you eat," she replied, but she looked again at Matariki's gaunt face and reconsidered. "I'll bring you some bread," she muttered. "Make yourself at home in the meantime."

Matariki sank down onto the pallet.

She felt utterly alone.

Chapter 3

Violet and Rosie waited in front of the harbor pub in Dunedin until it grew dark. They watched as the first-class travelers boarded cabs or were picked up by friends or relatives, and observed the immigrants from steerage getting their bearings. Lastly the sailors disembarked—some of them heading into the pub where her father had also disappeared. Violet ventured speaking to a steward whom she had seen at church service. He promised to look for her father and brother and remind them of the girls in front of the pub, but it was several hours before he came out.

He shrugged his shoulders when he saw the girls. "I'm sorry, miss. I told him once when I came in and then again before I left. But he just grumbled something like, 'Aye, aye.' He was already drunk when I got there. He's not good for anything else today."

That did not surprise Violet, but she didn't know what to do. Her father would remember them when he left and punish her if he did not find them right away. After all, she was watching his luggage too. Helplessly, she kept waiting, long after Rosie had fallen asleep on the duffel bag.

Finally, the last few customers staggered out of the pub, and a man moved to shut the door. Violet gathered all her courage.

"Pardon me, sir."

She approached the barkeeper. She hoped he did not mistake her for a loose girl and, more importantly, that he was not looking for one.

The man, however, smiled at her amicably. His round face looked gentle and tolerant. "No need to be so formal, dear. I'm not 'sir,' just Fritz."

Violet curtsied, feeling foolish as she did. So much time and so many miles lay between her mother's instructions on manners and this encounter.

"I'm Violet Paisley," she said politely, but then her desperation broke through. "Please, sir, please, you need to let me in or bring my father out. Maybe he's not even in there anymore. I mean, since you're closing. But he really couldn't be gone, or do you have a back door?"

Violet did not know whether she was afraid of her father and brother clandestinely making tracks, or whether she wished for it.

Fritz shook his head. "Nay, dear, I suspect he's still inside. I always let a few new arrivals sleep here if they've run up a hefty bill first. Where'm I supposed to send them anyway if they can hardly walk?"

"You mean he . . ." Violet felt betrayed, and at the same time, a powerful rage welled up in her. "You mean he completely forgot about us? He looked for a place to sleep and . . ."

"Well, I wouldn't say he 'looked for' it. He just fell asleep. I can go in and wake him, but I don't know what good that would do. At this hour and in his condition, he won't be able to find a hotel for you."

The man looked at Violet and Rosie regretfully and seemed to consider whether he should have them come sleep in the pub as well.

Violet shook her head. "It's not necessary, sir," she said, and showed him the paper with the reverend's address. "Is that far?"

Fritz whistled through his teeth. "That's pretty far away. It'll take you half the night on foot, especially with the little one. And a cab—"

"I have this." Violet showed him the pound.

Fritz laughed. "Better not let your dad see that. Otherwise, I won't get rid of him for a week," he joked. "But it's certainly enough for a cab to Caversham. No more will be stopping here tonight. My customers can't afford them. You'll have to go up a few streets, but I'll come and help with your things."

The barkeeper pointed to the suitcase and duffel bags. A stone was lifted from Violet's heart. She might not have found the way to the nearest cab, and she would have been afraid in the dark streets of the docks. Fritz, however, was as honest as he looked. Violet woke Rosie, and he hoisted the bags on his wide shoulders, so Violet could concentrate on pulling her sleepy sister over the cobblestones. Rosie cried a little when she saw she was still in front of the pub.

"It's all right. We're going to ride to Miss and Mrs. Burton and the reverend. They won't turn us away, that's certain."

She was not actually so sure, but the address and the money were from Heather. And you did not give someone that much money if you did not mean it.

Fritz led the girls past a few cranes and landing places, storage depots, and warehouses, but they arrived quickly in a lively part of town. Violet kept her eyes down again. The women strolling about at this hour were surely not churchgoers. Most of the men lurched and hollered obscenities at the girls. Violet wanted to disappear when one of them looked at her, but as she was in Fritz's company, no one dared to speak to her. Fortunately, a cab soon arrived. Fritz knew the driver, and the men spoke amicably about the girls' destination.

Fritz and the driver loaded the luggage, and Rosie fell back to sleep as soon as Violet helped her onto the cushioned seat. They had never traveled in such style. Violet marveled at the city's wide streets and lavish buildings. After a little while, the regular rocking of the cab lulled her to sleep as well. She did not wake up until the driver stopped and addressed her.

"So, miss, here we are. Saint Peter's. But there's no light on in the parsonage. Shall I wait for you in case no one's home?"

Violet was wide awake at once, her heart pounding with fear. Where was she supposed to go if the Burtons really had not driven home but were perhaps spending the night at Kathleen's friend's?

She shook her head. There might not be enough money for a trip back to the harbor, and if she had to sleep outside, this was certainly better than the docks. The house beside the small sandstone church made a good impression. It reminded her a bit of her grandparents' house. There was a garden with flowers so bright, she could make them out in the night, and a bench too. At worst, she and Rosie would sleep there.

"We'll manage," she said.

Violet paid the cabdriver after he had placed the bags in front of the house. To her surprise, she received a whole handful of coins back. At the front door, she relived that day a few weeks before when she had knocked on her grandparents' door. How happily it had begun. And how horribly it had ended.

Here there was no lion-headed door knocker but a bell that rang melodically. Exhausted, Rosie snuggled against Violet's legs while they waited. But it did not take long. Violet saw a lamp come on inside. Right after, Peter Burton opened the door.

"Violet! How did you end up here?"

***

Violet had thought she was long past hunger, but when Kathleen placed bread, butter, marmalade, and ham in front of them, she could hardly stop eating. Rosie forgot all her manners. She immediately stuffed bread with honey into her mouth, using both hands. Violet scolded her when she burped, but the Burtons only waved it off with a laugh.

"She can be well-mannered tomorrow. We'll make an exception tonight," said Peter. "But please, Violet, tell us: How did you get here, and where is your father?"

Violet summarized her first day in Dunedin. Heather could not get over how Paisley acted.

"They can stay here, can't they? We're not going to send them back, are we?" Heather looked imploringly at Peter and Kathleen.

Kathleen nodded, but Peter Burton hesitated with his answer. Then he said, "They'll stay here tonight. As I told the two of you in Wales, if it were up to me, they could stay here, or the parish would find a place for them. But the fact of the matter is still that this"—Peter swallowed a curse word—"that Jim Paisley is their father and guardian. Does he even know where you are, Violet?"

Violet pursed her lips. "Fritz knows," she answered, "the barkeeper. He'll tell him in the morning. He wouldn't have understood it tonight, anyway."

"So, you two ran away?"

"Were they supposed to have sat there outside the pub all night?" Heather asked.

Peter sighed. "We'll just wait and see what happens tomorrow. But everyone prepare herself for an angry drunk at the door insisting on the return of his kidnapped daughters."

***

Violet and Rosie slept soundly in Kathleen's clean, rose-scented guest room. They did not wake until around nine when the smell of coffee and waffles wafted upstairs.

Heather called the girls into the kitchen. Kathleen cast a glance over at the church. "Is anyone else sleeping there tonight besides the boy?" she asked her husband. "If not, why not bring him in too? Surely he'll be glad the girls are here."

To Violet's great amazement, Bulldog lumbered into the kitchen, grinning like an idiot when he saw Rosie again.

"The reverend let me sleep here," he explained, bouncing Rosie on his knee. "Before I set out for Queenstown. There are hostels, but—"

"But I don't like sending thirteen-year-olds there," said Peter. "Though Bulldog no doubt knows how to look after himself. Besides, you need your money for shovels and pickaxes." He nodded amiably at the boy. "Come, Violet, give the boy something to eat."

Bulldog nodded eagerly. Violet knew that he had savings—after all, even on the ship he had managed to make money, which led her to believe that he had hardly made his money honestly in London. But it was better not to ask about that, or why he was traveling alone. Violet would have guessed he was fifteen or sixteen, but hardly anyone that age set out for a new country without any family or friends. Violet shoveled waffles and ham onto Bulldog's plate and smiled at him. Even if he was a ruffian, she felt much better now that he was with her. The reverend was a good man, to be sure, and Heather and Kathleen wanted the best for her. But the only one who had ever really protected her from Fred and her father was Bulldog.

***

That morning, however, there was no need for Bulldog's special skills. By midday, Jim and Fred had still not appeared at the Burtons'. Kathleen and Heather prepared a bath for the girls and later took them into town; Kathleen wanted to visit her shop, and Heather took the sketches she had done in Europe to her studio. She made use of a few rooms above the shop—an apartment Kathleen and Claire had once shared. After her marriage to Jimmy Dunloe, Claire had moved into his apartment one floor higher, but the generous bank manager had not sought any new renters, instead leaving the apartments that belonged to the shop to Chloe and Heather. During their studies, both had lived there, but now Heather used it almost exclusively as a studio. She usually rode back to Caversham to sleep; without Chloe's company, the apartment on Stuart Street made her gloomy.

Today, though, she was in a good mood. She enjoyed showing her work and the big, bright rooms to Violet. Perhaps the girls could even move in with her.

Violet could work in the shop, and Heather could care for Rosie while Violet worked.

Violet admired Heather's pictures and the fine dresses in Kathleen and Claire's store. Claire almost intimidated her more than Kathleen had at first. The petite, dark-haired woman was a true lady. All the fine manners that Kathleen possessed, but which did not stand out because of her shyness, seemed comfortable on Claire Dunloe.

Mrs. Dunloe was very friendly to Violet and Rosie. Violet blushed when Claire praised her extraordinary beauty.

"Look at this girl," she said to Kathleen. "Sure, she's still growing. How old are you, thirteen or fourteen? These eyes, they're so big."

"Because she's half-starved," said Kathleen. "In that gaunt face—"

"The girl will always have a slender face, just like you, Kathleen. She has the same aristocratic features. High cheekbones, a small, straight nose, and her lips are a little more sensuous, fuller, and look at this natural red color. With her wonderful auburn hair, she looks like Sleeping Beauty. We should consider a fashion show for next year, like in Paris. Would you want to do something like that, Violet?"

Violet blushed again. She was ready for the earth to swallow her whole when Claire insisted that she try on a turquoise-colored dress, which had just been tailored for a wedding. Kathleen had been designing bridal gowns for years, and now that ever-bigger weddings were taking place in Dunedin—the first generation of children of the immigrants who had struck it rich were saying their "I dos"—there were more and more orders for bridesmaid and flower-girl dresses. One such order was the long dress in which Violet turned breathlessly before the mirror. Claire loosened Violet's braids and placed the flower crown that went with the dress in her full hair. Violet did not recognize herself.

"What did I say? Sleeping Beauty. Someday you'll turn all the young men's heads in Dunedin, my dear Violet. Just don't fall for the first one that comes along."

Heather insisted on painting Violet like this. Claire and Kathleen were happy to lend her the dress to make a few sketches, and so Violet and Rosie passed a dreamlike hour in Heather's studio. Violet sat at the window and looked out onto Stuart Street while Heather sketched, and Rosie even painted a picture using watercolors.

***

Peter, who had accompanied Bulldog into the city to advise him on the purchase of his gold-mining equipment, now directed the parish's team of horses toward the harbor. As much as he would like to welcome Violet and Rosie into his family, he worried about where Jim and Fred had gone.

He found Fritz, the friendly barkeeper, right away.

"Oh, hello, Reverend. I'm happy the girls arrived safely at your door," he said when Peter introduced himself. As for Jim and Fred, he could not help the pastor. "They left this morning. Of necessity, my wife comes at nine to tidy up, so I chased the fellows out then."

"And did you tell them where the girls—"

Fritz rolled his eyes. "Of course. But that did not seem to concern them. They were on fire to make for Queenstown."

"For where?" asked Peter, confused.

"Well, Queenstown, the goldfields. They were bragging about it all last night. It's the only reason those fellows came."

Peter shook his head. "Mr. Paisley is a coal miner. From what I know, he wanted to go on to Greymouth or Westport."

Fritz shrugged his shoulders. "I guess he changed his mind. But you're right. He said something like if anyone could find gold, it would be him with all his experience mining coal."

"His last mineshaft collapsed," Peter said curtly.

Fritz grimaced. "Doesn't surprise me, but I can imagine how it went. Most aspiring gold miners are clueless. And then a fellow comes along, boasting about how much 'black gold' he's dug out of the earth. So, everyone thinks he knows the business. However it is, Reverend, those men are gone."

"We have all their luggage." Peter was dumbfounded.

"But certainly not the money, assuming they have any left," Fritz said.

Peter Burton thanked him and directed his team back to Caversham. Heather and Kathleen would be happy about the news, probably Violet too. He had an uneasy feeling. Someday, Jim and Fred Paisley would resurface. And probably not with a sack full of gold.

Chapter 4

The morning after her arrival in Hamilton, Matariki felt better. True, her room was awful, but not nearly as ghastly as the night before. Matariki reassured herself she would not stay long with the McConnells. She wondered whether maids were paid weekly or monthly. Whether she had to work a week or a month, eventually she would have enough money to send a telegram to Otago. And then it would only be a matter of days until her parents would come.

While Matariki scrubbed the two steps in front of the store under Mrs. McConnell's watchful eyes, she happily pictured Michael and her mother alighting onto Victoria Street. They would all hug one another, and Lizzie would regard the McConnells with a stern gaze and place a soothing hand on Michael's arm when he wanted to rage at the sight of her chamber in the cellar. Lizzie would thank the McConnells with tight lips, and her face would express contempt. Michael would buy or have tailored the most beautiful dress for Matariki, so she would not have to travel in a large green housedress.

The food in the McConnells' house was meager, and not just for Matariki. Archibald and Marge McConnell seemed to view the intake of nourishment as a necessary evil on which they spent no more time than absolutely required. Their insignificant selection of dresses and fabrics soon no longer amazed Matariki, and the McConnells themselves only dressed in black. They were members of the Free Church of Scotland—a community of fanatical Christians who had splintered off from the main Scottish church and emigrated in large groups. The most important city they had founded in New Zealand was Dunedin. How the McConnells had ended up in the backwater town of Hamilton on the North

Island, Matariki never learned. She gathered, however, that the two of them didn't get along with their religious brethren any better than they did with the other people around them.

As storeowners, the McConnells had to be polite, but it was evident they felt they were better than the other residents of Hamilton. Their general store was not the hub of the town's business as such a store had been in the former gold-mining town of Lawrence. If people chatted there, it was only in hushed tones behind the shelves. No one wanted to risk a dirty look from Mr. or Mrs. McConnell; instead, one made his purchases and moved on. "Have a nice day" and similar friendly comments were not part of the exchange.

Though Matariki was never allowed to help in the store—she only worked in the house under Mrs. McConnell's supervision—she recognized that opening a competing business in Hamilton would be a sure path to wealth. Since no one liked the McConnells, if there had been any other option for shopping, everyone would have taken it.

The optimistic Matariki, however, determined to view this positively. After all, the obvious isolation of the McConnells was one reason they offered her work. Doubtless, no *pakeha* girl wanted the joyless job she now held.

At least the first days with Mrs. McConnell were not boring. The Scotswoman was downright talkative, or at least she liked to hear herself speak. She informed Matariki thoroughly about her religion: "We're God's chosen people. The fate of a person is predestined from birth: some will be raised up, the others cast down into the pit of hell." She left no doubt whatsoever that she belonged to the former group and Matariki to the latter. Matariki sometimes thought about presenting to her employer the philosophy of the Hauhau, according to which the celestial distributions would be precisely reversed. Yet she held herself back—Mrs. McConnell would certainly not tolerate any contradiction. The girl took it that this attitude had also driven the McConnells' sons from home. They apparently maintained no contact with their parents. To Matariki's question about their whereabouts, Mrs. McConnell only replied with an angry snort. From a conversation of Mr. McConnell's with a customer, she did glean that one of them served in the Armed Constabulary. Where the other one was, she never learned.

Regardless, Mrs. McConnell revealed what had agitated the citizens of Hamilton so against the Maori. Matariki dared not ask about it directly, but her employer quite liked to direct her deluge of words against the blasphemy of other races.

"King Country, I can't believe it. As if these savages were capable of choosing a king. Kings, girl, are anointed by God. A horde of wild beasts can't simply get together and set a crown on one of their own. And then resist when upright people settle here and till the soil as God has commanded them. But the English taught them. There's plenty to be said against them, but they did that well, and went straight for the troublemakers without dithering."

Matariki learned that the Crown had supported the settlers in the Waikato region with soldiers after the Maori tribes had united and protested the land seizure. Right had undeniably been on the Maori side; the Treaty of Waitangi secured their land ownership. Twenty years after the signing of the agreement, however, the whites had not quite been able to recall the wording. Matariki was slowly coming to understand Kahu Heke and his men better. Still, the so-called Waikato Wars had ended with the *pakeha's* victory. The tribes were all dispossessed where the whites wanted to settle, and to secure this, the military had been stationed in the region. That led to the founding of towns, one of which was Hamilton.

In 1864, the soldiers of the Fourth Waikato Militia Regiment and their families arrived and built their town on the grounds of Kirikiriroa, the old Maori fortress. They immediately tested their strength on the surrounding villages; the chieftains and their tribes withdrew without a fight into the woods of Waikato, where they were left in peace. The soldiers and their families, however, sat secure at the end of the world. No doubt they got bored and frustrated with their deployment. And for sure they held the recalcitrant natives responsible.

Matariki, however, was no longer confronted with the hate of the people of Hamilton because she hardly ever left the house. Mrs. McConnell kept her busy making sure the house was spotless. After the store closed, she had to clean it and restock the shelves. Matariki longed for the end of the first week of work, and when no one hinted at her pay then, she set her sights on the end of the first month.

When that time arrived, she raised the subject. It was now truly time to compensate her work.

"You want money?" Mrs. McConnell stared at Matariki with a confounded expression. "You don't really believe you're owed money, do you?"

Matariki nodded. "Of course," she said calmly. "I've worked for a month. I should receive at least a pound for that."

"And your food?" asked Mr. McConnell. "Your shelter? The clothes on your back?"

"And don't think we haven't noticed that you've been feeding that mutt as well," added Mrs. McConnell.

Dingo had gotten used to sleeping outside the barred window to Matariki's room. She could reach through to pet him, and she always set aside some of her food rations to feed him a bit. Mostly, however, he had to beg or hunt for himself. He was as thin and shabby as when Matariki had found him.

"I work more than ten hours a day," Matariki defended herself. "I've earned more than a little food and a pallet in a cellar closet. And as for my clothes, I traded you for them before there was even talk of work."

"I clothed you out of pure compassion when you were practically naked," said Mr. McConnell.

It was a mistake to discuss these matters at the dinner table with the McConnells. She would have done better to attempt it in the store with witnesses, although the customers had no idea how much she did for the McConnells, and they probably would have avoided taking sides.

Matariki squared herself. "Then I'm leaving tomorrow," she declared.

She did not particularly want to go. It would soon be winter, and even if there was no snow in Otago, it rained almost daily and could still get rather cold. Auckland was a good seventy miles away. She would manage. Her ancestors among the tribes had made it through considerably worse. She should have gone straight there after she had fled the Hauhau. But at the time, she had still thought the forests were full of Maori tribes that would likely bring her back to Kahu Heke. Now she knew better.

The McConnells laughed. "And where will you go, sweetheart?" asked Archibald, at which Marge gave him an angry look. She hated when her husband called Matariki sweetheart.

"The armed constables will have you before you've stepped outside of town."

Matariki frowned. "Why would they be after me?" she asked.

Mrs. McConnell laughed. "Because you stole from the register, girl. Because you ran away from your employers without working off the clothes you have on your back. And there are plenty of witnesses, dear, who saw how you arrived here half-naked."

"But that would be a lie," shouted Matariki. "Your, your faith forbids you from that. That, that's not pleasing to God."

There was renewed cackling, this time from both McConnells. "How do you claim to know what's pleasing to God? You with your idol."

Mrs. McConnell reached for the *hei-tiki* Matariki always wore around her neck. She pulled on it hard, but the leather band did not break. Matariki felt a burning pain in her neck as it dug into her flesh, but she managed to free herself quickly.

"Watch out, or I'll curse you."

Matariki held the small jade figurine in front of her without really expecting anything to happen. It would have worked among the Hauhau to invoke the spirits, but the McConnells were a different caliber. They made even God dance to their tune.

"There, you see, a little heathen. That's what they say, even in the mission school: the savages let themselves be baptized, so we'll feed and clothe them. But then they run off again and dance around their totem poles."

"It certainly pleases God to keep you here, Martha," said Archibald. "No doubt he sent you here to take part in the life of a Christian family and perhaps to one day truly repent."

"Like hell I will," Matariki spat back, and stormed to her room.

She was gathering her few possessions into a bundle when the key turned in the lock.

***

For the first few days, Matariki tried to treat her imprisonment by the McConnells as lightly as her abduction by the Hauhau. When she had been among the Maori, it had been clear to her from the beginning that she would be able to escape eventually. Maori warriors were simply not prison guards. When the tribes went to war, it did happen that prisoners were enslaved, but no one needed chains to keep them. Whoever let himself be taken prisoner lost his spiritual rank, his *mana*. His own tribe was ashamed of him and would not have accepted him back. So, the slave remained willingly among the victors where he had to do menial labor but was mostly treated well. Matariki had not felt herself a slave, and she never believed she was bound by such *tapu*. She had not been afraid among the Hauhau until bullets started flying. And then she had escaped.

In Hamilton, however, the situation proved different, although at first glance it did not look as hopeless. Matariki determined that very first night her cell was locked to run the risk of capture by the constables. At least then she would have the possibility of telling her story to the commanders. Perhaps someone would make the effort to follow up on it. And besides, it could not be worse in a reformatory than it was at the McConnells'.

However, the matter was anything but easy. The McConnells were not stupid. The very next morning, Matariki heard Archibald tell every customer of his Maori maid's attempt to steal and disappear with the money.

"Thanks be to God we caught her. And now we've locked her up. No, no, we probably won't report it. After all, the poor thing can hardly help being made to lie and steal since she was little. But naturally, we'll try to drive it out of her. With the goodness of Christian people, but also with the sternness the Lord teaches us. I think you can help us with that. If the girl ever shows up somewhere without our permission . . ."

Matariki suddenly saw herself surrounded by a whole town full of watchmen eager to catch her in a mistake. Over the first few days, she tried twice to get away but was stopped quickly.

The man who brought her back the second time scolded Archibald, saying he should chastise his ward. The storekeeper did not do that. The only thing one could say for Archibald McConnell was that he never laid hands on Matariki. He did not hit her or attack her sexually, and that remained true even though Matariki developed into an exotic beauty over the next few months. Despite the meager food, her breasts grew, and her hips rounded. She now fit into the old green dress, her only possession. However, there was no one to compliment her.

The McConnells completely sealed away their house slave.

***

Winter passed. Spring came and gave way to summer. Not a ray of sun reached Matariki in the cellar. She was pale and constantly felt tired. To be sure, she missed the light, but she suffered even more from the loss of hope. Still, she constantly told herself that there had to be someone in Hamilton who did not hate her and her people, who would believe her when she told her story, and who would risk everything to help her.

This someone, however, did not appear. At most, she would glimpse a customer who wouldn't give her a second look and talked about her dismissively with Mrs. McConnell: "How is little Martha getting on?" or "It is truly Christian what you've taken on with the little savage." Matariki could have screamed with rage, but she would only make her situation worse. If one of these customers ever heard her, it would only be when she shouted her cry for help.

Every few weeks, a pastor of the Free Church of Scotland came by to pray with the McConnells. A fuss was always made about it, and naturally Matariki was presented. The first time, she tried to ignore the McConnells' instructions: "You'll say your prayers, be humble, and be thankful. Pour your heart out to the pastor." In hurried, desperate words she confided in him that she was being held against her will, and he shook his head.

"My child, you must learn to accept your fate with humility. It may not please you to be here and unable to give in to the sinful drives of your tribe. Yet, for your immortal soul, it is beneficial. So, be grateful and try to be a true Christian."

Matariki wanted to ask how this coincided with the McConnells' beliefs that who was blessed and who was damned was fixed from the beginning of time. But it did not seem worth the effort to ask. Besides, the McConnells' expressions made clear what awaited her after the cleric's visit.

During the pastor's next visit, she showed herself tractable and humble, and she was as excited as a child when he gave her a copy of the Bible. The McConnells allowed her to keep it, and Matariki realized to her shame that she was moved to tears at that and truly thankful. Though she had not found the Bible such exciting reading before, now it was the first book she had held in her hands for months. The McConnells did not tolerate reading. The Bible was the only exception.

Boredom added to Matariki's hopelessness and desperation. The McConnells locked her up immediately after her work was done. She received her food in her cell. And then there was nothing to do but ruminate. If Dingo had not appeared every evening to receive her caresses and listen to her complaints, she probably would have gone mad.

Matariki began to read to him from the Bible, just to hear her own voice. The scrawny dog listened patiently. And the girl again created a little hope from new dreams. If she could scrounge a pencil from somewhere, she could write a cry for help on the edge of a page and tie it around Dingo's neck. If he then ran into the only nice person in town, who knew Dingo in turn because he occasionally gave him food, then perhaps she could be saved.

Matariki did not find a pencil stub in the McConnells' rooms; they wrote as little as they read. She dreamed of animal-loving citizens who opened their hearts to imprisoned girls, and sometimes of a fairy-tale prince who suddenly appeared to set her free. The longer her imprisonment lasted, the more often Maori warriors ghosted through her imaginings, men with spears and deadly war clubs, guns and frightening tattoos. She pictured an army of Hauhau fighters storming into Hamilton, razing houses, and throwing people into the river. She finally understood Kahu Heke's argument for fortifying the men spiritually, and she spent nights thinking up ceremonies with which she could send warriors into battle with the *mana* of a chieftain's daughter.

Matariki felt herself more and more a part of the Maori people, and as such, she had every reason to hate the people who had stolen her land and enslaved its true owners. After a long time with the McConnells, she felt the power of the chieftain's daughter rising within her.

Matariki wanted to see blood. No matter the price.

Chapter 5

For Violet, the happiest time of her life began when her father disappeared. She and Rosie moved into a room in Heather's apartment and studio.

Heather asked her stepfather to sign registration papers so Violet could go to school. She suggested Peter Burton claim Violet as his niece.

"If Paisley stays away, we'll do it," he declared. "For now, I know you don't want to hear it, Heather, but I don't trust this peace. The man could make life hell for us if he does come back. Besides, you should ask Violet if it's what she really wants."

Violet was fourteen years old and could not read or write any better than a young child. How were they supposed to explain that a niece of Reverend Burton's could hardly write her own name? In what class could they place her?

After she thought about it, Violet decided she preferred to work her way through the lessons in Heather's books by herself. She also worked in Kathleen and Claire's shop. At first, the women let her make tea and take care of small duties, but soon she was helping the seamstresses, and Kathleen praised her for her skills. No one screamed at her; no one frightened her. Instead, the seamstresses and often the customers, too, complimented her for her beauty and her good manners. Ellen Paisley had always urged her daughter to be polite, courteous, and friendly, and when she grew brave enough to smile at the customers, she was irresistible. Claire insisted that when Violet was working at the shop, she wear a skirt and blouse from the Gold Mine Boutique's collection.

"Admit it. This is a trick to increase sales," one of their regular customers said, laughing brightly. "You want to make us believe we can look as delicate and beautiful as your shopgirl in your clothes."

Violet also continued to model for Heather when they both had the time. However, word had already gotten out that Heather Coltrane was back in town, and her portraiture schedule was full. The city dwellers came to her apartment to have themselves painted, but when someone from an estate wanted a portrait, Heather also went traveling—though usually she had several commissions to fulfill at the same time.

"Barrington Station: the woman of the house, a horse, and a dog," Heather said as she packed her bags. "They're still thinking about the ram. It depends on whether it wins at the agricultural exhibition."

Violet and Rosie stayed at the Burtons' when Heather was traveling. Violet almost liked it better in the small house with its garden than in Heather's elegant apartment. She loved gardening and enjoyed helping in the pastor's soup kitchen, but most of all, she was happy when Sean Coltrane, Kathleen's firstborn and Peter's stepson, came to visit on Sundays.

Until then, Violet's heart had never pounded when she spoke with a boy, but this serious, dark-haired man had caught her eye. Sean was so quiet and friendly—very different from the men in Treherbert or on the ship. He had gentle, pale-green eyes, which always seemed lost in a lovely dream, and curly black hair. He did not speak much with Violet—what would a well-read young attorney, who was much older than she, perhaps nearly twenty years older, have had to say to a young girl from Treherbert? But when he did talk to her, it warmed her heart. Naturally, it was hardly more than, "Thank you, Violet," or "Did you really bake this cake yourself, Violet? It's exceptional." Sometimes, though, he would compliment her appearance with something like, "What a lovely dress, Violet." That would make her happy for days, and she would dream about his deep, friendly voice, which, in her imagination, said, "And how gorgeous you are, Violet. Would you consider kissing me?"

Sean always smiled when he saw the girls, and when Violet brought herself to ask him something, he answered very seriously. On a previous visit, he had mentioned an interesting case about a dispute between the Maori and *pakeha*. A tribe wanted to sue because a land buyer had cheated them in the negotiations.

Violet had thought about the case, and her response to it, for days. "But if they agreed to the sale," observed Violet, "then they can't change the contract later."

"That's precisely the question," said Sean thoughtfully, "and one could argue that the Maori were at fault if they sold too cheaply. However, they could not know what this piece of land would normally have been worth. It's a bit like in horse trading. If the seller is a scoundrel and sands the horse's teeth to make it look younger, then the buyer would have to know horses well to notice that. You can't assume that, and at trial, the buyer would be in the right as far as that went."

"But the seller could say he didn't know, especially if he bought the horse from another trader," Violet argued.

Sean laughed. "He'd probably do just that. And in that case, it would be good for the buyer if he had a witness to the sales conversation. For example, if he heard the trader say that the horse was born exactly three years ago in his stables." Sean briefly thought of Ian Coltrane, whom he had long believed to be his father, and his disreputable horse-trading practices. But then he found his way back to his conversation with the lovely young girl who clearly hung on his every word. "You've recognized the principle, Violet," he said amiably. "It's his word against theirs, and naturally, our land buyer will try to talk himself out of it. Although the argument on both sides is a balancing act. We have to argue that the Maori are a bit foolish but not too foolish—we don't want them to look completely incapable of business. It's very difficult. And it's an important case. Such a case sets what people call precedence. If we win for the tribe, others will refer to this judgment when they submit similar complaints."

Violet nodded. She noted every word of this first real conversation with Sean. She would have to think about it quite a bit and come up with more questions to keep the conversation going next week.

Now, however, Sean turned to his mother. "While we're on the subject of horse trading . . . You spoke in London with Colin? He really wants to come back?"

Kathleen shrugged. "He's hoping for better opportunities at being promoted here, in the Armed Constabulary."

Sean furrowed his brow. "With the constables? Does he want to shoot Maori? Well, he's out of luck there. They're resorting more and more to justice than show of force. There are a few exceptions, but, according to what

I've heard, they're now employing the armed constables by having them build bridges and roads."

"Swords to plowshares," said Peter.

Sean grinned. "As long as Colin doesn't sell the horse that pulls the plow."

Kathleen laughed, although her laughter was somewhat forced, and Violet laughed because she laughed at every joke Sean made, regardless of whether she understood it. She felt as if she were in a fairy tale: a family that talked and told jokes, with no screaming, no fighting about money, no beating.

***

Violet's fairy tale did not quite last six months. And then her luck turned bad, as it had so often in her life before the Burtons. When Violet later thought back to the day on which her father and brother appeared before Reverend Burton's house, she would ask herself over and again what would have happened if the Barringtons' ram had not won in its show class. If it had lost, Heather would have returned a week earlier from Canterbury. Violet and Rosie would have been living in the city, not in the parsonage in Caversham, and Heather would doubtlessly have pulled out all the stops to protect the sisters.

As it was, it was hardly possible to hide Violet and Rosie's presence, and the pastor could not afford any scandal. Traditionally, the church and parsonage stood open to all who came back impoverished from the goldfields. That applied to Jim and Fred Paisley as well as to Eric Fence.

"Many thanks again for taking my daughters in." For once, Jim Paisley was sober, and he tried a humble approach. Sheepish as he talked to the reverend, he turned his hat in his hands, which astonished Violet. She had not seen this pose in years—not since her father had developed the habit of drinking liquid courage before confessing a renewed bout of unemployment to his wife. "We, er, decided rather suddenly to go to the goldfields."

"You left us in front of a pub," Violet said. Previously, she would not have dared, but in six months, no one had glared as evilly at her as her father did now.

"Well, it doesn't seem to have been so bad." He played it down. "I knew that you would be welcome in the house of this, hmm, gentleman, and wouldn't you say yourself, Reverend, that it was for the best? Two girls in the goldfields, it'd be rough for them, I tell you, very rough."

Peter Burton pressed his lips together. "In Tuapeka, there used to be families who stuck together and cared for their children," he said calmly. "I ran a school myself. And in Queenstown—"

"Oh, Reverend, we weren't in the fields around Queenstown," Paisley interrupted quickly, as if to defend his honor. "My partners and I were seeking new claims. We—"

"So, you found gold and are rich now?"

Peter could not refrain from making his remark as he let his gaze pass over Paisley's filthy shirt and his threadbare work pants. The three men did not even have shovels and pickaxes on them anymore. Peter thought it likely they had pawned them.

Paisley made a face. "Poor men have no luck," he said, trying to garner sympathy.

"And the money from the sale of your house?" asked Kathleen sternly. "There must still have been some after the crossing."

Paisley shrugged his shoulders. "Money comes and goes; luck comes and goes, and some only have their own hands' work to rely on. I learned from it, Reverend," he said ponderously. "I was seduced into risking everything, and I won't deny it: I failed."

A cold flash ran down Violet's spine. His show was familiar; she had witnessed her father like this many Sundays after a boozy Saturday night. Her mother would point out that he had drunken half of his week's pay. Even though she had only been ten or eleven, Violet wondered at the time how her otherwise smart mother could fall for his whining and his useless excuses.

The pastor looked as unimpressed as Kathleen. "What are you thinking of doing now?" he asked Paisley sternly.

Jim rubbed his forehead. "I'm going to look for respectable work," he declared. "Just like my son. We're headed to the, the . . ."

"West coast," Eric helped him.

"That's right. That's where we're going, to the coal-mining region. I can feed my family, Reverend, believe me."

"You want to go to Greymouth or Westport?" asked Kathleen. "Without money or horses or a wagon? How do you plan to get there?"

Jim shrugged. "Someone may take us a piece of the way now and again. We'll manage. With, with God's help." He crossed himself.

"So, you'll leave the girls here," Peter said.

Kathleen and Violet held their breath.

Jim Paisley shook his head. "Of course not, by no means. How could I? We want to be a family again, you see. We need to stick together, and for that we need a woman in the house. Just look at us."

"And Violet's supposed to be this woman?" asked Kathleen. "She's supposed to cook, wash, tidy up, and keep your clothes in order?"

"What else?" inquired Paisley. "Don't you do that for your husband? Wouldn't you have done it for your father in his old age? Since my beloved wife was taken from us, Violet is the woman of our family. Get ready, Violet, we're leaving soon."

Kathleen gave her husband a desperate look.

Peter tried again. "Mr. Paisley, why don't you go with your son first and then send for the girls? A family, as you just said, naturally belongs together, but it also requires that a father build a nest, so to speak, for his family."

Jim Paisley grimaced. "You see, now we understand each other. A nest, exactly, that's what we're making, right here and now. We're going to rent a cute miner's house. Fred and I'll earn money. Violet'll make it homey. It's not that hard, Reverend. Usually there's already furniture inside."

In England and Wales, that was true. A miner did not make much, but the mine looked after good people. Did the mine owners in Greymouth or Westport think so progressively? The west coast wasn't particularly friendly to families. The typical coast dweller was a whaler or seal hunter. Miners mostly came without families, and though they were paid properly, they were otherwise on their own.

"Violet!" her father said, his voice booming.

Violet stood as if frozen. When her father had appeared, she had been puttering around the garden, harvesting winter vegetables. It had been completely unreal to see his heavy form emerge in the clear air in front of the silhouetted mountains and the homey little church. Even worse, Jim had hardly made an effort to greet her. They had not exchanged two words when the pastor and Kathleen stepped out of the house. Rosie had fled under the garden bench when she saw her father coming, and she was still hiding there.

"I don't want to," said Violet. She had not considered it. The refusal simply burst out of her. "I don't want to go to the west coast. And Rosie doesn't either."

Jim Paisley grimaced again. "Violet, that wasn't an invitation. It was an order. We're a family; I'm your father, so let's go."

"You don't even know where you're going," Violet yelled desperately.

"Of course we do," Eric Fence jumped in. "First to Canterbury, then straight across the country and into the mountains, and there we are."

"That's more than three hundred miles," said Peter. "And it's still winter. There might be snow, and you have to make it over the mountains. You should have better considered where you wanted to go before booking your passage. It's closer from other ports. You could also go by ship."

Jim Paisley did not give the pastor another glance. "Pack your things, Violet."

***

Violet cried, and Rosie screamed when Jim Paisley pulled her out from under the bench. Kathleen briefly considered calling for the police, but Jim Paisley was Violet and Rosemary's guardian, and he was not drunk at the moment.

"Can't we ask Sean if there's some option?" asked Violet desperately as Kathleen packed a few household objects and blankets into a bag. "We could sue and—"

Kathleen shook her head. "The Maori," she said bitterly, "may have some rights. They're still negotiating that. We'll see how it turns out. But women, Violet, don't have any rights. Your father is not allowed to beat you to death, but even if he did, he could probably talk himself out of the charge somehow. Otherwise, he can do just about anything. You have to hang on until you're an adult. Try to write us, Violet, best as you can. Writing mistakes don't matter. We should keep in touch."

Violet looked at Kathleen desperately, and an idea flashed through her eyes. "What if I marry? I mean, if someone married me?"

She was thinking of Sean, of course. At age fourteen, it had to be possible. If he did that for her, just to save her, they could always divorce later. The idea was too crazy. She dared not suggest that Kathleen ask him. If Heather were there, she would have asked him.

Kathleen's face assumed a hard expression. "Marrying doesn't help anything, Violet. Don't even think about it. If you flee heedlessly into marriage, you'll go from the frying pan into the fire."

"It could, you know, be a sort of trade," Violet whispered.

Kathleen snorted. "It often is, dear," she said, thinking of her own story. She, too, had once agreed to a trade: Ian Coltrane had given her son a name, and, in return, she gave him the money to emigrate. "But you're rarely the buyer or seller. You're the horse."

***

The Burtons ended up paying for the Paisleys' train travel to Canterbury. They paid for Eric Fence, too, once Jim declared they must all travel comfortably or no one would. Peter Burton would not have been extorted, but Kathleen was determined to do what she could for the girls. The pastor drove the family to the train station, purchased the tickets, and insisted on overseeing the boarding.

"No doubt he would have sold the tickets a moment later and drunk the money away," he said when he returned home and explained his long absence to Kathleen. "Leopards like that never change their spots, no matter what he pretended in front of us. Did you give Violet money?"

Kathleen blushed. Her husband knew her well. Still, she hoped that Jim Paisley had not seen anything.

"Maybe he didn't notice that you gave her something, but he's likely to guess," judged Peter. "He'll try to beat something out of her."

Kathleen tried not to think about it. She could still recall all too well how Ian Coltrane had taken the first money she earned with her sewing. She hated delivering Violet to a similar fate. If she made it through a few years, Violet and Rosie both had a chance of escaping misery. If only Violet did not fall in love, or marry just to be free of her father. If only Violet did not seek a way out that wasn't one.

Chapter 6

Kupe did not have the same concerns as Matariki about stealing laundry from a clothesline. He had no intention of arriving in Hamilton wearing the garb of a Maori warrior. During the last few battles, the Hauhau had reminded themselves of the tradition of going to battle half-naked, wearing only hardened flax fastened to a belt. That tradition, however, had proved just as useless as every other attempt to coerce Tumatauenga, the war god, onto the side of the Maori.

Kupe started seeking out *pakeha* settlements before reaching the city, and he found one near an abandoned *marae*. There was a tiny sheep farm with a primitive wooden house, a few sheds, and fenced-in pastures. Kupe felt a twinge of his old rage when he figured that the owner had likely taken part in the dispossession of its former inhabitants. Perhaps he should go inside and massacre them. Then he could gloat about it, and likely he would find some money.

Kupe quickly gave up the thought. He wouldn't be any good at massacring people. He had felt nothing but disgust when his tribal brothers cut out the heart of a dead soldier to eat it. He was slowly coming to face facts: he was no more a warrior than Matariki was a priestess. Heritage was not enough. One grew into these roles. While Kupe's upbringing in the orphanage had incited his rage, it had not prepared him to shed blood.

Kupe's luck was good in regard to a clothesline. Men's clothing, and only men's clothing, was drying in the sun. Work pants, shirts, everything in one size. When evening finally descended and lamps were lit in the house, he cautiously approached the line. The garden seemed abandoned, but when he moved to reach for a shirt, a grim voice sounded through the twilight.

"Stay where you are, boy! And hands up, show me your hands, no war clubs."

Kupe startled. His *waihaka* did hang from his wrist, but he did not hold it at the ready. After all, he had not counted on a fight. His opponent seemed familiar with traditional Maori weapons and how quickly a practiced warrior could strike with war clubs. Kupe turned, hands up, in the direction of the voice.

"Good. Now, come into the light, so I can see whom I'm dealing with."

The voice came from a shed to the side of the house. A gun barrel glinted. Kupe hesitated.

"I wouldn't try my luck in your position."

Kupe stepped closer to the house until the light coming through the window from inside partly illuminated him. He hoped he looked at least a bit dangerous, but he had lost all his weapons except for a knife and his *waihaka*. For this man with his gun, Kupe made the perfect target. He surrendered.

"Don't shoot," he called. "I'm, I'm almost unarmed."

The man laughed and now stepped out of the shed. He wasn't young, and he was considerably shorter than Kupe; however, he looked stronger and surely capable of protecting himself. And then he spoke to Kupe in Maori.

"Who'd believe it, a warrior. If a lost one, where's your *taua*, young man? Your *iwi*?"

Unfortunately, Kupe understood the words for "regiment" and "tribe" but no more. He bit his lip. "Pardon me, sir," he said politely. "Could we, could we perhaps speak English?"

The man laughed even louder and lowered his weapon. "Well, aren't you a strange warrior? And here I was seriously worried you were the scout, and a whole *taua* of berserk Hauhau warriors was lying in wait in the woods."

Kupe thought about bluffing and claiming this was the situation, but there was no point.

"You are alone, right?" asked the man in a somewhat friendlier tone.

Kupe nodded.

"Well, then come on in. I'm sure you're hungry. Take some of the clothes if they're dry. If not, I have more inside. *Piu-piu* skirts are *tapu* in my house." Again he laughed.

A few months before, Kupe would have gotten angry if someone had compared his warrior's belt with a girl's dancing clothes, but now he didn't care. He seemed ridiculous to himself. The *pakeha* soldiers' uniforms were much more suitable for war than the Hauhau's near nakedness. And a gun was superior to any spear.

"Oh, my name is Sam, Sam Drechsler. No need to call me 'sir'; no one does."

Sam Drechsler let Kupe enter first, likely to eye him for hidden weapons. The door opened into a single room. Sam's cabin was solid but small. He and the yawning old dog were clearly the only occupants. A stew bubbled in a pot above the fire. In front of the fireplace, there was a rocking chair on a flax-fiber mat, Maori handwork.

"My wife weaved it," Sam said when he noticed Kupe staring at it. "Akona, a Hauraki."

The man had married a Maori? Kupe was surprised, and immediately he felt safe.

"Well, go ahead and change. I won't look. That thing you've got on doesn't hide much, anyway. You don't need to hide your knife. I noticed it a long time ago."

As if to show he did not fear Kupe, Sam turned to a shelf, taking down a jar of flour. He poured some of it into a bowl, added water, and prepared the dough for flatbread.

Kupe slipped into the clothes. A little big and unusual after the many months among the Hauhau, yet comforting and warm.

"Your wife passed?" he asked shyly.

Sam Drechsler shook his head.

"No," he said, chagrined, "she didn't want to leave the tribe. We were neighbors as it were, the tribe and I, when I came here to look for gold."

"There's no gold here," said Kupe without hesitation. The Hauhau would have known about gold veins. Kahu Heke was always in search of funding sources for his campaigns.

Sam laughed. "I know that now. But back then, nearly twenty years ago, I thought I'd be the second Gabriel Read."

Gabriel Read was a geologist, and it was he who had discovered the first goldfield near Dunedin two decades before, making a fortune.

Sam Drechsler took out a pan and prepared flatbread the Maori way. "Go ahead and take the pot off the fire. I hope you like mutton stew."

Kupe did as he was told.

"Well, instead of gold, I found Akona. She was a beauty. The tribe was friendly, took me along to hunt and fish—and Akona took me to her bed. When more whites came, I bought a few sheep and built this house. Things went well for us, Akona and me, and our son, Arama, or Adam. But then the wars started down in Waikato. Here, near Hamilton, there wasn't any real fighting, but there were strife and quarreling among the *pakeha* and Maori. Ultimately, the tribe moved away. Akona went with her people. She took Arama with her. It wasn't the wrong choice. If I think about it, he must have gone to school over there." Sam gestured with his chin in Hamilton's direction. He stirred the stew once more and filled Kupe's bowl. "Where they spit at every Maori." He sighed.

"Why didn't you go with them?" asked Kupe, taking a spoonful of stew, which tasted better than anything he'd ever eaten.

Sam shrugged. "They didn't want me," he said simply. "After ten years of good neighborliness and friendship. I'm not blaming the tribe. The *pakeha* started it. They stoked the hatred, and even the most dignified chieftain and the coolheaded elders lost their patience. It hit me. It always hits the wrong ones." He fell silent for a moment and blew his nose. "But now, what's your story, young man?" he asked. "And don't leave anything out."

Kupe looked at Sam's round face where a shaggy beard grew. His head was bald in some places, while in others hair grew abundantly. Most of all, his gaze was friendly and open.

Slowly Kupe ate the rest of his stew and then lowered his spoon. He told of the dispossession of his tribe and of the last few nightmarish months with the Hauhau.

"Kahu Heke called it a war," Kupe reported. "But you can't lead a war with thirty people."

"That's not even half a canoe," said Sam.

Kupe looked at him questioningly.

Sam rolled his eyes at needing to explain to Kupe some of the history of his own people. "*Waka taua*—a war canoe. About seventy warriors and their leader fit in each."

Kupe nodded, then continued with his story. "Kahu Heke hoped more warriors would join us if we had success, so he waged his 'war' only against the most helpless of opponents. We spent all winter moving up the coast, where there were old whaling stations and isolated farms. We attacked those." Kupe looked at the floor.

"You're not proud of it," Sam said.

Kupe shook his head. "Although usually not much happened. At least, not in the beginning. It was intimidation more than fighting. We would appear as if from nowhere. That's already enough for most *pakeha*. Then we ran around screaming and making faces and waving our weapons. Mostly people ran off and hid until we were done."

"Done with what?" inquired Sam, collecting the plates.

Kupe rubbed his nose. "Plundering and stealing," he said bitterly. "We took what we needed, and sometimes broke furniture or drove away livestock, but that was all."

"Ultimately, what the *pakeha* did to your villages," Sam said.

Kupe nodded. "That's how the *ariki* explained it also," he said. "That doesn't make it right. It's not even really *utu*."

"Well, thank God," remarked Sam. *Utu*—recompense—in its true sense of designated blood vengeance. "So, how did it end? Go on, tell me what happened."

"Well, mostly not much. But then, a few of the warriors were unhappy. Actually, we were all discontent. You see, we were always on the move, always hunting. No *marae*, no women, and it was winter. It was cold. For a few months, that sort of thing is fun, but then—"

"Maori tribes fight from late November until early April." Sam nodded. "Then they go home and tend to their fields. If there's trouble the next summer, they start all over. But mostly there isn't. Maori wars are short. That irritated the *pakeha* at first as well—and unfortunately gave them the impression the tribes were weak and gave up easily."

"Really?" asked Kupe. "How do you know all this?"

For Kupe, the usual strategy of the tribes was new. Kahu Heke had told his warriors of Te Kooti's sensational campaigns, but they had sounded more like fairy tales than history.

"I've been around a while, young man," said Sam. "I was in Wanganui in 1874, if that means anything to you."

"It's a city north of Wellington," Kupe said.

"Right, an important port and originally Maori land. At first, they bought out the tribes, but then they overreached, taking more and more land and exhausting the patience of the Maori people—until things escalated. The tribes resisted, and they ought to have driven the entire population of Wanganui into the sea, and Wellington along with it. They would have earned respect. But no, your people had a few warriors march up and wave spears around. They kicked the *pakeha* out of the territory taken from them, but then they went back to being nice. Typical Maori, and that's what the *pakeha* don't understand. They take goodness as foolishness. So, Wanganui belongs to the whites. There's a giant military base. The tribes have been vanquished. And that's how it always went at the beginning of the so-called Maori Wars—really until today. Whenever it got more serious, it was always because a chieftain was waging a private war."

"Like Te Kooti," said Kupe.

Sam nodded. "Or Hone Heke before him. Sometimes several ran amok at once, like with the Hauhau now. But it never was an all-encompassing movement of the people and never will be either. Bad for you all, good for the whites. But go on, what happened?"

"A few warriors were discontent," Kupe repeated. "They wanted to see blood. What's more, they really wanted . . . I think some people are simply brutal by nature."

Sam rolled his eyes. "I was a soldier once," he remarked as if that might explain some things. "So, you all killed a few people."

"Worse. They, they ate them," Kupe finally blurted out. "They cut off their heads. That's some kind of tradition. They're dried, but they didn't quite get it right. It was just horrible."

"And it called the militia to action," Sam said. "They couldn't let that continue. Where did they find you?"

Kupe began to shake. "Near our old camp by the mouth of the river. Kahu Heke didn't really want to go, but he had lost some *mana*. His daughter and then the *ariki* rejected the cutting off of heads and the eating of hearts. He was against cannibalism. But they did anyway. It—"

"The great chieftain's own campaign got out of hand," Sam said. "I think I remember that now too. In Hamilton, they were talking about punitive expeditions. A few constables had to go. Was that ever an outcry in the city, especially among the womenfolk—as if their men had a right to an easy, well-paying job for the rest of their lives. The men, on the other hand, were happy to get out. Since the Maori have kept the peace, they've been assigned to building bridges. They don't see that as a favor. So, they were enthusiastic about their victory."

"Victory?" asked Kupe. "There were thirty of us. There were maybe two hundred of them, militia and settlers. The people of the coast had joined together."

"The incident is hardly likely to go down in history as an example of the British Army's bravery. So, they crushed you. Are you the only one to escape?"

Kupe shook his head. "No. I, I don't believe in acquiring invincibility from the eating of body parts. I didn't take part in that. And when the shooting started, I ran away. Like many others. Kahu Heke escaped as well."

"The troublemakers always get away," Sam remarked.

"It was horrible to watch how our people fought. As if they really were invincible. They screamed and ran into the bullets. I shouldn't have ducked out. But it was so senseless."

"Most wars are." Sam Drechsler stood up and pulled a whiskey bottle from the cabinet. "Here, take a drink. And forget all that. It wouldn't have done any good to let yourself get shot. How many dead were there?"

"Three dead, and others wounded," said Kupe. "A few are gone, a few were taken prisoner. Kahu Heke wanted to rally us together again. But I've stayed away. I've had enough." He took a big gulp of whiskey and coughed.

Sam laughed. "Before you die, you need to learn to drink like a man," he said, and poured him another one.

Kupe grimaced. "In the orphanage, they told us we'd die from it."

Sam raised his hands in resignation. "You have to die from something, young man. But there's still time for you. And now, tell me about the girl. What was that about the chieftain's daughter who cost Kahu Heke his *mana*?"

***

"She didn't turn up here," Sam said after Kupe had told him about Matariki. "At least I haven't heard anything, but I don't often go into the city. Sometimes to Potter's whores, I'll admit; I'm only human. But he doesn't have any Maori girls."

"She's no whore!" Kupe became outraged. "She's—"

"Hey, here's someone deep in love," Sam teased. "Face the facts: a girl can't earn money in a backwater like Hamilton except in establishments like Potter's. If she came here without money and proper clothing, Potter's would be the first place I'd look."

"She wanted to go to the police to tell her story. She wanted to go home."

Sam shrugged. "Then she needed to go to the regiment commander. And maybe she did. Could be they put her in the next coach, and she's been with her family all this time. It is hard to imagine, but anything's possible. Kupe—or should I call you Kurt?—how about sticking around here a few days and working for me? I have to take the sheep up into the hills around the lake for the summer. I can do it with old Billy"—he pointed to the collie, who was already gray around the muzzle—"but a little help from younger legs wouldn't be bad."

The dog wagged his tail. Kupe thought of Dingo.

"I pay properly," said Sam. "I won't trick you. Once we've got the sheep safe and sound up there, I'll go with you to town. We'll go to the constables and ask about the girl. Maybe we'll learn something. How's that sound?"

"I'd rather just go," said Kupe.

Until then, he had not really worried about Matariki. She couldn't have gotten lost, and he assumed that she had found help in Hamilton. But after the way Sam depicted the town . . .

"I understand. And I won't keep you from going," said Sam, "but I'm warning you. They won't give you the time of day in town. And you need money. Have you given any thought at all to what you want to do in the future?"

Kupe shrugged. "Maybe go back to school. In the orphanage, they said that if someone studied medicine or law, he'd be a useful member of society. Even the Maori. I don't believe we could drive the *pakeha* into the sea with our *mere* and *kotiake*. But if we have lawyers who can draft and read and interpret treaties, maybe we can get paid for the land."

Sam smiled. "A clever thought. You've got brains, so use them now. Accept my offer. Then I'll put you on the next coach to Auckland with the money you've earned. There's a university. Come on, put 'er there." He held out his hand to Kupe.

Kupe grinned. "How many sheep?" he asked. "The first rule of treaties: always know exactly what it's about."

***

Sam Drechsler had about two hundred sheep, and it took three days to drive them into the hilly areas around Mount Pirongia. Kupe had to do it by foot. He had never ridden before, and Sam only owned one mule, anyway. The young warrior was well trained. It was nothing to him to run for many hours of the day, and soon he discovered that working with the dog and the sheep was fun. He enjoyed hiking over the hillsides and the stillness interrupted only by the bleating of sheep and the dog barking.

Kupe could hear his own thoughts again after a long time. He even felt closer to his old tribe, the traditions of his people. Kahu Heke had taught him battle and the alertness of the warrior. Sam sharpened his senses for different things. He showed him plants from which the Maori *tohunga* made medicine, pointed out places to him that really had been *tapu* for hundreds of years, and gave him time to sit and feel the spirits. Sometimes, when the wind rustled the leaves or a lively brook babbled like a happy child, he felt as if nature were speaking to him.

Sam laughed when Kupe admitted that to him. "That would have brought you a lot of *mana*. The tribes appreciate people who become one with Tane or Papa. Tane is the god of the forest, you know. He is very wise. Look at this tree: a horoeka. It lives the life of a warrior. In its first years, it looks like a thin spear, and its branches are like lances. Later, it gets wider and more peaceful, and it sprouts leaves like a normal tree. It grows big and strong, gains *mana* like the eldest in the tribes, and sends out its fruits to grow to be warriors again."

Kupe laughed. "And over it, the kauri grows like a god. What did you say, how tall is the Tane Mahuta?"

The Tane Mahuta, named for the forest god, stood in Waipoua in the north. To the Maori, it was sacred. It even astonished the *pakeha* as one of the tallest and oldest trees in Aotearoa, if not the whole world.

"More than a hundred fifty feet," Sam exclaimed. "I'd like to see it once. I don't know how it is for you, but I feel very small underneath kauri like that. And very young. Some of them saw the first Maori canoes come, then the whites. Perhaps they'll still be here when we're all washed away."

Sam looked up to the mountains. To Kupe, he seemed more melancholic here, in the wilderness. Kupe could imagine why. He had probably driven his sheep up here with Akona and Arama, and listened as his wife told their son these same stories.

"You need to know your stories, young man, your roots. Only that way will you find your way back to your people. Listen to the sagas of your people. Learn your language. Akona always told Arama that his ancestors were the stars watching over him."

Kupe thought of Matariki—the child of the stars.

"We should get going," Kupe said. "I'd like to get to Hamilton."

***

As soon as Sam's mule pulled their small cart into Hamilton, it became clear to Kupe that he had been smart to listen to the old man and not to venture into town alone. Even with Sam, people stared at Kupe and cursed at him. There was no police station—apparently, in Hamilton a person only found an officer when he knew where to find one.

Sam steered them toward the nearly finished bridge over the Waikato River. Construction would have gone more quickly if the men worked harder, but it was clear that they considered the work beneath them. They almost all wore uniforms of the Armed Constabulary. Their leader, a young captain, was exceedingly happy to interrupt the work to talk with Sam when he asked about Matariki.

"A Maori girl? Here? No, I'm sorry, none reported to me. Yet you say she would have had information? About the Hauhau? Well, if she wanted to talk, they probably caught and ate her." He laughed.

Kupe shook his head reluctantly. "They wouldn't have killed a chieftain's daughter. She was *tapu*. They—"

The captain looked at him skeptically, and Sam urged him to silence by shaking his head. It did not bear considering what would happen if Kupe said he had also been with the Hauhau.

"The girl is a daughter of Kahu Heke," Sam informed the captain. "So, high-ranking and important enough to the devil that he kidnapped her from the South Island and dragged her here. He wouldn't just kill her."

The captain shrugged. "Who knows what goes through their heads? Maybe she died in the wilderness. Or is hiding out with some tribe. There are still plenty in Waikato. I'm sorry I can't help, but she's not here." With that, he turned back to the bridge.

Sam directed Kupe to climb into the cart. "Is that possible, what he said?" he inquired, directing the mule toward Victoria Street.

Kupe shook his head. "Unlikely. I mean, I didn't know her all that well. But she said she had spent a lot of time with the Ngai Tahu. They would surely have taught her to run a few miles along a riverbank without drowning, starving, or any of that. She spoke perfect Maori."

"So, a tribe's not out of the question."

"Stop, Sam. That dog there."

Kupe pointed excitedly at a scrawny mutt, which the butcher was just kicking away from his doorway.

"Dingo!" Kupe called to the dog.

The dog looked up, wagged his tail, and raced over to Kupe as he exited the cart. Howling and barking, he greeted the young Maori. Kupe hugged him, almost equally excited.

"This is her dog, Sam. She must be here."

Sam furrowed his brow. "Well, if that mutt's got an owner, she doesn't take great care of it. Not exactly like a girl to let the fur mat like that. And look at how scrawny it is."

Dingo licked Kupe's hand euphorically. Undoubtedly, he recalled that Kupe had cooked in the camp.

"But it's him, Sam. I'm sure. And he recognized me too."

Kupe stroked Dingo and looked around. Surely the dog would never have gotten too far from his mistress. Kupe was certain that Matariki would step out any moment from one of the house or shop doors.

"Perhaps she left him here," said Sam. "Or something did happen to her, and he strayed to here."

"She never would have left him," explained Kupe, "and I don't think he would leave her either. She must be here, Sam. We need to search."

Unfortunately, Dingo did not demonstrate much skill at tracking. Though he wagged his tail happily when Kupe said Matariki's name to him, he did not lead Kupe to her.

"Let's buy the mutt something to eat," Sam determined. "And then we'll ask around. Don't get your hopes up. A Maori girl would stick out here like a sore thumb. So if no one knows anything . . ."

The first woman Sam asked gave them information. "I don't know any Mata-whatever, but the McConnells who own that store, they have a Martha. A little hussy, that girl. They always have to keep an eye on her so she doesn't clear out the register. But they see it as their Christian duty."

Kupe was immediately agitated when he heard the name. "That's her. Martha is her *pakeha* name, but what could she be doing?"

Sam shrugged. "Working, if I understood her right, as a maid."

"This many months?" yelled Kupe. "It can hardly take that long to earn enough for passage to the South Island. Something isn't right here, Sam."

"Now, calm yourself a moment." Sam held him back. "We'll both go in there now and ask about the girl. If you show that kind of anger, it'll only bring trouble. Stay calm, and follow me."

"Martha?" Archibald McConnell was visibly surprised. "What do you want with her?"

Sam raised his eyebrows. "To pay her a visit. The young man is a friend of hers." He gestured to Kupe.

Archibald shook his head, his lips tightened. "I'm sorry, but we can't allow that. We're trying to keep Martha away from all bad influences. Especially from people like him."

"How do you know I'm a bad influence?" Kupe asked.

Sam was more direct. "What does it matter to you with whom your employee speaks? Matariki is your maid, isn't she? She's not your property."

Mr. McConnell was visibly nervous. "You're quite right. She's our maid," he finally answered, "and she's working now. So, leave us in peace. God knows she doesn't work hard enough for us to let her off in the middle of the day."

Sam raised his hands calmly. "No problem, then we'll just wait until she's free. How long do you make the girl work? Until sundown? That's just a few more hours."

With that, he tipped his hat and walked outside. Kupe followed him.

"I don't want to see you here again," McConnell yelled after the Maori.

"Looks like your nose led you right, Kupe," Sam said. "Something's rotten here. We should have left the sheep to themselves and come here sooner. But there's nothing for it. They can't lock the girl up, and she must be healthy or she couldn't work. So, let's just wait and see."

Sam treated himself to a cigar at the local import store and bought two pastries for himself and Kupe, along with a growler of beer from the nearest pub.

"You need to relax," he said, handing Kupe the jug. "Here, drink; it'll calm you down. She's not going to run away from you again. In a few hours, you'll be holding her in your arms. So, start thinking about whether you're going to kiss her or exchange *hongi*."

Kupe blushed as Sam had intended and then, somewhat embarrassed, told Sam about their first kiss. "But it's true, Maori don't kiss. Why did she let me kiss her?"

Sam listened, amused, as Kupe considered whether he had really kissed Matariki or maybe Martha. Whether she really liked him or if she had only wanted him to help her escape. Whether she perhaps did not want to see him at all.

"It could be she told that man to get rid of me. Maybe she's had enough of the Maori for good and—"

Sam slapped his forehead. "We'll know soon enough, Kupe. The sun's going down. And if I haven't missed my guess, those charming McConnells are about to close up their shop. But not before I've spoken with them again."

Kupe stayed with Dingo in the cart while Sam went to the shop door. Mrs. McConnell threw herself against the door to try to keep him out, but Sam pushed it open.

"Under no circumstances will we allow you to see Martha," she said sharply. "The girl can't come and go here as she pleases. She abused that privilege. Martha owes us money, Mr. Drechsler. We clothed her and fed her, and as thanks, she tried to rob us."

Sam scratched his head. He had taken his hat off and now, like a well-mannered supplicant, he held it in his left hand in front of his body.

"You sure must have dolled up the girl if she's been working this long for a few duds. And the money she robbed, did she spend it before the police caught her? Wouldn't she be in jail, then?"

"It's our Christian duty—," began Mr. McConnell.

His wife held up her hand to silence him. "Martha is still very young," she explained. "That's why we decided to give her a second chance, though under close supervision. She did break out of an orphanage, didn't she? Or was it from a reformatory?"

Sam put on a friendly smile, but rage flickered in his eyes. "I'm afraid that's where you're wrong, Mrs. McConnell," he said with the sweetest voice he could muster. "Matariki Drury was abducted from Otago Girls' High School in Dunedin. She's a chieftain's daughter—and what we *pakeha* might call a sheep baroness."

***

After Sam had disappeared into the McConnells' store, Dingo got increasingly agitated. Kupe held the dog firmly between his legs, so he wouldn't get away, but Dingo was whining and trying to break free. Eventually, Dingo became so angry that Kupe let him go. Dingo bolted around the row of houses. Kupe took off after him.

The houses on Victoria Street stood tightly side by side. Kupe and Dingo had to round a whole block before they reached the back of the houses. Most of the houses had gardens or backyards; a few were delimited by low barriers, others with high picket fences. Dingo aimed at one of the latter and left Kupe behind when he disappeared through a hole under the fence. Kupe looked at the fence more closely. It seemed likely that the yard behind it belonged to the McConnells. And he was sure Matariki was in their house. Kupe did not think long. He reached for his war club and struck the fence hard. The already somewhat rotten wood gave way immediately. After the second swing, the hole was big enough to allow Kupe through.

Kupe heard the same enthusiastic yipping with which the dog had greeted him earlier. And then a girl's voice calming him, praising him, sweet-talking him. Kupe ran after the voice.

"Matariki!" He was close to bursting into tears when he saw her face gleaming in the last light of day behind the barred window. "Matariki, I'll get you out."

***

Kupe quickly found an iron pipe, and with one powerful movement, levered the bars out of the window.

"Will you fit through?" he asked.

Matariki was already pulling herself through the window. "Like a warrior between a chieftain's daughter's feet. How did that go again? It removes compunction about killing and makes you invulnerable? I've been dreaming of it a long time."

Kupe took her arm and pulled her the rest of the way. Only Matariki's hips stuck for a moment. She was no longer as slender and childlike as she had been a year before.

Kupe stood dumbfounded by the transformation of his little friend to a young woman. He thought his heart would burst with happiness when she suddenly hugged him.

175

"I'm so happy you're alive," Matariki whispered. "I was so afraid for you. And I never thought that you'd come looking for me." Matariki laughed. "Listen, I've thought through just about everything in all this time, but a tattooed fairy-tale prince—I didn't think of that." She ran her finger gently over his *moko*.

Kupe smiled. "You're very *pakeha*," he replied hesitantly.

Matariki shook her head. "No. I'm Maori. I wasn't before, but I am now. And I'll never be anything else. Now, how do we get out of here?"

Kupe led Matariki to the hole in the fence while Dingo jumped on her, full of excitement.

"Do you want to take off or kill these McConnells?" he asked.

Matariki looked up at her massive defender. Kupe, too, had changed in the last few months. A grown warrior stood in front of her.

"The latter," she decided. "My mother has a *mere* of pounamu jade. I believe, I believe she killed someone with it."

With a shrug, Kupe handed her his *waihaka*. "Dog leather, you know," he said apologetically.

"That dog," Matariki exclaimed, "will take revenge for Dingo."

Kupe forced open the door to the shop once they had rounded the block.

Mr. McConnell, full of hate, looked at him. "You—"

"He's allowed to be here. I invited him," Matariki interrupted. "He's a Hauhau warrior, you know. And I've asked him to enforce all the *tapu* you've violated. The spirits, Mrs. and Mr. McConnell, you see, are quite angry."

Matariki went into the shop, let her eyes glide over the shelves, and swept all the pots and all the earthenware for sale to the ground.

"I touched all of that, Mrs. McConnell, and moreover, as a chieftain's daughter, cursed it. Everything's very *tapu*. Be happy I'm freeing you of it."

With her next swing of the *waihaka*, she knocked a few bottles from the shelf, and they smashed on the ground. Matariki cast a wrathful glance at them and then at the used clothing in the next corner. "Those actually need to be burned," she remarked.

"No." Mrs. McConnell's voice sounded choked. She and her husband seemed completely demoralized. Sam Drechsler's words had already made them fearful enough—war clubs and raging spirits did the rest. It was one thing to lock up an anonymous Maori girl, but a sheep baroness from the South Island? And now worse seemed to be coming.

176

"Here, however, it's not so bad," Matariki said calmly. "Here, I didn't touch that much. You're in luck, Mr. McConnell." She strolled through the store, taking up an ax. "But in the house, there I toiled away."

Matariki kicked open the door to the living quarters. Kupe followed her like a colossal angel of vengeance. Sam vacillated between amusement and concern.

"The furniture here—I had to polish that, an unbelievable *tapu*. Kupe, would you be so nice as to sacrifice it to the gods with me?"

Matariki assumed a pose and with all her might roared out a curse. Had she really not believed she could let out the *karanga* a year ago? Now she could. She raised the ax and let it fall on Mrs. McConnell's carefully preserved buffet. Then she gave the tool to Kupe.

"Would you please complete the work of the spirits for me? It's time a proper sacred fire was lit in the fireplace." She laughed as she swept Mrs. McConnell's beloved tea service onto the ground with one swing of the war club. "I occasionally drank from it," she said apologetically, "when you weren't looking, Mrs. McConnell. I shouldn't have done that, only—now it's *tapu*. But don't you worry. Once we throw everything into the sacred fire, it won't bring nearly as much bad fortune. And now—"

Sam shook his head. "That's enough now, Matariki," he said amicably but firmly. "I think the spirits are quite satisfied. If these people pay you your wages, I believe you'll be done, won't you?"

"Her wages?" screamed Mrs. McConnell.

Kupe raised the ax, and Mr. McConnell retreated in horror.

"No, leave it," Matariki said, trying for the broad, ponderous tone of a priestess. "These two are *toenga kainga*."

With that, she turned away.

Kupe looked at her reverently. *"Tapu?"* he asked, confused.

Sam Drechsler struggled not to laugh. "In a certain sense," he said. "And now, let's go. I hope there's still a coach for Auckland. Mr. McConnell, would you now please pay Miss Drury. We really must leave."

Matariki could hardly comprehend her luck. In all seriousness, she held ten pounds in her hand as she left the McConnells' house. Beyond that, Sam Drechsler had discovered the chieftain's cloak in the shop and immediately reclaimed it.

"Tapu?" grumbled Archibald.

Matariki smiled gently. "Very, very *tapu*," she replied, and allowed Sam to wrap the cloak around her shoulders. In the manner of a true princess, she left the shop with her head held high.

Sam couldn't stop laughing when she boarded the mule cart with just as much grace. "Hopefully there really is a coach now. Otherwise, tomorrow they'll get the idea of suing us," he said. "But my compliments, little lady. You've got *mana* enough for three. Someday you'll be *ariki*."

That was not out of the question. There certainly were female chieftains of other tribes.

"What did you say to them?" asked Kupe. "That was a curse, wasn't it? You set the spirits of the ancestors on their heels, right?"

Matariki shook her head. Now, she had to laugh.

Sam launched into an explanation. "*Toenga kainga* is more of a curse word. Or an assertion. It's a traditional way of telling someone what you think of them."

"What does it mean?" Kupe asked impatiently.

Matariki giggled. "You're not worth eating."

She wondered why Kupe did not find the saying funny.

Chapter 7

The train ride to the west coast was a nightmare. Jim Paisley dealt roughly with Violet, threatening her until she had to give up half of her money. The other half was still hidden, fixed with a safety pin to Rosie's undershirt. Jim remained sober in Christchurch long enough to find a cheap hotel. Probably he did not want to risk losing the girls and the luggage again.

"Make yourselves comfortable. We're going to go see about the rest of the trip," he said after depositing the girls and the bags in the sleazy room. Rosie stared ahead of her as fixedly as she had on board the ship.

Violet was not surprised when her father locked them in the hotel room. She had never managed to fool him, and she was sure he sensed there was more money. Until then, Violet had never planned an escape. If she had been alone, she would have gathered all her courage and made an escape plan. With Rosie, however, it was hopeless.

***

Naturally, her father and the boys had spent most of the money by the time they came back that night. In the pubs, the men had hardly received encouragement that they could easily get to the west coast on foot and without money.

"Make sure you go with someone," a farmer from the plains advised. "I'm driving to Darfield, and I have space in my wagon, but how you'd make it farther is a question of luck."

The next day, the man had departed long before Jim and the boys got out of bed. However, they soon found a wood trader bound for Springfield; he offered to take them along if they helped him unload his wagon.

The wood trader was surprised when along with Jim, Fred, and Eric, the two girls climbed into his open wagon. There were no seats except on the box. The other riders had to arrange themselves around the load, and Violet and Rosie froze half to death even though they were huddled up in Kathleen's blankets.

"Just wait until we get to the mountains," the driver said when they stopped for a rest. He lit a fire and was making tea. Clearly, he felt sorry for the girls. "In truth, it's madness to travel now, in the winter," he said to Jim. "Why don't you look for some kind of work in the plains and go to Westport in the spring?"

Violet wondered what sort of work there was in the area. They had yet to see villages or even houses. The Canterbury Plains seemed to consist solely of grassland, interrupted now and again by a copse of trees or a lake, and as they got closer to the mountains, there were boulders strewn here and there. It was similar to Wales: grass, sheep, hills, and mountains. Even Treherbert was nothing more than a great sheep pasture before the coal mining began, but in Wales, everything was contained and fenced in, and you knew which land belonged to whom. Here, there were no fences—just land and more land, over which the wind whipped the rain and which seemed contained only by the mountains that jutted up somewhere in the fog.

"I, for one, could use some help," said the wood trader as if he had heard Violet's unspoken question. "There's a lot of building along the future train tracks. My business is going well; a few extra hardworking hands would be more than welcome."

Jim Paisley and the boys murmured something incomprehensible. It was clear to Violet that they had fixed the coal-mining towns in their heads and did not want to deviate from their plan. Plus, miners were paid better than construction workers.

It didn't matter anyway. When he saw Jim, Fred, and Eric's "hardworking hands" in action, the wood trader reconsidered his offer. The three men were lazy, clearly more committed to the bottle than work. Springfield did not have a bar, so Fred acquired a bottle of whiskey at the local grocer's, and the bottle emptied more quickly than the wagon. Another circumstance arose that only encouraged the men to stop working completely.

A few hours before the wood trader's heavy rig, a wagon of coal miners had arrived, bound for Greymouth. Joshua Biller, owner of the Biller mine in Greymouth, had hired the men in Lyttelton, which was the port for Christchurch and closer to the coal-mining locations than the Dunedin port. Still, few men took the arduous road over the mountains. Most of them sought work in Christchurch or the plains first—only adventurers made it to Greymouth on the west coast. Biller intended to change that and all summer had offered transportation. In the winter, there were fewer wagons, and though this one was already full, the driver knew the mine could not pass up three strong men like Jim, Fred, and Eric.

"Everybody squeeze in," he ordered the men already in the wagon, and then waved the Paisleys to get inside.

Jim and the boys jumped in without a care that the wood trader's wagon was only half-unloaded.

"Please excuse my father, sir," Violet said. "I can offer you a bit of money for the ride."

"Oh, it's all right, girl. Hold on to your money. Your men won't earn much, not here and not in Greymouth. I'm already sorry for the foreman who has to deal with them. But for you, this wagon is a blessing. Alone with those three do-nothings, the little one might have frozen in the mountains." He pointed to Rosie. "You'll need provisions, though."

Violet looked over at the store. Should she run over and buy something with the money she had worked so hard to hide? Violet was torn. At that moment, the wood trader's wife came running up and pressed a packet into Rosie's hand.

"Here, I just baked some bread. I cut a few pieces for you, for the trip."

Rosie looked at the woman like she was Santa Claus. Violet thanked her. She was ashamed of her father and of having to start off in this new country as a beggar.

She pushed Rosie into the wagon and saw the next danger. Aside from an old, careworn woman in the front, only men were on board. And most of them were young men who began immediately to look Violet over and then make crude comments.

For Violet, it was an early sign of what Reverend Burton had warned her about on the west coast: "There are practically no women there, so watch out, especially at night. Stay home. Don't let anyone convince you to a rendezvous.

I know about it from the goldfields: a girl is lured into the wilderness, and then six men attack her."

Violet sat beside Rosie, and the sisters ate the bread ravenously. Violet did think about saving some, but then she would have had to share it. It was better to eat while the three men were still full of whiskey. As they ate, they looked out at the landscape, which grew increasingly bizarre and beautiful and frightening. They went up into the mountains through beech forests in Arthur's Pass. The rain turned to snow, and Violet and Rosie looked with fascination at the trees, seemingly dusted with rock sugar, and at the partially frozen ponds and streams. The higher they went, the worse the road became. At times, the passengers had to get out because the road was too icy for the horses to pull a fully loaded wagon.

So far, though, the other travelers were still in good spirits. They were strong, young men, and Jim Paisley was not the only one who had stocked up on whiskey. Violet, who had carried Rosie over the worst stretches of road, was exhausted by the first evening. They weren't prepared for the weather either. It was too cold for their clothing, and neither of the girls had shoes that kept their feet warm and dry.

Violet was relieved when they reached that day's destination, a primitive hut in the woods even though there was hardly space for the twenty-seven men and three women. The husband of the older woman insisted on his wife's sleeping close to the fireplace. Violet's own shy request that she and Rosie join the woman was met with lude responses from the men about how they would keep her warm.

Violet and Rosie fled to the stables, where they found the driver, who had made himself comfortable near his horses. Violet wanted to turn around and leave; one man could be more dangerous than a whole group. The middle-aged driver pointed to a corner covered with straw, near where he had lit a small fire.

"Go ahead and lie down there; I won't touch you," he said. "Got a girl in Greymouth."

Violet wrapped herself and Rosie in their blankets. The man slid a cup of coffee in her direction.

"They say there aren't many girls in Greymouth," she said shyly.

The man nodded. "Another reason I'd better stay true to Molly," he said.

Violet sipped her coffee and discovered with horror that it was laced with whiskey.

"Warms you up," said the driver, "but no worries, I'm not getting drunk. Have to keep an eye on the fire. It's dangerous here in the stables. I just don't want to freeze to death, or stink to death." He gestured with a crooked smile toward the hut.

Violet smiled. The stench of the men in the hut had made it hard for her to breathe.

"What is Greymouth like?"

The driver shrugged. "It's a town. Three mines, a pub, lots of filth."

Violet hadn't expected anything different. Snuggled against Rosie, she finally fell asleep. The driver had told her the truth: the whiskey warmed her, and he did not come too close.

***

The horses' warm bodies weren't enough to stave off the icy cold, and Violet woke early. The driver had let the fire go out during the night—otherwise he would hardly have dared fall asleep. Violet tried unsuccessfully to relight it. Rosie was awake, crying because of the cold.

"It's better than her sleeping," the driver informed her. "Before you freeze to death, you fall asleep."

Shocked, Violet determined to keep Rosie awake no matter what. She also forced her to drink the bitter coffee the driver brewed, for which he sought milk and sugar in his bags.

"I prefer it black," he said, "but this is for the little one."

Violet stirred in as much sugar as possible into her coffee—she had once heard it kept you warm.

In the meantime, the men were stirring.

Violet looked fearfully in the direction of the connecting door, and Rosie was almost in a panic. The driver figured they did not want to go inside and ask for breakfast. He shared his bread and cheese with the girls.

"I have enough," he said when Violet thanked him profusely. "And you two'll ride with me on the box. At least no one will paw you there, pretty one that you are."

Violet blushed. So, he had gotten a look at her.

***

Despite their new privileges, the two days of the journey were difficult. In the beginning, things were passable: the foothills, in which the beech forests slowly gave way to snow-covered rocks and scree, looked almost as beautiful as in a fairy tale. The gray-green birds with crooked beaks impertinently rocking on the tree branches and seemingly cursing at the travelers amused Rosie. A few landed on the wagon or the horses' harnesses, and the driver shooed them away when they tried to peck at the horses' backs.

Violet could hardly believe her eyes. "They, they look like parrots."

The driver grinned. "Keas," he said, "rude little bastards. Watch this."

He wrestled a bag out from under the seat and stuck a piece of bread inside. Then he tied the bag to the whip's mount. Violet and Rosie watched as two birds lunged at it, working at the tie with their crooked beaks. Finally, one of them slipped the strap over its head, pushed open the bag, and fished for the bread. As the keas fought over the hunk, they fell from the box and had to fly, losing the bread. Their screeches sounded as if they were blaming each other for the disaster.

Rosie laughed.

"Don't parrots normally live where it's warm?" asked Violet.

The driver shrugged. "Nothing's normal in New Zealand," he said.

By midday, the heavily laden wagon struggled up increasingly steep paths. Once again, the travelers had to get out, and now there was an added danger of slipping and falling into the chasms, which gaped to the left and right of the road. Bridges led over immense ravines.

When all the passengers were allowed in the wagon again, Violet asked, "Are they all miners from Britain? I mean, do they come from mining towns?"

The driver, who had finally introduced himself as Bob, made a face and shrugged. "So they say. I'm supposed to hire strong-looking fellows. With experience if possible. But if they don't have it, they'll get it in the Biller mine. I always look to see who doesn't seem scared. And it seems to work. I've been doing the job a year already."

Jim and Fred Paisley naturally met the requirements. Eric Fence probably lacked the imagination to be scared. The three bragged about their experiences underground and so made friends and gained admirers among the novices. The old miners rolled their eyes.

The trip was torturously slow. Violet would freeze to death on the wagon box, only to pour sweat when she had to trudge through the snow. Bob let

Rosie stay in the wagon when all the other passengers got out; she did not weigh much, after all. Around midday, she fell asleep, which set Violet in a panic. They rested for a while on a mountaintop, which Violet imagined would have offered a breathtaking view of the peaks all around if not for the snowstorm.

"It's better in the summer," said Bob.

Violet slid from panic to lethargy. Nothing mattered. She no longer had any objection to the whiskey in the coffee. With a guilty conscience, she forced the drink on Rosie too.

"Arthur's Pass," Bob finally said, leading his team along a particularly dangerous series of bridges and narrow paths, which mostly fell off sharply to the left and right.

"From here on, it's downhill."

"So that was the worst of it?" asked Violet hopefully.

Bob shrugged once again. "Depends on what you mean."

Indeed, the descent did not exactly prove easy. The passengers often needed to get out, now so the heavy wagon did not slide into the drawbar and make the horses stumble. Inching downhill through the snow was almost as arduous as trudging uphill. But, at the end of the day, a proper inn greeted them. In Jacksons, a tiny mountain village, the travelers could rent rooms or sleep in shared lodgings. For Jim and his entourage, though, there was only enough money for a beer before bed. Then they holed up in the stables. The innkeeper only permitted it because Bob assured him he would tend the fire.

Bob looked after Violet and Rosie again. They slept deeply and soundly under Kathleen's blankets. When they awoke, it was raining. It rained while they ate breakfast and hitched the horses, and it rained as they continued downhill.

"It's always raining here," said Bob when, after hours had passed, Violet asked when it might stop. "In Greymouth too."

Violet wondered if from now on she would only see the world through a curtain of rain.

The landscape grew wooded again. They drove through thick mixed forest, past streams and gorges. By the afternoon, all their blankets and clothing were soaked, and Violet longed for a dry place, even if it was cold like the stables in the mountains. It would not be granted to her quickly, however. It was evening by the time they reached Greymouth.

***

Violet had expected a town like Treherbert—sad, boring, but a proper town, at least. But Greymouth looked like a coastal village at first glance. Though the rain muted everything to grayscale, the town lay between the sea and a river whose mouth, she later learned, gave Greymouth its name. Violet had never heard of coal-mining towns on the sea before, but as Bob had said, everything in New Zealand seemed to be different. Most of all, everything in Greymouth seemed still to be under construction. On the main street, there were only a few buildings, one of which housed the pub. Violet didn't see any inns.

"They're building a few hotels," said Bob when she asked. "On the coast. They're going to be gorgeous but much too expensive for you, girl."

Violet saw no hope of a dry shelter if the Biller mine did not assign them a miners' lodge first thing. Bob looked at her quizzically when she asked about one.

"What kind of a lodge? Housing for the miners? First I've heard of it."

Violet stared at him. "Then where are we supposed to live?" she asked. "If there are no inns and no houses?"

"The miners build something for themselves," said Bob.

Bob had been instructed to take the men directly to the Biller mine—not that they might instead hire on at the national mine, which offered the best safety precautions but the worst pay, or with Marvin Lambert, who had just opened his second private mine next to Biller's. Marvin Lambert gladly lured away Biller's best people after it had become clear who was really useful for the mine.

In that respect, Biller had to rely on the men immediately signing a contract—and the path to the mine led straight through the workers' lodgings. Violet was horrified. No one thought of a master plan, of streets or drainage. Men built their huts where they pleased and with whatever materials were at hand.

There were cabins, but most of the lodgings were rather shacks made of waste wood or barked timber that had been taken home from the mine. Some men simply slept under oil-soaked tarpaulins. Violet was certain no structure contained more than one room, and in spite of the rain, the cooking fires burned outside. Inside, then, there were no fireplaces, or at least no chimneys. The air was stuffy; it smelled of smoke and excrement—presumably there were no proper toilets either, private or public.

Tears filled Violet's eyes. It must be awful to live in these huts—but it was still more awful to have no shelter. That was precisely how things looked for her, at first in any case. Her father, Fred, and Eric wouldn't build a hut that night.

The three of them would disappear into the pub and surely find someplace to sleep there too. And they would forget her and Rosie.

She remained seated in the wagon as if in a trance while Bob steered his male passengers into a newly built office next to the conveyors. The mine looked like the one in Treherbert: simple buildings, a tower, storehouses. And, here, everything was behind a curtain of rain. Violet looked at the older woman in the wagon and hoped she might know of a solution, at least for the coming night. But the woman, who had seemed imperturbable until now, had completely broken down crying at the sight of the settlement. Violet turned away.

In the meantime, the men came back from the office, all of them in high spirits and with a small advance. They would have the next day off, Fred and Jim said, overjoyed.

"We're going to build a house here," Violet's father boasted when Violet asked where they were supposed to live. "The mine offers wood to use. This Biller fellow is unbelievably generous. Should we drink a glass to him first, boys?"

Violet herself found no reason to toast the mine owner. Even if the workers did not have to steal the wood for their huts, they were miners, not builders. Violet blanched at the thought of the "house" Jim would build.

"Well, to the pub?" asked Bob. The men shouted their agreement. Bob looked at Violet and Rosie sympathetically.

Violet marveled that her tears did not come as the wagon rolled through the mine workers' slums. Violet felt only rage—wild, impotent rage.

Chapter 8

There was a mail carriage bound for Auckland, and the driver was willing to take the two Maori and the dog along with him.

Matariki giggled as Kupe lifted Dingo inside. She had rediscovered her positive attitude. "I'm so happy we made it out. I thought for sure I would have to work for the McConnells until I was old and gray. And in this awful town. Hopefully Auckland is better."

Even in Auckland—a burgeoning city with paved streets, wide sidewalks, and stone buildings—people looked at Kupe and Matariki with curiosity. Matariki's ragged, ill-fitting dress and her chieftain's cloak drew attention.

"First to the telegraph office, then to the store," Matariki said, steering Kupe down Queen Street.

Auckland reminded her of Dunedin, though it was more colorful, younger, and less structured. That was no wonder. Dunedin was planned by members of the Free Church of Scotland on a drawing table, while Auckland grew organically with the importance of the port for trade and immigration. Matariki was already looking forward to a shopping trip.

The men in the telegram office were reserved toward Kupe but were friendly toward Matariki. The girl blushed at the compliments that people gave her and their flirtatious jokes and comments. Kupe, on the other hand, looked sullen. He would have liked to defend Matariki but now had to admit that she knew her way around city life better than he did.

"We'll send two telegrams," she said. "It's not that expensive. One to my parents and one to Reverend Burton. The Burtons live in Dunedin, so they'll receive it right away. We'll come back for his response. For now, I need new clothing as soon as possible."

"It would be better to save the money," Kupe said. "We need to sleep somewhere."

"And we can with my pay. There'll be enough." Matariki wasn't worried. "What do you bet we are wired more money tonight? And if not"—she smiled in the direction of the telegraph office employees—"these good men will know of an affordable inn for us."

The employees had two or three suggestions ready, although they did hedge. "Are you thinking of a shared room? Or, two rooms in a respectable establishment?"

"Do we not look like respectable people?" she asked, which made Kupe blush.

Kupe had learned in the orphanage that respectable people did not wear old clothing that did not fit them and did not walk around as a couple unless they were married. Plus, he and Matariki and Dingo all needed a bath.

"There's an inn for women a few streets from here," one of the men said. "Maybe—"

"That sounds acceptable. But for now, we're going shopping. Let's go, Kupe, Dingo."

Matariki wanted to find a ladies' shop like the Gold Mine Boutique, but Kupe pulled her into a general store. Kupe found pants and shirts that fit him, and Matariki insisted he also purchase a leather jacket and a hat.

"And now you need a barber," she said. "That hair has to go."

Kupe looked at her, horrified. It had taken a long time for his hair to grow long enough to tie into a traditional warrior knot, and now his *tikitiki* was his pride and joy.

Matariki rolled her eyes. "Kupe, you can't run around like that here. The people get scared. You—"

"You're the one who said you're Maori," Kupe blurted out, "but now you're behaving like a *pakeha*."

Matariki bit her lip. She had not thought much about it herself, but Kupe was right. When she was imprisoned in Hamilton, she had sworn to be Maori from now on, one with her people, with all the advantages and disadvantages of that oath. Yet now she was slipping back into the role of a *pakeha* schoolgirl, as soon as a few *pakeha* were nice to her?

She sighed. "Fine, leave your hair long. But I wouldn't necessarily tie it up if you're not on your way to battle, agreed?"

Kupe nodded halfheartedly.

Matariki disappeared into the women's clothing area of the small store. When she approached him a while later in a new dress, his eyes beamed. It was a simple linen dress, brown with light-gold threads. The color emphasized Matariki's natural, warm complexion—even though it was now a bit pale from being locked up so long—and her golden-brown eyes. The dress had a long row of ivory-colored buttons as fasteners and black embroidery. The corset emphasized Matariki's already narrow waist. Ivory gloves concealed her fingers, chapped from the soapsuds during scrubbing. A cream-colored little hat sat atop her thick black hair.

"I know it's *pakeha*," Matariki apologized, "but—"

"It's beautiful," Kupe said hoarsely. "You're beautiful. You couldn't wear a *piu* anymore; otherwise, well, I couldn't even look at you without—" He broke off, embarrassed.

Matariki smiled. "Now, that would be very *pakeha*, Kupe. You need to work on that. A Maori can look at half-naked women without immediately getting stupid ideas in his head."

***

When they returned to the telegraph office, Reverend Burton's answer was already there: *Matariki, stay where you are. Parents being informed. Money at Bank of New Zealand, Queen Street.*

When they entered the luxurious bank building, they were treated in the friendliest manner and furnished with a sizeable amount of money.

"Where is all that from?" Kupe asked, staring at the pound notes in her hand. "Are they lending you that, or what?"

Matariki smiled, somewhat embarrassed. "Money transfer," she replied, "from the Dunloe Bank to the Bank of New Zealand. It's as simple as a telegram. Mr. Dunloe is a friend of the Burtons, and my parents have a business account there. But I think Mr. Dunloe did not wait for them to agree and just sent me something straightaway. In that sense, it's a loan, yes. But my father—that is, Michael, my real father, not the *ariki*—can pay the bank right back."

"So much money just like that. You're rich, Matariki." Kupe's tone was as reverent as the voices of the Hauhau when they spoke of Matariki's power as a priestess.

Matariki nodded without any shame and flashed her impish grin.

***

Matariki and Kupe strolled through Auckland and admired the port and the ships from England and Australia. Matariki told Kupe how her parents had first been in Tasmania before coming to New Zealand. Kupe pointed to the terrace-shaped slope of Mount Eden and explained that the Maori had undertaken agriculture there. Tamaki Makau Rau, Auckland's Maori name, had been a big city long before the *pakeha* came.

Matariki could easily picture that. She liked the natural harbor and the sea, the green hills, and the warm weather. By evening, they started to search for lodgings. The bank manager had recommended the Commercial Hotel, Auckland's first and most renowned hotel, and Matariki was fascinated by the playful and yet radiantly dignified wooden structure.

"You want to stay here?" asked Kupe, awestruck.

Matariki nodded. "Why not? Now we look quite respectable."

Kupe shifted his weight nervously from one foot to the other. "Matariki, I've never been in a hotel."

Matariki rolled her eyes. "It's not difficult, Kupe. You give them your name, they give you a key to a room, and the next day you pay your bill."

Kupe bit his lip. "But which name, Matariki?" he asked hoarsely. "I call myself Kupe. They called me Kurt at the orphanage. But I don't know the name of my ancestors. Nor the canoe in which they came to Aotearoa."

Matariki suddenly felt bad for him, though she was fairly certain that they had also given "Kurt" a last name—her own mother had received the last name of the man who had found her. Still, it seemed heartless to her to remind him of that.

Instead, she gently and shyly put her arms around his neck. "Kupe," she whispered, "your ancestors are gone, but they watch over you as stars. Let's go somewhere where it's not so bright from the gas lamps. And together we'll look up at the sky. When one of the stars looks down at you, laughing, you'll bear its name."

Matariki pulled the resistant Kupe in the direction of the botanical gardens. In the last light of day, they saw the silhouette of the mountains and hills, but the sea already reflected the stars. It would be a clear night.

"Where are your stars?" asked Kupe.

Matariki laughed. "Still in conversation with the gods behind the gods," she claimed. "I have several, you're right about that. Matariki is the mother of a constellation. But it's not visible until June, at the Touhou Festival. You ought to know that, Kupe. You did live among the Maori."

Kupe's sad face suggested that the Hauhau movement did not place much value on New Year's festivals and constellations. This strange religion had developed its own rites—far from goodness and peacefulness.

"Well, come now and pick one," Matariki said.

He pointed to one of the brightest stars, which seemed to shine down specifically on him. Kupe ventured smiling at it. The star seemed to blink back.

"That one," he said, pointing again at the shining star to the north.

Matariki nodded. "I know that one," she said, pleased, "and his line of ancestors. That is Atuhati, a child of the stars Puanga and Takurua." She pointed to Sirius.

"That's Takurua. Your ancestors must have exercised a great deal of *mana* to become such bright stars."

Kupe rubbed the tattoos on his face.

"Welcome to Aotearoa, Kupe Atuhati, son of Puanga and Takurua who did not come in a canoe but in the beam of a star direct from the sky."

Matariki smiled her mother's smile, which had always won her a place in every heart. And Kupe could not resist. He pulled her into his arms and kissed her. Much more strongly and possessively than back under the kauri tree. Matariki returned the kiss.

"That was lovely," she said softly. "And now, let's go into the hotel. We'll drink wine. We'll celebrate your name with wine. That's something special. My mother—"

"Your mother celebrated your name with a man on New Year's Eve," Kupe blurted out. "The girls of the tribe, Matariki. Would you, would you, with me . . . ?"

Kupe's gaze was pleading. Matariki again saw the sensitive youth behind the warrior. Briefly, she thought of giving in to him. He was right, a Maori girl did not make much of the loss of her virginity. Matariki's friend Keke had already slept with a boy from her *iwi* when she was thirteen. But here? Now? Matariki wondered if she loved Kupe. She liked him. But love?

Promise me you'll only do it out of love. Matariki thought she could hear her mother's voice. It had been at one of the wild, ebullient festivals of the Maori, and Matariki was still quite young. Lizzie had taken her to the bushes to relieve herself, and the two of them almost tripped over a couple making love. Matariki had asked what they were doing, and Lizzie had explained. There wasn't any point in doing otherwise; Lizzie's children grew up too close to the Ngai Tahu not to witness their liberal custom of making love. *It can be wonderful, Matariki. But don't do it lightly. Don't do it to receive anything. Don't do it just because the man wants to. Only do it when you're completely sure and when you want to do it so desperately, when you want him so much, you feel you'd burn up otherwise.*

Matariki was far from burning up. On the contrary, despite the temperatures in Auckland, she was beginning to shiver. It had been a long day, and she had not slept much in the mail coach. Matariki wanted something good to eat and then a bed to herself.

"Let's go to the hotel," she said calmly. "This isn't New Year's Eve."

Chapter 9

With few exceptions, the newly hired miners packed into the only pub in Greymouth, the Wild Rover. The place did justice to its name. From inside came unmelodic songs sung by tipsy men with strong Irish accents.

The others—the woman and her family and three or four young men who had been quiet during the journey—had asked to be dropped off in the settlement. No doubt they were doing the only thing they could think of to have a roof over their heads that night. There had to be one or two families whose houses were big enough to take in the new arrivals for a bit of money. When Violet asked if they could try the same, Jim, Fred, and Eric waved her away.

"We can ask in the pub," said Jim. "The barkeeper will know a thing or two."

Violet sighed. Half the night would pass before Jim asked, if he wasn't too drunk then to remember. Bob went into the pub, and Violet watched through the open door as a girl immediately leaped into his arms and he happily shouted, "Molly!"

Violet wondered whether his girlfriend worked at the pub.

Rosie was tired enough to fall over, and Violet looked around hopelessly. Next to the Wild Rover was the workshop for the local gravedigger and coffin maker. It had already closed, and Violet didn't think the owner would mind if she and Rosie sought shelter on the covered veranda while they waited for Jim, Fred, and Eric. She looked for dry clothes in her bag, and she and Rosie changed into them in the shadows. Oil lamps lit the pub's entrance, but the rest of the town lay in pitch blackness. Rosie whined a bit because there was nothing to eat, but then she fell asleep on her father's old duffel bag. The drive through the rain had exhausted her. It was no different for Violet. She was so tired that she even considered sneaking into the workshop and sleeping among the coffins. That happened in one of Heather's books. Violet sat on her bag and leaned against the workshop's wall, nearly dozing off as she tried to recall the story of Oliver Twist, but then voices from the pub woke her from her half sleep.

"I already told you, Clarisse. Maybe again on the weekend, when it's full here and the bastards are too drunk to tell black from white. But not on weekdays when no one's going to pay me for such a used-up whore."

The door opened, and a short, strong man with a red face pushed a woman out. She was heavily made up, and her hair was coiffed into a showy tower with ribbons and frills. The woman was slender and round in the right places, but she was no longer young. Her almost-white makeup grotesquely emphasized her wrinkles.

"I thought, now that Molly—" Her voice sounded vexed. "Damn it, Paddy, I wanted to do you a favor."

The man snorted and shook his head. "A favor my arse, you had your eye on a dry place to work," he mocked. "And Molly's only going to do it with her Bob tonight, but he's going to pay for it. Lisa and Grace'll take care of the rest. You cost more than you bring in, so go."

He threw the woman's shawl after her. She pulled it over her hair—insufficient protection from the rain but better than nothing. With a sigh, she made her way in the direction of the miners' settlement, but then she saw Violet under the sign that said "Gravedigger."

"Hello, girl." She smiled lopsidedly. What are you doing here? Working on your own?"

Violet shook her head. "I'm not doing any work," she muttered. "I don't have any money, and, and if I did, I wouldn't buy a coffin."

The woman laughed. "I didn't really mean it like that. I can see you're not one of us. You belong to one of Biller's new boys, eh? Dear Lord, you're still half a child. Did the louse marry you and drag you here, and now he's getting drunk instead of building you a house?"

Violet shook her head. "My father," she said quietly.

Rosie stirred. "Our father," she corrected Violet.

The woman came closer. "God, look at that one," she said. "Cute little thing."

Violet didn't think there was anything threatening about the woman, even if the barkeeper had called her a whore. Perhaps he only had been cursing. Violet remembered that her father had sometimes cursed at her mother like that. And Ellen had been the best woman under the sun. Tears welled up in Violet's eyes at the thought of her mother.

"Dear Lord, girl, are you crying?" asked the woman. "Well, I suppose you've got every reason to. Now come, that's enough. I'm Clarisse. And I'm not dependent on him." She gestured in the direction of the pub. "I work for myself. I'm not so poor. And most of all, I've got a warm place to sleep. If you want, I'll take you home. You can sleep in Molly's bed. She won't be coming home tonight."

Violet bit her lip. Ellen would not have allowed her to go with this woman. Yet Molly lived with her, and she must be respectable if Bob wanted to marry her.

"Your dad will find you tomorrow, though he might be angry if you hole up at our place," Clarisse said.

Violet shrugged. "He'll be angry no matter what," she said. "Especially tomorrow when he has to build us a hut. He doesn't like that sort of thing. He always yelled at my mother when she asked him to fix something around the house."

"The hangover he'll have tomorrow won't improve things. Who cares—tomorrow is tomorrow, and today is today. Today you and the little one need to get somewhere dry, so come on. Leave your dad's things. Nothing gets stolen here. In Greymouth, we're poor but honest. Most of us, anyway."

Violet rubbed her forehead. "I'm not supposed to follow strangers," she said, repeating one of her mother's commandments.

The woman laughed. "Didn't I already introduce myself? I'm Clarisse. Clarisse Baton. What are your names?"

"Violet and Rosemary Paisley. And we don't have any money." Violet blushed because she was lying, but she didn't want to reveal the money from Kathleen.

Clarisse offered her hand. "And I don't tend to take it from girls," she joked.

Violet curtsied, and Clarisse laughed again.

"A well-bred girl," she praised her.

Violet blushed again. Perhaps she should finally stop this courtesy.

Clarisse led the way down the dark, muddy streets. From the city to the miners' settlement was more than a mile, and Violet had to drag Rosie who was crying again.

"I have something for you to eat," Clarisse soothed Rosie. "There won't be much. We get our food in the pub, but there ought to be some bread at home."

Clarisse lived outside the miners' settlement. Her house was almost in the forest, a strange forest where ferns grew instead of trees. The ferns reached the height of a fruit tree, and birds seemed to live in them. Or were they monkeys? The noises sounded more like croaking and laughing than tweeting and singing, but Violet hadn't heard of monkeys in New Zealand.

She would investigate the next day. For now, she looked favorably at Clarisse's house, a surprisingly solid construction. Naturally, this shelter was built of waste wood and looked incomplete, but it was bigger than most of the other huts, and it had a chimney.

"Did you build this yourself?" asked Violet. Clarisse had not mentioned a husband.

The woman made a face and smiled impishly. "Well, you might say we worked it off," she answered. "The boys from the mine did the work. It was the only way they could afford a girl. They're always happy to do some more when we want to add on."

Violet bit her lip. "So, um, do only women like you live here?"

Clarisse laughed with her whole face. It was rounded. She surely would have been a heavy woman if she had more to eat. Yet, the women weren't rich. For provisions, there was barely half a loaf of old bread and some cheese. Clarisse shared it amiably with the girls. She gave them water to drink while she sipped gin.

"I wish I could tell you this is the local nunnery, but then I'd be a liar," she remarked. "No, we're not 'good' women. We're whores. And this here's the local brothel. It's nothing special, I'll grant you that." She grimaced, but as she spoke, the expression turned into a wistful smile. "Someday, dear, someday we'll build something proper. A pub in the middle of town, just to give old Paddy some competition, with stables and a kitchen and proper rooms—one for every girl. We're saving for it. I am, anyway. The others want to marry. And they almost always do. Even Molly's got her Bob now."

Violet was shocked but bit hungrily into the bread. Clarisse's house was warm, likely from the smoldering remains of a fire. There was little furniture, just four chairs, a table, and the fireplace. Otherwise, every corner of the room was screened off with thick velvet curtains.

"A little privacy for everyone," Clarisse answered Violet's unspoken question. "True, it doesn't help much. You do hear what's going on. But better than nothing. That corner is Molly's. Close the curtain tight, and don't come out until morning, no matter what's going on. I still need to find a couple boys tonight, and Grace and Lisa each might bring someone. No one will bother you. Molly's working, and then she'll sleep at Bob's. Tomorrow she'll be back on cloud nine. Good night, dear."

Clarisse stroked Rosie's little head gently. Then she tossed her wet shawl back on her shoulders and disappeared into the darkness. Violet vaguely imagined Clarisse standing on a street corner and calling to men—she had seen women do this when she accompanied her mother to pubs to look for her father. Sometimes she had seen one of the girls leave with men. It was embarrassing for Violet to even think about what the couples did, but she knew how it went—miners' houses were not so big that parents could hide anything from their children. And she had even heard people on the ship. In the cabins, so the noises carried into the corridors, and on deck. It seemed to be fun for the men. Otherwise they would not have paid.

Molly's area was clean, and the bed was freshly made. Violet tucked Rosie in and considered whether to take out her nightshirt or to just sleep in her dress. She decided on the latter and cuddled with Rosie under the blanket. She did not note much of what transpired during the night. She only heard the door open and close. She was attuned to this noise. In Treherbert, it had announced her father's arrival and, often, one of her parents' fights. In Clarisse's hut, there were only giggling and whispering, which did not stop Violet returning to her slumber. In the morning, she was awakened by the smell of fresh coffee and the sound of sleepy women's voices.

Nervously, she pulled aside the curtain, expecting garishly made-up night owls. Instead, she saw three normal women who did not even look bleary-eyed. Now that she had combed her hair straight and tied it into a bun at the nape of her neck, Clarisse looked almost motherly. She was surely over thirty, though the other girls were clearly younger. Dark-haired Grace was rather pretty. Without makeup, the blonde, Lisa, looked somewhat plain, but she gave Violet a friendly smile.

"These are your foundlings?" she teased Clarisse. "Admit it, you just want to hire the dear. Pretty as she is, she could make a fortune."

Violet blushed again.

"And then at thirty, she'd look as worn out as me," Clarisse concluded bitterly. "No, no, don't tease her. You see, she's embarrassed. Go buy bread, or did you bring some home?"

Grace and Lisa shook their heads. "Nah, it didn't go late last night," replied Grace, reaching for a few coins lying on the table. "There's never much happening on Wednesday. Sure, the new ones got here, but they wanted a beer—they have to save for a girl." She stood up. "Well, I'll get going, then. I'm hungry."

Clarisse and Lisa laughed as if Grace had made a joke.

"Really, she's got an eye for the baker's son," Clarisse revealed. "I'll guarantee she doesn't enter through the shop but through the kitchen."

"And gets the bread with a little love at no extra charge," Lisa said with a wink.

Violet was confused. "But I thought, I thought, wh—um . . ."

Clarisse smiled. "Sweetheart, we're the only girls far and wide. There are some married women, but most of them have a past similar to ours. Only a very few came with their husbands. The fellows take what they can get. You'll be spoiled for choice, Violet Paisley." Clarisse looked to Lisa and asked, "Am I wrong, or is she the only respectable girl in town?"

Violet was horrified. Things were even worse than the pastor had said.

Lisa nodded. "It may be that in Lambert's or the government mine there's one or two miners with daughters, but not in Biller's."

"Make sure you aim for a foreman, dear, or one of the people from town. Don't take one of the miners. No one gets rich here," Clarisse said.

Clarisse gave the inside of the pantry another glance. It was completely empty.

Lisa stood up. "I'll go over to Robert's. Maybe I can get a little milk," she said. "Or eggs. Eggs would be good."

Clarisse explained that a few miners kept sheep or goats and hens in their huts. With their milk and eggs, they improved their paltry pay.

"But you have to be born for it," she sighed. "I mean 'in their huts' literally. As soon as the critters get out, someone roasts them for dinner. Robert stinks like his goats, but Lisa is sweet on him anyway. Who knows, maybe she's a country girl."

Violet was surprised Clarisse did not know.

Clarisse used her friends' absence to count out the money she had earned and to deposit it in a hiding place in her area.

"It's not much, but I'll have the money for the land soon," she said happily.

Violet remembered that her new friend was saving for a building in town. She would have found it horrible to own a pub, but likely it would make you rich.

"Do, do you make a lot as a—?" Violet could not bring herself to say the word.

"You can say 'woman of easy virtue' or 'prostitute.' It doesn't matter what you call us." As Clarisse spoke, she opened the window to air out the little house. It was not cold outside, and, finally, it wasn't raining. It was even bright enough to seem as if the sun wanted to come out. The ferns, still heavy with rain, cast feathery shadows. "And as for money—" Clarisse took a deep breath of the fresh air. To Violet, it smelled peculiar, earthy and a bit sweet. The air was heavy with moisture and coal dust. She thought unhappily of Dunedin, the clear air there, and the fresh, cool wind from the mountains. "You earn more than a maid," Clarisse continued, "but you won't find that kind of job here. So, don't think a working woman has much choice, but as a whore, you spend more. Most do, anyway. Dresses, makeup, some gin to make the men and life look better . . ."

Violet frowned. Really, she ought to pull herself together and worry about breakfast. Rosie would be up soon, and they would have to go look for their father. But the conversation with Clarisse was too interesting.

"The women pay for men?" she asked, confused.

Clarisse made a face and rubbed her forehead. Without makeup, she really did look like a normal woman. She had friendly, light-brown eyes, and her wrinkles were hardly noticeable.

"Not directly," she answered. "That is, not like the men pay for women. It's like this: A fellow acts like he loves one of the girls, really, truly, for who she is. And then she melts away, buys him a shirt here, some nice suspenders there. A little tobacco and a good bottle are always ready when he comes to visit. He'll need money sometime—for some small business, for a bet. He says he'll pay you back. With interest. And he asks, wouldn't it be nice if he really won at poker once? Or at the races? Then you could marry."

"But they never win," Violet said knowingly.

Clarisse nodded. "As a rule, no, and if they do, they bet it all again, without giving the girl anything back. Ultimately, there are only tears and an empty purse."

Clarisse grabbed a broom and began to sweep the hut. Violet looked for an opportunity to help but saw nothing to do. The house was too small and already very clean.

"That doesn't happen to you?" asked Violet curiously.

Clarisse laughed. "No. I don't fall in love so easily, and I'm saving my money. I don't have to drink to make life look better. I already know the next day it'll be just as sad as today. I'd rather plan for a better future." She sighed. "Dear Lord, just once to have a place of my own, where no man could enter."

As if on cue, men pounded on the door, and they did not wait for Clarisse to invite them in. Jim and Fred Paisley stormed the house as if to save Violet's virtue.

Rosie woke up and pulled the blanket over her head when she heard them.

"Violet, I can't believe it," Jim roared. "We're not even here a whole day, and already people are talking. Have you lost your mind? Bringing the child into a—" Jim raised his fist.

Violet retreated fearfully into the corner.

Clarisse rushed in between Violet and her father. "A what?" she asked angrily. "A dry, warm place? So that she didn't catch her death in front of the coffin maker's in the rain? Did you even think of what could happen to the girl? Fifty men live here alone, Mr. Paisley, isn't it? And near the other mines, at least a hundred more. All of them go to the pub, and many haven't had a girl in bed in weeks. They're lusty as the neighbor's dog, Mr. Paisley. And you left your daughter in front of the pub like a corner girl. And with the little one too."

Jim Paisley looked like he might strike Clarisse, but before he could blink, she had a knife in her hand. Violet wondered how she could have drawn it so quickly, but she undoubtedly knew how to use it.

"Don't even think about it, Mr. Paisley. You won't threaten me in my own house. And now, thank me kindly for at least saving your older daughter from a fate worse than death." She grinned, but then made a face. "And probably the little one along with her," she added bitterly. "See to it that by tonight you put a roof over your children's heads. And even better, a door to close behind them. And a hellhound to guard that door." She only murmured the last statement.

Violet looked anxiously to her father, but a change had taken place in him when Clarisse mentioned the house.

"I already have a house," he exclaimed, grinning triumphantly. "Oh yes, Violet, you think I never do anything right and no business gets done in pubs, but your old man knows what's what. I talked one of the drunks out of a nice house. He says he's had enough of mining and is leaving tomorrow for a whaling station in Westport. And I'm getting his hut."

It was better if Violet did not ask how much of Jim's advance was left. Surely the house was not worth half of what Jim paid for it. But it was a weight lifted off her shoulders. Whatever it cost, it was standing, so she did not have to wait for them to build something.

"Now, come on. I'll show it to you. You'll need to tidy it up a bit. A bachelor's place, but otherwise fine."

Violet gathered her things. She would have preferred to stay, especially since Grace returned just then. Her cheeks were rosy, she smiled contentedly, and she had a loaf of bread under her arm and a bag of sweet rolls in her hand.

"Are you going so soon? I brought extras for the little one."

Rosie cast covetous looks at the bag. The baked goods smelled irresistible.

"I think you can take them with you," Clarisse said. "We would have liked to invite you to breakfast, but we have strict rules: no men in the house until the moon rises."

Grace giggled. Jim Paisley gave the women wrathful looks. Violet shyly thanked them and followed her father outside before he could cause more trouble. Rosie was already biting into a sweet roll.

"I'll be seeing you," Clarisse called after them. Violet wondered whether she meant her and Rosie or their father.

***

The "house," a ramshackle hut, stood in the middle of the coal-mining settlement. Violet had expected no different. The paths in front of it were so muddy that her feet sank into them. There weren't any outhouses, and the houses stood only a few feet apart, so people just went behind their houses, and the rain washed the urine and excrement into the streets. The settlement was one big sewer. And the stench was worse from the fires and coal dust. Almost all the people they passed between Clarisse's hut and their new lodging were coughing. Most of them were men. Violet saw only two women and two children; the women were carrying water through the muddy streets, and the children were playing in the filth.

Violet tried to ignore all that and only think of her new home. A retreat. Surely she could find flowers she could dry to fight the stench. She could also steam vinegar. If only—

"As I said, you'll have to clean up a bit." Jim opened the door to their new home.

Violet recoiled in horror. She had not wanted to cry, but this was too much. Whoever had lived here had never cleaned, never thrown out table scraps, and had not always made the effort to do his business outside. Likely too drunk for that. Dried vomit didn't vouch for a healthy lifestyle. Violet doubted the owners of this hut were leaving the settlement of their own free will. Probably the foreman had kicked them out.

"Get to work," said Jim Paisley. "We're going to go help Eric build a hut."

It was the first bit of good news since her arrival in Greymouth. Violet tried to buoy herself with the thought that they would not have to share this hut with Eric Fence. She found him unsettling, especially so because of the lustful looks with which he regarded her. She searched for a broom, a mop, and a bucket. Naturally, there was nothing of the sort. Should she ask her father for money for the supplies or dig into her emergency money? Jim, Fred, and Eric had found a building site three houses down and were uncorking their first bottle of whiskey to celebrate this decision.

Resigned, Violet looked for her money. She would not make it through another confrontation with her father.

Chapter 10

Miss Matariki Drury and Mr. Kupe Atuhati, her cousin, occupied two single rooms in the Commercial Hotel. Since neither of them had any papers, Matariki had given the name of the bank manager as a reference and guarantor. By coincidence, the man was eating dinner at the hotel restaurant with friends and vouched for Matariki. "The . . . niece . . . of Jimmy Dunloe, an esteemed colleague in Dunedin. I believe she is his niece, though the relations are a bit convoluted. Nonetheless, a princess."

He winked at Matariki. Later, she heard bits of a conversation with the hotel owner, in which the bank manager mentioned South Island, Canterbury, sheep barons. After that, the hotel owner was much friendlier and even allowed Dingo in Matariki's room. He did, however, lodge the "cousins" on different floors.

"Probably he'll patrol all night," Matariki said with a giggle, "to make sure we act honorably."

Kupe didn't reply, and he was quiet the rest of the night. He did enjoy the food—Kupe had never tasted anything like the beef medallions in pepper sauce and fingerling potatoes—though the wine did not do much for him.

After dinner, they went to their own rooms. Matariki washed Dingo and then blissfully sank into a bubble bath. Kupe longed to be back in the common lodge of the warriors.

The next morning, Kupe was gone when Matariki came down to breakfast.

"Without eating anything," the hotel manager remarked almost a bit reproachfully. "The young man—"

"Is a bit shy," Matariki interrupted. "He'll turn up again. I, for one, am hungry. And so is he." She gestured to Dingo.

"You'll be staying another night?"

Matariki nodded. "Of course, we're waiting here for my parents. We'll be taking in the sights until they arrive."

For Matariki, the highlight was walking through the shopping district—she had to admit that her *pakeha*-self was triumphing over her inner Maori rebel. She also looked at the buildings and returned to the botanical gardens to see them in the daylight. She marveled at the variety of plants—including palm trees—that grew in the warm climate. Matariki strolled with Dingo through the meadows and over the green hills that bordered Auckland, enjoying the view of the natural harbor and small coves.

When she returned to the hotel around evening, it was to a telegram from her parents—*Stay where you are! Will arrive soon. Overjoyed, Mom and Dad*—and a very anxious Kupe, who was waiting for Matariki in the lobby.

"There you are. Where were you? I thought for sure you'd run away. You—"

Matariki frowned at him. "You left this morning without a note," she said. "I was out for a walk. What else was I supposed to do? Weave flax or make a tasty dog stew?"

Kupe laughed. "Sorry. I just thought—"

"Where were you?" asked Matariki. "I was worried."

"First, the university," Kupe said. "They won't take me just like that. In principle, it's a matter of references. However, they said it wouldn't be a problem. They're writing to the mission school for the papers. I told them that I ran away from there, but the boy at registration was kind. He said he would have run away from there, too, and asked if I'd been at Parihaka."

"Where?" asked Matariki.

"Parihaka. They have several Maori students from Parihaka. It's a village on the coast, between Mount Taranaki and the Tasman Sea."

"A Maori village?" It was unusual for a single village to send several young people to school, though the children of the Ngai Tahu now almost all learned English, reading, and writing. In a few years, some of them would surely want to study, and as rich as the tribe was . . . "A well-off village?"

"Almost a town, Matariki." Kupe was excited. "Fifteen hundred residents, a hundred *whare*—houses—already, and two big *marae*. They're building more. Someday perhaps every tribe will have a *marae* in Parihaka."

"People from different tribes live there?" Matariki asked, amazed.

Large villages were rare on the South Island, but more Maori lived on the North Island, and the tribes often consisted of a few hundred people. Large *pa*—fortified villages, similar to fortresses—were rather common, mostly before the arrival of the *pakeha*. Now, only a few remained. The wars with the whites, and the diseases they brought, had reduced the Maori population. That several tribes were joining together to live together or to form a new tribe, however, was news to Matariki. She hadn't heard of anything like that except among the Hauhau, where the common religion unified the warriors.

Kupe nodded enthusiastically. "Yes, no more fighting among the tribes. Te Whiti is preaching solidarity, peaceful coexistence, and mutual respect—between the Maori and *pakeha* and the Maori with one another. He doesn't want to fight but to promote our rights to our land and to maintain it with spiritual means."

"The archangel Gabriel again," said Matariki. "You don't mean to tell me that you're going to fall for the next prophet, Kupe. This—what was his name?—is just looking for more trouble, just like Te Ua Haumene."

Kupe shook his head wildly. "The opposite, Matariki. I spoke with the men who are studying here in Auckland. And with the girls. They grew up in part in Parihaka. The village has been there twelve years. Te Whiti o Rongomai founded it in 1867 with Tohu Kakahi. Right after the first of the Maori Wars. He fought in them, but he realized that the killing had to end. Just like us, Matariki. Patariki came into being as a countermovement. The government had confiscated Maori land. The founding of the village was Te Whiti and Tohu Kakahi's reaction to that. No *pa*, Matariki, no fortress. An open village where everyone is welcome. The *kingi*, Tawhiao, sent him twelve men, twelve apostles."

"I knew it," sighed Matariki. As they talked, she and Kupe had walked to the restaurant, and now she was studying the menu. "Salmon steak, Kupe, that's what I want."

"Forget food for now, Matariki." Kupe could hardly sit still. "Parihaka has nothing at all to do with the Hauhau. Te Whiti doesn't even preach a religion. It's just about living together. The *kingi* wanted to reinforce the bonds between Waikato and Taranaki Maori. And Te Whiti would like to see everyone united under one roof: the Ngati Maniapoto, the Ngati Porou, the Ngati Pau, even the Ngai Tahu. We have to confront the *pakeha* as one people—a clever, rational, strong people. Only then will they stop stealing land and respect us."

"Should I order that, Kupe?" asked Matariki, still focused on the menu. "Or do you want something else?"

"I want to go to Parihaka," Kupe said, "and I want you to come with me."

Matariki tapped her forehead "Mount Taranaki is more than two hundred miles away. You can't just go there on a day trip, and my parents are coming here. I have to wait for them."

"Then I'll go without you," said Kupe sullenly. "But you said you wanted to be Maori. And to fight against the *pakeha*. In Parihaka, we could do that. We could—"

"What about your studies, Kupe?" Matariki asked. "I thought you wanted to be a lawyer."

"I want both. But something like Parihaka, it gives me courage. It's a starting point. At least come with me and speak to the students at the university, Matariki. They meet regularly."

"To *rire, rire, hau, hau*?" Matariki teased.

"No. Just to talk, study, and read. Sure, also about traditions. Just come with me, Matariki, please. They're all people like us."

Matariki shrugged. "Sure, fine. But not today; today I'm too tired. And I need something to eat." She waved to the waiter.

"In Parihaka, they raise all their food themselves according to the most modern agricultural methods. Te Whiti wants to show that the Maori aren't backwoods hicks or—"

"Cannibals. What does he say about dogs?" The waiter placed bread and butter on the table. Matariki ate a slice and immediately seemed in a better mood. "If you tell me they raise special breeds for eating, I'm going to change my mind."

***

The next morning, when Matariki came downstairs, she was astonished to find Kupe in an animated conversation about Parihaka with the hotel manager.

"I've heard of the project from journalists," said the manager when Matariki joined them. "Haven't you heard about it? All the newspapers in the country have written articles."

Except in Hauhau training camps and in Hamilton, thought Matariki.

"Recently, reporters from the South Island who had just been to Parihaka stayed here. They were quite impressed, especially with Te Whiti who runs the whole thing."

"Te Ua Haumene is also supposed to be very impressive," said Matariki, still skeptical.

The hotel manager frowned. "He's the one with the Hauhau. No, you can't compare the two. Te Whiti is a distinguished older gentleman. The journalists were full of praise."

Matariki decided to ask the bank manager about the matter. She needed money anyway.

"Again?" asked Kupe as they went to the bank. "What did you buy?"

Matariki shrugged. "Another dress, a riding outfit. Oh, don't look like that—even in Parihaka, they won't be running around in *piu-piu* skirts all year."

As grateful as she was to Kupe, he was getting on her nerves. If the conversation with the students from Parihaka really did turn to the traditions, they should put "Among the Maori, a woman is not the property of a man, especially not if he has only kissed her twice" on the agenda.

The bank manager handed her more money without hesitation. To Matariki's surprise, he had heard of Parihaka.

"An acquaintance of mine helped them open a bank," he explained. "He owns a bank in Wellington and wanted to talk them into a branch of his bank, but they wanted to do everything. They certainly do have some smart ones among them. Money transfers function seamlessly."

"They have a bank?" Matariki marveled. "With a Maori manager, Maori tellers?"

The banker nodded. "Yes. White people are welcomed as visitors, but only Maori can live and work in Parihaka. They have their own police, craftsmen, and industrial agriculture."

Matariki wondered what her parents might think of it, but she was curious herself. In the evening, to meet with the students at the university, she put on a simple dress and braced for anything from a *haka* to a Bible reading. Nothing of the sort awaited her. The seven students, four boys and three girls, met in a tiny apartment the boys shared.

"It was cheaper than rooms in a boardinghouse," Hori, the oldest, explained. "Plus, those are hard for us to find." He pointed to the tattoos on his face. Hori and Eti had many, and they twined around their eyes, nose, and cheeks. The other boys were decorated with fewer *moko*. Of the girls, two had *moko* around the mouth.

"Girls are only tattooed around the mouth to show that the gods gave women the breath of life," Kanono explained, grinning, "not men, as the Bible says."

Matariki laughed. She hadn't expected to like the young people. They had welcomed Matariki and Kupe graciously and happily shared beer with them as they talked.

"The Ngai Tahu rarely tattoo themselves anymore," said Matariki.

"We don't do it much anymore in Parihaka either," said Kanono, "particularly since it's not without its dangers. Our doctors and nurses complain whenever they have to treat another screaming child with inflamed *moko*."

Kanono studied medicine. She wanted to be a doctor in Parihaka.

"It's a shame, though," said Arona, a tall girl with black hair that fell straight down her back. "It's something of ours; it's part of our tribal rituals, *tikanga*, you know. If we don't do it anymore—"

The others groaned.

"Arona is our *tohunga* when it comes to tradition," Kanono teased. "If it were up to her, she would spin flax while she reads Shakespeare."

Arona was studying English literature.

"Someday people will also read our poets and study our customs," Arona said. She was not easily perturbed. "*Pakeha* and Maori art and literature will stand side by side, of equal value. We're fighting for that in Parihaka as well."

"For a Maori Shakespeare?" asked Matariki. "And for that you need to study English?"

"She's already studied Maori," Keke, the youngest of the girls, said. Keke was very pretty and not tattooed. She was lighter skinned than the others. Perhaps one of her parents was *pakeha*. Matariki liked her most. "Arona really is a *tohunga*. She's the daughter of a *matauranga o te*"—a high-ranking priest or priestess—"and she studied with her mother before she came here. During the *powhiri*, she lets out the *karanga* in the *marae* of the Ngati Pau."

Matariki eyed the girl with newfound respect.

"We're all pretty young in Parihaka," Arona said. "The old aren't going to leave their tribes, but many of us were sent by our elders. My mother wanted me to represent the Ngati Pau. Others come on their own because they want to try something between the Maori and *pakeha*, the best of both worlds."

Kupe glanced at Matariki. She looked impressed.

"But it's not a religion?" Matariki asked.

Keke shook her head, scratching Dingo. "No, you can follow any religion you want. The philosophy is naturally influenced by various religions, though, especially Christianity."

A few of the others booed her, but Keke would not be deterred. Philosophy was her passion, although she actually studied law. "Te Whiti says things like, 'When a *pakeha* hits you, don't hit him back.' Do you really believe he would have come up with that without reading the Sermon on the Mount first?"

"Who is this Te Whiti, anyway?" Matariki asked. She still had her reservations about the charismatic leader of the Parihaka. She kept thinking of Kahu Heke and the dependence of his preaching on Te Ua Haumene. He, too, had jumbled together Christian and Maori traditions.

"He's a chieftain's son," explained Eti, "from the Ngati Tawhirikura. His father was not an important *ariki*, but he had his son educated by Maori elders—by Maori who could read and write—and then by a Lutheran missionary, too, a German. Te Whiti was chosen chieftain, fought in Taranaki, but it became clear to him that bloodshed is not a solution."

"Certainly not when the others have guns," said Matariki.

Arona laughed. "A good *ariki* is also always a good diplomat," she said. "Te Whiti might have had that very thought, but he did better not to speak it. The Romans had more spears than the early Christians. And who won?"

"But we're not the chosen people, are we?" Matariki rolled her eyes.

"Of course," Keke giggled, and passed the beer around. "Especially those of us in Parihaka. We're going to change the world."

Chapter 11

Violet had tried hard to make the house in the miners' settlement halfway habitable, but she couldn't do anything about the fact that it was a primitive hut without ventilation, a latrine, or a bathtub. They could have gotten a washtub, but Jim and Fred didn't much care, even though they returned from the mine every day black with the greasy coal dust. In Treherbert, Ellen had always had a bowl of hot, soapy water waiting for them. When Violet did likewise on the first evening, she earned only curses and a slap instead of praise. Water had to be carried from a central location, and it was expensive. The alternative was the river, but it was half a mile away, and the wastewater from the camps, the town, and the mines was deposited there.

"Could you wash up at the mine?" Violet asked shyly. They could not go without cleaning themselves. Violet thought of her mother's cherished linens, which she had brought along. If Jim and Fred went to bed as they were, the sheets would be black within a night.

Jim Paisley laughed. "In that mine? What a joke, Violet. This mine is a shithole. Biller runs the business as cheaply as he can. No washrooms, hardly any lamps, and the ventilation is miserable. I don't know if I want to grow old here, sweetheart. There has to be something better, and I told the foreman that too."

Violet groaned. Problems from the start. Her father should have expected that the working conditions in Greymouth would be worse than in Wales. One only had to look at the settlement and compare it with the simple but solid mining houses in Treherbert. Violet would never have thought that she would look back with nostalgia on her life there, but she was already at her wits' end.

Worse still was having hardly any furniture. Violet had scrubbed the old table and two chairs, but the primitive wood beds were simply too filthy to use. She had made herself and Rosie a nest of blankets, but she needed to figure out something better. She thought of curtains, like those Heather had in the cabin on the ship and the ones Clarisse and her friends had in their house. A little privacy would be nice, but she couldn't get money from her father for that.

Jim and Fred were never too tired or poor to go to the pub. Without a word of thanks, they spooned down the vegetable soup Violet had cooked on the open fire, and then they went on their way. Neither the rain nor the long road to town bothered them.

Violet watched them go, and she thought how unusual the quiet was. She hardly heard any voices, let alone fighting. In Treherbert, you always heard the neighbors, and you could hear every noise coming from the ship's cabins, but in Greymouth . . .

Violet closed the door anxiously when she realized that most of the men in the settlement simply had no one with whom to argue. Other than her own, there were only three families with women and children. The men lived alone or shared a hut with a friend. In the evening, hardly any of them were at home; they thought of the pub as their living room.

When they came back, it could be dangerous for the girls. Violet decided to invest a bit of her money in a good padlock—even at the risk of her father beating her for not getting up fast enough to answer the door when he returned home at night.

***

Neither the passing of time nor trying to adapt improved life in Billertown. Violet continued to suffer from the filth, the stench, and the long distances. She had to go to town daily to shop, and her father made her beg for every penny she needed to take care of them. Often he would not even cough that up until he came home to no food on the table and then punished Violet for her negligence. Walking to town in the evening, however, was worse than the slap. She had to leave Rosie alone, and although Violet usually made the trip there with Jim and Fred, who were heading for the pub, on the way home, she was alone. She fled fearfully into the woods on the side of the road whenever men approached. Thankfully, they weren't usually drunk at that hour, so nothing more happened than a few catcalls. Occasionally, there were even polite greetings.

Not all the miners were idiotic drunks. Actually, it was mostly the opposite. Most of the boys had departed England and Wales to seek their fortune in New Zealand. They had saved money and gathered their courage and strength to work hard, seek a wife, and start a family. They had no way of knowing what awaited them in the new country, but still, most did what they could to get closer to their dream. They went to the pub, too, but only for a beer or two. Like Clarisse, they saved the rest of their money for a small house or a business in town.

There was a serious boy who always joined Violet on the way to church and told her about his plans for the future. She ignored his offer to formally escort her to church, just as she ignored the double entendres and flattery of the more forward boys. No foreman or craftsman from town ever chatted with her. Probably she looked too young for the men from better circles.

You only have to make it through a few years. Just don't fall in love. Take care of yourself. Kathleen and Clarisse's warnings shot through Violet's head every time she saw a young man, and she was determined to heed those warnings.

***

A few months after her arrival in Greymouth, Violet's money had run out. Her last coins went to medicine. The whole spring had been rainy, and Rosie had been fighting a bad cough for weeks. One of the three small children in the settlement had died of the same cough in October, and the thought of the same thing happening to her sister made Violet panic. Children did not die from a cold, but Rosie was running a high fever. Violet took her to the grave-digger's wife, who worked as a midwife and doctor's assistant. People joked that she helped her husband's business, but Violet had a good impression of Mrs. Travers, who was professional and friendly. She examined Rosie gently and carefully, and then gave Violet sage tea and cough syrup from the blossoms of the rongoa bush.

"I grow the sage myself, and the cough syrup is a Maori recipe," she said. "Make her tea, give her the syrup, and most of all, keep her warm and dry. See if you can't come upon a flue for your hut. Smoke is the worst. It settles in the lungs. And give her plenty to eat. She's still all skin and bones. You, too, of course."

Violet desperately made a hole in the roof of the hut herself. It did not help much, particularly now that the rain got inside, which made the fire smoke more. But, at least in dry weather, the air in the hut was slightly improved.

How she was supposed to feed Rosie better, however, Violet did not know. Her father was not willing to put out more money than he did for food even though there was hardly enough for bread, a few sweet potatoes, and bones, with which Violet made soup for the men. Jim and Fred demanded something warm in their stomachs after work, but they complained about the soup. What they did not eat, Violet gave to Rosie. She mostly went to bed hungry herself. Violet did not need Mrs. Travers to tell her that it could not go on like this. With her own money long gone, she contemplated how she could help feed the family. While trying to fish for trout, which were supposed to be plentiful in summer, she came upon Clarisse.

"You're not even curtsying anymore," Clarisse said in a tone between questioning and teasing when Violet gave her a tired greeting.

Violet stood barefoot in the freezing stream, watching the occasional fish rush by. How was she supposed to catch them?

"No time," Violet sighed. "Can you fish, Miss Baton?"

Clarisse sat down on the bank of the stream and smiled. "No. I only know that the Maori do it with traps and the *pakeha* with hooks. They're good at it here. We always get fresh fish."

Violet could imagine what the fishers got in return. But that no longer shocked her. She wondered about asking one of the well-mannered boys about his knowledge of fishing.

Clarisse played with the ferns on which she had sat. "You don't look well, dear," she said sympathetically.

Violet soldiered on with her fish catching. She thought a trap was a good idea and held her shawl in the water, hoping to catch a trout that way. Clarisse did not think it likely.

"Why didn't you ever come visit us?"

Violet shrugged. "There are only three women in the camp," she said bitterly, "but they're replacement enough for all the gossipmongers in Treherbert. If I visit you, they'll tell their husbands the next day, and then my father'll hear it during his next shift."

Clarisse nodded knowingly. "And he's just looking for an excuse to take his mood out on you, isn't he?" She noticed a swollen blue area under one of Violet's eyes.

Violet did not respond.

"Does he touch you?" asked Clarisse.

Violet furrowed her brow.

"Does he touch you or Rosie, um, improperly?" Clarisse reformulated her question.

Violet shook her head.

"You're lucky," the older woman said.

Violet looked up in disbelief. That was the first time anyone had viewed her father as a stroke of luck.

"It could always be worse," said Clarisse. "Believe me."

She sounded as if she had experience with that. Violet did not inquire further.

"Mine did it from the time I was six," Clarisse continued, "and Mother kept quiet. For the family's honor. I don't come from nothing, you know. My father was a cabinetmaker in Christchurch. He made good money, could have stuck to corner girls when my mom did not want to. But they were too old for him."

"Didn't you tell anyone else?" asked Violet, stepping out of the stream.

It wasn't worth freezing her feet off for the tiny chance of catching a fish. The ferns on the bank were warm from the sun.

Clarisse shrugged. "The priest. Afterward I had to pray five Our Fathers first; then my father made me really beg for mercy. People don't believe these things. Especially not from girls of 'good' families." She spat the last words out.

It was becoming clear to Violet why Clarisse was determined not to fall in love and to start a brothel rather than a family.

"I need work desperately," Violet said quietly, sitting next to Clarisse.

"A moment ago, you were scared to even visit us, and now you want to join us?"

Violet shook her head. "No. No, I, I can't. My, my mother was an honest woman."

Clarisse sighed. "And you don't want to mar her memory. I understand. Besides, your father'd kill you. So, why are you asking?"

Though still ice-cold, Violet's feet were dry now, at least. She put her stockings back on while trying not to let Clarisse see the multitude of runs in them. Clarisse was dressed a bit unreservedly, but cleanly and properly.

"I thought you would perhaps know of something else," she said.

Clarisse shook her head. "Nothing, I'm afraid. You could have asked the baker. He's making deliveries nowadays. But his son is going to marry Grace."

"Really?" Violet was happy for the dark-haired girl.

Clarisse nodded. "She's over the moon, and his mother'll come to terms with her. Either Grace or no grandchildren. The choice of possible daughters-in-law isn't big. So, they have enough workers in the bakery. There's a bed free at our place."

Violet didn't respond directly. Instead, she asked, "When will the hotels be done? They'll need maids, for sure."

Clarisse made a face. "That may be a while. You could knock on the doors of the mansions. The Billers just built a palace outside of town. And the Lamberts, they own the other mine; they have a mansion. It could well be that they're looking for maids. True, they usually take Maori, but if you can recall your nice curtsy and your 'Yes, sir, no, sir'—"

Violet beamed. "I'll try," she said, and curtsied. "Thank you very much, Miss Baton."

***

Violet put on her best dress, braided her hair, and left Rosie at home, though she cried pitiably.

"If I take you with me, they'll never hire me," Violet said. "Just sit here and play with your doll and don't open the door for anyone. I'll be back before Fred and Daddy get home. And if I get a job, I'll bring home something to eat."

The promise was a bit daring. There was no reason to believe she would get an advance. But she knew the thought of sugar rolls would soothe Rosie.

Violet was so worried about leaving Rosie alone that she almost ran the entire way to the Billers' house. She was out of breath and overheated when she finally reached the magnificent compound. The two-storied house stood in the middle of an unfinished but extensive garden, bordered from behind by the river. The villa was a country home, but it would have fit in a city as well.

Perhaps Joshua Biller anticipated that the growing town of Greymouth would someday incorporate his house.

Violet almost lost her courage. Could she really knock on the mine owner's door and ask for a job? Just then, she saw a short, stocky man working in the garden. Violet approached him and curtsied.

"Pardon me, I, I wanted to speak with Mr. or Mrs. Biller. I—"

The gardener turned toward her, and Violet startled at his round, tattooed face. He pointed to a path around the house.

"Mr. Joshua Biller and the Mrs. Her-hcr-mi-ne Biller both behind," he said, struggling a bit with the names. "Is trouble with Mahuika, not understand, but missus loud."

Violet was dealing with a Maori for the first time. Did the Billers hire only Maori? She thanked the gardener and headed to the path. Indeed, she did hear an argument.

"I do not care if there are advantages. She took off her clothes. In front of your son," a woman said shrilly.

The speaker, a petite, elegantly dressed woman, immediately came into view. She stood on a small dock that jutted into the river. Beside her were a strong-looking blond man in a waistcoat and suit, a brown-skinned girl, and a little boy. To Violet's astonishment, the girl was bare breasted, and she had only a light cloth slung around her waist. The man devoured her with his gaze while the woman struggled with her shock.

"She wanted to teach me to swim," the little boy objected. He might have been six or seven years old. He had his father's light-blond hair and his mother's slender figure and somewhat elongated face. "And what's more—"

"What's more, a respectable woman wears a bathing suit," his mother said. "In so far as a respectable woman swims. There's nothing wrong with a modest dip at a seaside resort, but not like this."

"We always swim so." The girl justified herself. She was not tattooed, but she had the same thick dark hair as the gardener, and her figure also looked a bit stocky. Her expression was gentle and reflected neither shame nor guilt. "And children always—"

"I told you, didn't I? They're savages." The woman spoke agitatedly. "Joshua, please stop staring at her. And, Mahuika, cover yourself. That is not for innocent eyes, the poor boy."

The boy did not seem distressed or to understand what the problem was. He did not even look at the bare body of the Maori girl, though she now pulled on her dress.

"She also speaks her strange language with him. Who knows what she's saying. No, really, Joshua, I must insist. We need an Englishwoman."

"What nonsense, Hermine. In half a year, he'll be going to boarding school. Sending for an English nanny before then would be madness. There's no time."

"I don't need a nanny," said the boy. "I got along on my own just fine. I'd rather have a globe and a dictionary."

"You hold your tongue, Caleb," his mother commanded. "You hear that, Joshua? He lacks any decorum whatsoever. The savages are rubbing off on him. He talks back, he looks at his naked nanny, and the gardener lets him 'help.' Yesterday he came into the house with filthy clothes and told me he caught a 'weta.' Heaven knows what that is."

"It's an insect, like a giant grasshopper," the boy said, earning himself another punitive look.

"Missus complains because of mud on clothing," the nanny said, presenting a new argument. "That's why undress today. Is better for playing."

"You hear that?" Mrs. Biller said accusingly to her husband. "He's going to arrive in England completely feral. What will they think of him in boarding school? He—"

"We could send him half a year early," Joshua Biller said.

His wife reacted hysterically. "Now, already? Even earlier? My baby." She moved to pull the boy to her. This was visibly embarrassing to him. Plus, he had just spotted Violet, who had crept closer.

"Who are you?" Caleb asked.

Violet smiled at him and looked apologetically at the Maori girl; then she approached Mr. and Mrs. Biller and curtsied with her gaze lowered. When she looked up, she sought Caleb's mother's watery-blue gaze.

"I'm Violet Paisley," she said firmly. "And I cannot swim."

***

For Mrs. Biller, it was enough that Violet was white, spoke English, and did not intend to fill her son's head with anything exotic like Polynesian languages. Mr. Biller asked questions and seemed satisfied with Violet's answers. Yes, she had experience with children; she took care of her little sister. And she had already served in a manor house, so she would not drop any porcelain and knew how to use a faucet. Mr. Biller nodded when she mentioned Reverend Burton in Dunedin, and Mrs. Biller seemed downright charmed when Violet referenced the Gold Mine Boutique. Kathleen and Claire's collections were known far beyond Dunedin.

"And your father works in my mine?" Biller finally asked.

Violet nodded. This question caused her the most concern. If Mr. Biller asked the foreman about Jim and Fred, he wouldn't likely give the best reference. For now, however, the mine owner seemed satisfied.

"Very well, we'll give you a try. We expect you—well, Hermine, you tell her, please. I must get to my office. This unfortunate business has already cost me too much time. And find some occupation for the Maori girl. We don't want to aggravate the tribe by letting her go."

A load lifted from Violet's heart. She would not have liked to take away the girl's post.

Mrs. Biller snorted once her husband had turned his back. "Aggravate the tribe," she muttered. "I'd say you've become keen on her."

Violet pretended not to hear and curtsied once more in front of her future employer. "Thank you very much, madam. When shall I return?"

***

Mrs. Biller requested Violet come at seven the next morning. She was to wake Caleb, serve him his tea, help him wash and dress, and then hand him over to his tutor.

"The reverend teaches him from nine to twelve. At one, we eat as a family; then you'll see to Caleb's afternoon rest, after which you'll supervise him with his homework."

Violet decided not to mention that she had not mastered reading and writing. Likely Mahuika hadn't either. She smiled at Caleb, who looked at her with a serious expression.

"He eats his dinner at six." Mrs. Biller spoke of her son as if giving feeding instructions for a pet. "Thereafter you may go."

That would be tight. Jim and Fred came home around seven. She would manage it somehow. It would be best if they never learned of her new job. At most, she would let on that she helped out a bit at the Billers'.

"Thank you very, very much, madam," she said again before turning to go. "Then, then until tomorrow, Caleb."

The boy did not answer.

Violet was in the best of moods when she ran home, though it suddenly occurred to her they hadn't spoken about pay. She had no time for the baker today, but maybe tomorrow he would sell her rolls on credit.

***

Caleb was already dressed when Violet arrived the next day. He sat at his desk in his study. Three rooms belonged to his domain: the study, a playroom that doubled as a living room, and a bedroom. Each room was bigger than Violet's whole hut.

Violet was nervous when she saw he was waiting. "Am I late?"

Caleb shook his head. "No, and I'm not a baby. You needn't wash me and dress me. I'm seven years old."

"Almost a man," Violet laughed.

"You also needn't make fun of me," the boy responded. "I'm lucky. Other children have to start working at seven."

"What should I do now, since you're already dressed?" Violet asked.

"Whatever you want," replied Caleb. "Well, breakfast first. You'll need to get that. My mother does not like me to eat with them."

Violet was surprised. "Why not?"

"My mother thinks I'm a baby. You've already seen that. And babies dribble and babble and whatever else. No one wants a baby at the table. Will you fetch the tea now?"

Violet hurried to the kitchen and met the cook. Agnes McEnroe was a Scot in her middle years. Her husband worked for the Billers as a coachman.

"So, you're the new nanny?" she asked amiably when Violet curtsied to her. "Y'look as if you could use one of your own. But the little Maori's hardly much older—just better fed."

At that, Agnes laid two more pieces of toast on the platter. Violet was never to know her as anything but generous.

"You can break your fast with the little gentleman. That'll cheer him. He's a good lad, the little Caleb, but always bored. See to't you brighten him up."

Violet nervously took the tray, onto which the cook had placed another plate and a second cup of tea. She had felt up to the job of a nanny, but would she succeed in entertaining the precocious boy? Most of all, she was worried about encountering Mrs. Biller. She would recognize that she intended to drink tea with her boy, and that was surely not permitted. Yet her mouth watered at the sight of the full sugar bowl, the creamy milk, the butter, and the two kinds of jam. She had only had a hunk of bread for breakfast in the morning and had not made coffee because Rosie was asleep and she did not want to wake her. Rosie would be alone all day, which made Violet worry.

Caleb had already cleared a table in his playroom and patiently awaited Violet with his book. He did not find anything amiss when he saw the second cup and the extra toast.

"You are rather thin," he said when Violet reached for the first piece of toast.

"Everyone in my family is thin," Violet said, blushing. "Would you like strawberry jam or orange marmalade?"

The boy rolled his eyes. "I. Am. Not. A. Baby." He repeated his favorite phrase slowly and more than firmly. "You don't need to butter my bread. I can even pour my own tea. Here." He proved it by standing up, draping his napkin over his arm, and gripping the teapot like a practiced waiter. Head upright and back straight, he approached Violet from the left, poured tea expertly in her cup without spilling a drop, and then in a servile tone asked, "Does the lady desire milk and sugar? Or does the lady prefer lemon?"

Violet laughed. Caleb took his seat again and reached for his own toast. "You can eat my other piece," he offered generously. "And you like, hmm, strawberry?" he decided. "You have a sweet tooth, don't you?"

Violet furrowed her brow. "How did you know that?" she asked.

Caleb shrugged his shoulders. "You look the type." He laughed. "And now, tell me: What do you want to do? We have more than an hour before the pastor comes for my lessons."

Violet bit her lip. "I don't know," she said. "What did Mahuika do with you?"

Caleb pursed his lips. "Nothing. Well, she fetched breakfast. But then she went to the garden. The gardener is her sweetheart, you know."

Violet wondered if Mrs. Biller's concerns about the Maori girl might have been justified. Who knew with whom besides Caleb she had shared her nakedness?

"That's why I also had to play in the garden a lot, which wasn't a big deal. I like weta."

"What's a weta, again?" asked Violet.

Caleb grinned. "An insect, like a grasshopper. Here, look."

He fetched a book from his shelf and opened it. Violet recognized a long block of text and a picture—although the bug depicted there did not improve her estimation of the fauna in her new homeland.

"Where do you find them?"

Caleb skimmed the text. "Depends. The tree weta like to jump around, but the cave weta will come in the house. Here, you can read it yourself." He pushed the book over to Violet.

Violet hesitated. "I can't read very well," she said quietly. "I'd like to, but—"

"But you're at least thirteen," Caleb marveled.

Violet bit her lip. "I'm fifteen," she said. Her birthday was at the beginning of the year, but it had gone uncelebrated. Her father hadn't even remembered the date. "But you don't learn it by growing older. And it's, it's rather hard."

Caleb shook his head. "It's not hard," he said confidently. "Shall I teach you?"

Over the next few weeks, Caleb Biller opened a whole new world to his fifteen-year-old nanny.

Apocalypse

Parihaka, North Island

1879–1881

Greymouth, South Island

1880–1881

Chapter 1

Since they had met with the students from Parihaka, Kupe wanted to see it and to meet Chieftain Te Whiti. Matariki had no illusions: if Te Whiti was half as charismatic a leader as he seemed, Kupe would fall for him and would want to live in Parihaka.

She didn't care. Matariki was not in love with Kupe. It was true she felt something for her savior, but even if he had freed her from her slavery in Hamilton, Kupe didn't have enough in common with the man she'd imagined. He was nice and lovable, but also puppylike. He stumbled more than strode through life in Auckland. Matariki did not exactly feel sorry for him, but he didn't impress her. Once again, her Maori and *pakeha* sides were in conflict: while a Maori woman thought nothing of being superior to her man in matters of *mana*, the schoolgirl dreamed of a hero.

What was more, he pricked her conscience. During her time in Hamilton, the girl had sworn to live as a Maori in the future and to fight for the rights of her people. After just a few days in Auckland, however, she admittedly fell for the charms of pretty dresses and soft beds. If she followed Kupe to Parihaka, he would compel her to stay, but she was excited about the coming academic year at Otago Girls' High School.

Then, Kupe found support from a side she would never have expected. He and Matariki had been in Auckland two full weeks before her parents finally arrived. They had traveled as quickly as possible from the South Island, and now Lizzie Drury wanted to visit Parihaka.

***

Kupe stood by, awkward and uncertain, during the emotional reunion among Matariki, Lizzie, and Michael. Until then, he had always seen Matariki as a chieftain's daughter, but she threw herself without hesitation into the arms of this tall, blue-eyed *pakeha* she called Daddy. And even Lizzie, the famous *pakeha wahine*, did not meet Kupe's expectations. He had imagined a powerful, spiritual personality, a tall, majestic chieftain's wife. Instead, the short, delicate Lizzie alighted from the carriage Michael had rented in Wellington in her elegant traveling clothes and her bold little hat. She was cordial and friendly— even to Kupe whom Michael eyed with suspicion at first—but not at all like the woman he'd pictured at Kahu Heke's side.

Lizzie spoke fluent Maori and addressed Kupe in his language. She didn't look twice at his tattoos. Kupe's admission that he had only a limited mastery of his people's language earned him Michael's sympathy. Over dinner, Matariki's parents questioned Kupe at length, and Michael asked the decisive question: "What, young man, do you intend to make of yourself?"

Lizzie laughed at Michael's serious question. To her, it was clear that no kind of romantic relationship existed between their daughter and this gentle giant— at least they were not sleeping together. Lizzie believed she could pick up on attraction between two people, and she had the sense that Kupe was getting on Matariki's nerves. Then, however, the young man mentioned Parihaka—offering the opportunity to bring the conversation around to another subject.

"Oh yes, I've heard of it," Lizzie said. "Or read, rather. Even the Ngai Tahu talk about it, though it's not as important to them because they don't have serious problems with *pakeha* like the Maori here. Why don't we drive there, Michael? We can bring Kupe to his new home and see the whole place."

She looked to her daughter for approval. Lizzie was going to free her of her nice but unsuitable admirer with the skill of a diplomat. Matariki, however, seemed unsure. Didn't she want to go to Parihaka? Lizzie would talk to her about it later.

***

Michael had nothing against a side trip to Mount Taranaki, and he hadn't the slightest concern about losing his daughter to the venture. He was certain Matariki would return with them to Dunedin and take up her old life. If she got rid of this Maori boy in the process, all the better.

Unlike Lizzie, Michael wasn't particularly attuned to emotional nuances, and he did not notice the tension in the carriage when the four of them made their way south the next morning. If anything, he attributed Matariki's unease to the fact that she was again traveling the route by which she and Kupe had fled Hamilton.

"Are you sure you don't want to press charges against the McConnells?" he asked Matariki. "For false imprisonment or whatever it's called? We could go to the police."

Matariki smiled. To make that suggestion, he had to swallow his pride. Even three decades after his deportation to Australia, Michael Drury had a strained relationship with authority.

"Oh, forget it, Dad. We gave them enough trouble already. Not to mention, Hamilton doesn't even have a police station. I never want to go there again."

Michael nodded in relief, steering the carriage carefully over the bumpy side roads that led past Hamilton. He would have liked to stay far away from the town, but there were only a few well-paved roads on the North Island. The road led through farmland, mostly pastureland, none of which seemed nearly as vast as the Canterbury Plains, or through shrub-covered hills. Occasionally they also crossed through beech or fern forests and marveled at the giant kauri trees.

To Kupe's astonishment, Lizzie knew a lot about them. She had lived a long time on the North Island where a Maori tribe in Kororareka had befriended her.

"The Ngati Pau," she told Kupe, "Hongi Hika's tribe where I got to know Kahu. Even back then he was a rebel, although not as fanatical or cold-blooded as you two describe. I like Te Whiti's idea much better. I'm so excited for Parihaka."

Lizzie smiled at Matariki. The girl had opened her heart up to her the night before their departure: "I feel like a traitor. On one hand, I know that Kahu Heke is right. I never took all that about oppression by the *pakeha* seriously. But Hamilton—"

"That was an experience," Lizzie soothed her. "You have to consider that on the North Island there were quite a few deaths during these disastrous wars and conflicts caused by madmen like Te Ua Haumene or fanatics like Te Kooti. Every side has victims to mourn, and they don't forgive each other easily. You don't have to take sides if you don't want to."

"But I do." Matariki stood up and paced—followed by loyal Dingo—restlessly around the room. A mannerism she had picked up from Michael. "It can't go on like this. Things like what happened to Kupe's village. They can't just happen, and—"

Lizzie smiled. "You'd like to make it right because you like Kupe," she responded, "and he's done a lot for you."

Matariki nodded.

"But you're not in love with him," Lizzie asserted, "and you blame yourself for that."

Matariki looked at her mother in amazement. How could she know that? It felt good for someone to say it out loud. Matariki bit her lip. She was almost ready to cry.

Lizzie pulled her daughter onto the sofa next to her and into her arms.

"Matariki, that's how it is with love," she said softly. "You can't direct it. Sometimes people fall in love with the wrong person and often with someone who doesn't return their love. And then there's someone who could love you with all his heart, but you don't feel anything for him. No one needs to feel guilty about it. Just don't pretend to him or yourself. You're doing everything right, Matariki. Don't worry."

"But I've never been in love," said Matariki. "And I really want to be. I'm afraid something's wrong with me. I—"

Lizzie could not help herself. As much as she understood the girl, she had to laugh. "Riki, it'll happen," she assured her. "Probably right when you least expect it, and when you have no use for it."

It would not be all that long before Lizzie's words would prove true.

***

During the journey, Kupe gained respect for Lizzie and Michael. Until then, *pakeha* had always seemed inept and inflexible. The whites he knew had almost never set foot outside their city, and every little trip necessitated ample preparation. Lizzie, Michael, and Matariki, however, sloughed off civilization as soon as they set out. The former gold miner and the friend of the Maori knew how to build a fire and how to catch fish and hunt. They thought nothing of overnighting in a tent. The tents were new; Michael had purchased one for himself and Lizzie and now two small ones for Matariki and Kupe in Auckland. Cost wasn't a concern; they bought the highest-quality equipment—Lizzie even complained that they had not rented a covered wagon.

"We wanted to get to you as quickly as possible, and we thought the roads would be in better condition."

The South Island seemed to be ahead of the North Island in that regard, though naturally the gold rush sped up the construction of roads, particularly in Otago. Lizzie and Michael proved themselves true pioneers and Matariki a child of the Ngai Tahu. To Kupe it was embarrassing that they knew more about surviving in his country than he did.

"Tattooing," Matariki teased, "doesn't make the Maori warrior."

They left the main road between Auckland and Wellington and turned to the west toward the Tasman Sea. Matariki and Lizzie were overjoyed when the sea came into view.

"This is where we sailed from, Kahu and I," Lizzie recounted, sounding almost wistful. Michael gave her a jealous look. "The coast is gorgeous."

That was true. The west coast of the North Island was varied: flat bays alternated with sheer cliffs; some beaches had dark sand and others had light; there were rocky sections, though sometimes the fern or mixed forests reached all the way to the sea. The weather was clear, and Mount Taranaki came into view, its snow-capped peak glimmering in the sun.

"Another piece of land they took away from us," Kupe said, looking at the mountain, "confiscated during the Taranaki Wars."

Lizzie frowned. "Didn't the government give the mountain back last year?"

Michael nodded. "Yes, once the settlers discovered the land wasn't good for anything. The volcano still erupts from time to time. Under those conditions, the settlers could afford to be generous."

To Kupe's amazement, the Drurys showed understanding for the situation of the Maori and their anger toward the white settlers. When he mentioned this, Michael spent half a day giving them an extensive history of Ireland and his people's struggle for freedom.

"We know full well what oppression is, my boy," Michael assured him, and recounted his own banishment to Tasmania for stealing grain during the famine.

In Kupe's eyes, Michael had earned points with regard to his *mana*. "You were a freedom fighter, Mr. Drury?"

Lizzie smiled to herself. Actually, Michael had been a whiskey bootlegger, and he had taken the grain for illegal distillation so he could use the profits to flee Ireland with his pregnant girlfriend, Kathleen.

"Is there any freedom fighter who doesn't have personal motivation?" she asked quietly.

Matariki, the only one who heard her whispering, shrugged her shoulders. The coastal road led along a beach that reminded her of her favorite cove in Dunedin, and she thought of school and Elizabeth Station. Would her life ever be so simple again? Was anything as it appeared?

***

Their first glimpse of Parihaka was the fields alongside an exceptionally well-built and -maintained road. Sweet potatoes and melons, cabbage and grain lined acre after acre.

"To farm that, you would need hundreds of people," Kupe marveled.

"Or very modern plows and other farming equipment," Michael said. As if to confirm his point, a heavy horse team pulling a massive plow came into view, the driver cultivating new land. The young Maori waved, and Michael returned the greeting. "Or a bit of both," he added, nodding toward a few women pulling weeds at the edge of a field. "But this here looks grand. If it goes on like this . . . What was this Parihaka originally, anyway, a *pa*?"

Kupe shook his head. "Specifically not a fortress," he said. "An open village. Te Whiti planned it that way. It's supposed to look inviting, not threatening. Everyone should feel welcome. It—"

"It was originally planned as a shelter for the people uprooted by the Maori Wars," Matariki said. She, too, had noted what the students had told them, but she was not enthusiastic about their prophet. "Many were driven out during the land confiscation."

"Gathering them here was an act of protest," Lizzie added. "Te Whiti had to be cautious, another reason surely for the open construction. The *pakeha* would have seen the construction of a *pa* as an act of enmity. Here everyone was and still seems rather thin-skinned."

***

And then all four of them fell silent, losing themselves in awe when Parihaka came fully into view.

"It's so pretty," whispered Matariki, who had been determined not to be impressed.

The village was constructed in a clearing—apparently no one had wanted to chop too many trees. Nature was sacred to the tribes. Past the village, the forest covered low hills. Above them, the majestic peak of Mount Taranaki shone forth. It looked as if the spirits of the mountain watched over the people gathered here. The sea, too, held Parihaka in its embrace, and Waitotoroa Stream provided the settlement with clear water.

Michael directed his horses on wide, clean streets through town, which consisted, like every Maori village, of common, sleeping, and storage lodges. Some buildings resembled the log cabins of the *pakeha* whereas others were decorated in the Maori way with intricate carvings. Lizzie recognized two large common lodges in the middle of the village. Carved stylized ferns and big images of the gods testified to the skill of the craftsmen. Small, well-tended gardens surrounded the sleeping lodges. They, too, were properly fenced and very well tended.

"It's like the area of the Germans I worked for," Lizzie said, amazed. She had spent her first few months in New Zealand as a maid in a village occupied by Lower Saxon farmers.

"Where do we find this wonder-worker, Te Whiti?" Michael asked.

The village was well populated, though Lizzie noticed it was lacking old people. It was afternoon, and Maori men and women would be in the fields or busy with other work. Typically, children would be lovingly watched by their elders in the village. Here, children were playing, but they were supervised by young women and girls.

Matariki nervously kept an eye out for overattention to tradition, but the *ariki* did not have a separate fire and the girls did not wear traditional clothing. Most were dressed in Western clothing—even on the North Island, the Maori had realized that *pakeha* clothes were better suited to New Zealand's climate than the light skirts and shawls of the Polynesians.

Michael stopped in front of a few women peeling sweet potatoes, and Lizzie asked about Te Whiti.

"Oh, he'll be in the fields," one of the girls answered, smiling. She seemed to be happy Lizzie spoke Maori. "If you're visitors, you'll be welcomed in one of the *marae*. You're a little early for the gathering. Most probably won't arrive until tomorrow or the day after. The *ariki* will speak when the moon waxes round. But please, feel at home, whether or not you speak to one of the chieftains. We are all Parihaka. Anyone will gladly answer your questions." With that, she pointed the way to the *marae* in the middle of the village.

"The people are all very nice," Matariki said, "and I'm already looking forward to the food. They're heating the *hangi*, did you see? I haven't seen that in a long time."

Hangi were traditional earthen ovens, heated with warmed stones, but here, close to Mount Taranaki, they were likely also heated by volcanic activity. One made holes and lowered in meat and vegetables in baskets. After a few hours, the food could be dug back out, fully cooked.

Kupe could not remember ever having seen such a thing.

At the *marae*, a group of girls was turning the common lodge into a guest house, cleaning and laying out mats.

"You're early," this welcome committee also declared. "Most guests come just before the gathering. But we're happy for you to take part in village life until then. Please forgive us for not greeting everyone with an individual *powhiri*. If we did, we'd never finish singing and dancing. Up to a thousand guests come to the monthly gatherings."

Michael smiled at the girls. "Do I look like I could dance the *wero*?" he teased them.

The *wero* was a war dance belonging to the greeting ceremony. An especially strong warrior performed it, and his movements signaled whether the visitor came in peace.

"You, no, but he could," one girl laughed, and pointed to Kupe, smiling flirtatiously at him. "You're tattooed. That's rare. Are you a chieftain's son?"

"No, I, it's really more because it's *kitanga*."

If the girl was surprised by the warrior who could not even pronounce the simple word for "custom" properly, she did not let it show.

"It's become fashionable among the Maori again, but I wouldn't have it done. It hurts terribly. But you know that. You must be very brave."

Lizzie noticed that Kupe seemed to like the girl's flirtation and that Matariki didn't seem at all jealous.

Lizzie descended from the carriage. "*Kia ora*. We're happy to be here," she said. "I'm Elizabeth Drury—in Maori, Irihapeti. Originally from London, but I lived with the Ngati Pau, and now we share the *wahi* of an *iwi* of the Ngai Tahu."

The oldest Maori girl approached her and exchanged *hongi*, pressing her forehead and nose to Lizzie's. "*Haere mai*, Irihapeti. I'm Koria of the Ngati Porou. I hope you do not see an enemy in me."

The Ngati Porou were old rivals of the Ngati Pau.

"I don't have any enemies," Lizzie said amiably. "And if I've properly understood the spirit of Parihaka, there's not supposed to be enmity among the individual tribes. Meet my daughter. She is half–Ngati Pau."

Matariki beamed at Koria and likewise offered her nose and forehead. "Let's be friends," Koria said enthusiastically once the girls had hugged.

Matariki nodded. "Can I help with anything here?"

Lizzie picked up a broom. Koria pressed a stack of blankets into Matariki's hands.

"You can place one of these on each of the mats. And Pai will show the men where they can unharness the horses."

She glanced at Kupe and winked impishly at Matariki. Pai was the girl who had spoken to Kupe about his tattoos and could not take her eyes off him.

***

When evening came, quitting time seemed to be its own festival in Parihaka. The people ate and drank, danced and made music, and the guests were naturally made a part of it as was customary among the Maori.

Matariki enjoyed being with girls her age. They laughed and clapped as she tried to perform the tribal *haka* of the Ngai Tahu of Tuapeka all alone. Pai clung to Kupe, plying him with food and beer. Lizzie was amused and concerned when she noted that despite Pai's attention, he had eyes for only Matariki.

Neither Kupe nor Michael felt excluded because they spoke no, or very little, Maori. Almost all the residents of Parihaka spoke English, many fluently. That confirmed Lizzie's supposition that the town was not a refugee camp for the displaced of the Maori Wars. It might have begun like that, but now Parihaka was home to young Maori who were unhappy about the *pakeha* intrusion into their world but did not want to respond with force of arms. Almost every one of them had a story—rarely one as dramatic as Kupe's—of wandering between the two worlds, which led to the desire to unite in peace.

"For peace to happen, we must show the *pakeha* that we're not stupid savages," Koria said. "We won't impress them by dancing a *haka*, sticking out our tongues, and threatening them with spears. They need to see that we can organize our community, cultivate our land, manage our affairs, and direct our schools—just as they do. We're not ashamed to adopt things from them, but hopefully they will see that they can also learn something from us."

Kupe was excited by this philosophy, and even Matariki seemed impressed. They caught each other slinking around the second *marae*, next to which there was a small sleeping lodge. They had learned that Te Whiti o Rongomai, the spiritual leader of Parihaka, lived here. It wasn't long before they spotted a white-bearded man who had a big head topped with dark hair. He wore a *pakeha* hat and poorly fitting *pakeha* clothing.

Te Whiti was talking with two other men. One was his representative, Tohu Kakahi; the other was his friend and relative, Te Whetu. When Matariki stumbled slightly on a rock, she drew the men's attention, and all three smiled at her. Matariki immediately noticed that Te Whiti was not tattooed, and she found that comforting.

***

Over the next few days, the village of Parihaka filled with visitors coming to the meeting, the monthly gathering at which Te Whiti and Te Whetu spoke.

On the second day, Koria and Pai asked Matariki to sing and dance with them. They lent her a *piu-piu* skirt and a top, into which the special pattern of Parihaka was woven. Matariki wore it proudly, dancing with the others, though the steps were not yet familiar to her.

Te Whiti and Tohu Kakahi were rarely seen before the full moon, busy as they were with speaking to the leaders of the various groups and advising them to work together. For the Maori tribes of the North Island, the thought of *kingitangai*—the unification of all tribes under one king—was not new. With Tawhiao there was a second king in office, and they still found it difficult to see themselves as one people. Te Whiti often had to ease minor strife.

Koria and the other villagers who spoke fluent English concerned themselves with the visiting *pakeha*, of whom there were many. Some were sent by the provincial government and the military, and there were journalists too. Others were just enthusiasts, people who were as excited as the young Maori about community life in Parihaka and would gladly have lived there. While *pakeha* were welcome as visitors, the village belonged to the natives.

***

By the day of the meeting, the population had grown by more than a thousand people, and the Drurys noted with respect how the residents mastered this crowd. The cooking houses and bakeries worked double time. Brigades of fishers and hunters went out to ensure provisions. Kupe went with them. He learned how to catch birds in the traditional way with snares, and proudly showed his prey to Matariki.

"And they even have the spirits on their side," Lizzie said when they all gathered at sunset to listen to Te Whiti in a clearing in front of the village. "At least those responsible for the weather. Isn't this light beautiful?"

Indeed, the sunset tinged the sky and the snow on Mount Taranaki with a symphony of colors. Varied shades of red mingled with ocher. The sea looked struck by arrows of gold and silver. The waves played with the last light of the sun. Even the dancers and singers, who greeted the visitors at the beginning of the meeting, seemed enchanted. They spoke the traditional prayers, danced their message of peace, and finally, an older woman let out the *karanga* with impressive fervor. Matariki thought her own attempt to unite the worlds of the gods and people must have sounded blasphemous. Now, however, she felt protected and blessed—and did not even resist when Kupe, moved, reached for her hand.

***

Finally, Te Whiti stepped before the crowd, wearing traditional chieftain's clothing. His ceremonial weapons were simple, and his assistant arranged them unobtrusively beside him. His wool cloak was not half as costly as Kahu Heke's feather cloak, with which Matariki protected herself from the evening chill.

Te Whiti, though diminutive, seemed to grow before his audience. He spoke Maori but paused every few sentences so Koria could translate his words into English.

"My name," said Te Whiti, "is Te Whiti o Rongomai. I belong to the Patukai, a *hapu* of the Ngati Tawhirikura. My family has represented for generations the chieftains of our tribe. I, too, was chosen for this, and like every *ariki*, I am a warrior. I was born and raised to fight, and I was present many times when my people awoke Tumatauenga, the war god, against the invaders who wanted to take our land. I bravely paid homage to that god, but as I shed my blood, doubt stirred within me. Killing is not what the gods had in mind. That's what our faith tells us, and that's what the *pakeha* tell them. Through violence, my friends, nothing good has ever come into this world. Violence changes us, and not for the good. Through violence a foreign force has gained power over us. Through violence we become slaves—slaves of death and the god Tumatauenga. I learned this, friends. I felt this, and I would like to pass this message on to you: Free yourselves from killing and from violence. There is no reason why war should have power over us. Be free. Let peace set you free."

Matariki and Kupe cheered with the others while Lizzie and Michael looked at each other skeptically. They had not always had the experience that the world belonged to peaceful people. Usually it was the opposite.

Te Whiti smiled at his audience. "I'm happy that many of you understand me and hear the admonition of the gods. But I also see fretful faces. In many of your hearts, darkness still reigns, and I understand that. I feel your sorrow when you see your land ravaged by the gold digging and coal mining of the whites. I feel your rage when they devour more and more from the ground that is sacred to your tribes. It is a justified rage, and I agree that we must stop them. But not with violence, not by taking up arms. The weapons of the *pakeha* are stronger. You cannot win a war against them with your *mere* and *waihaka* and *taiaha* and the few weapons for which you've traded with the enemy. The British Crown has fought for centuries, friends. It has subjugated as many people as there are stars in the sky."

"Not all that many," Michael grumbled.

Lizzie shrugged. "When he's right, he's right," she said. "*Taiaha*, as important as the speared clubs are for the Maori warrior, can't hold up against cannons. That uneven fight results in dead Maori and land for the whites. The question is what to do instead. The Maori can't wish the *pakeha* away."

"The *pakeha* are sure that they'll gain victory with their weapons," Te Whiti continued, "but I, friends, I am sure that we can win by the strength of our spirit. Our spiritual strength illuminates this land, and from this village the light will emanate. We will show the *pakeha* how we live. We will invite them to call the spirits with us. We will convince them that peace grants strength, much more strength than the violence of all the weapons in the British Empire."

The audience cheered as Te Whiti finished. Many of them, Matariki and Kupe included, sprang up singing and dancing.

Lizzie raised her eyebrows. "As long as it doesn't go awry," she remarked.

Lizzie Drury had her own experiences with a life pleasing to God. As a young woman, she had often tried praying, but she came to the conclusion that God largely stayed away from her affairs. Lizzie had been forced to lie and deceive. Once she had to use force to save her life. Though in that case, she had the Maori spirits on her side. When she had smashed the war club into the temple of her attacker, she believed her hand had been guided by one of the legendary female warriors of the tribes.

"You can't eat illumination," Michael said. "We Irish didn't lack for priests during the famine."

Matariki looked at her parents. "You don't understand him," she said. "Even though it's so simple. It's wonderful, I—"

"Shh, Te Whetu's speaking now," Kupe admonished. "He's imposing, isn't he?"

Te Whetu was younger and taller than Te Whiti, his voice more resonant. He introduced himself as a relative and confidant of Te Whiti and as a veteran of the Taranaki Wars. Then, he spoke to his concerns. "Te Whiti, our great chieftain, has heard the voices of the spirits. You, however, hear the voices of the *pakeha*, and I know they are often masters of eloquence. The spirits counsel us peace, friends, but they don't counsel us to give up. So, be watchful, be friendly, but not trusting. The *pakeha* will try everything to move you to give up your land, and sometimes their reasoning cannot be cast lightly aside. Trains now connect people across the country. Pasturelands assure the supply of meat. We know that these were concerns for our forefathers and that the tribes went to war for the sake of their hunting grounds. But all this should benefit us as much as the *pakeha*. There is no reason their sheep should graze on our sacred sites or even on land that simply belongs to us. If they want our land, they must pay fairly for it. And they must ask if we even want to sell it. Be smart, friends, and do not fall for the bribes offered to your chieftains. Don't let them pressure or convince you; don't let them drown out your voices. Show the whites that we have dignity. Receive them with politeness, but do not give an inch when it comes to what your tribe has decided about its land."

Te Whetu also earned loud applause—even from many tribal members who had still been skeptical before. After his speech, the visitors and villagers separated into smaller groups to discuss what they had heard. Then everything flowed into a festival with song and dance, food and whiskey and beer.

"A whiskey distillery would be worthwhile here," said Michael with an expert glance around. Matariki glared at him.

"You don't take any of it seriously," she said bitterly. "What's with the two of you? Don't you believe Te Whiti?"

Lizzie arched her brows. "It's not a question of belief. The man certainly has honorable intentions. But I fear he's not going to convince Her Majesty's army."

"If we receive Her Majesty's army with flowers and children's laughter, they will sing and celebrate with us just like the warriors of the tribes," Pai said. "Look, over there: the Ngati Pau dance with the Ngati Porou, and the Te Maniapoto exchange *hongi* with the Ngati Toa. That's the wonder of Parihaka, the wonder of Te Whiti."

"I'd attribute it more to the effect of the whiskey," said Michael. "But either way, it's better than the *pakeha* and Maori fighting. I don't really believe in wonders, and instead of spirits, I'd seek out lawyers to represent the tribes against the government. But Parihaka is a nice village, and I like Te Whiti a lot more than Kahu Heke."

"Then you won't have anything against my staying here," Matariki said sharply.

"You want to do *what*?" Michael yelled. "Have you lost your senses?"

Lizzie sighed. "No. I'm afraid she's found them."

Michael glared at mother and daughter. "Forget the expression," he said sternly. "Matariki, you can't stay here. You're too young to get by on your own. You—"

"I've had to get along on my own for months," Matariki interrupted, "and I'm not alone here, anyway."

"So that's the direction the wind's blowing. You're in love. This Kupe—"

Michael looked around, and he saw Pai and Kupe together not far away.

"Kupe has nothing to do with it." Matariki threw back her hair wildly. "I just want—"

"What about school, Riki?" Lizzie asked calmly. She had known since their arrival in Parihaka that her daughter had made her decision, but she wanted to at least talk it through. "Don't you want to finish school before you decide to be solely Maori?"

"I can go to school here," Matariki said. "I already discussed it with the teachers. And I'll even get to teach English to the little ones."

"Can the teachers here bring you to the same level as finishing high school?" Lizzie was skeptical. "You should think everything through once more, Matariki. Anyone can work the fields and show the *pakeha* how diligent and proper the Maori people are. But you can go to university. You know Dunedin accepts women in every subject. You can study medicine and work as a doctor here, or specialize in land sales as a lawyer. You could really change things, Matariki. In a few years—"

"It might be too late in a few years. I want to change things right now."

Matariki walked away confidently, every inch a chieftain's daughter. Her father's *korowai* hung on her shoulders. Lizzie finally recalled where she had previously seen the cloak. The great chieftain Hongi Hika had worn it when he gave Kahu Heke permission to take the *pakeha wahine* to safety from her *pakeha* pursuers in the chieftain's canoe. Everything had begun with that. And now her daughter was grown, and she strode with sure steps to the fire in the middle of the gathering place. Calm and self-assured, Matariki approached Te Whiti and bowed before him.

Lizzie watched him address her in a friendly manner, and she held her breath when her daughter took off the valuable feather cloak and laid it in Te Whiti's hands. Kahu Heke had wanted to use it to declare war and stoke hatred. Now, instead of a goddess of war, a prophet and peacemaker would wear it.

Lizzie did not believe in Te Whiti's message, but when she saw the dignified old chieftain in conversation with her daughter, she teared up with emotion.

Michael likewise observed the gesture.

"A present chosen smartly," he observed. "She's introducing herself as a chieftain's daughter from the first."

Lizzie frowned. "I don't think she has hidden motives. She's completely under his spell."

Michael bit his lip. He watched as Matariki bowed to Te Whiti once more and then went back to her friends. The girl sat down at ease beside Pai and Kupe.

"Do you think she'll marry him?" Michael asked.

Lizzie looked at her husband as if he'd lost his mind. "Te Whiti? For heaven's sake—"

"Lord, no." Michael waved that notion away. "Kupe, the boy. He's head over heels in love with her."

Kupe was just then handing Matariki a cup of wine. She thanked him with a laugh.

Lizzie rolled her eyes. "But she's not for him," she observed. "She doesn't have any feelings for the poor boy. But maybe he can hold his breath and hope longer." She smiled and cuddled against her husband. She, too, had to struggle for her at first hopeless-seeming love. "Who knows the ways of the spirits, after all?"

Michael put his arm around her, and for a while they watched their daughter. She did not look back at them. She joked with the others and finally began to dance with them. Her body swayed in the moonlight.

"Do you think we've lost her?" Michael asked. His voice sounded choked.

Lizzie shook her head. The night over Parihaka was beautiful. Starlight made the snow on Mount Taranaki shine like silver, and where earlier it had been the last sun's rays, now the moon's kiss brushed against the sea. It grew cold. And Lizzie mistrusted the magic.

"No," she said with another look at Matariki. "She'll come back. Someday she'll wake up from this dream."

Chapter 2

Seven-year-old Caleb Biller proved a much better teacher than Reverend Clusky in Violet's old Sunday school or even Heather Coltrane. Maybe it was because he recently had learned to read, or perhaps it was natural talent. From him, Violet learned reading and writing at breathtaking speed. Granted, she had plenty of time for it. Caleb showed little interest in typical boys' games. He did not climb trees, thought racing childish, and preferred analyzing grasshoppers with the help of a reference book rather than ripping off their legs. He left the house only when he had to, and even then, he took a book with him. Violet followed suit.

During Caleb's preferred activities like reading and piano playing, he did not need company, and he was pleased that Violet liked to read while he pored over reference books.

Violet preferred newspapers. Though she liked to read stories, she wasn't yet a proficient enough reader for great literature, and Caleb's children's books and Hermine Biller's women's journals were too different from her daily life. Violet was not interested in princesses and did not believe in heroes. She wanted to discover what was happening in the real world. She made a habit of taking the Christchurch and Dunedin daily newspapers off the Billers' breakfast table when she retrieved tea from the kitchen for herself and Caleb. Joshua Biller had already looked through the papers by then, and Hermine did not read them, so it did not bother anyone when Violet made off with her "instructional reading." Caleb patiently helped her through them once they finished their morning tea.

"'Dunedin. Renewed pro-protests before the public houses.'" Violet sounded it out. "'Last Saturday evening, three large taverns in Dunedin became targets of the ab-abstinence movement.' What is that, Caleb?" Violet looked up from the newspaper.

"Abstinence." Caleb said the word fluidly and looked it up in his dictionary. "'Anti-alcoholism.' Those are people who want to ban whiskey."

Violet understood, but she could hardly believe it.

"Seriously, Caleb? There is such a movement? Will it ever happen? I mean, can it be that they'd really outlaw the stuff?"

Caleb shrugged. "I don't know. Keep reading. Maybe they say."

"'The, the emotional women around Mrs. Harriet Morison pat-patrolled from opening until closing in front of the public house entrances after joining together at the Anglican church in Caversham and breaking into groups. The alco-alcohol opponents preached against whiskey and violence. They see the frequent visits of their husbands to the public houses as the root cause of their poverty and the destruction of their families. While singing the hymn "Give to the Winds Thy Fears," they waved banners and tried to prevent drunks from visiting the establishments. Two of the barkeepers requested help from the police, who could do no more than warn the bell-bell-i-bellicose women.

"'"No wonder their husbands flee to the pubs," the police officer in charge said, "but as long as they remain on public streets and do nothing more to draw attention than sing church songs out of tune, our hands are tied." The officer appealed to Reverend Peter Burton, who offered his church as a meeting point for the women, to no avail.

"'"The intentions of the women are serious and respectable and completely in line with our parish," said Reverend Burton. "If fewer men took their money to the pubs, fewer needy mothers and children would be seeking relief."'

"Hey, Caleb, I know him, the reverend." Violet beamed. "And if Reverend Burton throws himself into it, then maybe they really will ban whiskey drinking."

"My dad drinks a glass of whiskey every night," he said. "What's bad about it?"

Violet sighed. How could she explain to him what whiskey did to a man who was not content to stop at one? She tried it first with cautious words, but then the truth burst out of her.

"It's not just that they're drunk in the evening." Violet fought back tears. "Sometimes in the mornings, they don't wake up right when they've overdone it. Recently my father was sent home from work because he still couldn't walk straight. That's dangerous in a mine. He was angry because that cost him his pay for the day. Usually he'd beat me, but I was here, with you, so his anger fell to Rosie because she did not want to make him lunch, even though she can't do that yet, and besides, there was no food in the house. The teetotalers and Reverend Burton are completely right: men drink their pay away, and women and children go hungry."

Caleb chewed on his lip. Clearly, he had never heard of such difficulties before.

"You should bring her with you," he said.

"Who?" she asked, confused, wiping her nose. Under no circumstances could Mrs. Biller see that she had been crying.

"Your sister," said Caleb. "How old is she? You can say she's here to play with me."

Violet looked at him, uncomprehending. "You want to play with a little girl?"

Caleb rolled his eyes. "I don't play with anyone. I am not a baby," he repeated his standard line. "Though my mom seems to think so. She'll be overjoyed, since I don't ever play with anyone. Look." Caleb opened one of the cabinets in his playroom, and an array of stuffed animals, wooden horses, and toy trains tumbled out. "She can have all of it," he said generously. "She won't scream all day, will she?"

Caleb was suspicious of other children. With the invitation to bring Rosie, he was swallowing much of his pride. Violet appreciated that. She was touched. "Rosie doesn't scream at all," she assured Caleb. "She's a well-behaved girl and almost six years old now. You'll hardly notice her, believe me."

***

Rosie did indeed prove herself impeccably well behaved, and at the sight of the toys, she fell into a sort of stupor. Besides her little doll, she had never owned a toy. Naturally, she did not go unnoticed in the house. Mrs. McEnroe fell in love with her at first sight.

"Just call me Auntie," she cooed. "Will you come visit me in the kitchen sometimes?" The cook added a third kind of jam to the breakfast tray. "You could even help me. Do you like to bake scones?"

Rosie did not know what scones were and was so intimidated by the fat, warmhearted woman, the giant house, and the unbelievable breakfast that she did not answer.

Mrs. McEnroe did not take offense. In fact, she baked some scones that afternoon, which even excited Caleb, who loved scones.

"Why doesn't she ever make them just for me?" he asked, stuffing scones into his mouth at almost the same rate as Rosie.

Violet laughed. "Because you've managed to make her stop thinking that you're cute. When you were still a baby, I'm sure she spoiled you."

***

Violet had feared the first encounter between Rosie and Mrs. Biller, but Hermine was enthusiastic. "Violet, you truly do apply yourself on Caleb's behalf. You noticed that he was lonely, didn't you? He really must play with other children. A little boy would have been better." Somewhat mistrustfully, she eyed Rosie, who had shyly curtsied but now turned her attention to the train set, which Caleb was building for her on the floor. He even lowered himself to call out, "Toot-toot." "But you don't have a little brother, and we don't want some stranger's child, do we? Thank you, Violet. It really is touching that you go to such lengths."

Caleb rolled his eyes when his mother rushed out.

"I told you. She thinks I'm a baby," he said, leaving Rosie to play with the train herself.

Violet breathed a sigh of relief and glanced happily at her sister, who just then murmured a barely audible "toot."

***

Over the next few months, Violet and Rosie finally found peace again. The nights were still horrible. Violet got too little sleep, since she was always nervously awaiting Jim and Fred's homecoming. As she had planned, she bought a lock to keep out drunken neighbors. Jim had a key, but when he was drunk, he often couldn't find it and accused Violet of locking him out. Naturally he punished this offense with a beating, so Violet half slept as she listened for her father's steps and ran to open the door before he even tried to open it. Usually that worked, but sometimes he accused her of waiting for a lover at the door. There were blows for that as well.

The days were calmer and lovelier. As soon as her father and brother had left, she and Rosie fled the cramped, evil-smelling hut for the Billers' villa and its world of wonders: Caleb's books and toy chest, Mrs. McEnroe's cooking and baking, and even Mrs. Biller's vague friendliness. Until early fall, Violet took the children to the river in the afternoon, and often Caleb watched Rosie when tiredness overcame Violet. It always amazed her how lovingly Caleb treated Rosie. Though he did not like to play with Rosie, he read to her or played the piano for her. Violet was moved to tears when he played a children's song and Rosie suddenly sang along with her sweet voice, which she had not done since their mother died.

***

"We should teach her to read," Caleb said one day.

Violet now read fluently and followed with interest the reports about Mrs. Morison and her battle against alcohol. That it was about other things, too, did not become clear to Violet until she became witness to a bitter debate between Hermine and Joshua Biller.

"I repeat, Hermine, it might be printed ten times in your supposedly harmless housewives' magazine, but I will not tolerate such radical texts in my house."

"I haven't even read it, Joshua, but, but it cannot be so radical. She is right: All laws apply to women. Women can be judged for crimes and even receive the death penalty, just like men. And if you look at the schools—are girls really worse learners than boys?"

"So, you didn't read it, eh?" scoffed Mr. Biller.

"Maybe I read a bit," Mrs. Biller admitted. Her voice suddenly sounded fuller. "And I don't find it radical. What makes the woman great? She remembers everything women have done for this country. She points out injustices."

"She demands the unnatural," insisted Mr. Biller. "She's mad. And you'll throw this pamphlet away this instant. I don't want to think about someone seeing it here. People would think I didn't have control of my wife. Do you hear me, Hermine? This instant."

Joshua Biller did not wait for his wife to obey. Instead, he reached for the periodical, which was on the buffet, and threw it into the trash can.

Violet fished it out when he had left and Mrs. Biller had withdrawn to her bedroom with a migraine.

She carried it up to Caleb's room and read the article in question while the boy had his "afternoon nap." He was also flipping through some book during this time. Mrs. Biller insisted that Violet take her son to his bed, so they both obeyed. Rosie was the only one who slept during naptime, and she was stretched out on the rug in the playroom.

"Some 'Femina' wrote it, but that's not her real name, right?" Violet asked when she had finished.

Caleb pointed to the dictionary on the shelf without saying anything. Violet soon discovered that it was the root of "feminine."

"So, that just means 'woman' or 'female,'" she said. "And Femina says women should be able to vote."

This demand astonished Violet. Until then she had never thought about voting. She had heard of it, but her father had never taken part in an election.

Caleb shrugged. "They would have to if they want to ban whiskey," he said.

Violet looked at him uncomprehendingly.

"Well, if you want to forbid it, you need a law for that, and Parliament makes the laws, and representatives sit in Parliament, and they're elected. Don't you know anything, Violet?"

Violet felt stupid again. Yet in this light, Femina's demand was understandable.

"Why haven't women been able to vote before?" she asked.

Caleb shrugged. "I don't know," he said, disinterested. "Probably because they're not smart enough. I don't think my mom is especially smart."

Violet was pleased that at least he did not present her as an example of female inadequacy. Although from Caleb she would have accepted it. Compared to the strange boy, other people—men and women alike—were not terribly smart, and they did not think quickly enough. She had even heard the pastor complain to Mrs. Biller that soon he would not be able to teach the boy anything more. Caleb was almost better at Latin than the pastor himself.

What about people like her father? Or Fred and Eric? They could barely read or write—although Eric was better than the other two. Ellen Paisley had been smarter than her husband by a long shot. And even if the acknowledgment made Violet's heart pound, she was smarter than her father too.

So why should her father vote and not her? Why was Joshua Biller allowed to decide what periodicals his wife read? What gave Jim Paisley the right to treat his daughters like slaves, to drink away the family's money, and to beat Violet?

Violet decided to fight for the right to vote.

Chapter 3

Matariki led a busy life in Parihaka. In the morning, she and two other girls fluent in English watched a group of small children and taught them English. Week by week, the group grew. The people in Parihaka had faith in the future and loved one another, driving the birthrate high.

In the afternoon, Matariki and her friends dedicated themselves to their studies, working diligently through the secondary-school syllabi in preparation for graduation exams in a high school in Wellington or Auckland. So far, no student from Parihaka had failed the exams, so there was pressure on the young people.

Really, however, there weren't many worries, particularly since everyone in Parihaka was completely dedicated to its mission. No matter how hard they worked during the day, they spent their evenings enjoying dancing and music, or practicing traditional Maori arts.

The longer Parihaka existed, the more willingly the tribes of the North Island participated. They sent *tohunga* to teach the villagers how to make and play the old musical instruments, and they built their own *marae* where their tribal gods lived.

Kupe had a particularly memorable encounter when an *iwi* of the Hauraki arrived. The tribe had been driven from the region of Hamilton and lived nomadically ever since. Everybody greeted one another with the customary *powhiri*, and Kupe noticed that the young man who performed the *wero* was not a pure-blooded Maori. He spoke to him shyly because it was not polite to remind mixed-race Maori about their ancestry. Many were ashamed of their *pakeha* fathers. Arama, however, was open and friendly with his answer.

"I wasn't happy to leave," he admitted. "I would have preferred to keep going to school and then probably become a farmer like my father. I don't have much talent for hunting, let alone for being a warrior."

"But you do for being a dancer," Kupe laughed. "The way you made that face—it almost made me afraid."

These gestures were part of the war dances of the tribes, and Arama had mastered them. Solely by reason of his stature, he already garnered respect. Sam Drechsler's son was a giant.

Now, he grinned. "You see, in Hamilton they would have sent the army after me. It was the right thing to go. But I miss the farm. Maybe things will change someday."

Kupe nodded. "That's why we're here," he said seriously. "You can write to your father, you know. Parihaka has a post office. And a school. And a farm. Is your mother here too? I would like to tell both of you what your father did for me."

***

Arama's mother was a *tohunga* in jade carving. She instructed Matariki and the other girls in carving *hei-tiki* and *mere*. Matariki also tried to improve her playing of the *putorino*, a type of flute. Kupe was proud when, after a year, he was allowed to dance the *wero* at the *powhiri* before Te Whiti's speech. Like his new friend Arama, he was a gifted dancer and musician—and his Maori got better every day now that he did not limit himself to focusing on the chanting of nonsense syllables. Kupe was the smartest of the young people, and soon after arriving in Parihaka, he took the graduation exam and passed with high grades. He could have gone to university in Auckland, but he remained in Parihaka. It was exciting to watch the village grow and the movement expand with more members.

The gatherings were now attended by around three thousand people. While the message of peace was always communicated, the people at the meetings hoped to gain better understanding by airing their grievances. Just as Parihaka's population grew, so, too, did the population through the plains and the hills around Taranaki. White settlers poured in by the thousands. They were greedy for land, and the provincial government did everything it could to offer it to them. The tribe representatives reported on the occupation of land and the destruction of fences and other property. Tribes drove away the land surveyors, which became another reason for the *pakeha* to accuse them of revolt and confiscate their land "as punishment."

***

Te Whiti and Te Whetu did not mince words when they spoke to the people at the full moon. They had collected evidence against the *pakeha*, who attempted to bribe the chieftains in Taranaki with alcohol, clothing, and perfume into giving away their land. Te Whetu exposed the false promises of the *pakeha* to avoid the fishing grounds and *tapu* sites of the Maori and to reimburse the natives fairly in land sales.

"Friends, they make no secret of their intention to profit from the sale of our land and cheat us. They are offering more than six thousand acres of our land for sale to the settlers."

It was no wonder that the reporting on Parihaka and its spiritual leaders in the *pakeha* newspapers was slowly changing. It was rare now for journalists to write enthusiastic stories of Te Whiti's peaceful and friendly intentions. Instead, they called his speeches blasphemous and rebellious, and they reported on dangers emanating from Parihaka and the fateful influence of its leader on the tribes.

Nothing about Te Whiti's approach had changed. Just as before, the speakers at the meetings called for understanding, politeness, and the peaceful setting aside of conflicts.

"Above all, do not take up arms against the settlers," Te Whetu advised the tribes when they complained about sheep grazing without permission on their hills. "They cannot do anything about it. They bought and paid for their land. The money went to the wrong people. Try to make that clear to the settlers. Try to make them see that they, too, were cheated. There are clear rules among the *pakeha*: when they buy jewelry from a purveyor of stolen goods, then they have not committed a crime, but they cannot keep the jewelry either. The purveyor is guilty and so is the thief. We must find ways and means to explain this to the settlers. But without awaking Tumatauenga."

***

The Maori tribes understood this argument, though their concept of land ownership diverged starkly from that of the *pakeha* and based itself more on temporary use than on property. The settlers did not want to hear it. After all, they had saved for years for their farm in Taranaki. Now, it seemed so much easier to them to defend themselves against a handful of natives than to ask for their money back from the government.

Matariki was as outraged as the other citizens of Parihaka, but there wasn't a clear solution to the problem. The tribes began to grumble about Te Whiti's strategy of stalling. Further negotiations faltered, and the patience of the Maori reached an end.

At one gathering, Te Whetu detailed the future strategy.

"Friends, Parihaka has more than a hundred oxen, ten horses, and a matching number of plows at its disposal. We will now offer them to our neighbors. It is certainly so that the tribes that came to Aotearoa in the Tokomaru possess all the land in Oakura and Hawera, where the *pakeha* farms are springing up. The land has lain fallow, grass grew on it, and now the whites want to graze their sheep on it. But if our friends among the tribes decide to plow their land? It is their right. Maybe they want to raise potatoes and cabbage, or they just like to look at a few lovely, straight furrows."

Te Whetu and the other chieftains smiled sardonically as laughter spread through the audience. So that was what the men had in mind. Peaceful protest through use of the land. Once the pastures were plowed, they would be useless to the sheep farmers for years.

"We will begin tomorrow. The best plowmen will go to Oakura. Bear in mind, we're plowing, not fighting. Be polite to the settlers, inform them in a friendly manner. Do not defend yourselves even if they lay hands on you."

***

"Are you going to volunteer?" Matariki asked Kupe. They were celebrating the chieftain's speech that evening. The first plowmen could hardly wait to set out.

Kupe nodded. "Of course. Though I've never plowed before. But I think they'll soon start teaching people. The first ones will be gone soon, after all."

"Gone?" Pai asked, horrified. "You don't really think they'll shoot at the men?"

Kupe shrugged. "It's not without risk. They'll certainly threaten us, and you never know when someone will pull the trigger. Primarily they'll probably stick to arrest, though. I'd bet Te Whiti has already alerted all our lawyers. When the plowmen are arrested, the plows will be abandoned, so more people will need to be taught to use them."

"Oh, a lot of time will pass before that," Matariki said. "The farmers will long since have left, and our plowmen will be free."

Kupe arched his brows. "I wouldn't count on that. This is going to be a long struggle."

***

The next morning, a long train of oxen and plows moved toward Oakura, cheered on by the villagers who stayed behind. Te Whiti, Tohu Kakahi, and Te Whetu remained in Parihaka, but other chieftains, including those of the affected tribes, traveled with the plowmen. Kupe went along as a translator.

A few days later, he was back. Weary and exhausted but enthusiastic as ever, he reported on the first events.

"At first they did not even notice us. Even though we really made enough noise with our singing, the construction of the camp, and the oxen and horses. The *pakeha* don't pay any attention to anything not happening in front of their own door. On the farm where I was stationed, we worked the first three days unmolested. We plowed eight acres. The farmer almost went berserk when he finally noticed. Luckily, he was halfway understanding. When I explained to him that was a political action, and he should turn to the government, he went straight to New Plymouth. Before he left, we promised him we would not continue, and the plowmen went to the next farm. I'm here to report to Te Whiti. I'll be off again tomorrow. And I'm supposed to take a few girls as translators. The chieftains said the farmers wouldn't have such itchy trigger fingers then. Want to come?"

He looked at Matariki, but naturally Pai was the first to join him. Matariki still saw the young man as a friend, not a lover, and she worried about her apparent inability to fall in love. She did not lack for admirers. Both villagers and visitors courted her, but Matariki could not warm up to any of them. She tried, even letting some Maori boys caress her and *pakeha* visitors kiss her. She particularly liked a university student from Dunedin with soft blond hair and brown eyes. But her joy in his appearance did not exceed what she felt at the sight of a beautiful picture or the performance of a good dancer. While his kisses and compliments were pleasant, her heart did not beat faster at them, nor did she have feelings to match those Koria poetically described as belonging to love.

Matariki wanted to be in Oakura, so she set out the next morning with Kupe, Pai, and Koria. According to Kupe, the plowmen meant to work their way from Hawera in the south to Pukearuhe in the north. They plowed wide swaths through farmland that belonged to the tribes. In Hawera, they ran into the first group of plowmen and heard about the governor, Sir Hercules Robinson.

"The fellow almost exploded with rage," said Tane, a square-built young man who hardly spoke English but knew how to direct his oxen with few words. "They've also informed the premier. The farmers seem to know who's responsible."

Unfortunately, this notion quickly revealed itself to be a lovely dream. The government made no effort to return the farmers' money. Instead, Major Harry Atkinson, member of Parliament, promised military training to any interested farmer. The magistrate of Patea announced that the Maori had exactly ten days to stop their action; otherwise, the citizens would begin shooting the plowmen and oxen.

On the second day of their translation work, Matariki and Koria had a dangerous encounter with a hundred armed men who stood in the way of the plowmen. Matariki and Koria approached them, smiling. "Do lower your weapons. We won't continue plowing this space if you want to stand or walk here," Matariki said gently. "We can plow elsewhere. You see, all of this land has belonged to the Ngati Ruanui tribe for hundreds of years, and they have only now decided to cultivate it, doing as the *pakeha* do. We see what good yields your farms produce, and we are prepared to learn from others. We don't care if we plow here today or tomorrow."

"This land is mine, miss," one of the farmers declared, a tall, skinny man who did not actually seem unkind. "I can prove it. I have a deed signed by the governor."

Matariki nodded. "I believe you, sir, but please ask the governor again if he also has a deed for the land signed by the chieftain of Ngati Ruanui. You see, he doesn't. Nor can he claim he dispossessed the Ngati Ruanui because they started some war. They didn't. I'm terribly sorry, but the governor sold you land that didn't belong to him. And you can't keep it."

"Oh, I can't, can't I?" The young man raised his gun helplessly, but he seemed to have scruples about aiming it at the girl standing before him.

"Alternatively, you could appeal to the governor to purchase the land from the Ngati Ruanui after the fact. We have nothing against you, sir. On the contrary, you have our respect. It testifies to great courage to pick up from England, or whencever you come, and sail into the unknown to acquire new land. We did that too, sir. We Maori come from far away, from Hawaiki. We sailed far and took on great hardships to take possession of this land. You understand why we won't simply let it be stolen from us. So, please, lower your weapons. You wouldn't achieve anything by shooting us, anyway. The Ngati Ruanui tribe has many members who can all plow. And a *pakeha* court would not have any sympathy for you if you shoot unarmed farmworkers and two girls. Please speak with the governor, Sir Robinson. In the meantime, we'll gladly plow elsewhere."

Matariki and Koria spoke a few words to the oxen drivers, at which they saluted politely and turned their teams away.

The young farmer addressed the girl again, confused by what was happening. "What, what is all this? We thought we'd have to hold you off with guns, but it's enough just to show up? First you cause trouble and then you wander off?"

Koria smiled gently. "This is a political act, sir. We just want to point out the property situation. We don't want a war. And as my friend already said, we can plow anywhere. If you want to stop us, you'll have to stand in our way everywhere. Perhaps if you place a man every two yards, then we wouldn't be able to get through. The governor sold sixty-four hundred acres of our land. You can go ahead and calculate how many men you'd need for that."

***

Over the next few days, the plowmen worked their way north. They were left alone by the white settlers thanks to the diplomacy of the interpreters. Nevertheless, the atmosphere became more aggressive. Major Harry Atkinson began teaching the settlers how to use their weapons, and the *Taranaki Herald* wrote that the man wanted a fight and ultimately the extermination of the whole Maori people. The premier, Sir George Grey, did not give such militaristic interviews, but he was also far removed from accepting any blame for illegal land sales. At best, the government would speak of misunderstandings, but more often of unruliness and revolt.

***

After a month of plowing, the government had to give in or negotiate. Matariki, enlivened by her successes among the settlers, was almost convinced the premier would come around. She was completely dumbfounded when their plowmen were suddenly confronted by the armed constables.

"You are all under arrest," the sergeant announced to the men behind the teams of oxen. "Resistance is futile."

"We won't be resisting." Matariki smiled sweetly, but this time she was unable to talk them out of the situation.

"Come with me," the constable ordered the plowmen without acknowledging Matariki.

"Us too?" asked Koria.

The man looked at her as if she were stupid. "Of course not, our orders don't mention any girls. You can get lost."

"And the oxen?" asked Matariki.

The constable looked confused. "I don't know. They—"

"You can't arrest oxen." Matariki seized her chance. "Arrest our people, but I'm taking the oxen."

The soldiers were astonished when the delicate girl reached for the reins of the lead ox and tenderly stroked its nose.

"Come, we're going home." Matariki smiled at the soldiers and turned the team around. The massive animals lumbered dutifully behind her, and the arrested team drivers nodded at her assured air of victory.

They were replaced the very same day with new plowmen. The Armed Constabulary arrested them too. A few hours later, Koria and Matariki secured the oxen again.

"It's a shame it requires so much strength; otherwise we could just plow ourselves," Matariki laughed. "Then the poor sergeant would be completely lost, since he's not supposed to arrest either girls or oxen."

The next day, instead of more plowmen, a delegation of chieftains and dignitaries appeared.

"The men with the most *mana* should be the first to put their hands on the plow," Te Whiti announced, and Matariki showed the great *ariki* Titokuwaru and his subordinate chieftains how to hold the reins of an oxen team. The warriors did not get much done before they were arrested. The prisons of Taranaki filled with prominent prisoners like Titokuwaru, Te Iki, and Te Matakatea.

In the meantime, the regular plowmen tried to avoid the soldiers' patrols and continued to plow. If the plowmen were arrested, the tribes immediately sent replacements. Soon the prisons of Taranaki were overfilled. They took men to the Mount Cook fort in Wellington where almost two hundred plowmen were incarcerated.

The government then stopped selling the land in question. In exchange, the Maori stopped plowing. The examination of the legality of the land seizures was to be left to the high court.

"So, a truce," Matariki said. "And Te Whiti agreed to that?"

The young translators were a bit sad they would have to return to their quiet life in Parihaka after the excitement in the plowmen's camps.

Kupe nodded. "Te Whiti wants peace. It would not have ended well if he continued now. Besides, we're running out of plowmen."

***

Lizzie Drury sighed with relief when she read the report about the compromise in the *Otago Daily Times*.

"I was afraid every day that they would shoot Riki," she admitted to her husband.

Michael nodded. "But this doesn't mean it's over. There's a lot more to this Te Whiti fellow than I thought. If the negotiations don't go his way, he'll think of something else—he lives dangerously. The Crown won't be bossed around for long."

"What if he remains peaceful?" Haikina asked. She had come to pan for gold with Hone, and Lizzie had invited them in for coffee when she discovered the news in the paper. "There could be isolated incidents of attacks. I've been worried for Matariki. But what could they do?"

Michael shrugged. "That I don't know," he said. "I only know there's one thing the English absolutely hate more than any revolt."

Hone nodded and smiled grimly. "They have that in common with all the warriors of the world," the Maori said wisely. "They don't like to be made fun of."

Chapter 4

Violet hurried home. It had been a later night than usual at the Billers'. Caleb was supposed to celebrate his eighth birthday the next day, although he had mixed feelings about the giant party his parents had planned. All he really wanted was the microscope he yearned for so much that he had handed his mother a list of options, complete with brands and model numbers. The idea of a party, and the tea and games with all the socially appropriate children between Greymouth and Westport, made him shudder.

Still, Caleb had done his best to help Violet inflate balloons and hang garlands when Rosie didn't want to help. Rosie had been allowed to take a red balloon home with her, and she was now back at the Paisleys' hut, waiting for Violet, who had to run to town.

She would have sent the letter to Heather Coltrane another day—she had been corresponding for weeks with her friend and was very proud that she could read Heather's letters and answer them with very few mistakes—but when she and Rosie returned home, Violet discovered, as she often did, that the family's food stores were completely gone. She had thought there was bread, but her father and brother must have eaten it during the day. Really that could only mean one thing: one or both of them had not been allowed to go down into the mine that day. They had likely been too far gone from drinking the night before.

Violet sighed, thinking of the lost wages that would result and, in turn, the anger. At least it was Violet's payday, so she didn't have to get the groceries on credit.

If only the blasted town were not so far from the miners' camp. It did not bother Violet to run back and forth, but the spring evening was already getting dark, and she was afraid of the path through the forest. It wasn't the shadowy ferns or the eerie cries of the birds that scared her but instead the men she might encounter. Violet's heart beat faster at every bend in the road, but she told herself that at this time of day she did not have anything to fear. The miners on the day shift had just gotten off work. Violet would be long home before they made their way to the pub.

Then halfway to Greymouth, Violet ran into a group of miners and lumberjacks. The men had just arrived in Greymouth, and they had turned their advance from the mine not only into wood and nails to build shelters, but also into whiskey.

"Now, who's this running our way? Such a pretty girl here at the ends of the earth?"

The man spoke with an Irish accent and had a nice smile. Violet lowered her gaze and tried to pass them quickly. However, another man immediately put himself in her path.

"Don't flirt, Paul. Just think of your Mary waiting at home," he said to the first man. "Me, on the other hand, sweetie, I'm all alone with no one to kiss."

The men laughed.

"Today, anyway," the man specified, "and the three months on the ship. It makes a man real sad, cutie. What do you think, would y'like to cheer me up?"

He reached for Violet's arm, but she shook him off. He let her go, which gave Violet hope. The four men were certainly tipsy, but not very drunk, and besides a few lewd remarks, they did not seem to mean her any harm.

"Cheer yourself up," Violet said firmly. "I need to get to town, and I'd like to be back before dark."

"I'd be happy to accompany you," said the third man, a blond with a soft, deep voice. "Tell me if you need protection. I'll be your knight."

"He's no knight, just a dreamer," the fourth man said. "Right, Sir Galahad?"

Rolling laughter made Violet think the young man had earned the nickname on many occasions.

"What do you think? Will you get to kiss the girl, or are you just talking again?"

The blond looked at his pals with gentle rebuke, frowning comically. "A few pretty words, gents, conquer a woman's heart quicker than a kiss, which here I'd have to steal anyway. Or would you be willing, princess?"

Now Violet had to laugh. This strange miner would almost have been able to touch her heart. But now she had to go. She was about to make a suitable riposte meant to let her depart in friendship—when the young man in front of her was brutally yanked backward. In the half-light, Violet could only see the outline of someone seizing him by the shirt, yanking him around, and punching him powerfully in the chin.

"D-d-don't you talk to my little sister like that." Fred Paisley slurred the words in a hiss.

Eric Fence was right behind Fred—no less drunk and spoiling for a fight. After the blow, "Sir Galahad" sank at once to the ground. It would not have surprised Violet if his jaw had been broken. The other three men formed a front to defend their pal. Paul, the oldest, went after Fred, but received a blow from Eric that struck him in the kidney and left him groaning. That was all it took for the six men to become entangled in an embittered brawl.

Violet, who at first had looked on in shock, finally tried to stop them, but it did no good to scream at Fred and Eric. They did not seem to hear her. They were in the rush of the fighting and appeared to have the upper hand on the new arrivals. After Sir Galahad and Paul were knocked out, the fight was evened out, though the new immigrants were surely weakened after the long journey by ship. Fred and Eric were rested from a sleepy and boozy day.

"I, I'll teach you t-to feel up m-my sister." Full of rage, Fred thrashed his opponent, and Eric did no less.

"Th-the girl is, is sacred to us," he shouted histrionically, and seemed to spur himself on with those words. "Like, like family, get, get it?"

With that, Eric sent his next opponent to the ground. The man moaned once more before losing consciousness.

Fred's adversary now grew visibly afraid. "We didn't do anything. Girl, girl, tell—"

The man turned desperately to Violet, who had been maintaining the entire time that the men had not hurt her.

It clearly did not matter to Fred and Eric whether they were striking the innocent or the guilty. Violet was almost happy that they unloaded their anger on the strong men rather than on Rosie or Violet herself.

It was clear to her that was not yet over when the last of the men fled into the darkness of the forest. Fred seemed to consider whether it was worth chasing after him, but then he turned to his sister instead.

"Well, Vio? How were we?" He grinned triumphantly.

Violet did not know how she was supposed to answer. Was it better to soothe the boys with praise, or would a sobering rebuke be more effective? No matter what, they should all get away as quickly as possible. The men on the ground had not moved for some time, and she hoped they weren't dead. She also hoped the fourth man would take care of his friends once Fred and Eric were out of the way.

"We saved you." Fred beamed.

Violet bit her lip. "I, I was not really in danger. I—"

"Ooh, look at her play coy. Little Violet, she's so brave, she could have defended herself. Or were they not bothering you at all, little sis? Maybe you wanted to make a little deal with the men?" Fred's voice became threatening and serious.

Eric, however, grinned. "Nonsense, Freddy, our little Violet, she's, she's much too fine for—" He boomed with laughter. "Nah, nah, Freddy, she just doesn't want to be grateful. That's it. She's too fine for a little gratitude."

Fred looked at his sister searchingly. "Is that it? You don't want to say thanks? It's real easy. Try it. 'Thank you, dear Fred.'" He grabbed Violet's arm hard.

She forced herself to breathe deeply. "Thank you, dear Fred," she said through clenched teeth.

Fred laughed derisively. "That was very nice," he praised. "And now: 'Thank you, dear Eric.'"

Violet swallowed. "Thank you, dear Eric," she spat out. "Can I go now? I need to get to the post office and to the store. Otherwise there will be trouble with Dad when he comes home. There's nothing to eat."

She did not really want to go to town. She would have preferred to run straight home and crawl with Rosie into their shared bed. Yet the road to Greymouth was the only possible escape path if the boys really let her go. Besides, then she could tell Mrs. Travers about the wounded men on the road. The gravedigger's wife would send help.

Eric Fence scratched his nose. "Anyone can say it," he said, "but if you're really thankful, you'll show it too."

Violet tried to tear herself away, but Fred held her tight. She could only try diplomacy.

"I'd be happy to show you, Eric," she said as amiably as she could. "Tomorrow, tomorrow evening, you, you'll come to eat, right? I'll cook something extra good. Tomorrow's Caleb's birthday, so I can also bring something from the mansion. There will be leftovers. Roast and cake."

Eric grinned. "Something sweet, yeah, now we're getting closer. But not tomorrow. I've got a craving for something sweet now. How about you, Fred?" He laughed. "You really can't because, because she's your sister. That's bad luck, Fred, but, but you can give us something like your blessing. Eh, Fred? Give me your sister's hand. Then we'll let you watch."

To Violet's horror, Fred did not stop his friend from threatening his sister's innocence. Instead, he grinned lasciviously.

"What d'you want with her hand, Eric?"

Both men laughed.

Violet saw with a mixture of horror and relief that her admirer—"Sir Galahad"—seemed to be coming to, which was a good sign but also dangerous.

"Maybe we could talk about this at home?" she asked desperately.

Eric and Fred looked at each other. Then they nodded.

"Just a question of your house or mine," Eric said, placing his arm around Violet.

His arm gripped her body like a vise. She had no chance of escape.

"Come along, lovely."

The boys moved to take their prize home. Shadows were stirring in the direction of the mining settlement. The first of the miners were making for the pub.

"We'd better get out of here," said Fred, glancing at the men on the ground.

Suddenly it seemed to have occurred to them that they ought not to get caught among their unconscious victims.

"Not a sound," Eric hissed at Violet.

She nodded hesitantly. Would it do any good to scream and draw other men's attention to her situation? Fred was her brother. No one would believe he was threatening her. He put his arm around her too. Violet planted her feet instinctively in the ground, but the boys lifted her effortlessly and dragged her along between them.

"A bit, bit too much to drink," Fred said with a grimace to the approaching men.

Violet squeezed out a desperate, "Help," but her already weak call was silenced when Eric kicked her shin.

"You ought to be ashamed getting the girl drunk if she doesn't know how to control herself," an older miner chided.

"Slut."

Violet swallowed when she heard the word. Her reputation in the settlement would be ruined. The only thing that mattered was that the Billers did not catch wind of it. Her fear of losing her beloved post and refuge briefly overcame her fear of Eric. But so far, only two miners had seen her like this, and they would be distracted the moment they stumbled on the victims of the brawl. Maybe they would forget Violet.

"Let me go. I can walk on my own." Violet struggled against Eric and Fred's grip. "I don't want people to think I, I would—"

"Always thinking about her reputation," Fred laughed. "A real little lady, my little sis."

Eric seemed more agreeable. Perhaps he did not really like forcing women to do things.

"Don't you dare say a word. Don't you dare try to run," Eric said.

"We'd catch you anyway," Fred reprimanded her. "Certainly by the time you crawl back to your little Rosie. You wouldn't leave her alone with Dad."

Something else to worry about. Even now, without a doubt, he would be taking out his anger at the lack of dinner on Rosie.

"I'll do what you want," Violet said. "But quickly. I need to get back to Rosie. She'll be afraid. You, you won't hold me longer than necessary, right?"

Eric whinnied laughter. "Sweetheart, no one's complained until now. You can rely on ol' Eric. I'm always up for it."

Violet did not know what he meant, but she didn't care. Whatever the boys had planned for her, she would get past it. She would survive. She had to.

Trembling but resigned, she followed Eric into his hut. It was even more primitive than their own, and the place was filthy. It stank of rotten food and dirty, sweaty clothes; the sheets on the bed were stained and stiff. Violet shuddered when Eric directed her to lie there. Uncertain, she sat.

Eric grinned and fiddled with his fly.

Violet looked at him with horror in her eyes.

"Well, what is it?" asked Fred. "Take off your clothes." Fred was standing by the door, and he seemed excited for a show.

"I—"

"Do you want to get back to your baby or not?" Fred asked.

Eric let his pants fall down to his knees. He did not undress any further, but that was enough to fill Violet with disgust. She had glimpsed men and women having sex, but she had never had a male member in front of her like that, and never had a man looked at her so lecherously.

Violet closed her eyes and pulled her dress over her head. He yanked down her underpants and pulled up her camisole. Apparently, he had no interest in exchanging kisses—no "Sir Galahad." Violet thought of the young man's lovely words and almost giggled hysterically. Instead, she cried as Eric closed his lips and then his teeth around her nipples. Then he pressed himself into her. Violet screamed in pain. She heard Fred laugh.

"That's what I call gratitude," panted Eric, "and that, that, and that." He rode her like a horse, only she had no chance of throwing him off.

"Drive that pride out of her," Fred encouraged him.

Eventually, it grew dark around Violet. She tried to hold tight to her consciousness. She did have to care for Rosie. But the pain was too much, and when Eric finally collapsed on her, his weight knocked the wind out of her, and his stench choked her. Violet was petite and only reached to Eric's shoulder. Her last thought was that she would be crushed under his hard, unwashed body. Crushed like her mother was under the collapsing mine.

She saw her mother's face before her as her consciousness ebbed, but this time the sight was no consolation. Her mother—and every other respectable woman—would despise her for what she had done here.

Chapter 5

The next few months in Parihaka passed in tense anticipation. There hadn't yet been an investigation, but the first trials against the plowmen were held. A judge sentenced forty plowmen each to two months' forced labor and a two-hundred-pound fine for destruction of property. None of them could produce that much money, and though the community of Parihaka could have, it did not recognize the judgment. The government left the sentenced men and the others who had been incarcerated in prison. When the protests against this did not quiet down, they sent the plowmen to the South Island and distributed them in prisons between Christchurch and Dunedin.

Near the end of 1879, an investigative commission was finally formed, although the people in Parihaka could hardly believe its composition. The premier appointed two *pakeha* to the council. Both had served as Minister of Native Affairs and were directly responsible for the land confiscations among the Maori. A Maori chieftain who was exceedingly friendly to the government was also appointed. He withdrew immediately after Te Whiti commented on the men's nomination: "A grand investigative commission: it consists of two *pakeha* and a dog."

Te Whiti boycotted the hearings, which began in 1880. The government countered: if the armistice compromise stipulated that all land confiscation must cease, they would begin with the construction of a coastal road.

"Just a few repairs on existing roads," insisted the *pakeha*, but Te Whetu knew better: "They've recruited five hundred fifty armed men. No, no, friends, don't believe that they're employing the Armed Constabulary here to build roads because they don't have anything else to do. These people are settlers without money. They lured them here with the promise of giving them land, our land, land they plan to steal from us."

At first, the new soldiers did nothing but build camps around Parihaka. The Maori noted camps at Rahotu and Waikino and a blockhouse manned by armed men in Pungarehu.

"I have no desire to go there and bring them food," grumbled Matariki as she filled a basket with food in the cooking lodge. "Ignoring them is hard enough, but feeding them?"

One of the cooks laughed. "You know Te Whiti: friendliness and politeness— he kills the people with kindness, as long as they don't attack him. We view the soldiers as our guests, invite them in, and offer them food. They haven't done anything yet. And it's not their fault they're here. They're the government's toys, just like the settlers."

Matariki saw things differently, although she followed the chieftain's orders. The settlers had been betrayed, and the men who now lay in wait would not hesitate to overrun Parihaka and put down its inhabitants.

Matariki shuddered as she walked with five other women along the sand path inland to Pungarehu and the armed constables' camp. Between Parihaka and the camp was the villagers' farmland. Every Maori man who worked there watched over the women sent to bring the soldiers gifts. Matariki would have wished for a warrior or two as an escort anyway, particularly as the men in camp lacked soldierly discipline. They had not gathered warriors here but scum. Whalers, seal hunters, gold miners—fortune hunters who now wanted to give buying land a try, even if they knew nothing about raising crops or animals. They tended to receive the Maori girls crudely, undressing them with their eyes before digging into the food with few words of thanks. They took Te Whiti's friendliness for granted, or as the fulfillment of a sort of obligation to pay tribute.

This time, however, the arrival of the girls in the camp took a different form. Instead of walking through the open gate, they were stopped. A uniformed guard asked the women what they wanted. The group of women pushed Matariki forward. She was their translator; the others normally worked in the kitchen and fields and spoke only broken English.

"Chieftain Te Whiti sends us. We offer the hospitality of Parihaka. Custom has it that our guests share our food with us. You've already diverted our water." Matariki cast an annoyed look at Waitotoroa Stream. The *pakeha* had erected their camp at the headwaters. Since then, the water had not arrived in Parihaka as clean and full of fish as before. "We invite you to the gathering at the next full moon to speak and call the gods together."

The man looked at Matariki uncomprehendingly. "I'll call the sergeant," he said, and left his post.

That could hardly represent the usual procedure in the British Army, but it was still markedly more soldierlike than the previous behavior of the constables. There were other signs, too, that things were more ordered in the camp. No one loitered around, ogling the girls. A few men repaired the fences; others were exercising. And the tall man who now approached the girls with sure strides wore a full uniform.

"How may I be of service to you good women?"

The soldier was not as tall as Kupe, but petite Matariki had to look up at him. She observed his slender physique and straight posture—a soldier from head to foot. The sergeant's uniform was excellently fitted and was scrupulously clean and proper. His face was somewhat pale, but his features were aristocratic. He reminded Matariki of someone she knew, but she could not put her finger on who that someone was. She smiled unintentionally when she looked into the man's brown eyes. His hair was blond and short. If he let it grow, it might curl.

Matariki forbade herself imagining the young man fishing or hunting with a bare chest and laughing face.

"I am Sergeant Colin Coltrane. I am in charge of this camp. What can I do for you?"

Matariki repeated her speech. She felt strangely self-conscious as she did, and more so when the sergeant smiled.

"Ah yes, the Parihaka strategy, I was warned of as much."

Matariki furrowed her brow. "You were warned of us? Well, true, the Crown must quake with fear at a welcome committee like ours. What are you afraid of, Sergeant? That we'll poison your men?"

The sergeant laughed. "No, not really. I might let you. They try to kill themselves with alcohol every day. No, Miss . . ."

"Drury, Matariki Drury," she said stiffly.

"What a handsome name." Colin Coltrane smiled winningly. "Miss Matariki Drury. It's not about guarding against attacks but rather avoiding a certain, hmm, demoralization. We call it fraternization, what your chieftain's trying here. A group that he's fed for months will only reluctantly fight him."

"So, you're thinking of attacking us?" Matariki asked sharply. Coltrane's words offered new insights into the English strategy, at least.

The sergeant shrugged. "Against you, Miss Drury, I could never raise arms," he said gallantly, "nor against the other women either." He bowed in the direction of the women behind her. "But regardless, we are soldiers, and we receive our orders from the government. I am here to see they are carried out. And for that reason, as sorry as it makes me, I must reject your friendly request and offer. We have our own cook, and I conduct the speeches and prayer services."

"You don't look much like a pastor," said Matariki coolly.

Colin Coltrane laughed. "You wouldn't believe how many facets there are to my personality. For my men, it suffices. British soldiers aren't as spiritual as your Maori warriors."

With that, he turned away, but Matariki still caught a glimpse of undisguised disdain in his facial expression. She watched him go. She was speechless and angry, but also fascinated, for which she chided herself. The sergeant despised the spirit of Parihaka—perhaps he even despised her whole people. Yet, still . . . Matariki shoved all fantasies aside and translated his words for the other women. Coltrane's message had been clear: they need not come anymore. She was happy about that. And she was happy to never see Sergeant Colin Coltrane again.

***

The roadwork began immediately after the investigative commission announced its decision: the occupation of land by a few of the whites was not entirely justified since the Maori owners had never taken arms against the *pakeha*. However, this was not the case, at least not entirely, on the coastline. The coastal Maori remained recalcitrant. One need only think of the obstreperous men of Parihaka. The road between Hawera and Oakura could be built without the permission of the natives. And besides, Te Whiti and other leaders had said themselves that they had nothing fundamentally against white settlers. The commission interpreted this to mean that they were willing to part with their land in exchange for suitable compensation.

"But that's our land." Matariki grew agitated as word got around Parihaka. Te Whiti had just called an unplanned gathering for the next day. They were expecting tribes from the whole region. "That's Parihaka farmland. What are they thinking?"

Kupe, who had just been leading a team of oxen, shrugged his shoulders. "They think that already-cultivated land can be sold more easily." He laughed bitterly. "Nothing will come of it. We have enough of these military training camps on our lands now. Te Whiti gave us the assignment of plowing the Armed Constabulary's camps."

Matariki, who suddenly had Colin Coltrane's first friendly and then flinty face before her eyes, began to worry about her Maori friends. The sergeant would not retreat from the plows without a fight. She would have liked to go as a translator, but now Kupe truly needed no help, and this time the *ariki* was explicitly not sending any girls. He would have to know that the situation was coming to a head.

For Kupe, who aside from some brief instruction had never worked in agriculture, the oxen proved at first more dangerous than the soldiers. His very first attempt to plow a straight line in the road leading to the camp in Rahotu went awry. Kupe pulled on the reins here and there, signaling his ineptitude to the animals. The lead ox tugged suddenly to the right; the others went along, and the plow went spinning. Kupe lost his balance and fell from his seat, ending up with a foot under a wheel of the plow. The doctors in the village determined there was no break, just a strain and heavy contusion. But for now, Kupe couldn't take part in further "cultivation" of the *pakeha* camp.

Though dispirited he couldn't proceed, he thereby avoided arrest. The government soldiers did not quite know how to react to the plowing. They resorted to the arrest of some plowmen but not combat, and no one was shot.

"Which no doubt we owe to the presence of the press," Kupe noted in a bad mood.

With a thickly bandaged foot and leaning heavily on Pai, he had dragged himself to the gathering the next day. Despite the short notice, thousands were already awaiting Te Whiti and the other chieftains in the clearing outside the village. Though the attendees were predominantly Maori, there was a large contingent of *pakeha*, almost all bearing notebooks and pens.

The opinion of the reporters was divided, though many supported the government's measures. It was, after all, a fact that the Taranaki District was filling with white settlers speculating on land that had so far been fallow. The journalists, many of whom were city dwellers used to streets and train lines, often did not understand why the Maori population declined modernization. Hardly one of them, however, could completely ignore the achievement of Parihaka. They all noted the village's cleanliness and order, its first-class organization, and the cheerful spirituality of its residents.

***

Te Whiti was dressed formally in Matariki's chieftain cloak when he appeared before the crowds.

"My heart," the chieftain said, "is full of darkness. You know I do not want a fight. But it seems the *pakeha* do. They deny it and instead speak of another hearing, another commission. The muzzle flashes of their guns have already singed our eyelashes, but still they say they do not want a war. How does a war begin, my friends? When one party sends its army to overrun the land of the other. The *pakeha* say it is not clear to them where the borders are, which land belongs to them, which to us, and which perhaps does not even have an owner. Now we'll make that clear, my friends. From now on, we'll fence in our land. We'll begin tomorrow. And we will not give an inch. If the *pakeha* tear down our fences, we'll build them again. We'll work our land—we'll plow it and build upon it."

The listeners were dumbfounded at first, but then they applauded. The incarcerated plowmen still sat in jail. The people of Parihaka knew what they were getting into when they offered renewed resistance.

"Remember, we are doing nothing illegal," Te Whetu later encouraged them. "The others will face punishment if they tear down our fences. Do not be afraid. Let the spirits of Parihaka overcome violence."

***

The next day the fencing began—and with it a dogged wrestling for power in Taranaki. Again, only men were sent to work on the fencing at first, and just three days later, Kupe explained the term "Sisyphean task." The Armed Constabulary had begun the construction of the road. Its land surveyors established its course without consideration of the Maori fields. They tore down the fences. The villagers built them back up. They did this wordlessly and repeatedly. Once, twice, twenty times. After a few days, the workers were exhausted. Others took their place.

At first, the government troops played along, but then at the next gathering, Te Whetu threatened to tear down telegraph poles. The government had him arrested when he was inspecting the fences with eight subordinate chiefs. Following that, many fence builders were arrested without real cause. The Maori did not resist but were constantly hindered by force from their work on the fences.

Again, the prisons filled. The government quickly pushed laws through both houses of Parliament that harshly punished disturbing the peace by digging, plowing, or changing the shape of the landscape. Whoever built fences risked two years of forced labor, but the flow of fence builders still did not abate. Maori men and women came from every corner of the North Island to stand with the people of Taranaki, and Matariki and her friends would have celebrated the spirit of Parihaka if they had not been so exhausted.

After the first weeks of fence building, there was no more dancing and drinking in Parihaka. The population, having shrunken starkly through arrest, simply slung down its dinner and then fell on the sleeping mats, exhausted. Fence building was no longer limited to the men. Everyone who could summon the strength took part. Matariki and the other women who taught English led their students into the fields. The four- and five-year-olds did not manage much, but they impressed the soldiers and the journalists whenever they picked up wood. Matariki's fences had more symbolic significance than defensive ability. The desperate struggle of the unarmed Maori against the Armed Constabulary, however, drew ever more attention. And there were bloody attacks. The former whalers and seal hunters had had enough of tearing down fences. They were not gentle when they pulled the Maori from their work.

Matariki and her friends noted with satisfaction that first English and then other European newspapers reported on their struggle. The premier was placed under increasing pressure, especially after attacks on children and elderly men and women helping with the fence construction became known.

"And the costs," crowed Kupe who had been reading the newspapers aloud. "It says here the land reclamation costs were originally assessed at seven hundred fifty thousand pounds, and now they've already spent a million, but without a mile of road to show for it."

***

At the end of 1880, the premier, George Grey, gave up and forbade his overzealous Minister of Native Affairs, John Bryce, from making any more arrests. In the first six months of the new year, they let all the prisoners on the North Island go free.

"Have we won?" Matariki asked.

She no longer dragged her students to build fences, nor did she teach regular lessons. Everyone—from schoolchildren to teachers, from doctors to bank tellers—worked from sunup to sundown in the fields. Then once more, a sort of truce prevailed in Taranaki. Though there were no more arrests and road construction had halted, the government did not restore the annexed Maori lands. Minister Bryce now focused his efforts on the land of Parihaka. He announced that they planned to divide the region into three sections: the coast and the inland should be settled by *pakeha*; the narrow strip in the middle would remain Maori.

"English settlements will be built on Te Whiti's doorstep," he announced, but found no real backing from the government.

Te Whiti did not react. The Maori chieftain remained silent while his people indefatigably built fences, plowed, and worked the land.

In January 1881, Bryce resigned.

***

"The children won," Lizzie said as she put down the *Otago Daily Times*. "Bryce is gone, but Parihaka is still there."

Michael reached for the paper. "It's just a question of what comes next," he said. "Bryce was a loudmouth, but his successor, Rolleston, you know him."

William Rolleston was a farmer in the Canterbury Plains—one of the legendary sheep barons who was not content with ruling over a few thousand sheep. In the course of his political career, he had represented several voting districts around Christchurch but usually lost them after only one term. For him, a nomination to Minister of Native Affairs was surely an unexpected promotion. Rolleston had a reputation as being quick to decide and combative. Diplomacy did not number among his strengths.

"But Arthur Gordon is governor," Lizzie objected. "And there the Brits have finally made a good choice."

The conservative farmers of Canterbury considered Arthur Gordon suspect. He showed clear sympathy for the Maori, and the Crown had sent him for that reason. Te Whiti's actions had made for bad press, and it was not in the queen's interest to have her model colony of New Zealand portrayed as a nest of racists.

Michael shrugged. "It's not enough that Gordon's a good fellow. He has to be able to keep Rolleston on a leash."

Chapter 6

When Violet came to, she decided that nothing had happened with Eric. She had ended up in his hut and must have fallen asleep, and she was beaten and bloody all over when she awoke. And naked. Surely there was a good explanation if she only thought it over thoroughly, but for that she lacked the strength. And the time. She had to take care of Rosie, after all.

Violet quickly pulled her dress back on and dragged herself to the hut, where she found Rosie asleep and the red balloon tied to the bed. Her father was surely at the pub, and Fred and Eric were probably back, or rather—Violet reminded herself—still in the bar in Greymouth. Violet washed herself as best she could with the last of the precious water. Her father would curse her for that. Her dress also had to be washed. It reeked of Eric and his filthy shack. She would do that the next day before work; upriver of the Billers' house, the water was clean and clear.

She snuggled next to Rosie and tried to turn off her thoughts. She did not wait for her father and brother's homecoming that night. She had left the house unlocked. What could she be afraid of now? Violet pushed the thoughts away. Eventually, she fell asleep—and ignored her aching body when she got up in the morning. She needed to make breakfast and send her father and Fred to work. Both seemed very hungover, and what was more, Fred looked at her strangely. Violet ignored him.

"We need to bathe ourselves first," she told Rosie who was grumpy because Violet got her out of bed earlier than usual. "We're going to the river first before we visit Caleb."

"Why?" asked Rosie, but then realized the answer. "Because it's Caleb's birthday today?"

Violet nodded. "Yes, that's right, it's his birthday, and all well-wishers have to be clean and properly dressed. Come, you can wear your good dress."

In truth, she had wanted to leave Rosie at home that day. Mrs. Biller surely would not be happy to see a miner's daughter mixing with the birthday guests, but there was too great a danger that the foreman would send Fred and Jim home early, and she couldn't risk exposing Rosie to them after such rebuke. She put her hope in Mrs. McEnroe. If the cook did not have enough time, Mahuika and the gardener would surely watch Rosie. The Maori couple were always lovingly attentive to the child—at worst, Rosie might see things for which she was still too young at six. What did that matter? Violet almost amazed herself at her newfound apathy, but she pushed the thoughts away again.

***

At the Billers' that morning, Caleb was staging one of his rare fits. Though the boy often had difficulties with his parents, he was at heart a patient child and usually bore the intellectual deficiencies of the people around him with dignity. With his birthday presents that year, however, Mrs. Biller had taken it too far. Instead of the microscope he had hoped for, Caleb received a children's book, some crayons, and a pony.

Caleb did not think much of horses. He hated sport in any form, and he screamed bloody murder when his father lifted him onto the little horse. Violet was then supposed to lead the pony around with Caleb on it, which normally would not have bothered her. She had held her grandfather's mare dear, and she had also liked to go with Heather Coltrane into the stables and had even sat, heart pounding, on her massive purebred. Now, however, just the smell of the horse made her sick and every step she took hurt. Usually this would not have escaped the extrasensitive Caleb, but that day he was preoccupied with his own irritation.

"I don't want to learn to ride," he declared angrily. "I wanted a microscope. I—"

"Sweetums, a gentleman must learn to sit dashingly on a horse," his mother chided him with a smile. "Remember that you'll be going to England soon, to boarding school. You'll have to ride there. And a microscope is so bulky. You couldn't even take it with you."

This comment was a painful reminder to Violet that her beloved job at the Billers' would soon come to an end, and Caleb made it clear that it would have been fine with him to begin his riding career in the motherland.

"Ignoring the fact that a horse is much bulkier than a microscope," Caleb said when Violet took him to his room for his nap, "am I supposed to take the pony to England with me?"

That afternoon, Violet struggled together with Caleb through the festivities. When all the guests were absorbed in what he called "baby games," she gave in to his insistence and retrieved the chessboard. They withdrew to the farthest corner of the garden, where he beat her in record time. The chessboard was for Caleb what barroom brawls were for Fred and Eric. He worked off his anger here, but of course, he did not hurt the chess pieces, and from his opponent he required respect rather than fear.

Finally, even this day ended, and Rosie came beaming from the kitchen.

"Without Rosie's help, I wouldn't have made it," Mrs. McEnroe said with a wink. "She worked so hard, cooking all that food with me."

Rosie was overjoyed by the praise and wanted to tell their father about her heroic deeds. Violet, however, could barely stand how tense she felt as they approached the hut. When they entered, Jim and Fred were sitting at the table.

"Daddy!" Violet could not stop Rosie from leaping happily onto her father, nor could she prevent the thump on the head he gave Rosie in return.

"Shut your mouth, Rosie. That noise'll give a man a headache," their father grumbled. "And you, pack your things tonight, Vio. But only after you make dinner. There's time enough for that."

Violet looked at her father uncomprehendingly—and felt vaguely guilty. Had he found out what she had done? But, then, she had not done anything. Nothing had happened.

Was he kicking her out?

"That son-of-a-bitch foreman let us go," Jim blurted out angrily, giving Rosie, who was crying, another slap. "And wants us off the company land. We're moving over to Lambert's. I'll be damned if they don't need good men to swing a pick."

***

The Lambert mine was the Biller mine's competition, and Marvin Lambert was hiring miners. There was a constant lack of coal diggers, and the foremen talked among themselves about the miners. The Lambert mine foreman was clear with Jim and Fred from the start: "If you two don't behave better here than you did for Biller, don't make yourselves comfortable."

The warning arrived, but as Violet already knew from Wales, every time a mine had let her father go, he pulled himself together a bit for the new post. Neither he nor Fred ever found it hard to make a good impression. Both were monstrously strong; they knew how to swing a hammer and pick, and they had a sixth sense for coal seams. On good days, they dug twice as much coal as a weaker worker. On bad days, the foreman had to watch them.

Eventually, the bad days would win out again, and there would be trouble and inevitably another dismissal. Not bad for the boys—after all, they always found new work quickly, all mines paid roughly the same wage, and they did not care where they dug coal.

For Violet, the dismissal was a catastrophe, just as it had been for her mother. As a rule, being fired was tied up with the loss of their home in the miners' housing, or, as now, the right to stay in Billertown. Usually, too, it took a bit of time to get housing through the new mine.

Here in Greymouth, no one managed the mining settlements. Although the foreman expelled the fired workers from the mine property, surely nothing would have happened if the Paisleys had stayed until they found new lodging. Jim rejected that in favor of his pride and his own comfort. The Lambert mine lay on the opposite end of Greymouth. He would have to walk four miles to work, and that was too difficult for both him and Fred.

In the new settlement, which was just as filthy and disorderly as Billertown, they found a shack that had been abandoned by its previous occupants. Surprisingly, the previous owners had swept it out before moving away. The new hut's roof wasn't well sealed and would hardly keep out the rain or keep in the warmth, though Violet could no longer complain about the fireplace smoke, which dissipated through the drafty roof.

"You need to seal it," Violet implored Fred and Jim, "before we move in the furniture."

The furniture—the primitive beds, a table, and four chairs—was not valuable, true, but the rain would completely ruin it.

"This weekend," Jim promised.

Violet hoped to speed that up by placing her father's bed where the rain leaked through the worst. She no longer worried about the linens, which were gray and ruined.

Luckily, for a few days, it was fairly dry, and on the weekend, Violet borrowed a hammer and ax from the neighbors, chopped wood scraps into little pieces, and bought nails to mend the roof. One of the neighbors even helped. Mr. O'Toole was a square-set Irishman who shared his shack with his wife and a gaggle of children; it seemed they had added one every year. The family was friendlier than any of the Billertown neighbors had been.

Eric had not been fired and still worked for Biller, so Violet no longer had to see him every day. Two of the new miners had been seriously injured in the brawl, and they were looking for the perpetrators. Greymouth's police officer didn't exert himself on such matters, but Fred and Eric thought it was safer not to go to the pub as often or to appear together in town.

Violet also went to Greymouth more rarely, although it was easier to get there from Lamberttown. The path was shorter and only led a quarter mile through sparse forest. Still, Violet avoided the path as much as possible and tried to get by with the groceries Mrs. McEnroe gave her. On Saturday, she made her purchases during the day and wondered why she always felt completely exhausted after the short trip. Until then, after all, she had managed the stretch effortlessly, even after work, but now Violet was struggling against an omnipresent tiredness. She also increasingly felt disgusted by this or that stench, which once she could have easily ignored.

Fortunately, neither her father's dismissal nor feeling sick had any effect on her as Caleb's nanny. On the contrary, Mrs. Biller seemed overjoyed that Violet still had a good relationship with her son, who was growing more difficult by the day. Caleb did not forgive the matter of the microscope easily, and he hated his daily riding lessons for which Joshua Biller had hired the local police officer. He had once been in the cavalry and colorfully related his adventures in India. At times, Officer Leary boasted shamelessly, and this was especially true when Violet was among his listeners.

As a riding instructor, Officer Leary was strict and unrelenting. He didn't explain technique well, so Caleb quickly came to dread his riding lessons. Worse still, the boy often fell off, which Leary greeted with mockery instead of concern. The relationship between student and teacher was soon completely frayed. Caleb didn't get any help from his parents either. Instead, his father felt confirmed in his judgment that his son was a weakling, and his mother feared for his future as a gentleman.

"Can't you try at least a little?" asked Violet somewhat angrily when Caleb once more complained to her. "If you keep on like this, they'll send you to England on the next ship. I'm serious. Mrs. McEnroe heard something to that effect."

Violet did not want to rebuff her little friend, but it was becoming increasingly difficult to have patience with his moods, although Caleb was not the only one who got under her skin. Even when Rosie whined or misbehaved a little, Violet had to hold herself back from screaming at her. She fought more often with her father and Fred, which was not smart since the arguments inevitably ended with a beating. Violet could not stop herself; her nerves were raw.

"I wish they would," Caleb said angrily. "Perhaps school in England would not be nearly as bad. The teachers have to be better than the pastor; they couldn't be stupider."

Violet sighed. This disrespectful behavior of Caleb's was also new, even though it was true that the reverend had reached his limits with Caleb's thirst for knowledge. Since the little boy had discovered Darwin, teacher and pupil had been in open conflict.

Violet did not entirely comprehend why. How life had developed on earth in the past was of no interest to her—she would have rather changed the future. She was still following the passionate actions of the teetotalers in the newspaper and kept her fingers crossed for the right to vote. Although Violet was counting on results soon, Heather wrote her that probably years of struggle lay ahead of Femina, Harriet Morison, and all their fellows in arms. There were naturally male comrades as well.

Violet's face glowed when one day she read an article by Sean Coltrane on the right of women to vote. When she found the paper in the trash the next day, she pulled it out and put the page with Sean's article in her pocket. At home, she stored it carefully in a hole in the ground she had dug beneath her bed where she hid her meager savings. Violet still thought of Sean's deep voice and his friendly eyes, his politeness and his patience. Sometimes she tried to imagine his face before she fell asleep, and when she did, she felt strangely comforted.

"What will happen to me when they send you to England?" she yelled at Caleb. "Would you think of me too?"

Caleb grimaced. "I have to go to England sooner or later. You'll have to look for a new job then. Or a husband."

Caleb was not far off. She was now sixteen. Many girls her age were already married and had children.

However, Violet did not want to think about any changes, and least of all about men and love. She was happy when she made it through the day. And although she was constantly sick and she could hardly eat anything, she did not lose weight. On the contrary, her breasts grew, and they sometimes hurt. Violet was increasingly worried and considered seeking out the doctor, or at least Mrs. Travers. If only that did not cost money.

She wanted to see Clarisse and the girls again. However, she would not just show up at their door. It had to be a coincidence. So, the next Sunday, she headed toward Billertown—presumably to fish in the stream or gather kindling—while Rosie frolicked around her.

***

It was no secret in Billertown that the prostitutes bathed in the stream on Sunday. After all, their boisterous voices carried far enough to tempt the adolescent boys to creep up and risk a peek at the women's naked bodies.

Clarisse had laughed when Violet had once revealed to her that Fred and Eric, too, sat among the thick ferns and watched the whores.

"It doesn't matter, my dear. Looking doesn't hurt. On the contrary, if it gets them going, they're more eager to save up so they can take a bite of the fruit they can only see from afar."

Violet pressed closer and saw the three women as naked as God had made them. They sat on the banks, drying themselves in the sun and combing one another's freshly washed hair. Violet cast an embarrassed glance at their breasts. They were soft, and Clarisse's even hung a little low. None looked as swollen and hard as Violet's.

She rustled around a bit to avoid startling the women. Clarisse spotted her immediately.

"Little Miss Curtsy," she said, laughing. "What's going on, need another job? You won't have any luck here. We don't have any children to watch."

"Thank God," said Lisa, theatrically making the sign of the cross.

"I'm still at the Billers'," Violet said, "but . . ."

Clarisse looked at her. "But something's up," Clarisse said. "You're not just here to visit. And you're, well, something's different about you. Did you grow some?"

Violet shook her head. She also blushed. So, people could see it on her. Soon, everyone would know she was sick.

"I don't know. I'm not feeling well. I—" She gave Clarisse a pleading look.

The older woman understood. "I'm going to take a walk with Violet," she said to her friends as she put her dress on and wound a towel around her still-wet hair. "In the meantime, play with her little sister. It's a good warning to experience children. This way you take the vinegar washes on the crucial days seriously."

The women laughed and received Rosie amiably. Violet suppressed her concern that Rosie was seeing other people naked. It would not kill her. Nothing killed a person that easily.

***

Clarisse and Violet wandered along the stream with Violet choosing the difficult, rocky way. She had to pay attention in order not to stumble, so she did not have to look at Clarisse as she reported her troubles.

"You're not sick; you're pregnant," Clarisse said plainly. "Why didn't you come by and ask how to prevent this before sleeping with the lad?"

Violet glared at her. "I didn't—" She stopped herself.

Clarisse laughed. "Come now, dear, you can tell me. You fell in love."

"I don't love anyone," Violet screamed. Her voice sounded shrill and desperate.

Clarisse put her arm awkwardly around Violet. "I'm sorry, dear. So, he—"

"Nothing happened. Nothing at all happened. I—" Violet sobbed. She pulled out of Clarisse's embrace, stumbling. Finally, she collapsed on the edge of the stream, shaking with sobs. Clarisse sat next to her and waited.

"If nothing happened, nothing can have happened. There's an explanation. There—"

"For what?" Clarisse asked softly. "Come now, you don't really mean to tell me that no man, that none of these swine pulled you into some bushes and stuck his prick in you? Even though you resisted? Even though you screamed? It's not your fault, Violet. It happens time and again. Who was it?"

Violet shook her head violently. "I didn't resist." She swallowed. "I didn't scream. He didn't pull me into any bushes. I, I went of my own free will."

Clarisse pulled Violet to her and stroked her hair. "Never, dear. Never. I don't believe that." Cautiously, she drew the whole story out of Violet.

Violet calmed down as she told Clarisse what happened. Now that she had admitted the truth, she could handle it better.

"So now what should I do?" the girl asked. "Is there, is there nothing that can be done?"

"Ever heard of an abortionist? They scrape it out of you before anyone sees it. But it hurts, dear. It's not simple."

Violet bit her lip. "I don't care," she said. "Can you do it, Clarisse? Right away. I can take it."

Clarisse rubbed her forehead. "Sweetheart, I can't do it," she said. "And you can't do it yourself either, so don't even try. There are considerably less painful ways to kill yourself."

"It can kill you?" asked Violet.

Clarisse nodded. "Certainly. Though if someone knows what they're doing, then girls don't die any more often than they would giving birth. But if it's a bumbler—it's a serious matter, dear, without even mentioning your undying soul. I mean to say you could forfeit it too. You'd end up in hell at the least."

Hell did not frighten Violet. She would end up there one way or another when she told her father about her pregnancy.

"I don't care about that," she declared. "So, who can do it? One of the other girls?"

Clarisse said no again. "No one here, Violet, I'm sorry. The closest person is a Maori witch, over in Punakaiki. Strange woman, but she knows her craft. Apparently, she was an herbalist in her tribe. Then she lived with a *pakeha* doctor. He did it too. That's how she learned. She is with her tribe again, up in Punakaiki, in the direction of Westport. It's not easy to find, but I can tell you how to get there. She does it in a hotel. The night porter organizes everything. It's expensive, though. Two pounds altogether."

"Two pounds?"

Violet looked at Clarisse, disheartened. She had no inkling how she would even get to Punakaiki. It was surely three or four days away by foot. And then the money—Violet did not have more than a few shillings.

Clarisse shrugged. "It's just that a lot of people are involved," she explained. "The porter, the manager, maybe even the maid if the sheets get bloody. And the woman herself. She probably gets the least. But she's good. I've never heard of anyone dying in her hands. She knows what to do, and the girls say she doesn't treat you like the scum of the earth. If you get it done, do it there."

Violet sighed. "And if I report the bastard? You said it yourself, that it's not my fault. Even if I did it of my own—"

"If you say 'free will' one more time, I'm going to scream," Clarisse said. "But I'm afraid it won't help to report him. Maybe they'll lock him up, but maybe not. Your brother will testify for him if I don't miss my guess. But it won't change anything for you. On the contrary. Then you'll have a baby. If you report him, you'll still have a baby without a father."

"But, but it won't have a father either way."

Clarisse furrowed her brow and shrugged. "That's up to you. You can report the lout. Or you can marry him."

***

Everything in Violet bristled against the thought of marrying Eric Fence, but charging him really was not a possibility. Violet dreaded living through her father's reaction. The only solution was to scrounge together the money for the abortionist. She suggested to Clarisse that she earn it as a whore.

Clarisse shook her head. "Girl, the way you look just saying it, you'd scare away the customers. In this job, you have to at least pretend you enjoy it. And if you can, you have to praise the blokes for how great they do it. You, by contrast, might well bite off their prized possession when they want to do it French with you."

"French? The French? They put it in the mouth?" Violet felt sick.

Clarisse sighed. "You lack all the necessary prerequisites," she said sympathetically. "We could teach you in a few weeks, but after what happened, do you hate men now?"

The answer caught in Violet's throat. If she was honest, she could have vomited at the thought of a repetition of that act with Eric. And to do that several times a night? With different men? She would die of shame and rage and fear.

"Besides, you don't earn two pounds in this profession in just a few days," Clarisse added. "And you won't be able to play the good girl again afterward.

Once a whore, always a whore. Someday there will be someone who marries you. I'm sure of that. But you can have that now if you marry this Eric fellow."

"You're serious," she whispered.

Clarisse nodded. "Look, girl, marrying for love, people overvalue that. Believe me, there's hardly a woman who really likes it when men, well, who, um, who really appreciate the pleasures of physical love."

"Pleasures?" Violet looked at Clarisse as if she had lost her mind.

"It's much easier when you're in love. Then, then you're inclined to forgive when it hurts. And when the fellow's in love, he's more careful than your Eric was with you."

"He's not *my* Eric," Violet protested.

"It hurts less. Eventually, it hardly hurts anymore. There are also a few tricks, but marriage hardly makes a woman happy. Most love their children, though, and it doesn't matter how they came to be or who their father is."

Violet thought of her mother and vaguely felt guilty about the little being in her own body. Her mother had despised her father, but she had done everything for Violet and Rosie. Violet, on the other hand, was only thinking about getting rid of the child as quickly as possible.

"With that in mind, if you marry Eric now or someone else in a few years, it'll most likely come to the same thing." Clarisse stood up. "I have to go. By Sunday afternoon, the boys have slept off their Saturday night, and whoever has money left, treats himself to a girl. It's my favorite day of the week. A few good lads who want to enjoy it sober come, too, because they've scrimped and saved for it. They even wash themselves beforehand. So, think about it, dear. If you get the money together, I'll tell you where to find the Maori abortionist. If not, well, I'd be happy to be your bridesmaid, though I think the offer comes too late for the 'maid' part."

Violet could not laugh at that, but she thanked Clarisse for her advice, grabbed Rosie, and ran homeward, exhausted and beaten by all the information.

Rosie startled her when they stopped for a rest.

"Is it true, Violet? Are you having a baby?"

Violet yelled in horror. "What? Where, where did you hear that? Who?"

She turned red and chided herself for it. The best reaction would have been to deny it with a laugh.

"That's what the girls said," Rosie replied. "You're definitely having a baby. You look like it. Where are you getting the baby, Violet? Is someone giving it to you? Do you have to buy it? Are girls cheaper than boys? We'll get a girl, then, won't we? I'd rather have a girl. Is she my sister, Violet?"

Violet pulled herself together. "Don't talk nonsense, Rosie. I'm not having a baby. And for heaven's sake, don't say anything to Father. He would, he would . . ."

"Does Daddy not want a baby?" Rosie asked.

Violet forced herself to be calm. She had to talk her sister out of the matter. And then she needed to gather the money and make it to Punakaiki somehow. While she was assuring Rosie that she must have misunderstood Clarisse's friends and that she should not expect a baby, she formed a plan. She was not capable of being a whore, but she could steal. She knew where Mrs. Biller kept the money for her employees' salaries. They did not receive even two pounds together, but with a little luck, Mr. Biller did not count out the money to his wife. And if she had to, she would steal twice. She just had to make it look as if she were not guilty. Thus, she could not disappear right after the theft. And she needed a safe place to store the money. Violet's head spun.

She lay sleepless in the night. She felt the need to toss and turn, but as always, Rosie slept in her arms, and she did not want to wake her. What might it be like to hold her own baby in her arms? Violet banished the very thought. Whatever was growing inside her and however innocent it might be, she did not want it. When she finally fell asleep, she dreamed of a little girl—with the gentle eyes of Sean Coltrane.

***

When Violet went to work the next day, she had a bloated face, her legs felt heavy, and she already had a guilty conscience. So, she did not notice at first that the Billers' house bustled with activity. Mrs. Biller called her over before she could go up to Caleb. Mrs. McEnroe took Rosie into the kitchen, seeming to glance sympathetically at Violet as she did. Violet's heart raced. Could it be that Mrs. Biller knew something? Did she notice her pregnancy?

Mrs. Biller did not give Violet's figure or swollen face a second glance.

"I have to share something with you, Violet, which you'll not like. You did know from the beginning that this post was not forever. We had intended to send Caleb to England no later than next year, but now, well, you know how he's been acting. It seems that . . ." She sniffled theatrically. "It seems that my baby is growing up. The reverend thinks that the best thing would be to enroll him in a good boarding school as soon as possible, and now an opportunity has suddenly come up for just that."

Violet couldn't bear the way Mrs. Biller spoke about her son, or worse, that her time with the Billers was about to come to an end.

"An acquaintance of ours is sailing for London at the end of the week on the *Aurora*. Yesterday we first learned that he's taking his entire family with him. Their son is two years older than Caleb and will be attending school in London. The Bradburys are prepared to chaperone Caleb on the journey. Mr. Biller is securing Caleb's passage on the ship. But that won't be difficult. If need be, he can share the Bradbury boy's cabin. The boys will have to acclimate to roommates anyway."

Violet could picture how this revelation would be received by the rather unsocial Caleb.

"Tomorrow we'll be taking Caleb to Christchurch. And given that, as sorry as it makes me, Violet, your employment with us ends today. We have thought about whether we could have you stay on. Mrs. McEnroe would gladly have kept you as a kitchen maid, but we don't really need that now. On the contrary, with Caleb's departure, our household will be shrinking. Here." Mrs. Biller produced a shilling from her pocket. "Please, take this as a small token of our gratitude. Everything happened so suddenly. Otherwise, we would have purchased a present for you. However, circumstances . . ."

Violet thanked her politely. She was numb. This was her last day of work at the Billers'. And surely there would be no opportunity to steal. Mrs. Biller had paid everyone on Friday. By now, Monday, her husband had surely not yet refilled the household cashbox. Not to mention that under the circumstances, suspicion would immediately settle on Violet.

"Please go up to Caleb and help him pack. Mahuika is supposed to arrange his things, but she'll need assistance with that. Comfort Caleb a bit. He'll be sad naturally—I still remember how, when I was to go to boarding school, I was homesick in advance. Oh yes, and dissuade him from wanting to take those books. The ship would sink under the weight. Tell him that."

Violet had no intention of troubling her clever Caleb on their last day with such stupid things. Besides, Caleb had already realized that he could not drag multivolume reference books to England.

"Surely the school has a library," he said calmly.

Caleb Biller was not unhappy that his parents were sending him away. On the contrary, he seemed to yearn for England.

"Now, don't be so sad," he comforted Violet. "I'll write you to be sure. And you'll write me. And besides, I'll give you my books."

Caleb beamed at this idea, and Violet summoned all her energy to look suitably happy. Normally she really would have been joyful. The dictionary alone was an unbelievable treasure—and all the storybooks for Rosie and, and . . . No, she would not have a baby to whom she could read fairy tales.

Caleb misinterpreted Violet's reaction, which was stiff despite her efforts. "You can have my chessboard too. Then you can always think of me."

"I, I don't even have anyone I could play with," Violet whispered, touched but also desperate and close to tears.

Caleb fished for his handkerchief. "You can play alone. Just imagine I'm on the other side. And place the pieces like I would. Just don't cry, Violet. Otherwise I will too."

Violet did not cry until midday, when she was with Mrs. McEnroe in the kitchen. It did her good to be able to cry her eyes out, although she could not let the cook know what really weighed so heavily on her soul. A new idea had come to Violet during her conversation with Caleb. "Letter" had been the key word. She could write to Heather Coltrane and depict her misery. It would be difficult, but perhaps hints would be enough. Heather would be able to help her. But would a pastor's stepdaughter send her the money for an abortionist?

She took her leave from Caleb that evening. He was as dry eyed as he always desired to be. Rosie, however, did not remain so calm, instead sniffling and even pressing a wet kiss to Caleb's cheek. The boy bore it with composure, only clearing his throat before turning to Violet. With his pale face and watery-blue eyes, he looked up at her expectantly.

"If you, well, if you want, Violet, then, hmm, then you can kiss me too."

***

Violet decided not to tell her father and brother about her dismissal yet. She would find a new job as soon as possible, and it was better to tell them once she had it. Who knew what her father might come up with otherwise to keep her at home. He complained often enough that dinner wasn't ready when he returned from work, though he never said a word about who paid for the food.

That evening, Mrs. McEnroe once again had cooked a feast. Plenty of roast and vegetables had been left over from Caleb's farewell dinner, and the whole family was departing for Christchurch the next day, so the cook sent Violet home with all the food. It was customary to accompany the children one was sending to England to the ship. Mrs. Biller was already distressed at his leaving. Violet believed her. She would not see her son for years. When Caleb returned, he would have finished college and perhaps university. He would be an adult.

The Paisleys feasted that evening, but Violet felt so sick, she barely ate for fear she wouldn't be able to keep the food down. She clung to her hope in Heather. Violet did not know whether it was Heather's interest in women's suffrage, or her concern for women and children, or something about Heather's personality, but regardless of what Reverend Burton would say, Heather was no moralist. She was different. And she would be on Violet's side.

Violet was dreaming of how everything would be once she had Heather's help, when suddenly her father's loud voice tore her from her reverie. Beforehand there had only been Rosie's chatter, which Violet hardly noticed anymore. But now something had happened.

"What did you say, Rosie?" Jim Paisley's voice sounded alarmed. "What was that?"

Rosie smiled sweetly at her father. She feared him, but she also courted his attention. "I said I asked Mrs. McEnroe if Violet was having a baby. And where'd she get it? And she looked at me strangely. But then she said you didn't just get a baby. Didn't I say that, though, Violet? You definitely have to buy them."

"Is this true, Violet? Are you pregnant?"

At that moment, Violet Paisley's world came crashing down.

Chapter 7

Even under the new governor, Arthur Gordon, Te Whiti and his people did not find peace. The sale of Central Taranaki continued, and buyers were found for the land of Parihaka. Matariki and her friends had less and less belief that the farmers were innocent victims. Even Te Whiti stopped preaching the idea.

"They know exactly what they're doing," Kupe said.

Kupe should long since have been in Auckland. Other students already had returned and were working the land of Parihaka without regard for whether new "owners" wanted to graze their sheep there.

"They're almost getting the land for free," Koria observed bitterly. "Two pounds for an acre of land. For that, who wouldn't betray a few 'savages'?" The girl stretched her aching back. Together with Matariki and Pai, she had been planting seedlings on the newly cultivated lands and picking weeds from the old fields.

"Who can't even maintain their own town," Matariki added, throwing down an issue of the *Taranaki Herald*. "Here: 'The town makes a dirty and dilapidated impression. The residents look unkempt.'"

Pai looked around. The young people had just come from the fields. They sat in front of one of the communal lodges, eating a simple meal of bread and sweet potatoes. It had been a while since they had daily celebrated the *hangi* in Parihaka, and the hunters and fishers no longer went out to provide the settlement with delicacies.

"You have to admit that it has looked better around here," said Pai. "The gardens go to seed when people spend all day in the fields, and the buildings need repairs. No one's sweeping out the *marae* or polishing the carvings. Te Whiti preached to us for years not to be slaves to the war god, but now we're slaves to peace. As soon as we stop to breathe, they take our land away. I never would have pictured it like this."

The others nodded. They were young and hardworking, but the months of compulsory labor had worn away their strength.

"Do you want to leave?" asked Matariki quietly.

If she were to be honest, she contemplated it herself occasionally. She was ready to take the high school exam, and sometimes she dreamed of doing so in Otago.

Pai shook her head. "No. Too many are leaving as it is. We just have to endure. And now, I'm going to polish the statues of the gods. Who's with me? Maybe the spirits will take pity on us and bring the *pakeha* to reason."

***

In the middle of September 1881, Governor Gordon went to the Fiji Islands—a long-planned state visit. In Parihaka, they hardly noticed his departure. So far, the Maori-friendly representative of the Crown had not done much for the village. He might not endorse the land sales, but the laws regulating them had been signed by his predecessor, and he could hardly take them back now. Nevertheless, he did not allow their enforcement with violence. The land the Maori worked would not be touched no matter who owned it on paper.

He did not have much reason to intervene in the situation in Taranaki either. The farmers' complaints did not reach him any more than the laments of Matariki and her friends about the enormous amount of work. These latter complaints did not reach the ears of the Minister of Native Affairs, William Rolleston, either. But the farmers complained loudly, and Rolleston did open his ears to their protests. He, too, was a landowner, after all, and he did not want to think about what uproar would follow if the Ngai Tahu on the South Island decided to check the correctness of the deeds of land sale.

With the governor out of the country, Rolleston seized his opportunity. On October 8, 1881, a beautiful spring day, he visited Parihaka right after he had succeeded in coaxing Parliament into the appropriation of a hundred thousand pounds to continue the "war."

Te Whiti ordered his people to meet in front of one of the lodges for welcoming rituals. A full *powhiri* was on the program, with prayers, dancing, and singing. The new minister was to be greeted with all honors.

The red-faced, squarely built minister, however, hardly seemed to appreciate it. He followed the girls' dances with a certain fascination, but he watched the men's war dance with abhorrence and the prayers of the elders with impatience.

"Can we get to the matter at hand?" he called out during the most sacred part of the ceremony: the release of the *karanga* by the priestess.

Arona, a young student who had been granted the honor of letting it out, was shocked at the sacrilege. She broke off the call, and the spirit of Parihaka was not summoned on that day.

Despite all of this, Te Whiti attempted to remain polite, but William Rolleston did not mince words.

"It really is a nice estate you have here," he said, glancing around at the village and fields, "but it must be clear to you that you have to respect the government's decisions. You've played your little game with us long enough. It has to stop. You need to face the facts, you, the angel of peace. If the fighting escalates and a new war breaks out, the government won't take the blame for it. The fault will be yours alone."

***

Te Whiti had listened to Rolleston in silence, and he did not speak to his people in the following days. When he walked through the village, he hung his head.

"What are they going to do?" Matariki asked as she and her friends talked over the situation.

Matariki felt exhausted, disconcerted, and now abandoned. Without Te Whiti's encouragement and Te Whetu's clear announcements, everything seemed to lose its meaning. More and more people left Parihaka. And the word was that the Minister of Native Affairs planned to flatten it.

"Did he really say that?" Pai asked.

The news that came to Parihaka was often contradictory. Nothing was documented, but that William Rolleston was making plans to storm Parihaka was considered certain.

"He can't do that." Kupe, who had by now studied his first books on juridical questions, tried to comfort her however he could. "He has no legal basis. We haven't done anything, and the governor wouldn't sign off."

"What if he doesn't even know?" Matariki asked.

Koria shook her head. "He knows something. Or *will* know. We wrote to him. As soon as he receives the letter, he'll do something."

***

James Prendergast, chief justice of New Zealand, often served as a government administrator. He was originally an attorney on the South Island, where he became friends with Rolleston. With Governor Gordon away on Fiji, Prendergast went to the North Island to serve as the governor's deputy. However, his attitude toward the natives was well known—in trials he always decided against them and had previously called the Maori primitive barbarians whom one could not allow under any circumstances to take part in decision-making. To bring such a man to ratify invasion plans of Parihaka was not difficult. However, time was working against Rolleston. It simply took time to convince all the decisive men to set aside the money and to formulate the documents.

The Minister of Native Affairs called a session on October 19, 1881, at eight o'clock in the morning. Prendergast, Rolleston, and his executive committee released a proclamation: Te Whiti and his people would be rebuked for threatening settlers and their uncooperative attitude. Moreover, they presented them an ultimatum: within fourteen days, the chieftains would have to accept the revision of land allocation, cease all protest actions, and leave Parihaka; otherwise, consequences of a military nature would follow.

Two hours after the signing of the writ by his deputy, the real governor arrived in Wellington. He had broken off his state visit at once after word had reached him of Rolleston's unilateral action.

But it was too late. Rolleston had already authorized the publication of the ultimatum and the delivery of the writ to Te Whiti. Two hours had sealed the fate of Parihaka.

***

"The governor fired Rolleston at once," Arona explained to Matariki and her friends. As priestess, she had attended the reading of the proclamation to Te Whiti—and listened to the governor's subsequent apology. Gordon's messenger had caught up to Rolleston's man, and the two riders arrived in Parihaka at the same time. Te Whiti had received them with all honors. After all, neither messenger was responsible for the message he brought. "Or at least he suggested he resign. He can't really fire anyone. Just as he cannot withdraw any proclamation his deputy signed. In any case, not officially. Maybe it all transpired under the table, but Rolleston knew every trick in the book: the signatures under the text weren't even dry yet, and it was already in the *Government Gazette*."

"Gordon could have resigned," Kupe said, "in protest. Then there would have been a hubbub in England. The queen could have nullified the proclamation."

Matariki laughed bitterly. "What does the queen care about us?" she asked, scratching Dingo who snuggled against her. "And Mr. Gordon is attached to his pretty little post. They'll throw Te Whiti in prison and make Rolleston a knight."

Kupe shrugged. "Maybe, but what do we do now? Has Te Whiti said anything? Or Te Whetu? We're not really going to give up Parihaka, are we?"

Arona shook her head. "No. We stay and we await what happens. But they will make good on their threats; they will come. We should prepare ourselves."

"To die?" asked Pai.

***

At first, the *pakeha* in Taranaki reacted with more panic at the ultimatum than the Maori in Parihaka. They had gotten used to peace and feared a new war. Major Charles Stapp, commander of the barely existent volunteer army of Taranaki, immediately declared that every male citizen between seventeen and fifty-five had to prepare to be called upon. In other parts of the North Island, the expected battle met with more enthusiasm. At a single call of the *Government Gazette*, they succeeded in forming thirty-three units of volunteers. The army, which ultimately took up position outside of Parihaka, consisted of one thousand forty-seven armed constables, one thousand volunteers from all over New Zealand, and six hundred men from Taranaki—four *pakeha* armed to the teeth for every adult Maori in Parihaka. The units established camps around the village and immediately began with exercises and target practice.

The current and former Minister of Native Affairs—after Rolleston's ouster, John Bryce had been reinstated—demonstrated his agreement with the actions of his at-once successor and predecessor by riding out to the troops every day, inspecting them, and encouraging them.

On November 1, 1881, Te Whiti gave his last speech before his assembled people.

"The only ark that can now save us is to endure with strength of heart. Flight means death. Don't think of fighting. We were peaceful, and we will remain peaceful. That is the will of the gods. We are not here to fight but to honor the gods and hallow the land. We will not defile it with blood. So, let us wait for the end. There is no other option. We remain to the last on our land. No one fetch his horse or his weapon. He would die by them."

"So, what do we do?" asked Matariki again. "I mean, we have to do something. We—"

"We'll do what we always do," stated Arona. "We'll greet our guests with music and dance."

***

The invasion began early in the morning of November 5. Matariki almost lost her nerve when she saw the men marching toward them. The troops were armed as if for a battle. They carried heavy weapons and rations. The artillery marched forward, and an Armstrong gun was positioned in the hills overlooking the village. Bryce commanded everything on the back of a white horse. He seemed to like the role of the hero.

"That's not exactly how I pictured my prince," Matariki joked uneasily. "Hopefully they won't do anything to the children."

Pai shook her head. "Nonsense, the children just have to remain calm, and that's what we practiced. Look, here come the troops."

The gate of Parihaka was wide open. The troops did not need to storm it or fire warning shots from their guns as they galloped through. Bryce had sent the cavalry in advance. The men hardly managed to halt their horses in time before they crashed into the first line of the Maori defense: on the street leading to the village's gathering place, two hundred little boys and girls sat, supervised by an old priest who now had them sing a song of greeting. Behind the children, girls were arranged in rows. They sang and danced while they kept an eye on the children.

Matariki and Pai, who were not to give their performance until later, had climbed onto the roof of a building and followed the events from there.

"The children are wonderful." Matariki was excited when she saw the little ones showed no fear and did not give way even though the riders almost galloped over them.

It had rained recently, and the mud sprayed from under the horses' hooves. It struck the children in the face and in the eyes, and some of them cried quietly, but they did not run. More troops followed the horses on foot. The children and the girls kept singing but switched to a sad tune. The old priest called for the protection of the gods.

When the riders passed the children, they encountered Matariki, Pai, and other young women, who blocked the soldiers' path by swinging and skipping over jump ropes. None of that seemed hostile—only Dingo hid himself behind the corner of a building, growling. Apparently, the dog felt the threat, even if the people tried to ignore it.

"Would you like to play with us?" Matariki asked the invaders—and at that, her heart almost skipped a beat. The leader of the riders was a tall, slender man on an elegant black horse. Hazel eyes stared at her: Colin Coltrane.

The young sergeant twisted his mouth into a smile, although no cheerfulness shone in his eyes. "Why not?" he asked. "Miss Drury."

Matariki's heart beat faster. Was it possible he remembered her? The man turned his horse, gave himself some distance, and assessed her with a cool gaze. The horse leaped elegantly over the rope. The other girls were so astonished that they let their ropes fall.

"Come, men." Colin Coltrane grinned as he brought his horse to a stop behind the barrier of jump ropes. "And you, miss, should take care. I've overcome other hurdles."

With that, he galloped toward the village center, followed by his men. Matariki let her rope fall in front of their horses.

She flashed hot and cold at the thought of what Colin Coltrane had risked there. In the middle of the village, directly behind the girls with the jump ropes, sat twenty-five hundred people. Residents of Parihaka and delegations of other tribes of Taranaki. In the days since the ultimatum, no one had fled. On the contrary, like *pakeha* to the governor's weapons, the Maori thronged to Te Whiti's troops of the peaceful. It was a quiet final triumph.

Colin Coltrane now made his horse prance between them. Matariki noted that he had complete mastery over the animal, far better than most of the other riders who had solved the problem of the jump ropes by riding around the girls. The sergeant's black horse moved sideways and backward, and even reared on command. Colin Coltrane had him do that again and again to scare and provoke the people frozen in motionless protest.

Matariki wanted to despise him for that, but she was spellbound.

***

The frontline soldiers seemed unsure of what they were supposed to do with the silent villagers, who were still seated. Just behind them, the foot soldiers ran into the girls' jump rope, and their leader made a fool of himself by insisting on moving Pai, who was a stout girl, out of the way by himself. He yanked the jump rope out of Matariki's hand, and when Pai held on to it angrily, he lifted her up and hauled her to the side. Pai acted like a sack of flour. The other girls and the soldiers all laughed. Then, one of the soldiers reached for Matariki, when suddenly hoofbeats came up beside her.

"No one is to touch this girl," said Colin Coltrane, who reared his horse in front of the dumbfounded infantryman. "I'll move her myself." Before Matariki could even react, he bent down, put an arm around her hips, and swung the petite girl up in front of him on the horse. Matariki resisted, but he only laughed. "Where does my lady wish to alight?" he asked.

Matariki fidgeted and moved to grab his reins. Her dog—Colin recalled that the animal had also accompanied her on her visit to the camp—nipped angrily at the horse's fetlocks.

"Well, well, aren't we feisty, girl? Do recall that you invited me to your meetings."

"Between a visit and an invasion lie a host of differences," Matariki hissed. "Let me down. I—"

"Sergeant Coltrane," the commander of the foot soldiers furiously addressed Colin, who was beneath him in rank. "What's all this? What do you intend to do with the girl?"

Coltrane laughed. "Just lending the infantry a hand, sir."

Matariki tried to bite his hand. "I'm a chieftain's daughter," she screamed. "I'm *tapu*."

The scream had the desired effect. A few warriors of the more conservative North Island tribes stood up threateningly.

"Set the girl down this instant," roared the commander.

Colin Coltrane followed the directive, but Te Whiti had noticed the unrest and strode toward Colin, the officer, and the girl.

"I hope you'll respect our customs," the chieftain said calmly. "Even if you don't respect our lands. And please show respect to this girl. Not just because she's a girl—even among the *pakeha* it is, I believe, forbidden to abduct and violate a woman—but also because of her rank. Among the tribes, the daughter of a chieftain is elevated to a war goddess. She sends the men to battle. But you do not see our daughters amid our warriors. You see them singing and playing and dancing in front of their houses. Respect her and respect us. Come, my daughter." He laid his hand gently on Matariki's shoulder and led her to his fire.

Colin watched the old man and the girl go. Was she really his daughter? He could have sworn that she was no pure-blooded Maori. Granted, her hair was black like that of most of the girls in the tribes. It fell in soft curls down to her hips—like all the other girls, she wore it down that day and decorated with flowers. And she had played her skipping game in the traditional *piu-piu* skirt. Colin looked with pleasure at Matariki's swaying gait; her long, slender legs; her narrow hips. He would surely see her again.

Chapter 8

Violet married Eric Fence soon after Caleb Biller left for London. The pregnancy was barely visible, but it would not have bothered anyone if it had been. Most of the miners' wives had married their husbands because a little one was on the way.

After the truth had come out, to Violet's amazement, Jim Paisley had not directed his rage primarily at his daughter but at Eric Fence. It was not the rape he held against him but his presumed lack of readiness to marry Violet right away.

"What is that supposed to mean: he's not about to marry you? I'll have a word with him. You can count on that, even if I have to haul him to the altar myself."

Violet fought with the courage of desperation. "I don't want to marry him either, Dad. Please, listen, he, he doesn't even know that—"

"Oh, you haven't told him yet." Paisley laughed, relieved. "Then it's about time, Vio, if the womenfolk can already spot it." He eyed his daughter as if he were undressing her. "Well, I still don't see anything. But no matter, you'll tell him now, and he'll be happy, such a young love." Her father's voice almost sounded touched. He must have had whiskey before dinner.

"It wasn't love," insisted Violet. "He, he forced me. I didn't want to—"

"You went willingly," Fred Paisley interrupted. "We'd saved her from, hmm, well, what you call a fate worse than death." He laughed salaciously. "A few blokes were hounding her on the way to Greymouth. And after, she was so grateful to Eric that she—"

"Grateful?" Paisley frowned. "Well, who cares now, the baby's in there. And Eric's a good man, a proper miner. He'll be able to feed you."

Violet thought briefly about an escape toward Dunedin, but she would not have made it over the mountains with Rosie, and she would not leave the child with their father and Fred.

Rosie was the only condition Violet made to her bridegroom before the wedding. Her little sister had to be taken into their household. Eric did not put up a fight about it. He needed a wife, and he would not find a more beautiful one than Violet. She was a stroke of luck. Eric knew that better men with more savings had been interested in Violet. Perhaps he had even nursed the thought in a final calculating turn of his alcohol-addled brain when he forced her into his bed. Once she was no longer a virgin, his prospects improved. Most good men wanted an untouched bride. And then he had even landed a bull's-eye in the act, as Fred noted with a smirk. Eric was more than ready to play the proud papa.

Violet spent her arduously saved money on a dress she could wear for the wedding and then during the pregnancy. She hardly spoke a word to Eric during their engagement and did not look at him when she walked beside him through the church. The church service was well attended. Even Mr. and Mrs. Biller were there, and they gave the young couple timbered wood, with which to make furniture. Even if it only produced rough chairs, tables, and beds, it was better than the waste wood miners usually scrounged, and it helped Violet furnish her hut in Billertown. After Jim and Fred were fired, Eric left his shack for the Paisleys' previous hut. At least Violet and Rosie had a roof over their heads.

If only they could have sectioned off a small area for Rosie. Violet was afraid of the wedding night—not just for herself but for her little sister too. When the time did come and Eric, drunk again, jumped her, she tried to lie perfectly still and make as little noise as possible. Nevertheless, she occasionally moaned in pain, and Eric grunted like a wild animal. When he finally fell asleep, Violet was pinned underneath him. She did not get the opportunity to crawl back to Rosie and comfort her. Violet heard Rosie sobbing all night until she was able to convince the child the next morning that she was all right.

"Nothing happened. At least nothing that doesn't happen to other women," she said to Rosie. "Those are strange noises, I know, but it's normal when people are married."

***

Violet's life as a married woman did not differ much from her life as Jim Paisley's daughter. Eric, too, was thrifty with the household money and behaved as if he were giving alms whenever Violet asked for it. He also ordered Violet around like a slave.

Violet wept bitter tears at Heather Coltrane's first letter. She had not written to her friend about the rape and pregnancy as planned but only announced her engagement with brusque words. Heather sounded disappointed in her letter but politely congratulated Violet and sent a present—a practical set of cooking pots and very beautiful fabric.

Violet thought bitterly that with these she would almost have been able to afford the abortion. As it was, however, she suffered Eric and the changes in her body. She hated becoming fat and inflexible. Pregnancy seemed to be causing the water in her body to gather, and Violet felt bloated and exhausted. That did not seem to bother Eric, however. Whenever he came back from the pub and was not too drunk, he jumped her, and he was really only too drunk on Saturday.

Violet realized Eric drank less than her father and brother. He rarely stank of whiskey, just of beer, which was cheaper. Yet he spent more money in the Wild Rover than Jim or Fred, which irritated Violet. After three months of marriage, she finally dared to ask him about it. She still hated and feared him, but she had grown braver in her interactions with him. In contrast to her father, Eric had not beaten her since the night of the rape.

Though he caused her pain with his nightly "visits," once her panic at being used so mercilessly subsided, she ascribed her pain more to her tension and his lack of patience and skill than true cruelty. The pain subsided when Violet confided in Clarisse, who gave her advice to purposefully relax her muscles and to use oil as a lubricant. As her discomfort decreased, so did her fear, if not her disgust. She eventually spoke with Eric as with a halfway-normal person.

Surprisingly, he wasn't angry when she asked about the money he spent at the pub.

"I, it, well, it's your money of course," she said meekly, "but I do need to buy things. Things for the baby and food for us, and Rosie has outgrown her clothes again." The last remark was daring, as she feared that it would prompt Eric to send Rosie back to their father. "I wonder, since you don't drink that much, what do you spend the money on?"

Aside from beer or whiskey, she could only imagine the money went to whores. But she knew from Clarisse that he was not one of her or her friends' customers. Besides, Clarisse had told her that a man couldn't usually manage sex more than once a night.

"Aye, sweetie, wouldn't you like to know?" Eric grinned. To Violet's relief, he made no move to hit her. "But I didn't really want to bring it up until it panned out. That's to say that I'm spending the money for us, Violet, sweetheart. For you and me and our little one there." He pointed to Violet's stomach. "And for Rosie, too, for God's sake."

Violet looked at him incredulously. "You're saving?" she asked. "You're taking it to the bank?"

Eric laughed even louder. "Nah, sweetie, certainly not that. For what you get in interest, it's not worth the effort. That'll keep you poor your whole life. There's something better. Ever heard of harness racing?"

Violet sighed. Eric had always bet on horses. She remembered he had paid his passage to New Zealand with race winnings. However, she had not known that even here, at what seemed like the end of the world, there were races worth mentioning, let alone betting on.

"But of course, sweetie," he replied importantly when she said as much. "And the future, I'm telling you now, is harness racing. It's just getting started, and your Eric, beautiful, he's got an eye for it. I know who is going to race the others into the ground."

Pleased with himself, he waved around a red notebook, which Violet recalled seeing before. Eric had used it to look important to her father and Fred. He could read and write a bit, and he made notes about his winnings, though not the losses.

Violet bit her lip. "Shouldn't you then be winning more often?" she asked cautiously.

Eric grimaced. "Yeah, and I would," he explained, "but I don't settle for small change, Vio. I don't just bet on the winner or that a horse will place in the top three. I put my money where my mouth is: the trifecta."

It was not all that hard to understand. Eric tried to predict which three horses would achieve the first three places and in which order. One did not need to be a racing aficionado to know that this was difficult. Surely it was not easy even to recognize the three favorites, let alone to order them properly, so it was clear to Violet that one would almost need clairvoyant abilities. Or an exorbitant amount of luck. Eric certainly did not have the former, and as for luck, Violet did not believe that Fortuna could grace her braggart husband a second time.

"I know what I'm doing," Eric assured Violet when she didn't reply. "I'll pull us out of the mud here one day, Vio. Believe me."

Violet shrugged. There was not much she still believed.

Chapter 9

Colin Coltrane found the invasion of Parihaka unsatisfying, as did most of the other soldiers and armed constables. The men had expected a fight, or at least prepared for one. Yet now two thousand Maori enemies sat in front of their lodges, looking at the invaders accusatorily. The men formed a ring around the assembled villagers whom the girls and children had since joined, and felt like fools. No one intended to flee. The military force of the *pakeha* was unnecessary if not downright embarrassing.

John Bryce was obviously trying to make the best of the situation—although Colin thought his appearance rather more comical than heroic. The Minister of Native Affairs leaped on his white horse to read aloud to Te Whiti and the Maori the justification for the invasion. It overflowed with words like "rebellious," "obstreperous," "lawless," and "disturbance of the peace."

"If there's an opposite of a rebellion, then this is it," whispered Colin to another sergeant. "The only sensible thing the man did today was to ban the press. Thank goodness he hasn't made a fool of himself in front of reporters."

Te Whiti and the two other chieftains were arrested. Still there was no protest. Matariki and a few girls cried as Te Whiti strode slowly and evenly through the crowd of his supporters. He wore the valuable ceremonial cloak but left behind the other regalia of a chieftain.

"We seek peace, and we find war."

No one commented on Te Whiti's last words to his people. No one moved; no one left the gathering place until sundown.

Bryce finally withdrew. The soldiers stayed but did not know what to do. Colin and other soldiers organized guard shifts and pleaded to send the volunteers home. That, however, met with their commander's protest. Clearly, he had hoped for more from the whole matter.

"We can't just have the whole force standing around here, sir," Colin Coltrane said when the commander yelled at him rudely, insisting he keep his soldiers at their posts as well. "Otherwise it'll get out of hand; there will be assaults if the men don't have anything to do."

Already the volunteers were releasing their tension by plundering the more secluded buildings. The Armed Constabulary could keep them under control, but its members, too, felt their frustration and wanted something to do. The seated and still Maori were causing increasing annoyance, rage, and bloodlust among the soldiers and the volunteers.

The commander shook his head. "What can you be thinking, Sergeant? We're occupying this land. We're not going to give it back to them. No, for once they need to have a taste of our resistance. For all I care, they can sit here until morning. We can wait."

Colin rolled his eyes but changed his orders. Instead of sending the men back to their camp, he commandeered two of the sleeping lodges and ordered his men to take turns resting.

"You will not steal anything, and I had better not see any girls, willing or not. We're still at war, men."

Colin Coltrane had taken command of his old unit after the quickly assembled cavalry brigade clearly served no additional purpose. He could only shake his head at his superiors—he was anything but an angel of peace, and he did not see himself as a diplomat. Still, what he saw in Parihaka defied all reason. Even the ultimatum had been a mistake.

Colin had spent the first fifteen years of his life with his father, one of the country's craftiest horse traders. He had learned to play with people's ideas and sensitivities, to discover and exploit their pride and their longings—and most of all, never to do anything that put him in the wrong. Colin's father had been able to sell his customers even the lamest nag, and he always had managed to make his deception unnoticeable or to appear as a mistake. Ian Coltrane had even mastered a form of blame reversal: sure, the horse could not be tamed, but hadn't the buyer insisted on getting a particularly lively animal? And did not the buyer of the draft horse with four lame legs want an inexpensive animal? Ian

Coltrane reminded the buyer he had offered him about ten more valuable and thus, naturally, healthier horses, but so be it.

Colin had often made use of this tactic—in horse trading but also in rigging bets or card games, which had been forbidden in the cadet academy. When Colin got into mischief, he rarely carried out the deed himself, preferring to put others up to it. And that was precisely, in his opinion, what should have been done in Parihaka: no warnings, no threats, for which Te Whiti and his people could prepare. Instead, there had been the deliberate provocation of individuals, especially the field-workers. Colin was sure it would have been possible to enrage them. They could have turned fistfights into a rebellion, and by the first dead settler, people's anger would have boiled over, and they would have stormed Parihaka without forewarning. Now, however, Colin saw no opportunity for the government to come out of this on the moral high ground.

***

The Maori maintained their position the next day and the day after that. The men did not move. The women and girls only got up to retrieve prepared food from the *marae*. This ultimately offered the tense and frustrated officers of the Armed Constabulary an excuse to act.

"It's not acceptable that the people come and go as they please," said the commander. "At least not when it could harm the occupying army. Men, search the houses."

Neither the armed constables nor the volunteers needed to be told twice. Before their superiors could organize their soldiers, they stormed the houses, where some women and children could still be found.

The Maori hunters had not hidden their guns inside the houses, so the soldiers quickly found weapons. This quick success spurred on the men, who began to plunder. Soldiers ran out of the houses with weapons, *hei-tiki*, and jade amulets or figurines—and screams came from the cooking lodges. The men assaulted the girls preparing the food.

Colin Coltrane, who was as blindsided by the commander as the other sergeants and corporals, wasn't sure where to begin, which inspired him to take action. The first Maori men were already coming to the women's aid, and the priests were agitated over the defacing of the statues of the gods. A few armed constables emptied their bladders on the *marae*. If this continued, there would be deaths, and not only among the Maori. Coltrane saw trouble ahead: investigative commissions, questions, reputations destroyed forever, and no opportunities for advancement for anyone involved—the last thing he needed.

From one of the nearby buildings came women's screams, a dog barking, and sounds of a struggle. A giant, tattooed young Maori warrior approached the lavishly decorated building. No doubt, his orders had been to remain peaceful in the gathering place. Colin saw him disappear between the figures of the gods at the entrance of the building. A *wharenui*, Colin remembered, a gathering lodge—surely weapons were stored in there, if only for religious purposes. Ceremonial weapons could still be sharp.

Colin leveled his gun and followed the warrior. The building was large and sparsely furnished. A few statues of gods cast ghostly shadows on the two girls who opposed four soldiers. One of the girls was armed with a spear, the other with a war club of jade. The men laughed, threatening them with their bare hands.

Colin felt burning anger rise in him when he recognized the girls. One of them was the stout girl the officer had struggled to move out of his way two days ago. The other was Matariki. And at her side was her dog, which had the courage of a lion. The mutt barked, growled, and snapped at the attackers. Matariki held her club but froze when the men disarmed Pai of her spear. It took two of them to throw Pai to the ground, but they managed it, and Matariki saw no way of coming to her friend's aid.

Pai kicked and bit at her attackers. And then she saw the Maori man who had entered the building moments before Colin had. So far, he hadn't even started to intervene.

"Kupe!"

Pai called for the warrior, but he had eyes for Matariki alone. Without looking at Pai, he moved to hit one of Matariki's attackers in the temple with the butt of a rifle. He must have found the soldiers' weapons.

"Kupe, no."

Matariki seemed to be more afraid for the boy than herself. Or had she already seen Colin in the building's entrance?

When the young Maori hesitated, Colin swung his weapon, thereby knocking the man aside. When Kupe tried to aim the gun, Colin stepped on his hand, and the warrior screamed. Colin had likely broken a few bones. All the better.

"You're under arrest," Colin said to him. "Resistance, insurrection, breach of the peace, take your pick. And you . . ." Colin Coltrane stepped over to the men with Pai. "You will stand up this instant and behave like soldiers." He glared at them until the chastened soldiers got up. "Private Jones, Private McDougal, there will be consequences. Now, get out of here. Everything all right, miss?"

Colin held out his hand to the girl lying on the ground, but she did not take it. Instead, she scrambled to her feet on her own and went over to the Maori warrior who sat dazed and holding his hand.

"Kupe, Kupe, I called to you."

Pai's face was expressionless, but in her eyes shone a combination of incomprehension, shattered hope, and naked hate.

"Pai." The boy seemed only now to recognize the girl. "I—"

"I was fighting with two men," Pai continued. "I was on the ground. You didn't even see me. You've shared my bed for two years, Kupe, but you still only had eyes for her." She gestured with her chin to Matariki. "I don't hold it against you, Matariki. I know you didn't encourage him. You don't even want him now." The girl spat the words out. "May the gods curse you, Kupe Atuhati. May you go to hell; may your worst nightmares come true." The girl let her gaze pass over those gathered there as if she were mad, and as she fled, a gust of wind seemed to sweep through the *marae*. "May the spirit of Parihaka leave you, Kupe, as long as you bear the name she gave you."

With that, she pointed at Matariki and ran out of the *wharenui*. Shocked, Kupe and Matariki watched her go.

"She doesn't really mean it," Matariki murmured.

Colin squared himself. "Regardless of who meant what," he said, "your friend, miss, is under arrest. Assault with a deadly weapon on an unarmed man."

"Who was only unarmed because you can't hold a gun and hold a girl down on the ground at the same time," Matariki shouted.

Colin shrugged. "A judge will decide that. But it may well be that he ends up on the gallows, your little boyfriend—or is he your friend's?" He smirked. "And here I thought, in the uncommonly peace-loving wonderland of Parihaka, no one knew jealousy. I seem to have been mistaken."

"You can't accuse him of that. It was self-defense. He only wanted—" Matariki looked at Kupe, who was still too shocked to defend himself.

"Well, at least he has an eager defender, Your Highness." Colin smiled. "And very well, I don't want to be like that either, but one hand washes the other."

Matariki glared at him. "You want, you want me to, damn it, I wouldn't have thought that. An officer. You should be ashamed, Sergeant Coltrane."

Dingo growled, and Colin grinned. So, she had noted his name. Not bad, one could build on that. But for the moment, he had something completely different in mind than spending a night with Her Highness.

"Miss Drury," he said curtly, "you insult me. I am an officer, as you rightly noted, and a gentleman. I don't want you, Miss Drury. What I need is your—what do you call it?—*mana*, your influence over your people. Use your status as a chieftain's daughter to help me end this."

***

Chaos broke out throughout Parihaka. Though the majority of the residents held still, the soldiers' destruction was now unrestrained. The women under attack screamed and resisted, and men came to their aid. Sheep, cattle, and horse stables had been opened, and the animals ran freely around the village, further irritating the soldiers, who occasionally fired their weapons.

The men's leaders faced the situation rather helplessly—most of them were hardly better schooled than their subordinates, and very few of them had a horse.

If something did not happen soon, there would be fires and panic.

***

Matariki stared at Colin. "You want peace?" she asked. They still stood in the *wharenui*.

Colin nodded. He had neither the time nor the inclination to explain his motives to her. He did not even know exactly how to take hold of the situation, but he needed to gain recognition—and the girl was ideal for that.

He forced himself to be patient. "Miss Drury," he said in his most sincere tone, "we all want peace. Believe me, the majority of *pakeha* regret these events, but our army is not exactly the elite of Aotearoa." Colin noted that the girl's ears pricked up when he used the Maori name for New Zealand. "We must stop them. I, my people, and you, yours. So."

He made a welcoming gesture while regarding Kupe with a warning look.

Matariki followed Colin outside as if in a trance. Only her dog showed a spirit of resistance and snapped at Colin. But Colin was disciplined. It was not in line with his plans to kick the dog, let alone shoot it.

Colin's black horse was in front of the *wharenui*. The young sergeant swung into the saddle and helped Matariki up in front of him. He was surprised at how light of foot and skillfully she slid on. Clearly, she had experience with horses.

"Please, touch me as little as possible," she said, and grabbed the horse's mane to balance herself.

Colin urged the horse into a gallop, and then a jump into the middle of the gathering place, which was slightly elevated. The Maori stared as if spellbound at the rakish blond young *pakeha* and the chieftain's daughter. Colin noticed that the weather was also contributing to the scene's impact. The sun had just set over the sea, the air was clear, and Mount Taranaki rose like a tragic memorial behind them. The sergeant reared up his horse and fired his gun as a signal. The Maori ducked; the plundering soldiers paused briefly.

Matariki used the time. She focused hard to try and touch the spirit of the gods—the *karanga* had to come from her innermost being; otherwise it would not reach the people. At least, that was how Arona had explained it to her, though she agreed that breathing technique played an important role. Matariki hoped that her long practice would finally pay off—and that the gods would listen.

Indeed, her cry filled the camp. It froze the plunderers, and it gave the women time to escape their attackers. It called the men who had gone to rescue the women back to the circle, and it urged the other Maori to rise up as well. The old *tohunga* bade the children sing. A troupe formed for the *haka powhiri*, the greeting dance.

Colin waited patiently, but before more ceremonies could begin, he raised his hand. "Peace," he said with a voice that carried, "and war to those who would break it. We will now restore proper order. The men of the Armed Constabulary will return at once to their units, confiscated weapons will be brought to the collection point, and all plunder will be returned." This last point was a fantasy, but it sounded good, and that was what mattered. "The rebellious Maori under arrest will be placed in that building"—he pointed to the *wharenui* they had just left—"gathered together, restrained, and transported away tonight. The rest . . ."

Colin's speech faltered. If he called upon the people to disperse, they would not follow his orders.

Matariki spoke up. "Go home," she said calmly. "It will be necessary to clean and to catch the animals. Sleep. Pray. We all need rest. But tomorrow we'll be here to call the spirits again. Our power secures peace."

In truth, there was no reason for the people to follow the girl's directions, but they must still have had Te Whiti's words about the value of the chieftain's daughter in their heads. And they needed someone to whom they could listen. To Matariki's complete amazement, the village residents rose up and silently returned to their homes. With relief more so than amazement, Colin watched as the soldiers and volunteers also obeyed. His calculations usually bore out, but not always.

***

"Most of all, it looked beautiful," Koria said later as Matariki, completely drained by the events, curled up on a mat beside her. She was seeking explanations. "It was like, like a picture, like a fairy tale. That *pakeha* looked like a prince. Seriously, don't laugh, Riki, but with his golden hair and his handsome, serious face, and then you, the princess who fit right in front of him, so delicate and as if saved. Your hair was blowing in the wind—I was just waiting for the prince to kiss you. And behind you, the mountain, a backdrop from a dream. Shakespeare could not have thought up something more beautiful."

"But it wasn't a performance," Matariki insisted. "I had goose bumps myself. It was strange. It was as if some power, some spirit came over us."

"That is how it's supposed to be," Arona said, but she sounded skeptical.

Arona was deeply religious, but she was also a priestess of the third generation. She had been taught how to impress people. Moreover, she had studied Shakespeare, the master of all staging. Arona knew how to summon spirits.

And Colin Coltrane—a horse trader since childhood—knew as well.

That night, Matariki dreamed that he took her into his arms.

Chapter 10

Rosie fell completely silent the night Violet gave birth.

The cheerfulness the girl had regained during her time in the Biller household had disappeared since Violet's marriage. Rosie now stared blankly for hours and whimpered when the noises came from Violet's bed at night. She slept poorly and sometimes wet the bed, which made Violet anxious.

Violet found it hard to remain calm and endure Rosie's complaining. She really ought to be more understanding now that she was almost seven. But instead, she seemed to revert farther and farther back to the level of a very young child. With Caleb, Rosie had already read her first sentences, but now she sometimes had difficulty answering simple questions sensibly. Fortunately, Eric hardly noticed. He did not speak to Rosie. In general, he viewed her as hardly more than a piece of furniture as long as she did not, as had happened a few times in the beginning, crawl into his and Violet's bed at night. Then he slapped her and sent her back to her bed, where Rosie then cried the whole night long.

Violet regretted it, but she knew their father would have punished her more brutally. Eric, at least, did not look for excuses to let out his anger on the child. He was predictable. If Rosie behaved calmly and did not bother him, he did not do anything to her either. Violet pointed this out to Rosie, but she didn't answer.

***

None of that, however, was about the horrors of the birth—a terror for which neither sister was prepared. Naturally, Violet had been told it would hurt. Friendly Mrs. O'Toole, her former neighbor, had mentioned what awaited her.

"You're going to need help," she said with concern. "Can you pay Mrs. Travers? Otherwise, I'll come. I'm not a midwife, it's true, but I have brought six of my own into this world. I know the most important things. Your husband just needs to come get me."

"By the time Eric reaches you, the baby will long since have arrived," Violet said.

"I hope so for your sake, girl," Mrs. O'Toole said, "but when I take a good look at you, such a delicate little person and your first baby, I suspect it won't be easy, Violet, and it won't go fast."

Mrs. Travers, the midwife, expressed herself with far more concern. "Dear, you are so small and have such a narrow pelvis. I just hope the baby will pass through."

Violet did not ask what would happen if it did not fit. Eric, however, brushed her concerns aside with a laugh.

"Particularly since you're so young, it'll be simple," he declared, bursting with confidence. "Don't listen to the old crows. A young mare foals easy. Everyone knows that."

Violet tried to believe her husband. There was not much else she could do. She had not been able to save a penny in the months of her marriage, so there was no question of calling Mrs. Travers. As for Mrs. O'Toole . . .

When her contractions began on an ice-cold autumn day in May 1881, Eric was at the pub. Violet had just brought in wood to light a fire and drive the dampness out of the house a bit, when she felt a sharp pain and water ran down her leg.

"I think the baby's coming." Violet tried to remain calm. Rosie looked confused and afraid at the puddle that was forming beneath Violet's dress. "Don't worry, Rosie, we'll wipe that up in a moment."

Another pain made her collapse. She managed to clean the floor before hauling herself to the bed, and she thought feverishly as she did.

It was early and, worse, it was Saturday night. Billertown was swept clean: the miners were celebrating the weekend at the Wild Rover. Rosie wouldn't know where to find help.

Violet tried to relax, but against the pain of the contractions, it did nothing. She wanted to be brave and not scream, and she managed that for a whole hour. Then it became too much. Violet allowed herself a groan, and she sighed when Rosie snuggled against her.

"I'm scared," the little girl murmured. "I want to sleep next to you."

Violet pushed her sister gently away. "Rosie, you can't anymore. You have to be grown-up now, Rosie. Can you do that? Look, today you're the big sister. Get me—" Another contraction made Violet groan. "Get me a glass of water, would you?"

Rosie went to the pitcher where Violet kept the drinking water. "There's not much left."

Now this. Violet had asked Eric to fetch water before he went to the pub, but he must have forgotten. Of all times.

"I'm cold, Violet, really cold."

Rosie was crouching next to the bed. Violet was rather warm herself. Her futile attempt not to show her pain made her break out in a sweat.

"Will you make a fire?"

Violet shook her head. "Take a blanket from your bed, Rosie. I can't make a fire now." Desperately, she tried to estimate the time since the last contraction. Eric would come back from the pub and could then fetch help. Violet was slowly giving up the idea that she could do it alone. The time between the contractions was getting shorter and shorter. Mrs. O'Toole had said something about that. Yet the baby did not seem to move. Nothing moved. It was as if someone were sticking knives in her abdomen.

And then, after several more hours during which Violet barely managed to choke down her cries by biting her blanket, the baby was pushing against her pelvis. It seemed to want to come out, but Mrs. Travers had been right: the passage appeared to be too narrow. Violet was sure the baby would rip her up.

Maybe, maybe if she stood up and walked around? The baby did have to go downward. Maybe it would tumble out if she got up? Violet sat up. She was dizzy, but she tried to haul herself from the bed to the table, supporting herself on a rickety chair, but she fell to the ground. Rosie whimpered, and Violet began to cry—until a new contraction made her scream. She needed to get up; she needed to get back into bed or prop herself up on the table, or . . . Violet screamed again.

She forgot about Rosie entirely. She only felt pain still and a maddening thirst. Then her thirst passed, and she forgot that she had ever felt anything but pain. Violet screamed. Then she became one with the pain, a whimpering, screeching bundle of flesh. She turned on the floor of the hut, pressed her legs to her body, spread them, and she ripped her dress in tatters from her body. The wood of the floorboards chafed her back, but she did not feel it. She only felt the something that was ripping up her abdomen. Then blood shot from her body.

***

Rosie watched all of this, her eyes open wide, her lips forming a silent cry. When something bloody and blue appeared between Violet's legs, Rosie could no longer stand it. She fled.

Rosie ran blindly through the rain-soaked settlement and the outskirts of the fern forest. She knew almost no one, only the women who lived together in the house just outside of town. Rosie could not have named her destination, but she found herself in front of the hut that belonged to Clarisse and her friends. She flung open the door without knocking—only to be horrified anew.

From one of the beds came the same grunting noises that she heard from Violet's corner when Eric lay with her. Here, though, an oil lamp was burning, and in the oven a fire flickered. The house was dimly lit, but Rosie still made out a big man who had hair covering his whole body. He lay on top of Miss Baton, wheezing, and seemed to be trying to kill her. So that was what was happening every night with Violet. She was fighting with Eric for her life.

Rosie screamed. The tortured lament startled Clarisse and her customer.

"What in heaven's name was that?" asked the man.

Clarisse covered herself as fast as she could. "Put on your clothes, Geordie," she called to the man. "Dear Lord, you see that the little dear's scared. What is it, Rosie? Did you come here on your own? Where's Violet? Rosie, is something wrong with Violet?"

Rosie did not answer. Her cry was the last noise she would make for many years. Now, she simply stared straight ahead, seeming to see neither Clarisse nor her customer.

"Something must have happened." Clarisse closed her dress and threw on a shawl. "Come along, Geordie. We might need help. You don't need to pay this time. But come with me, and take the kid."

Clarisse did not know if that was the right decision, but she could not let Rosie stay there, and the little girl did not seem capable of moving herself in any direction. She was on the ground, with her legs pulled close to her body, rocking herself back and forth.

Geordie carefully loosened her grip and picked her up. Clarisse sighed with relief. Geordie was a good man; he had a wife and children in Wales to whom he sent money. Whenever he took a whore every few weeks, he always decided on Clarisse. Apparently, she looked like his wife, Anna. Clarisse hoped his fatherly feelings spoke to Rosie.

For now, he followed her at a quick pace through the forest and the settlement, talking calmly to the little girl. A weak light shone outside Violet's hut. The door stood half-open; wind and rain blew inside. Rosie pressed her face into Geordie's chest. Sobs shook her body, but she made no noise.

Clarisse found it difficult to orient herself in the hut. The light of the sole lamp was weak, and in the room, it looked like a fight had taken place. The bedsheets lay on the floor, a chair had fallen over, and there on the floor lay Violet. She did not move, but between her legs, in a puddle of blood, something stirred. The bloody, slimy baby was still attached to the umbilical cord. It did not let out a sound, but it moved its little arms. Clarisse ran to it, wrapped it in her shawl, and wiped the blood and slime from its little face. Only then did it take on human features. It balled its tiny fists and seemed to look at Clarisse. Clarisse smiled.

"Do you have a knife?" she asked Geordie.

Geordie nodded. "In my pants' pocket."

He could not reach in himself. He needed both hands to hold Rosie. Clarisse laid the baby on the ground, took the knife, and inhaled deeply before she cut through the umbilical cord. Then she picked up the infant again. At that moment, it began to cry loudly.

"What about the girl?" Geordie asked.

He was still standing in the doorway, uncertain whether he should help or continue protecting Rosie from the sight the room offered. She had fallen asleep in his arms but was now sobbing and shaking again after hearing the newborn's cry.

Clarisse laid a hand on Violet's cheek. She was pale as a corpse. Her face was strangely sunken with dark rings under her eyes. Her lips were chewed and bloody.

"She's bleeding; she's alive," Geordie observed. The lake of blood between Violet's legs was growing. "But when a woman is still bleeding after the birth, she'll not live long."

That sounded knowledgeable but not encouraging. Clarisse wondered whether Geordie had stood by his own wife in childbirth. Could he have helped Violet?

"Water," whispered Violet, choking. "Thirsty."

Clarisse stood up. Would she rely on Geordie's smattering of knowledge, or should she try to reach the midwife before Violet died?

"Fetch the midwife, Geordie," she said. "The wife of the gravedigger. Take the little girl with you. I don't need her here. I'll look after Violet."

Geordie frowned. "But you need help, the way it looks here. And I have—"

"Are you a doctor?"

Clarisse had to exert herself not to yell at him. He shook his head, chastened.

"We need someone here who knows a lot more about all this than you or I. So, go on. I'll manage here."

Geordie left but was there again in a few minutes. Clarisse had just had time to establish that there was no water there to give Violet to drink, let alone with which to wash herself. She tried unhappily to get at least a few drops from the pitcher, but there was nothing there.

Geordie shook his head in disbelief. "Who leaves his very pregnant wife here alone without fire and water?" he muttered. "The man ought to be beaten to death. I ran into little Jeff Potters," he reported eagerly. "He had just come from the pub but was halfway sober. He's gone to town to fetch Mrs. Travers. Don't cuss, Miss Baton. Jeff's much faster than I am. And he knows what's at stake. His mom died in childbirth."

Clarisse nodded. Deep down, she thanked heaven. Alone she would never have managed with this calamity.

"Fetch water, Geordie," she directed her assistant. "Put Rosie in her bed. Nothing worse than what she's already seen today can come. I'll make a fire. Fortunately, there's wood here."

"I'll do it quick, Miss Baton."

Geordie reached for the pitcher after he had set Rosie in her bed. And he proved his worth. Long before Mrs. Travers arrived—wheezing, she seemed to have run the whole way—Violet lay on a freshly made bed. A fire burned in the fireplace. Clarisse had heated water and washed her. Violet was still losing blood, but now there were only slow drips. Clarisse and Geordie, clearly taken with the little creature, bathed the baby.

"A boy," the man said reverently.

"Lucky for him," Clarisse blurted out, and then turned to the midwife. "Dear Lord, Mrs. Travers, am I happy to see you."

Before Mrs. Travers could even reply, Violet reared up with a cry.

"Looks like the afterbirth is coming," noted the midwife calmly. "Do we have hot water, missus, umm, miss?"

At that, Violet's tormented body was torn by yet another contraction. Later she could not recall it, but she was not completely unconscious. She was conscious enough to feel the pain, although it did not come close to what she had experienced before. Violet feared it would never end. Even when the afterbirth came, she could not calm herself.

"Poor child," sighed Mrs. Travers. "But she'll survive. We told that fine husband of hers on the way. He's buying a round for everyone."

"But how did he know it was healthy? And a boy?" asked Clarisse.

"He assumed," Mrs. Travers grumbled. She was a tall, strong woman whose giant red hands didn't suggest she would deal so gently and lovingly with newborns and women in childbirth. "Nothing less'd do for a splendid bloke like that. He's certainly not lacking in self-confidence. Poor woman. Hopefully he won't get her pregnant again right away." She carefully tucked Violet in and glanced at the bucket with the afterbirth. "The father can bury that later."

Geordie reached obligingly for the bucket, but Mrs. Travers shook her head. "Oh no. Thank you, but he should at a minimum get to see a little blood."

Violet stirred. She drank greedily when Mrs. Travers gave her some herbal tea.

"Rosie?" Violet asked weakly.

Mrs. Travers assured her that everything was all right with her little sister. Violet did not ask about the newborn. Clarisse, who had swaddled the baby, moved to lay it in her arms, but Mrs. Travers stopped her.

"In cases like this, that hasn't proved wise," she said quietly. "When they're halfway children themselves, and the birth is so hard, they aren't happy about it so soon. I gave her something to help her sleep. That'll help her forget the worst. When she sees the little thing tomorrow, hopefully she'll love it."

Eric Fence did not get to see any blood that night. When he came home completely drunk, he had Jim and Fred in tow, apparently just dying to see their grandson and nephew. They had expected to be welcomed at the door by a beaming Violet. Instead, they met with the stern Mrs. Travers, who was watching over Violet that night, just to be on the safe side. The midwife insisted they be quiet and only reluctantly let them inside. All three looked at the baby and decided wordlessly that under no circumstances could Eric be left to Mrs. Travers's harangue. Father, grandfather, and uncle left for Lamberttown after Fred and Jim generously offered Eric asylum in their hut.

∗∗∗

Violet saw her baby the next day. She took it in her arms and bravely withstood the pain that the first suckling caused her swollen breasts.

But she would never learn to love the child.

Chapter 11

"I'm sorry, Miss Drury, but I'm no longer in charge here."

Colin Coltrane sounded regretful, but in truth he was thankful that John Bryce had assumed command of the troops in Parihaka. If things went wrong, it could no longer be pinned on him as one of the highest-ranking armed constables or on the commanders of the volunteers. Bryce was doing everything he could to make the invasion one of the most embarrassing performances in the history of the British Army. The press embargo was the only thing really functioning.

The Minister of Native Affairs ordered the Maori tribes not located in or around Parihaka to return home. The Maori had assembled anew at sunrise. Things were just as they had been: the villagers and their visitors did not react to Bryce's orders.

So, the minister turned to his soldiers. "Men, remove and send away all subjects who do not belong in Central Taranaki."

"How are we supposed to do that, sir?" asked one of Colin's subordinates.

Colin shrugged. Matariki, who stood beside him after he had explained the situation, smiled.

"You recognize the tribes by the weave of their clothing and their tattoos," she said with a honey-sweet voice.

She was annoyed at Colin because Kupe was still under arrest. The soldiers also had hauled away his friend Arama and a few other young warriors after they had tried to stop the plundering. Colin's attempt to explain to Matariki that he could not do anything did not impress her, though his second attempt soothed her somewhat: "Miss Drury, it is for your friends' own good that they're now in protective custody. Who knows what might still happen here. They won't be kept. As soon as Parihaka is cleared, they'll be let go." Naturally, she was concerned about the impending clearing. However, Colin really did not have anything to do with that. For all the mistakes that were made, John Bryce alone was responsible.

"You wouldn't perhaps help us identify those people?" he asked.

Matariki glared at him. "Like hell I will," she declared.

Colin shrugged his shoulders again. He hadn't expected anything different.

Over the next few hours, the soldiers tore people from the crowd. They did not resist, but they also did not reveal anything about their tribal affiliation.

Colin Coltrane sent two of his best riders to the nearest Maori tribe friendly to the government. They could send people who knew their weaving techniques and tattoos. Coltrane smiled to himself. Matariki did not need to betray her people. Her words had sufficed to set the wheels in motion. And he hoped he would reap the reward himself.

Bryce took harsher measures. "All *marae* belonging to the foreign tribes will be destroyed," he said the next day. "Tribes that don't reside here cannot be allowed to settle in this region."

Indeed, a sort of village within the village had come into being in Parihaka. The various tribes had founded their own spiritual centers where delegations of their people lived and honored the gods. The buildings were easier to identify than their residents. There had originally been two *wharenui* in Parihaka. The newer constructions erected around them belonged to foreign tribes.

A lament arose from the people as the soldiers' axes felled the statues of the gods at the entrance of the first building. It was easy to destroy the wooden buildings.

"They're modeled on whales," Matariki whispered to Colin as she stood next to him again. Something about him attracted her. It was possible, too, that he sympathized with her; he had said the day before that he did not approve of what was happening. "Our lodges are meant to breathe and feel like living beings. That's why we build them of wood, not of stone."

Colin nodded. It was important to show himself sympathetic now. "A beautiful idea. But I'm sure they can easily be rebuilt. The statues of the gods, however . . ."

He thought there surely must be collectors—if not here, then in Europe—who would have paid good money for such primitive art.

"We call them *tiki*," said Matariki, "and the little ones are *hei-tiki*." She slipped one of the three amulets from her neck: the present from Haikina and her own two best efforts. "Here, take this," she said shyly, and placed one of the amulets in Colin's hand. "It'll bring you luck."

Colin furrowed his brow. He ran his finger over the jade figurine and felt strangely touched. "I, I can't accept this. I, these things must be valuable."

Matariki shook her head. "The jade is worth a little something, but not much. And besides, I carved it myself."

Colin looked at her warmly. She was charming and sweet, so innocent. And so beautiful. "Then it will always remind me of you," he said softly. "Of you and the spirit of Parihaka."

He knew that he had said the right thing when Matariki smiled radiantly.

***

Bryce had the men and women in the assembly place observed. Anyone who showed outbursts of feelings over the demolition of the buildings was arrested. In some of the *wharenui*, there were still women and children he had gathered together. The next day, a man arrived who was knowledgeable about *moko*. He could effortlessly assign tribal members with tattoos to their *iwi*. However, not all of them were tattooed, and most of them now wore Western clothing, so it wasn't possible to differentiate them by the weaving pattern of their clothing. Still, hundreds were transported away.

As for the rest of the protesting Maori, Bryce resorted to starvation and further demoralization. His soldiers destroyed Parihaka's fields—forty-five acres of sweet potatoes, taro plants, and tobacco. The land surveyors resumed their work.

Matariki and her friends cried quietly.

"Where will you go when this is over?" asked Colin. Overseeing the transportation of the people numbered among his duties. The invasion was now two weeks old, and every day a few dozen to a few hundred people were exiled from Parihaka. Colin listened to Matariki's complaints with understanding and performed his work discreetly. She did not need to know that he made the decisions about who had to go and who might stay. Passes were being issued to the "legal" village residents. "Or do you hope you'll be able to stay?"

Matariki shook her head. "No, I'll go back to the South Island. That's where my parents and I live."

"Your father the chieftain is an *ariki* of the Ngai Tahu?" Colin asked, amazed. He would not have thought that. The Ngai Tahu were considered peaceful.

"My parents have a farm in Otago," Matariki said. "The chieftain was just my sire. I first met him only a few years ago."

"And?" marveled Colin. "The encounter so impressed you that you at once made the Maori cause your own?"

Matariki grew angry. "It is my cause, as it should be the cause of every thinking and feeling person in this country. What does parentage have to do with it? I also sympathize with the Irish in their struggle against their oppressors, and—"

"My parents were Irish," Coltrane interrupted her.

Matariki smiled. "My father is too. My real father, not the chieftain. Your parents died?"

She noticed how his gaze became veiled. Matariki did not quite understand, but all the feelings Colin displayed seemed to burn in her heart at once. She had always been an empathetic person, but this intensity of pain, and rarely even triumph and joy, was new to her.

Colin Coltrane shook his head. "My father's dead. My mother is alive and living on the South Island. She's remarried. I didn't fit into that family. So I was sent to England."

Matariki looked at him, horrified. "They kicked you out?" she asked. "You had to go to England, you had to do this here because your mother didn't want you anymore?"

Colin lowered his gaze. "Not entirely," he said. "We're not on bad terms. On the contrary, I'm thinking of transferring to the South Island. So many years have passed. Sometimes I long for my family."

Matariki nodded. "Me too," she admitted. "But for now, I'll remain here. I'll stay until the last day. Have you heard anything new about Kupe?"

Matariki asked the question every day, and every day Colin replied, "No," but he promised to ask at every opportunity. Matariki believed him, but she was the only one. Koria and the other girls met her excuses for Colin Coltrane with laughter and warnings about the two-faced nature of the *pakeha*. None of them liked to see Matariki with the sergeant.

In truth, Colin knew where the prisoners from Parihaka—and especially Kupe—were housed. He was keeping an eye on Kupe Atuhati, and he knew how to keep him from being freed too quickly. It was not in Colin's interest for Matariki to meet the young man again as soon as she left Parihaka. Even if she appeared not to have loved him yet, she could still. And if that happened, Kupe would have stood in Colin Coltrane's way—something the self-assured sergeant could not tolerate.

Colin Coltrane had his own plans for Matariki Drury. But he would only reveal those when Parihaka really came to an end.

***

The crowd of protesters in the village had shrunken considerably, and the people whom the daily removals affected seemed almost relieved. No one continued to hope they would achieve anything by enduring more. By the third week, only stubbornness and dutifulness kept the people in place. The younger among them fed off the growing frustration of their guards. The soldiers now stood under better control, a portion of the volunteers had moved out, and members of the Armed Constabulary possessed a modicum of training and discipline. That prevented them from serious assaults—but not from provocations. Again and again, the men pointed their guns at the waiting Maori and threatened to shoot them if they did not reveal their tribal affiliation. Bryce spoke of firing the cannon still aimed at Parihaka.

"He doesn't really believe he's scaring anyone with that," snorted Matariki as the soldiers on the hill prepared the cannon for use. "They're out of things to wear us down, and they can't shoot at a crowd of people who aren't doing anything."

Koria shrugged. "You know that, and I know that. But the children in the square always flinch when that bastard Bryce talks about the canon, and the old people duck every time the soldiers wave their guns around. No one here can rest easy, and that's exactly what they want. Hopefully the newspaper people are at least getting that."

Journalists had begun to return to Parihaka, and they now represented the independent press. In that regard, the critical voices increased. On November 21, Bryce called his troop commanders to a final council.

"Tomorrow we'll be ending this," he declared curtly. "Arrest the last hundred fifty nonresidents, and let them out somewhere other than Central Taranaki. They'll find their way back to their tribes, and if not, then I can't help them. The rest will be issued their passes and can clean up here. Or disappear. I don't care, as long as they follow the rules. The strip of land on the coast is—what do they say? Taboo?—and inland too. They can build their village up again in between and plant something. It should suffice for six hundred people. If not, they'll have to go elsewhere. We're moving out tomorrow night."

Colin went straight to Matariki with the news. He met her in the girls' sleeping lodge. Since the looting, the female villagers tended to gather together at night. This arrangement resulted from Colin's suggestion, although he had been careful to ensure Matariki thought it was her own idea. He did not want to risk her being violated. Although it was rare for Maori girls of her age, he hoped that she was still untouched. Once Matariki and the others had gathered in one of the remaining lodges, he ordered the doorway guarded.

Matariki was grateful to him for that, even if she did not say so. The other girls still proved dismissive, and she did not dare show her fondness for him openly. Nevertheless, the women brought the guards food again, which they took from their own meager rations. Maori showed their gratitude through gestures—Colin remembered having heard that once. He requited this by a special allotment of provisions and smiled when he heard Matariki and the other girls fighting. He did not understand Maori, but it was clear what it was about: Koria and the other girls wanted to reject the food, but Matariki argued for its acceptance. This was another little wedge between her and her friends; everything was going according to Colin's plan.

Ultimately, Matariki prevailed—or the smell of fresh-baked bread emanating from the baskets of provisions did. The girls took the food and distributed it demonstratively among the hungry in the village square. Colin did not care, and luckily, Bryce did not notice.

Now that the final night had come, Colin, who knew what was acceptable and who did not want to negotiate with Matariki in front of the females of the village, called the girl outside.

"Miss Drury, I'm sorry to have to inform you," he began in a soft tone, "but we're approaching the end. Minister Bryce will have the last villagers without a pass arrested and removed tomorrow. And, and I fear that will not go easily for them. They will be incarcerated elsewhere. Who knows when they'll be set free again. I don't want to think about it. I say this reluctantly. After all, I do serve this country, but they make people disappear, often for a long time. Think about the plowmen on the South Island."

"And Kupe," Matariki said, as always more concerned for her friends than for herself. "Do you know where he is now?"

Colin shook his head. "Unfortunately not, Miss Drury, as I said. Please don't hold it against me, but I worry about you."

"About me?" Matariki looked taken aback, but her heart leaped for joy. She must mean something to him. If only he weren't the enemy. But was he an enemy? "You don't need to worry about me. My parents have influence. If it's a question of bail, that's not a problem."

Colin noted her carefree attitude about money. Her parents' farm on the South Island must not be a small homestead like the one his father had once worked. Did the chieftain's daughter hold other surprises? Perhaps her stepfather numbered among the sheep barons of the Canterbury Plains.

He contorted his face into a concerned expression. "That reassures me, Miss Drury, but what if your parents can't find you? Consider that no letter from your incarcerated friend has reached you yet."

Matariki frowned. "Our post office is closed," she said curtly.

Colin tried to look insulted. "I know that, Miss Drury, but mail still arrives. And I, though I should not, would not have kept a letter from your friend from you."

A warm feeling of gratitude spread through Matariki. Colin Coltrane was so nice, so considerate. Still, she tried to remain cool.

"What are you suggesting, Sergeant Coltrane? Do you want to issue me a pass? That would be unfair. There are people here in greater need."

Colin shook his head. "Issuing a pass is beyond my power." He hoped she believed that. If not, she would ask him for ten or fifteen passes for her friends. "Meet me an hour before midnight. I'll get you out of here. And you won't be leaving anyone in the lurch. You did what you could, Matariki. Now, let me do what I can." Colin Coltrane looked her straight in the eye.

Matariki thought about his offer briefly, though her cool assessment of the situation was limited by how weak her knees grew when she looked into his shining green-brown eyes. Warmth welled up in her along with a spark of longing and love of adventure. What had Koria said? Matariki and Colin had looked like a prince and princess when they restored peace to the village. And now the prince wanted to save her.

Colin was right: she had done her best to save the spirit of Parihaka. If she now disappeared into a prison . . . they would never let her write a letter. She would never get out.

Matariki swallowed. "All right, Mr. Coltrane. I'll do it," she said decidedly.

Her prince smiled at her. "Colin," he said in a pleading tone. "Please, call me Colin."

***

Matariki told no one of her escape plans and had a guilty conscience about it. It would have been the right thing to inform the other girls of the danger looming the next day. They all knew Parihaka like the back of their hand. Even without the accompaniment of a *pakeha* sergeant, they had good chances for a successful escape. But Matariki was afraid of her friends' comments, especially because they had become distant since the situation with Kupe. And Colin. And the performance at the village square.

Matariki sighed when she stood up, taking her tiny bundle. She left Parihaka with one change of clothes and a few mementos. If Colin provided horses, they could be in Wellington in a few days—and then on the ferry to the South Island. Matariki wanted to go home.

***

Naturally, the guards around the sleeping lodge smirked when Matariki slipped out around eleven. They did not stop her, though. The women were not prisoners, and every night one or two of them left the *whare*—and their men got up from the village square. In this way, some couples offered each other at least a little comfort at night.

Matariki tried to keep Dingo quiet. Since the looting, the mutt had developed an outspoken hate for *pakeha* soldiers, and he growled at the guards. Her canine friend was another reason to accept Colin's offer of help escaping. If Matariki landed in some prison, no one would care for Dingo.

Colin looked less enthusiastic when he saw the growling mutt with Matariki.

"Does he have to come, Matariki?" he asked, but then composed himself quickly. "I hope he doesn't draw any attention to us."

He tried to pet the dog, but Dingo snapped at him. Colin seized Matariki's hand.

"Come, Matariki, we'll sneak off under tree cover."

He put his finger to his mouth and pulled the girl along behind him as if she needed guidance. Yet Matariki knew the village much better than he did. She knew about the side gate in the fence that provided the workers quicker access to the fields. Now, that did not matter. The fence had been pulled down, and the buildings on the outside had been the first to fall victim to the looting and destruction. The area could not be seen from the village square, so the soldiers could look for valuables in peace, though there had long been nothing left to find or guard, not for two weeks, at least.

Colin knew that, and so his escape with Matariki was risk-free, but he played the role of rescuer perfectly. The girl sighed with relief when the two of them slipped through the gate, but then looked with horror at the destroyed fields.

"This is awful," Matariki said quietly. "We worked so hard, and now—"

Colin urged her to turn her gaze from the fields and look at him. "Don't look, Matariki. Leave it behind. Today a new life begins, and it can be just as lovely."

His voice sounded gentle at first, then hoarse. He slowly raised his left hand and ran it tenderly over her cheek to wipe away her tears. Matariki blinked, amazed but also a bit comforted. There were so many new feelings. She did not know what she should think. About one thing, though, Colin was right: she had to leave Parihaka behind.

Silently she followed him farther inland, toward Mount Taranaki. Behind one of the hills, Colin had hidden horses. But they would not ride straight to Wellington.

"I've secured us tents and provisions," he explained. "It won't bother you to spend a few days in the hills, will it?"

Matariki shook her head. "Of course not," she replied. "We'll likely have to do that on the way to Wellington, too, won't we? Only, I don't understand why. Wouldn't it be better to put as many miles as possible between us and Parihaka as quickly as possible?"

Colin smiled at her. "That's how everyone thinks, Matariki," he said with a slightly chiding undertone. "If they look for us, it'll be on the road to Wellington. And how would that look? A British sergeant helping a Maori girl escape? I would lose my post, and you'd be compromised."

Matariki frowned. Really, she was already compromised enough. And the switch from "Miss Drury" to the familiar use of her first name had happened a bit too fast. But it didn't worry her. She felt comfortable in Colin's presence. Her hand was warm in his, and it did not bother her to call him by his first name. On the contrary. But this strange escape plan . . .

"We'll make camp somewhere on Mount Taranaki, and you'll stay there and wait for me. I'll take my leave with the proper ceremonies, and then I'll take you home."

Matariki's heart pounded. Did he really mean to leave the army? For her sake or for Parihaka's? Did the destruction of her dream touch him so deeply, and did he really intend to accompany her not just to Wellington but to the South Island? It would not have bothered her to spend a few days in the city until her parents' money arrived. She had already practiced that thoroughly in Auckland. But she had not been alone since then—nor among the *pakeha*. She had still been able to suppress her experience in Hamilton, but her Parihaka experiences ran deep. She did not trust the *pakeha* anymore—she almost feared them.

Matariki forgot for a moment all her considerations regarding Colin's discharge from the army. It was time for her final good-bye to Parihaka. She and Colin stood on one of the hills above the village and looked down at the ruins that shone ghostly in the moonlight.

Matariki saw the razed fields, the rubble of the fences, and the last intact buildings amid all the destruction. She thought of her first sight of Parihaka more than two years before. All the hope, the speeches of Te Whiti. Matariki could no longer control herself. She cried, and she did not resist when Colin Coltrane pulled her to him for comfort. Matariki sobbed on his shoulder. Then she looked up into his understanding, gentle, sad eyes.

Matariki parted her lips.

Colin Coltrane kissed her.

Later she followed him down the hill with a feeling between happiness and resignation. He was right; that night something new began.

While Dingo yapped in front of the tent, trying angrily to free himself from the leash that tied him to a kauri tree, Matariki lay in Colin's arms.

No Choice

Dunedin, Greymouth, and Woolston,

South Island

1881–1882

Chapter 1

"Now you're going to be related to Mary Kathleen," Lizzie Drury teased her husband. "Is there a term for being a partial mother- or father-in-law?"

Lizzie had been over the moon since Matariki and Colin had arrived in Dunedin. The Drurys had met their daughter there; they could not wait for the young couple to ride up to Elizabeth Station, especially since Colin had some things to do in the city. Judging by Matariki's letter from Wellington, the young man had resigned from service with the Armed Constabulary. This pleased Lizzie, who, like Michael, looked at anyone in a uniform skeptically. So, it surprised her that Michael did not seem enthusiastic about Matariki's marriage plans.

"Now, stop being a wet blanket. Instead, help me lace this. The dresses from Kathleen and Claire are lovely, but they demand a certain amount of suffering."

Lizzie had been shopping that afternoon at the Gold Mine Boutique. She was determined not to play second fiddle to Kathleen Burton's beauty on this special evening. Jimmy and Claire Dunloe had invited Kathleen and Peter, Michael and Lizzie, and Colin and Matariki to a celebratory dinner in one of the best restaurants in the city. They had to celebrate the return of the "prodigal son," as Jimmy had said with a smile. He was as proud as ever to have convinced Kathleen years ago to send Colin to England. Lizzie had gladly accepted the invitation, but she was prepared to welcome Colin Coltrane without reservation. His father had been a scoundrel, but the boy did not have to take after him, and so far, Colin had made only the very best impression. Lizzie had always felt guilty with regard to the boy. She had killed Ian Coltrane in self-defense, though no one besides Michael and Reverend Burton knew. She was not sorry, but she had taken away Colin's father. If the boy now started a new, happy family with her daughter, that would be a relief to Lizzie. Proof that God, too, forgave her.

***

"Return of the prodigal son," Peter Burton snorted as he dressed in a distinguished brown suit. "Jimmy Dunloe citing scripture! With the character in question, we don't know what becomes of him later. Honestly, I've always found the metaphor somewhat dubious."

Kathleen laughed. In her simple dark-green evening dress, she was captivating. She merely hoped she did not outdo Lizzie Drury, who had invested a fortune that afternoon in a dark-red dream with white sleeves and a light-brown, gold-laced belt.

"Just don't let the bishop hear that—he'll send you back to the goldfields. Or this time into the coal mines, closer on the way to hell."

"That doesn't change anything about my bad feeling about this relationship between Colin and Matariki," said Peter. "He's started by not telling her the truth. He didn't really resign his service, or did he?"

Kathleen shrugged and tucked back a lock of her hair. "Not directly. But transfer to the South Island comes to the same thing. Here there just aren't any Maori uprisings. So, there's no need for armed constables—except in the police service, but there aren't many posts." Most police officers in the small towns of the South Island were elected by the residents or named by the government, and as a rule, they were interested in keeping the climate between the *pakeha* and Ngai Tahu peaceful. A veteran of the Taranaki Wars or the invasion of Parihaka was the last person they would choose. "So, they'll put Colin to work building roads or train tracks. He'll find out today. He has an appointment at the barracks."

"Then, we'll hope for the best," sighed Peter. "But that doesn't change the fact that he's lying to Matariki. And I can't imagine that in Parihaka his heart suddenly opened to Maori causes. Matariki does portray him as a hero of peace. I just can't believe it."

Kathleen bit her lip. "Perhaps we should stop attributing the worst motives to him. I include myself in that. Jimmy Dunloe seems to be the only one to believe in his wondrous transformation. But he really is charming with Matariki. Whatever else he has in his head, he loves her, without a doubt. He can hardly take his eyes off her. She shines like the stars she's named for. Lizzie is also happy. I think she's glad her little girl fell in love with a *pakeha*, no matter how close she is to the Maori. I always thought that was important to Michael too."

Kathleen put a valuable headdress of feathers and flowers in her hair. Whenever she and Claire went out in public, they always advertised for the Gold Mine.

Peter laughed. "I don't doubt Michael would rather have a *pakeha* son-in-law, but Colin wouldn't have been his choice. After all, he remembers him from Tuapeka, and he knows what you went through with him here. Lizzie doesn't know him, and she's a good soul. She won't condemn the son for the deeds of the father. We'll see if she doesn't regret it."

Kathleen cast a last look in the mirror. "Perhaps we simply shouldn't take such a dim view of things," she said, trying once more to encourage herself as well as Peter. "Like I said, he loves the girl. And love can change people."

Peter rolled his eyes. "You can give my next sermon, dearest. Faith, hope, and love, as seen in the example of the prodigal son. Or shall we wait a year or so and see how things go?"

***

That evening, there did not seem to be anything troubling the relationship between Matariki Drury and Colin Coltrane—perhaps because they had banned Dingo to the stables for the night. For Matariki, Dingo's obvious dislike for her beloved was the only drop of wormwood in her happiness. The dog had become a bit aggressive. If he ever bit Colin, it would force a decision that wouldn't land in Dingo's favor. The thought of separating from her companion of many years broke Matariki's heart.

Colin appeared in the lobby of the hotel where the Drurys were staying so he could accompany Matariki to the table. Rather than the gala uniform of the Armed Constabulary, he wore an elegant gray waistcoat and suit his mother had financed. He kept proper posture and wore his curly blond hair a bit longer than military norms required, and in his beautiful eyes shone genuine love and admiration for Matariki.

Even Peter had a good impression. He finally saw more than a fleeting resemblance between Colin and his beloved Kathleen. Usually Peter thought that Colin's good looks made one miss the warmth and gentleness that were part of Kathleen and that elevated her radiant appearance above the beauty of a perfect marble statue.

It was similar for Michael, even though the young Colin had reminded him more of Kathleen's brothers than Ian Coltrane. Lizzie, by contrast, observed Colin completely free of prejudice. Though Ian Coltrane had caused more suffering for Kathleen than for the men, she had hardly known him. And when she saw Colin for the very first time beside her radiantly happy daughter, she could only smile.

"Well, what do you think of your girlfriend?" Lizzie teased Colin. "I had to drag her to the Gold Mine Boutique, but then her guilty conscience about the starving Maori or whoever else could use the money better disappeared pretty quickly."

Lizzie winked at Matariki, to whom the business was rather embarrassing. She was happy not to have Kupe around her. He would surely have admonished her for putting forward her *pakeha* side again so quickly. Matariki still mourned Parihaka, but Wellington's stores, restaurants, and cafés had pulled her back into their gravity, and now, in Dunedin, she bloomed. Matariki had not been able to get enough of looking at her own image in her new dress in red and gold tones. She saw the admiration in Colin's and her parents' eyes. Matariki felt a little like a traitor, but she could live with the guilt.

"Matariki always looks beautiful," Colin said. "This dress emphasizes her charm, but when I fell in love with her, she was wearing a hemp skirt and looked like a queen."

"So, what's the news with your post, Colin?" asked Jimmy Dunloe once the first course was served. "Where will you be stationed?"

Matariki looked at Colin, confused.

"I'll take a post overseeing railroad construction," Colin answered. "The stretch from Christchurch to the west coast, you know."

Matariki lowered her fork. "But then you'll be traveling weeks at a time," she objected. "I thought you were looking for a job in Dunedin."

Matariki had been intending to first complete her high school matriculation exam. There had been differences of opinion between her and her parents about what came after that.

Michael and Peter exchanged conspiratorial looks, which rarely transpired between them. But "Let's see how he talks his way out of this" was written all over their faces.

Then, however, Jimmy Dunloe took over the explanation. "Oh, he doesn't decide that himself, Miss Drury," the banker said amiably. "The Armed Constabulary decides that."

Matariki frowned, and Michael marveled that she did not get angry. Before, the girl had always been impulsive and easily riled. "Just like her father, Irish temper and all," Michael tended to joke. Now, however, she remained astoundingly calm.

"Didn't you resign from the service, dearest?" Matariki asked.

"From active military service, love. But otherwise, it's not so simple, Riki. We do need for me to earn a living."

"You wanted to find work in Dunedin," Matariki said. "That has to be possible."

Colin bit his lip. He had asked around to determine whether there really weren't any police posts or other jobs more suited to his military education and experience than railroad construction. Colin Coltrane had tried a variety of apprenticeships but had never left a good impression. Even though that was more than fifteen years ago, there were still plenty of businesspeople who remembered him. Neither Reverend Burton nor Jimmy Dunloe wanted to put his reputation on the line by recommending the young man. Colin had caused enough trouble back then. Now, he needed to prove himself.

"Love, I'm going to first try my hand in the service with railroad construction," Colin said. "And in a year or so, I'll look again."

Matariki looked a bit unhappy, but she acquiesced to Colin's decision—again to her parents' astonishment. Only later, after the main course had been served, did Matariki return to the subject.

"And, and what about us when you're somewhere between Christchurch and Greymouth?" she asked unhappily. "What about the wedding?"

"Give that time," Lizzie interrupted. "Sweetheart, you're barely eighteen years old. And Colin, as much as we all like him"—she gave him an honest smile—"he ought to establish himself before he seriously considers a wife."

Colin was about to get heated, but Kathleen calmed him by placing her hand on his. "Lizzie's right about that," Kathleen said, casting a meaningful glance at Colin's elegant clothing. It had not pleased her that her son had turned up without any savings. He must have earned a fair amount in the military. Naturally, she did not lack for means and had not bristled at helping him get his feet on the ground. Yet she wondered where his pay had gone. Spent? Lost in gambling? "You have a first-class education and were surely an exceptional soldier, but you've decided to orient yourself in a different direction. Which is also what Matariki wants. After all, you did make the decision for her sake. Make the best of the situation with the railroad, and save your money. They'll keep you well fed, so you should soon be able to save up enough to think about a wedding and a family. Matariki can study in the meantime. What were you thinking of again, Riki? Law, like Sean? Or was it medicine? You taught children in Parihaka, didn't you?"

Matariki pulled herself together and chatted politely about her work with the children. Yes, it was fun, but really she wanted to accomplish more. Yes, she thought law was exceedingly useful but could not get much out of law books. She was a practical person and would surely make a better doctor than a lawyer.

Lizzie and Kathleen nodded, satisfied, and Matariki felt a little guilty. In reality, she had long since given up her plans to study. She did not want to sit in Dunedin while Colin was working elsewhere. She had only been with him a few weeks, but she could not imagine a life without him.

During the day, things were fine. Colin was always polite and obliging; however, her conversations with him often seemed no deeper than what she was having here with the Dunloes and Burtons. She had more in common with Koria, Arona, and Kupe. At night, though . . . it was completely different. Had she really believed just a few weeks before that she could not love?

With Colin, Matariki's feelings seemed to explode like fireworks of bliss. What she had not been able to identify before was simply a lack of attraction to available partners. But now that she had found the right one, she had no restraint. Matariki gave herself to Colin with the joy and inhibition of other Maori girls. She loved to experiment, exploring new touches and positions, stroking and kissing Colin, bringing him to climax again and again, and encouraging him in games that almost made him blush. Colin was almost taken aback by Matariki's wildness, but he was happy to play along, and he had no reason for concern. She was a virgin when they spent their first night together in the tent at the foot of Mount Taranaki.

Matariki did not have any intention of giving up these new pleasures just because they were in civilization. On the way to Wellington—and even before, when Matariki waited for Colin in the hills, observing the removal of the last residents of Parihaka with a bleeding heart—they had made love every night. It had been uncommonly romantic to set up the tent next to lively babbling streams and to listen to the rush of water, or to spend nights in thick fern forests surrounded by the cries of the nocturnal birds. Matariki would not have had anything against continuing this wandering life. When she was married to Colin, she could accompany him; the landscape between the Canterbury Plains and the west coast was supposed to be gorgeous.

Matariki could easily imagine leading an itinerant life along the train line for a few months or even years. Perhaps they would even need her as a translator. Surely there were also Maori tribes in the mountains with whom it would pay to come to an understanding. Yet Matariki did not create any illusions for herself: if this dream was to become real, she needed a marriage certificate. Even in Wellington, she had taken a risk in slinking into Colin's hotel room at night, and even to Colin, it seemed just barely within limits. He was concerned for Matariki's reputation, and his own. Under no circumstances would it be acceptable for her simply to follow her boyfriend along the railroad. Matariki, however, was optimistic. They would find a way to marry soon.

***

Colin Coltrane was good-natured in his dinner conversation with the Dunloes and Drurys, but deep down he was seething. Though Matariki was a bit assertive and more exotic than he would have imagined for his wife, he loved Matariki, and the match was not entirely unsuitable. Colin had rejoiced in the beginning when he learned of Matariki's origins.

Michael Drury was not exactly a sheep baron, but he was clearly well off. Matariki enchanted his nights and could change his life otherwise as well. No doubt she was expecting a large dowry, perhaps enough starting capital to build their own farm or business. Colin thought vaguely of horse breeding, an idea that Matariki had been enthusiastic about when he mentioned it in passing. She had talked for hours about horses—including an expensive present from her adoptive father, a Kiward cob mare that cost a small fortune. Matariki rode very well. Colin was certain she would not oppose investing her dowry in horses.

Colin had a plan: a year of service constructing the railroad, at which point Matariki would hate the separation and be bored at university, which would lead to his brilliant suggestion of officially starting their life together.

Now, however, the Drurys were undermining him, and his mother seemed to be behind them. Did they really expect him to build Matariki a nest before they agreed to the marriage? This vexed Colin, but when Matariki parted from him unwillingly after dinner—she was staying in a hotel suite together with her parents, and she could not slip out—he recovered his spirits. He would find ways to speed up this marriage. If nothing else, he would get her pregnant.

Chapter 2

Violet Fence was a good mother.

She breastfed her son, whom she had named Joseph after Eric's father, although she hated when the baby sucked on her. She was constantly reminded of Eric's abuse, and because she could not relax while he fed, it hurt. Yet Violet endured. She breastfed Joe, swaddled him, rocked him, and sang to him. She did what she was supposed to do but did not feel a spark of joy. She spent day after day alone with the insatiable baby and the silent Rosie, who clung to her but never made a sound. Whenever she wanted something, she pointed. Mostly, though, she did not want anything.

Rosie ate when someone put something in front of her, and she crawled under her blankets when someone laid her in bed. But she no longer did anything on her own. Violet sometimes thought Rosie had lost her mind and that she was well on her way to that herself. She was filled with sadness, and it took all her energy to get up every day and be a good mother.

Yet she could not talk to anyone about it. She only talked to Eric when absolutely necessary, and all the women she met could not stop talking about how cute Joe was and how well he was growing. The only thing that saved Violet during this time was Caleb Biller's dictionary. She read it from beginning to end, even when she did not always understand the definitions. Sometimes she read aloud, which she preferred to singing lullabies. Rosie seemed to listen closely, though she didn't care what "arithmetic" or "autodidact" meant, and Violet's voice seemed to soothe Joe.

Nevertheless, she wrote letters increasingly rarely. Baby Joe alienated Violet from her friends. She did not want to answer her friends' questions about Joe's size, weight, and hair color. What did it matter to Kathleen Burton whether Joe was brown haired or blond? Nonetheless, Kathleen's excitement and the reverend's well-wishes sounded completely genuine. Even Heather seemed happy for Violet. She was always sending little presents for the baby. Violet's lack of interest brought her to the conclusion that something was wrong with her, and so she worried all the more about Joe.

Caleb Biller was not particularly interested in Joe. He did not ask about the baby but depicted vividly his everyday life at boarding school. He seemed to like it there, shone in Latin and Greek, and even made friends among the older boys. His letters to Violet became less frequent, evidence of his dwindling interest in her life. After all, what did she have to report? That Rosie was silent and Joe screamed loudly? That Eric gambled away most of his pay, so Violet would have to breastfeed as long as possible to avoid buying milk?

Violet buried herself in Caleb's dictionary and finally understood the word "paradox." While she feared losing her mind, she also gained knowledge.

Eric was proud of his son but hardly took care of him. This was no surprise to Violet. All the miners left the raising of their children to their wives, although patriarchs like Mr. O'Toole at least tried to feed their offspring and create the necessary conditions to keep them warm and dry. Eric, however, did only a minimum. At the center of his world stood the pub and the horse races.

Violet was shaken anytime she thought of Eric trying to sleep with her again. She could hardly imagine it; her whole body was sore, and she was constantly exhausted. But Mrs. O'Toole and Mrs. Travers had made cautious allusions to Eric about a wife's being accorded a grace period of at most six weeks. And indeed, after barely a month, Eric had forced his way into Violet's bed again.

Violet had readied herself, had made plans, and had even discussed with Clarisse whether it might hold him off if the baby slept next to her.

"If it cries, maybe he'll lay off," she argued.

But Clarisse shook her head. "Or he'll slap it around until it stops. When men are horny, nothing will stop them. It'd probably turn some of them on to see the baby suckle."

Violet did not think it unlikely. Eric had sucked on her breasts often enough himself. If he did that now, if he liked the taste of her milk, she'd die of disgust.

She had decided to remain calm and lift her nightdress for Eric, but allow him as little as possible. When he was not completely drunk, he had to recognize that she needed a bit of relief and that her breasts belonged to the baby first of all.

When it did really happen, Violet's mind completely failed. Violet could not speak, let alone argue amicably. Even as Eric was approaching her, she froze in fear, and when he grabbed her, she screamed. The noise that sounded from her had nothing to do with pain. Violet shrieked in sheer panic. She was no longer mistress of herself. Eric laid off her when their frightened neighbors flung open the door. The two workers seemed to have expected at least one ax-swinging murderer. Now, embarrassed, they stood, facing Eric's naked man-hood and his screaming wife on the bed, her hands wrapped around her body and completely beside herself.

In the other bed, Rosie crouched in a similar position, pressing the baby to her like a doll. For his part, Joe reacted to his rough treatment by wailing.

"We'd, uh, better go," muttered the elder of the two men, his head lowered. "Sorry, uh, sorry about that."

When the men left, Eric beat Violet until she was quiet.

"And you keep the brat quiet," he hissed at Rosie.

The little girl holed up with the baby under the covers and tried to hold his mouth shut. Luckily, Eric was quick. He satisfied himself before his son suffocated. Three months later, Violet was pregnant again.

***

Some eight weeks before the birth of Violet's second child, three horses caused a small sensation in the Canterbury Plains. One of them was Spirit, a small black purebred stallion that had never galloped particularly fast but showed an exceptional gift for harness racing. Spirit was considered the favorite for the harness race on Easter Sunday. A few gamblers, however, had placed their bets for Danny Boy, the powerful cob of a milkman from Christchurch. Danny's owner occasionally let him run in harness races, but his placing depended on his mood that day. If Danny did not feel like it, found his rider too heavy, or was too tired from the week's work, he reached the finish line in last place. If he made an effort, he could definitely win.

No one other than Eric bet on Lucille, a gray mare who belonged to an animal farmer in the plains. Lucille had never appeared in a harness race, so no one knew anything about her. Eric put her in second place on his trifecta bet for sentimental reasons. He was already drunk when the betting slips were given out in the Wild Rover, and he wistfully recalled a whore named Lucille for whose services in Treherbert he had scrimped and saved. Lucille had been his woman, and she had not acted coy or lain tense beneath him. On the contrary, Lucille had praised and encouraged him. He had ridden her like, like . . .

Eric briefly considered putting Lucille in first place, but he had heard rumors that Danny Boy's owner wanted to have the horse ridden by a pro. The easygoing gelding no doubt had potential. Eric entrusted him with victory. That left third place for the favorite, Spirit. Eric's bet puzzled Paddy Holloway, the Wild Rover's owner.

"You're never going to have your stud farm in the plains," he said.

Eric liked to talk about his dream of winning big money and breeding horses in the Canterbury Plains.

"You'd do better to buy milk for your brats," Mr. Travers said to needle him.

Mrs. Travers complained about Eric Fence. Violet had not fully paid her for her help during her first birth. She doled out the money in tiny payments, and often Mrs. Travers would not even take it. She saw how starved Violet and Rosie looked, and the second child would be there soon enough. Violet was not under any circumstances to be left alone again when that happened. Mrs. Travers and Mrs. O'Toole had offered her to move in to either of their houses when the birth was imminent. Violet did not know whether Eric would allow that, and wondered if she could burden the women with Rosie and Joe as well. Leaving the children with Eric was unthinkable. Clarisse, whose help was not proper but who at least lived almost next door, was otherwise occupied. She had finally gathered enough money to buy the site for her "hotel"—in the middle of town, just as she had dreamed. Now, she was neck deep in plans and negotiations with carpenters and construction-material sellers, whose wives suspiciously watched to see if they were paid with something other than money.

"I take care of my brats," Eric angrily replied to Mr. Travers.

"Good-for-nothing," Mr. Travers said about Eric to his wife. "The little woman'd get on better without him." His gaze passed over his collection of coffins as if he would have liked to measure one for Eric. "Why in the world did she pick him, a beauty like her?"

***

On Easter Sunday, the beauty and magical attraction of a different female creature changed everything. Although the lady in question had four legs and Lucille was recognizably in heat when her owner, Robby Anders, rode her to the starting line, he didn't care; nor did anyone else. Lucille also proved well-mannered—in stark contrast to Danny Boy, the gelding, and Spirit, the stallion, who fell for Lucille's intoxicating scent right away.

At the beginning of the race, it was not a problem. Lucille ran with incredible speed, and the head-over-heels male horses followed. Later, it was said this was the fastest harness race ever run in Brown's Paddock in Woolston. Lucille, Danny, and Spirit left the rest of the field hopelessly behind in the second half of the race. For two and a half miles, they trotted in the same formation: Lucille in front, the gelding and the stallion next to each other, just behind.

Then, on the straightaway to the finish line, they all tried once more to speed up, but Lucille's reserves were exhausted. Danny and Spirit could have pulled past her. However, Spirit's young jockey was only a mediocre rider, and after almost three miles in Spirit's saddle, he lacked the energy to force the reluctant stallion past the mare.

The milkman in Danny Boy's clumsy saddle had a better hold on his horse. All rumors to the contrary, he hadn't engaged a jockey and rode his cob himself. Though he wasn't all that good, Howdy Miller had long worked with his horse, and on Danny's broad back, he sat more comfortably than the rider on the purebred Spirit. Miller knew how to make Danny run. The gelding brought himself neck and neck with the mare. Then he pushed ahead by a nose—finally trotting beside her across the finish line.

***

At the finish, amazed silence awaited the riders. The race attendees were too surprised to applaud. Danny Boy, Lucille, and Spirit—a trifecta no one other than Eric had believed in.

Chapter 3

The planned Midland Line, the railroad between Christchurch and the west coast, would travel through gorgeous terrain. The southern mountains formed a grandiose backdrop, and the forests and lakes along the future tracks were like a fairy tale in the sunlight. The path also represented a mighty challenge to architects and construction workers. Colin was almost speechless when he saw the chasms to build bridges across, the slopes into which the tracks would have to be driven, and the creeks they would have to bridge or redirect.

"It will take years," he said when he and two other armed constables reported for duty with Julian Redcliff, the leader of the current construction segment.

Redcliff was a compact though strong young man, and his dirty clothing indicated that he liked to roll up his sleeves. He greeted the men amiably.

"Undoubtedly," he answered as if Colin had addressed him openly. "That's part of technical marvels. They don't just spring out of the ground. The Midland Line is a challenge. I'm convinced that in a hundred years and beyond, people will still be marveling at what we did here. We can all be proud to have taken part." Redcliff glowed with pride and drive to action. "So, gentlemen, let's conquer Arthur's Pass. Does anyone here have experience as a construction worker?"

"As a what?" Colin looked at him, taken aback.

Redcliff returned his gaze reluctantly. He had to look up at Colin, but that did not seem to be what irritated him.

"As a construction worker, or a gold miner. We're happy when the boys of the Armed Constabulary have even held a shovel. Granted, it's work a little foreign to the profession, but it's better than shooting Maori."

Colin looked at things differently. "Mr. Redcliff, we were told we would be assuming leadership posts here. We—"

Laughter broke across Redcliff's broad, weathered, brown face. "Well, if you can construct bridges and explode tunnels, Mr. Coltrane, I won't stop you."

"Sergeant Coltrane," Colin said stiffly.

Redcliff rolled his eyes. "Well, Sergeant Coltrane, show me a few useful construction sketches, and you're my man. I'll provide a team of workers for the next section. If you only know iron in the form of bullets, and your experience with explosives is limited to firing your gun, then better grab a shovel and focus on the important work."

"I had assumed we would be overseeing the men." Colin did not give up.

Redcliff sighed and pointed to a team of construction workers who were leveling the ground for a rail track. Some were striking at the hard substratum with pickaxes while others were laying ties.

"We're not in Australia, Sergeant," observed Redcliff, nodding at one of the men who looked up briefly from his work. "These aren't chain gangs; they're free laborers who're prepared to earn their money with hard, honest work. They don't need oversight, least of all armed. They respect their foremen because they work even harder and know a little bit of the business besides. Whether they used to be armed constables, gold miners, or gravediggers doesn't interest me."

"But—" Colin wanted to make further objections, but Redcliff waved them away.

"So, boys," said the stout construction manager, clearly thinking that was enough with the formalities, "welcome to the Midland Line. If you put your backs into it, you'll be foremen in no time. You must have good heads on your shoulders; otherwise you wouldn't be sergeants or whatever else you are. Here, anyway, there's work for everybody. Except smart-asses. Them we send straight home." With these last words, he fixed his eyes on Colin.

"I haven't finished what I have to say," Colin said, coldly returning Redcliff's stare.

Redcliff handed him a shovel. "Here, let action do your talking." He grinned. "And complain all you want. You wouldn't be the first, nor are you the first they've sent me from your club, but it won't do you any good. Look at the facts. The government hired loads of you boys to have at the Maori. But they've proven to be peaceful little lambs." Redcliff laughed. Word of the dubious victory in the invasion of Parihaka already had gotten around. "So, now they need to assign you to other work. Do your duty here where they sent you, or quit and look for something else." With that, Redcliffe turned away.

Colin Coltrane reached for the shovel, gritting his teeth. He would quit this service as soon as he figured out an alternative. He needed to see Matariki as soon as possible.

***

It took more than two months for the train company to give the men more than a few hours off. And when the time finally came, Colin would have most liked to do the same as his colleagues in construction: ride the relatively short distance to the next settlement with a pub, get drunk, and otherwise sleep, sleep, and sleep. None of the armed constables had ever worked as hard as they did on the Midland Line.

In time, the pain of the physical work lessened, but he never quite got used to the hard and often dangerous work. There were always injuries during explosions or bridge construction: the Midland Line drew defiance from nature, and the mountains seemed to resist it desperately. After a short time, Colin no longer had an eye for the beauty of the forests in which he chopped wood or the sublimity of the mountains against which men like Redcliff measured their strength. This was not the life he had pictured. He was used to giving orders—and as a boy he had learned to sell. He didn't want to organize like Redcliff or break his back like the other railroad workers.

Even as an adolescent, Colin had thought less of gold mining than horse trading, and he most certainly would not grow old here working on the Midland Line. Yet he still lacked a clear business idea for setting up a new life all his own. Colin brooded as he directed his horse's steps first to Canterbury, then to Dunedin. In any case, Matariki should now be free for him. She ought to have successfully passed the matriculation exam, and probably she was dying for a wedding soon. Colin looked forward to her laugh, her kisses, and her lithe body. He also thought of her dowry. His love for Matariki Drury was a gift in every sense. She warmed his heart, and she would open the gateway to a new life for him, a life in which Colin Coltrane could be his own master as his father had once been on his farm on the Avon River.

***

To see Matariki, Colin had to ride into the mountains of Otago. As he had expected, the girl had passed her exam and had only just returned home. Colin was tense on the Drurys' farm. He had since become halfway knowledgeable about the conditions on the South Island, and according to his information, Michael Drury could hardly be a sheep baron like, for example, the Wardens or Barringtons in the Canterbury Plains. Otago and the region around Lawrence was sheep land, but all the big breeders found themselves rather in the vast plains in Canterbury or farther into Otago in the foothills of the highlands. Lawrence, under the name Tuapeka, had been known for gold finds rather than animal breeding, and according to what Matariki had hinted, the money for Elizabeth Station seemed originally to have come from gold mining. Colin thought he recalled rumors about Drury's spectacular gold find. There had been a death, and somehow the diggers in Tuapeka had connected his father's name with it. He did not know anything more. Ian Coltrane had died shortly afterward, and the loss had left the then fifteen-year-old Colin completely distraught. Immediately afterward, he had been forced to leave Tuapeka and move into his mother's household in the city. About the circumstances of his father's death, he still knew little. Back then, he could not have cared less about Michael Drury. Now, he was quite interested in him, even though he was not Matariki's birth father. There once had been an intimate relationship between Drury and Colin's mother. The family history was opaque, but Colin would have time to get to the bottom of it.

Colin spent a night in Caversham just outside of Dunedin, where he rode straight into a family tragedy. He did not really comprehend how the death of a young banker on the North Island so affected his mother and even more so his sister, Heather. The man had been married to Chloe, Heather's best friend.

Terrence Boulder had died in a boating accident. The young man never returned from one of his sailing excursions. Chloe was completely destroyed and was now planning her return to the South Island. Heather and Kathleen did not talk about anything else. They only occupied themselves with comforting Claire Dunloe and thinking about how they all could best help Chloe move past her loss. For that reason, Colin's hardships building the railroad hardly interested Kathleen. Only Reverend Burton listened to his complaints.

"That's what I was hinting at in England," he said. "The Maori are not a rebellious people. The unrest on the North Island couldn't last. A few charismatic madmen incited something for which everyone had to suffer, the Maori and *pakeha*, but now things are calming down. We don't need an army or a large police force. Mr. Redcliff is right: in the long run, you'll either have to come to terms with railroad construction or look for something else. Although, the railroad certainly has a future, and you do have brains. Why don't you work hard for a year or two and see if they would send you to university? Engineers are in demand. I'm sure the railroad companies offer scholarships."

Colin shook his head. Under no circumstance would he consider studying again. No, his way out of this dilemma was Matariki. Full of hope, he set out early the next morning for Lawrence. Perhaps he would even find a new direction on the farm. Anything was better than railroad work.

Colin and his fast horse traveled the forty miles from Dunedin to Elizabeth Station near Lawrence in good time. Thanks to the gold seekers, the road was well paved, though now that the fortune hunters were gone, Lawrence was just another town, the center of a community of farmers and livestock breeders. Elizabeth Station counted among the larger farms. The people in town spoke with respect and some envy of Michael Drury's estate.

The road led Colin farther into the mountains and into virgin land. All around Lawrence, the gold seekers' destruction of the forests and plains was evident. In the worst years, Gabriel's Gully, the center of the goldfields, had been nothing but a mud waste. Now, grass was growing. It would be years before the trees grew again, the birds returned, and nature resembled even distantly the glory of the highlands.

Colin directed his horse down convoluted paths between rocks and along crystal-clear streams, noting untouched, lush, green grasslands and sparse southern beech forests. Gold miners had not lodged anywhere near here, which was strange. Matariki had told him that Elizabeth Station was built on Michael Drury's old claim, or above it. Thanks to the relations between her mother and the local Maori tribe—Colin grinned at the thought of the similarities in Matariki—the Drurys had been able to buy the land.

"Why didn't you keep mining the claim?" Colin had asked, but Matariki had shrugged her shoulders. "Oh, there just wasn't any gold."

Colin found that exceedingly strange. The money for the land purchase had to come from somewhere. The Maori might have offered Lizzie a special price, but they did not just give it away. And then came the purchase of the sheep, the house construction, and so on.

As Colin passed a former gold miners' camp, he brooded over it. That must have been the first hut Michael Drury erected on his claim. Colin vaguely remembered that Michael and his partner had not lived in Tuapeka but a few miles outside of the main camp. Did the wealth of Matariki's family originate here?

Colin suppressed the impulse to look more closely at the stream. It would not do any good. He knew nothing about looking for gold. Back when he panned for it, he merely dug aimlessly like most of the fortune seekers. He rode farther up into the forest. The path here was well traveled, but the landscape was otherwise unspoiled. The trees seemed to strive high into the heavens, but the grassland was quite often cut through with rock. The slopes reminded Colin of the landscape around Arthur's Pass, but this region was far less raw and hostile. On the contrary, the valleys and streams seemed inviting to him, and clearings and gentle slopes overgrown with grass offered themselves for the construction of a farmhouse. Finally, Colin encountered the first flocks of sheep—rather small animals but all of exceptional quality. As he rode alongside a stream, he stumbled upon a waterfall that poured into a tiny pond. In the grassland next to it, five rocks jutted up like needles from the ground, and on the hill above them rose Elizabeth Station. It was no manor house like many of the stations in the plains, but a solidly built farmhouse with stables and pastures.

He was reminded a little of his parents' old farmhouse on the Avon, but Elizabeth Station looked more resilient and sturdy and, above all, beautifully tended. Flowers bloomed in the garden along with rata bushes, and wine grapes grew on the slope to the side. Colin recalled that Matariki had told him of her mother's effort to make wine in New Zealand and to achieve the same quality as the large estates in Europe.

He did not think much of such hopeless enterprises. A wife, as his father had taught him, was to care for the household, livestock, and children. He had seen what happened with his mother when she was given too much slack. He wouldn't let it come to that with Matariki. It was better to marry her right away. More university would only fill her head with nonsense.

The Drurys' house and gardens seemed unoccupied at first glance, but suddenly, a powerful-looking Maori stepped out from between the grapevines. Instinctively, Colin reached for his gun even though he had not carried one since he had been deployed to construction. When he looked more closely, the man did not look threatening. He was not tattooed. The ax he carried was a tool, not a weapon. Still, he looked suspiciously at Colin and his horse, and then called something into the vineyard. A moment later, Lizzie Drury appeared. She told the Maori in a few words that it was all right, and he followed her down to where Colin was.

"Ah, there you are, Mr. Coltrane." Lizzie Drury looked at him amiably, yet her smile was not half as radiant and heartwarming as her daughter's. At least not at the sight of Colin. "Matariki will be happy. She's talked about nothing for days except your visit—whenever she's not talking about the race, that is."

Meanwhile, Colin had dismounted, and Lizzie offered him her hand, then introduced the Maori.

"This is Hemi Kute, a friend of our family. He has been helping me in the vineyard this morning while Michael is sorting a few sheep and Riki is training her horse."

Matariki's brothers, as Colin already knew, had been attending a boarding school in Dunedin since last winter.

Colin did not quite know what was expected of him, but the strong Maori calmly wiped a dirty hand on his pants and held it out to Colin.

"Pleased to meet you," he said, although his facial expression was grim. "We're all very excited to meet the man Matariki has chosen. The Ngai Tahu will be happy to welcome you to our village sometime."

Colin was somewhat taken aback but then shook his hand. If all of the Maori here were like this, he understood what Reverend Burton meant. One did not need an army to keep the tribes of the South Island within their bounds. So far, Colin had hardly seen any Maori. Apparently, Redcliff negotiated with the tribes to whom the land for the tracks belonged, but he did not need any armed support when he did.

Lizzie turned toward her house. "Come with me, Mr. Coltrane. You must be thirsty after the long ride. Matariki will be back soon. She's expecting you today, but she's also taking this race very seriously. Though she has a Kiward cob, as she says, so she won't be outrun in harness racing. Hemi, how about you?"

"I need to go. We want to send a few sheep to Dunedin with Michael's shipment, and I promised to help sort them out. I'll just catch a few fish and then head home."

Colin watched as Lizzie furrowed her brow when Hemi turned toward the stream. Couldn't the man fish elsewhere than in front of his employer's house?

Lizzie laughed when he made a remark along those lines. "Hemi doesn't work for us," she said, and then explained further. "He's just a friend, as I said. Unlike most of his tribe members, he's interested in viniculture—he likes to drink wine, in any case. So, I take advantage of that." She smiled, her expression more relaxed as soon as she spoke about her vineyard. "But otherwise—"

"Otherwise he raises sheep?" asked Colin.

That, too, was unusual. Apart from exceptions like the community of Parihaka, Maori tribes practiced little agriculture and rarely had their own livestock.

Lizzie nodded. "His tribe," she specified, "and they're good. Michael sometimes spends sleepless nights wondering if they'll be able to sell their rams for more at auction this time than he will."

Colin determined not to spend more time thinking about this strange tribe, but if he decided to trade in livestock again, the natives might be an interesting new customer base—particularly as Matariki's ancestry could smooth a few paths there. For now, however, he was more interested in what Lizzie had been saying about his fiancée and horse racing.

While she offered Colin a glass of water and set the table for the family's luncheon, Lizzie readily told him about it.

"Oh, it's another of Reverend Burton's ideas about which the bishop will not be happy. Kathleen's pulling out her hair. Peter thinks that since people gamble anyway, they could try combining a horse race with a collection for the poor. It won't be dangerous; he's looking out for that for the riders and the gamblers. If someone's tempted to bet his week's pay on Matariki and her Grainie, Peter will keep them from it." Lizzie laughed.

Colin cast a brief, appraising glance at his horse waiting in front of the house. It was a fiery, long-legged animal; surely someone could win a race with it. But with Matariki's pony?

"That's precisely the joke," Lizzie explained when he gave voice to his considerations. "It's a harness race. It comes from England, and it's a new trend in the plains. It goes over a few miles instead of a short course like normal races. The horses can only trot. Anyone who gallops is disqualified or has to start over. Matariki knows all about it. And there she is now."

Matariki's small mare approached at a walk, but when Matariki saw Colin's horse, she immediately spurred the mare to a gallop. She threw the reins beside those of Colin's gelding on the hitching post and hurried inside straight into Colin's arms.

"Colin, dearest, you have no idea how much I've missed you."

Matariki was radiant, and Colin was instantly back under her spell. He kissed her, and she returned his affection by snuggling her lithesome body against his. Matariki's face had tanned and grown somewhat fuller since the last days of Parihaka. Her long black hair was braided, and she wore a brown riding dress. Matariki's waist was so narrow that she had no need of a corset. A good *pakeha* girl would have worn one, but Colin pushed the thought aside. She was a child of nature, and for now she could remain one.

"You have to tell me everything about the railroad," Matariki demanded breathlessly. "It's supposed to be exciting. Real pioneer work. Until now, people could hardly make it over the mountains with horses. Are you working under this Redcliff fellow? At the university, they talk about him as a genius."

Colin did not have the slightest desire to talk about the railroad construction and even less about his boss who remained unimpressed with his efforts. Harness racing sounded much more interesting. It did not take much to bring Matariki around to her current favorite subject.

"You can't just win with a Thoroughbred horse. It depends on the trot, not how fast you can canter. In England, they don't ride the horses either. There, they're pulled in sulkies, those little two-wheeled carts."

Michael and Lizzie exchanged quick glances. Colin Coltrane did not interrupt Matariki, but he knew what a sulky was. Had he told her nothing about his past as a horse trader?

"Naturally, you need a flat racetrack for that. The course here only goes a mile and a half in the direction of Dunedin and back on inland roads. In the plains, they've already repurposed a normal racetrack."

Matariki began to rave about her horse, and Colin started to take an interest in this strange new sport. One would need particular horses for it. Different from those for normal racing, but surely still Thoroughbreds. With little cobs, one could perhaps compete in charity events, but not serious races. Colin already had the right horse in mind: more delicate than Matariki's Grainie, but with the same trotting strength, although one could certainly consider crossing them with cobs. Combined with Thoroughbred stallions, they might produce the right type if perhaps only in the second generation. The breeding, however, could grow with the sport. Surely it would take a few years to establish a racing-sports scene with qualified horses.

Within Colin Coltrane a plan was ripening. For now, he would return to Arthur's Pass to work at laying the railroad for another few weeks. But when the racing got going in Dunedin, he would be there. Maybe he would see a similar event in the plains. After that, he would know more precisely what had to be done, but he could already see the sign at the entrance to his stud farm: "Coltrane's Trotting Winners."

Chapter 4

The victory of Danny, Lucille, and Spirit did not make Eric Fence rich. It would have been possible, since the odds had been astronomical. However, the month was coming to an end when Eric placed his bet, and Travers's remark about milk for his children had dampened his will to bet. He had only put down ten shillings and with that won slightly more than twenty pounds. Nevertheless, that was more than Eric and Violet had ever possessed.

"We can buy a proper house," Violet said breathlessly. "In town, maybe with a small shop in it. I, I could sew and sell clothing." With regard to her sewing abilities, she was still profiting from her short time in Dunedin with Kathleen Burton. Naturally, her sewing did not suffice for a collection like that of the Gold Mine Boutique, but she could handle basic tailoring. "Rosie and our children could go to school." There was talk of founding a school in Greymouth, although miners' children would rarely attend lessons. It was too far to town from the settlements like Billertown or Lamberttown for the younger children, and the adolescents worked in the mines.

Eric laughed mockingly. "While I go dig coal? That'd suit you, wouldn't it? No, Violet, this money here, it's not meant for a life in this shithole. This'll help us get out. We're moving to the plains, Vio. From now on, I'll be doing something with horses."

***

Eric's first act was to buy a rickety brown horse that he claimed had potential for harness racing. Violet thought the horse looked short and gaunt, but he was well behaved and could pull a wagon. Eric purchased him along with a hay wagon that had seen better days but was still good enough to bring the family's household across Arthur's Pass.

It was autumn when they set out on their journey. The beech forests along the paths blazed red, yellow, and orange. Snow already lay on the mountains, and along the streams they sometimes found enchanting ice formations in the morning when the nightly rainfall froze on rocks and plants.

Violet, however, had no eyes for the natural beauty. She was almost dying with the fear that her contractions could set in on the way. And she had her hands full keeping Rosie and the baby warm. Except for a troop of workers whose members were doggedly wresting a train line from the pass, Violet and Eric did not meet a soul on their way.

"Just a few years, my good woman, and you'll be able to take the train through here quite comfortably," said the leader, a friendly, red-faced man named Redcliff who obviously pitied the very pregnant woman and her frozen children.

He invited the Fences to eat with him and his workers. The field kitchen offered a rich stew, which warmed them all, at least inside. The tents where they ate were also heated. Violet would have liked to stay, but there were no midwives among the railway workers.

The young woman sighed with relief when they finally reached Springfield. It was a tiny village but still an outpost of civilization. For the first time, Violet felt a vague joy at having left Greymouth. Although she had not wanted to part from Clarisse, Mrs. O'Toole, or Mrs. Travers, here the air was not heavy with constant rain and omnipresent coal dust. The handkerchief Violet used to clean Joe's little face every evening no longer turned gray, and Violet felt she could breathe more freely.

All of that improved her attitude, and she felt cautiously optimistic. Perhaps everything would get better in the plains. Eric was steering them toward the small town of Woolston near Christchurch, where there was supposed to be a racetrack. Perhaps even Eric would change once he fulfilled his dreams. Since collecting his winnings, he had left Violet in peace. She had not asked Clarisse but presumed he was treating himself to a whore to satisfy his desires. Or maybe it was her advanced pregnancy. Violet did not care why. She was happy not to be harassed. Maybe Eric would become calmer—perhaps taking her less often and less roughly. Maybe it was good for him to be separated from Jim and Fred. Violet had left her father and brother behind without any regret.

***

After five grueling days—the little horse pulled the heavy wagon over the mountains with great effort, and Violet wondered during the whole journey whether Eric's horse knowledge was really so extensive—they reached the Canterbury Plains and found themselves in the middle of a sheep drive. In the fall, the big livestock breeders fetched the ewes that had been driven with their lambs into the highlands in the spring. Violet and Rosie and even one-year-old Joe happily observed the flock held together by a few dogs. Only a few riders accompanied them, and some of them were Maori. Violet, who had learned a few words of their language from Caleb, greeted them with a shy "*Kia ora*," which met with fervid enthusiasm.

"You soon baby," declared one of the shepherds seriously, pointing quite unabashedly at Violet's stomach. "Better you in village, better not have in wagon."

"I still have more than four weeks," Violet objected, but the man gave her another probing look and then shook his head. "No, me believe. I five children. And get sheep babies since"—he counted off on his fingers—"since twelve spring."

Violet bit her lip. The man might be right. She had felt occasional pains for two days but had attributed them to the rattling of the wagon. What would happen if her labor really did start? If she had to give birth in the wilderness all alone with Eric and the children?

"Nonsense," Eric said when Violet raised her concern.

For once, though, she was in luck. Around evening, they ran into the sheep drive again. The Maori men invited them to set up camp for the night. Violet feared Eric would refuse to join them, but he knew their supplies were almost exhausted. Too, the journey was uncomfortable. The roads in the plains were even but not well paved, and the wagon hardly had any cushioning. When its rattling stopped at night, Violet only wanted to stretch and sleep. She was as exhausted in this pregnancy as in her first, if not as bloated. Despite the hardships, one could recognize that she was a beautiful woman, and when Eric accepted their invitation, the men treated her well. They complimented her in their language and were baffled that Eric did not understand them. Violet enjoyed the friendly attention. In Greymouth, there had been nothing of the sort, at least not since she married Eric. The workers had neither time nor energy for flirting. In the plains, life seemed to be friendlier.

At first, Eric viewed the men's playful wooing of his wife suspiciously but then found them interested listeners when he started talking about harness racing.

"You saw that coming?" One of them laughed. "Our Lucy getting second place? Hey, Robby, d'you hear that? This fellow bet on you and won a fortune. Let him pour you some whiskey."

A blond young man who had just been standing at the cooking wagon over a stew approached in disbelief.

"Robby Anders," he said, introducing himself.

"And that's the miracle mare." Robby's friend pointed to a bony gray mare standing at ease next to the other horses. "May I introduce you? Lucille!"

Robby laughed because Eric was so excited just seeing a harness-racing horse in the flesh. Violet was less interested but recognized the difference between the slender, well-muscled mare and Eric's half-starved little brown. Eric surely had not made an exceptionally good purchase. Exhausted, Violet sat on a blanket, leaning against a saddle, and almost had the feeling that it made the baby inside her cozy too. It turned and lolled. Something seemed to be happening inside her, but Violet did not want to think about that for now.

"You're taking her out herding sheep now?" asked Eric after he had admired Lucille sufficiently. "I thought you could make money with her on the racetrack."

Robby Anders shook his head. "Nah, buddy, I'm not the type for it. Making money off horses, only scoundrels have ever managed that. It's the same with racing as with trading. I gave it a try, and it was fun. We won us a pretty penny, Lucy and me. But the gambling—in Woolston, they wanted to lynch me because I had the gall to show up with an unknown horse and then almost win. You see, it seems it was agreed that the black stallion was supposed to beat the milkman's nag by two horse lengths. In any case, that's what I heard. And what they do to the poor things to get them to trot at all. Lucy does it on her own and behaves. If I say trot, then she won't gallop. But a few of the others always want to take off, so the blokes put chains in their maws to hold 'em back.

Or they tie their heads back, so they don't lower it to gallop. Nah, I'd rather herd sheep."

Violet listened halfway. Something told her that this information could be important and that Eric was hearing it for the first time. Horse aficionado, as if. The way it looked, he had so far always fallen for rigged bets. When they had time later, she would feel angry about it, but now Violet only feared she would fall asleep leaning on the stranger's saddle if she did not go to their wagon. Rosie was already sleeping there, holding the baby to her as always. Joe was comfortable with her, and despite Violet's original fears, Rosie did not treat him as if he were a doll. She handled him carefully and liked to help put on his diapers and bathe him. Violet was happy to leave that to her, and it made her worry less. Perhaps Rosie was not as slow as Violet had feared. Before they left, Mrs. Travers had insisted she seek out a doctor for Rosie. It could not be that a seven-year-old girl suddenly stopped talking for no reason. Yet, despite Eric's win, spending money on a doctor was out of the question. Violet hoped there might be some work for her in Woolston. Then she would save to pay for a doctor.

Violet sat up laboriously and let out a shocked cry as the sharp pain ran through her and water ran down her legs. It was unspeakably embarrassing that it had to happen here among all the men.

The shepherds were astoundingly calm.

The Maori man spoke. "Husband, Eric, you bring wife to my village. Is not far from here. But needs help."

Eric was indecisive. He wanted to get to Woolston, and every delay annoyed him.

"Can't it wait?" he asked angrily, thanks to the whiskey he had been drinking.

The Maori laughed. "No, children and lambs won't wait. You—"

"But—" Eric wanted to object again, but Violet groaned and held her back.

She stood up, supporting herself on the wagon, but she wouldn't be able to do that for long, and undoubtedly she would scream again later, no matter how much she didn't want to.

"Watch out, Eric." That was Robby Anders. "Your little wife's having a baby tonight whether it suits you or not. And I'll show you a very special honor by taking her to Eti's village with the legendary, world-famous Lucille. How about that? You can even drive and brag about it later in Woolston. That'll make a good impression right off."

Robby Anders did not await Eric's response before he started hitching his mare.

For the first time in her life, Violet felt the desire to hug a man.

***

Lucille was of a different caliber than Eric's little brown, and Eric was so enthusiastic that he immediately forgot Violet's condition and spurred on the mare until they were heading down the rough roads at breakneck speed.

"Careful! Your axles," Robby warned as he held tight to the box next to him. "Don't ruin your wagon even if you don't care about your wife."

At this pace, it took only a few minutes to reach the Maori village, which was on the edge of an idyllic southern beech grove. Eti had ridden ahead to announce them, and his friends had just opened the gate in the light fence surrounding the *marae*. The Ngai Tahu did not fear enemies, and the tribe received the late-night visitors willingly and hospitably. The Maori had not gone to sleep yet either. The fire in the small but beautiful and well-kept village was still burning. For the men, there was whiskey. For Violet, there was an ancient, very short woman who looked shriveled as a prune.

"This is Makere," a young girl said to Violet in English. "She must have already delivered a hundred babies or more. You don't need to fear, madam."

Robby moved to find a stretcher for Violet, but Makere rejected this.

"Just let her walk," the girl translated for Makere. "It's better for the baby."

Though Violet wanted a bed, she followed the Maori midwife without hesitation. Makere and the girl helped her to one of the buildings decorated with carvings and laid her down on mats.

The dry little fingers of the midwife danced skillfully across her stomach and pelvis. She gave Violet a juice that tasted bitter and said something to her assistant.

"The baby is in the right position, and it is small," the girl translated, although she seemed somewhat embarrassed. "But Makere says you are weak, madam. You don't have the strength to properly help it along. So, it might take longer. She's sorry."

"Will I die?" Violet asked quietly.

She had been afraid of that since she learned she was pregnant again. She would not survive another birth like Joe's.

The Maori woman shook her head as if she had understood. She probably had heard something similar in her own language and recognized the question solely by its tone.

"No," the girl said. "The baby is tiny; it'll come easily, not like the boy you brought with you."

Violet marveled. She had not realized that the Maori midwife had seen Rosie and Joe too. Sharp eyes and an alert mind lay between the deep wrinkles.

"The girl isn't yours," the young translator asserted.

Violet considered whether she should ask Makere about Rosie. Perhaps this Maori woman knew as much as a *pakeha* doctor, and she surely was not as expensive.

"My sister," Violet whispered. "Someone needs to look after her. She can't watch."

Makere said something, and Violet looked inquisitively at the translator.

"She's already seen too much," said the girl. "Now the spirits have closed her eyes."

Violet had a thousand questions, but at that moment another contraction seized her, and she fought against the pain.

"No fight baby," the midwife said softly in broken English. "Say welcome, *haere mai*."

Violet bit her lip but smiled as the contraction ebbed. "That's how you say welcome? *Haere mai?*"

The translator nodded. "And it would be best for you to stand up again, madam, and walk a few paces. Then the baby will come faster."

Violet got up with her help. "Don't call me 'madam,'" she groaned, "just Violet."

The girl nodded. "I'm Lani."

***

Violet suffered during the birth of her second child, but nothing like she had during the agony of Joe's birth. Everything went faster, and above all, she was not alone this time. Makere and Lani led her around, supported her, and comforted her when she had to scream because of a contraction. They gave her tea that lessened the pain, and most importantly, her terrible fear of being helpless fell away. Makere checked again and again how much Violet's cervix had dilated and how the baby was doing, and Lani translated Makere's reports. That helped Violet almost more than the tea: she knew what was happening to her, and she came to terms with it.

She didn't need to worry about Rosie this time either. Lani reported that Robby Anders had first let the little girl ride Lucille, which even made her smile a little, and then that the other women in the tribe were looking after Rosie and Joe. Eric had given himself wholeheartedly to the whiskey and wasn't worried about anything, but that did not bother anyone. Maori men seemed to participate in births the same way as *pakeha*.

The moonlight was just fading when Violet gave birth to a tiny baby with a long, final cry. Lani quickly wrapped it in a cloth and laid it in her arms. Violet looked into a red, wrinkly face and thought her baby was almost as creased as Makere. She had to smile at that. And the baby seemed to be smiling back.

Robby Anders stuck his head inside the building.

"The woman's not screaming anymore," he said, concerned. "Did something happen?"

Makere let him in and pointed to the baby. Apparently, she thought he was the father. Violet also gave him an exhausted smile. "I don't know how to thank you," she whispered. "He, he—," she said, gesturing outside with her chin.

Robby nodded. "Your husband would have let you give birth on the highway," he noted coolly. "Some people don't know how to appreciate their luck. But he'll fit into the world he's eager to get to. In Woolston, they'll lick their fingers when they see him." He grimaced. "Well, Lucille made everything right. Just look after yourself, madam, and your little sister." Robby made a parting gesture.

"I'd at least like to name the baby after you," Violet said before he turned away. "What do you think?" She looked tenderly at the little being in her arms. "Do you like Robert?"

The baby made a face. Robby smiled. He was clearly honored.

Lani shook her head. "I don't think she likes it. Didn't you see, Violet? It's a girl."

***

Roberta Lucille Fence was baptized two weeks later in Woolston. Robby, her god-father, insisted on appearing with her four-legged "godmother" at the baptism but declined to contest another race, even though the next race day was approaching as Eric importantly declared. He had, indeed, found a job. The recently founded Lower Heathcote Racing Club needed stable hands and did not look too deeply into qualifications. Eric had been working there for about a week and was boast-ing about it to Robby, already with insider information. At the very next harness race, he put the rest of his winnings on a chestnut stallion named Thunderbird. The horse made a valiant go of it, but just before the finish line, the jockey lost control. Thunderbird galloped across and was disqualified.

Violet was poor again.

Chapter 5

"Of course you have to participate. Write to Wellington and have the horse sent."

Heather Coltrane was ardently pleading with Chloe now that she had finally found something for which her friend showed at least a spark of interest.

Claire Dunloe's daughter had returned from the North Island two weeks before, and Heather had hardly recognized her best friend. Chloe, who had been an ebullient woman, looked broken, a mere shell of her former self. She seemed unable to comprehend the loss of her beloved husband about whom she still spoke in the present tense: what Terrence "likes" or "doesn't," what "interests" him. When she became conscious that she would never again laugh and talk with him, eat or ride with him, she sobbed and ran to her room to cry, or—worse—she sank for hours into a silent brooding. Try as she might to cheer her up or in any case distract her, Heather did not get any further than Claire and Jimmy Dunloe, who had retrieved Chloe from Wellington, where they had arranged the funeral and the reading of the will.

These tasks had been hopelessly overwhelming for Chloe even though she had been known for her organizational talents. She had taken joy in scheduling exhibitions and marketing Heather's paintings and those of other artists. Before her marriage, the two young women had planned to open an art gallery, and after Terrence's death, Heather had hoped that this dream might yet become reality. But now her petite, dark-haired friend who had always danced through life was tired, careworn, and desperate—an inconsolable creature who hardly ventured to leave the house and hid in public behind a widow's veil.

That morning, Heather had finally convinced her friend to pay a visit to the Burtons. When Peter had mentioned the harness race, Chloe seemed to come to life.

"I had a hackney," she said in a monotone voice. "Terrence gave her to me, a golden-chestnut type. She pulled the carriage, but she also would let you ride her. During the fall hunt—" Chloe suppressed a sob, then pushed to continue her story. Her voice grew livelier with every word about her horse, Dancing Jewel, and their adventures during the fox hunt.

Heather listened with amazement when this time Chloe was able to speak of Terrence and his black horse, Hunter, without breaking down in tears. She even laughed when she described how she and Terrence came up behind the hunting hounds, cornered the fox, and then how they succeeded with cunning to let him slip away.

"The fox was so darling. I would have preferred to take him home. I could not allow the hounds to tear him to pieces, and then Terrence . . ."

Chloe's eyes shone as she recounted how Terrence saved the fox. With that, an idea occurred to Heather about how she could pull her friend from her grief: Dancing Jewel belonged to the estate of Terrence Boulder and was to be sold in Wellington. However, if the mare was still in the stables there, Chloe could have her brought to Dunedin and ride her in Caversham parish's charity race. She would finally get out of the house, experience something new, and talk with other people about something other than her sorrow and loss. Heather just needed to convince her.

"And if she's already gone?" Chloe asked despondently. "With my luck—"

Heather shook her head. "Such an unusual horse wouldn't sell that quickly, especially since it's so expensive. But you'll only know if you write as quickly as possible to the executor. It'd be best if you sent a telegram. Let's go. We're off to the telegraph office. And on the way back, we'll buy you a new riding dress—nothing black, something blue. Otherwise, even the horse will get depressed."

***

Heather hardly had dared to hope, but her idea paid off. Chloe had loved horses her whole life. Her mother, Claire, had taught her to ride as soon as she could walk. When Claire and Kathleen finally had turned a profit through their shop, Chloe received a pony, for which Heather had burned with jealousy. It had been important to Chloe that Terrence shared her passion. Surely it had only been shock and her deep sorrow that had allowed her to leave her Jewel on the North Island when her parents brought her home. And just as surely, the executor had known that. He had not sold the mare; instead, he had researched how to ship a horse at the best price.

He responded to Chloe and Heather's telegram immediately with a message that the chestnut mare would be sent the same day. Chloe's reaction exceeded Heather's greatest hopes: she immediately made plans to meet Jewel when she arrived. The two friends took the train to Christchurch, where Chloe let herself be talked into a shopping trip and a visit to the plains' racetrack until Jewel's arrival.

The track was located in Woolston, two miles from Christchurch. Woolston was a tiny village consisting solely of a general store and a few wool-processing businesses when races were not happening at Brown's Paddock. A stable owner had the idea to lay a racetrack, and it sparked the attention of well-off investors and brought in additional income on the weekend. A racing club, which offered a few trainers and racehorses a home, was across the street.

Heather and Chloe arrived on a race day and were hoping to watch a harness race. Those, however, were infrequent, and the Thoroughbred breeders did not take them seriously.

"The harness races draw crowds," said Lord Barrington, a sheep baron and one of the first racehorse breeders in New Zealand. "People come with their workhorses, milk-wagon horses, and who knows what else. Sometimes the fellows drive them more than fifty miles here, just to make them trot three more miles, so the horses are tired. In England, the sport's supposed to have its supporters, and here, well, the common man wants his fun too."

Barrington looked at the farmers, riverboat men, and craftsmen crowding around the racetrack, eager to gamble on the day's main race. Behind them, a women's group was demonstrating. They waved banners pointing to the dangers of gambling and alcohol, but the crowd either ignored them or mocked them, to which the women didn't pay attention.

The better-society members of Christchurch filled the stands, wearing elegant dresses and extravagant hats as if they were at Royal Ascot. Heather and Chloe learned that for harness races, the racetrack was in the hands of the lower classes and brought in a different crowd mainly made up of the factory workers living around Woolston. Apparently, things got loud and anything but polite when they cheered on their favorites and now and again got in fistfights with the bookmakers. The bet was generally a tenner.

When it came to the main race, Barrington wouldn't take no for an answer about placing a bet with his own money for the women. To be diplomatic, the two women decided on Thoroughbreds from Barrington's stables and were not disappointed: Heather's horse won, Chloe's was second, and they pocketed the winnings. The business paid doubly for Heather: Barrington engaged her at once to paint the victor's portrait, and she passed the time waiting for Jewel's arrival with making sketches and first drafts.

"On the next race day, we should arrange an exhibition of your pictures in Woolston," Chloe said.

Heather sighed with relief. Chloe was slowly finding her way back to her former self. And now, she followed Heather's lead by donating her winnings to the women for their fight against gambling and alcohol.

"I've heard they're fanatics," said Lord Barrington. "They even want to ban Communion wine in the church."

Heather laughed. "My stepfather's trying to talk them out of that, but they're correct about their cause. For you, my lord, ten shillings is pocket money. For a worker, a tenner is half a week's pay. If he drinks it up and gambles it away, his children starve."

***

When Chloe's horse arrived, the first thing she did was purchase a two-wheeled gig; she had gotten the idea from harness racing where the horse trotted, pulling sulkies. In Dunedin, they rode the horses—as in most of the races at Brown's Paddock—but the idea of driving in a harness race seemed more interesting to Chloe. Trotting proved an uncomfortable gait, and sitting through a harness race taxed the rider. In a sidesaddle it would be hell, but Chloe did not want to go too far by presenting herself before the parish of Dunedin in a gentleman's saddle. In contrast, the idea of driving during the race appealed to her, and on the well-paved road from Christchurch in the direction of Otago, she astounded Heather with Jewel's incredible speed while trotting. Jewel was a born carriage horse, and she rarely slipped into a gallop. Chloe wouldn't have trouble keeping her mare at the predetermined gait.

"What's more, she's beautiful," Heather said enthusiastically. "She really is like a sculpture of pure gold. You'll stand out as the loveliest couple in this race."

Chloe laughed—perhaps for the first time since Terrence died. "It's not about beauty, Heather. It's about pace. And I am focused on the win."

Chapter 6

Colin Coltrane left his post in railroad construction two weeks before the First Caversham Welfare Race, and he had fallen out with Julian Redcliff before that. Colin was intelligent and easily comprehended the fundamentals of explosives and bridge construction. Redcliff had finally and against his will promoted Colin, who came to lead a construction team of six people, two of them Maori. On the dangerous construction sites in Arthur's Pass, Colin's attempts to speed up the work by circumventing Redcliff's instructions repeatedly brought his men into precarious situations.

When one of his Maori workers had fallen after Colin had neglected to secure him during the construction of a bridge, there was trouble. Fortunately, the man survived, but he had been seriously injured, and his rescue from an inaccessible ravine had put more workers in danger and delayed work along the construction site. Redcliff mercilessly chewed out Colin in front of his men and revoked his promotion, at which point Colin tried to attack him, but Redcliff knocked him to the ground.

Colin left the construction site crestfallen, but his mood improved when he rode down into the plains. The railroad chapter of his life was behind him, as was the Armed Constabulary chapter. Attacking one's superior was a serious violation in the military. To avoid being discharged or demoted, Colin resigned at the rank of sergeant and decided to introduce himself to the racing enthusiasts and horse breeders of the South Island as Sergeant Coltrane. The title sounded trustworthy and authoritative—no one would doubt his qualifications.

***

Colin was in luck in Woolston and was able to watch a harness race. He reached Brown's Paddock the week before the next race day and immediately got along quite well with the resourceful stable owner.

"If you open a stud farm, build a racetrack first thing," advised Brown, a square-built, red-faced horse trader from Manchester. "But not here, young man. I'd ask you that. Show your favor to the area 'round Dunedin or up in Otago. It should work there, too, what with all the gold miners. Harness racing isn't a sport for the money bags. The working people like to bet a little of their earnings. And they like to get drunk. Next thing, I'm opening a pub too."

The Thoroughbreds were usually delivered Friday for the main races on Sunday, but the competitors for the Saturday afternoon harness races arrived just before noon. There were no professional jockeys, and the field was a wild mix of horses of all races and sizes.

Most of the horses came from the surrounding sheep farms, and they were ridden by shepherds or by their owners. Petty traders and drivers from Christchurch and the surrounding towns sometimes appeared with their horses in Woolston. Some of the farm horses had also never been driven before, and some of the carriage horses had never been ridden. The chaos on the racetrack took shape accordingly.

It was not always obvious if one of the horses took a few paces at a gallop. This often led to fighting among the event hosts, participants, bookmakers, and the crowd. The trotting races were not orderly, but Colin saw the potential in the new sport. The stands were packed, the small bets amassed to a small fortune, and the victors received respectable purses. Colin Coltrane saw his loftiest hopes confirmed: his and Matariki's future lay in the breeding and marketing of harness-racing horses.

***

The First Caversham Welfare Race hardly offered any surprises with regard to the participants and the horse selection. Everyone who had a riding horse participated, even though there weren't any money prizes. There was only a trophy cup, which the pottery group of the housewives' organization had crafted.

"Where are we going to put that if Heather wins?" Kathleen Burton asked in feigned exasperation.

Heather was walking her handsome, black Thoroughbred gelding to the starting line. Next to his sister and Matariki, Colin noted another female participant, a dark-haired young woman who was the only one driving her horse instead of riding it. She seemed familiar to Colin, but Matariki took up so much of his attention that he did not ask his mother about her. Matariki was in a dazzling mood and bursting with pride.

"Don't you worry about the trophy, Kathleen. Grainie and I are going to win."

Laughing, Matariki patted Grainie's throat. Colin noticed that she had not put a sidesaddle on the mare that day, and that irritated him. On their journey from Parihaka to Wellington, it had not bothered him. After all, there were no sidesaddles to be had. Yet, here, in front of the whole church parish, Colin found it rather unsuitable for his fiancée to be sitting on a horse with her legs splayed and her ankles exposed.

Matariki only laughed when he pointed that out to her. "Everyone knows I have legs, so why should I hide them? I'm about to ride three miles at a brisk trot, Colin. If I did that in a sidesaddle, I'd die of back pain. And you don't want me to be stiff tonight, do you?"

Matariki let go of her horse briefly and snuggled like a kitten against Colin. It wasn't a particularly appropriate gesture in public, but Colin and Matariki's mother saw past that. Michael was not among the crowd—he, too, had a horse and wanted to ride.

"So, I'm running a double risk of having to put such an ugly pot on my mantel." Lizzie Drury smiled with a glance at the prize. "There, look, Peter's taking the stage. I think you need to get to the starting line, Riki."

Peter Burton welcomed his parish to the race and to the picnic and charity bazaar that would follow. "As always, we're hoping for generous donations for the needy in our parish and for the immigrants. You all know that the influx of gold miners to Otago hasn't abated, and they're not all scoundrels. Rather, many of them see no more hope in their homeland. Many of you also followed the promise of gold before you found opportunities more pleasing to the Lord to earn your living. Who are we, then, to judge the dreamers who now come to our city, worn, poor, and often sick? I would like to thank you for your help tending the soup kitchens, advising the new arrivals on their tools and equipment for the winter in the goldfields, giving work to those disheartened and desperate returning from the goldfields, and taking in the children who are sometimes orphaned during their ship's passage. You all do God's work, but food, medical care, blankets, and warm clothing cost money. For that reason, we had a new idea: the First Caversham Welfare Race. Anyone in the Dunedin region with a quick-trotting horse can race, and the audience can place small donations on the riders. A passion for gambling is a vice that throws many families into poverty every year, but just as the enjoyment of a glass of good wine does not make someone a drunk, neither will a small bet on a harmless game lead directly to the loss of your mind and money. The bets are limited to a shilling. Two-thirds of the proceeds go to the parish; the other third to the 'women against alcohol' initiative, whose president, Mrs. Harriet Morison, will now say a few words."

A short, round woman ascended the podium and began to speak.

"Peter must have a silver tongue to have convinced that woman of the godliness of this event," Lizzie said to Kathleen.

Kathleen nodded. "Though she's right in principle, with regard to gambling and alcohol. We appreciate Mrs. Morison and her women, even if she sometimes overdoes it. These women are bitter. Their men drink away their pay. The children starve, and the families can't pay their rent. It's a tragedy. No wonder she's developed a hatred of whiskey. Personally, I don't believe these men would be better spouses if they closed down the pubs. It's always possible to get whiskey."

She cast a meaningful glance at Michael, who came from a dynasty of bootleggers, after all. Lizzie smiled.

"Women just need more opportunities to take action." A deep, friendly voice joined in the conversation. "They need better access to the family wealth, support when it comes to divorce, and a right to the upkeep of their children. Did I miss anything, Mother? I couldn't get out of the office any earlier."

Sean Coltrane was again wearing his gray waistcoat and suit instead of lighter casual clothing like most of the men at the event. His shirt, however, looked wrinkled, as if he had slept in it. Kathleen believed that was possible. Her eldest son was still wearing himself down in his law office, in which he had risen to partner. He no longer needed to work day and night, but besides the lucrative cases with which his firm was primarily concerned, Sean represented indigent clients. He advised charity groups, fought cases for abandoned women and children, and was counted among the few advocates who would represent women in divorce proceedings. Sean had been eleven years old when Kathleen left her first husband. He could still recall her situation and wanted to spare other women from the same experience. He was somewhat taken aback when he spied Colin next to his mother.

"Well now, Colin, what brings you here? And without a horse. I would have expected you to race, at least."

Colin grinned condescendingly at Sean. "Would you have placed a bet on me, then, dear brother? Or do your morals forbid you that? I'm not going to ride my rear sore so you can win a few coins. Besides, the riders here don't get anything, so forget it." He turned away, and Sean did likewise.

The half brothers had never liked each other. They had little in common. Sean first had suffered from Ian Coltrane's preference for Colin and later from Colin's escapades in Dunedin. He had been overjoyed to watch Colin sail off for England and even now could not quite believe that he had turned into a useful member of society—armed constable or not.

***

Colin sauntered over to Matariki to wish her luck once more before the race started. Sean eyed him suspiciously.

"Is he always slinking around the Drury girl?" Sean asked his mother before spotting Lizzie.

"Oh, forgive me, Lizzie. I hadn't noticed you. I, uh . . ."

Sean blushed, which drew a friendly smile from Lizzie. The serious, friendly Sean had won her over even as an adolescent. Now, he looked like Michael, with his dark hair, angular facial features, and tall stature. Sean was not a man of action like Michael, but rather of a contemplative nature. His eyes were not shining blue like Michael's and those of her own sons by him, but rather pale green. He always looked a little like he was daydreaming. That must have been irresistible to girls, but so far Sean had not found the love of his life.

"You have certain qualms about your brother's relationship with our daughter," Lizzie observed. "You're not alone in that. We view this rather quick engagement with skepticism. But clearly they are in love."

She pointed at Colin, whom Matariki was leaning down to kiss again just as the pastor lowered the flag to start the race. Matariki had to sit up quickly as Grainie began to trot along with the other horses.

369

The riders—and the one driver—were soon out of view. Reverend Burton and a few other observers followed them on horse to identify rule violations. Since no racetrack was available, the race was on the road to Dunedin. It was well paved. On the first half of the course, the driver had even chances with the riders. The return stretch, however, led over uneven ground. Matariki had considered hitching her horse to a cart, but with an eye to the condition of the roads, she had decided to ride instead of drive.

Colin watched the riders go, but rejoined his family until they came back into view. He needed to make a good impression on Lizzie Drury. After all, his plans for the future hinged on her, among others. He had come prepared: in his saddlebag was a bottle of good Australian wine to which a large portion of his last paycheck had gone. He knew that Lizzie would not resist a sip, but for discretion, he procured a few teacups before he opened the bottle and offered Lizzie and his mother a taste. After all, Mrs. Morison might be nearby.

***

Matariki had made a good start, and positioned Grainie behind one of the horses that had immediately broken into a gallop. That at least set the pace, whereas the other horses were held by their riders to a slow trot. Matariki had to rein Grainie in, but she hardly had any trouble keeping the mare from a gallop. The only other participant who achieved that so effortlessly was the woman in the gig with a picture-perfect chestnut mare. The purebred hackney quickly made itself known: another exceptional horse for trotting and Grainie's greatest rival. Added to which, the driver had her own pacesetter. Ahead of the hackney, Heather Coltrane's Thoroughbred galloped easily.

Matariki trotted Grainie beside her. "It's not exactly fair what you two are doing here," she complained, somewhat short of breath.

Grainie's massive trotting motions shook her mercilessly while Heather sat at ease in her sidesaddle. Her horse obviously had a soft, pleasant gallop.

Heather shrugged. "No one's stopping you from following along."

Matariki glared at her. "And if I'd rather go faster?"

Heather laughed and gave her friend in the gig an animated look. "Is Jewel warm enough now?" she called to her.

The young woman nodded and lightly raised her whip. The hackney mare pulled forward at once, and Heather let her Thoroughbred go. The powerful brown gelding now galloped at a middling pace, and the mare followed effortlessly at a trot. Matariki could hardly see enough of her powerful but still light movements, and the driver seemed to feel the same about Grainie. The mare trotted with tall, giant strides, and Matariki suddenly had an idea about how to avoid the shocks: she simply pushed herself up more in the stirrups, thereby making herself lighter and letting Grainie trot effortlessly.

Neither Matariki nor the woman in the gig had eyes for their pacesetter. The two mares were now trotting side by side and goading each other onward. Their owners exchanged looks. The race had become secondary. Both were now enjoying the rush of speed.

"Fantastic horse," Matariki called over to the gig. "Hackney?"

The woman nodded. "And yours?"

"Kiward Welsh cob," Matariki proudly replied, and began to rein in Grainie's pace.

Ahead of them stood an assistant who was checking the gait of the horses and showing the riders the way. The stretch down the main road ended here, meaning they needed to turn and trot back to Caversham along the side roads. Immediately Chloe's decision to drive instead of ride proved fateful. The return path was rough and so narrow in places that Chloe had to slow to a walk to maneuver her little vehicle through. As a rider, Matariki did not have these problems. True, Grainie did not keep the pace to which the mares had accelerated on the street, but she continued at a brisk trot. Matariki hesitated before she left Chloe and Heather behind.

"It's not fair," she said regretfully. "Really, you ought to win."

Chloe shrugged. "So far the horses have kept the same speed. Who would have won would have been determined on the way back. Anyway, it's my fault. I could have ridden. But I hope I've left all the others behind up to this point."

Matariki giggled. "You have, except for one."

Chloe laughed at her and raised her whip in salute. "Then ride on before someone else catches up to us."

Matariki did not need to be told twice. She cracked her whip at Grainie, and Matariki rode her across the finish line.

Matariki's mother and the Burtons cheered for her. Lizzie and Kathleen seemed a little tipsy. Colin received Matariki at the finish line, and she fell into his arms.

"I won! Did you see?"

The crowd laughed as the good-looking blond young man kissed the victor. Matariki looked lovely. On the wild ride, her hair had come loose and now tumbled down her back. The wind had reddened her cheeks, her golden-brown eyes flashed, and her full, red lips glimmered moist, especially after she downed the teacup of wine Lizzie had handed her.

Matariki laughed without inhibition. Peter Burton's parish celebrated her. Bigotry had never flourished under this pastor, and Matariki's joy was infectious.

"We should wait for Heather and her friend," said Matariki when a few girls wanted to hang a floral wreath around the winning horse. "There they come."

The hackney mare was just then pulling the gig over the finish line. Heather held back. She had long since disqualified herself from the race and did not want to rob her friend of her triumph. Colin observed that Matariki had encountered a true rival here. It was a marvel that Grainie had beat the hackney. The picture-perfect chestnut did not look tired at all.

And the same went for the young woman at the reins. Impressively cool and ladylike, she sat upright in her gig; her dark-blue riding dress was impeccably clean and modestly covered her ankles. In contrast to Matariki, whose dress had flown up so much on her spirited ride that one could see a strip of her lower leg's bare skin above the tight riding boots, the driver barely showed the tips of her dainty laced boots. She, too, had dark hair, but not a strand had loosened from under her hat. Though her tulle veil had surely flown up during the race, it now fell neatly over her face, slightly obscuring her delicate features and her pale complexion.

"Who's that?" Colin asked Matariki.

She shrugged. "Don't know. Really, she should have won. Her horse is grand, but the way back was too difficult for the gig."

So that was it. Colin could only shake his head. Harness racing would only be marketable if the crowd could view the race on a track throughout.

"Ask your sister," Matariki said. "She rode with her. She seemed familiar to me but—"

Colin stopped listening. At the mention of his sister, a light had gone on. As Matariki turned to the driver, he did, too, and then offered his hand to help her out of the gig.

"Please allow me, Miss Dunloe, um, pardon me, Mrs. Boulder. That was a fantastic race. My name is Colin Coltrane, Heather's brother. Congratulations on your gorgeous horse."

Chapter 7

To Violet, it was clear that the rent for the little house she and her family had occupied since their arrival in Woolston was too high for Eric's earnings as a stable hand. In the beginning, she had not thought much about it: there had still been money from his winnings, and Eric had claimed he would climb quickly in the hierarchy at the racing club and that he could supplement his income with gambling winnings.

"Sweetie, when you work there, you know who's going to win," he'd said with bravado when they first walked through the handsome house.

It was a cute little cottage, painted sky blue, and it even had a tiny garden in which Violet could grow vegetables and the children could play. From the neighboring house, a young woman waved over amiably, so perhaps Violet could even find friends. Except for her time with the Burtons, she had never lived anywhere so lovely or comfortable. For those reasons, she suppressed the question of why, under those conditions, all the stable hands in the racing club did not become rich in a short time. She just wanted to believe Eric. For once something had to go well in her life.

Then, however, the stallion Thunderbird lost, and the old, hard struggle to survive began again. She had gotten new clothes for Rosie and Joe before the loss of the money and bought some material to sew more clothes. However, after she had paid the rent, only just enough remained for food, and Violet now needed more groceries than ever. Since giving birth to Roberta, she had not been breastfeeding Joe, so she needed to buy milk. What was more, the little boy was developing a healthy appetite. He already ate more than Rosie, who increasingly resembled a shadow, hanging on Violet's skirts, ghosting through life, and staring into the void. The girl did not say anything, did not play, and did not read, although she was more than old enough and had already almost mastered reading at Caleb's. Violet did everything to reteach Rosie her letters and open the world of books to her, but to no avail.

Violet's attempt to enroll Rosie in the nearest school ended in a fiasco. When Violet left her at the school, Rosie opened her mouth in a soundless scream and threw herself on the floor, where she rocked herself back and forth to an inner rhythm. By the end of the morning, the young teacher, a volunteer from the abstinence movement, whose members often engaged themselves with parishes and cared for women and children, had reached her wits' end.

"I tried everything I could, Mrs. Fence," insisted Miss Delaney. "I was friendly—and then also a bit strict, but just a bit. She is already scared to death, plain to see. Rosie doesn't even look at me. You should take her to a doctor, Mrs. Fence. She's disturbed."

Eric waved it away when Violet told him of this diagnosis. "She is sick herself," he said. "I don't like you going around with these shrews, Violet. Teetotalers! But that's just a pretense. In truth, they're suff-suffra-suffratittes. That's what they say in the pub, anyway."

"Suffragettes," Violet corrected him. "They want women to have the right to vote. But that's not what Miss Delaney or Mrs. Stuart is even talking about."

Mrs. Stuart was Violet's new neighbor, with whom she had indeed formed a friendship. She was also a member of the abstinence movement, like her husband. Mr. Stuart did not gamble, which was why he could easily afford the rent for their little house even though he did not earn much more as the stable master of Brown's Paddock than Eric. To Violet's question as to why Mr. Stuart did not use insider knowledge about the races, he laughed.

"I'm there like the three monkeys. I don't see nothing, hear nothing, or say nothing. It'd be mostly off target, anyway. The trainers run their mouths, but the nags have their own heads. If just one of 'em farts wrong, or some mare's in heat and can't think of anything but a nice stallion, suddenly they're running clear across the field. Sometimes literally."

Naturally, Eric declared such incidents as the rare exceptions to the rule. He thought Mr. Stuart was an idiot and Mrs. Stuart a dangerous rabble-rouser.

"I'd prefer you didn't have anything to do with these suffras," he declared, then set down his spoon, stood up, and took his jacket. "Work a little harder at cooking. This vegetable mush'll never fill a man up."

Eric went to the pub. He did not have to go far. Brown had realized his plan and opened a tavern next to the racetrack. Eric had been a regular ever since. And only rarely did his small winnings cover what he drank.

"We're going to protest there next week," Julia Stuart declared, encouraged when Violet aired her grievances.

The week was only halfway through, but she had no food left, and the grocer did not want to put more on her tab. Even the milkman was threatening to stop deliveries, having so far only relented because of how the children looked. Rosie touched his heart most of all when she shyly came out to take the milk bottle.

"Just come along, Violet." Julia Stuart had been trying to convince Violet to join their organization. "If we don't do anything, nothing will happen, or it will turn worse. Brown's pub is a catastrophe for Woolston. All the factory workers take their money there. Until now, they had to walk almost to Christchurch to drink. No one was going to do that after work, so they went home to their wives like good men. But now: a beer in the tavern, and that turns into two or three, a game of darts, a little wager on the horses, and before you know it, half a week's pay down the drain. Families are starving, Violet. Carrie Delaney has started collecting for school lunches. The children can't learn when their bellies are empty."

Violet sighed. She, too, was starving, which Julia seemed not to have noticed or did not want to know.

"You could lend a hand, you know," Julia said, seemingly making a casual observation. "Carrie is a gifted teacher, but she can't cook. If you'd take care of that, you could bring your children along."

Violet accepted the offer—full of repentance and admiration for Julia's diplomatic abilities. She was not offering her friend alms; instead, she was offering her an honorable solution. As a cook, Violet could eat the food at the school and fill her children's stomachs for free.

***

Not long after that, Carrie Delaney achieved what Julia could not: she convinced Violet to attend a gathering of the Women's Christian Temperance Union.

"Forget the 'Christian' and concentrate on the 'Women,'" said the lively young woman.

She had gotten into a conversation with Violet when she had discovered a new article by Femina in a newspaper among Violet's things.

"We need someone like you. We have enough church wives; we need women who read this and understand it." Miss Delaney pointed to the text. "We're not going to change anything by singing hymns. We need power and influence; we need the right to vote. But you can't talk about that with the tee-totaling goodwives." She grew heated. "For them, it'd be enough if the blokes stopped drinking and betting and instead prayed and worked."

"But wouldn't that be progress?" asked Violet shyly.

Carrie rolled her eyes. "Sure, it'd be good. But it'd be hard to implement. And we present it as if it were an act of mercy on the part of the men. What's worse: a few of them even believe that only the 'devil alcohol' and gambling are to blame. The poor man is a victim. That's not how it is, Violet. Personally, I don't believe an alcohol ban would be effective. We need completely different laws. A duty to pay upkeep for example, a proper right to divorce, one that doesn't throw women and children into poverty. Welfare laws when the fellow won't pay or can't. But fine, let them ban booze, too, for all I care. The problem is this: Parliament won't do it, not as long as only men elected by other men sit in it. That's why we need to change that first. We need the right to vote, actively and passively."

"You want to be elected to Parliament?" Violet asked, taken aback but also awed.

Carrie laughed. "Why not? Wait a few years, and we'll have the first female premier. And you must come to the next meeting. Kate Sheppard will speak, and I'll introduce you. By the way, you're the first woman to whom I haven't had to explain the difference between active and passive voting rights. Where did you learn that, Violet Fence? Do you read parliamentary reports?"

Violet laughed. "I have a dictionary," she said, "and I just got to 'weather phenomenon.'"

Carrie grinned at her. The petite, brown-haired woman sometimes looked like a schoolgirl herself. She savored the actions of her women's group as an adventure.

"Then you're in for a storm. Sunday afternoon in the Methodist meetinghouse in Christchurch. Kate Sheppard from the Ladies Association of Trinity Church is speaking, and Harriet Morison is coming from Dunedin. Don't miss it!"

Violet thought nervously of the domestic storm Eric would unleash if she joined a suffragette movement. But on the other hand, who would tell him? Sunday was race day for the main races; he would be looking after the horses and betting the last shilling to his name.

Violet was determined to risk it.

***

On Sunday, Violet set out for the meeting. It would not be easy to carry Roberta and often Joe, too, the whole way to Christchurch, particularly as Joe was always whining. Despite the meager meals, he was a strong little boy and insisted on his right to walk on his own. That was impossible for over two miles, and his tiny footsteps slowed Violet down. She came close to screaming at him when, for the second time, he fell down and pulled himself up on Violet's skirts with dirty hands. It was the dress Heather had given her, and she still wore it.

Although she had given birth to two children, except for across the bust, Violet was hardly any more full-bodied than the fourteen-year-old girl from back then. Julia Stuart admired her slender physique, which the burgundy velvet dress particularly emphasized. Julia wore a simple taffeta dress herself—of good material but dark and modest. Glamor, she explained to Violet with slight regret, was not compatible with her husband's religiosity. Violet was slowly coming to understand why Carrie somewhat derogatorily called her neighbor a church wife. Julia's frequent moralizing often got on her nerves as well.

Still, she was happy to have her with her. Julia Stuart did not have any children yet, although she wanted some, and she was crazy about Joe. Violet found the delicate Roberta, who now had smooth, rosy little cheeks, adorable pink lips, and giant blue eyes, much cuter than Joe. She carried her in a sling in front of her chest and was grateful for Julia's efforts with Joe. Julia let him walk some more before picking him up and was ultimately over the moon when he fell asleep on her shoulder. This also pleased Violet.

"Now we can finally get moving," she observed. "At Joe's rate, it would have taken three hours."

Julia did not give the impression that this would have troubled her. "Well, Rosie isn't that much faster," she asserted, which simply was not true.

Violet held Rosie's hand, and the little girl followed easily as always, and without a word. Violet was worried about how she would react to a large gathering of people, but it would only be women. In general, Rosie was less afraid of them than men.

"There are always a few men who come," Julia noted when Violet expressed her thoughts. "My husband, for example. We all have the same goals. I don't know about this Kate Sheppard. She's rather radical in her views. Women's right to vote, I mean."

"Do you not think you could do it?" asked Violet.

Julia looked at her, taken aback. "That's not the question. The question is rather: Is it what God wants? I mean, he created Eve from Adam's rib, and the very first decision she made was wrong." Julia crossed herself.

"Maybe that's the reason," said Violet.

Julia frowned. "Hmm?"

"Perhaps that's just it. Because she, um, from the man's rib, if God had made the effort and used a little extra clay, or lopped a little off Adam's brain instead—"

Julia crossed herself again. "That is blasphemy, Violet Fence," she said, outraged.

Violet shrugged. "I think it was a little negligent. But just because Eve wasn't the brightest doesn't mean that all women make bad decisions. Adam and Eve's daughters, for example—they must have had some of Adam's reason."

Julia Stuart clearly did not want to get into such blasphemous contemplations. Instead, she told Violet a bit about Kate Sheppard.

"She has a young son around Joe's age. She's originally from Liverpool. And she's supposed to be religious. Even if she has these rather radical views. 'All that separates, whether of race, class, creed, or sex, is inhumane, and must be overcome.' That's her motto."

"That's really lovely," Violet said.

Julia snorted. "A world where all are equal? What would become of us?"

"We'd all have enough to eat," Violet said.

"Or everyone would starve," Julia crowed.

Violet thought about it. That could not just be brushed aside, though it surely was not the sense in which Kate Sheppard meant it.

Violet and Julia were a bit late to the meeting. The hall was already almost full, and some fifty women were already singing the movement's hymn, "Give to the Winds Thy Fears." Julia Stuart was wondering whether they could even enter, when Rosie began staring at a strange occurrence: two bicycles came rolling along—elegant penny-farthings like those Violet had seen in London just before her passage to New Zealand. Then, men with tall hats had ridden the bicycles; here, however, two women were approaching, one of them riding smoothly while the other occasionally wobbled.

The woman in front turned around. "There, you see, Harriet? It's easy to learn, it contributes to bodily strength, and it's quite enjoyable. And it's considerably cheaper to acquire a bicycle than a horse and buggy. What's more, you don't have to feed it. Now, it just needs a child's seat. And for that corset not to bother you so."

The woman stopped her bicycle gracefully in front of the meetinghouse and smiled at Violet and Rosie.

"You may try it if you like," she said to Violet, "although you do have much shorter legs than I. I'm not sure if you can adjust it for that."

Violet blushed. Not even Carrie Delaney would ever have used the word "legs" so unabashedly in public.

"Harriet, are you coming down from there?" the woman asked her companion.

This Harriet seemed unsure about how one dismounted a bicycle. She was, however, much shorter and heavier than her friend who was imposingly tall and slender and needed no corset to accentuate her figure. Nor did she wear one. Violet blushed again when she recognized that reality.

Meanwhile, the woman eyed her friend's bicycle. "You could try that one," she said to Violet, "but only after the meeting. They must be nervous that I'm running so late. I'm the keynote speaker, you see."

She smiled, checked whether her hair remained up beneath her jaunty little hat, and turned to enter the hall. Her friend was still putting her bicycle away. Violet helped her.

"There, you see, you're a natural talent." Mrs. Sheppard smiled, leaving open whether she meant Violet or her friend.

Violet slipped behind Mrs. Sheppard and into the hall. She pulled Rosie with her without looking back at Julia. Following Mrs. Sheppard, for whom the crowd naturally parted, she quickly made it to the front. Julia followed her, and Carrie Delaney came after them. She offered to take the children.

"I'll look after them in the back, where I've got crayons and picture books. Then there won't be any crying, and the mothers can relax and listen to the speakers."

Mrs. Sheppard smiled with satisfaction at the young woman from the podium when Joe, who had just woken up again, toddled after her. Surprisingly, Rosie loosed herself from Violet's skirt and followed. Usually, she never went with strangers. Violet marveled once again at her sister: she knew that Rosie felt something like responsibility for Joe, but she would not have thought that she would take such a risk just to keep an eye on him.

Violet forgot her son and his silent protector when Kate Sheppard began to speak. Mrs. Sheppard greeted the gathering, apologized for the delay, and began to present her points.

"Since mankind was driven out of paradise, it has struggled with God's help for the overcoming of sin, the cultivation of the world, and the seeking of happiness and justice. Much is said about this last point in particular, and much has been achieved since antiquity. We no longer have any slaves, we no longer judge sinners arbitrarily. Instead, we have laws and courts, and we care for the poor and sick. Human rights are being defined and, at least within modern states, recognized. Nevertheless, in practice, human rights are still men's rights. Men have work; men have money. The husband manages the wealth of a family, even when the wife brings the money into the marriage. And he may also keep de facto slaves: once a woman says 'I do,' she can hardly get out of the marriage to him again. He can beat her, starve her, force her to give birth to one child after another. Even if he kills her, the punishment is often mild, assuming he can portray it as an accident. If a woman pushes for a divorce, she loses her belongings and her children. Custody is almost always granted to the husband, even if he was the one who shattered the marriage by beating the children and drinking and gambling away the money with which he was to support his family.

"Surely all of you are, like me, of the opinion that this must be changed. We need new, more just laws, but we will not receive them because men make the laws. Only they may vote; only they may go as members to Parliament. And they react with total outrage when we ask them why this is so. Why, when it comes to voting rights, are women equal to the mad and criminal, who also are not allowed to determine the country's fate at the ballot box? They offer many arguments. We women are too sensitive, they say, too weak, too in need of protection, too emotional, too sentimental to make hard, difficult decisions. I hear some of you laughing bitterly. But we must stop suffering in silence. We must prove that we can do more than pray and, with our loving support, pave the way to heaven for our husbands. That, after all, is what one concedes to us: a high moral feeling, a natural dignity that ought not to be sullied with disgraceful, earthly political nonsense. These equate us with madmen, the others with angels. Both come to the same thing, for naturally angels cannot vote."

Julia furrowed her brow, vexed, but Violet and most of the women in the hall laughed.

"I do not need to provide any evidence that we are not angels, but our political opponents also have said that the intelligence of women does not exceed that of children, the mad, and convicts. In other circumstances, they concede understanding to us. The laws made by men, my friends, likewise apply to women. They concede we can enter into valid marriages and, at least in limited capacities, perform business. Perhaps a bank will not lend money to a single woman, but if it does, the woman has to pay it back without reference to her sex.

"Men and women are already equal here in our country and in all others—however, only when this equality serves men's interests. Where the women might use them, suddenly completely different laws apply. That is not just. And that cannot be the will of God."

"But would it be so if God did not want it so?" a woman behind Violet asked. Violet turned around and saw a careworn woman in a threadbare dress. The woman continued. "Mustn't we submit to his will?"

Kate Sheppard smiled at her. "God gave men and women reason and will to fight against evil, although it sometimes takes time until mankind recognizes that something is wrong. Just think of slavery. Even that lasted for many centuries. Many desperate prayers were directed at God before mankind saw that his neighbor's skin color did not make him a beast of burden. But even there, God did not send thunder or an angel with a flaming sword. He only kept his hands over those who fought, and so they triumphed. God loves and supports the just, but he has no time for the weak and hesitant who merely curl up and cede the field to the evil and unjust.

"We don't want to clip the wings with which men strive toward heaven. But we're tired of them standing on our shoulders to do so. We want equal rights for all. We want reasonable divorce laws, welfare laws that prevent children from starving. We want schools for boys and girls, for the children of the middle class and of workers. We want medical care—free medical care. No woman should ever die again in childbed because her husband drank away the money for the doctor.

"So far, my friends, the only right of a woman, the only domain in which she has been equal, has been her right in church to say 'I do.' Now we would also like to be able to say 'no,' and there's only one way to do that: we want, we *need* the right to vote."

Violet could hardly stop clapping when Kate Sheppard stepped down from the podium.

Julia Stuart was less enthusiastic. "My husband doesn't beat me," she said as Mrs. Morison climbed onto the podium in Kate's place to speak against the dangers of alcohol and in favor of prohibition.

"That's nice for you," Violet replied icily, "and one can see that he doesn't make you have a baby every year either, but I'm afraid you're rather alone in that."

***

"Violet?"

The gathering ended, as always, with a communal teatime. Violet had just summoned enough courage to inch in the direction of the group of women around Kate Sheppard, when Carrie Delaney approached her.

"It's about Rosie. I think you should come see for yourself."

As Violet turned around, Kate Sheppard noticed Carrie and greeted her. Carrie took the opportunity to introduce Violet.

"We met briefly outside," Kate replied with a smile. "Mrs. Fence was interested in my bicycle. Would you like to try it out now? It really is quite a lovely innovation, and it allows a woman to constantly prove absurd the arguments of male ignoramuses that 'women are not suited for bicycling due to their bone structure and physical disposition.' Apparently, we're too fragile to pedal. And these people call themselves scientists, doctors no less. I always wonder if they were ever present for a birth. Probably not, otherwise they'd forbid childbirth. After all, compared to bicycling, there they might have a point."

Violet would gladly have kept listening to her, but she was worried about Rosie. What might have happened? And who was watching the children with Carrie here?

Kate Sheppard noticed her unease. "Well, whom am I telling? You already have children of your own as I saw outside. Are all three yours? Heavens, when did you start?"

Violet blushed, but Carrie explained quite matter-of-factly that Rosie was Violet's sister. "And she's somewhat disturbed. She does not normally stir; she's very quiet. But today, well, perhaps you should see for yourself."

Violet wanted to die of shame at this offer. How could Carrie trouble this woman with her affairs? Kate Sheppard did not seem offended.

"Catatonia, you mean?" she asked.

Violet shook her head. "No, she moves. It's more"—she sought the word she had taken from Caleb's dictionary—"more that she's mute."

"Persistent silence without any underlying physical causes of the muteness? Did a doctor diagnose her?"

Violet shook her head. "No, it's just that—"

"I'd love to see for myself," Kate said.

She followed the younger women to the back of the room where Carrie had been watching the children and where Julia Stuart had taken over. She was sitting on the floor, playing trains with Joe and two other little boys while Roberta and two more babies slept nearby. Rosie sat at one of the tables, very still, but highly agitated. She had a focused, even grim expression, and she held a crayon.

Rosie had not colored since Caleb had left for England. Violet couldn't afford crayons. Now she looked with curiosity at her sister's work. What she saw shocked her. Rosie was pressing the crayon so hard while coloring that the cheap paper was ripped in several places. Violet saw four more pieces of paper similarly torn. In quick, almost enraged movements she continued. The crayon was already broken; she was coloring with the stump.

"For heaven's sake, Rosie, the table, the crayons. You're breaking everything. That costs money." Violet sounded critical, but at heart she only felt naked, ice-cold fear. Rosie seemed to have gone completely crazy. And everyone could see it.

"What are you doing there, Rosie?" Violet heard Kate Sheppard's calm voice. "Do you want to tell us what that is?"

Rosie scrawled across another piece of paper while Kate waited patiently. Then she raised her head and stared into nothing.

"Red. Blood," she said suddenly, then lowered her head and began to cry— silent as ever. After a while, Rosie stopped. She seemed to have fallen asleep.

"At least she said something," Kate remarked.

"She should see a doctor," Carrie said.

Kate shook her head. "Just because someone doesn't talk, it doesn't mean that person's sick," she said. "Maybe this is just Rosie's way of saying no. She was overwhelmed by our world. So, she sought a different one."

Julia shook her head, and Carrie looked confused. Violet understood.

"We don't need to change Rosie; we need to change the world," she said. "Thank you, Mrs. Sheppard. Where can I sign up? I'd like to become a member of the Women's Temperance Union."

Kate smiled. "Don't forget the 'Christian,'" she said. "We need God's help."

The next Saturday, Violet met with twenty other women. While Julia watched the children, the women sang hymns and waved banners in front of the Racehorse Tavern.

"Ban alcohol! Renounce the devil! Bread instead of whiskey!"

When Eric saw her there, he dragged her home and beat her black and blue in front of a horrified Julia. The next day, he told Violet that he had ended the rental contract for the little house because they could not afford it, which, of course, Violet had said often enough herself. They moved into a shed behind Brown's Paddock that was hardly big enough for a dog. No one would have considered placing one of the valuable racehorses in there.

"You can even earn a little something yourself." Eric laughed. "Brown'll let you clean the pub tomorrow."

***

Violet cleaned the Racehorse Tavern, although she could have died, it was so disgusting. Nevertheless, on Saturdays, she took the children to Julia and made her way to Christchurch alone. The Temperance Union demonstrated in front of different pubs every weekend.

Though Eric still disapproved of Violet's engagement with the opponents of alcohol, he was not going to sacrifice his Saturday night in the pub to look after his wife. Violet took her chances. Sometimes she was home before him and could pretend already to be fast asleep. Sometimes she had bad luck, and Eric caught her with her banners. Then she let herself be beaten. After all, the children were safe and sound at Julia's. Eric came to her bed drunkenly again, but to her astonishment, she did not conceive any more children. She was small and undernourished, and she was still breastfeeding, which, according to one of the women in the group, was supposed to help prevent conception. The women around Kate spoke candidly about men and children.

"Best is to marry a good, morally firm man who is prepared to live abstinently," one of the women said as she lectured on the subject of contraception.

"Like from whiskey?" Violet blurted out. "Can't we just push for abstinence right along with prohibition?"

Then she laughed with her new friends. After all, if that sort of abstinence had stood on the Temperance Union's program, no man would have been won over to membership.

***

On race days, Violet made the pilgrimage to the meetinghouse and listened to the speeches from the supporters of prohibition, or when she was lucky, from women like Kate Sheppard. She listened to Ada Wells, Harriet Morison, and Helen Nicol—and once even to John Hall, one of the few men who engaged in women's right to vote. And then her heart almost stopped when Carrie Delaney showed her the announcement flyer for the next event.

The keynote speaker was Sean Coltrane, attorney from Dunedin and Liberal candidate for a seat in Parliament.

Chapter 8

"No," said Michael Drury. "The answer is no, Matariki. No ifs. No buts."

"That's unfair. There's no reason whatsoever to say no. The gold's there. And it's my inheritance anyway," said Matariki, her amber eyes flashing.

Lizzie Drury turned her eyes to heaven. "Maybe you could just wait until you receive it?" she replied.

"Sorry. I meant that it's my dowry. I have a right to my dowry. I—"

"You don't have a right to a damned thing," Michael said sternly. "You're eighteen years old. You can marry without our permission, but you won't get a dowry. We won't finance a horse-trading business for this shady Colin of yours."

"It's not a horse-trading business. It's a stud farm," Matariki yelled. She was asserting that for the umpteenth time. She had expected enthusiastic agreement when she laid out Colin's plans to her parents. After all, who would not think it was a good idea to open a racetrack and horse-breeding business in Otago? "We want to breed horses—from Thoroughbreds and cobs—for harness racing. We've thought it through, and it'll be a good business."

Michael frowned. "With that sort of crossbreeding, I have seen too many horses with big, strong bodies and short, thin legs. I'd at least ask Gwyneira Warden on Kiward Station before I started something like that. She'd lop off your heads if you bought horses from her and then attempted dubious breeds."

"Michael, this isn't about the horses," Lizzie said.

Lizzie intervened before the conversation degenerated into a discussion of trotting versus galloping breeds. It did not matter from what stock Colin wanted to breed trotting horses. She did not intend to deliver her daughter to a dowry hunter. In her opinion, that was what this amounted to. Unfortunately, neither Michael nor Matariki really listened to her.

"We don't even need to tell her," Matariki said. "We'll pay her for two or three mares, and once we buy them, it's not Mrs. Warden's business what we do with them."

"And so it begins," Michael replied. "The fellow doesn't even have a single horse in his stables, but he's ready to lie and cheat, and even the most important people to start with. He'll get off to a great start."

"Fine, then we'll ask her," Matariki said, backing down. "Probably she wouldn't have anything against it. Colin knows loads about horses. He—"

"That's all well and good," Lizzie said, trying anew to launch an objection, "but it's still no reason to put a fortune in his hands to gamble with."

"You're not giving it to him. I'm the one getting it," Matariki yelled. "Without me, nothing would happen. We're running the stud farm together. We're making decisions together, picking out the horses—"

"But the whole thing will bear his name," said Lizzie. "Watch out, Matariki. The moment you marry him, he has control over your money. And you hardly know him."

"I hardly know him?" Matariki exploded. "I've been with him almost, almost half a year. And we"—she blushed slightly but defiantly continued— "we've long since been man and wife."

Lizzie rolled her eyes. "You mean to say you know how the lad looks naked. But he doesn't reveal his thinking to you by dropping his trousers."

"Lizzie," Michael yelled, horrified.

Lizzie shrugged. "That's how it is," she responded. "I'm sorry, Michael, but sometimes respectability gets in the way of the truth. A bed, Matariki, is not a confessional. And I've heard tell you can even lie in the latter without God smiting you with a lightning bolt on the spot. I don't trust Colin enough to invest money in him."

Michael looked at his wife in amazement. Until then, she had always been the one speaking up for Colin while Kathleen, Peter, and Michael himself had looked at Colin's relationship with Matariki skeptically. He wondered about her sudden change of mind.

"Then we can't get married," Matariki said, crestfallen, "not now that he's resigned from railroad construction."

Michael sighed. "Matariki, no one forced Colin to resign. If his intention to marry you hinges on how much money you're bringing to the marriage, you're better off letting him go."

***

Matariki fled to Hainga, one of the Ngai Tahu elders and something like a grandmother to her.

"If your man doesn't have any money, bring him with you and live with him among the tribe," the Maori said.

Matariki shook her head in horror. "Colin would never want to spend the night in the sleeping lodge with all the others. He—"

Hainga nodded understandingly. "Of course not. He's *pakeha*. Then build yourselves a cabin. Or move into Michael and Lizzie's old cabin. You can breed a few horses there if you want. The land belongs to us, and since there's no gold on it, no *pakeha* will care if someone else lives there. We can also give you a few sheep and vegetable seeds."

For a Maori tribe, this offer was exceedingly generous. Most communities couldn't afford to give anything away, and even this *iwi*, which was rich from the gold find, did not generally make presents to individual members.

"He doesn't have a cabin in mind, Hainga, but a farm breeding first-class horses. Even a single Thoroughbred stallion will cost a fortune."

Hainga shrugged. "Does he want you, or does he want horses?" she asked, eyeing Matariki. Until then she had only half listened to the girl while she wove flax.

Matariki sighed. "He wants me, but, but if he doesn't make a proper living, then, then he can't marry me. He's very proud, you see. He—"

"You mean his *mana* depends on his possessions," she said. "Yes, I've heard of such things. That's how it often seems to be among the *pakeha*. But then he should acquire those possessions himself, shouldn't he?"

Matariki became indignant. "It doesn't matter, Hainga," she said, "whether it's my money or his, as long as we get married."

Hainga now gave Matariki her full attention. "You want to pay him to marry you?" she asked, alarmed. The thought of a dowry was foreign to the Maori. "That doesn't seem smart to me. Just leave it. You're young. Maybe you'll find someone better."

Matariki turned her gaze to heaven. "But I love him, Hainga," she yelled.

Hainga furrowed her brow. She took her time formulating her words. "You give him your love," she finally said, "but you have to buy his?"

***

Matariki returned, pouting as she considered what options she still had available. One was to pan for gold secretly, like back when she wanted to secure Dingo a place to live in the stables. However, for the dog she had only needed a few ounces. To finance a whole stud farm, she would probably have to pan for weeks. That was hardly doable in secret. So, her second option . . .

Matariki smiled to herself. She liked the alternative better anyway. It would be lovely to have a baby. She mounted her horse and spontaneously pointed Grainie in the direction of Dunedin. Let her parents worry a bit about her when they came home. She wanted to spend this night with Colin. And then as many nights as possible for the foreseeable future.

***

"Where else would she be? Probably with the Maori."

Michael and Lizzie's concern about their daughter stayed within reason, especially since, after their argument, they had watched Matariki ride in the direction of the mountains. "She'll get a little sympathy and come back tomorrow."

Lizzie shook her head. "I don't think so. Particularly since no one in the village is going to sympathize with her. Haikina and Hemi can't stand Colin, and that's just the beginning. The elders won't give her money no matter how much she begs. The Maori want to be sure the public doesn't know about the gold find on their land. If there was even a rumor there was any gold left, another rush would start right away. The same goes for us. There'd probably be talk if we gave our daughter such a royal dowry now."

Michael grimaced. "Well, she didn't ask for a royal dowry. We could raise what she wants from the farm's profits. After all, the lovebirds also mean to milk Kathleen and Peter. Kathleen and I already financed one Coltrane farm. We certainly won't do that again."

Ian Coltrane had built his first horse-trading business with Kathleen's dowry, a stash of money that stemmed from Michael's whiskey bootlegging.

"I am, however, interested in why Sergeant Coltrane has suddenly fallen out of Mrs. Drury's favor." Michael grinned at his wife conspiratorially. "What happened, Lizzie? Until now you really did like him."

While Lizzie was still thinking about her answer, he went to the cupboard in the living room and brought out a bottle of red wine. That evening both Drurys could use something reviving, and though Michael preferred whiskey, wine would cheer Lizzie up. She smiled as soon as he uncorked the bottle.

"So, nothing stood out to you at the parish festival?" she asked mischievously. "Or to Peter? Kathleen and I saw it at once. And so did Claire Dunloe."

Michael frowned. "What am I supposed to have seen?"

"The looks our future son-in-law was giving Chloe."

***

Colin's strict Scottish landlady would not allow Matariki to wait in the tiny apartment Colin had taken in the back of a building in Dunedin. She reacted indignantly to women visitors. When Matariki spent the night with Colin, she had to slip in under cover of darkness. Since Colin was not home, the landlady sent Matariki away, and she did not even tolerate her waiting on the street in front of the house.

"We're engaged," Matariki said, giving the landlady a crushing look.

"A young lady meets a young gentleman in one of their parents' homes for tea. Perhaps her parents will allow them a short walk or boat ride in public. A visit to a bachelor's apartment is improper, miss, and this is a respectable house."

Matariki sighed and finally backed down. She went to the parsonage, where she found his horse hitched in front of the stables. Heather's Thoroughbred was also waiting for its owner. Matariki tied Grainie next to them, pausing when she heard angry voices from inside.

"If I were you, I wouldn't go in," Heather said from the garden, where she was pulling weeds. "Help me instead. When the seas have calmed, we'll both go in and hope there's tea."

Matariki gladly joined her. "What's going on?"

Heather shrugged. "Peter and Mom are fighting with Colin," she said. "Just don't ask me what about. I have my suspicions, but—"

"Colin wanted to ask your mother to invest some money in our horse-breeding business," Matariki said. "However, that seems to be a red flag to everyone involved. My parents' reaction was extreme. And yet I have a right to my dowry. I want—"

Before Matariki could make her complaint yet again, the front door opened, and Colin stormed out. He looked more enraged than Matariki had ever seen him, and when she addressed him, he gave her a wild look.

"Riki, what, what are you doing here? Dearest, I'm not in the mood for flirting. I need to get to Mr. Dunloe's. My mother has just rejected our finance plan. Perhaps the bank will give us the money for the stud farm. Or have you managed to speak with your parents?"

"They don't want to give me my dowry," Matariki said sadly. "But, Colin, we can get married anyway. The Maori will give us land and sheep. If we manage that well for a few years—"

"The Maori." Colin spat out the word. "Do you think I'll let them support me? No, Matariki, we won't do anything halfway, and we can't wait a few years. It's just a matter of time before someone else takes the matter in hand. It's now or never, Matariki. Think about it."

Colin's words almost sounded threatening, although Matariki did not know what she could do to further Colin's plan. Unless she became pregnant. Then she would have to marry Colin quickly, and her parents would not deny her the dowry.

Matariki went to Colin and snuggled against him. "Colin," she said softly. "The bank can wait. Why don't we go for a little ride? To the beach perhaps. We could swim, and then we could indulge ourselves a little."

At first Colin seemed as if he wanted to rebuff her, but then he changed his mind. His smile seemed somewhat forced, but he nodded.

"Very well, sweetheart, we really ought to treat ourselves to something. Come, then."

***

Matariki was startled by Colin's desire and by how assertively his tongue shot into her mouth. He had never before made love to Matariki as hard and with such wildness as on that afternoon on the beach from where Matariki had been abducted years before. She had wanted to tell Colin that story but had never found the time

391

to tell him about her bizarre experiences among the Hauhau. On that day, however, he did not want to talk, and he barely bothered with tenderness before he pushed into her. Matariki willingly accepted the new version of the love game. She preferred it to be tender, but if he wanted to experience the wildcat within her . . .

Laughing, she reared up beneath him and acted as if she wanted to resist, scratching her fingernails into his back and biting his shoulder. Matariki pulled away from him, ran to the sea, and dove into the waves. Colin had to run after her, catch her, pull her back to the shore, and throw her onto the sand. Out of breath, they rolled across the warm beach, their hair almost white with sand. Matariki laughed when Colin made a comment about it.

"Well, now you know how I'll look when I'm old and gray," she teased him.

Colin sealed her mouth with a kiss. He wanted to enjoy her beauty and wildness as long as he had her. He did not believe he would be growing old with Matariki Drury.

Chapter 9

Sean Coltrane was campaigning for the Liberal Party in Parliament—surely one reason why on the day of his speech in Christchurch, more than 50 percent of the audience in the Methodist meetinghouse was male. A few of the attendees were protesting against the children's corner in the back of the hall, which Carrie Delaney was providing as usual.

"This isn't a playground; it's a political event," one of them said. "Where'd we be if everyone brought his brats?"

"Somewhere with more women in the audience," Carrie informed him calmly. "Where are your children, sir? At home, I imagine, and you let your wife look after them."

"Our children are under the care of their nanny," the man said. "My wife is at tea with friends. As a sensitive, good woman by nature, she has no interest in spending time in stuffy halls or pondering objectionable subjects as the idea of women's right to vote."

Carrie shrugged. "Well then, she's lucky she can afford it. The women here don't have a nanny, and they'd also rather be having tea with their friends. Unfortunately, they can't even afford bread to serve with it, sir, because their husbands drink away their pay. Yet they see it as their duty, as good women, not to let their children starve. That's why they're here, sir, and why they need the right to vote."

Sean Coltrane was amused by how politely and yet sharply the petite blonde teacher responded. This ought to be an interesting meeting. After all, Sean was on the stomping grounds of the ardent Kate Sheppard. Although he acted on behalf of women's issues, rarely did so many female listeners fill the halls where he spoke. Kate was right: there was a need for the Women's Christian Temperance Union where women were among themselves and fought for themselves on their own. He did not accord much meaning to the "Christian" in the organization's name.

Reverend Burton had shaped Sean Coltrane from a young age, but the pastor was more scientifically than spiritually oriented. In truth, Sean had never understood why Peter remained loyal to a church that was always chastising him for speaking the truth. Burton had repeatedly had trouble with the bishop because he acknowledged Darwinism and occasionally preached about it and because sometimes the physical well-being of his flock was more important than the spiritual. With Reverend Burton, there had always been more soup kitchens than prayer circles. Sean thought that made sense and ultimately had decided to study law instead of theology. Surely that had caused Peter some pain, although Sean knew his mother was happy about it. Kathleen Burton had converted before her marriage, but at heart she was still an Irish Catholic. She could not picture her son as an Anglican cleric.

Reverend Matthew Dawson introduced Sean, and the lawyer joined him on the podium. While he did his best to sing along to the hymn "Give to the Winds Thy Fears," he glanced at the audience. The men stood in the front, the women in the back. Only Kate Sheppard and Ada Wells were in the second row; between them sat a young woman he could not place.

Sean Coltrane was not easily impressed by feminine beauty. He had grown up around the Gold Mine Boutique, after all, and the girls of Dunedin courted the good-looking young lawyer. Among Sean's clients were beautiful women, often touching in their helplessness, and self-assured Maori girls who represented their tribes in legal matters because they spoke better English than the young warriors. Until then, no woman had touched Sean's heart, and now he marveled at how much the girl in the second row fascinated him. Was it that she seemed vaguely familiar? Sean asked himself if and where he might have seen the young woman with the chestnut-brown hair.

"Well, Sean," said Reverend Dawson, "I leave the podium to you. Convince the good citizens of Christchurch of your progressive ideas."

Sean pulled himself together. He smiled winningly as he stepped forward. "There once was a girl," he began, "who had a true love. So begin all fairy tales and, alas, almost all the tragic stories I hear in my law office. I'd like to tell you a story today."

Sean paused dramatically, and the men in the audience exchanged reluctant looks with one another before giving their attention to the speaker. The women hung on his every word. Sean tried to look past the second row. He would only lose his train of thought if he looked into the eyes of the delicate woman with the marble complexion.

"The girl in my story lived in Ireland many years ago, in the dark days of the hunger. Her beloved stole a few sacks of grain and for that was deported to Australia. The girl remained in Ireland without him, carrying his child in her womb. The young man left her with a bit of money, and if this world were a different and better one, she would have been able to lead a good life with it. She was a gifted seamstress. She might have opened a small shop. She would have been able to raise and feed the child, and no one would have bothered about whether it bore his father's name or his mother's. But the world was as it still is: her father found the money and took it for himself. She was lucky that he did not drink or gamble it away, but he married her off to the first man prepared to take 'used goods' in exchange for a sizeable dowry."

In the hall, an indignant murmur rose. Sean smiled. This was the desired effect.

"Does my choice of words bother you, gentlemen? I believe I heard the protests from the men. Among the women, I see faces blushing with shame. Without reason, I might add. No one should feel ashamed for being vilified. The ones who vilify should feel ashamed. And, hand over your hearts, gentlemen: Have you never used such terms? Have you ever spoken derisively of 'fallen women'? Whereby I always ask myself: How did they fall if no one pushed them? But that's another matter."

Sean permitted himself a glance at the dark-haired girl and saw her laughing. She no doubt had a sense of humor and understood innuendo. Sean had to keep himself from smiling.

"Our girl must have felt betrayed and traded away, but she politely said, 'I do' at the altar. She followed her husband into a foreign country. Her money allowed him to escape his hated life. But don't think he thanked his young spouse. No, he made his wife pay for her failings. He frightened her, beat her, and he did her violence. When she earned money, he took it from her. The man cheated all his friends and neighbors so that soon no one wanted to speak with him or his wife. And there was nothing this woman could do. There was no one to whom she could turn to in need; even priests took the man's side—the same church, I should note, that condemns slavery as unchristian. There was no divorce; the Catholic Church still does not accept it. And the woman could not press charges against her husband for his crimes against her and others. A wife testifying against her husband was and is unthinkable. No one would have been surprised if her husband were to beat her to death for that. Some might have excused him.

"Now, I don't want to make you any sadder, ladies. I already see tears in your eyes. And this is not because women are so sentimental that just a story touches you but rather because more than one of you recognizes yourself or a friend in this story. Is it not so?"

Sean looked into the audience and reaped calls and applause. Naturally, the women recognized themselves, and even the men looked more concerned.

"My story, I'm glad to say, has a happy end. One day, the woman fled from her marriage. She left behind everything to which she was attached: her house, most of her worldly possessions, and even one of her children. Yet she succeeded in bringing her other two children and herself to safety. Today she's doing well.

"And now, you're probably asking yourselves why I would begin this speech with such a story, which maybe I've made up—after all, it did begin like an age-old fairy tale. However, it is no fairy tale, and it is not age-old. It's the story of my mother, and I am one of the children she could save. I had unbelievable luck. I was able to go to school, which was made possible by her indefatigable work and, too, her fears and lies. To pass for a good woman, she had to present herself as a widow, and she spent years fearing her husband would find and punish her. My mother lived through hell, and I stand here today in order to make the world a place where such stories will never happen again. Or if not the world, then at least New Zealand. All of you here, gentlemen, have it in your hands, for ultimately you will decide whether to grant your wives, your lovers, your friends, the mothers of your children, the right to go to the ballot box and occupy political office. You will not seriously contend your wives lack the maturity. You don't really believe that the women who birthed your children lack the strength. It is to your credit that you want to protect these women, to feed and clothe and be there for them. You build them a house where they find sanctuary even when you're not home. You care for the education and nourishment of your children and secure this in the case that, God forbid, something happens to you. Yet, the greatest security you can give, not just to your own wives, but to all women, is granting them the right to vote. Place all women under the protective roof of laws that make their lives easier, and let women take part in shaping these laws. Just as you let your wives share in shaping your house and as you complement each other in raising your children. Women will not abuse their rights. Has letting women vote on the Liquor License Committees these past two years not proven its value? You know as I do that fewer drunks now brawl in our streets. Many communities have silently offered their female citizens the right to vote, and they do well by it. The time has come for us to spread this through all of Parliament. I'm calling for the active and passive right to vote for women, immediately if possible. Make history, gentlemen, history of which we can be proud."

With that, Sean, bowed and stepped back. In looking up, he met eyes with the young woman in the second row and was cheered by the admiration that filled them. He suddenly recalled where and when he had seen her before. She had worn the same velvet dress back then and had looked at him just as admiringly. Then her narrow face had still been childlike, and her splendid hair tied in tight braids. The dress had been his sister's.

Violet Paisley. She had asked clever questions back then, and now she counted among the first who raised a hand when Reverend Dawson opened the floor to questions. The reverend called on a gentleman in the third row, and Sean politely answered his question about the general stance of the Liberal Party toward prohibition. After that, Reverend Dawson chose someone else. He seemed to be ignoring the girl in the second row. After Sean had answered his third question from a man, he called on the girl himself.

"Mr. Coltrane." Her voice was somewhat breathless, but very pretty and lively. "Mr. Coltrane, if I understood you correctly, you are demanding both the active and passive right to vote for women. Whereby you are exceeding the demands on some female activists like Mrs. Nicol in Dunedin. She is of the opinion we should first settle for the opportunity to vote at all. The opportunity likewise to be elected would be—"

She became stuck, and Sean smiled at her.

"Reaching for the stars. I'm familiar with the argument," he said. "But why shouldn't you reach for the stars? Miss Paisley, isn't it? I'm very happy to see you again."

Violet blushed with embarrassment but also with happiness. He remembered her.

"It's like this, ladies and gentlemen: if women may vote, but men still determine for whom they may vote, then we damn the freshly baked voters to another hard struggle. Again they will have to do what many of them do see as all too feminine, but which must be felt as unworthy among all people of equal rights: courting the favor of a man, dancing carefully around a representative who is perhaps prepared to do something for them, but then again perhaps not. And if no one at all is prepared to promote what is dear to the hearts of female voters, then the right to vote is of no avail. That is why I say let's strike while the iron is hot. I hope one day to sit in Parliament with heads as beautiful as they are smart. For example, beside Mrs. Kate Sheppard, Mrs. Ada Wells, Helen Nicol, or you, Miss Paisley."

Sean signaled the women to stand. Kate Sheppard and Ada Wells did so; they routinely spent time in public, but Violet remained seated and blushed deeply. He remembered her, but he knew nothing about her marriage. She would have liked to flee. Naturally, that was not possible. The room was full of people. What would she do if he came to talk to her after his speech? No doubt he would, perhaps to take greetings to his sister. Violet was afraid she would die of nerves.

Sean answered more questions, but glanced again and again at Violet. When Reverend Dawson finally ended the gathering, Sean Coltrane turned to Kate and Ada—and Violet. She blushed again when he greeted her first.

"You must forgive me. I did not recognize you at first glance, Miss Paisley. Naturally, you've grown up, and so beautifully that I'd almost have to accept my opponents' argument: a woman like you in Parliament, and the speakers' breath would catch, one after the other."

"Well, that would be progress," Kate Sheppard observed. "Now, stop your sweet talk. You're going to make the girl faint. Besides, you're speaking to a married woman and mother of two. Your Miss Paisley is our Mrs. Fence."

Violet thought she saw a hint of regret flash in Sean's eyes, regret and amazement.

Sean furrowed his brow. "Aren't you still rather young for that?" he asked. "But it's none of my business, and as I said, almost all stories of women begin with true love." He smiled, that expression perhaps also a bit forced. "I hope yours is a happy story."

Violet struggled for words. She wanted to say something in reply and vacillated between a polite generality and an urgent wish to scream out the truth. However, then someone else addressed Sean, and he had to turn away from her.

A few women now brought in tea, and Kate poured some for Violet.

"Here, with lots of sugar, dear. You look like you've just seen a ghost."

She laughed and looked at Violet probingly. "Even if one you rather fancy. How do you know Sean Coltrane? Are you from Dunedin?"

Violet told Kate and Ada about her acquaintance with Heather Coltrane and the Burtons.

"Oh yes, Reverend Burton." Kate smiled. "And Kathleen of the Gold Mine Boutique. I should reject her collection vehemently. For one, it's just for the rich, and for two, it's to be worn over tightly laced corsets. But it's sooo lovely."

She eyed Violet's burgundy dress. "That's from her, too, isn't it? There's something unmistakable about the cut."

Ada Wells frowned. "Kate, I must protest. This is a political meeting, and you're talking about fashion."

Violet almost had to laugh.

Kate shrugged. "Well, yes, female representatives can't walk into Parliament in waistcoats," she said. "We'll have to dress appropriately." Her face beamed. "Now that I think about it, we should talk to Kathleen Burton about it. She could consider it for her next collection: dresses for women to catch the breath of parliamentarians. Whether at her sight or heckling, the main thing is the gentlemen shut their mouths." She laughed and patted Violet's back. "Now come, Violet. We'll find Mr. Coltrane, and you can give civilized conversation another try. His sister will surely want to know how you're doing. Perhaps you could even introduce your children to him."

***

Sean Coltrane did not mind leaving his conversation with Reverend Dawson and some male citizens of Christchurch. Violet was astounded by how willingly he followed her to the play corner to see her children. Kate was less astounded. She had, after all, just witnessed the sparkle in his eye when he faced Violet. And Violet looked different. Even Ada Wells had noticed how often Violet checked the hold of her hair, which was put up especially elaborately. Her cheeks looked as if she had pinched them to redden them, and her eyes were filled with more anticipation and excitement than a political speech might usually inspire.

Sean Coltrane really might only have recalled Violet Paisley at second glance, but Violet had been dreaming of meeting him even if she was fueled only by a childish infatuation—she could hardly have been more than fourteen when she came with the Burtons to New Zealand.

"A nice young man," Sean said of Joe, "and what a charming little girl."

Sean insisted on picking Roberta up and rocking her. Violet beamed at him. So, even he found Roberta cuter than Joe, who despite the meagerness of his diet was already showing signs of someday being as stout as his father. Roberta took after Violet. Already her first chestnut locks were curling over her delicate face.

"And that's Rosie?" If Sean was shocked at the sight of her, he hid it well.

Rosie had gotten hold of crayons, although Carrie Delaney usually avoided letting her color. Kate Sheppard had spoken in favor of it, but Carrie was frightened by the way Rosie colored page after page with red scribbles. She did that now, too, without looking at Sean or anyone else.

Violet nodded. "She's, she doesn't speak. People say she's slow." She bit her lip.

Sean eyed Rosie. It was not the first time that he had encountered such a child. In the charitable institutions, too, there were such children who clung silently to their mother's skirts or stared absentmindedly into space. Almost always they were children of women who had fled abusive husbands. Sean's eyes wandered from Rosie to Violet. He had almost expected her to lower her gaze. Most women felt guilty for what happened to them and their children. Violet, however, did not lower her eyes but instead looked at him directly. Sean felt he could read her thoughts: *Not a nice story, Sean Coltrane. And no true love.*

Sean cleared his throat. He had to say something about Rosie. "I don't think she's slow," he said. "She was such a bright child. She's scared."

"A Maori wisewoman once said the spirits closed her eyes to, to protect her, and apparently, her lips too."

She never told anyone about that. Although talking about it with Sean seemed entirely natural, she immediately chided herself for her openness. Sean Coltrane was the stepson of Reverend Peter Burton. Surely as fanatical a Christian as Julia.

Sean smiled at her. "Don't we all occasionally wish we could have such friendly spirits?" he asked softly. "Don't lose hope, Mrs. Fence. Someday her eyes will open again. And maybe she's even well on her way to that."

He gestured to Rosie, who now briefly paused and seemed to waver between the different colors of the crayons. Violet looked at Sean and felt strangely comforted, and happy.

"You'll give your sister my greetings, won't you?" Violet asked. "I haven't sent her a letter in a long time."

She had not written to Heather since she had been forced to exchange her dear wooden house for the shack behind the pub. She had convinced herself she could not find any more time to read and write with all the singing and demonstrating with the Temperance Union. In truth, though, she had only been ashamed.

Sean returned her gaze. "We won't lose contact again," he promised her, "not now that we, that we've—" He broke off.

"Mr. Coltrane." Reverend Dawson had come over with a few notables of Christchurch who wanted to speak to the future representative.

Sean had to go. He was already spending an unseemly amount of time with the women and children. Violet, too, girded herself to depart. Sean saw her pull Rosie away from the crayons and take Roberta in her arms. Kate had revealed to him that the Fences lived in Woolston. That was far. He would have most liked to offer Violet his carriage, but that would not do. People would talk about him. Still, he could not simply leave her like this.

"We'll meet again, Mrs. Fence," he said quietly before turning away.

Violet gave him a slight smile, but her face seemed to radiate from within.

"Violet," she said.

***

With Violet's next wages from cleaning the pub—Brown paid the money to her directly instead of putting it in Eric's hands—she bought crayons for Rosie. At first, Violet's sister filled page after page with the color red. Then she began to use the black crayon. Rosie did not talk again while coloring, but she now became calmer and at least did not break the crayons anymore. Violet let her do as she pleased, although Julia complained, and Eric declared his wife was just as crazy as her sister.

"She doesn't even know what she's doing," he mocked.

Makere, the Maori midwife, would probably have said that the spirits were guiding Rosie's hand.

Chapter 10

"Riki, you can't just sit around all day. You should do something—didn't you want to study?"

Kathleen Burton was happy to let Lizzie and Michael's daughter live with her for a time, but her inactivity could not go on, and after nearly a week, Kathleen finally worked up the nerve to do something about it. After her fight with her parents, Matariki had remained in the city. She appeared in the early morning—although Kathleen had her suspicions that she arrived in the garden an hour before and waited there until it was appropriate to enter. And in the evening, she disappeared, usually just after it grew dark. The reason for this was easy to uncover: Colin's strict landlady got up early and went to bed with the chickens. The girl matched the landlady's hours.

This was not compatible with Kathleen and Peter's ideas of morality, and it did not please Michael or Lizzie. No argument, however, reached Matariki. And she defended herself by referring to the customs of the Maori, which allowed her to see a lover when she wanted.

"What they're up to doesn't have to be done in a bed at night," Lizzie said pointedly. "Who knows what those two would do if we forbade them. Probably they'd do it in public."

Lizzie was right. They could not lock up Matariki, let alone Colin. The best thing would be for them to marry soon, but that would again pose the question of her dowry, and there, all parents were in agreement: they would not finance a horse-trading business for Colin, whether he called it a racetrack, stud farm, or whatever else. Moreover, he no longer seemed in such a rush to get married.

"We're putting that off while Colin tries to raise money," Matariki said when Kathleen asked her about a wedding. "As for my squatting here all day, Kathleen, I wanted to get a job, but Colin prefers I don't."

Matariki flipped through a magazine. She did not seem entirely pleased with her life, but Colin disapproved of her attempts to gain employment. She would have gladly helped Kathleen and Claire in the shop, for which the two of them also would have wanted to pay her. At this suggestion, Colin had made quite a scene, which led to a heated argument.

"You remind me a lot of your father, Colin," Kathleen had hurled at him. "He also would have liked to lock me up, although he was quite welcoming of my money. I should tell you the whole story sometime, Matariki. You don't know what you're getting into."

Matariki was no submissive Irish Catholic; she was more than self-confident. Before she finally resigned herself, she and Colin fought.

"Just what will happen when we finally have the stud farm, Colin?" she spat out. "Will I not be permitted to show myself in the stables, let alone make any decisions?"

Here, however, Colin could calm her, mostly by pointing out that women on other big farms managed on many occasions to gain respect. Matariki's great model was Gwyneira Warden on Kiward Station, the breeder of Grainie, her mare.

"Do you think Mrs. Warden worked as a saleswoman or barmaid before her wedding?" Colin said. "That would have been beneath her dignity, and you don't need to do it either. As mistress of your own farm, you can act very differently."

Matariki let herself be assuaged by this argument, but her discontent grew with her boredom. Moreover, Colin had already twice rebuffed her in the evening.

"I could go with you," she said when he revealed that he needed to go to a reception with Jimmy Dunloe. "I can buy a dress from Kathleen, and then—"

Colin smiled indulgently. "With what would you buy a dress, my little lamb? Do you think you still have an account? No, no, my dear, your parents are cutting you off. You said so yourself. Receptions like these are boring. Just sleep at my mother's. It's better for her pastor's soul, anyway."

Matariki did not want to think about whether her parents really had cut off all support. A few days before, the Drurys had suggested she pay the entry fees for the university but declined to hand her money. Matariki was determined not to back down, even if it was hard, as it was in regard to this evening.

Kathleen and Peter were going to the opening of Chloe and Heather's first exhibition at their new gallery.

"Are you sure you don't want to come along, Riki?" Kathleen inquired, concerned given how she was sulking. "Or are you doing something with Colin? Heather invited him, too, so why aren't the two of you going together?"

Matariki did not have an answer to any of her questions. She withdrew into the guest room with the newspaper. She did not feel well anyway and had not all day. Maybe she had eaten something bad. She paged listlessly through the *Auckland Herald*, wondering how it ended up in Kathleen's living room. The news from the North Island did not really interest Matariki, even if she had lived there a long time. Nevertheless, she hoped for information about Te Whiti or other incarcerated leaders of the Parihaka movement. As expected, however, she found nothing. The chieftains were still incarcerated, the protests of the Maori against the government's land grabs largely silenced. People expected Te Kooti and Te Whiti to be released soon, but their influence on their people was without a doubt broken.

Then, however, a name Matariki had heard before caught her eye: Amey Daldy. It took a moment for her to remember how she knew the name. Amey Daldy worked for women's suffrage—for the *pakeha* and the Maori. The girls in Parihaka had often talked about suffrage, debating the controversy. Among the tribes, women had largely equal rights. They could freely choose their husbands, own land, and acquire the status of a *tohunga*. Men and women alike belonged to the villages' councils of elders, and a woman was occasionally elected chieftain, particularly on the largely peaceful South Island. Arona had told the girls that female chieftains had appeared at the famous meeting in Waitangi. On the treaty signed there, however, no women's names were found: the *pakeha* had sent away the female tribal leaders.

The girls in Parihaka were not in agreement about whether Maori women had to fight it out in Parliament for this long-held prerogative or whether they could force the *pakeha* to accept them without needing further legislation. The invasion of Parihaka had proved the latter question, in any case, academic: the Maori could not force the *pakeha* to do anything, and the rights of women were the last thing for which the men of the tribes were prepared to reach for arms. Matariki's own experiences with Kahu Heke confirmed this sad observation: the fundamental attitude of the Maori people was a pragmatic one. Whatever roles the Maori needed women to fill, be it as priests, healers, or even warriors and chieftains, they were allowed to take up that profession. Yet that did not mean men would condescend to cook, clean the lodges, or raise the children. If the *pakeha* were of the opinion that women should not own land or have a voice in Parliament, then tribal warriors would happily accept real estate and the status of representative. After all, no one had scruples about taking away the rights of chieftains' wives and covering chieftains' daughters with restrictive *tapu*.

In this regard, Matariki had the highest respect for women like Amey Daldy, and she read what the *Auckland Herald* wrote about her with interest. Daldy's Ladies' Seminary wanted to open itself to Maori women. The journalist smugly noted that the ladies in question would have to learn English first. Matariki clenched her fists with rage. After all, many more Maori spoke the language of the *pakeha* than the other way around. Nevertheless, she was interested in Mrs. Daldy's ladies' seminary. What did the women learn there? Housekeeping and proper conduct? Or writing petitions, singing protest hymns, and fighting for rights?

The article did not provide any information about this, but farther down the page, a notice caught Matariki's eye:

Seeking well-bred young lady of Maori ancestry as colleague in Daldy's Ladies' Seminary. Conditions: good knowledge of the Maori language as well as English, takes joy in teaching, knowledge of the conventions and customs of the tribes as well as their traditional crafts, music, and culture.

For a moment, Matariki forgot Colin and their marriage plans. This employment seemed made for her. She could apply what she had learned in Parihaka—from hardening flax to peaceful resistance. Matariki briefly pictured herself at a podium beside women's rights activists like Amey Daldy or her great predecessor, Mary Wollstonecraft. She would translate the words of the speakers for the women of her people and teach the children English without letting them forget their roots. Te Whiti would be proud of Matariki Drury. Then, she remembered Colin and the stud farm. No, under no circumstances could she leave him alone in that—plus, she missed him when she had to spend even one night without his embrace.

Matariki pushed her daydream aside and instead considered which of the other girls from Parihaka might be interested in this position. The girls had been taken prisoner the day after Matariki's escape with Colin, but Colin's warning they would have to spend months in prison had not come true. The last residents of Parihaka had been incarcerated for a night before they were freed near their home tribes. Arona had even remained in Parihaka. The young priestess came from there and was now doing her best to hold together the shrunken, unsettled, and depressed community until Te Whiti returned.

Through Arona, Matariki had also resumed contact with her other friends who had mostly done as she had: whoever passed the high school exam began studying to become a doctor, teacher, or lawyer. Matariki knew from Koria that Kupe, too, had been freed and was studying in Wellington. She had written to him, but he had not answered. Koria revealed to her that her relationship with Colin had struck him hard:

> He was in love with you. We all knew that. And he had accepted that you could not return his love. He would have gotten over another Maori man at your side. But a pakeha! Don't be angry, Matariki, but none of us find it easy to accept your relationship with an English officer. You love him, and I know there's not much anyone can do about that. But an armed constable, Matariki? An enemy?

Matariki had blushed when she read her friend's letter—and hurried to assure her that Colin had long since resigned his service for the Crown. She did not feel entirely comfortable repeating his lie, but the other girls didn't address her relationship with Colin further. Instead, they told her about their studies and about the hearings for the defenders of Parihaka. Others were in love and colorfully depicted their happiness. Matariki responded with reports of the harness races and made up stories about her vague plans to study. Only Kupe remained silent.

Matariki could not think of any girl who was free to take the post in Auckland. Still, the contemplation had distracted her, and it had gotten late. Matariki extinguished the light and curled up under her covers. The next morning, she would see Colin and forget Amey Daldy.

***

Kathleen and Reverend Burton had come home late and were still asleep when Matariki woke up early, well rested. She went shopping and surprised her hosts by making breakfast.

Usually Kathleen would have been happy about this, but that day the Burtons spoke only in monosyllables.

"Is something wrong, Kathleen?" asked Matariki after Kathleen failed to answer the second of her questions about the night before. "Are you mad about something? Or at me?"

Kathleen shook her head. Matariki noticed that she looked like she had not slept much.

Reverend Burton cleared his throat. "Kathleen, I think you ought to tell her. There's no point in not saying anything. Heather will tell her straight. She was ready to burst with rage last night."

Matariki furrowed her brow and stopped drizzling honey on her roll. "Heather was angry with me?" she asked, confused.

Kathleen shook her head, looking in anguish at the girl. "No, Riki, not at you, at Colin. You see, it wasn't that he was going to some reception with Jimmy Dunloe. Or, well, it was to our reception, that is, Heather and Chloe's. As Chloe's companion," Kathleen said.

Honey dripped from Matariki's roll as she stared at Colin's mother in disbelief. "As her *what*?"

***

"Matariki, it has nothing to do with us." Colin Coltrane maintained his innocence even after Matariki struck him across his face with her wildcat paw. "Look, you know I have to court her father if we want credit."

"Jimmy Dunloe is Chloe's stepfather," Matariki corrected him, "and as far as I know, he doesn't work as a panderer. It would be too early anyway. She hasn't even been a widow six months. So, why?"

"For that very reason, Matariki," Colin said. "Because she was widowed such a short time ago. She needs a companion, rather a family member so to speak."

Matariki laughed mockingly. "You see yourself as a member of the Dunloe family? You're not seriously trying to convince me of that? And if so, then why wasn't I to know about it? You could have just told me you were chaperoning poor Chloe Boulder for business reasons. Not that I understand why she needs a companion. You recall that it's her own gallery, Colin, don't you? She organized this reception, and as hostess, she surely would have had plenty to do selling the pictures to visitors. Or did you help her with that too?"

Colin looked at Matariki, who burned with anger. Good God, she was beautiful, and he loved her. Naturally, Chloe Boulder was beautiful too. Her cool attractiveness, her ladylikeness, her impeccable comportment, drew him in. Matariki, in her worn riding dress, not evenly properly laced in her corset and her hair once again loose, was such a strong contrast. Her skin was tanned by the sun, and Colin still recalled all too well her long, brown legs, framed by that *piu-piu* skirt while she skipped rope in Parihaka. If only it were possible . . .

Colin pulled her into his arms and silenced her with a kiss. Matariki bit his tongue and pushed him away.

"Colin, I want an explanation." She spat the words. "What was that with Chloe?"

Colin tasted blood and grew angry. Could Matariki not behave like a normal woman for once? Submissive, coddling? Until now, he had always believed he could tame her, but perhaps that was not possible. That would make his decision easier.

"Matariki, I don't have to explain myself to you. I told you it meant nothing. I did it for the stud farm. For us."

"Colin . . . ," Matariki said, looking at him with incomprehension. She then spoke more calmly. "Colin, you kissed her. Don't deny it. Heather told me so herself. And don't claim now that Chloe seduced you. Heather said she was completely confused. And I doubt Jimmy Dunloe was guiding your hand in that, was he? So, what is all this, Colin? We're engaged."

Colin stood up straight in front of Matariki. So, his damned sister knew. Heather had stuck to Chloe the whole evening. Only after one of the visitors roped her into a sales conversation about one of the pictures had he been able to lure Chloe away and try a first kiss. Chloe had not been opposed. Then, however, she had to go and tattle.

Colin unloaded his rage at his sister on Matariki. "We are not engaged, Matariki. We share a bed. Go on and look at me like a dying doe, but it's the truth. I would gladly marry you, Matariki, but your parents are undermining our relationship. Thus, you have to permit me to look elsewhere."

Matariki's hand struck his face again, but this time her nails left behind deep red tracks on his right cheek. Before she could also scratch the left one, he seized her hand.

"Enough of this," he yelled at her.

Matariki looked at Colin with tears in her eyes. Still, she kept an iron composure. "You said it, Colin," she said firmly.

That same day, she wrote to Amey Daldy.

With Open Eyes

Dunedin and Invercargill, South Island

Auckland, North Island

1883–1893

Chapter 1

"What does he have that I don't?"

Heather Coltrane had not wanted to ask the question, but now, on the day before Chloe meant to marry her brother, she could no longer contain herself.

Chloe eyed her friend sympathetically.

"He is," she said, "a man." She tried to reply in a ladylike way.

"Yes, and?" asked Heather. "Can he love you more than I can? Does he understand you better? Can he offer you more? Do you have more in common with him?"

"Of course not."

Chloe sighed. She did not know how to make Heather understand, at least not without hurting her more. She should not have let it go so far, anyway. Chloe and Heather's relationship had always been intimate, but in the months since Terrence's death, it had grown in intensity. Chloe and Heather had exchanged caresses, Chloe had snuggled against Heather when the sorrow threatened to overcome her, and, ultimately, it was Heather, and not Colin, who had helped her move past the loss. Chloe loved Heather deeply, but Heather could not love her like Terrence—or Colin. Heather was not a man.

"Heather, I want to marry again. I want children."

"We could adopt children," noted Heather. "As many as you like. The charitable institutions are overflowing with orphans. One word to Sean or Peter, and we'd have the apartment full."

Chloe continued packing her dresses. Colin had just come from Invercargill where he was overseeing the work on the stables and the new racetrack and redecorating the house. The next day, after their wedding, they would travel to their new home.

Heather kissed the nape of her neck softly. "Chloe—"

Chloe spun around. "Do you really think Peter, a pastor, would approve of that?"

It sounded sharper than she had intended. She did not want to upset Heather—and there was nothing truly forbidden about their friendship, even if it was unusual for two women to kiss and touch each other in places on the body that one hardly looked at herself. Chloe had taken joy in Heather's affection, but Chloe had never been able to quite feel like Heather, who seemed to burn under her own kisses. She missed the body of a man—firm everywhere.

"I'd like my own children," she said now in the hope of assuaging Heather. "You have to understand. And Colin, he's good-looking. He's polite."

"He left Matariki Drury when her parents did not want to finance his racetrack."

"One decision doesn't necessarily have to do with the other," Chloe said for the hundredth time.

It was not just Heather who was anything but confident about Chloe's relationship with Colin. Jimmy Dunloe, her mother, and even Kathleen and Peter had raised objections.

"He's my brother, but I don't trust him. He was never what you call a good fellow."

"Dear God, Heather." Chloe was clearly irritated. "I've been listening to this for months. I should wait longer, and I should be careful, and should this, and should that. Not that any of you can say we didn't stick to the rules. We upheld the year of mourning. We hardly ever met in public. We had long conversations." Most of which had ended in Colin's arms, but Chloe would not reveal that to Heather. "We even once spent weeks apart."

"During which time he bought a farm in Invercargill with your money without even showing the property to you first."

"I trust him," Chloe said.

Heather should not have been having these conversations. She was the last person to whom Chloe would attribute any reasonable motivations in warning her about Colin Coltrane. Heather knew she spoke at least in good part out of jealousy, but she could not keep it inside. This evening was her last chance.

"So much so that you're giving him all your money?" Heather asked bitterly.

Terrence had been wealthy, and Chloe was his sole beneficiary. Jimmy Dunloe had offered to manage the money for her, and Sean advised her to sign a prenuptial agreement that would at least limit Colin's control of the money. Chloe would not hear of it.

"We both want the stud farm. It will belong to the two of us, and we'll both manage it. I gave Colin the money because I want the same thing. It's not only his dream."

"I thought your dream was a gallery," Heather whispered. "You loved art and wanted to promote painters and sculptors in New Zealand. What about the exhibition of Maori art? What about that female Russian artist? We were to have the gallery together. And now? Am I supposed to do all that alone?"

Chloe hugged her friend. She could not bear to see Heather sad, but she had to be firm.

"You'll manage it alone if you want to keep working on it," she said. "The gallery was, well, a sort of girlish dream, but now—"

"Now you're all grown up," Heather said bitterly. "I understand. And I hope you're happy, Chloe. I really hope you're happy."

***

There were women in Reverend Burton's congregation who gossiped about Chloe's new union so soon after Terrence's death. Kathleen and Claire did their best not to listen, but the two friends were of the same opinion.

"I'm happy that we're related," Claire said, "but couldn't she have married Sean?"

Kathleen smiled ruefully. "Sean seems to have lost his heart in Christchurch," she revealed to Claire. "He hasn't said anything, but since his speech there a few months ago, he's different. Hopefully she's not some fanatical suffragette."

Claire laughed. "I found Kate Sheppard quite nice. And our Mrs. Morison is easy enough to get along with, as long as you pay women a proper wage." Harriet Morison applied herself on behalf of the seamstresses in the factories. The forming of a union was imminent, and Mrs. Morison would lead it. Claire and Kathleen had always paid their seamstresses properly, and most of them had worked at the Gold Mine Boutique for years. That was not the case, though, in the textile factories that had popped up in Dunedin over the last few years. The women often worked under inhumane conditions, and Claire and Kathleen were glad Mrs. Morison gave them her support. "We need women who speak up for women's suffrage. And I'll vote for your Sean first thing."

Kathleen smiled. She, too, was proud of her son, and she would not begrudge him his happiness no matter what the woman who had his heart was like. Until recently, the matter of the girl in Christchurch had been more of an intuition for Kathleen. Sean seemed to think about her incessantly, but it did seem he was avoiding the Canterbury Plains.

***

Colin and Chloe were blissful on their wedding day. Chloe looked beautiful in her dress of gold-colored brocade. Kathleen had put a great deal of effort into the design, and she knew the dress would cause a sensation in Dunedin. Claire and Kathleen were also wearing sumptuous gowns. Heather wore a green-apple dress, her hair gently framing her face; she would not have been bested by the radiant bride if her eyes had showed a little gleam instead of melancholy. Kathleen sympathized with her daughter. Heather would be lonely again.

At least she had renewed her correspondence with Violet. Kathleen would encourage Heather to visit her. She had talked about it for a long time, really since Violet had moved to Woolston.

Kathleen looked around for her husband, who was chatting with Sean at the well-stocked bar. The reception was taking place in Jimmy and Claire Dunloe's apartment—and neither of them thought anything of the prohibition efforts. Whoever wanted whiskey got some. In this, fortunately, Jimmy Dunloe, Michael Drury, and Reverend Burton were of one mind. Banning alcohol would only stimulate the black market and further burden the poorer families.

Neither Sean nor Peter looked enthusiastic as Colin approached them with Chloe blissfully smiling on his arm. Kathleen stepped beside her husband.

"We must take our leave," Chloe said in a regretful tone. "This reception is wonderful, but Colin wants to take the night train to Christchurch. Tomorrow is race day in Woolston, and before we go home, we want to look at one or two horses Colin thinks might be right for the stud farm." She gave her husband an adoring look.

Sean arched his eyebrows. "I keep hearing stud farm," Sean said, "but if I recall correctly, it takes a foal eleven months to be born. Have you even mated any mares yet? Or are you still just trading horses like before?"

Kathleen shot her older son an admonishing look. Sean was the gentlest, most polite person she knew, but when Colin appeared, the devil got into him.

Colin simply laughed. "Three mares have been mated, dear brother. My wife's hackney mare is one of them; she's been covered by a Thoroughbred stallion with a strong trot. And I'm afraid I can't escape horse trading, but I have to acquire a certain breeding stock. Occasionally one of the animals will prove ill-suited, and we'll have to part ways with it."

"However, we'll discuss that together at the time," Chloe interrupted him.

Chloe surely understood a thing or two about horses, but she also was sensitive and did not like parting with them. Kathleen still could not picture Chloe as the wife of a horse trader.

"There, you heard it, Sean," laughed Colin. "I'm not even lord of my own land. Next thing, my wife will want a voice in everything, which must please you. After all, you're in with the suffragettes. Come along, Chloe. We should leave, or we'll miss the train."

Chloe said her good-byes graciously, and Colin steered her energetically in the direction of the exit before she could chat with someone else.

"A wedding night on the train to Christchurch," Kathleen mumbled. "Wouldn't you picture something more romantic?"

Sean shrugged and took another sip from his glass. "She doesn't seem to have a voice in anything."

Peter, who rarely drank but was persuaded by the quality of Jimmy's whiskey, grimaced. "Looks more like a newly bought horse he's leading home from market."

Kathleen gave Peter a warning look. "What a thing for a man of the cloth to say."

Peter laughed. "I'm tipsy, Mrs. Burton," he admitted. "But not so much that I confuse what's yours and mine like your son, lord of *his* land. Even though not a shilling of his own went to it. The 'newly bought horse'—forgive me, dear, I'll express myself more clerically tomorrow—paid for its own stable."

***

Indeed, Chloe was not especially pleased by her wedding night on the train. She hardly got any sleep and felt beaten when they reached Woolston early in the morning. Colin was wound up and lively. His eyes shone as he stepped into the racetrack. Chloe kept an eye out for acquaintances in the stands, but she did not see any. In the morning, a few less important races took place. The main events of the day were the harness races in the afternoon. Chloe recognized that two of the galloping horses wore Lord Barrington's colors.

"Lord Barrington must be here. Let's go to the owners' box and say hello."

In the owners' box, there would surely be a royal breakfast and first-class champagne. Those two things could have reinvigorated Chloe's spirits.

Colin, however, shook his head. "Not now, dearest. First, I'm not for more small talk with better society. We had plenty of that yesterday. And second, we did want to look at horses. There're apparently a mare in the racing club and one just like her here at Brown's. We should go before someone snatches them out from under our noses."

Chloe reluctantly obliged. Colin was right, but this was their honeymoon. She would have liked to show off her good-looking husband in the owners' box.

Instead, Colin led her into the rather dark stables of Brown's Paddock. The mare in question was a handsome cob. However, she seemed unfriendly and bit at Colin when he wanted to look in her mouth. Chloe did not like her for their stables.

"I thought we wanted to breed with mostly Thoroughbred horses," she objected when Colin began negotiations with the mare's owner. "Cobs are sure-footed and fast on uneven ground, but harness races are now mostly run on special tracks. On even ground, Jewel would have beaten that Maori woman's horse."

Chloe blushed. She tried hard not to mention the name Matariki Drury to Colin.

Colin shrugged. "We can always get rid of the horse, but one or two foals, just to try."

He paused when he saw Chloe frown. They had different ideas about horse breeding. Chloe preferred the British model, which was planned across generations. Colin found crossbreeding interesting and hoped for lucky accidents.

"Very well then, let's take a look at the other." There was no point aggravating Chloe on the very first day.

The grounds of the Lower Heathcote Racing Club were busy. Finally, they found a stout, blond young man who seemed prepared to show them around.

"Horses for sale? Mares? Oh, right, Beasley's brown." The man led them along one of the spacious aisles and pointed to an elegant dark-brown Thoroughbred mare. "And then across the way over there is a chestnut pony. But"—the man lowered his voice—"if you ask me, sir, I wouldn't take either."

Colin furrowed his brow. "You work here?" he asked. "For one of the horse trainers?" The club provided stables exclusively for regular racing horses.

"For the club," the man said. "Eric Fence is the name. But my heart, sir, is in harness racing. I follow it closely. And these mares here, neither'd run a mile faster than five minutes."

"But that horse over there is supposed to have already won a race," Chloe said.

She had not liked the cob mare, but she liked this man even less. She challenged him on principle.

Eric Fence nodded. "Sure, after the three favorites galloped. The chestnut trotted, so she won. She would have come in fourth. That's how it goes, madam."

His presumptuous tone annoyed Chloe. "I know how it goes," she said.

Fence was no longer looking at her, however. He had turned back to Colin. "If you ask me, sir, the only horse for sale here worth his salt as a trotter is the black gelding over there." He pointed two stalls down where a rather small horse with a handsome wedge-shaped head, longer mane, and soft eyes waited. "He's supposed to go because he gallops too slow. But I've seen him trot before. A stableboy got on him, you know, for fun—"

"Without the knowledge of the trainer or owner," Chloe completed the thought.

Fence smirked. "Doesn't hurt the horse none," he said. "In any case, did he ever take off like a cannonball. And he's soft to sit on, too, so the jockey has it easy when he trots."

Three miles at a strong trot demanded quite a bit from a rider, and if the horse had a particularly uncomfortable gait, the jockey might occasionally lack the strength—or pain tolerance—to spur the horse faster to the finish line.

"The future of harness racing lies in sulkies," Chloe objected. "Ridden harness racing is dying out. We need horses that can move in the tackle, which does not seem to be the case with this horse." The gelding stuck his head out of the stall, and she stroked him. She liked him, but he was the opposite of what they needed. "Besides, we're looking for mares. We're setting up a stud farm."

Eric Fence shrugged his shoulders. "Well, when you look at it that way, I suppose someone else will soon be winning with him. Doesn't bother me. I'll give the tip to the horse trader who once discovered Spirit. Does that name mean anything to you, sir? Spirit? The black Thoroughbred stallion?"

Colin nodded. "He's in my stables," he said curtly. "I bought him for a stud."

Eric Fence looked at him with shining eyes. Chloe thought his smile looked honest for the first time. "Seriously, sir? Spirit? You won't find a better one, sir. And this one here." He pointed to the little black horse again. "Man, he goes right with him, sir. Buy him, and when he wins, say he's the son of your stud. What do you think? Then the mares will pour in. You won't need to buy as many yourself."

Chloe wanted to laugh at the idea, but then she realized that Colin was considering it.

She tried to object. "Colin, we do need to think long term. The future—"

"The future is this afternoon, sir." Eric Fence grinned. He felt he had already convinced the wealthy gentleman. "Buy the gelding and sign him up for the harness race. He's well trained. It's all the same to him if he canters two miles or trots for three. If you put down three or four tenners, and he wins, you'll already have almost made your money back."

Chloe bit her lip, but Colin was now seriously considering it. "Does it really go that quickly? With signing up for today, I mean? Will I be able to find a jockey?"

Eric laughed. "If I put in a little of the ol' elbow grease, sir," he boasted. "Or you could ride yourself."

Colin puffed himself up. "I was in the cavalry, Mr. Fence. I can handle any horse."

"Now, that won't work." Chloe glared at her husband as well as the impertinent stable hand. "We would ruin our reputation. No breeder here rides his own horse. People would think we couldn't afford a jockey. You decide: either a professional rider or none at all, Colin."

Only after she had said it out loud did it become clear to her that she had essentially given her blessing for the purchase of the horse. That was probably exactly what the men wanted. She was irritated but tried not to let Colin sense it.

A "professional" jockey did turn up: Eric gave the stableboy a few shillings to sit in the black horse's saddle. The boy was inept. Colin saw red as he followed the race from the owners' box but tried not to let Chloe sense it. The black gelding—he was actually named Lancelot, but Colin signed him up as Spirit's Pride—did his job phenomenally. With the shaky boy on his back, he came in third. Colin could effortlessly have ridden him to victory himself.

Eric Fence met Colin and Chloe in front of Pride's stall. He was breathless with pride and excitement. He had bet on the horse and made a handsome profit. As had Colin, although Chloe did not consider it gentlemanly to bet on one's own horse.

"I can organize the transport too," Fence offered enthusiastically. "However, I'd like, I mean, perhaps we could work out a small commission?"

Colin pursed his lips. He knew he would upset Chloe with his next words, but this man was exactly what he needed.

"Bring him yourself. I'm offering you the post of stable master at Coltrane Station. Will you accept it?" He held out his hand to Eric.

Eric shook it.

***

That night, Colin and Chloe Coltrane fought and made love in the White Hart Hotel in Christchurch. As ladylike as Chloe seemed, she had a temper that Colin then got to soothe in bed. In that way, Colin thought, she resembled Matariki. But Chloe was older, and much more conservative. She did not lie stiff and resistant beneath him, but she did not show the wildness and imagination of the lithe Matariki. Well, one could not have everything. Colin poured Chloe another glass of champagne and tried to arouse her once again.

***

Eric Fence celebrated his new job in Brown's Tavern but went home early enough to discover that Violet had slipped out to another meeting of the teetotalers and suffragettes. Well, that was going to stop. He hoped Coltrane's stud farm was out of the way enough that she wouldn't be able to join up with another group. His satisfaction at that prospect did not hinder Eric from letting Violet feel his displeasure when she returned home. He beat her ghastly little sister, who had withdrawn to a corner to smear paper with red crayons, along with her. Rosie cried soundlessly, Joe bawled, and Roberta screamed as if being roasted on a spit. Eric hoped there would be a bedroom with a door he could close in Invercargill. For now, he took Violet despite the noise. The prospect of a new job had given him wings. He was not ready to sleep yet.

"Pack our things tomorrow," he ordered. "Mr. Coltrane is expecting us. We're moving in as soon as possible."

***

Three days later, Sean and Heather Coltrane stood in shock before the shack where Violet had dwelled for almost a year. Sean had been contemplating for a long time how he could arrange to see Violet again without compromising them both. Heather's desire to visit her friend had been a convenient excuse for him. He bought crayons for Rosie, a dress for Roberta, and a stuffed animal for Joe. It would not have been proper to bring Violet a present, but she would be happy about the gifts for the children, as well as the basket Heather had filled with groceries. Though Violet had only vaguely mentioned her economic situation in her letters to Heather and even more cautiously to Sean, they both did enough work with charities to imagine Violet's situation. Still, the shack behind the pub thoroughly horrified the siblings.

Their landlord merely shrugged. "What do you mean, inhumane?" he grumbled. "It was rather nice of me to let them live there. And now don't come to me about the tavern and the whiskey and tell me that I led the man astray. That Fence doesn't booze more than the others. He gambles his money away. And I don't get a penny of that."

Heather and Sean looked at each other helplessly, but there was nothing more they could do. Violet, Eric, and the children were gone. A new job, somewhere to the south. They would have to wait for Violet to write them again.

If she did.

Chapter 2

Amey Daldy was fifty-four years old, but she had never had a stranger introductory conversation than that with Matariki Drury.

The girl had come to her on Hepburn Street in Ponsonby and got caught up in the confusion of eight children moving into a new house. Mrs. Daldy had been widowed four years earlier, but then she married the merchant and politician William Daldy, a widower himself. Apparently, she had planned to devote herself entirely to her political goals and duties, but something had interfered: William's daughter and shortly thereafter the daughter's husband had died, leaving the care of their eight children to the Daldys. Right away, Amey rented the house next to her and her husband's residence and hired a housekeeper. The children, some of whom were still quite little, were just moving into the neighboring house when Matariki arrived in Auckland. It was a long trip with a crossing by ship from the South Island to Wellington on the North Island, and then a ride on her trusted horse Grainie from Wellington to Auckland; Dingo was with them the entire time.

Amey preferred to delay the introductory interview while the children were moving in, but Matariki shook her head and laughed. "Not at all, Mrs. Daldy, you need help. And since I'm here, I can read stories or cook or help the children settle in. All I could do in my hotel would be to sit around. And they don't like having Dingo there."

To Mrs. Daldy's horror, she pointed to the mutt following her. The animal seemed well behaved. Two of the children immediately sat next to him on the ground and stopped crying the moment Dingo offered them his paw. Matariki already had one of the little girls in her arms.

"Mrs. Daldy, let me make myself useful. You don't need to feel obligated in return." Matariki flashed a mischievous smile at the stern matron. "If you can't use me as a teacher, perhaps you can recommend me as a nanny."

***

Matariki had originally feared that her return to the North Island would depress her. After all, she had last crossed the island with Colin, enjoying their love. And her memories of Parihaka's conquest weren't cheerful. Nonetheless, she was quickly engrossed by the landscape and the greater activity of the North Island, where there were larger cities, more *pakeha*, and markedly more Maori tribes, which she found especially interesting.

Matariki took her time on her ride through the country. This time she and Grainie did not ride along the coast but along the new rail line from Wellington to Auckland. She thought wistfully of Taranaki and rode around Hamilton, shuddering a bit. She thought of Kupe, who was likely still studying in Wellington; she knew that Koria, whom she hoped to meet soon in Auckland, had no direct contact with him. However, Matariki had heard he was back together with Pai. If Kupe was with Pai and Matariki's relationship with Colin was over, there was no reason for any ill will, and perhaps they could be in contact. Colin, however, would never entirely be in the past, and Matariki was not sure what Kupe would say about what the *pakeha* had left her to remember him by.

She reached Auckland and was again fascinated by the city between the Pacific Ocean and the Tasman Sea. Matariki had liked Auckland when she had been stranded there with Kupe. She would be happy to live here—assuming Amey Daldy took a liking to her. She wasn't sure whether the strict Congregationalist would be accepting of a young woman who visibly had not taken seriously the question of chastity before marriage.

Matariki was pleased that the interview was delayed by moving the children into the house. She seized her chance; by evening, Amey Daldy knew Matariki Drury was useful.

To Amey's amazement, Matariki had gotten the little children to bed without any back talk: "Of course you can sleep alone. You don't need to be afraid of anything. We'll leave Dingo with you. He'll make sure you don't have any bad dreams, and if any ghosts come, he'll eat them."

She had taught the slightly older children a song in Maori, and they were drawing pictures to illustrate it. The eldest were unpacking suitcases and filling drawers.

"Good job, doing that on your own," Matariki encouraged them. "When you go to high school or university, you won't have a maid then either. What, you're already in high school? What year? Oh, that's when you start reading Shakespeare. Are you performing *Romeo and Juliet?* My friend wanted to play Juliet, but let's just say she didn't look the part."

Matariki laughed and chatted with the children, who forgot their sorrow and their fear of the new house and their strict step-grandmother.

***

Only after calm prevailed and the housekeeper no longer felt overwhelmed did Mrs. Daldy take Matariki next door to her own home to interview her. As for her education in Dunedin and her time in Parihaka, she found the answers highly satisfactory. Did the young woman, however, lead the virtuous life expected of a teacher?

"Miss Drury, am I correct in my perception that you have been blessed?" Amey Daldy glanced with clear displeasure at Matariki's belly, which was beginning to show evidence of her pregnancy.

Matariki nodded. "Yes, but that won't affect my work. On the contrary, I am supposed to work with Maori women, and almost all of them have children. The *pakeha* practice of not allowing teachers to marry is completely incomprehensible to them. A *tohunga* is proud of passing on her knowledge to her own children and grandchildren."

"But you are not married," Mrs. Daldy said sternly.

Matariki shook her head. "No, but the Maori women won't find fault with that. Every child is welcome in the tribes, whether or not the mother takes the father for a husband."

Amey Daldy tried to maintain her composure. "Miss Drury, I am seeking someone who understands native customs. But you don't have to practice everything, you know."

Matariki smiled. "It wasn't quite planned this way," she said. "I did want to marry."

"Did the father leave you in the lurch?" asked Mrs. Daldy, sympathy and disdain in her voice. "When it became clear you were going to be blessed?"

Matariki chewed her lip. "Not quite," she admitted. "When I noticed the baby—by the way, the Maori simply say 'pregnant'—I could still have married him. But, you see, well, the best way to prevent trouble in a marriage is to wed a man who holds Christian values and who is capable of moderation."

"And?" Mrs. Daldy asked, interested despite herself.

Matariki shrugged. "I found out just in time that mine was a scoundrel."

Amey Daldy tried to stifle a laugh. "Just in time? Rather a bit late, I'd say."

Matariki arched her eyebrows. "Better late than never," she said.

Mrs. Daldy regained her composure. "Very well, Miss Drury, the Maori women you will primarily be working with may accept that. However, you will also have to deal with the English. You'll live among whites, you and your child."

"*Pakeha*," Matariki said. "We call them *pakeha*, and they'll flap their gums, um, forgive me, Mrs. Daldy. I meant to say I run the risk of becoming the object of gossip. However, I've thought of that." Smiling, she drew a small silver ring out of her pocket. "Here, we'll say I'm a widow. And in a certain respect, that's true. The fellow's dead to me."

Amey Daldy was a very serious woman, a good Christian, an upright tee-totaler, a powerful fighter for the rights of her gender. Yet Matariki Drury over-taxed her capacity to control herself. She shook with loud laughter.

"Very well, Miss Drury. How does one say your first name again? Mar-tha-ricky?"

Matariki smiled at her. "You can call me Martha."

***

Matariki occupied a room in the Daldys' rented house next door to their own. She took care of the orphaned children, placed Dingo on the night watch against nightmares, and found—although Mrs. Daldy only permitted it with reservation—a place for Grainie.

"Why do you need a horse?" Mrs. Daldy asked. "This is a large city. There are cabs."

"That's too involved," said Matariki. "You'll see, Grainie will make herself useful."

Amey Daldy later had to admit it. While only a few Maori women ventured into the city to attend Daldy's Ladies' Seminary, Matariki rode Grainie to their villages, where they greeted her warmly. The region of Auckland had been densely settled by the Ngati Whatua and the Waikato-Tainui, and the *iwi* of these and other lines still lived in the Hunua and Waitakere Ranges. To Amey Daldy's great amazement, the men there did not disapprove of their women and girls learning English or letting Matariki bring them into town when there were political gatherings on the subject of female or Maori suffrage.

Matariki celebrated it as her first success when one of her students spoke up at a gathering.

"I do not quite understand," said Ani te Kaniwa, a musician of the Hauraki tribe. The women's rights activist Helen Nicol had just announced from the podium that, in her opinion, women did not necessarily need to be members of Parliament but should still have the right to vote for them. "Why women should not want be chieftain?"

"Is it true that there are female tribal leaders?" Mrs. Nicol asked Matariki afterward.

She confirmed this. "You see, we do have an advanced culture." Matariki laughed. "It's about time the *pakeha* learned from us."

***

Matariki brought Maori and *pakeha* women together and tried hard to overcome the gulf that the Maori Wars had opened between the new and old settlers. Though there had been little bloodshed in Auckland, the governor had used the city as the base of operations, and the natives were frightened by the strong military presence and the often less-than-diplomatic behavior of those in uniform. Also, the *pakeha* had brought with them diseases like pox and tuberculosis, which had decimated the Maori population. Matariki started giving presentations on diseases and fighting them. She led the women through the English schools and made it clear to them that hardly anything better could happen to their children than to be educated. On the other side, she invited the Anglican and Methodist women to visit the tribes and had them experience a *powhiri* ritual and communal cooking in the *hangi*.

At first, the *pakeha* women were shocked by the appearance of the Maori women, so Matariki convinced the tribal women that it was better to cover their breasts when visitors came from Auckland—at least at first. They were always amused when the proper Englishwomen finally relaxed and communicated with the Maori by gesture. Everyone laughed and sang together, and the English matrons even tried to draw notes from the *koauau* flute with their noses. "Give to the Winds Thy Fears" met with the greatest appreciation among the Maori women. Their *tohunga* could easily imagine entrusting all their fears to the wind. Matariki translated the hymn into Maori, and the women around Amey Daldy astounded the guest speakers at gatherings by performing the song in both languages. Matariki—and later the women to whom she had taught English—usually followed the song with a few remarks about Maori suffrage: the same country, the same concerns, the same needs for women and children—suffrage for all!

The thoughts on abstinence, however, offered little to the Maori. Only a few women were won over to the Temperance Union, and they were either married to *pakeha* or to Maori men who worked in factories and had adopted the habits of their *pakeha* colleagues. Otherwise, the natives remained inclined toward the sensual and did not shy away from whiskey. That worried Mrs. Daldy, but Matariki felt considerably more comfortable among the tribes than under the strict Christians of the *pakeha* communities—although she always prayed properly for her husband, Colin Drury, sadly taken too soon.

For the birth of her daughter, Matariki went to the Ngati Whatua. Mrs. Daldy told the *pakeha* women that Mrs. Drury preferred to be in the safe harbor of family for the birth.

"It is true in a sense," said Matariki, thinking of her birth father, Kahu Heke. He was certainly related to the Ngati Whatua somehow.

In the care of a *tohunga* of the *iwi*, she gave birth one autumn morning to a girl just as the sun rose over the village and bathed it in a tender reddish light.

"Atamarie," said the midwife as she laid the baby in the arms of an exhausted but happy Matariki.

The word for sunrise was a favorite girls' name among the Maori.

Matariki sighed. "A beautiful name. But I'm afraid the *pakeha* will call her Mary."

Chapter 3

Chloe and Colin Coltrane's stud farm was near Invercargill, a small city in the Southland Plains. The fruitful plain offered grassland for the horses, and the Main South Line connected the South Coast with Christchurch and Dunedin, so the racetrack was easy to reach by train from the cities.

It was near Invercargill that Colin bought a vast estate that suited his designs. Desmond McIntosh, a descendent of a Scottish noble line, had built it a decade before but then lost his taste for sheep breeding. The man was an eccentric bachelor rumored to have an intense relationship with his young secretary; he now lived in Dunedin and was a patron of the arts. Colin had met him at Heather and Chloe's gallery. The estate offered a manor house that resembled a Scottish castle, pastures, horse stables, and a coach house.

Desmond McIntosh had clearly been thinking more of living as landed gentry than breeding sheep when he planned the estate, so it had proved difficult to sell—especially so since he wanted to try to recover some of the astronomical construction costs, and hardly any New Zealander could afford that. So, Colin seemed heaven-sent to Lord McIntosh.

"The grounds are ideal for you. The house will please your wife, and with a bit of refurbishing, the stables would have space for a hundred horses."

Colin was enthusiastic about the estate, though it was not cheap. Ultimately, all of Chloe's inheritance went to the acquisition of the estate and the construction of the racetrack. Only a small portion remained for the purchase of horses.

The mare stock of the future stud farm also seemed rather thrown together as Chloe determined on her first walk through the stables. The stallion was promising to be sure, but Colin had bought quantity over quality when it came to the mares. Only Dancing Jewel and a Thoroughbred mare met Chloe's standards. She would not even have coupled the others with the Thoroughbred stud. Although she did not want to get into another fight right away, she was close to expressing her concerns. But when Colin led her through the house, her recriminations caught in her throat.

"Very tastefully furnished," Desmond McIntosh had assured him with slight regret.

He was obviously happy to part with the estate but not with the furniture. After stepping into the living room, into which the sunlight fell through large, tall windows, Chloe understood why.

"It's unbelievable," she marveled as she touched the thick brocade curtains and the furniture crafted of old kauri wood. "These pieces don't come from England or Scotland."

Colin shook his head. "No, Desmond had the furniture made, from his own designs, or those of his secretary. Come upstairs; you must see the bed. So decadent, you'd think kings were conceived in it."

"Well, perhaps not so much," Chloe joked, thinking about Desmond McIntosh and his secretary, "but we could certainly try for little Coltranes."

They tried amply, which made Chloe struggle against feelings of guilt when she thought about Heather. Would McIntosh have exchanged his secretary for another woman as inconsiderately as Chloe had Heather for her husband? Surely the wealthy lord did not have a lack of candidates. The secretary was no makeshift solution, and no one seemed to take it as such. When women lived together, people spoke of old maids or late bloomers who lacked suitable husbands and offered each other platonic company. No one seemed to imagine they might share a bed.

In Colin's arms, Chloe forgot Heather and her concerns about the horse breeding. The next morning, she was again convinced the marriage was the right thing, even when confrontations loomed about the mares and she dreaded the arrival of the new stable master.

Chloe thought first of gypsies when Eric's hay wagon rolled onto the estate. Laden with household belongings, it was pulled by a scrawny pony and steered by a woman to whom a frightened-looking girl and two small children clung. The elegant Thoroughbred gelding, Lancelot, renamed Spirit's Pride, followed them. Eric Fence sat proudly in the saddle, pulling inexpertly on the reins to stop the horse. Anger seized Chloe, who watched the whole scene from her dressing room. She had not imagined the transportation of the valuable horse like this. If the man had tugged the whole time, the sensitivity Pride needed in a race was probably gone—at least temporarily. A callous-mouthed horse could not be kept at a trot when others passed it. It would take the reins from the rider and gallop forward. Eric Fence did not seem to know anything about riding, and as for horses in general, his pony needed more feed. Just like his children. Excepting the rather fat little boy, everyone looked famished.

Chloe had wanted to prepare for an evening event in Invercargill—the notables of the small city had immediately invited their new neighbors to festivities, surely to test whether they belonged to better society. For Chloe, a good presentation was second nature, and Colin, too, could be charming. However, he did not like making small talk with factory owners and sheep barons. He only played along because he hoped to make relationships with new customers, and he was usually successful.

Colin made it clear to the often nouveau riche owners of wool factories and warehouses that owning a racehorse was among the things that made a gentleman a gentleman. Already two of his new acquaintances were seriously considering acquiring either a galloping or trotting horse and ordering it from Coltrane. Chloe hoped they would really be getting their money's worth. Though the main races were the domain of high society, with harness racing, the opposite had so far been the case. That evening's event was a dinner given by a factory owner, and Chloe had already laid out her gown. For the moment, she quickly slipped into a house dress. She had to watch over the invasion below.

***

The hay wagon and harnessed pony were still in the yard when Chloe came down. Colin and his stable master had taken Pride to his stall. The handsome black horse was in a stall next to Spirit, and the stallion was agitated about this. In every other male horse, Spirit saw a rival. The stables were half-empty. Could they not have found a different stall for the gelding? Chloe's annoyance gave way to sympathy when she saw the young woman and her children standing fearfully in the stable aisle. Mrs. Fence carried the little girl. The older girl clambered onto her, and the boy held tightly to her skirt. Unlike his mother and the girls, he looked more interested in the raging stallion than fearful.

Mrs. Fence seemed unsure about whether to follow her husband and Colin in the direction of the tack room, which would have required passing by Spirit. Chloe smiled at her, and she halfheartedly returned the friendly acknowledgment. She was extraordinary-looking despite her exhaustion. She also seemed strangely familiar to Chloe, but she was sure they hadn't met before. This delicate woman with chestnut hair and giant blue eyes wouldn't be easily forgotten.

Chloe indicated the stallion. "You can go ahead and walk past. Don't be afraid of Spirit. He's putting on a show, but he's very peaceful. He can't get out of his stall anyway."

The woman and the little boy looked at her with equal skepticism.

"He don't spit?" asked the child.

Chloe laughed but again could not help wondering: Was that how the son of a stable master would react? It did not look as if the little boy had been raised in horse stables.

"Horses don't spit. You can trust me on this," she assured him before turning to his mother. "I'm Chloe Coltrane. And you are?"

"Violet Fence," the young woman said, reaching awkwardly for the hand Chloe held out. "My husband is going to work here."

Chloe nodded, hoping Violet did not see her concern. "I know. However, no one told me he was bringing his whole family right away. We need to see where we can lodge you. In any case, you don't need to stand around the stable trying to tame spitting stallions." Chloe smiled at them. "Come with me. We'll unhitch your horse, and we'll go into the house and consider where you can live."

Violet pointed at the tack room. "I think we're supposed to live there," she said.

Chloe furrowed her brow, recalling the apartment for the stableboys next to the tack room and feed room. Colin could not be serious.

Chloe left Violet and the children where they were and followed the men into the living quarters. The small apartment had the essential furniture, and in the feed room was a stove. The arrangements were sufficient for a stableboy.

"It's a bit small," Colin said matter-of-factly. "After all, I couldn't know you already had a family. But—"

"My wife is used to thrift," Eric Fence said. "Her sister can also sleep in the feed room if you give us a cot to put in there. The little ones, too, certainly. It'll work."

Chloe cast an incredulous eye at Colin and Eric. Violet finally ventured past Spirit and now looked at her new domicile with horror. She seemed to want to say something, but a threatening look from her husband made her remain silent. The little girl seemed to have caught the meaning of his expression and hid her face in Violet's skirts.

"At least it'll probably keep the rain out," Violet said resignedly.

Chloe glared at her husband. "Have you lost your mind?" she asked angrily. "Five people in this room? A whole household, children? A baby in a dusty feed room? And where are the children supposed to do schoolwork? In the tack room? Come, Violet." Everything in Chloe bristled against calling this submissive young woman Mrs. Fence. "I'll make us tea, and then we'll take a closer look at the house. There must be servants' quarters."

Colin was annoyed. Chloe should not have spoken to him that way in front of his new employee. Besides, Eric seemed to have a handle on his own family.

Colin couldn't let Chloe get away with her insubordination. "I don't care," he said sharply. "The stable master must sleep near the horses. That's how it's always been. Just imagine if a mare were to foal with no one here to help, or if a horse were to have colic."

Chloe rolled her eyes. "Mares foal in the spring, Colin," she replied, and resisted asking how many foals Eric might have helped birth. "And rarely as a surprise. Mr. Fence can sleep in the stall when the time comes, and then really in the stall, Mr. Fence, not in the feed room. You'll detect colic by making a tour every night. We'll likely run into each other. I like to check on the animals before I go to bed."

Chloe withstood Colin's angry gaze. The day before, they had already argued about her nightly inspection tour. Colin did not think a lady had any business in the stables at night.

"That would not be necessary if Mr. Fence were to sleep here," Colin insisted.

Eric Fence nodded while Chloe felt the rage boiling within her. It had to be clear to the man that the lodgings in the house would be more comfortable for his family than this shack within the stables. Yet Fence seemed determined to echo his new boss. Colin and Eric Fence seemed to be taking position against Chloe as a lone warrior. This was a power game, but Chloe did not intend to play along.

"Very well," she said with a sardonic smile. "If you insist, Colin. Then Mr. Fence will sleep right here, and I'll house Mrs. Fence and the children in the house. We do so appreciate it, Mr. Fence, that you take your job so seriously. Please bring the gelding to the second stall, so the stallion will stop screaming. And then unharness your pony and give him a proper helping of oats. That wagon is much too heavy for him. You ought to know that as stable master. Violet, collect your children and come with me."

Chloe observed the effect of her words. Eric and Colin clearly had not expected this solution. Certainly, Fence would not like it, but Chloe saw he looked too dumbfounded to make a counterargument. She tried not to let her triumph show, and now turned to Violet and her children to observe their reactions. Were they sorry to be separated from husband and father?

The expression Violet and the older of the girls now directed at Chloe, however, did not testify to displeasure. They looked as shocked as if Chloe had just summoned a genie from the bottle. As if they had been set free.

They still hesitated in front of the stallion's stall. Violet gripped her son's hand, and Chloe was startled when small, ice-cold fingers—those of the older girl—closed around her own. She might be nine or ten years old. Chloe squeezed her hand and smiled at her.

"And what's your name?" she asked amiably.

Violet was going to answer for the child, but then she paused, shocked as Rosie spoke.

Very quietly, and tonelessly, her sister said, "I'm Rosie."

***

The manor house of Coltrane Station had appropriate servants' quarters. Chloe found two rooms next to each other that seemed meant for the butler and a maid.

"Three would be better with all the children," she said while Violet eyed the rooms in disbelief. "But we'll also need a maid, and perhaps a cook, so we can only offer you these two."

In her household in Wellington, Chloe also had a lady's maid. But in Invercargill, the duties of appearance were less demanding. It would be enough if the maid could also occasionally help her dress. The usual Maori servants—her new acquaintances recruited their help from the surrounding villages—would not suffice for that. But perhaps . . .

In a maid's dress, Violet would make a pretty sight, and Rosie no less so. "Would you want to help around the house, Violet? Perhaps in time we could also teach the little one." She indicated Rosie.

Violet had already been looking at her gratefully, but now she seemed close to tears. "I didn't think," she whispered. "I didn't think anyone would give Rosie a chance. But if you—" Violet's voice threatened to crack, but she collected herself and forced a businesslike tone. "If you would be content to have me as a housemaid, I believe I could meet your expectations. I worked in Greymouth as a nanny, and the Billers would surely provide a reference. I have also worked in a ladies' boutique."

At the mention of the boutique, Chloe flashed on her commitment for that evening. If she wanted to make it on time, she would have to hurry.

"Very well, Violet," she said. "That you can care for children, I believe. We can speak about references later. But if you really have helped a lady dress before, then you can prove it to me this very moment."

The children followed Violet into Chloe's dressing room, and she breathed a sigh of relief when her new mistress did not object to her bringing Roberta along and laying her down on a chair. After a day or two, she could have Rosie watch the children while she worked, and perhaps she could even convince Rosie to stay with them in their new rooms. But that evening, everything was still too new. They would all be frightened if Violet left them alone.

"It's quite all right," Chloe said, fending off her apologies about the children. She was focused on getting dressed. "Have you laced a lady's corset before?"

Chloe moaned as Violet pulled on the laces. Then she laughed. "Oh, I see you have. Thank you, Violet. And now the dress. Careful, it's thin silk, and the ribbons run so easily."

Violet pulled the fine web over the crinoline and checked the decorative ribbons on the seam and below the waist. The dress was cream colored, the ribbons aquamarine. The label indicated the dress was from the Gold Mine Boutique.

"That's where I worked, madam," Violet said, overjoyed. "Shall I also put up your hair? I can't do it that well, but—"

Chloe nodded and was quite thrilled when she finally looked in the mirror. "The post is yours, Violet," she declared briefly, "as house and lady's maid. And Rosie, you'll help, too, won't you?

"How was it at the Gold Mine? Oh, we'll talk about that tomorrow. I must go now. I hope your husband made himself useful and hitched a horse in front of the chaise."

***

Eric had not hitched any horse, having instead gotten lost with Colin in shop-talk about trotters. Both earned another tongue lashing from Chloe, which immediately hardened the relationships further. Colin was in a bad mood all night and argued heatedly with Chloe when she insisted on going through the stables when they got home to check on the horses. Things escalated irrevocably when Chloe discovered a small cut on the stallion's forehead.

"He certainly didn't get that in the last two hours. This happened during that theater over the gelding. Your fabulous stable master should have noticed," she said angrily as she quickly rubbed a salve on the wound. "Hold the lantern for me. We need to look closely at the gelding. He didn't beat any less hard against the walls of his stall, after all. It won't do for your valuable racehorse to have swollen legs tomorrow."

It was one o'clock in the morning before Colin and Chloe finally got to bed—Eric Fence had either slept through their argument in the stables or consciously ignored it. Or had he been with his wife? Chloe decided to check whether he was really sleeping in the stables. And she would not give herself to Colin that night.

That decision, however, became shaky as soon as Colin stepped behind her and undid the complicated clasps on her dress. She shuddered with pleasure as he kissed the nape of her neck. Colin was a wonderful lover, more experienced than Terrence, Chloe's first husband. Despite her efforts to resist him that night, he brought her to the highest delights of desire, which was always the case when a fight preceded their lovemaking. Chloe almost did not recognize herself anymore in this. She had always thought tenderness and harmony determined fulfillment. Terrence had always stroked and kissed her a long time before he pushed into her. Colin, however, seemed bored during foreplay. He preferred to take her when she was still excited after an angry exchange of words. Occasionally she resisted his "attempts at assuaging her" before she let herself be convinced. When it was over, she was satisfied and pleasurably tired, but she was also frustrated with herself. After all, usually nothing was discussed. Sometimes it seemed like her honor was a contest Colin won every night.

That night, too, Chloe lay awake, wrestling with the bitter recognition that, though Colin did not leave her unsatisfied, the spiritual affinity she had hoped for in Dunedin, when he had ensnared her with plans about the stud farm and a family, would never come to be.

***

Chloe Coltrane's dislike of Eric Fence mounted to sheer hatred over the next few months. She could live with the fact that his knowledge regarding horse care and training did not extend far. Fine, her husband had granted him the demanding post of stable master, which involved cleaning out the stables, feeding and cleaning the horses, and putting on their harnesses and saddles. Colin was still too much a cavalryman to leave the last duties in particular to a stable-boy. Chloe checked on the feeding, even though this did not seem right to Colin. Here, Chloe would not compromise: she would not be shut out from the management of the stud farm.

Chloe quickly discovered and admonished Eric's mistakes and negligence, though he did seem capable of improvement. Worse was the influence Eric Fence exercised on Colin Coltrane, or was it Colin on Eric? The two outdid each other even with little white lies like the matter of presenting Pride as Spirit's son. Pride won one race after another, and people were willing to spend a lot of money to mate their mares with Spirit.

Chloe might have been able to look past this. Spirit was, after all, a strong trotter, and there was reason to hope he would pass on his aptitude. When, however, she caught her husband in a conversation with a customer on whom Eric had foisted an infertile horse as a broodmare, she became irate—and even more so as Colin remained completely calm.

"Really, my stable master told you that?" he incredulously addressed the new owner of the mare, Annabelle. "Yes, well, he hasn't been here long; he must have gotten mixed up. I am quite sure he did not intend to cheat you. Suitability for breeding is important—it's about distilling harness-racing horses, you know. Your mare Annabelle runs a mile in under two minutes. She's much too good for breeding. Have her race for two years, then try again."

The buyer tried to protest, but Colin merely shook his head condescendingly. "What do you mean? You don't get the impression she's that fast?" Colin lowered his voice as if sharing a well-kept secret with Annabelle's owner. "Have you driven the horse, Mr. Morton? No? There you have your explanation. With a rider, Annabelle isn't outstanding. I agree with you, but the future lies in harness racing with sulkies."

Chloe snorted with rage when the man had finally gone without returning Annabelle and without repeating his accusation of being cheated.

"Colin, we agreed to give the horse up because she was neither fast nor fertile. The best would have been not to sell her. In any case, Annabelle belongs in front of a light vehicle, perhaps in town. She is a good horse and could pull a delivery wagon or even a chaise, but Mr. Morton has a racing stable. He doesn't need a wagon horse. What got into you and Eric, fobbing this mare off on him?"

Colin laughed. "He's never going to get anywhere with his racing stables. Not as long as he has so little sense, anyway. But you gain that with experience, and viewed in that light—"

"You've helped the man to grow wise from loss. He ought to be grateful," Chloe exploded. "I don't believe it, Colin. You're acting like a horse swindler. Aren't you thinking at all of our reputation? Make him an offer to take Annabelle back if she doesn't win next Sunday."

Chloe sighed with relief when Colin did go after Mr. Morton. She had feared a renewed struggle for power, but Colin's acquiescence confirmed her view that Eric Fence was influencing Colin to fall back into bad habits. That this happened in horse trading did not really surprise her at all. After all, they had warned her sufficiently about Colin in Dunedin. She needed to keep a close eye on him.

Chloe left the stables calmer, but she was shaken when Annabelle won the next Sunday. In front of one of the new, light wagons with big wheels called sulkies, she trotted across the finish line first, followed by Pride and Rasty, another horse Colin had trained.

"Bad day," Colin replied to Chloe's suspicious question about how the mediocre Annabelle could win against fast-as-the-wind Pride and the promising Rasty.

His nonchalance stoked Chloe's suspicions. In general, Colin was a bad loser and got angry every time one of his horses came in second or third. After all, that reduced the winnings, which in harness racing were not high, anyway. Here, one could only make good money through betting. The next day, Chloe learned from Violet that Eric had won big. Had the stable master bet on Annabelle? And not just the obligatory tenner for himself, but more money for his boss? Had Pride and Rasty's drivers—both stableboys and apprentices of Colin and Eric—held their horses back purposely?

***

Despite how skeptical Chloe was about Eric Fence, she became all the closer with his family over time. Violet proved her worth around the house and as a lady's maid. Joe and Roberta were not difficult children. Chloe had found a soft spot in her heart for Rosie, especially after Violet had told her about her years of silence, which she had now broken for Chloe in particular. Rosie remained all but mute, but she did not leave the impression on Chloe that she was stupid or slow. Chloe was outraged when Eric presented his little sister-in-law as daft. And she was touched when after only two days at Coltrane Station, Rosie let go of Violet's skirts and took hold of Chloe's. No matter where she went, Rosie followed her like a little dog.

"She must be a burden," Violet said fearfully as her sister, covered in hay, followed Chloe out of the stables. "I'm sure she's afraid of the horses, and then she always wants to hold your hand."

Chloe laughed and considered Rosie with a downright proud look. "Afraid of horses? She just groomed her pony. And then she rode with me in a sulky. But not fast, Rosie, just a little endurance training, right? So Jewel doesn't get out of shape now that she's foaling."

Rosie nodded importantly and looked at Chloe as if she worshipped her. She was not afraid of horses whether they trotted fast or slow. What did she have to fear as long as Mrs. Coltrane was with her? Mrs. Coltrane had the power to save them. She had somehow made it so Eric Fence did not break into her nights like a monster. So he no longer beat Violet and no longer frightened Rosie and Joe. Rosie could still hardly comprehend the miracle: in the evening, Violet simply shut the door to the bedroom, and Rosie and the little ones slept the whole night undisturbed.

Joe sometimes had nightmares, or Roberta would cry, but then Rosie would hold the children in her arms and rock them without having to fear that Eric would scream at them or shake them. Though in the first nights he had sought Violet in her room, he arrived through the hallway without bothering Rosie and the little ones. Rosie had listened fearfully to every step in the hall. When he had gone, she slipped into Violet's room to make sure she was still alive. Though Violet repeatedly maintained Eric would not do anything to her, Rosie knew better. And now even these visits had stopped. Rosie did not know why, but she was convinced that Mrs. Coltrane had worked this wonder too.

Violet explained her husband's waning interest less supernaturally, but she was nevertheless prepared to thank the heavens for it. In truth, it was simply too difficult for Eric to slip into the house at night, particularly since Chloe had fun checking on his presence in the stables all night. Above all, however, his income had grown enormously since he started working for Coltrane. Coltrane paid him well, including bonuses for some "trivialities," and Eric also won with his bets. Thanks to Coltrane, he had access to insider knowledge. Colin and Eric manipulated the races sometimes so an outsider could occasionally win. However, then they really skimmed off the top, and Eric could easily afford a whore in Invercargill. The girls in Christchurch or Dunedin, where Colin occasionally raced his horses and where Eric traveled to place a lot of money on dark horses in transregional betting offices, were more fun than the fearful and always tense Violet.

***

Violet did not care if the money Eric had drunk and gambled away before now landed in prostitutes' purses. She earned her own money as Chloe's house and lady's maid, and her employer, who also had hired an uncommonly capable cook, made sure they were all fed. The better nourishment and less worrisome life did her and Rosie good. Both finally gained some weight, and Violet liked what she saw when she looked in the mirror. She wore a maid's uniform and thought she looked neat and competent.

Chloe bolstered her new self-assurance. She took more of a liking to the young woman all the time, and when the Gold Mine Boutique was mentioned for the second time, she realized why she recognized Violet.

"You're the *Girl with Flower* and the *Girl in Red* and the *Girl in the Forest*—Heather Coltrane's portrait series," she said, amazed by the coincidence. "Beautiful pictures, the best Heather ever painted. She sold some, but a few still hang in her apartment in Dunedin. I was . . ."

Chloe paused. She could not possibly admit she had felt something akin to jealousy when she had seen the portraits of Violet in the apartment she had shared with Heather. Even if not in the way she loved Chloe, Heather must have loved Violet, who was rendered so beautiful in the pictures, so young, innocent, and vulnerable. Heather had somehow succeeded in capturing the story of one whose trust in the world had been shaken but who was still able to marvel and love. Violet's gaze back then had been filled with painful hope. Heather had painted her like a promise to the future. Compared with that, it hurt Chloe's heart to look at the young woman today. Violet was still beautiful. Her expression still stark. Yet Eric Fence had needed only a few years to rob her of her hope and destroy her future. Violet Fence was hard, alert, and knowing. Chloe thought she sensed rage behind her resignation. She saw Violet as a warrior, even if Violet didn't see herself that way.

Chloe wondered how Heather would paint the young woman now. She often admitted to herself that she missed Heather painfully. She pined for the cocoon of harmony and mutual understanding that had shielded her and Heather since their childhood. Heather and Chloe had not always been of the same opinion, but their arguments had never been as bitter as the fighting that flared up again and again with Colin. Chloe didn't want to fight constantly. It was strenuous to weigh every word every moment of the day in order not to chide Colin constantly. She could feel his annoyance and suspicion when she entered the stables and watched the men as they worked with the horses.

Colin now acted as a trainer, which Chloe regarded skeptically. Her husband had no experience with racehorses even though his cavalry training was excellent and he was an exceptional rider. If the other horse owners entrusted their animals to him, they hardly had anything to which they could object. Yet her husband's often brutal manner of treating the horses did bother her, and a few of his training methods were questionable. Chloe knew that Eric and the apprentices called her a nitpicker and chronic know-it-all. Chloe was tired of the tension. She yearned to let herself sink down again, to feel Heather's cool hand on her forehead, and to be able to talk openly.

She could write her friend, and she often enough made an attempt to do so. But whenever she sat at her desk with pen in hand, she was frozen. Chloe simply could not manage to describe her daily life as she felt about it. Her letters fell into endless descriptions of horses and social events, a bit about Violet, a lot about Rosie.

Chloe's pride numbed her fingers. She could not admit that her life with Colin Coltrane was a singular disappointment, her marriage a singular folly.

Chapter 4

Heather Coltrane fought her way through the commitments Chloe had entered into for the gallery before her wedding. She felt tired and exploited. With Chloe, she would have even enjoyed the work to prepare the exhibitions and private viewings. But Chloe was the more extroverted of the two women. She had organized the viewings and receptions, and she graciously handled the artists and their often-difficult companions and family members. Chloe also had been the one to advise customers on their artwork purchases.

In the past, Heather had usually only helped hang the pictures and schedule dinners and entertainment for the artists and their companions. Now, however, all of these responsibilities fell to Heather. She tended to them but without real enthusiasm. She liked the gallery, but she wanted to paint more than anything. And she longed for someone close to her.

Heather wanted Chloe.

***

Her discontent and tension resolved in a flood of tears when Violet's first letter arrived from Invercargill. With the same delivery was a letter from Chloe.

Both women seemed happy. Heather tried to convince herself that she must likewise be happy because her friends had found their way to each other, and Chloe was taking care of Violet. Yet she was by no means happy, instead inwardly churning and cut to the quick. Chloe had her beloved husband, she had the stud farm, and now Violet and her children too. Heather had nothing.

Angry about her jealousy, ashamed of her resentment, deathly unhappy, and lonely, she barricaded herself in one of the gallery's side rooms. Between crates of unpacked pictures, she cried her eyes out. There were other things she should have been doing—most urgent of which was to hang the unpacked pictures for the exhibition of work by an artist from Paris—or rather, she was from Russia and lived in Paris. Svetlana Sergeyevna painted unique filigree landscapes, which enchanted the viewer. Heather imagined her as a sort of fairy who hardly touched the ground over which she walked. The London gallerist with whom Chloe had organized another exhibition had recommended that Chloe and Heather exhibit her work before she was too well known and her art too expensive. All the artist needed was a bit of money for travel and a place to stay in Dunedin.

Chloe had naturally seized the opportunity and offered the guest room in their apartment to Miss Sergeyevna. Now, without Chloe, Heather would have to deal with a total stranger who probably did not even speak English.

***

Everything had gone wrong leading up to the exhibition. The paintings had arrived before the artist. While Heather should already have hung them since the private viewing was that evening, she knew from experience there would be trouble. Artists never liked how the gallerist arranged their pictures. Plus, there were so many, there wasn't enough wall space to hang them all. Added to which, the wine had not yet been delivered, the cook who was supposed to prepare hors d'oeuvres had not been in contact, and the Dunloes' Maori housemaid who was to help serve the guests was late. If she did not come soon, Heather would have to polish the glasses herself. And now, these letters from Chloe and Violet.

Heather knew she had to pull herself together, but she simply couldn't. She cried, cried, and cried.

***

"Oh! Here is someone after all." A deep voice startled Heather. "And I thought they leave my pictures all alone with open door so that someone can steal."

Heather looked up and saw a large pale face, framed by an abundance of carrot-red hair. So red that the color could not actually be natural. Heather imagined only actresses and whores dyed their hair. And this woman wore her flood of hair loose. It fell in thick locks over her massive shoulders. Everything about Svetlana Sergeyevna was abundant. She was not fat, but tall and thick. Her face was broad, her lips full. Beneath strong eyebrows and long eyelashes, blue eyes popped out, round and soft. They gave her face a somewhat astonished, almost childlike and friendly expression. She eyed the sobbing Heather sympathetically.

"How one can cry when such beautiful pictures hang in next room?" The woman smiled, putting an index finger under Heather's chin and raising her head. "Is no reason to be sad. World is beautiful."

Heather could have said something to that, but she was about to die of embarrassment in front of this woman. Obviously, this was the artist, her guest of honor. And she—

"I . . . forgive me, Miss Sergeyevna. I was supposed to have picked you up from the train. And the pictures, they don't all fit in the exhibition space. That is, if I hang them all, they'll be too close together. They don't have the same effect, you know."

Heather had to stop crying. Svetlana Sergeyevna reached into the pocket of her wide dress. Clearly, she rejected corsets. Her gown resembled a caftan, and it shimmered in shades of blue. She produced a handkerchief and handed it to Heather.

"For that don't cry. No one must pick me up. I am not packet, am I? So far have I always found my way. And better too many pictures than few, right? We sell simply five, six, and then hang new ones. Not bad. For that you cry?"

Svetlana Sergeyevna smiled. At least she did not seem to be difficult.

Heather shook her head. Please excuse me, Miss Sergeyevna. You must think me hysterical. I wasn't crying for that. It's just, the cook hasn't come, or the maid, or the wine, and I haven't yet labeled the pictures, and . . ."

None of that sounded much more reasonable. Heather tried to breathe deeply.

The Russian laughed, the sound deep and booming like her speaking voice. She had more in common with a bear than a fairy. "Are the people coming for food? Are the people coming for wine? Nonsense, coming for pictures. And there is time. We can cook ourselves. We buy caviar; we make blini. Very Russian, people will love. You don't cry, Mrs. Boulder?"

Heather burst into tears again and found herself in a bear hug. Embarrassed, she freed herself.

"I'm sorry, Miss Sergeyevna. I'm Heather Coltrane. Mrs. Boulder, um, left me, us."

"Svetlana. You say Svetlana. Or Lana. Is shorter. What means 'left'? She dead?"

Heather sounded incredibly stupid again. How could she express herself so ineptly? Blushing, she corrected herself. "No, no, of course not. She just, she married."

Svetlana looked at Heather probingly. Then she smiled. "My dear," she blurted out. "My dear, the one often is not better than the other."

***

Half an hour later, Heather and Lana had already shared many laughs. Heather could not recall acting so boisterously with anyone since Chloe's departure. And now the problems seemed to solve themselves on their own. The cook did not appear, but the Maori girl did. Heather sent her straight to the wine merchant to remind him of the delivery while she went shopping with Lana. A gourmet grocer had salmon and caviar, the milkman had cream, and the tiny pancakes, which occupied Lana's time until the exhibition, only required water and flour. Before she took her position at the stove, Lana helped Heather label the pictures. The Russian artist thought Heather's selection brilliant.

"Yet you are not gallerist, you artist. Mrs. Boulder wrote me you paint portraits."

Lana seemed about to fall over with laughter when Heather admitted that most of her models had four paws or hooves.

"But you know they loved," she explained. "Friend of mine, Alicia in London, paints portraits of rich women. They often sad. Is hard to paint beautifully when not loved."

"Sad because they're married?" Heather giggled.

The wine had arrived in the meantime, and Lana had opened a bottle straightaway. After two glasses, the two women were already a bit tipsy.

"One can be happy married," Svetlana said, fluttering her eyes innocently and likewise giggling. "I believe we must eat a few blinis. Otherwise all people think we drunk vodka."

"I'll show you a few portraits of two-legged models soon," Heather promised. "When we're in the apartment. Heavens, yes, we should change. The guests are coming in an hour. Where are your things?"

Heather instructed the housemaid to polish the glasses, hoping she would leave the wine bottle untouched while she did. Lana, however, quickly solved that problem.

"Let's take wine. Helps select clothes."

Though Heather doubted that, she was so tipsy that she did not stop her new friend from sticking the bottle under her arm. Lana followed her a few streets to Heather's apartment over the Gold Mine Boutique and admired the décor.

"Here you lived with Chloe?"

Heather nodded, again a bit sad. To change the subject, she showed Lana her portraits of Violet. The Russian eyed them with unexpected seriousness.

"This beautiful," she said reverently. "You real artist. And this girl very beautiful, but very, very, I have a bit of fear for this girl. Is very good picture. Picture makes happy and sad. Touches the heart. Like girl has touched you."

Svetlana eyed Heather with a look she could not place. Questioning? Tender?

"I liked her a lot," Heather said stiffly, "like, like a daughter."

Lana nodded. "What happened to her?" she asked, and smiled when she saw Heather's face cloud over again. "Let me guess. She married."

Heather laughed a little bitterly. "I'll tell you another time. Now, we must hurry. Here's the guest room. I have an iron if your clothes are very wrinkled, but no housemaid."

Lana shrugged. "I also no housemaid. Too expensive. I can iron alone."

She ran into the guest room, only to emerge again at once. Over her arm, she carried a dress in various blue and gold tones—she was dressed in only a one-piece undergarment, the top portion of which replaced a bra; below, it turned into wide pants ruffled with lace above the knee. Lana's ample bosom showed through. Heather gasped for air.

"You are not shocked, are you?" Lana asked casually as she filled Heather's iron with glowing coals.

Heather was still wearing her afternoon dress. She was wavering between two evening dresses. She preferred the smoky blue to the dark red, but for that she would have to tighten her corset. She was not sure if she could do that alone. Perhaps if Lana was already running around here half-naked, it would not bother her.

Heather blushed as she asked her new friend to lace her corset. She and Chloe had always done that for each other. Heather smiled at the memory of their first corsets. The girls had tied them so tight that they thought they would suffocate.

"Me it doesn't bother, but you. Do you not know is unhealthy? Ruins whole body, say doctors."

"Whoever wants to be beautiful has to suffer. It's always been that way."

Lana had the laces of her corset in her hand, but she did not pull on them. Instead, Heather felt her warm breath on her neck. "You no need to suffer to be beautiful. You gorgeous. Always."

Heather held her breath as Lana's lips brushed her shoulder. Lana kissed her tenderly. Heather felt the hair on her skin stand up and warmth overflow from her. She felt light but also firmly rooted in the earth. Her body seemed to vibrate toward Lana's. Her heart raced.

"You like?" asked Lana.

Heather nodded.

"You done before? With Chloe?"

Heather did not know how to answer that. She had shared a bed with Chloe, had fallen asleep cuddling with her, had kissed her at night, and had stroked her a little. But this here? In the bright light of day, their bodies hardly covered?

"Not really," she whispered.

Lana laughed. "Then you virgin," she declared. "I will show you how goes."

Svetlana opened Heather's corset, and Heather thought she would collapse with desire as Lana's fingers moved in small circular motions along her spine while her lips caressed her neck. She had to pull herself together. In less than an hour, half of Dunedin would be expecting her in the gallery.

"Later, then," Lana said when Heather pointed out with a trembling voice how time was trickling away. The Russian laughed, reaching for the laces to Heather's corset. "Now I tie you up like mail packet, and later I unwrap you like present."

***

The viewing for Svetlana Sergeyevna's exhibition was a high point of Dunedin's social calendar—not just because of her artwork but also the painter's relaxed cheerfulness and openness and the easygoing, self-assured introduction by the gallerist.

Sean Coltrane had rarely seen his sister so excited and happy. He attributed her mood with slight amazement to the news from Invercargill. Chloe Coltrane was caring for Violet and her children. Sean would have expected Heather to be jealous, but his sister was even more bighearted than he could have imagined. For Violet, the move to Invercargill was surely an improvement. Compared to the shack she had dwelled in, the servants' wing of the "little castle" must have seemed like heaven. Fundamentally, nothing had changed about her situation. *No true love.* Violet's sad gaze would not leave Sean's head, nor would her touching beauty. Over the last weeks, he had repeatedly caught himself visiting Heather's apartment just to view the pictures of Violet even though she had changed since they were painted.

Now he could not even innocently suggest to Heather they pay Violet a visit: Sean had been elected to Parliament in Wellington.

"That's very good news," was all he had said when Heather showed him the letters. "Please, send both Chloe and Violet my love."

***

Heather and Lana returned to Heather's apartment around midnight, elated and intoxicated from success and the wine. The exhibition had been a huge success. Heather had sold eight of the thirty-two paintings already. Yet that was not all that made that evening unique. Much more exciting were Lana's fingers, which skillfully unwrapped her "present." It took endlessly long before all the laces and buttons of Heather's dress were undone, but all the while Lana's lips brushed over Heather's hair and her tongue caressed her ear. Among a thousand caresses, she freed Heather from her corset.

Heather blushed to her core when she stood naked before Lana in the candlelight, and she held her breath as Lana undressed.

"You so beautiful," Lana said in her deep voice, undoing Heather's hair with trembling fingers. "You Eve in paradise."

Heather led Lana into the bedroom. She could not wait much longer.

"If I'm Eve, then who are you?" she whispered between kisses.

"The snake, what thought you? This time we don't let Adam play."

447

Chapter 5

"You really want to leave?" Heather was close to tears.

The last few months, she had lived as if in a fairy tale. Though Lana did not look the part, for Heather, she had been the fairy who saved her. The artist had led her into the secrets of the love between two bodies at once so similar and yet so different. Feelings stormed through Heather she had never thought possible—she followed her friend into the realm of desire, and she learned how she could lead Lana there. In the beginning, she had been fearful and bashful, but Lana had made love to her ever more imaginatively and fearlessly. In comparison to what Lana and Heather did with each other at night, the little intimacies with Chloe had been harmless. No one seemed to find it strange that Heather went to evening invitations and theater performances with Lana. No one thought anything salacious about friendship between two women. Heather found that surprising and pleasing. It did not surprise Lana.

"They don't believe women capable of anything," she said in French, a language in which she expressed herself much more easily than English and which Heather also spoke. "We don't feel anything in bed. That's what even our mothers tell us. Just lie still and endure. Then, as recompense, we get a screaming brat."

Lana playfully traced the curves of Heather's body. They had just made love, and neither of them had lain still in doing so. Only now did Heather rest in Lana's arms.

Heather shrugged. "I wouldn't have anything against a baby," she said.

Lana tickled her with her long red hair. "Then find yourself a husband. There are supposed to be some men with whom it's fun. Just not for me."

"So, you've tried it?" asked Heather, shocked. She sat up.

Lana rolled her eyes. "I've tried just about everything. But so far no fruit has been as sweet as you." Laughing, she pushed herself onto Heather and began kissing her anew. "I can't get enough of you."

Heather felt all the more unhappy when Lana announced she planned to travel to Christchurch and see the plains—"Maybe I portray a few sheep"—and then continue to the west coast. "I want see mountains; I want see west coast. There supposed to be rocks that look like blini."

"The Pancake Rocks." Heather smiled through tears.

Lana looked at her. "You cry again already? Why? If you don't want stay alone, why you not come with me?"

Heather raised her head, confused. "You want to take me with you? But, but—"

"Gladly. Is more fun traveling when we are two. You can also portray a sheep."

"But the gallery, my work."

Lana shook her head. "At moment, you not have work. You only paint me."

That was true. Heather had made a few sketches of Lana and was thinking of a series similar to the portraits of Violet. Once again, she had the feeling she was able to capture a beloved person on canvas. It was intoxicating and confusing at once.

"Gallery don't make you happy. Now empty, anyway. So, come."

Lana was right. Her pictures had sold, down to the last watercolor, and there wasn't another exhibition soon. Heather could close the gallery any day. Besides, spring was almost over, and the art trade stagnated in the summer. Heather could even use the travel opportunity to buy Maori art. Although she had never been interested in the natives' pictures and artifacts herself, Chloe had always wanted to venture there.

"And you really want to have me around?" Heather asked once again.

Lana kissed her. "You little kiwi. You sometimes like this bird that digs in at night. I always have to dig you out again. But is nothing, is fun for me. We will see birds, Heather, and mountains and sea. We will have beautiful time."

***

449

For the first time in her life, Heather did something spontaneous and rash. She closed the gallery and went traveling with Lana. At Lana's request, they did not take the train, instead harnessing Heather's highbred horse to a light chaise, so they would be unconstrained. Heather showed her friend Christchurch— "Looks like England. Boring"—and then took her into the vastness of the plains. She knew several sheep breeders who always welcomed guests, and despite some nerves, she introduced Lana to the Barringtons and Wardens. The women stayed a few days at Kiward Station, where Heather painted portraits of two horses and a dog, and Lana created wondrous landscape watercolors.

To Lana's confusion, Gwyneira Warden paid Heather almost as much for the paintings of her animals as Lana's entire exhibition had made. Her own pictures found favor with Marama, a Maori woman who murmured something about them like, "You paint my songs."

Lana found the farm and its residents peculiar. Heather laughed.

"You're peculiar," she explained to Lana. "The others are normal."

In a way, that was true. Heather loved Lana, but she didn't see her as a part of herself or even as a true complement. That had been different with Chloe. Chloe was for Heather a sort of second self. A bit more open and lighthearted, true, but similar: modest and friendly, polite and proper, always disciplined. Lana, in contrast, sometimes seemed like a barely tamed wild thing. She spoke her mind and did so loudly. She could be moody, and she turned every guest room into a colorful confusion of scarves, jewelry, and exotic scents.

When they were in their room, she tended to walk around undressed. As a rule, she slept naked and urged Heather to do the same. In Christchurch, she made Heather's corset disappear and dragged her friend through the shops to find more comfortable clothing. Heather did feel decidedly comfortable in the empire-waist dresses on which she decided. She didn't look fat at all. Instead, the draped fabric emphasized her slender figure. However, these styles did raise questions from hostesses like Gwyneira Warden and Lady Barrington about whether these were the latest designs from the Gold Mine Boutique.

"My mother would kill me," Heather said.

Lara laughed. "Is nonsense. On contrary. Without corset, we live longer."

Lana did not possess even a hint of shyness when it came to men or women. She never lowered her gaze or even blushed. When the women turned in the direction of Arthur's Pass, Lana insisted on driving alongside the new train line and asked bold questions of the construction workers. She accepted an invitation to eat with them and laughed boomingly with the men, letting her gaze wander over their powerful muscles. Heather tried her hand at a few drawings of the crystal-clear streams in the beech forests while Lana unpacked her paints and drafted one of her crazy pictures, in which a train inched its way across a filigreed bridge between heaven and earth, mountains and lakes.

Julian Redcliff found the picture so accomplished that he bought it on the spot. Lana asked for just as much as Mrs. Warden had paid for a portrait of her dogs and was shocked when the construction leader accepted the price without negotiating.

Heather shrugged. "People will pay any price for a picture of what they love," she remarked, and made another sketch of Lana on her paper.

"Then I should take money from you for modeling," she said in French.

"Or paint me," Heather suggested shyly. Sometimes it hurt her that Lana made no attempts at that.

Lana gave her a kiss on the forehead with a laugh. "I'll paint you soon, dearest. I prefer painting something when it's complete."

Heather frowned. "So, you'll paint me in my coffin?" she asked.

Lana laughed again. "Just wait. Be patient. You'll see your portrait."

***

Heather's horse pulled the chaise effortlessly over the pass, and they were treated to the natural beauty of full summer. They reveled in the gold of the hills overgrown with tussock grass, traced the structure of the rocks that looked as if they had been polished, and let the cloud formations over the snow-capped mountains inspire them. When they reached the west coast, which Heather, relying on Violet's letters, had imagined covered in coal dust and Lana imagined inhabited by whales and seals, neither found confirmation. Lana and Heather kept their distance from the coal-mining towns and dove into the green fog of the rain forests. Heather portrayed Lana in a dress of ferns. Lana lay on the moist, lichen-covered ground and looked up at the tree-high, feathery green plants.

"Those are kauri trees?" she asked.

Heather shook her head. "No, those are ferns. The kauri trees are on the North Island."

"We'll go there next," Lana said.

She laughed boisterously at the whirlpool in the Pancake Rocks, was enthusiastic about the seals and the colony of boobies, and painted the birds as residents of their own city lost to dreams at the end of the world. The women floated along the coast on a fishing boat they had rented, admiring the forested cliff sides and waterfalls. Finally, their path took them to Blenheim, where they boarded the ferry to Wellington.

"I don't get seasick," Lana claimed, only to spend half the journey hanging over the railing.

Heather grew increasingly sure of herself and more easygoing. She stopped wondering what people thought of her. Lana did her good, though she still missed Chloe. Again and again, she caught herself viewing this lake, that rock, or some fern through Chloe's eyes, and now they were on the North Island, where her friend had lived with Terrence.

The capital, Wellington, almost seemed familiar to her. After all, Chloe had described it down to the last detail. Lana and Heather explored the city. They admired the government building, which was supposed to be one of the largest wooden buildings in the world, and visited Sean in his office on the second floor. Lana seemed a bit astonished when a strong-looking Maori, his face emblazoned with a warrior's tattoos, opened the door for them. Heather was not especially taken aback. After all, her brother had often represented the Maori tribes in Dunedin on questions of land. She was more astounded by the young man's perfect English and his exceptional manners.

While Heather and Lana waited, the Maori buried himself in the mountain of documents on his desk in Sean's anteroom. Apparently, he was serving as a secretary.

Sean was more than a little surprised at the visit. He did not know Heather to be someone who enjoyed traveling, and he marveled at her heartfelt friendship with Lana. Heather grew nervous under his probing gaze. For the first time, she had the feeling that someone sensed something of their true relationship.

"Have you heard anything from Chloe?"

Heather hated herself for it, but she blushed. Why was Sean suddenly taking such an interest in Chloe?

"I, um . . ."

She had written Chloe a few times, but always just postcards with information about the trip. She had not received any letters herself. How would she? Lana and Heather rarely remained in the same place longer than a few days.

"And, uh, from Violet?"

Heather relaxed again. So that was the way the wind was blowing. Sean's interest in her former ward had caught her notice in Dunedin.

"I haven't, but I'm going to visit her as soon as I return, and then I'll report back to you. I promise." Heather spoke quickly with feigned cheerfulness. "Are you, um, getting anywhere with women's suffrage?"

Sean shrugged. "First we need universal suffrage. As long as only landowners and taxpayers may vote, we Liberals are never going to win. And until we have a majority, there's also no chance for either the white or Maori women. Although, the Maori argue that their women already urgently need the vote because they do own land. We're doing our best in any case, and it won't be for lack of petitions. Amey Daldy is writing her fingers sore, not to mention Kate Sheppard. It'll happen, but it takes time. As with everything in politics." He sighed. "And so, now you're traveling around the North Island, Miss Sergeyevna? Looking for new motifs? I very much liked your exhibition back in Dunedin. And you, Heather, are you painting landscapes now?"

Heather blushed again. Sean was asking her why she was running around with Lana.

"Heather makes more portrait," Lana said. "These days paints me. But could also paint others, has great talent. Sees in soul. Heather, why you not try portrait from this, how you say, Maori? Your secretary, Mr. Coltrane, is Maori, no? Fascinating face. Why you have Maori as secretary?"

Heather did not know whether to be indignant at Lana's lack of tact or to marvel at her skilled change of subject.

Sean laughed. "Oh, Kupe is helpful because of his bilingualism. I wasn't, however, looking specifically for a Maori, just for a young law student. Kupe is still studying. The top of his class. His heritage was of secondary concern."

"Perhaps put in good word for us with him." Lana smiled. "We would like visit Maori tribe. Heather has interest in Maori art."

Lana casually laid her hand on Heather's thigh, and Heather grew hot under her loving gaze. Embarrassed, she shifted to the side.

Sean ignored the wordless exchange between the two women. He shook his head. "Kupe won't be able to help you there. Kupe doesn't have a tribe. He grew up in an orphanage. A tragic story, a victim of the thousand fights and misunderstandings in the relations between the Maori and *pakeha*. But you are traveling to Auckland, aren't you? You can speak to Matariki Drury there. She'll put you in contact with a tribe quickly."

Sean scratched an address on a piece of paper.

"You're in contact with Matariki?" Heather asked. "I thought she couldn't stand to hear the Coltrane name again."

For Heather and Chloe, it had seemed back then that the girl had left for Auckland above all to forget Colin Coltrane.

Sean furrowed his brow when Heather said as much. "I am in contact with Matariki almost weekly." Sean handed Heather her address. "She works for Amey Daldy; that is to say, she writes petitions. For women's suffrage, for the unions, for the establishment of relief offices. She's always thinking of something. Matariki is almost more ardent about it than Mrs. Daldy. Clearly, it's her dream job. Someday she'll probably take her seat as the first Maori woman in Parliament. And she's hardly likely to ever forget Colin—the kid looks an awful lot like him. Or our mother, as you'll see. It's going to be extremely good-looking someday either way."

"The kid?" asked Heather, blindsided. "You mean to say, he—"

Sean's eyes flashed. "Precisely," he said, "the little shit got her in a family way. Please pardon my language, ladies."

Svetlana shook with laughter. Until then, the young representative had seemed somewhat stiff, but now he showed some fire. "For that it takes two, Mr. Coltrane."

Sean nodded. "Matariki shares your perspective. She says she wanted the kid, that she was trying for one. Then, however, she realized Colin only actually wanted her money, and she left him. Then he fell in love with Chloe's money."

"Well, you like so much your brother, Mr. Coltrane," Svetlana teased. "You also speak so clearly in Parliament?"

"I try, Miss Sergeyevna." Sean smiled.

Heather sighed with relief when she saw the warmth in her brother's gaze. Clearly, he liked Svetlana. At that moment, there was a knock on the door, and Kupe entered.

"Excuse me, Mr. Coltrane, but Sir John Hall would like to speak with you in his office when you're done here. Can I inform his secretary when he can expect you?"

Sean smiled at him. "I'm coming at once, Kupe. By the way, you've just met my sister, Heather, and her friend Miss Sergeyevna. The two of them will soon be in Auckland to see Matariki Drury. Shall they take her your regards?"

A shadow crossed the tall Maori's otherwise friendly expression. "My thanks but no, Mr. Coltrane," he said stiffly. "I see no value in further contact with Miss Drury."

Sean shook his head. "Now, there's no cause to be so spiteful, Kupe. She knows you work for me. Every time she writes me, she tasks me with giving you her regards. We're all fighting the same fight. You can't hold a grudge against her forever."

The Maori bit his lower lip—a gesture Heather recognized from Matariki. Had the two of them once been close?

"You'll have to leave that to me, Mr. Coltrane," said Kupe.

Heather turned, embarrassed, to her brother. It was clearly time to change the subject.

"A child! Do Mother and Peter know? Does Chloe?"

Sean shrugged. "I'm sure Chloe doesn't know. She would not have kept it a secret from you, after all. As for Mother and Peter, I imagine it depends on whether Lizzie and Michael have told them. Matariki makes no secret of it, but she hasn't sent copies of the birth certificate either."

"What is it, anyway," Heather asked, "a boy or a girl?"

"A girl," Sean said, and was about to add something when Kupe interrupted angrily.

"Atamarie—sunrise. A Maori name for a *pakeha* child. A shame to Parihaka."

Kupe reached quickly for a few documents and left the room without another word.

Heather watched him go. "Impertinent fellow," she said.

Lana reached for Heather's hand. "I think he has simply very loved her."

***

"It doesn't matter to me, but perhaps you should not display it so clearly," Sean said a few weeks later. Heather and Lana had ended their trip across the North Island and planned to take the ferry to Blenheim the next day. They were spending their last evening with Sean. "If you always travel around with such a domineering woman, you're hardly likely to find a husband."

Sean had taken the women out for dinner, and the evening had so far passed quite harmoniously. Lana and Heather had described their North Island experiences. Lana raved about the beaches, the volcanoes, and the massive kauri trees to which she had devoted an entire picture cycle. Heather was most enthusiastic about her niece, Atamarie. She had just shown Sean the pictures she had painted of the little one. When Lana excused herself briefly, Sean asked Heather about her relationship to her friend.

"I've heard that women sometimes, with other women—I don't know how to put it. It seems your relationship with Lana . . . well, it seems rather intimate," Sean murmured.

Heather swallowed. "I love her," she said. "Do you have anything against that?" She tried to sound direct, but her words came out more like a girl asking her brother for permission.

Sean shook his head. "It's just," he continued, "it's strange. Women ought to love men, not other women. And I always thought you wanted children. Your devotion to Violet back then and now your excitement over Atamarie. You should marry."

Heather shook her head, letting her hair flap. She no longer wore her hair up primly, instead only tying it into a ponytail.

"But I don't want to," she said firmly. "I would never dare. When I think about marriage, I think about how Father used to beat Mother."

She pushed her plate away. As always when this image came to her, she felt sick.

Sean eyed her, shocked. "But you can't possibly remember that, Heather," he objected. "You were still so little."

"I remember it very well," Heather said fiercely. "I still remember how I hid under the covers and heard dull thumps. And the groans Mother tried to suppress. She did not want to frighten us by screaming. Besides, Sean, why aren't you married yet? Admit it: you're afraid. Just like me. Though I'm also afraid to be alone," she sighed. "I wish I could marry a woman."

Sean had to laugh and gestured with his chin at Lana who was walking toward them. All eyes followed her as she crossed the restaurant. Her breezy, colorful clothes, her height and her ample figure, her red hair, and her proud gaze seemed to spellbind people.

"Well, I wouldn't have it in me to ask her," he joked.

Heather smiled. "I don't need to worry about that. She already asked me if I'll go with her to Europe."

Sean looked at his sister. "And will you go?"

"Yes, she'll go." Lana seemed to have caught the last words when she reached the table. "She's artist. She cannot bury herself at end of world. You do not forever want to paint dogs and horses, Heather, do you? In Europe—London, Paris—there are so many like us. Women who paint and write. So many galleries, museums, art collectors. They will love you, little kiwi. We will have life that is big party."

Heather smiled and managed to allow Svetlana to lay her hand quite publicly on her own. One thing was clear: here, "at the end of the world," she could not pursue this relationship. Usually female friendships were not scrutinized as long as everyone involved preserved a modicum of discretion. Svetlana, however, seemed to prefer the straightforward and open. Perhaps that was not a problem in Paris, but in New Zealand, people would talk about them. And Heather did not want to be the subject of gossip and mockery.

"Should I go?" she whispered to Sean when she hugged him good-bye.

Sean kissed her softly on the cheek. "If nothing's holding you here."

Chapter 6

Letters from Chloe and Violet were waiting for Heather in Dunedin. Violet sounded almost euphoric: she liked working for Chloe; Rosie occasionally said a few words and helped with the horses; Roberta and Joe were thriving. She wrote nothing about Eric, but she had never written much about him. Heather still did not know how their quick marriage came about.

Chloe reported about the horses in great detail, about her neighbors in Invercargill, and about Rosie for whom she was head over heels. She seemed to have infected the little girl with her enthusiasm for horses. Both were looking forward to Dancing Jewel's first foal. Other letters were filled with landscape descriptions—the beauty of the fjord lands, the craggy mountains, the evergreen forests, even the diverse world of birds. She wrote practically nothing about Colin. Heather read the letters again and again to pick up attitudes, feelings, fears. The friends had shared everything their whole lives, but now there was nothing more there. Chloe's letters sounded like those of a stranger.

"We should go," Heather said to Lana after she had read Chloe's treatise on whether the high knee movement of a hackney was desirable in race trotters. "Something is off."

Lana shrugged. "When they marry, they become always off. Is way of world. You cannot change."

"But I—" Heather rubbed her forehead. Chloe's letters gave her headaches.

Lana took her in her arms. "Look here, little kiwi: she now has husband, has horses, has house. She thinks no more on you."

Heather shook her head. "That can't be. When she was married to Terrence, her letters sounded very different. Then they sounded happy."

Lana rolled her eyes. "And now?" she asked. "They sound unhappy? Look, kiwi: She does invite you? Wants to know about your life? Ask about me? She does nothing. Does only duty. Duty demand good girl write letters to friends. So is it, little kiwi. And now no more thinking of Chloe. Think of London. Here, look."

She shoved one of her own letters at Heather. It was from a gallerist in London. While they were traveling, she had sent him her latest work, and the paintings had created quite a stir in London. Everyone wanted something from Svetlana Sergeyevna. The gallerist urged her to come back to Europe and show herself in public.

"People are extraordinarily enthusiastic about you. They're just waiting to introduce you in high society."

Heather read this with a prick of envy. So, Lana would become truly famous, while Heather painted babies and animals.

Lana was ready to book passage on one of the new steamships. "And now you decide. You come with me?"

***

In October 1884, Heather Coltrane and Svetlana Sergeyevna boarded a ship—a direct route to London. Heather informed Chloe in a formal letter, and she answered with no less stiff wishes for safe and pleasant travel.

Heather cried again, but she realized there really was nothing holding her in New Zealand anymore. She was ready for love with Lana and for the most exciting time of her life.

***

As the gallerist had described, London welcomed Svetlana with open arms. There was a suite in one of the best hotels waiting for them. The days and nights were busy with exhibitions and viewings and concerts and theater. Lana introduced Heather as often as possible as a highly talented young artist.

Lana's gallerist was not yet fully convinced by Heather's work. "You have talent," he pronounced, "but you need to develop it further. So far, these works

Sarah Lark

are too cloying. The children's portraits are endearing, but they're not art. Go to Paris with Miss Sergeyevna, continue studying, and then we'll see."

Heather found London fascinating, but Svetlana was bored with the British metropolis after a few weeks. "It is always same," she said, complaining about the small talk in the palaces and elegant town houses to which people invited the artists. "What horse has won derby, who marries Princess So-and-So, and what does queen do. Queen does always the same. She is boringest person under sun. I yearn for Paris. We go to Paris and rent studio together."

Svetlana had earned more than enough money to afford a studio in the most sought-after quarter, and Heather had no need to do any less. Kathleen had furnished her with a generous monthly allowance although, or precisely because, she did not particularly like Svetlana.

"Don't become dependent on her," Kathleen had advised her daughter. "Don't cling to her. Because it'll turn out just like with Chloe. Eventually, she'll find a man." Kathleen blushed. She knew that neither Svetlana nor Heather was interested in men, but she was too much a lady to say it aloud. "And then you'll be written off again."

Heather had thought a lot about her mother's words. Had she really clung to Chloe? Had she been a burden? Heather took the warning to heart and expressly kept a distance from Svetlana in London. She hardly seemed to notice. Her life as a rich woman and famous painter took up too much of her attention. Her newfound wealth sent her from one shopping spree to another, purchasing clothes for Heather and herself and so many extravagant pieces of furniture that Heather could only shake her head.

"How do you mean to get all that to Paris? And where will we put it? Do you want to rent a palace? Just for the two of us?"

Svetlana laughed and spun her around. "Not just for the two of us, little kiwi. We will have company every night. We will celebrate. You will know great women painters. We will see big exhibitions, Salon de Paris and Salon des Indépendants. It is exciting; you will see."

Paris was the European art center in the 1880s. For the first time, Heather saw impressionist paintings and was fascinated. So, Svetlana invited Berthe Morisot, an impressionist specializing in portraits, to their housewarming party. Lana also invited Rosa Bonheur, and Heather was awed by the great painter of nature and animals. Mademoiselle Bonheur, who had known Svetlana for

460

a while, greeted her euphorically with kisses on the cheek and proved to be enraptured by Heather.

"She's just as beautiful as you described her." She smiled and immediately introduced Heather to her own companion.

In artists' circles, no one seemed to find it strange or shocking when female or male couples lived together. Exchanges of partners seemed to occur relatively frequently, and no one appeared to be familiar with discretion. Embarrassed, Heather followed an angry confrontation between the young sculptor Camille Claudel and Rodin, her mentor and lover. She saw how Svetlana's friend Alicia, the portrait artist who painted unhappy women and now lived in Paris, comforted her models. And she heard how no subject was too intimate to be talked about with all of their friends. Heather tried at first to befriend the women, but she soon learned that both Svetlana and Alicia were possessive and jealous. After that, Heather kept aloof of other women when she knew that they loved women.

Lana dedicated herself to the production of large-sized oil paintings, for which, until then, she had not been able to afford the materials and studio space. Heather finally ventured to show Mary Cassatt her pictures. Mary was an American and did not indicate whether she preferred the love of men or women. She lived with her mother and sister, so Svetlana did not react grumpily when Heather visited the artist alone. Mary Cassatt praised her new works, particularly a picture cycle of Violet.

"That's still a bit conventional. You need to paint freely. There's photography now; conventional portraiture survives in that. Express what you see within people, and you can certainly do it. This girl here"—she pointed to a picture of Violet—"is pretty enough to bring you to tears. But you could put more into the painting."

She laughed at Heather's portrait of Svetlana. "Oh no, dear, you're better off throwing that away. You're not looking at our Svetlana with the eyes of an artist. You're looking at her with love in your eyes. God in heaven, you paint her, and she's a whole lot of woman, like the Virgin Mary." Heather did not quite know what she meant by that but was too shy to ask. She was, however, overjoyed when Mary declared herself prepared to teach her. "Join our circle. I'll introduce you to Degas and the other *indépendants*. And go to the museums. Paint copies of the great masters, feel their genius. It takes a while to find one's own style."

***

461

The craze for Svetlana's work lasted about two years. During that time, Heather sat dutifully in the studio beside her and imitated paintings by Titian and Rubens. At first, she had no success, and, disheartened, she stopped painting her own works. After some time, however, her imitations turned out similar enough to the originals to fool someone.

"Now you're going to have to decide whether you're going to make a career as an artist or a forger," Alicia said. "Get to work. You're a portrait artist. So, show us what you can do."

Heather would have most liked to paint Svetlana again, but she still had Mary's laughter in her ear. So, she painted Alicia. A few days later, Mary and Berthe, Svetlana, and Alicia stood before the finished watercolor, discussing it.

"Everyone sees something different in the picture." Heather was surprised by the varied responses. "Sometimes more than I do myself. Is that—"

"That's exactly what you want, Heather Coltrane. You're on your way," Mary said.

***

While Heather slowly developed her own style, Svetlana's star began to fade. True, it had been her wish to fill big canvases with life, but as it turned out, she had little talent for oil painting. Svetlana's dreamworlds were miniatures. Her small pictures had worked like crystal balls the viewer could dive into, searching for secrets and discoveries. In large format, they seemed by contrast clumsy, unnatural, and tacky—of which no one dared make Svetlana aware. Only her friends' male companions showed deprecatory smiles, but since Svetlana reacted to every criticism with a hysterical fit, they, too, remained silent.

"Although really these studio parties are also supposed to serve for a bit of mutual critique," Mary observed regretfully. Her companion, Edgar Degas, had withdrawn silently with a glass of champagne to a corner where he did not have to look at any of Svetlana's botched efforts. "At Lana's, all we compliment now is the quality of the champagne."

There was nothing to hold against that in any case. Lana still made good money, and her pictures sold well, though the gallerist decided to forego private viewings and sold them directly to foreign investors. The hope was the value would increase, but the art world had no scruples, and one could sell anything on hand to an eager buyer. Occasionally, it reminded Heather of her brother's horse business, and she thought painfully of Chloe, with whom she still dutifully exchanged vapid letters. Violet wrote much more vividly, and here Heather thought she could also read something between the lines. Violet mentioned disagreements, sometimes expressing concern that Rosie could get caught in the middle of a quarrel.

> *I would never have thought it, but my shy little Rosie has grown into a really brave young groom. All that's lacking is for her to wear pants, but Mr. Coltrane prohibited that rather strictly when Mrs. Coltrane suggested it. Rosie cleans the horses and harnesses them, and she drives them on the track at a speed that scares me. She talks to the horses, too, though almost never with us. She can get by with pointing. Sometimes she seems to do things better than Mr. Coltrane's grooms. Mrs. Coltrane enjoys that, but I worry.*

Heather would have liked to ask for more details, but it took months for a letter from New Zealand to reach France and vice versa. This kept a real conversation from coming to be.

Besides, Heather was busy with her own life. Astoundingly, she profited from Lana's decline. The visitors to their studio expressed platitudes about Lana's work, but they were effusive about Heather's painting. Heather took in praise and censure, accepting help and making use of critique. She was shocked when Berthe suggested they exhibit together.

"Your pictures are good, but if you exhibit alone, it will fizzle. This is Paris. There are so many exhibitions that no one will come to see a novice. But if you provide the, let's say, sideshow for me . . ."

At first, Lana was upset by the arrangement. "You are good enough to do alone. And if you exhibit with someone, then do with me. What this person thinks of us."

"Berthe paints women's portraits," Heather objected. "Just like me. They go together. With your paintings—"

"You now want to say my paintings you don't like."

Svetlana flew into a rage. She must have recognized that she had passed the zenith of her fame but wasn't prepared to find her way back to her earlier style.

"I just mean your subjects don't match with my work."

"You not do it. I say it, the end," Lana said, shaking her head wildly.

Heather had tears in her eyes when she told Berthe of Lana's decision.

Berthe Morisot frowned. "Pardon me, Heather, but did she paint the pictures, or did you? Where you exhibit your pictures, only you decide. Don't be ordered around, Heather. Free yourself from Lana."

***

Svetlana reacted with an outburst of anger worthy of a great tragic actress when Berthe's gallerist sent for Heather's pictures. That night, Lana was throwing another party, and their first guests landed right in the middle of their furious argument.

"If you take away pictures, you can go with them now," Lana screamed.

Heather began to pack her things. Half an hour later, Lana begged her tearfully to forgive her. Heather unpacked.

Her exhibition with Berthe was a respectable entrance into the Parisian art world. Heather sold all of her pictures, which surprised Svetlana, who was both proud and irritated. Then, Heather announced her plans to travel to Verona, Rome, Siena, and Madrid.

"I need to study the old masters up close," Heather explained, "and now I have the money to do so."

She did not reveal that she also had the money before. She had still not come close to spending everything Kathleen had sent to her. Heather, however, wanted to support herself.

"You want to leave me?" Svetlana asked.

Heather shook her head. "Why don't you come with me? It's going to be summer, Lana. Nothing will be happening here. Close the studio for a few months and travel with me."

"And then will paint my pictures who? Who supposed to earn living?"

Heather was silent. The last few months, she had been shopping for them. Lana earned only just enough to pay for the studio.

"I came with you once," Heather said. "Now you come with me."

"That was very different," Svetlana declared. "You should prefer to stay here, work still a bit on your portraits." It sounded patronizing.

"I'm leaving in a week."

"All alone?" asked Svetlana. It almost sounded malicious.

Heather squared herself. "All alone," she said.

***

Heather would not remain alone. She was prepared to gather together all her courage to go alone, but her friends advised her against it.

"All alone, you'd fall into disrepute. They won't rent you a hotel room," Mary said.

The other women confirmed this.

"It's madness," said Alicia. "You can occupy any wedding suite in the best hotels with your lover and no one looks at you askance. Yet a woman traveling alone isn't acceptable."

"What am I supposed to do now?" Heather asked indecisively.

Alicia smiled. "We'll find you a companion. I have two suggestions right off: Mademoiselle Patout, a daughter by profession. Her father is a well-off merchant who caters to his favorite child's every whim. She's a student of mine, but I really would be happy to be rid of her. Now and again I do simply need some sleep. The second is Madame Mireille de Lys, high nobility, very, very unhappily married, and very interested in art. Still a bit prudish in bed. You really have to arouse her."

Heather had stopped marveling at Alicia's extravagant conquests. She decided on Madame de Lys—precisely because she hoped not to have to arouse her. She did not want to cheat on Svetlana. Though it did annoy her that Svetlana had remained away for several nights since Heather had announced her trip, and Mireille de Lys was a delicate beauty.

Heather's good intentions did not last long, particularly as Mireille was out for an adventure that went far beyond art. The first night she came to Heather's hotel room, and after that they booked a shared room. Mireille was desperate for love but completely inexperienced, and, for the first time, Heather was in the role of seductress. She quickly realized it was fun to carry Svetlana's techniques over to Mireille. She learned quickly—too quickly perhaps. By Verona, Heather was already too tame for the hot-blooded lady. At the very first studio party to which the women were invited—Mary, Berthe, and Alicia had given Heather a whole list of friendly artists who would be excited to meet her—Mireille disappeared with a blonde American woman, never to be seen again.

In the Castelvecchio, Heather ran into an "English rose" who did not speak a word of Italian and was completely lost in Verona; but she quoted Shakespeare wonderfully and wanted to study art. The girl was named Emma, but she hated the name, so Heather called her Juliet. Emma in turn called her Romea, and the two explored Verona on the trail of the famous lovers. Finally, they traveled on to Florence, rented a studio, and began to work seriously.

Unfortunately, Emma proved completely untalented artistically. Heather was almost relieved when, after three months together, Svetlana appeared, made a monstrous scene, and threw Juliet out. Heather protested but quickly fell back under the spell of the Russian, who now had a very short haircut. Their reconciliation went spectacularly. Heather and Svetlana celebrated with their new friends and enjoyed having Heather walk around in a suit with trousers but with her hair worn down and long while Svetlana put on a corset.

"You look like a whore in the Middle Ages whom they caught, then tarred and feathered," one of their new male acquaintances teased. "Afterward, they cut her hair."

Svetlana found the idea fascinating and did not leave the young painter's side all evening. She was kicked to the curb by Heather the next day when she returned after a night in his arms. Once again there were apologies, anger, tears, and reconciliation—but then it was fall again, and Svetlana had to return to Paris. She had taken a post as an instructor at an art school, another sign her artistic career was headed downhill.

Heather continued working in Florence through the winter. In the spring, she met an Italian woman whose face resembled a Madonna by Titian. Gianna looked delicate at first sight, but she had dedicated herself to sculpture and had muscles like a man from the hard work. She accompanied Heather to Rome in the summer, and the city kept them breathless for months. Then Gianna fell in love with a stonecutter. Heather had gotten used to women changing their preferences for men or women, or loving men and women at the same time. Gradually she ceased holding a grudge against Chloe for that. She had not betrayed Heather by preferring first Terrence and then Colin. She could just as well have had a Svetlana.

Heather was now experienced enough to be able to keep her lovers. Even Svetlana was surprised by her skill at lovemaking when she appeared the next spring—again unannounced.

"This time I did not catch you, but I know you were not true, little kiwi."

Heather did not answer. Svetlana was surely unfaithful. Were they even still a couple?

Svetlana convinced Heather for a few weeks that summer that she needed her more than anyone else. She was possessed by a new drive to create, and during this time, she was faithful to Heather. She occupied their tiny studio day and night, smearing giant canvases with her impressions of Rome and wanting praise. Heather was happy when fall came and the Russian returned to Paris, along with her artwork. The farewell was tearful.

"You must soon come back. Without you, I not can live, not can work."

Heather assured her she would think about returning home soon, but first, she went to Madrid, alone. She was no longer afraid of traveling without accompaniment. In general, the bloomers she had since grown fond of protected her from unwanted advances. They identified Heather as a bluestocking and a suffragette—no respectable man and certainly no good, modest woman came too close to her. Heather did not care. She no longer looked shyly at the ground when someone addressed her, and she no longer surrendered sheepishly when she was issued the worst room in the hotel or the table next to the kitchen door in a restaurant. Heather Coltrane remained polite and ladylike, but she knew how to assert herself.

Madrid was giant and exciting. Heather joined an art class for women to practice drawing nudes. She laughed at herself when she thought that even three years before she had blushed just thinking about it.

At school, she met Ana, a graceful little thing, lithe as a dancer and cuddly as a kitten.

"*Gatita,*" Heather said, tenderly testing her freshly acquired knowledge of a bit of Spanish.

At that, Ana dug her claws into Heather's back. "Never call a tigress kitten."

***

Heather did not return to Paris until the spring of 1891. She was alone but with a contract for a solo exhibition in one of the best galleries in the city. She had sent a few of her last works to Svetlana's gallerist, who ordered her to come back right away.

"Simply fantastic," Mary, Berthe, and her friends pronounced.

Alicia stood speechless in front of Heather's portraits of Mireille and Juliet, Gianna and Ana. She brought one after another of her friends to the gallery to interpret the pictures.

Only Svetlana seemed hardly to look at Heather's work. She still had their studio but shared it with a parade of students—mostly women from the art academy where she taught, but also occasionally young men. Heather started a fight when she found one of them in their bath, though Svetlana had assured her the young man came only to paint. In truth, the relationship in this case was innocent, but Heather took over the rent for the studio and forbade Svetlana any more private students. Svetlana felt she was being bossed around and now ran riot. Heather painted Lana anew—this time as a woman burning up in her own fire.

"Well," Mary said when Heather uncovered the picture to reveal it to the circle of *indépendants*, "are we celebrating the eyes of the artist or mourning the eyes of the lover?"

***

The next evening, Heather told Svetlana that she intended to leave her.

"I've paid three months' rent on the studio, Lana, but I'm going to London in a week to show my work, and then I'm taking the next ship home. It's better this way. It's over."

She had hoped that Svetlana would accept the matter calmly, but she reacted with her usual hysteria. "You not can me leave, little kiwi. You cannot. I not can live without you, and you not can live without me. Do you not understand? Kiwi!"

Svetlana clung to Heather like a woman drowning. Heather knew this was for show. Lana might need someone, but most assuredly not the woman Heather had become.

***

Heather spent her last week in Paris in a hotel. She packed her things when she knew Svetlana was at the academy. On the last day, she found the rooms empty. Svetlana, too, had gone.

On the easel in the middle of the studio stood a single, not very large picture, a watercolor. Heather gasped when she saw her portrait. Svetlana had kept her promise; she had painted Heather. The picture showed a young woman, stepping through a veil. She emerged from a dreamland formed from the beaches at Cape Reinga, the volcanoes of King Country, the massive kauri trees in the north, and she laughed at the wind that blew against her. Heather wore her hair loose. Her face looked radiant and young, determined and strong. Completely beautiful, completely free.

Touched, Heather opened the letter that lay beside it. It consisted of only five words:

Give my regards to Chloe!

Chapter 7

Heather Coltrane reached Dunedin in December 1891 after a calm crossing. She held her face into the summer wind of her homeland, enjoying the crystal-clear air and the beauty of the mountains that rose up behind the city, seemingly close enough to touch. Already from the ship she had felt a rush from the long, empty beaches, the cliffs, and forested hills.

"I'm no longer used to so much lonesomeness," she admitted to another traveler, a merchant from Christchurch, "after so many years in Europe, densely populated as it is."

"It's not all that lonesome here anymore." The man smiled. "The population's growing every day, new towns are being founded, and the railroad is being built up. The male population is still much bigger than the female. You won't be lonely here, Miss Coltrane."

He did not understand what Heather found so amusing about this remark.

***

In Dunedin, not much had changed—compared to Rome, Madrid, and Paris, all of New Zealand seemed a bit sleepy and backward.

"Not when it comes to politics," said Kathleen, who was celebrating the return of two of her children in two days. The next day, Sean would arrive from Wellington for a massive election campaign in Canterbury and Otago. "We have the most progressive social laws in the world since the Liberal Party took power.

And now we're hoping for women's suffrage. Kate Sheppard is mobilizing everything. There are more than seven hundred petitions to date. Unfortunately, it's so far run aground in the upper chamber, and that's full of conservatives. But Sean is optimistic that it'll finally pass next year. The day after tomorrow, there's a rally in Dunedin. You'll see what's going on here. Backward? I mean, really."

Seemingly as proof, Kathleen showed her Gold Mine Boutique's new collection. Even in New Zealand, they seemed about to banish the corset to the back of the wardrobe.

"Claire is having some trouble adjusting." She smiled. "She has put on just a little weight in the past few years and maintains she can make it disappear with a corset while clothes now show every little pound. Complete nonsense, but she's conservative on that point."

Heather used the mention of Claire to ask about Chloe. Kathleen's face clouded over.

"Dear, I don't know." Kathleen shrugged. "We see her so rarely. Invercargill isn't all that far away. Colin had horses run in Christchurch, but he never comes to visit us alone. Chloe brings him by once a year at most. They come for tea—always in haste, they're just passing through, you see. We talk a bit, everyone's polite, but what's really going on, no one knows. Claire and Jimmy drive to Invercargill now and again on race days. But I can't convince Peter to go. I've never even seen the house, but Claire says the whole estate is dreamy. Yet Chloe runs around in her riding dress, constantly concerned about the horses. Claire says the atmosphere is strange. Indifferent, as she put it. But that's all I know."

Heather found this information alarming. "She still doesn't have any children?" she asked, although she was sure that Chloe would have written her about a birth.

Kathleen shook her head. "No. And I think that burdens the marriage. She wanted children. Anyway, she pours that energy into horse breeding, and she mothers little Rosie."

"Well, she can't be all that little anymore," said Heather. Violet's sister had been five when she came to New Zealand. Now she must have been around eighteen.

"Are you going to pay Chloe a visit? Perhaps you'll get more out of her."

Heather nodded. "That's why I'm here," she said calmly.

***

She would have most liked to depart the next day, but she was also compelled by the rally at which Sean was expected. Aside from the fact that her brother would have been terribly disappointed, she wouldn't have missed hearing him speak.

"You'll also enrich the event," Sean said, looking at her appreciatively. "You look grand, little sister. And it's not just the new clothes. It's your whole aura. I'd like to pull you up to the podium with me. Voilà, New Zealand: the modern woman."

Heather smiled. "You'd scare away half the people with that," she noted. "But what's with you, my dear brother? Aside from your hair's being a little thinner, you haven't changed a bit. Do you still spend half the night in your office? With your secretary?" She winked at her brother. "Do you still keep that handsome Maori?"

Sean rolled his eyes. "Don't bring me into disrepute, Heather. Kupe and I have a collegial relationship. He hopes to be elected to Parliament soon. He campaigns actively for Maori universal suffrage, and the chances don't look bad. If he makes it, then perhaps they'll soon have more seats than the two that the *pakeha* graciously allow them."

"Don't change the subject," Heather chided. "I don't want a lecture on the situation in Parliament. I want a glimpse into your heart. What's going on with Violet?"

Sean's face darkened. "I haven't heard anything from her in all these years. She used to go to the Temperance Union gatherings, so I had hoped to learn something about her through Kate. But Invercargill seems to be the last hold-out, or, to take a more charitable view, extremely peaceful. Rural area, a single pub in which apparently no one drinks too much, or at least no one has had the idea of demonstrating in front of it. There isn't even a local group of the union yet, so at most, I hear about Violet from Mother when Chloe wanders into Dunedin once a year. According to her, she's doing well. So." Sean lowered his gaze.

Heather observed him searchingly. "But you still think about her?"

"I can picture her like it was yesterday," Sean admitted. "But it's nonsense. After all these years."

"I'm driving there tomorrow," Heather said. "Why don't you just come with me? We had planned that once, and now we've just put it off a few years."

Sean shook his head. "The day after tomorrow I have to go to Christchurch. This rally in Dunedin is just the start. We have a massive campaign in Canterbury.

New petitions, new signature collections, and all the important people will be there. John Ballance is coming."

"The premier?" Heather asked, impressed.

Sean nodded. "Yes, Canterbury is our center. It's where Kate started, and Sir John Hall likewise comes from the area. Now we're concentrating there—also to regroup for the final push. We really need to work together, with the Maori too. Kupe's staying there already. Hopefully he doesn't bump into Matariki, or all hell will break loose."

"Are they still on the rocks?" asked Heather.

Sean sighed. "Not a word between them."

Heather yawned and stretched—a gesture she would never have made in a man's presence before. "I stand by it: this country is sleepy. Sure, you yell into your microphones at demonstrations. But otherwise, not a word between Claire and Chloe, not a word between you and Violet, not a word between Riki and Kupe. It's time someone made some noise."

***

At the rally in Dunedin, there was plenty of noise. Hundreds of women—and a few men too—sang the movement's hymns, waved banners, and marched through the streets. Kate Sheppard read her "Ten Reasons Why the Women of New Zealand Should Vote" and was cheered. Meri Te Tai Mangakahia, an attractive and highly educated young Maori, spoke about the rights of women in her culture and expressed her hope that all issues in Aotearoa would be better represented, even to the queen, if women could work as ambassadors.

"She is, after all, a woman. She will listen to her sisters."

Sean Coltrane explained calmly and clearly what had caused the women's suffrage campaign to fail so far. The legislation had fallen just short of being ratified several times—and Heather was astonished at Sean's explanation.

"The question is no longer whether Parliament thinks women are intelligent and educated enough to vote. Apart from a few ignoramuses living in the past, people have accepted that women like Kate Sheppard, Meri Te Tai Mangakahia, Ada Wells, and Harriet Morison"—Heather noticed that he purposefully named women who were present, and the audience cheered for them—"can represent this country as well as any male politician. No one doubts their integrity or their public spirit. The question in the parties is this: For whom and what will women vote? What party would they support, what governmental program? In sum: Is women's suffrage useful for us or not?"

The audience responded with jeers.

"Now, so far, no one knows for what women will vote," Sean continued, "except on a single subject: prohibition. The movement for women's suffrage developed from uniting for moderation and against alcohol. One can assume that female voters will support legislation regarding the more strictly enforced closing times, fewer liquor licenses, and anything that moves in the direction of prohibition. And with that, ladies and gentlemen, we have made ourselves powerful opponents. The whole alcohol industry uses a great deal of money and skill to undermine the movement for women's right to vote. Its lobbyists work on the representatives. They fund campaigns and rallies against women's suffrage. The faction of anti-prohibitionists is large, and it reaches across parties. Even among the Liberals, many representatives are at least against a strict alcohol ban. And so, this vote for women's suffrage becomes a touchstone for the view of every single representative toward democracy: Will we deny half of the mature, thinking population the right to vote simply because we might not like its decision? Or are we honest such that we will put our arguments up to all people for a vote? I advocate for the latter, and I will fight for it in Parliament."

Amid the cheers of the crowd, Sean left the podium.

"No one's explained it like that before," said Lizzie Drury, standing next to Kathleen and Heather with Haikina, her Maori friend. "Does Sean really expect an alcohol ban?"

Kathleen nodded. "Draft legislation for it is ready." She smiled. "Peter is already quite concerned about his beloved red wine."

Lizzie winked at her. "There's always mine, you know. I'm sure not going to stop pressing wine. And if it comes to it, Michael can always fire up his distillery again. We'll get back to the Irish ways, Kathleen. Just watch out they don't catch Peter stealing grain."

The women of Dunedin responded to Sean's detailed explanations by forming the Women's Franchise League. It was the first time a union in which the word "Christian" played no role and in which it was about the right to vote from the beginning, not just abstinence and alcohol. The chair, Anna Stout, was greeted with thunderous applause.

***

Sean asked Heather to postpone her visit to Chloe by two weeks; he wanted to go with her as soon as the campaign in Canterbury was over.

"No. I can't. I'm sorry. I've waited long enough. Maybe too long. I'm taking the early train tomorrow and will be in Invercargill by afternoon. Assuming my luck holds, Colin might be busy with tomorrow's race, and I'll have Chloe to myself."

Chapter 8

"Why don't you just let Rosie drive?"

Chloe knew she was fighting a lost cause, but Dancing Rose was her horse, the last daughter of her beloved Dancing Jewel, and today she was running her first race. Chloe was less than enthusiastic about Eric Fence swinging onto the sulky's box.

"The horse is so sensitive," she argued. "If Eric pulls the reins too hard, it'll come out of its lane and might ram the side fence. Rosie drives with a lighter hand."

The question of who should introduce Dancing Rose in her first race had already been the subject of several arguments. Chloe and Colin had finally agreed on a young jockey from the racing club, but he had fallen during one of the galloping races and was out for the day.

Colin rolled his eyes. "If they realize we let a girl drive, there will be loads of trouble."

Chloe exhaled sharply. "That didn't bother you two weeks ago when the driver for the brown gelding fell out."

Rosie Paisley had already stepped in as a driver several times. When she wore pants and stuck her already rather short hair under the cap, the delicate girl could pass for a boy without any problem. But those horses had never been favorites; mostly, they were pacesetters for other horses from the Coltranes' stables. With Dancing Rose, it was different. The chestnut mare had a real chance of winning, and Rosie would hardly let others blow past her. The mare was not just named after her. Rosie had raised the horse, acclimated her to the harness, and broken her in. Now she was dying to race with Dancing Rose. No doubt Rosie's heart was breaking when Eric yanked the mare out of her stall without a friendly word. Dancing Rose held her head high and pranced nervously when the bit struck her front teeth during bridling.

Chloe saw how Rosie was struggling with herself. Rosie would have liked to stroke and soothe the horse, but for that, she would have to get close to Eric, which she simply would not do. Rosie had made enormous progress in the past years. She was still quiet, but no longer let out her fear, anger, and sorrow with red and black crayons on paper; instead, she drew horses. If someone asked her something, she answered, and in the stables and house, she was exceedingly helpful. To this day, though, she still hated and feared her sister's husband.

"But now it bothers me," Colin said curtly without dignifying his wife or Rosie with a look. "I don't want a girl on the box. The mare has a chance of winning. I'm not going to take the chance that she's driven timidly."

"Driven timidly?" Chloe yelled. "I can't believe my ears. Rosie is far and away the best driver on this track. If she were a boy, the trainers would be falling all over one another for her. She's calm and has a fabulous hand."

"Except she never uses the whip. And she's a girl. Enough, Chloe, end of discussion." Colin turned away.

"Checkrein, boss?" asked Eric as he fiddled with the leathers.

"No," said Chloe.

She strictly refused the use of this auxiliary rein, since it hindered the motion of the horse's head. It did, however, make it harder for trotting horses to begin galloping and thus decreased the risk of disqualification.

Eric was as insensitive a driver as ever, but nonetheless very decisive. At the finish, he tended to employ the whip too strongly, and often the extra rein was all that saved him from having his horse gallop away. Colin reluctantly agreed with Chloe this time, especially because Dancing Rose reacted fiercely to constraint. She had reared up more than once in front of the sulky, and Colin did not want to take any chances. Besides, it was not smart to get under Chloe's skin. The mare belonged to her. She could revoke the entry if she was prepared to risk the scandal.

"No. Without," he finally said, reluctantly.

"And be careful with the whip," Chloe added, but she doubted anyone listened.

Disheartened, she stayed behind in the stables when the men led the horse out.

"Are we not going over to watch the race?" Rosie asked quietly. When she was alone with Chloe, she sometimes volunteered speech.

Chloe shook her head. "You can go, Rosie. I won't. I have a headache."

Rosie left reluctantly. For her, it was a test of courage to go to the racetrack without Chloe, but for her favorite horse, she would do it. Chloe felt helpless rage against Colin and Eric well up within her. It was not fair. Rosie should have driven in this race and led the horse to victory.

It was not at all certain that they would have disqualified Rosie and her horse after a victory. So far there were no binding rules about participation in harness racing. The rules only said girls could not ride.

Chloe rubbed her forehead. Her head ached as always after these fruitless confrontations with Colin. She did not even know why she still bothered. Colin had put her in her place long ago, and for years there had been no more reconciliation and no compromises. Coltrane Station was completely under Colin's control. He was established as a horse owner, trader, and trainer—if not especially beloved—and the same applied to Eric Fence. No one spoke anymore about how the whole estate had been financed with Chloe's money.

Chloe bitterly regretted not having at a minimum insisted that her name be given as coowner on the documents. But she had not wanted to listen to advice to do so, and instead behaved like most well-bred wives. Colin had received her dowry and signed the deeds of sale for the house and land. Chloe really only owned a horse: when Dancing Rose was born, she had the foal registered under her name. Colin had always registered Jewel's offspring himself, and Chloe had not noticed until she once protested the mistreatment of a young stallion, and Colin showed her the papers, laughing. Shortly before her death, Jewel had foaled once more, and Chloe seized ownership of the little horse as her last effort at resistance. After that, she capitulated to Colin's strategy: malice and needling belonged to her everyday life.

In principle, this was Eric's strategy too: once he felt secure in the Coltranes' stables, he ignored Chloe's instructions, fits of anger, and interdictions. Naturally, she complained about this to Colin, but he did nothing to put Eric in his place. On the contrary, Colin began to ignore Chloe in the stables. He humiliated her in front of his apprentices and employees, and he smiled smugly when she yelled at someone, or tried to fire an impertinent stableboy.

The situation had escalated a few months before when Eric and Colin returned home from a very successful trip to Woolston. They had started two horses, placed winning bets, and sold one of the horses for a high profit in Dunedin. Eric had finally broached the subject that had been in his heart from his first day at Coltrane Station. He had done enough sleeping in the stables, and he wanted his wife out from under Chloe's wings.

Colin shared his decision with Chloe the morning after they had returned. "I'm allowing Eric to refurbish the old summerhouse for himself and his family. It's not right for him to be sleeping in the stables while Violet and the children sleep here."

"But he did insist on it," Chloe said, sweet as sugar.

Colin looked at her condescendingly. "Would you stop with the nonsense, Chloe? We both know what it was about. And I've had enough. I won't keep the man away from his wife any longer. And it's for your good. Perhaps he'll give her another baby, and you can drag it around like you did Rosie, since you haven't had one yourself."

Chloe glared at him. "And how do you know that the fault lies with me?" she asked. "Perhaps the problem is yours. Perhaps your seed's not worth a damn."

She was so enraged that she did not even blush when she used the expression she had heard in the stables about a stallion's inability to sire.

Colin smirked. "Nonsense, sweetheart," he said brusquely. "You can congratulate me. I heard it just yesterday—your dear mother let the cat out of the bag, even though everyone wanted to keep their mouths shut to spare poor Chloe. I have a kid, love. Little Matariki gave birth to my daughter. So, if we're not drowning in heirs, Chloe, it's on you."

At these words, something inside Chloe had died. She stopped opposing letting Eric move out of the stables and had largely kept out of the stud farm's affairs since then. She knew that Violet cried secretly, but she could not protect her. Chloe wanted Rosie to stay in the housemaid's room, but at that Violet only shook her head.

"Rosie will be afraid there," she said, "and Eric won't let her keep our children with her. So, I'll either have to take her with us to the summerhouse, or could she perhaps sleep near you, Mrs. Coltrane? Next to your rooms, as your lady's maid? I know that she's not the most skillful when it comes to help with dressing and all that, and your husband . . ."

Violet reddened. She had heard Colin and Chloe fighting loudly; she also had heard their reconciliations. Surely Colin would not permit Rosie to share his wife's suite.

Chloe waved these considerations away. "That is an excellent idea, Violet," she replied. "Thank you, I hadn't thought of it myself, but that's how we'll do it. And don't worry about my husband. He won't be setting foot in my suite again."

Since then, Rosie had slept in Chloe's dressing room, and Chloe locked her private suite. Colin had accepted it without protest.

Chloe rubbed her forehead and left the stables, heading in the direction of the house. She needed to think about the end of this marriage.

***

Heather asked about the Coltranes' estate at the train station and was directed to the racetrack.

"You can't get there on foot, madam," the newspaperman who was also offering the race programs informed her. "Take a cab. It's race day, so they're in front of the train station."

Heather did indeed quickly find a cab to the racetrack and shared it with a horse owner from Dunedin whose trotter was supposed to compete in a race in the afternoon.

"It's a young horse," he said to Heather. "Normally I keep it in Woolston, but it's promising. Over time, I'm going to have it start elsewhere, but first I want to try it here."

Heather was not particularly interested in racing, but there was something about the man's words that made her curious. "Why here first? Isn't the track established?"

"It's not so well regarded," he said. "Among aficionados, that is. There's betting enough. However, the major breeders don't start their horses here anymore. So, the number of proper races is decreasing. It's losing its glamor, if you catch my meaning."

Heather nodded. "Why are the Barringtons and Beasleys withdrawing their horses?" she asked, consciously letting the names of the breeders exert their influence.

The man beamed. "Ah, so you know a little, madam. Grand. But then you must also have heard."

"I've been abroad quite a while," Heather said.

The man nodded. "Alas." He seemed to wrestle with himself a bit, but the enjoyment of gossip finally overcame his discretion. "Well, you see, I don't mean to spread gossip, but the track's owner, Coltrane, doesn't have such a good reputation in horse circles. He's repeatedly sold horses with great expectations, which then, well, did not meet them. At least nowhere else. Here in Invercargill, one or two of them have won several times."

"You suspect rigging? Cheating?"

The man shrugged. "No one's proven anything. People merely talk about it. And that's enough for the crème de la crème to withdraw. We small players, however"—he smiled apologetically—"quite like to race here. Particularly young horses that still need experience. There's no shame in losing in Invercargill."

Heather nodded. This information didn't surprise her. She would have been astonished if Colin had been regarded as a model of integrity. But what did Chloe think? Did she know?

The cab finally stopped in front of the racetrack, and Heather's new acquaintance headed for the racing club, where guest horses were stabled. Coltrane no longer rented stalls for short periods. This, too, was a bad sign. Renting to guest horses brought in money. If there was nothing to hide, there was no need to shy away from the presence of strange riders, trainers, and owners.

Heather left the racetrack behind and went off toward the house and the Coltranes' stables. A grand sign with gold and red lettering pointed the way: "Coltrane Station—Stud and Training Stables." The sign clearly wasn't Chloe's taste.

As Heather made her way to the house, a girl came walking toward her. On first seeing her, Heather thought of Violet. Heather could still picture Violet's slender face, high cheekbones, and full lips as clearly as if she had seen her the day before. This girl, however, had lighter-colored hair, not chestnut but dark blonde. And she did not have Violet's shining turquoise-blue eyes but instead frightened light-blue eyes. Then, when Heather made to stop to speak to her, the girl looked away and set off at a fast walk as if to escape. Heather watched her go with irritation. The resemblance to Violet was unmistakable. But that could not be her daughter. So, was she Rosemary, her little sister? Rosie had been such a dear, open little girl. Heather smiled at the memory of her sweet voice when she had sung children's songs. Could she have become such a shy, mistrustful creature?

Heather tried to recall whether Sean had mentioned something, but then the path made a sudden turn, and the house and stables were in front of her. Heather's heart leaped when she saw a woman walking from the stables to the house. Somewhat colorless in her faded riding dress, and somehow bent and broken. But without a doubt Chloe. Heather could not hold herself back. She shouted her friend's name and ran toward her.

Chloe thought she was mistaken that someone was calling her name. Yet then she saw Heather rushing toward her, and she instantly felt transported back in time. Even as a child, Heather couldn't wait until Chloe had climbed down from the little donkey in front of the Coltranes' farm. And Chloe could still see Heather jumping down the stairs of the farmhouse and hugging her. *Chloe, Chloe, look what I found, I drew, I saw.* Later she had hurried to Chloe from the Burtons' parsonage and then in the halls of the university when they found each other again after attending different lectures.

But this Heather was less the modest, hardworking student who pinned up her hair chastely and wore dark dresses so as not to excite her professors or fellow students. The young woman who flew toward Chloe wore her hair loose. It fell in long tresses over her shoulders. Her loose-fitting, pastel-green dress billowed over dark-green culottes gathered at the knee and decorated with lace. Over everything she wore a short, dark-green little jacket. In her ears flashed long, ruby earrings—Chloe would at most have dared to wear something so extravagant at balls—and the necklace that went with them hung around her neck.

"Chloe!"

Heather paused when she arrived in front of Chloe, somewhat out of breath and unsure whether she could just hug her. Chloe was speechless. All she could do was stare at her friend and her shining eyes, her radiant countenance. For the first time in years, Chloe looked at a face where there was nothing to read but wholehearted love. She threw her arms around Heather's neck and began to sob.

***

Heather had anticipated a lot when she came to Invercargill but not such a fit of crying. Her first look at Chloe had surprised her, and now, as she read the weariness and desperation in her features, she was deeply alarmed. Had she come at just the right moment? Heather held Chloe tight and let her cry, just as she had once cried herself out with Svetlana. The memory had something eerie about it—or something magical?

Heather smiled when Chloe's sobs finally abated and her friend let her go.

"Better?" Heather asked softly.

Chloe rubbed the tears from her eyes. "I'm being impossible," she muttered. "Here, you come to visit—for the first time in years—and I don't have anything better to do than to wail. Come, I'd rather show you the house and the stables. It's all very lovely. Remember Dancing Jewel? She had a very handsome daughter. And one of her sons is a stud for us. She . . . or should I make tea first?"

Chloe turned busily toward the house. She chattered on and was annoyed with herself for doing so. Yet, she could not pour her heart out to Heather just like that. So far, she hadn't said anything to anyone. She always pretended she was happy. This way, she would not have to admit that everyone who had warned her about Colin had been right. And now with Heather of all people, she could not admit that her life and her love were one giant lie.

Heather seized Chloe by the shoulder and held her back. She turned her around and pulled her gently toward herself and forced her to look her in the eye.

"Chloe, I don't want to see your house or drink tea. No doubt Dancing Jewel's offspring are charming, but I didn't come for their sake. I came for your sake, Chloe Coltrane. I longed for you. And if you look me in the eye now and say that you didn't feel the same, that you didn't long for me, then I will just go." Heather looked at Chloe searchingly.

Chloe lowered her gaze. "No. No, don't go. I, I did long for you. I've missed you so."

Heather smiled. "Well, good, and to people for whom she longs because she, well, maybe she loves them a little bit, she wouldn't lie, would she?"

Chloe shook her head but still would not look her friend in the eye. "I won't lie to you," she whispered. "I don't lie to anyone anyway. Except myself."

***

As it turned out, Heather had really chosen the ideal day for her visit. The friends had the house all to themselves. Colin was at the racetrack, and Chloe had given the cook the day off.

"Colin goes to the pub afterward, anyway," she explained nervously. "Whereby, whereby I don't mean to say he spends too much time there. He's actually a homebody, though he has to travel around a lot. We do start horses in Woolston and—"

"You don't need to make excuses for him," Heather responded drily. "And please don't say 'we' when you're speaking of that whole business out there. That's not you, Chloe. That gaudy sign, the horse trading, and possibly the bet rigging. I hope your name doesn't appear in connection with that. Chloe, if that becomes public, you'll both end up in hot water."

"Bet rigging?" Chloe asked, confused. "I, I don't know what you're talking about."

Heather sighed. "I thought as much. But that's not so important now either. In any case, don't tell me what a jolly fellow Colin is. Instead, tell me how he ousted you from everything. Oh yes, and where is Violet?"

"She also has the day off. Women's Franchise League," she said, as if that explained everything. "Apparently, it was just founded, and Violet's part of it, although Eric makes her life hell because of it. Every day I hear new excuses about where the bruises come from. The bastard beats her black and blue. But yesterday, she went to Dunedin anyway. With a few other friends from the area, they all took the train to hear this rally for women's suffrage."

"But not you?" Heather asked almost accusingly.

"God knows I have other things to worry about," Chloe said. "In any case, Eric was traveling yesterday. They picked up a little stallion somewhere. He's supposed to start off today in the conditions race. But they don't tell me anything." It sounded embittered. "Violet hopes, with all that going on, her husband won't notice she's away. But there's no chance. Joe will blab as soon as Eric walks in the door tonight. The boy idolizes his father."

Heather sighed. It was always the same story. Now it was Violet's son, back then her brother Colin. He had grown up in his father's stables where he had learned horse swindling and his father's hate for his mother.

"Very well," said Heather. "We'll worry about that later. Now, tell me about you and Colin. Which of you was the first to stop loving the other?"

"I don't think, from the start, that Colin loved me," said Chloe. "I loved him. But if he ever loved anyone, it was Matariki Drury."

"And not even her enough," Heather said drily. Then she wrapped her arm around Chloe. "How is it that you no longer have anything to do with this racetrack? It was your money, after all. What happened?"

***

Chloe told her about Colin's horse buying, his employee policies, his opaque machinations.

"I discovered too late that my name was not on any ownership documents," she said.

Heather rolled her eyes. "But, Chloe, that was obvious, you know. When you finalize a purchase, you have to sign. Whoever doesn't sign doesn't get to be an owner."

I did once sign something," Chloe recalled. "A preliminary contract, with Desmond McIntosh. I did not need to be there for the second appointment with the notary. That was just before the wedding."

"That was before the wedding?" shouted Heather. "You must have been out of your mind. Sean or another lawyer needs to take a look. We'll have to see how we can get you out of this."

"Get me out of this?" Chloe asked helplessly.

The women had gone into the living room, and she remembered her duties as a hostess. She opened one of the cabinets and reached for her tea service.

"Chloe, you don't mean to stay with him, do you? You can't keep up pretenses to yourself and the world for the rest of your life. And besides, I'm back now. I want to ask you to live with me, Chloe. As, as my wife."

Chloe almost dropped the teapot. Confused, she stared at Heather who sat quite relaxed on the sofa. "As your . . . ?"

Heather stood up and took the teapot from Chloe. Then she pulled her friend down beside her on the sofa. She told her about Svetlana, and Mireille, about Juliet and Ana.

"Now I know, Chloe, what Colin had that I didn't," she said with a smile. "And he and all other men will always have something that I don't, but believe me, you won't miss it."

Chloe swallowed. She had listened wordlessly, at first disbelieving and then amazed. London, Paris, Rome, Madrid. Chloe herself had always been the friend who rushed from one adventure into the next. And now, shy Heather of all people had dared to take the leap and crossed borders. Not just those between England, France, and Italy, but also those guarded much more carefully.

"You mean, in France something like that is totally normal?" Chloe asked hesitantly. "For, for two women—"

Heather shook her head. "It's not exactly common for two women to love each other and live together," she admitted, "but it happens. More often in artists' circles. And they don't always stay together forever. Some only love women; some love men too. And I, well, I love you, Chloe. And I want you. If it's forever, good; if not, then someday another Terrence or Colin will come along. But I'd like to try in any case."

"A Colin will never come along again," Chloe said firmly. "As for how things would look with someone else, I don't know, but now, now I just don't know anything anymore, anyway. Except that you're here. And that I've always loved you more than any other person in the world. Even if, well, even if you didn't, or you did, well, if we—what are you doing, Heather? Do you want to kiss me?"

***

Heather seduced Chloe very softly and very slowly. She kissed her lips and her face, opened her riding dress and her bodice and caressed her breasts. Chloe let herself be swept away. At first, it was perhaps only curiosity or the joy of being loved, touched, caressed, and admired again. But then Heather unleashed feelings of lust in her. Chloe's body vibrated beneath Heather's lips and her skilled hands. Just before the climax, Chloe thought how it would have been better to take Heather with her into her suite. Here, after all, someone could discover them at any moment. But everyone was away. Even little Roberta, who was off with the cook. Nothing could happen.

And then Chloe stopped thinking. She only arched herself toward her friend, her soul mate, her love, her second self, her wife.

***

Colin was aggravated. Damn it, Dancing Rose should have won. He had bet on her. And she had been ahead by a mile as the horses headed for the finish line. Guaranteed, that fellow from Dunedin's stallion would never have passed her. But Eric had wanted to be doubly sure, so on the straightaway, he had used the whip, while pulling on the reins to prevent her from galloping. Colin had tried for years to get him to stop doing that, but in the key moment, Eric did it. And the effect on the sensitive mare was devastating. Dancing Rose had launched into a gallop, and she could not be brought back to a trot. She had run through the finish line and far past it, almost off the track and into the stables. Eric had completely lost control.

Fortunately, Rosie had been waiting at the exit, and she stopped and calmed the horse. Colin had first had a mind to shoot his stable master and the horse, too, but then the winner's owner had approached him. A dummy from Dunedin who absolutely had to tell him that it was clear to him how wrong all the rumors about the racetrack in Invercargill and race rigging had been. This race, as everyone saw clearly, had not been rigged. His stallion had won fair and square, but naturally, he was sorry the handsome mare had galloped.

At first, Colin had let the chatter wash over him. The race had not been rigged; he would have to be crazy or stupid to do that every race day. He and Eric carefully considered when they would hold horses back to let others win, or apply a few drops of the right liquid to the coronary band of an out-of-town champion's hoof, which then led to an irregular gait and galloping. Today, however, Colin Coltrane had bet on Dancing Rose's phenomenal talent, and, because of Eric's stupidity, he lost a hundred pounds. But then he listened more closely to what the merchant from Dunedin was telling him. He was in the process of building up a small but fine racing stable. He was still buying horses. This sparked interest in Colin. Perhaps he could still make up for the loss with the stallion they had picked up the day before.

Colin had no idea how fast he was, but he had signed him up for the conditions race. Not an important race, and aside from two rather hopeless competitors, only horses Coltrane had been training were starting. Three of his apprentices would be driving them—or no, he could put the best of the boys behind the young stallion and Eric behind the fastest of the other horses. The horse could then run neck and neck with the new one, and at the last moment, Eric could make the same mistake he had with Dancing Rose.

"I might have a horse for you," replied Colin. "Something of an insider secret, you see. I bought him on a whim, so I don't have any idea myself how he'll race."

A short time later, he knew that the merchant from Dunedin was one of those who believed races were won with pedigrees, just like Chloe. It was a stupid prejudice that the horses' pedigree ultimately made them good or bad trotters. English racehorse breeding was based on the idea that the coupling of especially fast horses would lead to ever-faster horses, and long term, this also promised success. However, Colin did not think long term. Colin believed in flukes. And the greater the fluke, the higher the rate of return.

"Perhaps you'd like to look at the stallion's papers, Mr. Willcox? I'm not sure, but as I recall, he has Thoroughbred ancestors on the mother's side, the Godolphin Barb line."

Mr. Willcox took the bait. And now Colin just needed to keep him interested until they got to the house. Colin hoped there was champagne there. If the man was a bit tipsy, the horse's victory would seem even more wondrous, and the price would not be too high for his means. Colin only planned to ask for double what he had paid for the horse himself.

***

Heather and Chloe jumped when they heard footsteps in the receiving room.

"Come in, Mr. Willcox; have a seat. I'll get the papers for you."

The pedigree certificates were in the office in Colin's apartments. To reach those, he had to cross the living room.

Chloe, who had been on top of Heather, trying out the new techniques she had just learned, tried to quickly throw a blanket over her and Heather's naked bodies. It was too late. Colin could not miss them on the sofa. And his reaction made everything worse.

"I'll kill the bastard."

At first glance, Colin only recognized two bodies intertwined and his wife's dark hair bent directly over her partner. He pounced on the two of them in a frenzy, grabbing Chloe's hair and brutally yanking her from atop her lover. Then he looked down at his sister.

Heather sought salvation in impertinence. "Hello, dear brother," she said.

Colin hit her in the face. He beat her heedlessly and kicked Chloe. Chloe retreated from the kicks and tried to pull her husband off her friend. And then she saw the second man in the entry to the living room, observing the scene as

487

if frozen. Chloe forgot that she was naked, and now realized that this situation probably compromised her forever.

"Well, do something," she screamed at the man. "You see he's going to kill us."

"But that's, that's a woman," the man stammered.

Chloe's fists hammered desperately on Colin's back.

"Exactly," she roared. "She can't defend herself. Please!"

Finally, the man took action. And luckily, he was strong and apparently trained. A single tug sufficed to pull Colin from Heather. Then Colin moved to attack her rescuer, but a left punch from the man made him see stars for a moment. Colin fell to the carpet.

The man resumed staring at the two women. "This is, quite unnatural," he muttered, "and you, you . . ."

In that moment, he recognized his traveling acquaintance. The young woman in the jaunty culottes. Perhaps he should have thought something was funny before.

Chloe bent down to Heather to help her. Her lip was busted and bleeding, as was her cheek. Without Chloe's help, Heather could not have sat up. Colin's fists had struck her in the ribs. The Dunedin horse owner suddenly found himself across from two naked women.

"Who, what's this?"

In his confusion, Willcox turned to Colin. He was coming to and picked himself up.

"If I may, my wife," he said biliously, "and my sister. Damn it, do you always hit like that? You should box instead of racing horses."

"But what, what do we do now?" Willcox still found himself in a sort of shock.

Colin stood all the way up. "I suggest you go to your horse, and I'll continue here."

He balled his fists. Until then, he had never beaten Chloe. Today, however, he would. And afterward he would take her. He was going to beat any thought of his sister out of his wife, and then he would—

"Mr. Coltrane, not that I don't understand you're upset. But you can't beat a woman."

The situation was almost comical, and much, much later, Heather and Chloe would also laugh about it. The proper Mr. Willcox's image of the world had just been shaken to its core, but his upbringing as a gentleman triumphed over the outrage he likely shared with the cuckolded husband.

"Oh, can't I?" asked Colin, and moved to pounce on the women again.

This time, Mr. Willcox's fist struck him under the eye. Colin fell like a ton of bricks. Willcox gave him an almost apologetic look. Then he turned to the women.

"Mrs., uh, Miss Coltrane. I think with that I've given you some, hmm, breathing time. Perhaps, uh, you ought to, hmm, put something on. And then, well, I could remain here until you've gone. Because I'm sure you, uh, no doubt will want to leave. Or might you be able to explain this somehow? Is this some kind of a, hmm, misunderstanding?"

"No," Chloe said calmly, and picked up her and Heather's things. "If you'd pardon us for a moment, Mister . . . ?"

"Willcox," said the man, and bowed formally.

Heather could not help herself. As Chloe pushed her out of the room, she began to laugh hysterically. Her whole body hurt as she did. Colin had certainly broken a few ribs.

Chloe, anything but amused, helped her into her culottes. "Stop that, and get dressed before he changes his mind. My God, Heather, didn't you see Colin's face? He's lost it. He really will kill us."

Heather nodded, now serious again. "I saw my father's face," she said quietly, "when he'd beat my mother. Do you want to take anything with you, Chloe?"

Chloe hesitated briefly but then grabbed Dancing Rose's papers. "She belongs to me beyond a doubt," she said. "We'll have to send for her. And Rosie and Violet and her children, we have to take care of them too." She trembled.

Heather nodded. "Tomorrow we'll organize all that," she said. "For now, we need to get to Dunedin as quickly as possible. Maybe Sean's still there. You're going to need a very good lawyer."

Mr. Willcox was still sitting next to the unconscious Colin when the women returned.

"We'll be going now," Heather said. "Thank you very, very much."

Chloe walked by their rescuer with her eyes downcast, but then she turned around and looked him in the eye.

"Mr. Willcox, I don't know what horse my husband wanted to foist on you, but it's better you don't buy it."

Chapter 9

When Violet returned from Dunedin, she discovered the races weren't over yet, and she breathed a sigh of relief. Eric most likely had not missed her. Rosie was waiting for her in the summerhouse, hidden in a corner like during her worst days. Violet was immediately frightened. What might have happened? If Rosie was not talking again, it could take hours to find out. But the moment Rosie saw her sister, a torrent of words came from her.

"Rose lost; he hit her. Mrs. Coltrane is gone. With another woman. I'm supposed to tell you she's coming back to get us. But I don't believe it. She ran away from Mr. Coltrane."

Violet understood only half of it, though it seemed possible Chloe had left. She had complete faith that the mistress she admired would leave her husband eventually. But so suddenly? Without any preparation? As if escaping? Because someone struck her horse?

"Stay here, Rosie. I'm going to the house. I have to look for the children anyway. Are they with Mrs. Robertson?"

"Roberta, yes. Joe was in the stables."

Violet sighed. She could have guessed. She had instructed the children to stay with the cook. On her free days, Mrs. Robertson visited her sister, who had children of her own. Roberta loved playing with them, and this time the children were even supposed to stay the night with their friends. Joe, however, preferred to stay with Colin and his father, and apparently, he had once again convinced Mrs. Robertson. That meant he would know that Violet had stayed the night in Dunedin. And he would tell Eric.

To her amazement, Violet met her son in the house. He was standing in front of Colin, who sat slumped over on the sofa, holding a bag of ice to his cheek.

"Joe, what are you doing here?" she yelled.

Colin Coltrane turned a rather battered face toward Violet, dominated by a massive swelling below his right eye. It was already nearly swollen shut. Violet almost felt sorry for him. She knew from personal experience that the next day his eye would be red and circled in green and blue. She thought of Eric at once, but surely he had not done that.

"He's making himself useful," Colin mumbled with an appreciative glance at the boy. Colin's lips were also thickly swollen.

"Because the whore ran away," Joe added.

Violet glared at the boy. God forgive her, but she still had not managed to feel love or even fondness for him. Particularly because the older he got, the more he resembled his father. She thought she could already recognize Eric's devious look in the boy. And now this.

"Joseph Fence, another expression like that, and I'll wash your mouth out with soap," she said sternly, although he was sure to say something else. "Please don't teach him such things, Mr. Coltrane. He doesn't even know what a, what that word means."

"I sure do," said Joe. "A whore's a woman who does it with others in the bed. Overnight?" He looked at his mother inquisitively.

Violet was not certain, but it sounded as if the men had been blabbing about taking women to Dunedin overnight. And Joe had picked it up. But who had laid Colin out like that?

"I'll use whatever words I want in my own damned house," Colin snapped at her. "Whether Mrs. Fence approves or not. You can clean up here, Violet. I'm not going to the pub tonight, but the boy here is going to go for me. Be a good boy, Joe, and fetch Mr. Coltrane a bottle of whiskey. Have the barkeeper put it on my tab."

"Sir, you don't really mean to send a child to the pub?" asked Violet, horrified.

She had heard so much the day before about the connection between prohibition and women's suffrage that she was almost inclined to make allowances on the question of abstinence. The right to vote had to pass first. Then they

could discuss whether it made sense to close the pubs. Colin's behavior immediately convinced her of the contrary.

Colin grimaced. "The pharmacist is closed on Sunday. And I need something for the pain. I'm sending him for medicine, Mrs. Fence, no more, no less.
Go, Joe."

Joe smirked triumphantly at his mother before going on his way. Violet
began cleaning up the living room, which showed clear signs that a fight had
taken place.

"Where is Mrs. Coltrane? Rosie said something—"

"There is no Mrs. Coltrane anymore."

Violet discovered the glass and the empty bottle on the side table next to
the sofa. So, Colin had already been drinking and only needed a new supply.
Why send Joe, though? The Coltranes always had whiskey, wine, and champagne in the house.

"As your son said, the whore is gone. And Eric's going to have it out with
you. You think he didn't notice you were gone last night? You've got another,
right? Cute as you are, you could have ten. Or is it a woman? Have you all gone
mad?"

Violet did not say a word. It would be bad enough to have to answer Eric
later. It seemed Rosie was right. Some woman must have convinced Chloe to
go away with her. Heather? Violet's heart suddenly raced. If Chloe was with
Heather, it really could be that the two of them would come back to get Violet.
And where Heather was, Sean might also be.

***

The thought of Sean Coltrane helped Violet make it through the endless evening. Eric hadn't gone to the pub after the race. Instead, he got drunk in the
living room with his boss. That had never happened before. Chloe had always
somewhat managed to prevent a fraternity between Eric and Colin. Now, however, a new era was dawning, and Eric evinced an intuitive sense of it. First, he
approached Colin, crestfallen with more bad news. The new horse had failed
spectacularly. The potential buyer had left beforehand anyway. And the idiot of
an apprentice who was supposed to lose the last race had delusions of grandeur
and ran neck and neck with the designated winner until the very end. When
they then trotted across the finish line, his mare had her nose ahead. So, more

lost bets. It was better to forget the day had ever happened. With the help of the whiskey, master and servant made good on that thought. And Joe sat there, looking at the men and worshipping both of them.

Violet had sent Roberta straight to the summerhouse, and the cook, who slept in the servants' wing, was trying to convince Rosie to occupy a room there. Under no circumstances could the girl stay in her chamber next to Chloe's deserted rooms that night.

Colin got drunk enough to tell Eric about Chloe, Heather, and Mr. Willcox. In the story he related, he had first beaten the two "whores" out of the house and then the prospective horse buyer who tried to defend them.

Violet took it that it had not quite been like that. Rosie would have been much more disturbed if her beloved Mrs. Coltrane had shown traces of abuse. She also wondered what Chloe and Heather could have been doing together on the couch to get Colin so angry. Yet, in truth, she did not care. Violet would survive the night, and with a little luck, Eric would just drink himself into unconsciousness and not even molest her. Regardless of what happened, the next day she would take the early train to Dunedin with the children, though she already knew that would not be easy. Joe would want to stay with his father and Rosie with her horse. Violet had made her decision, and she was determined to prevail.

She sighed with relief when she succeeded in slipping out of the house late in the evening without the men noticing. She pulled Joe, who was almost falling asleep while walking, along with her. For a moment, she thought about fleeing to Mrs. Robertson. Then surely nothing could happen to her. However, Eric was likely to make a scene when he did not find her at their house, and he would drag her by her hair out of the servants' quarters.

So, she went into the summerhouse and hoped for a peaceful night, especially when she discovered Rosie and Roberta cuddled together in Roberta's corner when she put Joe to bed. She would have to bear it silently if Eric did something to her. She would not allow Rosie to be frightened back into muteness and blank stares.

***

Violet's hopes would not be fulfilled. Though Eric came to the guesthouse late, he was astoundingly alert. Probably he had fallen asleep with Colin in the living room and then come to, a little more sober, a few hours later. Now he stumbled into their house—a small building of two rooms and a kitchenette. The entry was through the larger of the rooms, where there were a table and chairs and where the children slept at night. The smaller room was Violet and Eric's bedroom. When he would come home from the pub, Eric would feel his way through the children's bedroom without making much noise or even lighting a candle. This time, he had a lantern with him from the main house. It was easy to see Rosie and Roberta, who slept tightly intertwined.

"Is it possible?" Eric roared. "In my house? My daughter! I'll show you, to seduce my child, you little whore. You probably did it with the missus, heh? Learned it from your Mrs. Coltrane." Eric tore Roberta and Rosie out of the bed and threw Rosie across the room. "And yet, you're pretty cute, Rosie. About time a man broke you in, not just the missus."

He approached Rosie, who retreated fearfully, but he pressed her against the wall and forced his tongue into her mouth. Rosie kicked him and screamed.

Violet was there in a flash and pressed in between them. "No, Eric, in God's name, not her. Take me. You're not mad at Rosie. You're mad at me. I ran away, Eric. I ran away with the women of the Women's Franchise League, but there were also men at the rally."

Eric let Rosie go. "So, you admit it," he said, sneering. "You admit it: there was always something you kept running to. Even back in Woolston. That highfalutin Mr. Stuart, right?"

Violet backed up toward their bedroom, trying to entice Eric and warn Rosie at the same time. *Don't hole up in the corner, Rosie. Run away. For heaven's sake, run away, and take Roberta with you. Don't let Roberta watch him beat me to death. Don't you watch.*

"Mr. Stuart was a nice fellow," whispered Violet, "very nice."

Eric followed her into the bedroom. His first blow knocked her onto the bed.

***

Violet did not take the early train the next morning. She survived the night, but she was hardly able to get out of bed. When she had woken before dawn, she convinced herself that Rosie and Roberta had disappeared. Joe, too, was gone, but she could no longer worry about where he was. She would have liked to wash or make tea, but she could not stay on her feet long enough. Her head and back hurt unbearably. Perhaps Rosie could care for her later? Or Mrs. Robertson? Violet was not sure how much the cook knew of Eric's rages, but she thought she had sometimes exchanged looks with Chloe when Violet could barely haul herself to work. She would have to regain her strength by midday. There was an afternoon train. Her last chance. She would not survive another night. Violet stumbled to Roberta's bed. She had hardly stretched out when she lost consciousness again.

***

Rosie groomed Dancing Rose. She had spent the night in her stall with her while Roberta, who was afraid of horses, had curled up in the hay. Roberta fled in the first light of morning into the kitchen. She loved Mrs. Robertson, and Rosie loved the mare. Dancing Rose was enjoying some time alone with Rosie, even if the quiet in the stables would not last. Colin gave the apprentices the day off after the races. Colin and Eric would come in early to train the horses as always. Rosie was afraid of that, but what could she do? Run away? Ride away?

Rosie was not very good at thinking. She had stopped a long time ago because thinking only caused pain. Because it meant remembering, remembering the screams and blood and death. But she had started thinking again recently. There were beautiful times and memories now: Dancing Rose and everything Mrs. Coltrane had taught her about horses. How to harness them, how to acclimate them to the bit and reins. *Always think before you do something, Rosie*, Mrs. Coltrane had said. *Try to think like a horse. Then you'll know what you need to do.*

A horse would run away.

Rosie considered which vehicle she would need and whether Rose could pull it. She had only ever pulled the sulky before, but if Violet and Roberta and Joe were to ride, too, she needed a chaise. And a different harness.

While Rosie tested the leathers in the tack room to see which of the harnesses might suit Rose, Eric entered the stables.

Eric was in a bad mood. Colin had barked at him when he came into the house to check on him. Colin was sick and would stay in bed. Eric would have to see to the horses alone.

Eric cursed. He would have to train all of the horses himself. At least the first one was already in the aisle, clean and ready to harness. Mrs. Coltrane's mare. So, Rosie had to be here somewhere. What had been with her last night? She had looked like a damned woman.

He found her in the tack room. And when Eric said good morning, Rosie looked at him as if looking at the devil himself.

"Finish readying the mare. I'm going to take her out first. Sulky, Rosie, with the harness she always wears. Oh, and a checkrein. The little shit got away from me yesterday. I'm going to teach her manners today."

Eric cast a glance at the mare and realized he liked that. It was fun teaching manners to females, whether they had two legs or four.

While Rosie harnessed the horse, he went to check whether she had fed Dancing Rose properly. The girl was guaranteed to have done something wrong.

Obey—do not think, Rosie told herself. Then the devil might leave her in peace. Or would he? He had never left Violet in peace, no matter what she did. And yesterday he had—Rosie did not want to think about it. *Do not think.* But he would beat Violet again. And now he would put that hateful checkrein on Dancing Rose. And then he would beat her. And the next day he would do it again.

Rosie reached for the racing harness. He could not be allowed to do that again. She had to stop him. Rosie begged the horse's pardon as she put on the checkrein.

"Just for today," she whispered to the mare, "just this once."

Then she led the mare between the poles of the sulky and harnessed her to it. She tied a leather strip around the shafts of the left and right poles, a light connection. In the case of an accident, highbred horses should be able to free themselves quickly from the sulky so they wouldn't become frenzied and break their legs. Chloe had shown Rosie many times how to tie the leather bands around the shafts: easy to undo but secure enough so they wouldn't come undone themselves. Rosie tied the left side as she had learned. On the right side, she slung the leather bands only once, carelessly, around the shaft of the pole. Then she led the horse and sulky in front of the stables. Her heart raced. Chloe would have checked the bindings. She always did. But the devil?

"Did you feed the new stallion, Rosie?"

The devil came out of the stables, snorting with rage. "A gallon of oats for that useless horse? What do you think, Mr. Coltrane has too much money? How long have you been feeding the horses, girl? For years. But there's nothing inside your stupid skull. Still too batty to put a few oats in a trough." Dancing Rose pranced nervously back and forth. Eric took the reins out of Rosie's hand. "We'll talk more later, girl. We're going to teach you to do things differently now that the missus is gone. You'll see. I'll teach you manners yet."

Eric swung onto the seat of the high-wheeled sulky and whipped Rose's back with the reins. He had her start at a trot, riding the approach to the racetrack with verve. Rosie followed him, her heart racing. It must not happen until he reached the racetrack. If it happened on the road, Rose would run away and sooner or later collide with another horse or a tree or whatever else. She could kill innocent passersby, and herself.

Rosie sighed with relief when Eric drove through the gate to the track, but she trembled again as he briefly stopped to speak with other trainers. Rosie recognized two other sulkies on the track. Apprentices were exercising the horses according to instructions from the racing-club instructors. If they noticed something now . . .

But the other trainers did not pay much attention to Eric. They had eyes only for their own protégés. One of them opened the gates to let Dancing Rose onto the track. He ought to have noticed something, but he stood to the horse's left, the side on which Rosie had tied it correctly. Eric had Dancing Rose trot again, and Rosie breathed a sigh of relief. At this speed, no one else would be able to see anything.

Dancing Rose trotted a lap and a half before the leather strap on her right side loosened. It might have held if she had not resisted. However, Eric did exactly what he had done the day before during the race: he whipped the mare on the straightaway. Rose wanted to begin galloping, lowering her head to do so, and came up against the stiff reins. The jerk in her mouth made her stop suddenly, a reaction Eric anticipated, and which he sought to avoid with another flick of the whip.

Dancing Rose reared up in the harness and, still on her hind legs, threw herself forward again to escape the whip. At that, the leather strip slid out of its fitting, and the simple slipknot loosened. Rose would feel the weight of the sulky only on her left side now. She spooked—at first from the uneven ballast and then from the leather, which now dragged across the ground to her left. The mare retreated to the right, then broke into a run. In her panic, she wouldn't likely feel Eric pulling on her reins, but it didn't matter. Eric lost the reins quickly. Being pulled on only one side, the light sulky quickly began to spin out of control. Rose galloped faster and faster. Eric was unsure whether he should jump out or try to keep his seat. And there were the side fences.

Rose veered toward the edge of the racetrack. Eric didn't have time to make a decision. He felt the sulky being thrown against the side fence, the wheel breaking, and the seat flying through the air. He saw the wooden benches of the crowd stands as he shot toward them.

Then he did not see anything anymore.

***

Violet awoke when someone knocked on the summerhouse's door.

"She must be in here." The cook's voice sounded strangely dampened. "She didn't come to the house, and she never goes to the stables. God in heaven, hopefully nothing happened here. That would be—"

"That would be as if lightning struck the same house twice," said Mr. Tibbot.

Violet did not recognize the calm voice in which these words were spoken. Violet forced herself to stand up. She was already doing somewhat better than early in the morning. It had to be that way too. She had to make the afternoon train.

When she opened the door, Mrs. Robertson stood there with a man whom Violet had seen before. At the racetrack. Mr. Tibbot of the racing club, a trainer. Chloe had spoken with him a few times.

Mrs. Robertson shrieked when she saw Violet's battered face. "Oh, dearie," she whispered. "Dearie, we, we have bad news."

"Rosie?" she asked.

Mr. Tibbot shook his head. "Your husband," he said. "Although from the look of y—is the news really so bad?" He cleared his throat. "Forgive me, Mrs. Fence. That was a slip of the tongue. Your husband had an accident. My God, Mrs. Robertson, how the devil am I supposed to tell her this now? Should we bring him here? Lay him out here, or in the main house?"

Violet looked at Mr. Tibbot. It was hard for her to see clearly. Both her eyes were almost swollen shut, and her tongue lay like a dry clump in her mouth. She had to try twice before she could get the words out.

"He's dead?" she asked.

***

The men brought Eric Fence to Colin's house, and a police officer questioned Colin gruffly. Two men who had been drinking together, one of whom had clearly been beaten and the other of whom broke his neck the next day because something was not right with a horse or its harnessing. It was suspicious at the least. Mrs. Robertson, however, confirmed that Colin had not left the house. Mr. Tibbot stated that none of the apprentices or stableboys had been occupied with the horse. Even now, he said, only the girl who took care of the horse after the accident was in the stables.

"Looks like it really was an accident," the officer said to Violet. After the questioning at Colin's house, the officer went to speak with Violet at the summerhouse. He explained that the men at the racetrack had called him after they had retrieved Eric and brought the frenzied horse to a stop with Rosie's help. The officer had looked at what was left of the sulky and the harness. "A little carelessness. Your husband—" The officer bit his lip when he saw Violet's battered face but then decided to calmly say his piece. The woman must know in what condition her husband had been the day before. She also seemed rather collected now. The cook had helped her wash and dress. "Your husband seems to have had a great deal to drink last night and did not devote the, uh, necessary attention to harnessing his horse. In any case, the sulky came loose, the horse panicked, and it ran against the fencing."

"Nothing happened to the horse?" Violet asked. She was concerned for Rosie.

"Nothing serious as far as could be determined." The officer seemed vexed. "Your husband, however, was flung over the racetrack's wall. He died instantly."

Violet nodded. She could hardly believe it. She would not need to take the train. Eric would not touch her again.

"If you want to see him, the men brought him into the house, but he's, hmm, not a pretty sight. The undertaker has been notified."

Violet nodded again. "I need to look after my sister," she said quietly. "If you'll excuse me." She hoped that Mrs. Robertson was taking care of Roberta and Joe. Especially Joe. With luck, he had not heard too much about it. Dear Lord, she should be taking care of him. She could only think of Rosie, however. She had been in the stables.

***

Violet tried to run, but she only managed to limp. She saw the chestnut mare tied in front of the stables—thank God, really nothing seemed to have happened to the horse. And Rosie was taking care of it, so she was not terrified and silent in a corner of the stables either.

On the contrary, as Violet came closer, what she heard made the blood run cold in her veins. Rosie was singing. A happy little song, a tune she had learned from Caleb Biller. She was washing the horse, smiling and singing.

She had not sung in years.

Violet wanted to think about everything alone somewhere. But then she saw Joe coming out of the stables. His face was pale as a corpse, his cheeks showed traces of tears, and his eyes looked unnaturally enlarged. He was going to run to Violet, but then he saw Rosie, and his eyes narrowed. Naked hate spoke from them.

"It was her," he yelled, pointing at Rosie. "She did it."

Violet slapped him in the face.

Chapter 10

The little horse snorted as Violet finally brought it to a stop in front of the parsonage. It was now not so scrawny, but pulling the hay wagon, it still did not move very quickly. Besides, Violet had gotten lost several times before she found the suburb of Dunedin where Reverend Burton's church stood. Thus, it was almost midnight and as dark as it had been back when Violet and Rosie first sought sanctuary here many years ago.

Peter Burton even had a sense of déjà vu when he saw the young woman and the girl standing before the door after their knocking had roused him from bed. This time, however, it was not Rosie clinging to Violet exhausted but Roberta. Rosie was with the horse, which had walked alongside, hitched to the hay wagon. Dancing Rose, she explained to Violet, had never been away from home before. She shouldn't get frightened.

"Is Heather here?" asked Violet, without pausing for a salutation or her once-so-common curtsy.

The light of the oil lamp the pastor held in his hand fell on Violet's face, and Peter saw the devastating traces of blows but also exhaustion and anxiety. He shook his head. Heather and Chloe had arrived in Dunedin, but they were living in their apartment above Dunloe's Bank and the Gold Mine Boutique. Heather was not feeling well. In any case, it did not seem to be bad. Sean had spoken with the women. After that, he had taken care of a few other things in the city that probably had to do with him pushing back his trip to Christchurch. In any case, he would be staying until the next morning. He was staying the night in the parsonage but had only come home when Peter and Kathleen were already sleeping.

"Sean's the only one of the children here," noted Peter without having the slightest idea what he thereby unleashed.

"Sean's here?" Violet asked disbelievingly. "Sean is here?"

Peter wondered what she found so aberrant about that. After all, this was more or less his parents' house, so why would he stay in a hotel?

"Can I, then can I speak with Sean, please?"

Violet sank down on the steps leading to the front door and began to weep bitterly.

***

The mention of Violet's name tore Sean Coltrane out of his deep sleep and set him into action. Get dressed? He could not appear in his bathrobe. Shave? Peter had said it was urgent, so better not. Heavens, hopefully he did not look like he had been out all night. Sean was no teetotaler. That evening he had drunk champagne with Heather and Chloe and then whiskey with his old colleagues from the law office. What would she think of him if she smelled it on him? *Brush the teeth, rinse the mouth.* What had happened that Violet was there in the middle of the night?

Sean already had agreed with Jimmy Dunloe to come back to Dunedin after fulfilling his obligations in Christchurch so they could go to Invercargill. By then, they figured, Colin should have calmed down enough that they could speak with him. Sean and Chloe's stepfather wanted to retrieve Chloe's belongings and her horse, and offer Rosie a post in Dunedin. Sean had planned to speak with Violet then too. Chloe had agreed to take her and the children in as long as Violet left Eric.

Now Violet was at the kitchen table, sobbing desperately, her head buried in her arms. He only saw her tousled chestnut-brown hair. Beside her, her well-mannered daughter sat straight up. The delicate girl was her spitting image. Roberta was primly dressed—why in black, however, escaped Sean's understanding. Even her long, chestnut-brown hair was tied with a black ribbon into a ponytail. She sipped a cup of cocoa and looked exhausted and concerned for her mother.

"Rosie is still in the stables with Chloe's horse," Kathleen said. "Peter, show her where she can put it up."

"And the boy?" asked Sean. He remembered clearly that Violet had three children with her when he had seen her at the rally in Christchurch.

"He ran away," Violet sobbed. "I slapped him, and he's gone, and now he's going to tell everyone. They can't lock her up. Sean, please, you're a lawyer. You—"

She raised her head and looked directly into Sean's pale-green eyes. His slender face showed alarm at the sight of her swollen eyes and her busted lip, and, too, heartfelt concern.

Sean's dark hair was somewhat thinner than before. He looked older, but more important, more distinguished. Violet felt better at once. It was like magic.

"Violet, why don't you give yourself a moment to calm down, and then you can tell me everything that happened? No one's going to be locked up any time soon. Unless it is whoever did this to you." He indicated Violet's face. "That man could be locked up quickly."

"He's already burning in hell," she said calmly. "And Rosie killed him."

***

"Well, there's no question of murder in any case," Sean explained after Violet had told him what she thought she knew and what she was sure Joe had seen. "If there's an inquiry, which I doubt, then the most someone could prove is that Rosie was negligent. Regardless, Mr. Fence would meet with an appropriate amount of complicity. He should have checked the harnessing. You always check the girth before mounting if a groom saddles it."

Violet nodded. Now that Sean was speaking with her, she felt secure. As secure as she ever had in her life. But she was dead tired. Violet just wanted to sleep, and she would have liked to lean on Sean's shoulder for that. She forced herself to keep listening attentively.

"Joe will tell Mr. Coltrane and maybe the police officer," she objected. "And Mr. Coltrane will say Rosie is feebleminded, and they'll send her to an institution."

Sean shook his head. "Nonsense," he said. "Likely he'll tell Colin—it was a mistake to hit the boy and then let him get away, Violet. You should have stayed until he reappeared. And it would have been best not to hit him. Oh well, you know that. My brother won't volunteer to bring the police back. It will all come out in the wash, Violet, believe me. But you should go back and attend the funeral. You need to retrieve your son. If you want, I'll come."

Violet looked up at Sean, disbelieving. "You, you want to come with me?" Her battered face formed a weak smile.

"I thought you need to go to Christchurch, Sean?" Kathleen said.

Sean squared himself. "They'll get by without me in Christchurch," he said. "But this here." He let his gaze pass over Violet and smiled. "This I've already put off too long."

***

Violet's battered body refused to work. The Burtons brought in a doctor who advised no less than a week of bed rest. Violet stayed with the Burtons. After that, Sean accompanied her, as promised, to Invercargill. Roberta rode along, wearing the mourning dress Mrs. Robertson had put on her immediately after Eric's death. Rosie stayed with Heather and Chloe.

As Sean expected, Colin did not mention the cause of the accident at the funeral. He had organized the burial without bringing the police officer in again, and at the graveside, the pastor spoke of bad luck, but he could not refrain from saying a few admonishing words about the devil's water. Joe stood between Colin and Violet and listened with a scrunched face. In his Sunday suit and his father's cap, which he had worn constantly since the accident, he looked hauntingly like Eric. Violet had to force herself to be nice to him.

"He behaved badly," Mrs. Robertson said. "I wanted to care for him, since you seem to have forgotten him. I'm not blaming you, Violet. It was all too much. But he was just angry and mean and said awful things about poor Rosie. That she was to blame for his father. Rosie! That girl wouldn't hurt a fly. I had to wash his mouth out with soap."

Violet gave her son an apologetic look. He did not return it. Mrs. Robertson's measures had been drastic but effective. Eric's death was not discussed. Joe revolted, though, and threw a fit in which he insisted on remaining in Invercargill.

"Mr. Coltrane will take me as an apprentice," he said. "He promised me."

"You're too young," Violet argued.

Sean scrutinized the boy. Joe was eleven years old—a bit too young for a post, but not all that young. What was more, the boy was tall and strong. Sean thought of Colin. He had been about the same age when he refused to leave Ian Coltrane when his mother and siblings did. Kathleen had given her son up then. And now Violet.

"You should be going to school," said Violet. She had been sending her children to the village school, but she knew that Joe often skipped in favor of helping in the stables.

"I'm not going anywhere," said Joe.

Now Colin was approaching, and Sean steeled himself for a new confrontation. Before the burial, the brothers had only exchanged a few words.

"Well, if it isn't my wonderful brother. Who sent you to serve as guardian angel to our Mrs. Fence? My beloved sister or my beloved wife?" Colin fixed Sean with a brutal look.

"Neither one," Sean said calmly. "I don't practice law anymore, but you'll be hearing from Chloe. Heather will forego a complaint about the assault. Circumstances were, after all, a bit, hmm, embarrassing."

"Embarrassing?" Colin rumbled. "Two naked whores on my—"

"Hold your tongue, Colin," Sean ordered. "Or do you want to let all Invercargill know that your wife left you for another woman? I'm here as Violet's friend. She wants to liquidate her household, which I'm sure is fine by you. And she's taking her son with her."

Colin shook his head. "The boy stays here. That was a promise to Eric. He'll learn from me."

"Horse swindling?" Sean asked with an ironic smile.

"This is a recognized racing stable," Colin said brusquely. "And really you should be happy about any child you can find work and bread for, Mrs. Fence. You'll have a hard enough time feeding the rest of your dependents."

Violet bit her lip. It was true. Eric had not left her any money. Roberta was only ten. Violet would have to find work and a place to live. She looked to Sean for help.

"You know best, Violet," he said calmly.

She hesitated.

"She's still thinking about it," Sean said to Colin. "Would you like to go to your house, Violet?" He carefully placed his hand on her shoulder. He would have liked to hug her. However, he could not move too quickly. Violet would need time. "You did want to take a few things, didn't you?"

Violet shook her head. In truth, she had thrown everything she needed into the hay wagon. Violet was used to relocating quickly, and she did not own much. Nonetheless, she let Sean lead her into the house. Perhaps she could make some tea. It would be nice to just sit there with Sean and drink tea.

"Mommy, is it true that we won't have anything to eat anymore?" Roberta asked shyly.

Sean looked around the summerhouse's small but tidy rooms. So, this was where had she lived. Considerably better than the shack in Woolston, but the children still would have heard what transpired between their parents.

Violet gently put her arm around her daughter and pulled her close. The girl looked astoundingly like her. Like Violet long ago, she seemed too serious for her age and too smart.

"We're poor, that's true, dear," Violet said softly. "But I'll find work, don't you worry. And as long—"

"You could just bet on horses," Roberta asserted, freeing herself from the embrace.

While Sean and Violet looked at each other, confused, and Violet searched for a reply that would not portray Roberta's father as a scoundrel but would indicate the depravity of gambling, Roberta fished a red notebook from the corner her father had grandly called his "office."

"Here," Roberta said, holding the book out to her mother. "Joe showed it to me. Inside it says which horse is going to win."

***

"This is unbelievable," said Sean after he and Violet had studied the entries.

At first, the names of the pubs and betting offices and the lists of horse names did not say all that much to them, but then Violet remembered.

"It was a sensation back then when she won," she said, pointing to the name of the mare Annabelle. "Chloe fought with Colin over it. He had sold her as a racehorse, but Chloe didn't think she was one. She was slow and not suited to breeding for some reason. Mr. Coltrane was supposed to take her back, and he said he would if she didn't come in first in a race the next week."

"And?" Something was dawning on Sean.

"She really did win. Chloe was flabbergasted."

"Mrs. Coltrane must still have been blindly in love," snorted Sean. "Violet, unless I've completely missed my guess, this here is a list of rigged bets. That Eric of yours noted down all of Colin's crooked dealings."

"But why?" Violet asked, taken aback. "I mean, he was involved himself. He was always going from place to place and making bets elsewhere. I thought something was rotten. After all, he could have just put his tenner down on Mr. Coltrane's horses here."

Sean laughed. "He put down more than that. Look here: a hundred pounds in Christchurch, fifty in Dunedin." He pointed to neat lists documenting betting amounts in various gambling offices.

"But he could not have bet that much. He didn't earn that much."

Sean shook his head. "He placed the bets for Colin. And the apprentices and jockeys they employed here probably had a hand in it too. Eric made the bets—as far from here as possible and probably under assumed names—and Colin pocketed the money."

"Eric had to do it because Mr. Coltrane could not bet on his own horse?" asked Violet.

Sean shrugged. "I don't know for sure; I don't gamble. But you're not allowed to rig races. And if you take a close look here, the victors are noted before the bets were placed. Roberta is quite right: the book says which horse will win."

"But why did he write it down?" Violet thumbed through the notebook. Eric had kept accounts for years. "It incriminates him as much as Mr. Coltrane."

Sean shrugged. "Maybe he just had a bad memory and had to note the horses he was supposed to bet on. Or he wanted to have something against Colin just in case he did throw him out someday—he was a thorn in Chloe's side, after all. Perhaps it was also aimed at her. She would have rather kept Eric or paid him hush money than have thrown her husband to the wolves."

"But Mrs. Coltrane would never have covered this up," Violet said, completely convinced.

Sean shook his head. "No, she would perhaps have left Colin once she found out. But she would have avoided the social scandal. She would not have reported him. And everything would have been back to how Mr. Fence liked it."

Violet rubbed her temples. Sean kept flipping through the notebook.

"It's a question of what we're going to do now," he said finally. "Shall we go to the police? Or to the horse breeders' association? We need to put a stop to Colin's swindling, but, to be honest, I'm also a bit hesitant about the scandal. It'd blow back on Chloe. She wouldn't come out of it unscathed. When I think of the press and now her relationship with Heather—"

"Why don't we just take a tenner and put it on the horse that will win?" Roberta asked innocently. She had so far been quietly sitting nearby, listening to the adults, if apparently not quite understanding them. "You will lend us a tenner, won't you, Mr. Coltrane?"

Sean smiled. "Two even, Roberta, but what you have in mind is not exactly fair, you know. Betting is like a game. You can't decide ahead of time who's going to win."

"Don't listen to him, Roberta," Violet said coldly. "Mr. Coltrane says that because he's always been lucky in this game of life. But this game isn't fair, Roberta, and unfortunately, it's almost always determined before a race who's going to win. People like us can only try to make the best of it, when now and again we're dealt a joker. Like this book. I'm sorry, Mr. Coltrane, but I can't just throw it away as you would probably think right. Or Mrs. Coltrane. I have to do something with it. It's the only inheritance Eric left his son. But you're welcome to come with us, Mr. Coltrane."

Violet stuck the book in her bag, left the summerhouse, and went to the racetrack. Sean followed her without further question. The track was deserted. Violet entered the racing club.

"Might Mr. Tibbot still be in?" she asked some boys cleaning harnesses.

A few curious horses stuck their heads over the stall doors. Sean stroked their noses.

The girl trotted obediently behind her mother, but she ducked her head in front of the horses. When they passed the stall of a somewhat nervous stallion, Roberta reached fearfully for Sean's hand. Sean was touched and held her hand tight.

"Who's Mr. Tibbot?" Sean asked Roberta.

"Mr. Tibbot trains the harness racehorses," Roberta said in her somewhat stilted, formal tone. "He's Mr. Coltrane's chief competitor."

A child to whom Violet had read the dictionary in the cradle. Sean had misgivings. Meanwhile, Violet had located the trainer. A short, square man with a red, open face and small blue eyes. Assuredly Irish in origin. Sean greeted him politely. Roberta curtsied.

"Mr. Tibbot." Violet formally extended her hand.

Tibbot bowed over it. "Once again, my heartfelt condolences, Mrs. Fence. If there's anything I can do for you."

"That you can, Mr. Tibbot," Violet said calmly, even though she wasn't at all sure Mr. Tibbot's offer was genuine. "I'd like you to take on my son as an apprentice. He's still a bit young, I know, but the jockeys do always start young, and I know that your apprentices live in your house and your wife cooks for them. I would like that for Joe, if it would please you."

"Mrs. Fence, I don't know. I already have two apprentices, and Joe, he's rather tall and heavy. He won't do as a racer."

"He can drive, though," said Violet. "Or train. Or clean out the stables, or I don't know what all. But I'd like him to work for you and not for Colin Coltrane. I'd like—"

The matter was visibly uncomfortable for Mr. Tibbot. He wiggled like an eel. "Mrs. Fence, I, I don't mean to speak ill of your husband and Mr. Coltrane, but those two have already heavily shaped Joe. I would not be able to rely on his discretion. And I can't risk him immediately talking in the neighboring stables about everything he sees and learns here."

Violet drew the notebook from her bag. "This would come with my son, Mr. Tibbot. And if you use it properly, there won't be a neighboring stable anymore."

**

Mr. Tibbot and the still-young trainers, riders, drivers, and breeders of harness racehorses did not want a scandal any more than did Sean and Chloe. Therefore, Eric Fence's notebook did not end up in the hands of the police or the press. While its contents did reach the trainers and horse owners in rumors, the bet rigging was never proven. It was, however, punished, and more harshly than the legal system of the scandal-mongering press ever could have done.

Tibbot dutifully said a prayer for Colin Coltrane and then passed the notebook to a bookmaker in Invercargill. This man then handed it on to other representatives of his profession in Christchurch and Dunedin. The men needed a few days to calculate their losses. Then their troop of executors appeared at Colin Coltrane's—and collected.

Chapter 11

Atamarie Drury's first word was "mommy," her second "granny"—that was what she called Amey Daldy, like the step-grandchildren among whom she was raised. But her third word was "petition," for that encapsulated most of her mother's work since Atamarie's birth.

"I'm coming, love. I just have to write this petition." "Atamarie, go straight to Mrs. Daldy and ask her if she's already signed this petition." "No, sweetie, we can't go to the beach Sunday. I need to collect signatures for Kate Sheppard's petition." After the third word, Matariki stopped keeping track, but she was quite certain that "women's suffrage" counted among the first ten words in her daughter's vocabulary.

Matariki had begun her work with Amey Daldy as a teacher and intermediary between the *pakeha* and Maori, but since the fight for the right of women to vote had entered its crucial phase, she was occupied almost exclusively with that, even though she found the work boring.

"Elsewhere the women take to the streets and attack the police with their umbrellas," she complained to Lizzie and Michael when they visited her in Auckland. "And they're locked up, singing hymns in jail. At least there's action in that. And what do we do? We write petition after petition after petition. All told, more than seven hundred, not counting all the letters to individual parliamentarians. We've probably cut down half a forest for all that paper."

Michael and Lizzie laughed. They were in high spirits. Lizzie wore a bold little hat atop her increasingly gray hair and with it, one of the new dresses from Kathleen's collection. She had put on a little weight in the last few years and was happy not to have to wear a corset anymore. Now she was sipping the champagne Michael had ordered as an aperitif and looking forward to a fine meal in one of the best restaurants in Auckland with Matariki and nine-year-old Atamarie. Matariki had protested because she thought the restaurant was much too expensive. Lizzie would not be dissuaded. If they were going to be in the city, Lizzie wanted to go someplace with a large and refined wine list, although it was becoming difficult to find a restaurant that served alcohol. Paradoxically, the Temperance Union met with success precisely where alcohol abuse rarely occurred. Whereas pubs continued to spring up from the ground like weeds, family restaurants ceased pouring beer and wine.

"Well, half a forest or a whole one, I feel better, anyway, having you running around and writing petitions. I can't come visit you in prison," Lizzie teased her daughter.

"Not to mention all the bail fees we'd have to pay to get you out again," Michael said, smirking. "We couldn't bear the responsibility for letting our beautiful granddaughter grow up in prison if you end up there."

He cast a content glance at Atamarie, who was sitting between her grandparents and studying the menu. Michael could hardly get enough of looking at the child, which prompted a few pointed remarks from Lizzie. Atamarie did not owe her clear skin and golden hair to her Maori ancestors. They contributed only the exotic features: her darker complexion and nut-brown eyes with flecks of amber. Otherwise, the girl resembled her paternal grandmother, the love of Michael's youth, Kathleen Burton. Today, however, Lizzie had other things to do than chide her husband. She studied the wine list intensely.

"I think we'll stick to champagne for the crab cocktails," she decided. "Then, if we get the lamb, the 'eighty-seven Bordeaux. Or do you want fish, Matariki? In that case, Chardonnay."

Judging from Lizzie's expression, she would have liked best to order both sorts of wine. Since she was no longer trying to grow grapes for heavy red wines, concentrating instead on light white wines whose grapes simply flourished better in Otago's climate, her results had been thoroughly drinkable.

"Chardonnay, Mom, but please don't strangle me if I drink it out of a water glass." Matariki grimaced. "Mrs. Daldy would kill me herself if she found out I drank alcohol. Worst of all in public." Amey Daldy was a strict teetotaler and also demanded that her coworkers not drink. Another thing that Matariki liked to get worked up about. "We'd long since have had the right to vote if it weren't tied to this prohibition disaster," she said. "Most men don't care if we vote, but when you tell them that we're going to shut the beer taps, they kick up a fuss. Even John Ballance is supposed to have said that he supports our right to vote, but women vote for the conservatives because there are more teetotalers among them."

Giving up alcohol did not matter much to Matariki, but she did not see it as the root of all evil. The McConnells, her tormentors in Hamilton, had been strict teetotalers, but that had not made them good people. Meanwhile, Reverend Burton, for example, had done good his whole life and nevertheless capped his day with a glass of whiskey.

"There is the Women's Franchise League, without 'temperance' in its name," said Lizzie.

Matariki nodded. "Yes, they finally did something sensible in Dunedin. And the new signature gatherings for women's suffrage are showing phenomenal results. Last month, we took twenty thousand signatures to Parliament."

"Yeah, Mrs. Sheppard really did push a wheelbarrow," Atamarie told them. "And we all went with them and painted banners and sang. Only we couldn't go into Parliament. John Hall did, though, and Uncle Sean." Apparently, there had been a fairground atmosphere.

Lizzie took notice. "Sean Coltrane?" she asked. "Are you in contact with him?"

Matariki nodded. "Of course, but mostly by letter. Last month, though, we were in Wellington and met with him. We had a good time, didn't we, Atamarie?"

Atamarie told them enthusiastically about the capital and their meeting with her uncle. Michael listened, full of pride, although it had at first seemed suspect to him that Sean—the son of an Irish rebel—now sat in Parliament with the Brits. He had moved past it. There were no Irish and English here anymore, just New Zealanders. And Sean did more for the simple folk than the Drurys in Ireland had ever done. Sean probably would have maintained that supplying the population with bootleg whiskey was not even a particularly socially minded deed. He had never really taken after his birth father, the freedom fighter.

Lizzie was motivated by very different concerns. "Isn't that young Maori also in Parliament in Wellington? Kupe, right? How is he doing?"

Matariki chewed her upper lip. It was typical of her mother to bring the conversation around to acquaintances. Lizzie was a little worried about her future. She surely would have liked more grandchildren, but the way things looked, she would have to wait until Kevin and Pat married, which could take a while. Both of Matariki's brothers were attending university in Dunedin. Not that Matariki was opposed to new acquaintances. Colin had not broken her heart as badly as Lizzie feared, nor had she been abstinent during her first years in Auckland. Back then, she was often a guest among the Maori tribes, and she had occasionally given in to the urging of one of the young men after sitting for an evening around the fire with her people, drinking and telling stories about Parihaka. However, she had not fallen in love with any of them, and she had ceased these adventures, too, when Atamarie was big enough to pick up on something and perhaps tell Amey Daldy about it. Despite her openness to Maori customs, the strict Congregationalist expected complete abstinence from her teachers, and Matariki could only be kept on as a pretend widow. Although Matariki had stopped her Sunday prayers for her departed husband once Atamarie began to understand more, she did not establish new contacts with *pakeha* men. Not that there was much opportunity to do so, anyway. Matariki's work was mostly with women. She occasionally met male politicians who supported women's suffrage, but apart from Sean Coltrane, they were all married, and under no circumstances would they have indulged in even a little flirting with a women's rights activist.

"Kupe doesn't want to have anything to do with me," she told her mother regretfully. "I wrote to Pai once. She and Kupe were together in Parihaka and then in Wellington. She wrote back, saying he didn't want to read my letter. He still holds it against me that I fell in love with Colin and ran away with him. Yet Kupe wasn't even in Parihaka anymore then. They arrested him beforehand, even though Colin tried to stop it."

"Did he really?" the keen-witted Lizzie inquired. "Or did he have a hand in it? Maybe he saw Kupe as a rival and had him cleared out of the way? By the way, Chloe left him."

Matariki nodded, not overly interested. "So I heard. Good for Chloe. They say he's sold the house and the horses and everything? Which she never saw a penny of, though. But please."

She gestured discreetly with her chin at Atamarie. The girl was not to hear too much talk concerning her birth father. Lizzie sometimes wondered what she even knew. According to Maori custom, Matariki ought to have informed her daughter about her father, but Atamarie had to play the half orphan for the *pakeha*.

"I'd be happy to meet Kupe again," Matariki said, returning to the original subject, "but he's obviously avoiding me. Maybe when we've passed women's suffrage. Then I'll be devoting myself more to Maori affairs. Those are still in disarray, after all."

***

Matariki intended to resign her job with Amey Daldy in the near future. Recently, Meri Te Tai Mangakahia, whose husband had just been elected premier of the Maori Parliament, was creating a stir. Matariki had gotten to know her in Christchurch and liked her immediately. Meri was just a little younger than Matariki, had likewise enjoyed a *pakeha* education, and was a chieftain's daughter. Her father was only elected *ariki* of his tribe in 1890, so she had been spared the strange customs of some of the North Island's tribes and the Hauhau. Now, she was fighting not just for women's suffrage but also for female representatives to be allowed in the Maori Parliament.

Matariki yearned to work with young people again instead of the sometimes-fossilized ladies around Amey Daldy. There did not need to be street battles with police, but Matariki did want something more than letter writing from her political engagement.

However, she had not expected that her meal with her family would catapult her into the center of events. Nor did she sense anything amiss when Amey Daldy called her to her office the next morning. Her boss received her in the living room but did not offer her a seat in any of the plush armchairs. Mrs. Daldy sat at a little secretary where she tended to manage her private correspondence. It was very tidy there, whereas in Matariki's office, petitions piled up and law books were scattered about.

"You were at the Four Seasons yesterday?" Mrs. Daldy asked sternly.

Matariki nodded. The Temperance Union had its eyes everywhere. "With my parents," she said conciliatorily, "and I only had a little wine."

"It was alcohol in public, Matariki. I've had two gentlemen speak to me about it. You drank champagne, wine, and cognac. And you laughed."

"Surely laughing in public isn't forbidden," Matariki said, astonished. "And I only sipped the cognac. My mother said I had to try it. My mother—"

"According to my informants, the man was also not your father," Mrs. Daldy said. "And your mother was described as an exceedingly frivolous person. Assuming she really is your mother. Matariki, this is not acceptable. We who are fighting for the right for equal treatment of women must be models of virtue and abstinence. With you, that's already questionable. True, you made no secret that Atamarie is a child born out of wedlock. However, we had agreed that, given the circumstances, you would present yourself as a widow. Now Atamarie's saying Sean Coltrane is her uncle."

It was so complicated that Matariki decided it best to dive in headfirst. "Sean Coltrane is her uncle on both sides. That is, he's my half brother through my father, Michael Drury, who, as you correctly determined, is not my biological father, while Colin Coltrane is Atamarie's father and Sean is Colin's half brother—"

"And the child is aware of these relationships?"

"More or less. Well, I don't believe she knows that Sean is Michael's son. But—"

"Matariki, this is unacceptable," said Amey Daldy. "I've always looked the other way for you, and you do exceptional work. But if Atamarie were to begin spreading the word that her father isn't even dead—"

"I can't force her to lie," Matariki responded. "I can tell her she should keep it quiet, but she's so proud of her uncle Sean, and she does also look like him, you know."

"Which further complicates the matter," Amey Daldy said. "There have been rumors about you and Sean Coltrane since the delivery of the last petition to Wellington. You were seen together—"

"We didn't drink any wine," Matariki assured her. "And of course we were seen. We were in a large restaurant."

"That doesn't matter. Moderation and abstinence must define our entire lives, Matariki. I've been thinking about this a long time, and I don't make this decision lightly. But with this business last night, I've decided to end our relationship, Matariki." At least she looked her assistant of many years directly in the eye as she said it.

Matariki was silent for a moment. "Me too," she then said. "That is, I actually wanted to resign. But just now? How will you manage everything,

Mrs. Daldy? The goal for the next petition is thirty thousand signatures. The law has to pass next year, and Mrs. Sheppard is counting on us. Who's going to write all the letters and send all the telegrams and—"

"Those who have always done it," Amey Daldy said abruptly. "Virtuous, Christian women. We will need a few more volunteers. I'm sorry, Matariki, but it's better we roll back our expectations a bit than betray our principles."

Matariki brushed her hair out of her face. She usually wore it up, but a few strands always broke free. Matariki had often been annoyed by that, but now, however, she felt something like joy and pride welling up about it. Her hair would not be bound, nor would she. She wasn't fighting for women's rights just to be locked in a corset of virtue and principles by members of her own sex.

"Then I'll be going," she said calmly. "I'll pick up Atamarie from school, and then we'll drive to Wellington. I'm going to keep fighting, Mrs. Daldy. I won't roll back my expectations. And you and your Christian teetotalers should consider whether you really want women's suffrage. Once we have it, after all, we might vote for something that doesn't suit you. Something like laughing and drinking wine, perhaps in the company of men. Maybe you've been fighting a false fight all these years, Mrs. Daldy. Maybe you don't just want to give women the right to vote but to take it away from men too. That way a few self-righteous goody-goodies can determine what's pleasing to God." Matariki glared at her boss who eyed her, uncomprehending. But she smiled at the old woman. "Regardless, we'll be seeing each other in September in front of Parliament," she said. "Now, the last thing we need is to be fighting among ourselves. It was a pleasure working for you, Mrs. Daldy."

Matariki left the gloomy room and stepped into the sunshine. She practically danced to Atamarie's school. Her daughter would be happy to get out of the strict institution. Then Matariki would telegraph Meri Te Tai. There was a lot to do. And Matariki was looking forward to it.

White Camellias

Wellington, North Island

1892–1893

Chapter 1

Matariki and Atamarie did not go to Wellington right away; instead, they went to Waipatu, where Meri Te Tai Mangakahia lived with her family and where in June the first Maori Parliament had convened. The Te Kotahitanga movement wanted to oppose the government of white settlers in Wellington with a representative body of the tribes. They agreed on bills, which the two Maori representatives who had sat in the *pakeha*'s Parliament from the beginning were to make universally valid. That only progressed to a point, and the collaboration was not perfect. So far, it had gone as well for Maori as for white women: they did not take part in the election of representatives to Wellington. In that respect, their representatives were elected by the whites who naturally chose yes-men over freedom fighters. That, too, was supposed to change with the next election, or so Meri and Matariki hoped.

"Why did you start by convening in the middle of nowhere?" asked Matariki. She was impressed by the beauty of the landscape, the white beaches, the almost tropical vegetation, and the very traditional Maori settlements. "Politics get done in Wellington, you know."

Meri Te Tai, a very pretty, dark-haired woman who always dressed in the latest *pakeha* fashion, shrugged. "You'd have to ask the men. I don't make those decisions. But I believe it has to do with independence. We can't let ourselves be ordered around by the whites when it comes to where and how we arrive at our decisions, and we don't want a Parliament Building. Our representatives will convene in a different part of the country every time and be hosted by other tribes."

"But that makes everything more difficult," Matariki said. "Don't you think we should have an office? Constant representation in Wellington?"

Meri smiled. "Sean Coltrane also advised us of that. Women should represent. After all, we are fighting on two fronts for the right to vote—as Maori and as women. Would you like to run an office like that? As for the financing, we're collecting donations."

Matariki nodded cheerfully. "I might know a tribe on the South Island that's provided with considerable means and has always generously supported the struggle for freedom."

She smiled, thinking of Kahu Heke's thinly veiled extortion attempts. The Ngai Tahu had cursed him but paid. Haikina and her tribe would prefer supporting peaceful emancipation efforts. It wasn't a hardship. There was still a lot of gold in the stream near Elizabeth Station.

***

The office on Molesworth Street, diagonally across from the Parliament Building, opened in November 1892, just in time to lend support to Kate Sheppard's last petition for the right of women to vote.

"Officially we can't leave our representation to any woman on her own," said an apologetic Hamiora Mangakahia, the premier and Meri Te Tai's husband. "It can't be just about the right to vote. It will be a proxy for the Te Kotahitanga Maori Parliament in Wellington, and we can't occupy that with just women."

Matariki had recruited a few of her former students from the beginning of her time with Amey Daldy to work with her. "I thought I was taking over the office management," Matariki said confidently. "Especially since I organized the largest portion of the financing."

Hamiora nodded. He had come out of his way to Wellington to open the office and speak with Matariki.

"And you will. But together with a man, you see? Sean Coltrane recommended an exceptionally capable young jurist to us, someone else who's spent a long time supporting the campaign for the right to vote, that is, someone used to women with *mana*."

Matariki smiled grimly. "But not a *pakeha*, right?" she asked.

Hamiora shook his head. "No, a pure-blooded Maori. Even if he doesn't know in which canoe his ancestors arrived in Aotearoa. He should be here any minute. I told him three o'clock." He looked at the wall clock.

"And why all this cloak-and-dagger?" asked Matariki somewhat indignantly. "Why couldn't you tell me ahead of time?"

"Sean Coltrane thought it would be better if we asked pardon rather than permission," he said sheepishly.

Matariki was not particularly surprised that they were placing a male coworker at her side, but she had hoped to be involved in selecting candidates. While she was looking for further arguments and objections, there was a knock.

Hamiora opened the door.

There stood a Maori whose powerful body almost burst out of his proper suit. His hair was short, but he wore the tattoos of a warrior.

Kupe looked at Matariki just as incredulously as she looked at him.

"You?" they asked each other almost simultaneously.

And then came a whining sound from under Matariki's desk. Dingo, now very old, struggled to his feet and greeted his friend. Contrary to how he felt about Colin, Dingo had always liked Kupe.

***

Kupe scratched the animal, giving him an excuse not to look at Matariki. Eventually, though, he would have to look up.

"I didn't know," he said.

Matariki shrugged. Then she smiled. "I didn't either. But I'm happy to see you."

Kupe wanted to make an unfriendly reply. However, he could not bring himself to do so. He would not abandon her. Besides, how would he explain to Hamiora Mangakahia that he was not going to take the work after all, which he had just called his dream job?

Matariki held out her hand. "To doing good work together," she said firmly.

Kupe was silent. He simply shook her hand.

***

Matariki and Kupe managed to work almost half a year together in the same office without ever exchanging one word with each other. Kupe was the one who wouldn't speak. Matariki found his attitude childish. After a while, she got annoyed and ceased talking to him, which would not have been so easy for her if Sean Coltrane had not added a position to the office, thus setting a buffer between the two representatives of the Maori: in February, Violet Fence occupied a desk in the office of the Te Kotahitanga.

"You do have space here," Sean had said, and he presented his plan to Matariki and Kupe. "And Kate Sheppard and her Women's Christian Temperance Union urgently need permanent representation in the capital for as long as the campaign lasts."

"And for that, someone had to come all the way from the South Island?" Matariki asked. She reacted as if allergic to the words "Christian" and "temperance." "Aren't there any teetotaling Methodists in Wellington who could work from their living room?"

He had expected a question like that and gave Kupe a pleading look. After the rally in Dunedin, Kupe had stood in for him in Christchurch. Kupe had to sense that Sean wanted Violet Fence near him for personal reasons as well.

"Violet is not a fanatic. She's a very reasonable woman. You'll like her, Matariki. And she needs to get out. She needs a job."

"And there are no jobs in Dunedin or Christchurch for a reasonable woman who can read and write?" asked Matariki. "Well, fine, what do I care? Hopefully it's just for a few months. I won't drink in her presence. I'll ask her not to pray. I'm sure we'll get along."

Violet wouldn't ever think of praying in the office, and after two months of working together, she let Matariki convince her to try the new wine Lizzie sent to Wellington with high hopes: "Tell me if this isn't as good as the Chardonnay at the Four Seasons."

At first, Violet found it a little strange to be between two people who had mastered both English and Maori and who liked to talk to people but never with each other. They tried not to communicate at all, but when there was no choice, the messages passed through Violet: "Please tell Kupe he should remind Sean of the copy of Sir William Fox's letter if he runs into him later." "Would you be so good as to inform Miss Drury that more signed petitions have arrived from Mrs. Daldy?"

Violet put up with this for a while. She wondered if this sort of behavior was normal among secretaries and clerks but could not imagine it was. However, she did not want to cause problems. She was happy about her work for Kate

Sheppard, which also kept her near Sean Coltrane and far from Colin's sphere of influence.

There had been some fuss before she convinced Joe to begin his apprenticeship with Tibbot instead of Coltrane. Violet had to admit that without Sean's support, she wouldn't have managed to face Colin and justify her decision. Naturally, Colin had raged when she accused him of having misled her son into dishonest business practices. He would charge her with slander and any damages to his business if she spread such accusations. That had frightened Violet, but Sean wasn't concerned.

"This isn't about whether you're a horse swindler, Colin," he finally had said. "You're not the guardian of Joseph Fence. The boy is a minor, so from a legal perspective, that means his mother decides about where he lives and apprentices. Joe would like to work with horses, and Mrs. Fence has found a trainer with whose family he can live during his apprenticeship. You can't offer him anything comparable since your wife did, regretfully, leave you, which, you have to admit, might relate to the question of whether you're a horse swindler. In any case, you can't offer your apprentices a family life. Therefore, Joe is going to Mr. Tibbot, or to Dunedin with his mother." He turned to Joe. "And you do not need to start screaming again, young man. Those are your two options, so decide."

Violet had looked at Sean in awe after this speech. She couldn't imagine the confidence to argue with such polish. Colin kept his mouth shut, as did Joe; Violet had never seen him so pliant as under the calm but definite guidance of Sean Coltrane.

"You'll be a good father someday," she had said shyly after Joe was delivered to his new master, having parted with a polite bow. "If you ever marry, I mean." She blushed again.

Sean acted as if he did not notice. "And you, Violet," he remarked with a smile, "are a very good mother."

***

Before she moved to Wellington, Violet had heard that Colin Coltrane found himself in great financial difficulties. Naturally, she assumed this had to do with the contents of Eric's notebook. How precisely, she did not know, nor did she care. Should Colin find out that she had something to do with it, however, well, she felt more secure at a distance.

Ultimately, Violet asked Sean about the strange conditions in his office. He sometimes picked her and Roberta up on the weekend—they had rented a room in a widow's large penthouse while Rosie had stayed in Dunedin to work for Chloe and Heather—and took them walking or for a drive. Only in busy areas. He would not dream of compromising her. Now he seemed about to topple from laughter at Violet acting as go-between for Kupe and Matariki.

"No, Violet, that's not normal. I can assure you of that. But what exactly happened between the two of them, I don't know."

"Atamarie says Kupe is in love with her mom," Roberta said. On their first day in Wellington, she had made friends with Matariki's daughter, who was one year younger than Roberta, and since then had lost some of her shyness.

Violet furrowed her brow, but Sean laughed again. "I suspected as much, Roberta, but it's not proper to say so directly to people." He winked conspiratorially to the girl, then to her mother. "Just ask the two of them why they don't talk to each other sometime, Violet. I'm curious how they'd answer."

After that, Violet took heart and spoke to Matariki, who then invited Violet to lunch at the nearest café, where she told her about Parihaka.

"We were always good friends," Matariki observed. "Sure, he was in love with me, and I wasn't with him, but that didn't burden the relationship. Until they arrested Kupe, and I went to Dunedin with Colin. What's eating him now, though, I don't know. But if that's how he wants it, I don't need to talk to him. We'll just see who lasts longer in silence."

This last point sounded defiant. Matariki seemed intent on making a sort of game out of the situation. Violet didn't think Matariki was truly indifferent toward Kupe, and she wondered if this was some form of flirting.

As their lunch continued, she learned about Matariki's relationship with Colin Coltrane and thereby a bit of the background to the marriage of the mistress she idolized, Chloe.

"He can be very charming. I can't blame Chloe for falling for his act," said Matariki. "And he has other qualities, too, if you know what I mean."

Violet did not know what she meant—at least not until that evening, when the women ended up telling each other secrets over glasses of Lizzie's wine.

"Colin was the best lover I ever had," Matariki said, "but an ass otherwise."

"So, you mean it can really be enjoyable?" Violet finally asked, doubtful, after Matariki had also commented on her other experiences with men. "You did it willingly? I only ever found it horrible." Her face showed repulsion and fear at the memory of Eric's embrace alone.

Matariki took her hand and led her to the window. "Look out there, Violet," she said, rather tipsy after three glasses of wine. "Outside is the night. It's part of life and inextricable at that. It sometimes seems threatening, and not always without reason. Somewhere there really are murderers and thieves slinking about. Sometimes it's horrid—when you have to fight through the dark while it's storming, and hail hits your skin like arrows. But it can also be beautiful: velvety and warm and lit by the full moon, and thousands of stars to show you the way. When everything goes right, Violet, when you can choose, then you only go out in starry nights like these, when you can bathe in the moonlight and your ancestors send you a smile through the stars. But when it's not going well, when you have to flee through dark, dangerous nights, or when you live in an area where it constantly snows and rains, then you learn to hate the night. It's the same with lovemaking. When you're forced, when the man is brutal, and when you don't love him, then it's horrible. But with a good man, an experienced man—especially one with whom you're in love—it's the most wonderful thing in the world." Matariki looked at her friend radiantly.

"And what's it like to be in love?" Violet inquired.

Matariki's ecstasy turned to confusion. "Don't you know? Oh, I didn't realize. What with the way you're always looking at Sean."

***

After this and more evenings with Matariki, Violet began to dress more consciously and colorfully, and she tried not to lower her eyes shyly when she encountered Sean. With every day that passed in Wellington, she felt younger and happier. For the first time in her life, she had a real friend, she was reading novels instead of the dictionary, and spending the money she earned on new clothes.

And she dared to admit to herself that she loved Sean Coltrane.

***

Kupe and Matariki stuck to their silence for the first months of 1893, though it was an exciting time for the suffragettes and their supporters. The list of signatures on Kate Sheppard's petition that year grew longer and longer, but at the same time, the opponents of women's suffrage mobilized. The movement's archenemy was a politician from Dunedin, Henry Smith Fish, a lobbyist for the alcohol industry. Fish wrote requests and petitions almost as ardently as the women, and he found it easy enough to gather signatures: one round through Dunedin's pubs on Saturday night, and he had just as many signatures as Kate in a month of laboriously knocking on doors. Once, however, he had bad luck and picked a pub where Peter Burton and a Catholic brother of the cloth not opposed to a well-poured beer himself were topping off their evening. The priest and pastor observed with equanimity as Fish first made a fiery speech—and then had every guest at the pub sign it three times. Burton and the priest went public with the story, and from then on, Fish was considered untrustworthy. Ballance, the premier, ordered him to his office and upbraided him. Ballance was avowedly on the side of the women, and everyone was counting on a victory in September.

But then, on a quiet day at the end of April 1893, Sean Coltrane rushed into the office of the Te Kotahitanga. He could hardly believe what he had to tell Kupe, Matariki, and Violet.

"He's dead," he blurted out. "John Ballance. In his office. A heart attack, we think. His secretary was on hand. All morning he was saying he felt under the weather, and then he seized his chest and fell over. The doctor couldn't do anything for him."

"But this is a disaster," Matariki said. "For him and his family, but also for us. What's going to happen now? Who's going to replace him?"

"Richard Seddon probably. Ballance already appointed him his deputy. In that respect, he's been formally presiding over the upper house for almost a year," Kupe noted, forgetting that he was thereby also addressing his words to Matariki. "But he—"

"He's no real Liberal," Matariki completed the thought. "It's not about political goals with him, just influence. And the Liberals are simply the party with the most supporters."

"He's a populist," Kupe added.

In her head, Violet thanked Caleb Biller for the hundredth time for his dictionary.

"You mean to say he doesn't have time for women and the Maori," she said timidly.

The others nodded gloomily.

"That's putting it mildly," Sean sighed. "The man is, well, one of the conservatives once described him as 'partly civilized.' However, it seems rather disrespectful to me to be talking about his successor now. John Ballance was a good man. We should say a prayer."

Violet lowered her head and joined Sean in saying an Our Father. Kupe and Matariki politely murmured the words to the Christian prayer but then looked at each other. As before in Parihaka, they did not need to say anything. At once and in harmony, they began singing a *haka*. Both had lovely voices, and the Maori lamentations for the dead sounded out onto the streets of Wellington. John Ballance had labored for understanding between the races. He had brought along many laws that benefited both the Maori and *pakeha* equally.

Whether Richard Seddon would continue down this path was written in the stars.

***

In the small office of the Te Kotahitanga and the Women's Christian Temperance Union, at least, John Ballance posthumously provided for reconciliation and peace: on the day of his death, Matariki and Kupe began speaking to each other. Not much, not often, and not over anything personal, but the ice was broken.

As Sean and Kupe had expected, the day after Ballance's death, the governor named Richard Seddon the new premier, a bitter setback for women, Maori, and other people struggling for recognition. Sean suddenly found himself confronted with the Chinese Protestant immigrants whom Seddon had described as monkeys. Sean had to wrestle with new ministers whose only qualifications for their posts were their friendships with Seddon, and he reported to Matariki and Violet on the heated debates on women's suffrage. Seddon rejected it forcefully and pleaded just as passionately against any bills regarding the sale of alcohol.

"He's being paid by every brewery and distillery in the country," Sean speculated, "and they're also torpedoing any push in the direction of women's suffrage."

"It's just a question of what he has against the Maori," Kupe sighed. "You really can't accuse us of lacking a taste for alcohol."

Matariki smirked. "My dad even taught the Ngai Tahu how to distill the stuff themselves," she remarked. "His friend Tane still delivers to half the South Island."

"I just think it's disgraceful," Violet ranted. She still could not laugh at whiskey-related jokes. "Equality of the races and sexes counts among the foundations of Liberal politics. This Seddon can't play the party leader and premier if he denies them."

"Robert Stout told him that to his face too." Sean grinned. "In just about as many words. You'll be giving speeches soon, Violet. Mark my words."

"We'll all be giving speeches," Matariki said. "We all have to redouble our efforts. From now on, it'll be one rally after another. We'll demonstrate so loudly that Mr. Seddon won't be able to hear himself think."

***

The Women's Christian Temperance Union, the Women's Franchise League, their Maori equivalents, and the Tailoresses' Union all made good on Matariki's threat. The women's organizations outdid one another in the writing of petitions and calls to rally. Women protested in front of Parliament practically every day and collected signatures. As a sign of their vocation, they decorated their clothes and hats with white camellias.

Atamarie and Roberta participated ardently. The girls painted banners together, helped carry them through the streets at the protest marches, and asked their mothers to let them gather votes together.

"If there are two of us, no one'll try anything. We'll be able to run around and gather signatures."

Matariki and Violet allowed them, at least at their own rally, and the girls almost burst with pride when first Matariki and then Violet as well took the podium and pled passionately for women's suffrage.

Violet began her speech with the words, "I'd like to tell you a story today," just as Sean had begun his address in Christchurch. Clearly and passionately, she described her marriage and how she had joined the fight through the Temperance Union for the right of women to vote. "I don't know if I would be standing here if this were a rally for a strict alcohol ban," she concluded. "There are arguments for and against that, and every woman and every man will have to weigh them when we really do hold a debate over whether the devil gets into our husbands through the whiskey, or whether there are also other reasons they mistreat us. But I know one thing for sure: men and women are equally capable of considering, weighing, and deciding. They must be equal under the law. So, give us the right to vote!"

Atamarie and Roberta hollered their excitement and yelled along when the women chanted, "Suffrage now."

"You little gals surely won't be voting any time soon. Is that any way to behave in public?" a curmudgeonly man said to them.

Roberta blushed, but Atamarie would not be cowed. She laughed in the man's face. Then she pointed to the women on the podium. "No, sir, we're too young. But we won't always be. Those women up there, our mothers, they want to vote. When we're old enough, we want to be elected. Sir, allow me to introduce Roberta Fence, premier 1920."

***

"Not a bad idea," Matariki said later when Atamarie told her about the scene. "Roberta in the *pakeha* Parliament, you in the Maori. Then we'd finally be able to work together."

"That'll be the day," Kupe snorted.

He left open whether he meant women's leadership overall or Atamarie in the office of Maori premier. She was, after all, anything but a pure-blooded Maori. Whenever Kupe looked at her, he recognized the features of his enemy.

Chapter 2

Two weeks before the upper house's decision in September, John Hall and a few other representatives brought the last petition of the women around Kate Sheppard to Parliament with more than thirty-two thousand signatures. All in all, a quarter of New Zealand's female population had spoken out for the right to vote, and Kate insisted on attaching all the signatures together herself and wrapping the list around a broomstick. John Hall presented it with all due theatrics, letting the list unroll from the broomstick down the long aisle in the middle of the legislative house. As he held up the petition before Parliament, the many thousands of names formed a row between the parliamentarians. At the end of the aisle, the bare broomstick stopped with a dull thud.

As expected, the bill passed the lower house with a large majority.

"We've managed that often enough before," Sean said. "It depends on the upper house, on September eighth."

***

A few days before that important date, Violet and Matariki could not find Roberta and Atamarie. They had agreed to a late lunch with the girls after school and planned to meet Kate Sheppard and Sean as well. Kate had arrived the day before. She wanted to be there for the decision in Wellington.

Violet grew nervous when Roberta had not arrived ten minutes after the agreed-upon time. "Just where is she? She's usually so punctual." Violet had already finished her work and was looking impatiently out the window at the street.

Matariki, who was still sealing letters, was less concerned. "I thought Atamarie was already here," she remarked distractedly. "Dingo was wagging his tail, anyway."

The old dog lay under Matariki's desk and was usually too tired to stand up and greet new arrivals. As a rule, though, he announced his friends by wagging his tail and whining, and he tended to notice their approach before they opened the door.

"Dingo wags his tail for just about anyone," Violet said, unconvinced.

Matariki sealed the last envelope. "Dingo only does that for us and the girls, Kupe, and Sean," she specified. "And Kupe went to eat with Hamiora an hour ago. Why would he come back now, walk up and down the street, and then just go again?"

"Why would the girls come and go again?"

She still worried about possible revenge schemes on the part of Colin Coltrane. Joe did not write about him anymore, but Joe rarely took up his pen. Heather, on the other hand, reported that when Chloe's lawyer had met with Colin, he was in a rather desperate situation. The stud farm was being liquidated. She did not mention anything more, and in truth, there had been nothing that suggested a concrete threat to Violet. However, she had lived in fear so long that she now—from Sean and Matariki's point of view, in any case—invented dangers.

Matariki shrugged. "How should I know what gets into Atamarie's head? Maybe they forgot their white camellias."

Atamarie and Roberta were exceedingly proud of the symbols identifying them as suffragettes. They would not meet with Kate Sheppard without a flower pinned to their clothes.

"Both of them?" Violet expressed doubt. While Matariki tidied up her desk, Violet paced back and forth between the two office rooms. "I'm going to go look for her," she said when the girls were almost twenty minutes past due. "Will you wait for them here?"

Matariki rolled her eyes. "We could also just go to the restaurant and leave a note for them on the door. I don't know about you, but I'm dying of hunger."

Matariki was not a bit worried. Atamarie was self-sufficient.

Violet shook her head. "How can you even think of food now?" she asked accusingly. "The girls are so reliable. Something must have happened to them." With that she stormed out.

Matariki stayed behind, shaking her head, but she used the time to write another letter. Violet was right when it came to Roberta. A person could set his watch by Violet's daughter. Atamarie, however, often talked Roberta into foolishness. Violet had to know that too.

***

Violet tried to think clearly. What could the girls have gotten into?

Violet scanned the broad street lined with tall trees to where it stopped at an angle across from the Parliament Building. The girls' current favorite game was "premier." What if they had stumbled on the idea of looking at their future workstations? Maybe a side door had been open, and the girls slipped inside and lost track of time exploring the building.

It was worth a try to look for a way in herself, and she was too nervous just to wait. She crossed the street and discovered a side entrance that was wide open to the gardens behind Parliament. Two Maori gardeners went in and out with watering cans, sacks of manure, and plants. The door must have led to the maintenance area.

The Maori greeted Violet with a friendly *kia ora*. Unfortunately, they did not understand English, so they couldn't answer her questions about the girls. Violet was almost sure of her hunch. Atamarie did not speak Maori as fluently as her mother, but she spoke enough to trick the gardeners about her and Roberta's business in the Parliament Building. Violet would not even put past her a "*Kia ora*, we're the future premiers and wanted to take a look around first."

She wavered between looking for the girls herself and going back to the office to ask Matariki to question the gardeners. She shied away from entering buildings closed to strangers and women, but the door was open. And it was her Parliament, belonging to all New Zealanders, man or woman.

The gardeners did not stop her from entering, and she didn't encounter anyone as she went through the maintenance area and storerooms. Now, almost more curious than concerned, she climbed the stairs to the main level, admiring the inlay work and columns in the broad corridors, and looking with awe into the large assembly hall. Finding no trace of the girls, Violet decided to continue up to the second floor, where she found archives, libraries, and offices. From one of the offices, behind a large, elaborately worked door, sounded the characteristic giggling of excited girls.

"Go, just have a seat in your chair, Robbie. So you get a feel for it. Roberta Fence, the premier. Or is it mistress premier?"

Violet looked at the sign next to the office door: "Mr. Richard Seddon, Premier." She flung open the door. Roberta had just settled into the premier's chair. Atamarie was enjoying the view out the office's large windows.

"Have you two lost your minds?" Violet yelled. "We've been worried sick about you, and you're in Mr. Seddon's office. What do you think he'd do with you if he caught you?"

She did not know that herself either, but there was guaranteed to be a heavy punishment for snooping around at the center of power. Roberta sprang up at once, but Atamarie would not be intimidated so easily.

"We just wanted to bring him a white camellia," she said. "We thought it'd be a good idea. He'd ask himself who put it on his desk, and then—"

"That's just about the stupidest idea I've ever heard," Violet shouted. "The man would think who knows what, and it's possible Sean and Sir William Fox and the other supporters of our law would have to answer for it. Now, get going, out. We'll talk about your punishment later."

"Shh, Mom."

Roberta put her finger to her lips and looked fearfully at the door. And now Violet heard it too. Heavy footsteps were approaching in the hallway. The three interlopers froze.

"Come into my office," a booming voice sounded. "We'll talk better over whiskey."

For a moment, Violet hoped the man meant a different office, but she knew better. Atamarie was already looking for a way out.

"In here," she whispered to the others.

Next to the cabinet on the wall was a narrow door that led to a tiny closet. There was barely enough space for the two girls and petite Violet. The three of them pressed in tightly, and Roberta closed the door just as the men entered. It was pitch-black in the closet. Violet hoped Seddon did not store his whiskey there.

"Hand on your heart, you're not opposed to a good swig yourself, Bromley. You wouldn't like it if we soon had to get the stuff under the table."

Glasses clinked.

"Cheers, my friend."

"Excellent whiskey, sir," Seddon's visitor declared. "And you're right. None of us wants alcohol prohibition. However, we don't have to vote on that. It's about the women's right to vote, and—"

"One's the same as the other," Seddon said. "The moment we let those hysterical women get their hands on the power, Sheppard and company are going to close our pubs."

"Naturally, that would be a shame, sir," Bromley said, "but the last word hasn't been said on that. And New Zealand is a democracy. If the people want to close the pubs—"

"The people absolutely do not want that," Seddon blustered. "Only a few moralizers want it, fanatics like that Daldy who would even ban wine in church if she could."

"Then the people will vote accordingly. I'm a Liberal, sir. I entered this party with the conviction that all men are equal before the law. And that means—"

"That next thing, we'll be letting ourselves be ruled by women and the Maori?" roared Seddon. "Fine then, Bromley, we're of different opinions here. You represent Liberal principles, which is praiseworthy, but I see our party most of all as the party of the little man. They want their families safe, and they want their pubs. Not feral suffragettes who won't let them enjoy their time after work. Can we agree on that, Bromley?"

The listeners did not hear anything, but they gathered Bromley nodded assent.

"In that case, I can assume then that you'll be reconsidering your attitude regarding the vote on the pending legislation, can't I? You know, several posts will soon be vacant. Until now, I've hardly changed anything, you see, for reasons of, of def-defer—"

"Deference," Bromley helped him. Seddon had not had any higher education. Without a doubt, he had never studied a dictionary.

"Precisely. But soon it'll be time to form a cabinet, Bromley. You can rest assured of that. And I tend not to forget my friends."

Silence in the office.

"Another glass?" Seddon finally asked.

"I need to go now, sir. But I'll think it over. Although the post of Minister of the Treasury might be of interest. You do know I come from a family of bankers?"

Violet swallowed. She could hardly believe what she was hearing.

"We'll work that out at the appropriate time," Seddon said. "Wait a moment; I'll accompany you out."

Violet prayed the premier would not lock his office. They only heard the heavy door shut, no key in the lock. Atamarie immediately opened the closet door and gasped for air. It was a warm spring day, and the three of them rushed out of their prison.

"Is drinking alcohol allowed here?" Roberta asked.

"They did something much worse," Violet exclaimed, "and they're planning something even worse than that. I have to speak to Sean. But we need to get out of here. It doesn't bear thinking about what would happen if they discovered us. Influencing representatives, bribing them even. There will be consequences."

Violet had the girls go ahead to see if the coast was clear. Whether the girls were discovered was no longer as concerning to her. Seddon would not be threatened by two guileless children in the Parliament Building. But a representative of the Women's Christian Temperance Union?

Atamarie returned to get Violet while Roberta watched the stairs. "The premier's gone," Atamarie whispered, no doubt savoring the adventure, "but the gardeners might be too. Then we'll have to climb out the window."

Violet prayed she was spared that, but the Maori were still there when the three left the building the same way they had come. Atamarie called a few cheerful words over to them; the men answered with amusement and waved at Violet and the girls as they went.

"You see, we didn't do anything wrong, Mrs. Fence," said Atamarie. "I asked them very nicely beforehand if we could go in, and they said yes. So—"

"Wrong is relative," Violet sighed, recalling one of Caleb Biller's favorite expressions. "It looks like by going in alone, you've saved our law. I hope, anyway. We'll see what Sean says about it."

***

Matariki had not waited in her office but had given in to her hunger, hanging a note for Violet and the girls on the office door:

I'm at the Backbencher. Come there if Violet hasn't already killed you.

"She doesn't take anything seriously," Violet said, then nearly ran with the girls to the Backbencher, a restaurant on Molesworth Street favored by representatives, lobbyists, and government employees. Matariki aside, Violet hoped to find Sean there.

The Backbencher was crowded. Violet looked around for Sean, but she spotted Matariki, Kate Sheppard, and Meri Te Tai Mangakahia first. Violet went over to them.

Matariki smiled at her. "Well, you found the girls. Where were you, Atamarie? Violet was worried sick."

"Tell them where you were," Violet said stiffly. "I'm looking for Sean, Matariki. It's an emergency. He needs—"

"Mr. Coltrane is over there," Kate Sheppard said, smiling. "But don't you mean to say hello first, Violet? Dear heavens, you look like you've seen a ghost."

"Not a ghost, just—" Atamarie started babbling.

Violet told her to be quiet with a gruff hand gesture. "Where's Sean?" she insisted.

Kate Sheppard gestured to a recess where Sean sat with two representatives from the upper house, drinking beer. Kate must have disapproved of that, but she probably saw it as a means to an end. The two men were opponents of women's suffrage. Sean was having a lively conversation with them—likely trying to change their minds.

Violet walked toward Sean with brisk strides.

"Mr. Coltrane, forgive me if I'm interrupting, but I've just heard something. I—"

Sean looked up with a furrowed brow. Usually he was happy to see her, but she could see her interruption came at an inopportune moment.

"I can speak with you in a moment, Violet. I'm in the middle of a discussion."

Violet shook her head. "We don't need to leave," she said in a clear voice. "These gentlemen are welcome to listen. Really, they should know too."

Sean and the two men listened spellbound to Violet's tale. When she was done, Sean did not look nearly as overjoyed and relieved as Violet had expected.

"Whew," he said with a look at the men. "I don't know about you, gentlemen, but I could use a whiskey. What do you say we head to the nearest pub and talk there about whether the Liberal Party can still be saved?" When the men involved nodded, he turned to Violet. "Mrs. Fence, please, could you keep this to yourself? Even from Miss Drury, and especially Mrs. Sheppard and Mrs. Mangakahia? If this gets out, Mrs. Fence, Seddon will fall, and all of us with him."

***

Naturally, the women bombarded Violet with questions. The girls had already told them about their adventure. However, they had not understood the implications of what they had heard. They had only told the women that Mr. Seddon had whiskey in his office and that Mr. Bromley really wanted to be Minister of the Treasury in the new government.

"And they talked about women's suffrage too," Roberta added when Violet came back.

Matariki, Kate, and Meri were on the verge of putting two and two together. Violet's silence disappointed them deeply.

"Won't you at least confirm what we think?" Kate Sheppard finally asked.

Violet shook her head. "I need to have something to eat," she said, only to play with the food on her plate. Atamarie and Roberta ate with enough appetite for her. So far, no one had upbraided them for sneaking into the Parliament Building.

"So, if it doesn't work out being premier, we could be spies instead," Atamarie said. "I thought it was exciting in that closet. I could do that every day."

***

Violet's landlady was incensed when Sean Coltrane knocked on her door late that night.

"Don't you know what time it is?" she asked indignantly, sniffing audibly. Sean smelled of whiskey.

As soon as Violet heard the knock on the front door, she was sure it was Sean, and she left her room. "It's all right, Mrs. Rudyard. It's important," she said. "Perhaps we could speak in your receiving room as an exception?"

The strict Mrs. Rudyard had often allowed Violet and Sean just that. She had nothing against the relationship between the young widow and the exceedingly distinguished member of Parliament. However, she was very sensitive about propriety, and he seemed drunk.

"Not here, Violet," Sean said before the landlady answered. "I know, Mrs. Rudyard, I'm compromising Mrs. Fence, but it's important. And it has to stay between us. Please, come, Violet."

Violet had already thrown on a shawl and hurried past Mrs. Rudyard before she could protest. She followed Sean down the stairs and onto the street. He stopped only when they were safely out of view of the old lady, who was surely watching them through the window.

"I'm sorry, Violet, about the whiskey as well," he began, "but such conversations are best had among men over a glass. And, and besides, I might otherwise have lacked the courage to steal you away from that dragon, Mrs. Rudyard, tonight."

"I almost died of suspense," Violet said. "Matariki and the others spent hours trying to talk me into telling them. They already suspect something. I'm sorry, but the girls talked."

"Keep it to yourself anyway, Violet. There are only three days left. And we, well, Mr. Leicester, Mr. Torrance, and I agreed that the public shouldn't catch wind of what you heard. Seddon stands for the Liberal Party. What he does comes back to bite the whole government. If you speak to the press, they'll force him to resign, and it might come to new elections—those would not help us either."

Sean looked at Violet imploringly.

"But if Bromley votes against the bill—," Violet said.

Sean shook his head. "I'm going to speak to Mr. Bromley tomorrow. And Leicester is speaking to Seddon. I've made a deal with Leicester and Torrance. I promised you wouldn't say a word or cast aspersions on the Liberal Party. In exchange, they will vote for suffrage for women and the Maori. We'll win twenty to eighteen. You just have to say yes, Violet."

Violet nodded. She was enraged at Seddon and would have liked to damage him. However, Sean and many others in his party were honorable men who had set out to make New Zealand a nation with the most progressive laws on earth. She could not allow the idiocy of an uneducated provincial politician whom fate had kicked upstairs to destroy everything.

Sean smiled with relief when she agreed. He had watched her attentively while she considered. He loved her serious face, the furrows her forehead made as she turned over a problem, and he loved her triumphant smile when she made her decision.

He should not have drunk the whiskey. But he never would have dared to kiss her if he hadn't. Sean bent down to Violet as she looked up at him, smiling. She was so small and delicate; yet she always protected everyone. Sean hoped she would let him take care of her.

Violet had often seen people kiss, but she had never kissed anyone herself. She had been forced to endure Eric's tongue in her mouth, but for her that had never been a kiss. Now, though, she parted her lips for Sean. And marveled that she hardly tasted whiskey as so often with Eric. She tasted peppermint, and alongside her rising excitement, she felt somehow touched. He must have gone home to brush his teeth. So, he had planned this.

Without thinking, she said something to him about it when they parted.

Sean nodded. "I'll admit it. I had to have some liquid courage. I've never compromised a woman before, Violet Fence. And tomorrow, Mrs. Rudyard is guaranteed to tell all Wellington. Not just your reputation will be ruined."

Violet fixed Sean with a mischievous stare. "There might still be a way to avert scandal," she said. "But then, then you'd have to ask me something else, and I would have to say yes."

Sean smiled. And then he asked the question.

Chapter 3

On the day before the passage of the law on women's suffrage, Richard Seddon, the premier, had an astounding conversion. He avowed the fundamental Liberal principles and declared that equality before the law demanded suffrage for women and the Maori.

His supporters in Parliament couldn't understand what had happened. Outside of Parliament, however, people celebrated the premier's change of heart. Seddon's popularity climbed, and women cheered for him in front of the Parliament Building.

"He really did manage to come out on top of the whole thing," said Sean.

He and Violet had agreed to let Matariki and Kupe in on their secret. Matariki had already coaxed out of her daughter nearly the precise wording of the conversation between Bromley and Seddon. She could piece together the rest. Sean needed an audience to whom he could let off steam.

"I've been telling you," Kupe said, "a born populist. With him we'll have our hands full in Parliament. Sean, I think we have some interesting years ahead of us."

Sean shook his head. "You might, Kupe, if you stand for election. With the Maori and the women's vote, you'd win for sure. But I'm done. Under Seddon, I'll never be on solid footing. It's no secret how he treats his opponents. And my heart's not in it anymore. If it continues like this, if I'm just having to fight against corruption and incompetence, I'm not made for that. I'll stay till November, but then I won't run again. I'll go back to Dunedin with Violet, open a firm, and support Peter's parish in legal matters."

"Specializing in divorce?" Matariki teased.

"And questions of land ownership," Sean responded seriously. "I think I'm going to take another look at the Parihaka affair. Maybe you all will get some sort of reparations."

"Sure, when heaven and earth meet," grumbled Kupe.

Matariki looked out the window. It was raining again. "Which is not impossible," she said. "If Rangi never stops crying," she said, referring to the rain, "maybe it'll move the gods."

***

On September 19, 1893, as the governor, Lord Glasgow, signed the Electoral Act into law, giving women the right to vote, the rain stopped and the sun shone over Wellington, and the women danced together through the streets. Matariki hugged Amey Daldy, who had traveled there to experience her triumph in person in the capital.

"We did it, Mrs. Daldy," she cheered. "Suffrage for us and for Maori women too. Would you have believed it when I started teaching them English all those years ago?"

Amey Daldy smiled at her graciously. That day Mrs. Daldy was acting almost frivolously. Instead of one of the black or brown outfits she usually wore, she came in a light-green one with a matching flower hat. In any case, she forgave Matariki her missteps, and for her part, Matariki suppressed the suggestion of drinking a glass of champagne to their victory. She was ebulliently happy and completely wound up following the strain of the days before.

As Sean had predicted, the law had passed on September 8, twenty to eighteen, but afterward another flurry of action surrounded the Parliament. Opponents of suffrage hoped until the end for a veto from the governor and tried to influence him to achieve that goal. Petitions and counterpetitions chased one another. The women at the front did not get a minute's rest. In the meantime, nearly every citizen wore either a white or red camellia on the street as a sign of agreement or rejection of women's suffrage. The governor, Lord Glasgow, did not allow any of it to impress him, however. Unlike Richard Seddon—now known by his nickname, "King Dick"—Glasgow had no weakness for the old lordly politics. The law had passed; his signature was just a formality.

Matariki wanted to share her excitement with Kupe by hugging him, but he rebuffed her stubbornly.

"I would like to know what happened between them," Violet whispered to Sean.

Matariki overheard her. "Me too," she grumbled. "Dear God, he can't really still be holding it against me that I fell in love with a *pakeha* more than ten years ago."

***

November 28 was another radiant early-summer day. *The flowers shone in competition with the colorful summer dresses of the women walking proudly to the ballot boxes for the first time,* a newspaper in Christchurch reported, re-creating the mood in the streets quite closely.

"I hope it won't come to riots during the election," Matariki said, concerned when she met her friends around eleven o'clock to cast their votes together.

Several newspapers had expressed corresponding fears, and the police presence near the polling stations had been increased.

"We'll make it through this now too," Violet said, smiling.

Violet shone in competition with the sun. Matariki had taken Roberta to spend the night before with her and Atamarie. Violet had been with Sean. After a celebratory dinner at the Commercial Hotel, they went to the apartment he had rented near the Parliament Building.

"We don't need to make love tonight," Sean said gently when he saw her pale face. "We can just as easily wait for our wedding night."

Violet shook her head. "I'm not a prude," she said. "I'm just—"

Sean kissed her tenderly. "You just can't imagine making love with me will make you happy. You can't imagine that—"

"That it won't hurt," Violet whispered.

Sean took her in his arms and then looked her straight in the eye. "I'll never hurt you. That I promise you. I won't lock any doors or hold you unwillingly. Whenever you want to stop—"

Violet shook her head. "Please, just hold me willingly," she murmured, snuggling against him as he lifted her up and over the threshold of his small apartment.

On his bed, she lay completely still at first, but then she helped Sean with the bands and hooks of her dress as he undressed her.

"You don't have to be completely, um," Violet whispered embarrassedly, particularly as Sean had not extinguished the light.

Sean laughed. "No, you don't have to be naked, but I'd very much like to see you, Violet. And you should see me too. We will see and hear and feel and taste each other—I'd like to become one with you, Violet."

Sean covered her body with kisses, and a night of enchantment began for Violet. She opened herself to him joyfully and explored his slender, wiry body. When she cuddled into Sean's arms to fall asleep, she had forgotten everything that had come before. Worlds lay between what Eric had done to her and what she and Sean had experienced together.

Violet blinked into the sunny morning when she awoke next to Sean. Election day. What a wonderful start. There were so many things she could look forward to, and Violet suddenly saw her life as a shining road of joy and contentment ahead of her. No wonder her beauty and her inner radiance outshone those of all the other women that day.

***

"That dress really suits you," said Matariki, greeting her friend and her half brother with a wink and a smile. "A morning gift?"

Violet turned red, but Sean nodded and laughed. "An engagement present," he corrected her. "And thank heavens it fits."

The aquamarine-blue empire-waist dress with its matching hat came from the Gold Mine Boutique. Sean had asked them to ship it to him. Kathleen had guessed Violet's measurements. Quite successfully as it turned out.

Matariki wore a dress patterned in gold and red that complemented her black hair and golden-brown skin. Kupe could not stop looking at her, though he turned away shyly when their eyes met. Matariki would have liked nothing more than to normalize her relationship with Kupe. Or maybe even more than that.

In their months of working together, she had gotten to know Kupe as an exceedingly competent attorney, obliging but persistent in dealing with the Maori and *pakeha*. He spoke both languages fluently, and he made a distinguished and self-assured appearance. He also impressed Matariki with his obstinacy. She did not know what she had done to wound him so badly that he still held it against her, but his determination to stay away from her motivated Matariki to try her arts of seduction on him. The new low-cut dress was part of that. It had been exceptionally expensive, but Matariki thought the occasion worth it. She found herself in agreement with the women on the islands who were wearing their most elegant clothes.

The women of New Zealand were turning their first vote into a summer festival. The feared protests did not materialize, and those wearing red camellias proved to be good losers: they left their flowers at home—white dominated the streets.

Seddon, the premier, handed the chair of the Women's Franchise League in Wellington a bouquet of white camellias after she had cast her vote. "For the Liberals, I hope," he said gallantly.

The chair of the league did not quite know where to look. Sean, who was strolling with his friends from one polling station to another, taking in the scene, rubbed his forehead.

"You really want to be part of this Parliament?" he asked Kupe.

He shrugged. He had not put himself on the ballot for the current election. He planned to go to Waipatu and work with the Te Kotahitanga. He had focused his studies on property law. The Maori Parliament had asked him to advise it on related matters.

"Someone has to do it. And now that we're allowed to vote, no more *pakeha* strawmen are going to sit in the lower house. Shall we find someplace to eat? I'm starting to get hungry."

Matariki, Violet, Sean, and Kupe ate in a café, which, to Matariki's dismay, did not serve champagne.

"It's so unfair," she complained. "The men meet in the pubs, talk about the results until the votes are counted, and then drink a glass to them. We, on the other hand—"

"I might still have two bottles of champagne in my office," noted Sean, winking. "I just didn't dare bring them before. After all, you know what Meri thinks about that."

Meri Te Tai Mangakahia had been with them in the morning. Though she wasn't yet permitted to vote—the vote for the Maori seats in Parliament was not until December 20—she had come to Wellington with her husband to experience the women's triumph. The Mangakahias had been invited to a lunch and had parted from the others after Matariki and Violet had voted. Before they left, Meri made some jabs about Matariki voting that day and not waiting to vote with her tribal compatriots. Matariki did not have a choice in that, though. Since she was legally Michael Drury's daughter, she was considered of Irish ancestry. Meri Te Tai had not known that.

"Good, then we'll go back to our office and drink there," Matariki said. "I can get the champagne from the Parliament Building. You just show me the way, Atamarie."

Violet smiled indulgently. Matariki still had not gotten over Violet having explored the Parliament Building with the girls while she herself had still never seen it. This time, however, Atamarie entered the building through the main entrance; although the prohibition on women had not been lifted, no one stopped them. While Sean and the others went on to the office, Matariki admired the entry hall of the Parliament Building.

"The offices are upstairs," Atamarie said as she dragged her mother up the stairs and began searching for Sean's office, which fortunately was not hard to find. Sean had described exactly where the champagne was.

"He even thought of ice." Matariki pulled a champagne cooler with two bottles of ice-cold French champagne from the cabinet. "I could fall in love with Sean too."

"Mom," Atamarie yelled chidingly.

At that moment, they had heard steps in the hallway—surely a parliamentarian on the way to his office. This man's steps, however, stopped in front of Sean's door as if he were reading the name of the representative located here. Matariki had an uneasy feeling when at that moment the door handle turned. It seemed to be the same for Atamarie, who suddenly ducked under Sean's massive desk. Noticeable was the reaction of old Dingo, who had patiently hauled himself up the stairs in Matariki and Atamarie's train. He puffed himself up in front of Matariki and began to bark and growl protectively.

The man who entered was blond, slender but heavier than Matariki remembered him. She gasped when she saw Colin Coltrane's face. His once-appealing features were destroyed: his broken nose had healed poorly, his jaw was crooked, and a thick scar twisted one eyebrow diabolically.

"Colin," cried Matariki, shocked. "What happened to you?"

Colin Coltrane was just as surprised as she, but he collected himself quickly and forced his face into a smile—or was it a sneer?

"Well, Matariki," he said. His voice sounded throaty, perhaps a result of the deformed jaw. When he opened his mouth, Matariki saw he was also missing several teeth. "That I should run into you here, cute as ever, and wild." He laughed and glanced at the champagne. "Don't tell me you're doing my brother."

"Your brother is engaged," Matariki said calmly, "and you're still married, or has Chloe divorced you now?"

Colin stepped closer. "I'm free again," he smirked. "Although the little bitch kept my name. Suits her, since now she shares a name with her whore. Whoever doesn't know them thinks they're sisters who are very loving to each other."

Matariki thought that was a good solution. "You did get to keep the house in exchange," she noted. "A stud farm, a racetrack, a manor house—not bad for a little name."

"The only thing I got is this here." Colin ran his hands across his ruined face. "I don't know how the bastards found out about the bet rigging. I could have sworn Chloe didn't know about it. Otherwise, she would have shoved it in my face amid all the trouble at the end."

"Bet rigging?" Matariki asked cautiously. She knew about Eric Fence's notebook, but it was best not to betray any of Violet's involvement in the matter to Colin.

Colin looked out the window at the summer day. "That's what they call it, anyway. Really, it was only half as bad. A little boost for a horse here, a poorly shod shoe there."

"You shoed horses so they'd go lame?" Matariki was outraged. Violet had not gone into details when she told Matariki about what Colin and Eric had done. "And then naturally they couldn't win. That's lousy, Colin."

Dingo growled.

"So, you've still got the mutt," observed Colin. "Does he put on this kind of show when Sean comes near you?" He pressed threateningly close to Matariki. "You're beautiful, my dear. I ought never to have let you go." Colin kicked at Dingo as he reached for Matariki.

She evaded him skillfully. "Enough, Colin," she said sternly. "What are you even doing here? Were you looking for Sean?"

Colin nodded. "Oh yes, sweetheart. I thought I'd ask my brother to whom I owe my betrayal. Someone must have given the information to the bookmakers. And the first one who sent his ruffians after me was in Dunedin."

Matariki pointed to Colin's face. "That's from people who wanted to collect money?"

Colin grimaced. "You got it," he said, "and now you know what happened to the farm, the track, and the house. Everything sold, sweetheart. 'As compensation for lost bets,' as the gentlemen put it. Requested with a great deal of emphasis." He touched his jaw again. "It's nice to see you here. Indeed, perhaps with your help, I can request some compensation from Sean? What do you think: Would he pay a bit for you if I take you with me now?" He reached for her arm and twisted it with a skilled motion onto her back. "We'll take the champagne and have a nice evening with it. Tomorrow we'll send Sean a note, maybe a dog's collar." He kicked at Dingo again. "Or a dead dog."

"You bastard." Matariki tried to tear herself free, but Colin held her with an iron grip.

"Sweetheart, doubtless you'd come with me willingly rather than look like me afterward?"

While Matariki was desperately considering how she could draw out information from him about where he intended to take her—Atamarie was listening and would have been able to inform Sean and the police—the door was thrown open.

"Let her go this instant," roared Kupe.

It was not the tattoos that made the warrior and certainly not the *haka* Kupe had danced in Parihaka. It was rage. Kupe leaped on Colin, pulled Matariki from him, and landed a fist in his face. Colin fell to the ground.

"No," he whimpered, trying to protect his nose, which was bleeding again.

Matariki almost felt sorry for him. He had not been cowardly before, but the bookkeepers and their brutes must have worn him down.

"Oh, so the gentleman doesn't want an honest fistfight," Kupe spat at him. "But you always had your difficulties with honest combat, didn't you, Sergeant Coltrane?"

"I had nothing to do with your arrest," Colin moaned. "You have to believe me."

"No," Kupe retorted, "but you did with the fact that afterward I spent six months lying in that shithole in Lyttelton and almost died. You certainly had something to do with that."

Matariki looked at Kupe, confused, and then let her gaze wander over to Colin. "I asked him," she whispered. "He said he didn't know where you were."

547

Kupe laughed. "And you believed him. You only had eyes for him. How could you take off with him, Matariki? How could you?" He turned to her with a distraught look.

Matariki swallowed. "But, Kupe, what good would it have done if I had let myself be locked up too? He said we were looking at months in prison, all of us. And he would smuggle me out, and I was so afraid. You had disappeared, and every day more people were taken away."

"And set free two miles from Parihaka," Kupe scoffed. "In the final days, they did not arrest anyone anymore, Matariki. Either they transported you the fastest way home to your tribe, or they set you free somewhere in the wilderness. With one exception." He looked at Colin hatefully. "What did you tell that Bryce bastard I was, Coltrane? A leader? A criminal hiding out in Parihaka? I suspect the latter, given the way they treated me. They sent me to the South Island, Matariki, in chains. In this shithole of a prison where they had kept the plowmen whom they didn't take to trial for months either. If a few journalists and churchgoers there had not become aware of us, they would have forgotten us there. With nothing but bread and water, although they liked to forget the first sometimes. Just like cleaning out the cell and heating fuel in the winter. It was cold and wet in the cells, Matariki, and the latrines overflowed. We had cholera and gangrene of the lungs while you were enjoying yourself with your *pakeha*. They pulled us out of there just before the first of us died. Straight to the nearest army hospital. We all just made it. While Miss Drury was planning to start a stud farm with Sergeant Coltrane. Probably with a few savage Maori as stable hands." Naked hate filled Kupe's eyes.

Matariki, nevertheless, held his gaze. "I didn't know any of that, Kupe," she said quietly. "I didn't hear about you again until you were studying in Wellington, from the other young women, first from Koria and then Pai. She wrote me that you didn't want anything to do with me, and I got the impression you were with her."

Kupe snorted. "Then you got the wrong impression. I actually wanted to see you when I heard that this bastard left you, first got you with child and then left you." He seemed about to kick Colin, but Colin turned, whimpering on his side before Kupe's foot even came close. Kupe laughed and spat at him.

"Kupe," Matariki called chidingly. Then, however, she looked at him doubtfully. "You looked for us?" she asked quietly. "But we weren't hard to find, Atamarie and I?"

"I received a letter from Amey Daldy," he explained wearily, "who strongly denied she was letting any fallen woman work for her. You were a widow. She had never heard of a Colin Coltrane. Well, so I gave it up. Two *pakeha* one right after the other, married to one." He smiled crookedly. "I had hoped I could come by like something of a fairy-tale prince to help you out of your troubles. I did have experience in that, after all. But then you never thought much of me."

Matariki looked up at him seriously. "In any case, you did save me again today," she asserted, letting her gaze—a gaze of contempt—wander over to Colin, who had turned his face from her. Then she collected herself. If Kupe was now finally talking, maybe he would tell her why he was so endlessly resentful toward her.

"But you must have found out later that I wasn't ever married," she drilled down, trying not to sound accusatory. "In Wellington at the latest, I am still named Drury, after all."

Kupe nodded. "I also only needed to look at your daughter's face to know that there was no one else other than this, this piece of shit." He pointed to Colin. "But it was too late, Matariki. Then I didn't want it anymore either." The expression in his eyes betrayed him.

Matariki smiled. "But maybe I'd like to," she said, "and I think it's time you forgave me. I was eighteen and in love."

"I was too," said Kupe, his tone hard. "When your father brought you to the Hauhau, I was eighteen and in love. And? What good did it do me?"

"It didn't do me any good either," noted Matariki. "And Mrs. Daldy lied to you, and Pai lied to me. Can't we just begin again?" She stepped toward him. "I'm Matariki Drury," she said, smiling. "A chieftain's daughter. In search of a warrior with loads of *mana*."

Kupe looked at her doubtfully. "I'm not a warrior," he said.

"Oh, but you are," Matariki said, pointing to his tattoos. "You fight for your people, don't you, Kupe? Didn't you just win a decisive victory?"

Kupe had to laugh at that. He had controlled himself so long, although he had never been able to resist her.

He squared himself, building himself up in the manner of a Maori warrior presenting his *pepeha*. "All right, fine, Matariki Drury. But I have a surprise for you. I'm not Kupe Something Something. My name is Paikeha Parekura Turei from the tribe of the Ngati Porou. My forefathers came to Aotearoa in the Nukutaimemeha. Hikurangi is the mountain—*maunga*—Waiapu the river."

"That's good, I don't need to know everything," Matariki said, interrupting the speech he had obviously learned by heart. A *pepeha* could go on and on, and Matariki was really not interested in Kupe's ancestry to the fifth generation. "But how do you know it? You always said—"

Kupe bathed in the successful surprise. "Hamiora told me before. They undertook inquiries in the area from which my tribe came. Since they could hardly send someone to Parliament who didn't know his old canoe. Well, and Te Kotahitanga does make quite a bit possible."

This time, he let Matariki come closer to him, and he seemed to be expecting her to embrace him. She did not do that, however. She pressed her nose and her forehead to his face in the traditional *hongi*.

"*Haere mai*, Paikeha Parekura Turei," she said tenderly, "and with that, the curse should be taken from you."

"Curse?" asked Kupe, confused.

Matariki rolled her eyes. "Heavens, Kupe. A woman goes and takes the trouble to curse you, and you can't even remember it?"

Kupe smiled. "You mean Pai with that childish fit? That the spirit of Parihaka is supposed to have abandoned me as long as I bear the name you gave me?"

Matariki nodded. "Don't make fun of it," she warned. "I, in any case, have not noticed much of the spirit of Parihaka recently. Or do you call that peaceable?"

Colin Coltrane moaned. He moved to get back to his feet, but a look from Kupe made him sink back down.

"Are you going to reproach me for knocking down this bastard?" Kupe asked.

Matariki made a face. "No. I was just thinking of forgiving and forgetting with regard to a certain chieftain's daughter."

Kupe smirked and put his arm around her. Matariki lifted her face toward his, but in that moment, Dingo began to yap.

"Not again," Matariki sighed, but then she saw the dog was only reacting to Colin, who had just seized his chance to pull himself up on the door in order to escape.

Kupe let go of Matariki, went over to him, and helped him up. "Get out of here, and thank the spirit of Parihaka," he grumbled. "Leave Matariki in peace. If you want to speak with your brother—come during business hours."

Colin practically crawled out the door; Matariki again almost felt sorry for him. Yet then, when Kupe kissed her, she forgot him just as she forgot everything around her. It was better than years ago under the stars in Auckland. She had felt sympathy for the young warrior. She loved the strong warrior of today.

***

Kupe and Matariki were startled when Atamarie crawled out from under the desk.

"Atamarie, I'm sorry," he murmured. "I didn't know that you were there, or I would have expressed myself more carefully. Speaking to Coltrane, I mean."

Atamarie cuddled against her mother. She hardly seemed to notice Kupe, and she was surely preoccupied with things other than his word choice. She was pale and trembling.

"Mommy," she whispered. "Mommy is, was, is that evil, ugly man my father?"

Matariki struggled for words. How was she supposed to explain? How much had Atamarie understood of everything she had said to Kupe? What did she know about Colin?

Kupe took the girl by the shoulder and separated her gently from her mother's skirt. Like that, he got Atamarie to turn to him, and looked at her carefully. For the first time, he saw not Colin's hated features, but Matariki's slightly slanted eyes, her raspberry-red mouth always just about to form a mischievous smile, and the golden glimmer of her complexion. From now on, he would only see Matariki in her. And now, he glanced up at Matariki with an expression between "please" and "sorry." Then he looked the girl in the eye.

"No, Atamarie," he said firmly. "I'm your father."

Chapter 4

"You want to live on the North Island, but you're bringing the girl to us?"

Miss Partridge, who was still the principal of Otago Girls' High School in Dunedin, wore somewhat thicker glasses than she had nearly twenty years earlier, but otherwise, though she seemed ancient to Matariki, she was still spry, and she gave her future student and her parents exceedingly stern looks.

"We'd like to go back to Parihaka," Matariki explained. She could easily imagine how her mother had squirmed many years before under Miss Partridge's gaze. Matariki nearly felt as if she were the eleven-year-old who had been summoned before the principal for torturous questioning. "You've heard of it perhaps."

Miss Partridge made a face. "I can read, my child," she said. "I'm old but not blind or deaf or ignorant. An interesting experiment. However, wasn't the settlement destroyed?"

Matariki nodded. "Yes, Miss Partridge. Forgive me." She pulled herself together. "But now Te Whiti is back, and his people are building the village up again. My husband and I want to help. He will be working as an attorney, and I'll be managing the elementary school. We bought land there. No one will drive us out again."

"Ah," Miss Partridge said as she eyed, somewhat disapprovingly, Matariki's outfit, which was a compromise between *pakeha* and traditional Maori clothing. Matariki wore a dark skirt but a woven top in the colors of her tribe, and her hair hung long and loose down to her hips. Not exactly how Miss Partridge pictured a teacher—not to mention that her former student seemed to be married. For Miss Partridge, a teacher with her own family was unthinkable. "Well, times change," she remarked. She did not sound enthusiastic.

Matariki nodded again. She seemed to radiate from within as she did. "We hope to expand, but we won't have a high school immediately—at the moment, there are hardly any children Atamarie's age." Her face clouded over. "Once, there were so many children."

"Atamarie's aptitudes cannot be adequately developed in Parihaka," Kupe said.

It would take a bit for the principal to get used to the sight of him. She tried to maintain decorum and under no circumstances to stare at his tattoos.

"Her best friend, Roberta Fence, will be living in Dunedin and attending this school starting next academic year, so it seems a good idea to enroll our daughter here," Kupe added.

"She can spend her weekends with my parents," Matariki said, "and my tribe. I would welcome her spending more time with Ngai Tahu. We've not yet lived in a *marae* together."

Miss Partridge's gaze now wandered from her former student and her husband, whose careful form of expression stood in stark contrast to his martial appearance, to their daughter. She eyed Atamarie's blonde hair, her by no means dark complexion, and her golden-brown eyes. Aside from the girl's somewhat slanted eyes and slightly exotic features, she would never have recognized the Maori in her.

"Is she your real daughter?" she asked Kupe. "I mean, she—"

"Oh yes. Atamarie Parekura Turei," Kupe said with absolute surety.

Miss Partridge sighed. She, too, felt returned to twenty years earlier.

"And a, hmm, child of the stars?" she asked with a slightly drawn mouth.

Atamarie shook her head and joined in the conversation for the first time. Until then, she had only observed with fascination how this old lady managed to intimidate her mother.

"No," she said energetically. "You've misunderstood. 'Matariki' has to do with the stars. 'Atamarie' means sunrise. One of my grandmothers says it's very beautiful. Although, she always calls me Mary."

Miss Partridge had to smile, even against her will. She did not know where this Maori warrior with a law degree fit in, but Atamarie was, without a doubt, Matariki's child.

"How many grandmothers do you have, Anna-Marie?" she asked.

Kupe suppressed a laugh. Matariki had told him about her own interview for this school, in which she had told Miss Partridge she had sixteen grandmothers.

"Two," Atamarie declared firmly, and Matariki sighed with relief. Atamarie had Lizzie and Mrs. Daldy in mind. Though she recently had gotten to know Kathleen Burton, she didn't yet grasp the familial relationships.

"That's progress, anyway," Miss Partridge said curtly, and played with her glasses in a way that made Matariki think the woman wished for her old lorgnette. "Although, I take it that will change once you've spent more time with your tribe."

"Do I need to take an exam now?" Atamarie asked eagerly. "My mother says she had to read and do math with you when she was my age. I can do those really well. And writing. Most of all, I like to make banners for demonstrations."

Miss Partridge frowned.

"You've recently adopted a student government here, isn't that right?" Kupe asked amicably. "To practice democratic decision-making, election processes, and all that? That is important to our daughter."

"It is also very important to us," Miss Partridge said firmly, and seemed to become twenty years younger. "Now that we women finally have the right to vote and are gaining influence. We are proud of Elizabeth Yates. You do know she has been elected mayor of Onehunga? Just a few months after women gained the right to vote—and we have the first female mayor of the British Empire."

Kupe and Matariki smiled at each other. Apparently during Roberta's interview, Sean and Violet hadn't informed Miss Partridge about what had occupied all of them for years.

"We know Elizabeth," Matariki said confidently. "For a while, I worked with her in Auckland on the suffrage efforts. We even drove to Onehunga to congratulate her."

Atamarie nodded with shining eyes. "Mrs. Yates is very nice. She gave me a camellia."

Miss Partridge gave her former and her future students the first open and enthusiastic smile of the day.

"So, surely you want to be a mayor someday too, Atamarie," she said.

Matariki noted with delight that she pronounced her name correctly this time. Atamarie also seemed to find herself in tune with the school's principal and beamed at her conspiratorially.

"Premier," she corrected her.

Miss Partridge indicated a bow and cast another glance at the name on Atamarie's registration form. "We will do everything we can, Atamarie Parekura, to help you with that."

Matariki smiled. No one would ever call her daughter Mary.

Afterword

With a law for women's suffrage in 1893, New Zealand proved itself the forerunner of progressive social legislation. In England and Germany, the suffragettes did not succeed until 1918 and 1919, respectively. Success with the passive voting rights of women, however, would not arrive as quickly as Atamarie hopes in this novel. Although they were allowed to participate in municipal politics practically as soon as the general right to vote was achieved, women first received the right to occupy the House of Representatives as representatives in 1919. The upper house (New Zealand Legislative Council) remained closed to them until 1941. The first female deputy prime minister was Helen Clark in 1989; the first prime minister was Jenny Shipley in 1997. Since then, several women have occupied the post.

This novel deals in many respects with emancipation. It spans a wide arc from the Maori Wars, to the general lack of rights and forlornness of women in the coal-mining settlements, and to the legislation of 1893, which made the sexes formally equal. As always, I have tried to set my fictional characters within a background that is as authentic as possible. Here is some additional information regarding certain plot elements:

Kahu Heke's role in the Hauhau movement is based on the historical figure Patara, who is occasionally also called the "true founder of the Hauhau." Like my fictional character Kahu, Patara was knowledgeable about *pakeha* society and deeply discontent with its dominance over his people. He ultimately committed to the Hauhau movement and went with a group of warriors to Opotiki to take revenge on the whites for a typhus epidemic that they introduced. In so doing, he killed the missionary C. S. Völkner, leading to hostilities between him and *pakeha* troops. Innocent Maori were killed, which made Patara controversial among his own people. There could no longer be a question of a serious office as a representative of the Maori people. The man hid himself away for a long time, whereby the *kingi* granted him asylum. Ultimately, his trail became lost in the darkness of history.

It was characteristic of the Hauhau to revive old Polynesian customs and mix them with confused ideas from Christianity. Among other things, they tried cannibalism—the atrocities portrayed did take place. I have tried to describe the customs of the Hauhau movement as correctly as possible, but nothing with reference to Maori customs can be generally applied. Myths and spirit summoning differ from tribe to tribe.

Kahu Heke's idea to carry over the traditional function of the chieftain's daughter as a warrior goddess to his construction of the Hauhau movement is completely fictional. There is no evidence that girls were involved in the rites of the Hauhau.

In contrast, all my descriptions regarding life in Parihaka and the downfall of this model settlement are precisely documented. Te Whiti was unequivocally a pioneer of nonviolent resistance, even if he did not attract the worldwide attention Mahatma Gandhi did later. It must be bitter for the Maori people that Mahatma Gandhi is today celebrated as a hero of peace whereas Te Whiti and his comrades have nearly been forgotten. Nevertheless, Parihaka was indeed rebuilt, and a historical site exists to this day. People still tend Te Whiti's grave there. Once a year, the area serves as the locale for the Parihaka International Peace Festival with music and rallies.

In the assault on Parihaka, volunteers and members of the Armed Constabulary were employed; among them I have placed my character of Colin Coltrane. Armed constables were a mixture of police and soldiers. In New Zealand, they recruited a large number of young men, mostly in the context of the Land Wars and Maori Wars. A certain hysteria no doubt played a role in the amassing of these troops. In relation to other colonial wars, the confrontations between the *pakeha* and the Maori cannot really be called wars. Rather, one can speak of battles or engagements, which rarely cost many lives, even when the parties met in the field with thousands of fighters. In the Battle of Ohaeawai on July 1, 1845, there were thirty dead to mourn. At the Wairau Affray on June 17, 1843, there were twenty-six.

By 1872, there was only a minimal need for armed constables. Aside from the few men who found work as police, the troops were employed constructing bridges and railroads, including the Midland Line. Julian Redcliff, the leader of the construction workers is, however, a fictional character. Devoted readers will perhaps recognize him from *Song of the Spirits* as the husband of Heather Witherspoon.

I found the fewest historically documented facts on the history of harness racing in New Zealand—namely, the development is impossible to establish chronologically. This is because reporters concentrated more on stories than on history. When and where the first race was run with sulkies instead of riders, or when precisely which racetrack was opened and by whom, however, was difficult to research. Brown's Paddock, the location of the first races in Woolston is, for example, just a name handed down. Whether a resourceful stable owner really did recognize the sign of the times and build a racetrack—which Colin Coltrane then mimicked in Invercargill—can be deduced from the name "paddock" but is not documented. The racing clubs mentioned in the text did exist. Some of them were, however, later closed, and the towns do not seem to have been so proud of them that they receive special mention in the city archives.

What is certain, however, is that in the time in question, there were racetracks in Woolston as well as Invercargill where regular and harness races took place. Harness races also occurred more or less as described. It was entirely normal for the milk truck's horse to race a shepherd's pony. In the very beginning, harness races were also held on public streets, but my charity race in Caversham is fictional. I do not know if there was anything comparable in New Zealand or elsewhere.

For those interested in horses, it should be noted that the auxiliary rein called a checkrein is still used in harness racing and gaited horse sports.

Without a doubt, Chloe and Heather Coltrane form the most unusual couple in this book, and to this as well I would like to offer some background information. Naturally, there has always been same-sex love among women—just as among men. While male homosexuals, however, were mocked and often persecuted, the love between women was rarely so. Sigmund Freud and his successors were the first to stigmatize it as unnatural and a form of hysteria. Outside of the avant-garde—artists like Rosa Bonheur were open about their lesbian relationships—the phenomenon seems barely to have been known. Neither was there a generally applicable term.

Only around the turn of the twentieth century did words like "lesbian" come into common use. Thus, the men and women in my book did not yet know them, which is why I also did not use them in my narration. Were the love between two women in bourgeois circumstances to become public, husbands may have reacted similarly to Colin; friends and relatives, however, may have reacted as liberally as Sean and Matariki. In the nineteenth century, it was entirely common for women to be very loving toward one another. The borders around the display of tenderness between friends and lesbian love were fluid.

Finally, a few words on that first women's movement of the suffragettes, in which both Matariki and Violet engage. Here I have portrayed Kate Sheppard, Amey Daldy, and other historical personages. A few times, Matariki butts heads with Amey Daldy. From today's perspective—as well as from the perspective of Matariki, who is strongly shaped by Maori traditions—Daldy the feminist seems sanctimonious and narrow-minded, nothing comparable to the attitudes of the lively multiculturalism of the modern women's movement. Amey Daldy was, however, for her time an exceedingly liberal and progressive woman, although she, like many suffragettes, particularly in New Zealand, came from the milieu of the Congregationalist Church and the temperance movement. These women were shaped by the strictest moral principles from youth, and they also saw in their social work with women and children the horrifying effects of alcoholism, which was widespread in the poorer classes in the New Zealand of their time. Violet's path to the women's movement is much more typical than that of the "child of the stars," Matariki. Strict adherence to the conservative image of women by Mrs. Daldy, Meri Te Tai, and others is understandable and should not be condemned. On the contrary, their fight for the right to vote is all the more admirable. They had to swallow their pride regularly.

Femina was writing her first feminist articles in 1869. Her husband was a member of the Nelson Provincial Council and would certainly have mounted the barricades if he had known of her activities.

Mary Ann Müller wrote anyway.

Acknowledgments

As always, many people helped me with this book. The collaboration with my first reader, Melanie Blank-Schröder, and my original editor, Margit von Cossart, was as exceptional as ever—thank you both!

Klara Decker was again helpful as a test reader and internet researcher with regard to driving horse trailers and harness racing. I thank Judith Knaggs for advice in the matter of coach lighting and authentic methods of killing with the help of a sulky.

A special thank-you to everyone who helps bring my New Zealand novels successfully to readers! From translation and editing to cover design and marketing to sales and distribution—really, all of your names belong on the bestseller list!

And naturally, nothing at all would happen without my wonderful agent, Bastian Schlück, and all his colleagues at the agency. Here again, a thousand thanks!

Sarah Lark

About the Author

Photo © 2011 Gonzalo Perez

Born in Germany and now a resident of Spain, Sarah Lark is a horse aficionado and former travel guide who has experienced many of the world's most beautiful landscapes on horseback. Through her adventures, she has developed an intimate relationship with the places she's visited and the characters who live there. In her writing, Lark introduces readers to a New Zealand full of magic, beauty, and charm. Her ability to weave romance with history and to explore all the dark and triumphal corners of the human condition has made her a bestselling author worldwide.

About the Translator

Photo © 2011 Sanna Stegmaier

D. W. Lovett is a graduate of the University of Illinois at Urbana–Champaign, from which he received a degree in comparative literature and German as well as a certificate from the university's Center for Translation Studies. He has spent the last few years living in Europe. This is his fourth translation of Sarah Lark's work to be published in English, following *In the Land of the Long White Cloud*, *Song of the Spirits*, and *Call of the Kiwi*.